THE ANXIETY OF
KALIX THE WEREWOLF

THE
ANXIETY
OF KALIX
THE WEREWOLF

MARTIN MILLAR

SOFT SKULL PRESS
AN IMPRINT OF COUNTERPOINT
BERKELEY

ISBN 978-1-59376-537-8

SOFT SKULL PRESS
An imprint of COUNTERPOINT
1919 Fifth Street
Berkeley, CA 94710
www.softskull.com
www.counterpointpress.com

Printed in the United States of America
Distributed by Publishers Group West

10 9 8 7 6 5 4 3 2 1

THE ANXIETY OF
KALIX THE WEREWOLF

CHAPTER I

Eighteen years in the past.

Markus MacRinnalch was used to being treated with respect. As the son of the Thane, he was an important figure in the werewolf clan, and he was popular at the castle. Women in particular were always fond of him.

Apart from Dominil, thought Markus. For a nine-year-old, she's certainly mastered the art of withering contempt.

His young cousin regarded him with scorn. "Don't you know *anything*?" she said. "I'm not an *albino*. I'm *leucistic*. It's a completely different condition."

"All right," said Markus, raising his voice against the wind. "You're leucistic. Now could you put some clothes on and get back to the castle?"

Dominil, standing in her underwear, in a snowdrift that reached up to her waist, showed no inclination of putting her clothes on.

"It's really a foolish mistake," she continued as the snow fell. "Albinism is a result of the reduction of melanin only. Leucism refers to the absence of all pigments. Hence my white hair and pale skin. But if I were an albino I'd have pink eyes. Clearly, my eyes are not pink. They're dark. Eye pigmentation derives from a different source."

Faced by this barrage of biology, Markus struggled for an answer. He attempted to steer the conversation away from Dominil's unusual genetic makeup.

"Why are you standing in the snow in your underwear?"

Dominil's long white hair perfectly matched the snowflakes that were settling all over her; her skin was hardly any darker.

"To see how it affects me."

"And?"

"It has very little effect."

Markus shook his head. The whole MacRinnalch Clan already knew that cousin Dominil was an odd character, and this only served as further evidence. He felt himself starting to shiver but stopped it by an effort of will, not wanting to show weakness in front of the nine-year-old werewolf who was apparently determined to prove that she was unaffected by the elements.

"Did he send you to look for me?" asked Dominil.

"No," said Markus.

He thought he noticed the faintest trace of disappointment on Dominil's features, but it vanished immediately.

"Then why are you out here, Markus MacRinnalch?"

"To get away from the childbirth. There are so many werewolves fussing around the chamber."

Dominil nodded somberly. "Is it really going to happen tonight?"

"So they say."

"It's most unusual," said Dominil, thoughtfully. "Werewolves are hardly ever born on the full moon. Unfortunately the clan doesn't keep proper statistics."

"I don't think we need statistics," said Markus. "Everyone knows how rare it is."

MacRinnalch children were almost always born in their human form. No one could remember the last time a child had arrived when the moon was full and actually been born in a werewolf shape. According to Doctor Angus, it was going to happen tonight.

"We should keep proper statistics," insisted Dominil. "I've told Clan Secretary Rainal time and again but he never listens."

Not wishing to be sidetracked by Dominil's peculiar obsessions, Markus tried encouraging her to return to the castle.

"Everyone in the castle is waiting to see the new cub. There will be a party when she's born."

Dominil was clearly unimpressed by the prospect of a party. Markus began to feel frustrated. The MacRinnalch werewolves were famously hardy, well used to the harsh rigors of the Scottish Highlands. That didn't mean they wanted their children to stand around nearly naked in the snow.

"Wouldn't you like to see the baby when it arrives? If it's really going to be born as a werewolf, you won't see that again for a long time."

Dominil considered this. "Perhaps I should observe it," she conceded. "I'll come back to the castle after the moon's risen and I've made the change."

Tonight, on the full moon, every MacRinnalch in the castle and surrounding lands would take on their werewolf shape. It was a welcome event. The clan could always feel their health and power being boosted by the moon.

"Why not come back now?"

Dominil gave Markus another withering look, something that, for someone so young, she seemed remarkably good at.

"I need to compare my resilience before making the change to my resilience afterward."

Markus was unable to prevent himself from shivering. The snow was coming down harder and the freezing wind was gathering strength.

"What for?"

"It's part of my regime," declared Dominil. "I'm charting my results on the computer I'm constructing."

Once again, Markus experienced the uncomfortable feeling of inferiority that could only be brought on by talking to Dominil. He wearied of the conversation. If the clan wanted Dominil to get out of the freezing cold they could fetch her themselves. He nodded stiffly to his young cousin, drew his long coat around him, and departed. As he marched back to the castle, his boots made deep imprints in the new snow.

Dominil wondered briefly why Markus had been concerned. She was in no danger. Her recent experiments had demonstrated quite clearly that she could stand in the snow for hours without coming to harm. Dominil didn't enjoy the freezing cold but was prepared to put up with it, both as a means of improving her self-discipline and as an interesting scientific observation.

She waited till night fell. When the moon rose, full and low in the sky, the change came upon her swiftly. There was no notable reaction on her part. One moment she was a human girl, the next she was a white werewolf, standing on two legs in the deep snow. Dominil made a brief entry in her notebook, then remained where she was, observing the differences she could feel.

As a werewolf, I'm almost impervious to the weather, she thought. The wind and snow can't penetrate my coat at all.

The snowdrift was now several feet deep, backed up against a row of tall ash trees. Dominil sat down and looked at her fur against the snow. Both were pristine white.

"I could hide in the snow," she mused. "No one could see me."

An hour later, she made her way back to the castle. If Doctor Angus had been correct, which he normally was in werewolf matters, Verasa should have had her child by now. Dominil had many cousins and couldn't raise much enthusiasm for the birth of another, but she did have some curiosity to see the child born in its werewolf shape. She entered the castle through the small post gate beside the portcullis. The tall werewolf at the gate barely acknowledged her. Dominil had once lectured him on his gate duties, and since then he'd never liked her. He wasn't the only adult werewolf in the castle with an aversion to the girl.

Dominil had expected to find signs of celebration, but the castle seemed quiet. There were lights on in the courtyard but no sounds of revelry from the chambers above. The Scottish werewolves were capable of raucous celebrations—on Hogmanay, the party generally got out of hand—but there didn't seem to be any exuberance in the air tonight. A few werewolves emerged from one of the stone stairwells. Mostly their fur was a dark, shaggy brown, but one of the younger werewolves had a coat with a slightly redder hue. Dominil recognized her cousin Decembrius. She greeted him formally and asked if the child had been born yet.

Decembrius nodded. "We've been to see it. It's funny, a baby were-wolf. Are you going to . . . ?" His voice trailed off as Dominil lost interest in the conversation and walked on by. She climbed the stairs that led to the Mistress of the Werewolves's chambers. She passed a few other were-wolves on the way. None of them seemed particularly happy. When she reached the west wing of the castle, the outer chamber had obviously been set up for some sort of celebration. The chamber was warm, with a great log fire burning in the grate, and there were bottles of the werewolves' favorite whisky, the MacRinnalch malt, standing on the tables. Plates of venison lay half-eaten beside them. Dominil frowned. It was unlike her clan to leave a celebration before the whisky and venison were finished, particularly on the night of a full moon, when appetites were at their strongest.

She wondered if her father, Tupan, was around. There was no sign of him. Nor was there any sign of Thrix, the Mistress of the Werewolves's daughter, or Sarapen, her eldest son. Dominil carried on toward the inner chamber where she met Doctor Angus. The doctor was a renowned physi-cian, both as a human and a werewolf. The clan depended on his services, as did his human patients in Edinburgh. Angus was frowning, but he forced a smile when he saw the young white-haired werewolf.

"Hello, Dominil. Come to see the baby?"

Dominil nodded. "What's it called?"

"Kalix. It's a girl. But I'd wait a while if I were you."

"Why?" asked Dominil.

At that moment, furious yells erupted from the private chamber beyond. The Mistress of the Werewolves was shouting, and so was the Thane. Their voices were clearly audible as they insulted each other. Dominil looked at Doctor Angus.

"How long has this been going on?"

"Ever since the birth."

Dominil nodded. No wonder the celebrations had been muted. The Thane and his wife had been on bad terms for some time; the werewolves in Castle MacRinnalch had come to dread their violent arguments, and they tried to avoid them whenever possible. She made to enter the chamber. Angus put a hand out to restrain her.

"You should wait."

"I came to see the baby," she said, removing his hand. She slipped through the great wooden door into Verasa's private chamber. Inside, Verasa was sitting on the edge of her bed, half shouting and half growling at her husband. Neither werewolf took any notice of Dominil. She stared at them without expression for a second, then walked into the small room next door. Behind her the argument intensified.

The room, like Verasa's chamber, was not as warm as the rooms outside. The Mistress of the Werewolves's private chambers were large but not particularly luxurious. There was a small, old cot in the center of the room. Dominil looked in the cot and there was Kalix, a werewolf baby, tucked up under a green tartan blanket. It was indeed an unusual sight. A tiny little werewolf, only an hour old. She had thick dark fur, which made it difficult to make out her features. Dominil studied the baby objectively. She wondered, in her inquiring manner, if the unusual birth might have any long-term effects.

Dominil could still hear the thunderous argument going on in the next chamber. She looked down at the tiny werewolf, who twitched in her cot and whimpered a little.

"Welcome to the MacRinnalch Clan," she said.

CHAPTER 2

Moonglow considered organizing a surprise party for Kalix's eighteenth birthday; Daniel persuaded her against it.

"Kalix doesn't like surprises," he pointed out. "We're liable to end up with an angry werewolf looking for someone to bite."

"Kalix has never bitten us!" protested Moonglow.

"She once knocked you across the room. You know she has a violent temper."

"Her temper's not as bad these days," said Moonglow. "But I suppose you're right. The surprise might upset her. We'll give her plenty of warning so she can get used to the idea."

As far as Daniel and Moonglow could gather, Kalix had never had any sort of birthday party before.

"It's a pity her eighteenth birthday's actually on the full moon," said Moonglow. "She'll have to make the change. So we can't invite anyone who doesn't already know she's a werewolf."

"I don't think she has any other friends anyway," said Daniel.

Moonglow looked slightly troubled. "I hoped she might make a few friends at college, but she doesn't seem to want to."

"Unlike Vex," said Daniel. "She makes friends with everyone."

Agrivex, the fourth occupant of the small flat in South London, attended the same remedial college as Kalix, who had never learned to read or write properly. Since meeting Daniel and Moonglow, the young werewolf's skills had gradually improved. Vex's literacy and numeracy were not that impressive either, but she had the excuse of English not being her first language. Vex was a Fire Elemental and had been born in a different dimension.

"Does Vex have a birthday?" asked Moonglow.

Neither of them knew. All matters of dates and times seemed confusing when transferred from one dimension to another.

"So if we can't have anyone human here for the party, who can we ask?"

They wondered about it, sitting at their table in the living room. It was a small flat, and very old, built above a small shop in Kennington that had been boarded up since they'd arrived. The walls were painted a dull cream, through which the pattern of some ancient wallpaper showed, and

8

the carpet was faded brown and threadbare, much like the couch. Despite the dilapidation of the flat, it was comfortable and warm, and even cheerful, due to the assortment of pictures, ornaments, flowers and candles Moonglow had distributed around the rooms.

They waited for their tea to brew. Moonglow was fastidious about her tea-making, and regularly produced a well-set-out tray containing a teapot, black china cups, a sugar bowl and a small silver milk jug. The tea had to be left for several minutes to brew properly, and Moonglow would chide anyone who tried to pour it too quickly.

"What about Decembrius? Should we ask him?"

"I'm not sure."

"Are they still going out with each other?"

"Were they ever really going out?"

Decembrius, another member of the MacRinnalch werewolf clan, had certainly been keen on Kalix. They'd slept together on at least one occasion, as far as Moonglow knew. After that, they seemed to have spent most of their time arguing, sometimes violently.

"What about Thrix?" suggested Moonglow.

Daniel shuddered. His dark, floppy hair fell over his face, as it did when he was troubled or nervous.

"I don't like Thrix."

Moonglow didn't much like Kalix's older sister either. Thrix MacRinnalch was a very notable werewolf but not a very congenial one. Thrix, often referred to as the Enchantress, was a powerful user of magic. That was unusual for a werewolf. Her sorcery wasn't her only notable attribute. She was a successful businesswoman, running her own fashion house in London. She was also the only blonde werewolf in the clan, and vain about it. Moonglow and Daniel both thought that she could have been more helpful toward Kalix in the past. Unfortunately, Kalix and Thrix had a history of ill feeling, and relations between them were now worse than ever.

"I'm sure Kalix wouldn't want to have Thrix at her birthday party."

"Well, on the subject of hostile, unfriendly werewolves, what about Dominil?" suggested Daniel.

That did seem more promising. Daniel's description of Kalix's cousin Dominil was accurate enough—to most people, she was hostile and unfriendly—but Kalix seemed to like her, or at least respect her.

"I think she gets on reasonably well with Kalix. We should ask her. And the twins too. I'm sure they're always up for a party."

Kalix's cousins Butix and Delix, twin sister werewolves, were older than Kalix by a few years. They lived a riotous lifestyle in Camden in the north of the city, playing in their own band.

"That's probably enough," said Moonglow. "Vex, the twins and Dominil are enough to create chaos anywhere." She paused. "But it doesn't include any boys. Can you have an eighteenth birthday party without any boys?"

At that moment the door banged downstairs and they heard the sound of heavy boots on the uncarpeted stairwell that led from the street up to their flat. Vex and Kalix trudged into the room carrying heavy orange plastic bags full of shopping.

"I have totally done my bit of the quota!" yelled Vex, and seemed delighted about it.

Some months ago, the household had threatened to descend into chaos because of unpaid bills. Moonglow, offended by this, had efficiently marshaled the previously disorganized resources of Daniel, Kalix and Vex, organizing a schedule to pay off their debts. They'd all worked through the summer, stacking shelves at a local supermarket, earning enough money to ease their financial crisis. Emboldened by her success, Moonglow had then organized them into a schedule of housecleaning and shopping. Given the complete disorganization of her three flatmates, this was working surprisingly well. Though there were complaints, everyone was doing their part. The house was tidier than it had ever been, and there was at least a reasonable chance of finding milk in the fridge and soap in the bathroom.

Work at the supermarket had now come to an end, giving them the last few weeks of summer to rest and enjoy themselves before their new academic years; Daniel and Moonglow at university, Kalix and Vex at college.

"We really did that shopping!" declared Vex. "I got everything on the list. Except a few boring things. But everything else is right here!"

She gestured proudly toward the plastic carrier bags. "And I got new hair dye because we've saved so much money on the budget."

New hair dye hadn't been on the shopping list, but Moonglow let it pass. Vex's aunt, Queen Malveria, made a vital contribution to their household, providing Vex with money for food and accommodation every week. Less generous, but still important, was the contribution from Verasa MacRinnalch, Kalix's mother. Verasa transferred money for Kalix's upkeep every month into Moonglow's bank account. Life as students in

London seemed to be becoming harder and harder: without the money from Malveria and Verasa, they couldn't have kept themselves afloat.

Kalix sat down on the couch. Though the late summer had not turned cold, she wore a long overcoat that stretched down past her knees, hiding the extreme skinniness of her frame. Over the shoulders of the coat her dark hair hung down in a huge wave, abnormally long for either a human or a werewolf. The MacRinnalch women, Moonglow had observed, took good care of their hair. Both Thrix's golden curls and Dominil's icy white mane were always beautifully conditioned. Butix and Delix, or Beauty and Delicious, as they had renamed themselves, sported extremely impressive hairstyles, pink and blue respectively.

"Would you like a party for your eighteenth birthday?" asked Moonglow.

Kalix looked unsure. "Uh . . . "

"Birthday? Is it Kalix's birthday?" Vex leaped from her chair. "We have to have a party. I want a party!" Vex's dark features lit up with happiness at the prospect. "We're going to have a party!" cried Vex. "I've never had a party before!"

"It's a birthday party," explained Moonglow. "For Kalix."

Vex looked disappointed. "Isn't it my birthday too? I'm sure it must be. Aren't I turning eighteen as well?"

"I'm not sure. When is your birthday?"

"The same day as Kalix!" exclaimed Vex.

"I'm sure it's not," said Moonglow, smiling at Vex's enthusiasm.

"But I'm the same age as Kalix! Kalix, we can have a party together!"

"I don't think I want a party," said Kalix quietly. "It makes me nervous."

Moonglow nodded. She'd been expecting this. Kalix was very prone to anxiety. The prospect of anything unfamiliar always upset her.

"Well, there's plenty of time to think about it," said Moonglow. "We won't have it if you don't want it. But if you do, we could ask a few people—Dominil maybe, and the twins. It wouldn't be a big affair. Just a little celebration for you turning eighteen."

"I don't think I'd like it," said Kalix, already defensive.

"We could go to the cinema!" yelled Vex, loudly enough to make Daniel wince.

"What?"

"In the afternoon. Kalix will be a werewolf on her birthday, after the moon comes up, right? So we should go out in the day, do some shopping, then go to the movies in the afternoon. Then we can come back here and have birthday stuff. Like cakes. You have cakes on a birthday, right? I read about it in class."

Vex looked pleased with herself for remembering about cakes. Her life in her own dimension as a Fire Elemental had been very different, and she was always pleased when she learned and remembered something new about life on Earth.

"Kalix can have a big joint of raw beef; you'll like that, won't you?" Vex looked eagerly toward Kalix, expecting the prospect of a large joint of raw beef to entice her. It didn't. Though Kalix had a very hearty appetite as a werewolf, at other times she wasn't keen on eating. Kalix had a difficult relationship with food. It upset her to think about how much she ate as a werewolf. Not long ago, the distress would cause her to be violently sick the next day when she changed back to human. This didn't happen so often, but if her eating problems were less severe, they were never far away.

Vex carried on enthusiastically. "We should go and see the Runaways movie!"

Kalix looked up sharply. "What's that?"

"There's a movie about the Runaways! You love the Runaways, right? On your birthday we should go see the film about them, then come back here and eat cakes. And drink beer. Is there beer at parties? Yes? This is going to be great. I'm so looking forward to turning eighteen!"

Vex already seemed to have convinced herself that she was turning eighteen too. Moonglow wasn't certain whether to discourage the notion or not. She didn't want Kalix's birthday to be drowned out by Vex's enthusiasm for her own. On the other hand, it was possible that Vex's enthusiasm might encourage Kalix to participate. She did seem a little keener on the idea after Vex mentioned the Runaways. They were Kalix's favorite band, and had been since the days when she'd wandered the streets of London, homeless and alone, with only an old tape of the all-female band for company.

"I would like to see the film," conceded Kalix.

A pleasant aroma of jasmine filled the air. There was a muted orange flash as Queen Malveria appeared. The sudden arrival of the Fire Queen, materializing out of nowhere, had at one time been a startling occurrence for Daniel and Moonglow; over time, they'd grown used to it. She was beautifully attired as always, in a smart gray dress with matching heels and handbag. Since procuring the services of Thrix MacRinnalch as her designer and fashion adviser, Queen Malveria had secured the position of best-dressed woman in the whole Elemental dimension, a position which she guarded jealously.

"Me and Kalix are having an eighteenth birthday party!" cried Vex.

The Fire Queen raised an eyebrow and looked questioningly at Moonglow.

"Kalix's birthday is soon," explained the young student. "We were thinking of having a party. Vex wants to join in."

Malveria paused to say a polite hello to Daniel, whom she had always liked, before turning her attention to Kalix and Vex.

"I see. Well, I suppose it could be said that Vex is approaching her eighteenth birthday, in your terms."

Vex squealed with delight and leaped around, her boots making thumping noises on the threadbare carpet. Vex had a liking for the heaviest of boots, as if they might anchor her skinny frame to the earth. The Fire Queen regarded her niece with distaste. "Unless my idiotic niece will ruin everything. In that case it could also not be her birthday."

"No, I think it's good," said Daniel. "Vex and Kalix can have a party together."

"Would you like some tea?" Moonglow asked the Fire Queen. Malveria smiled. She always appreciated Moonglow's hospitality and good manners.

"Not at this moment. I am on my way to visit Thrix MacRinnalch for an important shoe meeting, and must not tarry. I merely called in to check on my niece."

"Hey," protested Vex. "I don't need to be checked up on."

"You need to be constantly checked, dismal niece. One is relieved to find the house in one piece. Which does remind me, I must cast my eye over the sorcery that encircles this dwelling."

Though the flat above the empty shop seemed unremarkable, it had the secret distinction of being protected by the magic of both the Fire Queen and the Werewolf Enchantress. Malveria had altered the dimensions of the attic, making it habitable by her niece, and placed defensive spells around the house to keep Vex and Kalix safe from prying eyes. Thrix's sorcery likewise protected them, helping to keep Kalix safe from the guild of werewolf hunters. As an added protection, Kalix wore a pendant, a gift from Malveria, which hid her from any form of sorcery, no matter where she traveled. Without it, Kalix would not have survived long in London, where the hunters were active.

The Fire Queen vanished, traveling upstairs where she examined the sorcerous protection with her experienced eye, before appearing back in the living room, apparently satisfied.

"Everything is in order. No enemy will find you here. Kalix, are you remembering to wear your pendant?"

Kalix nodded and then, thinking this might not be polite enough, said, "Yes, thank you." The young werewolf knew that without the pendant the hunters would have found her by now.

"Good." Malveria turned her eyes on her niece. "Are you now in control of your monstrous debts?"

"Yes, Aunt Malvie," said Vex.

"Do not refer to me as Aunt Malvie, dreadful niece. It makes me sound old. Have you been making ready for your next foray into college?"

"Yes, Aunt Malvie."

"Good. As you have now been here for many months, and my sorcery that surrounds this house remains stable, I believe it will be possible for you to extend your stay on this planet to five days a week."

The Queen turned to Moonglow. "I apologize if this is inconvenient."

"No, it's fine," said Moonglow.

"You are so hospitable, Moonglow. Many people would tremble at the prospect. Agrivex, do not do anything which will disgrace the Hiyasta nation, annoy your hosts or cause me to lose sleep. Life in my palace is moving along in a most satisfactory manner at this moment, and I want no interruptions."

With that the Fire Queen bade them a polite farewell, waved a well-manicured hand and dematerialized.

"I can stay here five days a week!" said Vex, and grinned. Having long ago grown bored with life in the Imperial Palace in the land of the Hiyasta Fire Elementals, Vex was much happier to be living as a student in London, even if it had brought with it the unfamiliar terrors of unpaid bills and a housework rotation.

"And we're having a birthday party! We should start planning it right now! I'll get my marker pens."

Vex ran out the room, heading for the attic. There was a brief silence.

"I'm still not really keen on this," said Kalix.

"Sorry," said Moonglow. "I wasn't expecting Vex to go mad and start hijacking your birthday. Don't worry, we'll have a nice celebration. I won't let anything spoil it."

CHAPTER 3

Queen Malveria reigned over the Hiyasta Fire Elementals. Bordering her realm was the land of the Hainusta. The two Fire Elemental nations had never been great friends. Throughout their history, there had been many territorial squabbles and occasional outbreaks of war. The last major conflict had been a long time ago, but there were still occasional flare-ups, particularly in the Western Desert, where there was an endless border dispute.

Queen Malveria's relations with Asaratanti, Empress of the Hainusta, had never been warm, but as the centuries passed they'd developed a grudging respect for each other. Their subjects were reassured that warfare was unlikely to break out between them. Recently, however, the elderly Asaratanti had passed away in her sleep. Her son and heir, Prince Esarax, had died in an accident on the very same day. Much to everyone's surprise, Princess Kabachetka acceded to the throne. Fire Elementals everywhere now wondered what the outcome might be, because it was well known that Kabachetka and Malveria hated each other.

Empress Kabachetka's palace was situated on the edge of the Eternal Volcano, the huge raging natural furnace from which the nation drew its power. There the Empress was conferring on matters of state with her new chief adviser.

"Chief Adviser Bakmer, I am not at all happy with my new hair coloring. It is a shade too dark and I specifically asked them not to do that. I am considering a mass execution."

Chief Adviser Bakmer nodded gravely. "Executing your hairdressers might not go well with the population, your majesty."

"I don't see why not. Won't the population be outraged that they got my hair wrong?"

The Empress glanced in one of the many mirrors that adorned the walls and puckered her lips. "I mean, just look at it."

Bakmer experienced the feeling of hopelessness that was rapidly becoming familiar while talking to the Empress. He swiftly concealed his thoughts. Like all the most powerful Elementals, Kabachetka was skilled in reading auras. It paid to be equally skilled in concealing them.

The Empress looked suspiciously at the papers in her chief adviser's hand. "Why are you holding that bundle of documents? You know I don't like documents."

"The ratifying of your new officials in each district requires your signature, Great Empress."

Kabachetka sighed. Since becoming Empress, she always seemed to be signing some document or other.

"Put them down somewhere. I'll sign them later. Meanwhile, kindly initiate a search for a new hairdresser. Someone who knows what 'ash blonde' means."

Chief Adviser Bakmer looked blank.

"It's a hair color," snapped Kabachetka. "One that suits me well, and will go with this season's fashions. Approach stylists in the Earthly dimension if necessary. And don't look at me like that, Bakmer. I had enough trouble with Tarentia when I brought my shoe designers here from Milan."

The unfortunate Tarentia had recently suffered disgrace and demotion after proving himself unable to satisfy Empress Kabachetka's requirements in matters of style. Her new adviser, Bakmer, knew he could easily suffer the same fate. As an ambitious Elemental he didn't intend to let that happen.

"The population would most certainly not like to see the Empress in inferior shoes," he said, very convincingly. "Particularly with several important engagements on the horizon."

The Empress smiled. She enjoyed thinking about her upcoming social engagements.

"Absolutely. When I venture out to that designers' reception in London, I'll need the very best shoes that can be obtained in any dimension. The place will be thick with glamorous women from the world of fashion. Malveria will also be there. It is time to put the rapidly aging Fire Queen in her place. Shoes and hair need to be perfect. So find me a competent hairdresser."

"I will attend to it," said her chief adviser.

"And send in Distikka."

Chief Adviser Bakmer bowed, gathered his dark-red court robe about his tall figure and walked swiftly from the throne room. Moments later, Distikka appeared. The liveried guard saluted as she entered. Empress Kabachetka eyed her critically as she approached.

"Do you really have to wear that ancient piece of chain mail at my court?" demanded Empress Kabachetka. "It is quite unbecoming."

"I like it," said Distikka. "I grew up wearing it."

"And it shows. One does not expect you to be fashionable, Distikka, but there is no need to wander around like a refugee from the Western Desert."

"I am a refugee from the Western Desert."

Distikka was below average height, and her dark hair was cut very short by the standards of the women at court.

"I am considering executing my hairdressers," said the Empress.

"That's foolish," said Distikka.

"How dare you call me foolish!" cried Kabachetka, flaring up immediately. "Show some respect for the Empress!"

Distikka shrugged, something which no one else at court would have dared to do.

"It is foolish," she repeated. "No one deserves to be executed over some trifling hairdressing error. And the citizens wouldn't like it. Do you want them to regard you as a tyrant?"

"No, but—"

"So just discharge your stylists and find some new ones. Then you won't have a problem. Is that the only reason you called me here?"

Empress Kabachetka tapped her fingers on the armrest of her ruby throne, which twinkled from the reflection of the burning torches on the walls.

"Distikka, you really must show me more respect. Had I not given you refuge after the failure of your coup against Malveria, you would now be a homeless refugee. Or dead, more probably."

"You asked me to come to your court. You asked me to be your adviser. So I'm giving you advice. But I'm not going around bowing and scraping like your other advisers and ministers do. And I'm not giving you only the advice you want to hear either."

The Empress glared at Distikka, then laughed. As a princess, Kabachetka had not successfully negotiated the hazards of life at court by being unable to adapt. In the few months that she'd been Empress, she'd come to appreciate Distikka's qualities.

"Would it really be a bad idea to execute my hairdressers?"

"Yes."

"Well, I won't do it then," said the Empress. "Though I'm sure they deserve it. Ash blonde is not that difficult to achieve, I'm certain."

The Empress leaned forward. "That, however, is not the reason I called you here. Now that the realm is more or less in order, it's time I made progress with a few other matters. You are aware, of course, of my hatred for the Scottish werewolves on Earth, in particular Thrix MacRinnalch and her miserable sister Kalix?"

Distikka nodded. The Scottish werewolves were one of Empress Kabachetka's favorite topics.

"It's time for revenge. I'm going to destroy them with a plan of quite unparalleled cunning, a plan so intricate, devious and powerful that it will eradicate forever the dreadful werewolf sisters, and hopefully their annoying clan as well."

The Empress sat back in her throne and smiled happily at the prospect.

"What is this plan?" asked Distikka.

"I've no idea," admitted the Empress. "I want you to come up with it."

"Ah."

"My best attempts to defeat these werewolves have gone wrong," said Kabachetka frankly. "I admit I may not be the best planner. But you are good at it, Distikka. Cunning plans are your forte."

Distikka frowned. "My greatest plan was a failure."

The Empress waved this away. "You almost succeeded. It was a glorious scheme to overthrow Malveria, and you got very close. Much closer than I was expecting. Had Thrix MacRinnalch not interfered yet again, you might well have killed Malveria and taken the throne for yourself."

The Empress's eyes flashed with angry golden fire at the thought of Thrix's interference. She composed herself quickly. It was not the done thing to exhibit flames at court.

"I have confidence in you, Distikka. I want you to think up some plan for revenge. I now control the Eternal Volcano, and my power is much greater than it was. In London, I have access to the guild of werewolf hunters. That ought to be enough to deal a deadly blow against the poorly dressed Thrix and the scrawny Kalix." The Empress paused. "Scrawny is perhaps a little unfair. I rather admire Kalix's slender physique. Remind me I have to step up my exercise program. I want Kalix punished. Can you do this?"

"I'm sure I can," said Distikka.

"Excellent. Now leave me, Distikka. I have a nail appointment, and I have little confidence in my nail attendants. I foresee another very unsatisfactory session."

CHAPTER 4

The Fire Queen was noticeably maudlin when she arrived at her friend Thrix's apartment. Never one to hide her emotions, she sighed loudly as she settled down on the couch.

"Are you all right?" asked Thrix.

"I am perfectly fine, my dearest friend. I have arrived here to watch the Japanese fashion show in excellent spirits."

Malveria sipped from a glass of red wine and sighed loudly again. The Enchantress smiled.

"Tell me what's wrong, Malveria."

"Really, nothing is wrong. Apart from the most trifling matter. But not a matter the Queen of the Hiyasta would trouble herself over."

Thrix gave a little shrug and settled down to watch the program. The first model was no more than halfway down the runway when the Fire Queen uttered another sigh.

The Enchantress raised an eyebrow. "Malveria, stop sighing like a love-struck teenager and tell me what's on your mind."

"Well, really, Thrix, I would not dream of mentioning it had you not dragged it out of me in such a brutal manner, but the truth is I'm feeling old."

"Old?" Thrix was very surprised. Though Malveria was many hundreds of years old—the Enchantress wasn't quite sure how many—she was still far from elderly in terms of the Hiyasta, the most vigorous of whom could carry on brightly for thousands of years. Fire Elementals took a very long time to grow dim. "What brought this on?"

"My appalling niece. Kalix has an eighteenth birthday party approaching. The foul Agrivex has plunged headlong into the affair, declaring herself to be eighteen too, which is accurate, more or less. She will now share the party."

The Fire Queen looked downcast. "Hearing them planning their eighteenth birthday made me feel very old. No doubt the party will involve much foolish behavior, and Agrivex will drink too much and make herself ill. But really, I cannot help feeling jealous."

"Jealous? Why?"

"On my eighteenth birthday, I was hiding in a cave with a price on my head. Only good fortune and the assistance of Xakthan allowed me to escape."

"But you like these memories," said Thrix. "You were facing hopeless odds and you defeated them. You became Queen."

"Eventually, yes," agreed Malveria. "But it was a long, weary process and it took up my youth. I never had an eighteenth birthday party, or any sort of party. I was always running, hiding or fighting. And now, observing Agrivex, I suddenly wished that I had had some parties when I was a young girl."

The Fire Queen sighed again. "And now I feel old."

Malveria sank further into her armchair. "Look at that young model in her beautiful dress. I could not wear that. It is too young a style."

"You could wear it perfectly, Malveria," said Thrix sincerely.

"And now the model is pouting!" cried Malveria. "It is annoying!"

"What's wrong with pouting?"

"Only young people can do it gracefully. Agrivex pouts furiously. Many days she does little else. But on me it would be unbecoming."

Thrix was quite certain she'd seen Malveria pouting many times, quite becomingly, and didn't understand her friend's gloom. Though the Fire Queen was prone to excesses of emotion, it was unusual for her to exhibit depression. She lapsed into silence in front of the television. Thrix caused the wine bottle on the table next to her to levitate, filling both their glasses, and they sat mostly in silence, only occasionally commenting on the fashions on display. From the kitchen came the faint hum of the air conditioning. Though it had been an indifferent summer in London, the clouds had cleared in the past week, ushering in an unexpected wave of heat that now hung over the capital.

"There is much talk in the elemental lands of the new young Empress of the Hainusta," said Malveria, suddenly.

"Ah . . ." said Thrix and nodded. "Kabachetka."

"Everyone is talking about her!" exclaimed the Fire Queen. "The young Empress with her blonde hair and beautiful outfits. Ha! It is the same vile Kabachetka. Just because she has ascended to the throne—no doubt after poisoning the old Empress—does not mean that people should be making a fuss over her. I cannot tell you how it irritates me!"

The Fire Queen, Thrix realized, had been considerably younger than the previous Empress. Now the younger Kabachetka had taken power and it had obviously upset her.

"You know the bards on the borders are singing songs about her youthful beauty? Youthful beauty! The only beauty Kabachetka has came out of a clinic in Los Angeles. Her mother was bad enough with her visits to the cosmetic surgeon, but at her age, one could find some excuse.

Kabachetka has been hopping through the dimensions since she was a girl, getting this tucked and that altered. I swear she'll fall apart one day, hopefully in a most painful manner."

The Fire Queen drained her glass and snapped her fingers, tilting the wine bottle over her glass. Nothing emerged.

"Is there something the matter with this bottle?" said Malveria. "It seems to have emptied far too quickly."

"I'll get another," said Thrix, and headed for the kitchen. The Fire Queen followed her.

"So between the new young Empress and my foolish young niece, I am now feeling old. A relic from a past age, like one of these pieces in the museum that Dominil is so keen on visiting. Please tell me that my outfits for new season are ready?"

"They're ready," said Thrix.

As well as a good friend, Malveria was also a very important client. Her money and patronage had kept Thrix's business going when times were hard.

"Good." The Fire Queen was partly mollified. "Perhaps there may be one last flowering of my fashionable glory before I retire into my dotage."

Thrix couldn't help herself from laughing. "'Dotage'? When did you learn that word?"

"It was used in a harsh piece in American *Vogue* concerning a designer the editor did not like. I greatly admire that editor. She is so cruel." Malveria suddenly looked troubled. "What if she were cruel to me? I do not think I could bear it."

"Malveria, why would that happen? You're always the best-dressed person in the room."

"If that's the case, why have they never included me in their 'fashionable party people' page?"

It was a long-standing ambition of the Fire Queen to appear as a "fashionable party person" in *Vogue*. Her failure to achieve this was a source of constant irritation.

"Though I have appeared at many of the most fashionable events, and practically flung myself in front of the cameras, they have so far resisted me. It is most aggravating. Am I not fashionable?"

"You're very fashionable. But there's a lot of competition. Don't worry, we've got a lot of events coming up."

Thrix used a small piece of sorcery to bring up her social calendar, which hung in the air in front of them. The Fire Queen gazed at it approvingly. Since Thrix's business picked up, she was being invited to more events.

"Soon we will attend the designer of the year awards. Such a wonderful occasion."

The Fire Queen finished another glass of wine. "I feel my gloom lifting. I must be at my most fashionable at this event. *Vogue* will take my picture, and then the new young Empress will see what it really means to be an icon of style."

CHAPTER 5

The funeral service at the abbey had been a splendid affair, reassuringly traditional and full of ceremonial flourishes. As the burial proceeded at the cemetery in Chelsea, there was general satisfaction among the assembled mourners, many of them fellow members of the aristocracy, that the Countess of Nottingham had received a fitting send-off. The late afternoon sun lent an unexpected warmth to the proceedings, and the mood among the mourners as they made their way from the grave was not overly somber. The Countess had been very elderly, in poor health for a long time, and her death had not come as a surprise.

"A nice funeral," said Mr. Carmichael on the slow walk back to the car park. "The Countess would have been pleased."

Both of his companions nodded. They had been impressed by the ceremony and the rank of many of the guests. Mr. Carmichael, chairman of the board of the Avenaris Guild, was a well-connected man. He had good reason to be at the Countess of Nottingham's funeral. She'd had an association with the werewolf hunters' guild for many years.

Mr. Carmichael nodded politely to one of the Countess's sons, himself a wealthy man in the city, who paused nearby as his wife dabbed her eyes with a tiny lace handkerchief.

"Do we have the money?" asked Mr. Eggers.

Mr. Carmichael frowned, not quite liking the tone of the question. "Show a little respect, Mr. Eggers. "We're still at the funeral."

"Sorry."

They waited patiently outside the car park as the crowd dispersed.

"But yes, we do have the money," said Mr. Carmichael softly.

The legacy from the Countess had been expected, but its size had been a surprise. The Countess of Nottingham had made donations to the Avenaris Guild for many years. She believed that her youngest son had been killed by a werewolf in Scotland, many years ago. Mr. Carmichael had never been certain that this was actually the case, but the Guild accepted the money gratefully. Now the Countess had left them a large sum, which could hardly have come at a better time. The Guild had been hit by a recent severe downturn in the markets and had seen many of its investments shrink alarmingly. There had been talk at headquarters of laying people off, and even suspending operations in some areas of the country, but now the mood had changed. Bolstered by the huge sum left them by the Countess, the Guild had plans to expand.

As the crowd thinned, Mr. Carmichael and his companions made their way to their vehicles. As a family friend, Mr. Carmichael had been invited to the post-funeral reception at the Countess's town house in Chelsea. Carmichael was a little impatient at the thought of this. He had a hankering to be getting on with business. It wasn't only financially that the Guild had suffered recently. The MacRinnalch werewolves, their eternal enemies, had bested them again. The Guild had lost some good hunters. Mr. Carmichael had come under pressure. His position as head of the Guild was again being questioned. Strong action was necessary, and with the arrival of the Countess's money, action could now be taken.

"I'll be back later in the evening," Mr. Carmichael told Mr. Eggers. "Make sure you have the final list drawn up by then. I want the new hunters in as soon as possible."

Mr. Eggers nodded. Although he would have been rather pleased to have been asked to the reception, he was as keen as Mr. Carmichael to press on with their mission. The werewolves may have scored some successes against them in recent months, but that was soon going to change.

CHAPTER 6

Kalix wasn't sure what to think about her upcoming birthday party. Left to herself, she'd have ignored the occasion. She hadn't celebrated her birthday since leaving the castle, and those celebrations she remembered from her childhood weren't especially happy. The idea of having a party made her nervous. The flat would be full of people. She wondered if she might have to make a speech, or entertain them somehow, something she knew she was incapable of doing.

Moonglow assured her that she wouldn't have to make a speech, or do anything special at all, but Kalix still felt uncomfortable. She didn't like being the focus of attention. Kalix's chronic anxiety made her pessimistic. She had a fear of everything going wrong, and of being blamed for it. Kalix felt a brief surge of anger and briefly contemplated moving away from this house full of humans who gave her problems. She controlled the anger, with an effort, allowing it to fade, knowing that after it was gone she'd be able to look at things more rationally.

"I suppose it's nice of them to want to do something for me," she muttered.

Vex was bursting with excitement about their joint birthday. The young Fire Elemental had used her highlighting pens to mark off all the days on the calendar in the kitchen, putting huge crosses over every day that passed, and smiley faces on the days still to come, despite Moonglow's protests that Vex's marks covered up everything else on the calendar. Moonglow didn't want Vex's enthusiasm to overshadow Kalix's part in the proceedings, but Kalix was grateful for it. It took the pressure off her. If Vex wanted to make a lot of noise and be the center of attention, Kalix didn't mind.

She took her journal from the locked box in her bedside cabinet. She'd bought the small container for her journal after realizing that nothing was safe from the prying eyes of Vex, who seemed not to understand the concept of privacy. All of Kalix's deepest thoughts were contained in her journal and she refused to let anyone else read them. She carefully locked her bedroom door before opening the book and looking at her most recent entries. After a year at remedial college, her writing was still poor, but a little more legible.

Werewolf Improvement Plan. She frowned and wondered if that was a stupid title. The young werewolf glanced at the door, as if fearing that someone might be spying on her.

It had occurred to Kalix quite recently that perhaps, as she was often unhappy, she could do something to make her life better. The idea had come to her after she'd decided not to accept money from Dominil. Dominil had made an agreement with Thane Markus whereby he secretly paid her for any werewolf hunters she killed. She'd offered part of that money to Kalix. Kalix decided she didn't want to accept it. She felt no guilt over killing werewolf hunters, but she didn't feel comfortable being paid for it. This decision led Kalix on to a lot of unexpected thinking. If she'd made an important decision about something like that, perhaps she could make other difficult decisions too. Perhaps she could change other things in her life that bothered her. She was familiar with the notion of deliberately modifying her behavior, thanks to her time in therapy. She'd never felt that her therapist had helped her in the past, but she was stronger now. She might be able to help herself.

Kalix looked at the list she'd made under the heading of *Werewolf Improvement Plan.*

- be less violent
- be independent
- stop taking laudanum
- get on better with people
- stop being anxious
- stop being depressed
- stop cutting myself
- eat better
- don't throw up
- improve reading and writing and math

"I could make these things better. Some of them anyway."

Kalix wondered if she should include something about relationships. She'd been seeing Decembrius but it wasn't going well. Decembrius had strong feelings for Kalix, and she liked him in a way, but they never quite seemed to gel. Their encounters always ended in arguments, and sometimes in fights.

I'll leave that off the list for now, thought Kalix. After all, everyone has problems with relationships. Look at Daniel and Moonglow.

Kalix focused on the first entry on her list. Be less violent. Her short life had been full of violence. She'd killed werewolf hunters, many of them. She'd killed werewolves too, members of her clan who'd pursued her. Moonglow and Daniel knew some of her history, but Kalix wondered how they'd react if they really knew the levels of violence she'd been involved in. Would Moonglow be quite so keen to give her an eighteenth birthday party if she'd ever witnessed her ripping a fellow werewolf to pieces? Or killing three hunters in the space of a few seconds? Kalix's ferocity in battle was legendary in the MacRinnalch Clan. Once attacked, she lost control of herself. Her battle madness descended on her and nothing could stop her. She'd torn apart werewolves much larger and stronger than herself. Her speed and power were abnormal, even by the standards of her fellow werewolves. The madness in battle was just part of her general insanity, according to her detractors. Dominil thought it was more to do with her unusual birth at the full moon, and Dominil was a very clever werewolf.

Kalix wondered if she might be able to avoid violence for a while. Dominil didn't think that Kalix would suffer any more pursuit from the MacRinnalchs. Those members of the clan who still hated her had finally been brought into line by Markus and the Mistress of the Werewolves. While there were still many werewolves who still believed she should be brought to justice for her part in the death of the old Thane, the past was to lie quietly for a while.

That left the werewolf hunters. Here too, Kalix had some reason for optimism. Some months ago, the Avenaris Guild had sent hunters all the way up to Scotland. Kalix had defeated them. Others in the clan fell victim to the sorcery of their enemies, but Kalix had resisted it and killed the attackers. It had been a severe blow to the Guild. Dominil, who apparently was able to spy on them, had reported that they were quiet these days.

So maybe I can stay out of fights for a while, thought Kalix.

There was a violent crash as Vex attempted to burst into the room without considering that the door might be locked. Kalix hurriedly hid her journal.

"Hey, Kalix, let me in!" shouted Vex.

"Go away," shouted Kalix.

"Did you know your door's locked?"

"Yes. And don't you dare teleport in here!" yelled Kalix.

"OK, I'll just teleport in," shouted Vex.

Seconds later, Vex materialized in Kalix's room, looking pleased with herself.

"I am getting so good at this traveling through space stuff," she said. "Did you know your door was locked?"

"Of course I knew my door was locked! I was trying to keep people out."

"Really? Can I help?"

Kalix sighed.

"Our party is going to be the best thing ever," cried the young Fire Elemental. "I'm so excited! Do you think Yum Yum Sugary Snacks could play in the living room?"

Yum Yum Sugary Snacks, fronted by Kalix's werewolf cousins Beauty and Delicious, were Vex's favorite band.

"It would be great! We could get up onstage and dance with them!"

"I'd hate that!" said Kalix. "And where would the stage be anyway—in the living room?"

Vex looked puzzled. "I hadn't thought of that. Maybe we could dance on the couch?"

She grinned eagerly. Kalix found herself smiling, though she hadn't meant to. Vex's enthusiasm tended to be infectious. It was hard to remain completely uninvolved once Vex developed a passion for anything.

"It's going to be the full moon. Beauty and Delicious will be werewolves too. I don't think they can play guitar when they're werewolves."

The MacRinnalch werewolves were able to change into their wolf form any night if they chose, but on the three nights around the full moon, they all transformed automatically.

"Oh." Vex looked disappointed. "That might be a problem. These big werewolf claws are a bit clumsy. No offense, you can't help having big clumsy claws. We'll just have to make do with CDs. Daniel is showing me how to make a playlist!"

Vex shook her head, dancing to an imaginary playlist. Recently she'd been letting her hair grow, and the bleached spikes that once stood vertically in the air now enveloped her head in a jagged sphere. She wore one of her many Hello Kitty T-shirts and a small red kilt. Unusually, she was barefooted, having been discouraged by Moonglow from jumping around the house in her large boots.

"And we're going to the movies! I love the movies!"

Vex's suggestion about the Runaways film had been generally approved. Moonglow had already booked their tickets. Kalix was looking forward to seeing the film and felt more enthusiasm for this than any other part of the birthday celebration. There had been times in Kalix's lonely past when her two tapes of the band were all she had for company. She still loved the Runaways. When she'd learned that the band had never been all that successful, she'd felt quite angry about it and taken it as proof of the world's stupidity. According to Daniel, who was obsessively knowledgeable about music, the film was part of a process that had seen the band's reputation grow since their demise in 1980.

Why did people not like them till now? she wondered.

Vex jumped onto Kalix's bed. "I can't wait till our birthday! I've never been so excited! I'm the most excited a person can be! Unless there was some exciting news about *Tokyo Top Pop Boom Boom Girl*! Then I'd be even more excited!"

Tokyo Top Pop Boom Boom Girl was Vex's favorite Japanese cartoon. She was a fanatical devotee.

"I don't think you could take any more excitement," said Kalix.

Daniel put his head through the open door. "Hey, Vex, did you know there's a new spin-off from *Tokyo Top Pop Boom Boom Girl*?"

Vex gasped, and then fell over. She lay on the floor, panting.

"Now you've got her overexcited," said Kalix, helping her back onto the bed. It took a few minutes before Vex could speak again.

"What's the spin-off?" she asked.

"Tokyo Top Pop Boom Boom Girl has a sister—Nagasaki Night Fight Boom Boom Girl. She's getting her own series."

Vex squawked loudly, and fell on the bed in a faint again. Kalix looked at Daniel.

"You have to stop doing this."

"But I thought she'd want to know."

Moonglow appeared in the room. "What's all the noise?"

"Vex is overexcited because Daniel told her about a new *Boom Boom Girl* cartoon," explained Kalix.

"Daniel, you need to be more careful. Look, Vex's fingers are starting to glow."

The Fire Elementals were in complete control of the element of fire. Apart from Vex, who wasn't very good at it. She revived again, and grinned.

"I never knew Tokyo Top Boom Boom Girl had a sister. Did you know?"

"I think the sister just came along because the original is popular," said Daniel. "They wanted to make a spin-off."

"When does it start?"

"Next week," said Daniel.

Vex fell over in a faint for the third time. Kalix, Moonglow and Daniel looked at her prone figure, as did the cat, who chose this moment to wander into the room.

"If you have any more Japanese anime news, break it to her gently," suggested Moonglow. "Otherwise she'll never be conscious again."

Daniel nodded. "Lucky I never showed her the pictures."

"I want to see the pictures," came Vex's voice, faint but still excited.

CHAPTER 7

Mr. Carmichael sat alone at the table that dominated his office, an elegant piece from the Georgian era. There was a smaller table, also Georgian, in the corner of the room, and four antique chairs, all of which gave his office the appearance of a room which contained too much furniture. It was a common feature of the Guild's headquarters. The Avenaris Guild had been in existence for a very long time, and its headquarters was filled with old and valuable antiques, mostly Queen Anne and Georgian, with a few pieces from the Regency. Though the mahogany and walnut chairs, tables and cabinets now existed alongside computers and filing cabinets, the abundance of antique furniture still gave the offices an air of antiquity and opulence, and a slight aura of gloom.

If the Guild's furnishings were old, the Guild had finally brought its security into line with modern practices. The London headquarters of the Avenaris Guild was extremely well hidden. Mr. Carmichael had recently used some of the Guild's new wealth to boost its defenses, and the board was now confident that its headquarters could not be discovered, by magic, cyber-espionage or any other means.

It was disturbing, therefore, to look up and find a woman he didn't recognize sitting in the chair opposite him, apparently flickering in and out of existence. As the woman came into focus, she frowned.

"Odd," she said. "I can't seem to materialize properly."

Mr. Carmichael frowned in turn. "You shouldn't be able to materialize at all."

The woman became solid for a few seconds. She was still frowning. "Empress Kabachetka believed she could send me straight here."

"Ah." Carmichael nodded. "Kabachetka. That explains how you knew our location."

Kabachetka was an ally of sorts. She'd lent assistance to the Guild's hunters in the past, notably Captain Easterly. Not that the affair had ended well: Easterly was dead and sorely missed.

"Turn off your defenses and allow me to materialize properly," said the woman.

Mr. Carmichael shook his head. "I can't. It's a permanent feature. If you redirect your teleportation to the front door, I'll let security let you in. Who are you, by the way?"

"Distikka. Emissary from the Empress. Kabachetka sends greetings and wonders if her greatly increased power might help you destroy the MacRinnalchs."

The woman slipped out of existence again, and this time she didn't reappear. After a few moments, Mr. Carmichael's intercom buzzed, and security at the front of the building informed him there was a woman outside, asking to see him.

"Send her up," replied Mr. Carmichael. He was interested to hear what Distikka had to say. Since the money from the late Countess of Nottingham had been transferred into the Guild's bank accounts, Mr. Carmichael had had the feeling that things were finally turning in his favor. Only a few weeks ago, he'd wondered how the Guild was ever going to make progress against the werewolves. Now, plans were being made. There was a list of possible targets. Top of the list was Kalix MacRinnalch. Information on important werewolves was hard to come by, but the Guild knew quite a lot about Kalix. They'd encountered her several times and knew all about her savagery. They also knew she was an outcast, living in London, far from the support of her Scottish clan. Mr. Carmichael had developed a particular obsession with Kalix. She was an important werewolf: daughter of the old Thane and sister to the new one. She was strongly suspected of killing Captain Easterly, and possibly Albermarle as well. Not only that, she'd killed hunters here in London, right under the noses of the Guild. Kalix was a werewolf who had to be eliminated.

Despite the information the Guild held on Kalix, there was no clue as to where she might live. The Guild had been unable to track her down. For some reason, she was extremely difficult to find. It was partly for this reason that Mr. Carmichael had come under pressure. His failure to deal with her had not gone down well with the rest of the board.

Perhaps she won't be so hard to find with Kabachetka's help, thought the chairman.

Distikka arrived in his office in the company of two security guards. Mr. Carmichael greeted her and dismissed the guards. He was surprised at Distikka's appearance. It was unusual to meet a person wearing chain mail these days, though for all he knew it might be normal among the Fire Elementals.

"That was inconvenient," said Distikka brusquely. "Though it's no bad thing your defenses are working well."

Distikka leaned over the desk. She was a small woman, with a dark brown complexion, short dark hair and an air of intense concentration.

"There are werewolves in London that the Empress would like to see dead. Notably Thrix and Kalix MacRinnalch."

Distikka's voice was a little deeper than might have been expected from her small frame. Her accent was quite pronounced, though Mr. Carmichael couldn't have made a guess as to its origin.

"Kalix MacRinnalch is a target of ours," said Mr. Carmichael. "But I'm not certain of the other. Thrix, did you say?"

Distikka nodded. "Kalix's sister. A werewolf who uses sorcery and hides herself so successfully that you've already forgotten it was her who ensnared the hunter Easterly, leading to his death. She too must be killed."

CHAPTER 8

Kalix experienced a burst of optimism on the evening before her birthday. She was looking forward to seeing the Runaways film. Unusually, her excitement did not turn into anxiety. When Moonglow asked her if she wanted to invite Decembrius, she agreed.

"Then that will be Decembrius and Beauty and Delicious, and maybe Dominil," said Moonglow.

"Maybe?"

"I asked the twins to invite her," explained Moonglow. "But they said she wouldn't commit herself."

Kalix was disappointed. She liked Dominil, even if the white-haired werewolf was rather foreboding. Moonglow suggested that Kalix might call her herself, but Kalix demurred. It would be embarrassing if Dominil refused the invitation. Kalix had encountered a lot of rejection in her life and never voluntarily put herself in a position where it might happen again.

Daniel had agreed to drive them to the cinema where Moonglow had already booked seats. They were due to meet Beauty and Delicious, and if all went according to plan they'd be back home before darkness came, triggering the change into werewolves. It struck Moonglow that they were about to spend an evening with four werewolves in their house. Five if Dominil showed up.

"I hope nothing goes wrong," she said to Daniel.

"It'll be fine," said Daniel. "We've met them all before."

"But not all at once, as werewolves."

"Well, they all seem quite well in control of themselves. Apart from the twins, I suppose, when they drink too much. And Kalix can get a little agitated. But apart from the intoxicated twins and Kalix maybe going mad, we've got nothing to worry about."

"At least Dominil never goes mad," said Moonglow reassuringly. "She's always . . . uh . . . "

"Unfriendly? Violent? Murderous?"

"Maybe I was so keen to give Kalix a nice birthday I didn't think this through properly. Is the fridge full of meat?"

"Absolutely packed," said Daniel, who had responsibility for meat buying in the household, Moonglow being a vegetarian. "Enough for plenty of hungry werewolves. That's a nice dress, you're looking pretty."

Moonglow was surprised by the compliment, and pleased. Daniel had always been attracted to Moonglow and seemed recently to have been trying to win her over by way of compliments and helpful behavior. Which, Moonglow admitted to herself, was an improvement on his previous campaign of bad moods and displays of temper.

The next day there was an unusual amount of activity in the small flat as the four flatmates prepared themselves. Moonglow felt that she should make an effort, and she spent a long time in the morning drying and styling her long black hair and selecting a long black dress from her wardrobe. She put on a pair of high-heeled boots which, while not as pointed as the ones she wore on her occasional visits to Goth nightclubs, were still fancier than she'd normally wear out in daylight. She spent some time on her makeup and was looking very dramatic as she applied the finishing touches to her darkened lips.

Downstairs, Daniel was in conversation with Vex. "It's time I was going out with Moonglow. I'm going to make it happen today."

Daniel looked expectantly at Vex.

"Do you think this purple Hello Kitty T-shirt goes with this red kilt?" she asked.

Daniel pursed his lips. "No, it looks awful. But that's beside the point. Moonglow should go out with me, don't you agree?" He spread his arms wide, inviting the whole universe to agree with him. "It would have happened before now if we hadn't had all these distractions. But every time we got close there was some werewolf crisis and everything went wrong." Daniel looked pained. "And if it wasn't a werewolf it was someone from another dimension—"

"I'm someone from another dimension!" said Vex brightly.

"—butting in with some weird problem or a fashion crisis or something like that. Who could do any pursuing with all that going on? My failure with Moonglow has mitigating circumstances."

Vex took a bright red lipstick from her Hello Kitty bag and busied herself at the mirror. Her lips were already a brilliant red, but she liked to put on extra layers. Daniel, now in good voice, carried on.

"And then we've been working in that horrible supermarket all summer and I was so tired when I got home I couldn't do anything except lie on the couch."

Vex paused momentarily to nod in agreement. They'd all found it hard, working in the supermarket. For much of the summer, the commonest sight to be seen in their flat was Daniel, Vex, Kalix and Moonglow all strewn around the living room, tired out after their long day's work.

"It's time for it to end."

Vex looked around. Her lips were deep red. "What's coming to an end?"

"Moonglow not going out with me."

"Are you going to grab her in the cinema?"

"Possibly."

Vex burst out laughing, which deflated Daniel.

"What's funny?"

"The idea of you grabbing Moonglow."

"Just wait and see."

Vex grinned. She'd have been quite happy to see Daniel going out with Moonglow, but she didn't anticipate it happening anytime soon. The conversation ended as Moonglow came down the stairs.

Vex greeted her enthusiastically. "Hi, Moonglow you're looking nice. Look at my kilt. I'm wearing tartan in honor of Kalix's birthday. Because she's Scottish. They like tartan."

Moonglow smiled, admiring Vex's choice. Vex's kilt was tiny, displaying her slender legs from thigh to knee, beneath which they disappeared into her customary large boots, giving her the look of a character from one of her favorite Japanese cartoons.

"Do you think I might meet a boyfriend at the party?" said Vex.

Moonglow frowned. Moonglow had no objection to Vex having a boyfriend, but she didn't quite approve of the way Vex had been fixating on it recently. The young Elemental seemed to have developed the notion that she was somehow lacking without a boyfriend, a notion that

Moonglow was sure she'd picked up from the enormous amount of manga she read online.

"Just because girls in comics want boyfriends doesn't mean you need to have one," she'd told Vex. Vex hadn't paid any attention.

Daniel had brushed his hair and put on the new jacket selected for him by Moonglow a few months ago.

"Everyone ready for the cinema?" said Moonglow. "Where's our birthday girl?"

"I'm right here!" cried Vex and began hopping up and down.

"Right. I meant our other birthday girl. The werewolf."

"I'm here," said Kalix, appearing from her room upstairs. Kalix was smiling excitedly. She'd brushed her very long hair, and it shone as it streamed down past her shoulders, in contrast with her dull gray coat. As always, Kalix's outfit contrasted strongly with the bright and colorful Vex. The young werewolf was averse to wearing anything colorful. Beneath her coat she wore a pair of jeans that had faded to a neutral gray, bought from the local charity shop. She had a new Runaways T-shirt, a birthday present from Daniel and Moonglow. They knew that Kalix would only wear the T-shirt if it were either black or white, so they'd picked white, with the band's figures outlined in black. Kalix was very happy with the T-shirt.

"Everybody ready?" asked Moonglow.

"Wait!" cried Kalix. "I forgot my keys." Kalix hurried back up the stairs.

"I forgot my keys too," said Daniel. He headed back toward his room.

"Did I forget anything?" asked Vex.

"I don't know," replied Moonglow. "Did you?"

"I better check," said Vex, and rushed upstairs.

Moonglow was left on her own in the living room. Kalix was the first to reappear.

"I got my keys." She paused. "But I forgot my money."

Kalix bounded back up the stairs. Moonglow pursed her lips. It could be a difficult task getting everyone out of the house.

Daniel appeared. "Got my keys," he said.

"Did you bring your wallet?"

Daniel felt in his pockets. "I'll be right back," he said, and hurried off.

How did I become everyone's mother? thought Moonglow. I'm too young to be in charge of three idiots.

★

Beauty and Delicious were surprised at how easily Dominil had been persuaded to attend Kalix's birthday party. They'd assumed she'd refuse and had been preparing to assail her with a long string of reasons as to why she should attend. Kalix was a fellow werewolf, she was Dominil's cousin, and she had on one occasion saved Dominil's life. Besides, as Beauty pointed out, Dominil lived the most boring life imaginable, visiting art galleries and translating Latin poetry. It would do her good to let her hair down.

"Although her hair is pretty much straight down already," said Delicious.

"True. But it is a bit weird, being so white. She should let us dye it."

Beauty's hair was bright pink and Delicious's a vivid blue. The twins devoted a lot of time and energy to hair maintenance. It was worth the effort. Even in Camden, where brightly colored coiffures were common, the magnificence of the sisters' brightly colored tresses could still attract attention as they sauntered down the pavement. Their visits to a salon in Knightsbridge were expensive, but they could afford it. Their parents had died in an accident, making Beauty and Delicious wealthy at a young age. They'd wasted no time in decamping to London to engage in a riotous lifestyle. The rest of the clan didn't approve, but Beauty and Delicious didn't care what the rest of the clan thought.

"So why is Dominil coming to Kalix's party?"

It was puzzling. Even though Dominil had been acting as manager of the twins' band, she'd resolutely refused to join in with their lifestyle. Dominil would never visit pubs or clubs. But now she'd agreed to travel south of the river to Kalix's birthday party, and she hadn't even complained about it.

"Dominil likes Kalix, I suppose," said Delicious. "More than us, anyway."

"True. Though I wouldn't have thought she liked her enough to put up with a lot of drunken werewolves."

"What drunken werewolves?"

"Us. Dominil has this weird thing about not liking drunken werewolves. It's a flaw in her character."

"Maybe she's looking for a man?"

The twins roared with laughter. The twins amused themselves with the continual fantasy that Dominil was desperate to find a boyfriend. There was no reason to believe this was true, though Dominil had been

35

known to engage with the opposite sex. She'd once spent the night with Pete, their guitarist. Dominil had initiated this, and ended the relationship immediately afterward. Pete had never gotten over it. He still longed for Dominil, though she'd shown no interest in continuing the relationship.

The phone in the living room rang.

"I'm outside," said Dominil.

The twins rushed out to Dominil's car, clutching their bags. It was mid-afternoon and they were due to meet the others at the Odeon Cinema in Marble Arch. The twins weren't particularly keen on the Runaways, but they were willing to watch any film about a rock band.

"I hope there's lots of drugs and stuff," said Beauty. "And alcohol."

"And sex," said Delicious. "At the same time. Hi, Dominil, looking forward to the movie?"

"Not really," said Dominil, and pulled carefully away from the curb.

"Is there any chance you could not drive like a nervous eighty-year-old?" asked Beauty as Dominil carefully negotiated the turn into the main road in Camden. Her cautious driving was another target of the twins' mockery.

"Did the Mistress of the Werewolves call you?" said Delicious.

"Yes," replied Dominil. "Why do you ask?"

"We wondered if she nagged you into going to the party, to check up on Kalix."

Dominil halted at a traffic light at Mornington Crescent. She turned to stare at Delicious.

"I assume that you called the Mistress of the Werewolves yourself, to ask her to pressurize me into attending?"

"We may have," said Delicious.

Dominil scowled. The twins knew that Verasa MacRinnalch, Kalix's mother, held Dominil in high regard. They also knew that Verasa worried about her errant daughter, far away in London. Asking her to persuade Dominil to attend the party had been their idea of a cunning plan.

"There was no need," said Dominil. "I had already accepted the invitation."

"But why? You're so antisocial. Beauty, isn't Dominil antisocial?"

"The most antisocial werewolf in the clan," agreed Beauty. "I think she holds some sort of record."

Dominil's lips compressed slightly, but she didn't engage with the twins. It would be a waste of time. When Beauty and Delicious were excited, as they were now, there was no way of preventing them from talking nonsense. Since taking on the task of managing their band, Dominil had learned to ignore it. She followed the one-way system through Camden before taking the main road toward Oxford Street, bringing them to a large underground car park close to the cinema.

"Wouldn't it be funny if the car broke down?" said Delicious as they emerged into the street above.

"Why would it be funny?" asked Dominil.

"Because we're all going to turn into werewolves in a few hours, of course. We'd be werewolves in the middle of town. Owwooo!"

"It would not be funny at all," said Dominil sternly. "And the car won't break down. I had it serviced recently."

"Owwooo!" Beauty joined in with her sister, imagining themselves already to be werewolves. Passersby looked at the girls and smiled. It was odd behavior, howling in the street for no apparent reason, but given the brightness of the sisters' hair and clothes, it didn't seem out of character. Students, they imagined. Or perhaps some sort of alternative models, with their pink, blue and snow-white hair.

"Kalix and her friends are in the foyer," said Dominil. "Now stop howling and start behaving. I'm expecting this film to be tedious enough without having to listen to you making fools of yourselves all the way through."

CHAPTER 9

Sarapen MacRinnalch stood on the roof of the great palace, gazing at the lava that poured down the eastern slopes of the Eternal Volcano. Flames crackled above the molten rock and the air shimmered. The first time Sarapen had seen the approaching lava he'd felt a mild sense of alarm; it seemed that the palace would soon be overwhelmed and swamped by the molten liquid. He was used to it now. The Royal Palace of the Hainusta was connected to the volcano, existing with it in some sort of symbiotic relationship. Rather than causing harm, the fiery outpouring of the volcano gave power to the Empress and her people.

Sarapen knew that he shouldn't be able to stand so close to the boiling lava. The heat should have driven him back. He hardly felt it. Empress Kabachetka had worked spells on him, enabling him to exist in her land.

Since taking control of the volcano, Kabachetka's power had greatly increased. Here in her own land there seemed to be little she couldn't do. She could enable a werewolf to exist alongside the Fire Elementals. She could cause a werewolf to live when he should have died. Sarapen's fingers touched his chest, something he did quite often these days, unconsciously. Beneath his shirt there was a terrible scar. Even the Empress's healing powers couldn't get rid of that. But she had prevented him from dying, though the Begravar knife that had pierced his chest should have been lethal. No werewolf could survive such a strike. The weapon had been designed specially to confuse and kill any shape-shifting creature. It was always lethal against werewolves. It was also forbidden. No werewolf would use it against a fellow member of the clan.

"Apart from Kalix, of course," murmured Sarapen. "She had no hesitation about thrusting it into my chest."

The huge werewolf smiled. He despised his sister Kalix, but somehow he didn't hold it against her that she'd stabbed him with the Begravar knife. At the time, he'd been trying to kill her. Most probably he'd have used the knife on Kalix if he could. Clan traditions were important, but the most important thing about a war was to win it, and Kalix had done that.

"I'll pay her back one day," he muttered.

Sarapen was the eldest son of the old Thane. He was the strongest werewolf in the MacRinnalch clan. He should have been elected as leader when his father died. His mother had seen to it that he hadn't been. Thanks to Verasa, his brother Markus was the new Thane. His mother, his brother and both his sisters had all conspired against him.

"But I'm still alive," mused Sarapen. "That would surprise them. Alive and stuck in an alien dimension. That surprises me."

He heard a soft footstep behind him. Only the Empress had access to this part of the roof. She approached him from behind and put a hand on his shoulder. Sarapen didn't turn around.

"I still want to go back," said Sarapen.

There was a moment's silence. When the young Empress spoke there was a note of frustration in her voice. "I can't send you back yet. The after-effects of the Begravar knife will kill you if you return to Earth."

Sarapen remained silent, staring out over the streams of lava.

"Why go back anyway?" said Kabachetka. "What's in Scotland for you? A clan that betrayed you? Werewolves who don't appreciate you?"

"I should be Thane," said Sarapen.

"So what? How would that compare to staying in a palace with an

Empress?" Kabachetka edged her way to his side, placing her arm around his frame. "I know you miss your home. I'll be able to send you back sometime. My sorcerers are working on it. Meanwhile . . . "

The Empress stood on her tiptoes to kiss Sarapen, embracing him as she did. She liked to put her arms around Sarapen. His muscles felt like steel beneath his garments.

Sarapen kissed her back, not as passionately as the Empress would have liked. She withdrew her lips and gazed into his eyes.

"Your mind is elsewhere."

Sarapen nodded.

"Are you thinking about your clan?"

"You said you'd bring me news."

The Empress sighed. "I really have little business on Earth these days. It's difficult for me to bring news."

Sarapen nodded. He didn't know whether to believe the Empress or not. She always sounded sincere, but the werewolf found it hard to believe she knew nothing of his relations back on Earth. He turned to gaze out over the red rock landscape that fell away in a long slope beyond the volcano.

"Now you're thinking about going to fight in the desert!" exclaimed the Empress, and sounded cross.

"I thought you weren't going to read my aura," said Sarapen.

"I am not reading your aura. I never learned to read werewolf auras. It's perfectly obvious you want to go and fight in the desert. Or anywhere away from me, I suppose."

Sarapen didn't reply. There was a long-standing conflict between the Hainusta and the Hiyasta in the Western Desert. Sarapen was tired of the palace, and having no other prospect that pleased him, he'd asked the Empress to send him to the fighting. The Empress had so far demurred.

"I can't understand why you'd want to go and fight anyway. I have a beautiful palace and beautiful lands. And I'm beautiful too."

Sarapen looked at her. He nodded. "You are. But I don't belong in this palace."

For a brief second it seemed as if the Empress might flare up in anger. Instead, she laughed and put her arm around him again.

"You'll change your mind, Sarapen. I'm a much better prospect than fighting in the desert. Or a gloomy castle full of werewolves."

CHAPTER 10

Dominil's calm exterior showed signs of fraying as the twins prevaricated at the refreshment stand.

"I can't make up my mind," said Beauty.

"Me neither," said her sister.

"Maybe we should just buy everything?"

"I want everything too!" cried Vex, who had a very sweet tooth.

"Do you want anything, Kalix?" asked Daniel, raising his voice to compete with Vex and the twins.

Kalix shook her head.

"A hot dog? Maybe they could give you a raw one?"

Kalix looked outraged, and turned to Moonglow. "Tell Daniel to stop making jokes about me eating raw hot dogs!"

"Daniel, stop making jokes about Kalix eating raw hot dogs."

Moonglow and Dominil looked at the squabbling mass in front of the confectionery stall. Moonglow sighed.

"It's like taking children to the pictures."

"Indeed," agreed Dominil. "I'm not sure how I ended up in this position."

"I know!" said Moonglow. "That's just how I feel. How did I end up being the mother?"

Dominil and Moonglow shared a brief moment of empathy before shepherding their charges into the cinema. Fortunately for their state of mind, the cinema was quiet for the afternoon showing, and there were few people there to witness the loud behavior of their party. They trooped through the corridor, looking for the correct screen in the large cinema complex.

"Does everyone have their tickets?" asked Moonglow.

"I've lost mine," said Vex.

"How do you know? You didn't even check."

"I just assumed," said Vex, and started fumbling in her pocket. "Oh, here it is!" She brandished her ticket triumphantly.

"I've lost my ticket," said Daniel.

Moonglow scowled at him. "Stop making jokes."

"I'm not joking. I really have lost it."

Daniel started searching through all his pockets.

"How could you lose it?" asked Moonglow. "The ticket office is only twenty yards away."

Daniel looked around. "Maybe it dropped out of my pocket? Oh wait, here it is! I forgot I had a pocket there. It's this new jacket, I'm not used to it."

"Is everybody ready now?" asked Dominil.

"I've lost my ticket," said Beauty.

"So have I," added Delicious.

"You never had your tickets," said Dominil. "I have them."

They showed their tickets to the young woman at the door and entered the cinema.

"The previews are on already," said Beauty, as they walked down the aisle.

"Previews!" cried Vex. "I love previews!"

Vex had never been to the cinema before, so how she could love previews was a mystery. Moonglow and Dominil guided everyone to a row in the middle of the cinema. Before taking their seats, Vex looked around, and waved to some people in the next row.

"It's my birthday," she shouted. She pointed to Kalix. "It's her birthday too."

"Stop embarrassing me," hissed Kalix.

Vex waved cheerfully to several other people before taking her seat. After a few moments she turned to Kalix. "Is this the film now?"

"No, it's an advert."

"I hate adverts," said Vex.

There was a brief commotion as Beauty dropped a large bucket of popcorn on the floor and then scrambled to retrieve it. Delicious collapsed with laughter at the sight, and Beauty started laughing too, still scrambling on the floor. Moonglow had never seen Dominil look embarrassed before, but as she looked along the row, she thought that the white-haired werewolf might just have sunk a little further down in her seat, trapped as she was with the twins, in a public place, while they made an exhibition of themselves.

"Shove over, Daniel," said Vex. "Stop hogging the armrest."

"I'm not hogging the armrest!" protested Daniel. "I was here first."

"Moonglow, Daniel's hogging the armrest!"

"No, I'm not!"

Daniel was in no mood to give in to Vex. He'd already had to struggle with her to ensure that he sat next to Moonglow. For a few moments Daniel's plans had hung in the balance, but he'd finally managed to maneuver Moonglow to the outside of their group, with him next in line. He could easily put his arm around her without anyone else noticing.

Vex stared at the figures on screen. "Is this the Runaways?" she asked, loudly.

"Of course it's not the Runaways, it's an advert for potato chips!" said Kalix.

"Oh . . . will the Runaways be here soon?"

"Yes."

"Will they be in the next advert?"

"No."

"Don't they get to be in any adverts?" asked Vex.

"Why would they be in the adverts?"

"To advertise their film? Can't they do that?"

"The Runaways won't be in any adverts!" said Kalix, and started to feel cross. "They're only in the film. Stop being stupid."

Vex turned to Daniel. "They should have the Runaways advertising these potato chips. It would definitely make me want to buy them."

There were a few seconds of silence. Vex leaned over Kalix toward the twins.

"Did anyone buy any potato chips? Now I really want some."

There were a few dissatisfied mutterings from elsewhere in the cinema as other visitors started to regret being at the same showing as such a noisy party.

"Will everyone keep quiet!" hissed Moonglow.

"Sorry!" shouted Vex.

"I've dropped my popcorn again," wailed Beauty.

Moonglow and Dominil shrank in their seats and hoped, rather desperately, that things might calm down when the film started. As the adverts and previews came to an end, Kalix suddenly felt very excited at the prospect of watching the film about her favorite band. She focused on the screen, ignoring everything around her. Vex and the twins finally fell silent. Daniel inched closer to Moonglow. He felt the warmth of their arms touching.

I'm sure Moonglow's deliberately leaning on me, he thought. This is going to be perfect. First I'll put my arm around her and then I'm going to kiss her.

CHAPTER 11

"I've never been lucky in romance," admitted Thrix. "I got off to a bad start. The first disaster happened when I was nine years old."

The Fire Queen leaned forward eagerly. "Really? Tell me all about it."

"I had a crush on Bobby MacPhee. He sat next to me in class. He had spiky black hair. I was fascinated by it. And he gave me sweets at playtime."

Malveria nodded sagely. "A young Lothario, with his fascinating hair and generous ways. I can see the attraction."

"He was a popular werewolf," agreed Thrix. "All the girls at the castle liked him. But I had an advantage, sitting next to him in class. He asked if I'd like to meet up some time."

"For a date?"

"Well, sort of. A nine-year-old date."

"Excellent," said Malveria. "The other girls at the castle must have bristled with anger. What happened?"

"One evening when the full moon was out, Bobby shouted up at my window, asking if I wanted to come out. Which I did, obviously. For a play fight."

The Fire Queen was surprised. "A fight? Surely an odd choice for your first date? Was there no restaurant nearby?"

"Well, when werewolf children go out as werewolves, they have a lot of play-fights. It's normal behavior."

Thrix frowned, remembering the occasion. "Unfortunately, I got carried away and almost severed his jugular vein. If Doctor Angus hadn't been visiting the castle, poor Bobby would have bled to death."

"Ah." Malveria nodded. "I take it the romance did not continue?"

"Bobby's parents told my mother if I ever went near him again they'd make a formal complaint to Baron MacPhee. It was all very embarrassing. But really, I didn't know I was that powerful. We were strong children, the Thane's family." Thrix sighed. "I spent the next few years being called the 'blonde bully' by the other werewolves in class. I never had another date at school."

Malveria sipped from her glass of red wine. "But did you not once mention you'd had a teenage romance with an older werewolf?"

Thrix screwed up her face. "Only because I'd had too much to drink."

"Tell me all about it."

"I'd rather not."

"Of course," said Malveria. "But tell me about it anyway. You are quite diverting me from my previous unhappiness over the dreadful Kabachetka."

Thrix filled her wine glass. "His name was John MacAndris. He was an artist. Quite a good artist. He lived in Edinburgh. I really fell for him."

"Ah." The Fire Queen nodded. "An artist. They can be alluring, for a while. Was he handsome?"

"Quite handsome. He had this air of . . . " Thrix struggled for the correct description. "Well, he seemed exciting, with his exhibitions, and critics writing reviews in the Scotsman and the Glasgow Herald. I dated him for about three months. I took care to keep it secret. Because my mother wouldn't have approved, with him being a lot older than me."

"Did he paint you naked?" asked Malveria eagerly.

Thrix laughed. "No! Why did you ask that?"

"I just thought it might have happened."

"He was mainly an abstract expressionist. No naked models. Well, not me anyway."

The Fire Queen was disappointed. "Surely any artist with spirit would have attempted to scandalously paint you naked? One hardly sees the point otherwise."

"It didn't take any naked pictures to cause a scandal. I turned up unexpectedly at one of his exhibitions. Unfortunately, his wife did too."

"His wife? Did you know he was married?"

Thrix looked uncomfortable. "I pretended to everyone afterward that I didn't. But I did know really. I was only a teenager. I sort of thought it was all right, with him being an artist. I persuaded myself that him having a young lover was probably just normal artistic behavior." Thrix shuddered. "Apparently it wasn't. Mind you, I don't think that his wife traveling all the way from Edinburgh to the castle just to shout abuse at me was normal behavior either."

Thrix found that she'd finished her wine rather quickly, and refilled both of their glasses.

"It was a huge scandal. There were even suggestions of removing me from the Great Council, though Mother wouldn't hear of that." Thrix shook her head. "That was another early romantic trauma. But I was naive. Growing up in Castle MacRinnalch was fine for learning about being a werewolf but it didn't really prepare you for life outside."

Thrix looked thoughtful. "It was one reason I left to join Minerva on her mountaintop, to get away from the gossip. Minerva didn't care one way or the other about affairs or scandals. I appreciated that."

CHAPTER 12

Empress Kabachetka walked delicately over the bridge of blue crystal that spanned one of the great lava-filled gorges beside her palace. Adviser Distikka accompanied her.

"Should I send Sarapen to the Western Desert?"

"You asked me that already," said Distikka.

"So?" said Empress Kabachetka. "There is no rule that says an Empress cannot ask an adviser for an opinion more than once."

"Unfortunately for me."

The Empress laughed. "Distikka, you are amusing. Once your insolence would have upset me. Not any more. Have you noticed how I have rapidly matured since becoming Empress?"

Distikka declined to reply. The Empress checked her lips in a small mirror she carried in her handbag. The bag, a recent acquisition from Paris, had been sorcerously treated by the Empress to enable it to withstand the fiery temperatures of her realm.

"This lip coloring is not entirely satisfactory. Should I let Sarapen go and fight in the desert?"

"What you're really asking me," replied Distikka, "is do I know any way of making Sarapen fall in love with you?"

"That is not what I'm asking at all!" declared the Empress. She frowned and glanced in the mirror again. "But if I was asking you that, what would you reply?"

"I'd say that I have little insight into affairs of the heart," said Distikka. "Never having participated in them myself."

The Empress was dissatisfied. "You must have some experience, Distikka. Did you not seduce General Agrippa, and cause him to rebel against Queen Malveria?"

"I suppose I did. But the General was so blinded by ambition it wasn't hard to make him rebel. I don't think I really made him fall love with me."

"Fortunately for the General," said Kabachetka, "as you abandoned him at the scene of the crime, so to speak, leaving him to have his head chopped off by Queen Malveria. Which was the correct course of action by you, in the circumstances. But why will Sarapen not fall in love with me?"

Distikka looked blank.

"Stop looking blank," demanded Empress Kabachetka. "I don't like it. You must have some insights. Consider the facts. All independent witnesses agree that I am a remarkable beauty. My blonde hair alone is the wonder of the nation. I am also an empress. That has to count for something. Furthermore, I saved his life. One would think that was enough."

Distikka smiled, which she rarely did. "Presumably love does not run along logical lines, Empress. Which you already know. I really am at a loss what to suggest. Perhaps Sarapen, if facing hardship in the desert, might decide you were a better option?"

The Empress frowned, not liking to hear herself described as merely a better option.

"I will muse on it longer. But I'm not satisfied with your advice, Distikka. And on the subject of your unsatisfactory advice, nothing seems to be happening concerning werewolves."

"The Avenaris Guild is growing stronger. They have more money and more power."

"That is no use if they never encounter any werewolves. Are Thrix MacRinnalch and her annoying sister Kalix never to be punished?" The Empress's temper flared. "I had a hunter from the Guild on the very point of killing the Enchantress when Kalix intervened! And Kalix is still unpunished for attempting to murder Sarapen! *And* the Enchantress is still providing fashionable garments for Malveria! It is all most frustrating, Distikka. Something must be done."

They paused to admire a huge spout of flame that shot up from the gorge below.

"Something is being done," replied Distikka calmly. "Soon we won't have to worry about the werewolves avoiding the Avenaris Guild. They'll be rushing to confront them. And then they'll be killed."

"I hope so," said the Empress. "Your plan is no doubt very complicated and I'm suspicious of complicated plans. I will let it proceed and see what happens. But if we meet with another failure, I may forget my newfound maturity and introduce you to some of my own assassins."

CHAPTER 13

Although there were only eight people in Daniel's and Moonglow's flat, the small apartment had never been so noisy. Beauty and Delicious turned up the music, shouted over it to make themselves heard, and then turned it up again. Vex screamed at the top of her voice and danced in the middle of the floor.

Decembrius hadn't come with them to the cinema, but he'd arrived at the party. He was now talking to Kalix, or rather listening, as she enthusiastically talked about the film. Kalix had enjoyed the Runaways film and described all her favorite parts to Decembrius. They sat close to each other on the floor, leaning against the wall, drinking beer and looking, for once, like a couple who were comfortable in each other's company. Moonglow observed them with interest. She thought it would be nice if Kalix and Decembrius managed to establish some sort of stable relationship. Decembrius wasn't such a bad werewolf, once you got past his slight arrogance. Moonglow suspected that Decembrius put this on to cover a degree of natural shyness. When he forgot about being arrogant he was much more agreeable.

Dominil sat quietly in a corner. She seemed thoughtful and had hardly spoken since they'd left the cinema.

"My cup is empty!" yelled Vex, and hurried to the kitchen. There she found Daniel, who was drinking from a bottle of lager while putting another in his jacket pocket.

"Daniel! Wasn't that a good film?"

Daniel grunted.

"And isn't this a good party?"

Daniel grunted again.

"Why are you putting beer in your pockets?"

"So I can drink on my own in my room."

Vex looked puzzled. "You've looked awfully gloomy since the film ended. Almost like there's something wrong. What's the matter? No, don't tell me, I'm good at guessing these things . . . " Vex studied Daniel, trying to interpret his aura. "Did you have an accident?"

"No."

"Are you sick?"

"No."

"Did someone you know have an accident or get sick?"

Daniel shook his head and tried to escape from the kitchen. Vex blocked his way. She put her face an inch from his and grinned very broadly. "Tell me what's wrong. It can't be that bad."

"I tried to kiss Moonglow and it all went wrong," said Daniel.

Vex winced. "Oh. That's really bad. What happened?"

"She hit me."

"Hit you?"

"Well, more of a push really." Daniel looked thoughtful. "No, I think it qualifies as a blow actually. A violent push, say."

"When did this happen?"

"In the cinema."

"I didn't notice."

"You were singing along with the film," said Daniel. "I picked a moment when everyone was occupied."

"So you just grabbed her and kissed her?"

"Yes."

"And Moonglow hit you?"

"Sort of. And she told me never to do it again." Daniel looked crestfallen.

"Well OK," said Vex. "At least you've learned something. It was a bad idea to grab Moonglow and kiss her. But it was obviously the wrong time. I mean, you were both sober. That was bound to be embarrassing. Why didn't you just wait till the party when Moonglow had a few beers inside her?"

Daniel shook his head gloomily. "I expect you're right. I always get these things wrong. If anyone needs me I'll be up in my room, listening to depressing music."

"What use is that? I keep telling you, you're not going to get anywhere with Moonglow if you keep skulking around, doing nothing."

"What would you suggest?"

Vex looked thoughtful. "Have you considered kissing her?"

Daniel put a weary hand to his forehead. "Agrivex. Please never talk to me again."

"Why do people keep saying that?" said Vex, but Daniel by now had slipped past her, out of the kitchen.

As he slouched his way through the living room toward the stairs, Moonglow studiously avoided looking at him. She regretted that matters between them had come to a head that day, though she'd known they inevitably would at some point. She hadn't expected that point to be in the middle of a film about the Runaways, when they were sitting in a cinema with five other people. It had been a very poor time to attempt to kiss her. Moonglow had been shocked, and not very pleased. She'd pushed Daniel away quite angrily. Since then they hadn't spoken a word to each other.

It's going to be awkward living together now, she thought.

Vex arrived back in the room and began haranguing Beauty and Delicious about playing more gigs. Yum Yum Sugary Snacks were Vex's favorite band and she was eager to see them onstage again.

"We want to play more," said Beauty, raising her voice over the music, "but Dominil says we have to record something. Something good."

Beauty and Delicious had made some demos. Dominil had dismissed them as lacking in quality and demanded something better.

"Dominil is as big a pain as ever," yelled Delicious. "If we don't do what she says she starts sulking."

This was far from the truth. The twins knew that without Dominil's assistance they'd still be in the same position they'd been in a year ago: lying around their house in Camden, vaguely thinking about playing music again. Dominil now had them rehearsing regularly. Membership of the band was stable, and everyone was fairly well rehearsed.

"Even Pete is still on board," said Beauty. "Though he's still pining for Dominil."

Vex laughed. She knew the story of Dominil's one-night stand with Pete the guitarist. The affair had meant nothing to Dominil, who had merely wished to occupy herself for a few hours, knowing that the next day she faced the possibility of dying in the great werewolf feud. After the crisis passed, Dominil had shown no further interest. Pete could not get over the affair so fast. He pined for Dominil, privately at first, before going public at a gig, where he'd announced to the entire audience that he loved her. Dominil had not been pleased. Making everything worse, Pete had subsequently learned that they were all werewolves. This was serious. Hiding their werewolf nature was important to every MacRinnalch. Only the degenerate Beauty and Delicious could laugh when it went wrong.

"We've invited Pete here," Beauty told Vex. "We figure he deserves another chance."

"We thought maybe she might loosen up at a party," said Delicious.

They looked over at Dominil, sitting quietly in the corner.

"I've never seen anyone look less loose," said Delicious. "Let's get her some wine."

As any Scottish werewolf would have regarded it as shameful to arrive at a party without making some contribution, the kitchen was now well stocked with alcohol.

Decembrius and Kalix were still discussing the film. Kalix, in her enthusiasm, had edged very close to Decembrius and he was keenly aware of it. His attraction for Kalix had not waned, though recently he'd been frustrated by her diffidence and her reluctance to commit to anything. Even arranging a phone call with her could be difficult. Decembrius's patience was strained, but he knew that if he complained too strongly, Kalix would simply stop talking to him. He felt some humiliation that he seemed to be powerless in the relationship. After all, Decembrius wasn't a werewolf who had trouble finding girlfriends.

Vex, dancing nearby, stumbled into them. The impact pushed Kalix into Decembrius and he instinctively put his arm out to support her.

Vex grinned. "Are you having a nice cuddle?"

At that moment, the full moon appeared in the sky outside. Instantly, Kalix and Decembrius changed into their werewolf shape. Seeing this, Vex laughed. They heard howling from the kitchen from the twins, who had also changed. They didn't need to howl, but they knew it would annoy Dominil.

Decembrius received the customary boost brought on by the werewolf change. He noticed that he had Kalix in his arms, so he kissed her, feeling it was the only reasonable thing to do.

Kalix kissed him back, very briefly, but withdrew. "I have to get up early in the morning."

"No, you don't."

"Yes, I do."

Decembrius looked at Kalix suspiciously. As far as he knew, Kalix never had to get up early in the morning. She wasn't working and college hadn't started yet. He frowned.

"Well, so what if you have to get up early?"

"So you can't stay the night."

Decembrius felt his humiliation returning. "I didn't ask you if I could stay."

"You were going to."

"How do you know I was going to?"

"Because you're kissing me."

Decembrius's powerful feeling of well-being brought on by the werewolf change evaporated rapidly. Kalix refusing to sleep with him before he'd even suggested it seemed particularly humiliating. He suddenly felt too annoyed with Kalix to argue about it.

"Who'd want to stay with you anyway?" he said harshly. He pushed Kalix away, then stormed off to the kitchen. There he found himself in the midst of an argument, with Beauty and Delicious on one side and Dominil on the other.

Dominil was irate. "You invited Pete? When we're all werewolves?"

"Why not?" said Beauty. "He knows we're werewolves anyway."

"That doesn't mean we should invite him to see us. Are you both insane?"

"Moonglow said they were short of boys," said Delicious, who didn't see why Dominil was making such a fuss. "And he's one of the few boys who won't be shocked to socialize with werewolves."

Dominil shook her head. She was struggling to control her temper over the twins' idiocy.

"What about Kalix and Decembrius? Pete doesn't know they're werewolves. Don't you know it's taboo to give clan secrets away?"

Delicious shrugged. "I never thought about them," she admitted. "But hey, what's another werewolf or two? Pete won't tell anyone."

Dominil snarled in frustration. The bright light from the naked bulb in the kitchen reflected from her sharp teeth.

"He won't tell anyone? He's a guitarist in Camden. That doesn't make him trustworthy. And would you stop trying to force me into some sort of relationship with Pete? I've told you a hundred times, I'm not interested."

"Have you really given it a shot?" asked Beauty. "Maybe with a bit more werewolf passion?"

"Who's got werewolf passion?" asked Vex, who chose this moment to stumble into the kitchen. "Is it Decembrius?"

Decembrius looked uncomfortable.

"I don't think kissing Kalix was a bad idea," said Vex. "Even if she shot you down in flames."

The twins sniggered. Decembrius looked furious.

"She did not shoot me down in flames."

"Yes, she did. Hey, don't look at me like that. It's not my fault if she won't sleep with you. Don't be embarrassed. Kalix is really beautiful, anyone would want to sleep with her. Isn't that right, Beauty?"

"Definitely."

"You see, they agree with me," said Vex. "There's nothing wrong with wanting to sleep with Kalix. If she rejects you in a crushing manner, well, that's just unfortunate. And a bit embarrassing, I suppose."

Decembrius left the kitchen with an angry scowl on his face. Agrivex turned to the twins. "I could really do with a boyfriend. Do you know anyone nice?"

CHAPTER 14

With Dominil furious, Decembrius humiliated, Kalix moody, Daniel crushed and Moonglow uncomfortable, the party might have ground to an uncomfortable halt. As it was, Vex's and the twins' high spirits were enough to keep things active and noisy. During a pause in the music, the doorbell rang, with an insistence that suggested the caller had been ringing for a long time.

"I'll get it," cried Vex.

"Who could be calling?" Moonglow was worried. "We can't let anyone in with . . . " She looked around awkwardly.

Beauty and Delicious laughed. "With werewolves everywhere? Don't worry, it's probably Pete."

"He knows you're werewolves?"

"Unfortunately, he does," said Dominil. "It's still exceptionally stupid to invite him here."

With the full moon above, none of the werewolves were able to resume their human shape. This frustrated Decembrius. After his disagreement with Kalix, he'd liked to have departed, but it would mean skulking his way through backstreets and gardens. He had done this occasionally in London, but it was a risk he'd rather not take.

Vex appeared in the room with Pete in tow. "Look, it's Pete the guitarist! I said there were werewolves here and it was a secret, but he said he knew already so I said he could come in!" Vex beamed, pleased to have another visitor.

Pete greeted the twins, politely thanked Moonglow for having him as her guest, then attempted to sit on the arm of Dominil's chair. Dominil angrily brushed him off.

"Uh . . . hi," said Pete.

Dominil glared at him. "I have no idea what you're doing here and I'd advise you to leave. You're not welcome."

Dominil, as an angry werewolf, made for an intimidating sight. The atmosphere sank. Pete looked embarrassed and quite alarmed. Even the twins seemed surprised by the strength of her unfriendliness.

"Have some wine," said Vex. "I'm Vex! Or did I tell you that already?" She laughed, and Beauty put music on, masking the awkwardness.

Moonglow stood close to Kalix and whispered in her ear, "Are you really getting up early tomorrow? Or were you just . . . ?" She glanced at Decembrius.

"I am," said Kalix. "I've got to do something."

"What?"

"Something private, with Dominil. I didn't think it would happen so soon, but Dominil just told me she's got everything ready. That's why she came tonight. We'll be going away for a few days."

Moonglow was concerned.

"Don't worry," said Kalix. "I'll be fine."

"Is it going to be violent?"

"No. It's just something private."

Moonglow dropped the subject, knowing there was no point interrogating Kalix. But Moonglow remained worried because, in her experience, any time Kalix left the house for a few days, violence would ensue. She'd come back wounded, either from fighting other werewolves, or the hunters.

"It'll be fine. No fighting," said Kalix, confiding a little more than she might normally have. "I'll be back in a few days."

"Can you really not tell me where you're going?"

Kalix shook her head. Moonglow dropped the subject. At least Kalix would be with Dominil. Moonglow knew of Dominil's reputation. She was intelligent, competent and powerful. She would keep Kalix safe, if anyone could.

CHAPTER 15

Kalix yawned. She'd had only a few hours' sleep before Dominil had woken her. She looked down at the clouds below.

"I didn't know we'd be above the clouds."

Kalix had never flown before. She was nervous, but Dominil's presence was calming. Besides, she had more to worry about than a flight to Inverness.

"Do you know the way once we get to the airport?" asked Kalix.

"I'll find it. The rental car has GPS, I checked."

Kalix nodded. According to Dominil, they'd still have some hours of driving after reaching Inverness. It was the closest airport to Minerva's mountaintop, but Minerva's retreat was in a very isolated spot.

"I wonder what happened to Decembrius?"

Last night Dominil had slept in Kalix's room. Wakening early in the morning, they'd found the twins passed out on the couch downstairs, with no sign of anyone else.

"Do you think he might have gone out at night?"

"As a werewolf?" said Dominil. "Unlikely. How badly did you insult him?"

"I don't know. I didn't mean to insult him at all. But he was hinting about sleeping with me. I said I had to get up early in the morning." Kalix pursed her lips. "I suppose that does sound like an insult."

Kalix gazed down at the clouds again. She found it amusing to be flying above them.

"Do you think I should have slept with him?"

"I have no opinion," said Dominil.

Dominil fell silent. Kalix knew her cousin didn't want to talk, but found it difficult to remain quiet.

"I'm nervous. Not about flying. About . . . you know, Minerva."

"I am a little discomfited too," said Dominil. "But Minerva says she can help us end our addiction, and lessen the withdrawal symptoms. It's worth trying. We both know we've got to stop taking laudanum."

Kalix stared at the back of the seat in front of her. She wasn't looking forward to the next few days. Though she was only eighteen, Kalix had been addicted to the opiate for years. Her addiction was widely known throughout the clan, and was a large part of the reason for her disgrace. Kalix's mother burned with shame if ever the topic was raised. Kalix's brother Markus and her sister Thrix regarded her addiction with contempt. Throughout history, a few werewolves had exhibited a peculiar weakness for the drug. Becoming addicted to it was regarded as extremely shameful. Anything Kalix did was attributed either to her craziness or her drug addiction; as far as the clan was concerned, the addiction was worse.

Dominil's addiction was secret: Kalix was the only person who knew. Dominil had managed to keep it under control. Nonetheless, she was addicted. For months, she and Kalix had been traveling to Merchant MacDoig's shop in East London to purchase laudanum, and paying heavily for it. The Merchant knew he had a captive market and kept his prices high. This was a drain on Dominil's limited resources, and was worse for Kalix. There had been plenty of occasions in the past when she'd stolen to support her habit. Recently, she'd found herself tempted to steal from her flatmates, and while she had resisted the urge, it was this that had made her agree to Dominil's suggestion of appealing to Minerva for help.

It annoyed Dominil that she was so dependent on the opiate. Dominil had little empathy with the world, and a very powerful intellect that could not always be satisfied by her computer work, or her love of history. There were times when she was dreadfully, numbingly bored. During one such time she'd taken laudanum. It had warmed her inside and made her forget her boredom. It hadn't taken long to become addicted. Now she needed the substance, though the warmth it had once given her had mostly faded.

"Do you think it will hurt?" asked Kalix.

"Hurt? I shouldn't think so. Minerva isn't going to punish us."

"Is she going to work some spell?" said Kalix hopefully. Perhaps Minerva could easily make them better with magic.

"I'm not certain," admitted Dominil. "When I talked to her on the phone, she mentioned a herbal treatment to ease the withdrawal. But I'm sure we'll suffer for a while till it clears out of our systems."

"I wish she'd just use magic," said Kalix gloomily.

"By reputation and by my observation, you are very resistant to magic," Dominil pointed out. "Possibly because of your unusual birth."

"I hate my unusual birth," moaned Kalix and sank into her small chair. The closer they came to their destination, the more nervous she was becoming. Her head drooped and she stared at her boots.

"I'm scared of this."

"There is no need for fear," said Dominil. Kalix didn't think she sounded quite as confident as usual.

Inside their hand luggage, they each carried a bottle of laudanum. A brown, antique-looking bottle, as supplied by Merchant MacDoig. Minerva had advised them to keep taking their normal dose until they reached her retreat. Dominil had kept on carefully measuring out the amount she needed each day. Kalix had too, though she was gripped by a desire to take more, to use it all up before it was taken away, as if filling herself with the drug might somehow insulate her from the unpleasantness to come.

"Are you still helping the band?" asked Kalix.

"Yes."

"Do you enjoy it?"

"Not a great deal."

"Then why do you do it?"

"Partly because the Mistress of the Werewolves asked me to, to keep the twins out of trouble. And partly because I can't think of anything else to do. Since leaving Oxford, I haven't managed to establish a clear set of ambitions."

"But you're a computer genius," said Kalix. "Can't you do something with that?"

"There are a lot of computer geniuses. Plenty of them remain unsuccessful."

"You're a good artist too. And you can translate Latin."

"Once more, these are not immediately translatable into a viable career. It's a failure of mine that I don't seem able to decide what to do. And being a werewolf, job opportunities are limited. Possibly I haven't broken away from the clan's influence yet, which is another fault."

Kalix was surprised to hear Dominil describe herself so negatively. In Kalix's experience, Dominil was the most competent werewolf in the clan, as well as the most intelligent.

"Helping Yum Yum Sugary Snacks helps fill in the time. And it occurred to me that somewhere in the middle of the computer work I'm doing for them, and the design work, and the music contacts, I might find myself a career I'd be able to tolerate."

Kalix was on the point of asking Dominil if she needed a career. Most of the leading families of the MacRinnalchs were wealthy. Dominil's father Tupan was an important werewolf at Castle MacRinnalch, a brother of the old Thane. But she remembered hearing from the twins that Tupan was not generous with his money, so she kept silent.

A stewardess pushed a trolley up the aisle. Dominil bought two cups of tea and two miniature bottles of whisky.

"Should we be drinking?" said Kalix.

"Possibly not. But it can't do much harm. I'm really not looking forward to this any more than you."

Dominil and Kalix drank their whisky straight off, then sipped their tea as the plane approached the airport at Inverness. Kalix risked sneaking a look at her journal, guarding it carefully so her companion wouldn't see. She'd made her first addition to werewolf improvement list, putting a small tick next to *get on better with people,* and another tick beside *stop being so anxious*. Kalix had managed to go to the cinema and attend her party without panicking. She'd felt some anxiety, but it was definitely less than she once would have experienced. She felt it deserved a tick. She'd also managed to talk to people at the party and had been, for her, quite sociable. The only negative aspect had been her disagreement with Decembrius. That surely hadn't been her fault. She did have to get up early in the morning. If Decembrius got in a bad mood about that, she couldn't help it. All things considered, Kalix thought she'd made a good start on her werewolf improvement plan.

She glanced at another item on the list. Stop using laudanum. She was about to attempt that, much quicker than she'd anticipated when she first made the list. Kalix wasn't feeling very confident about it.

CHAPTER 16

After the party, Moonglow slept late. She would have slept later had Vex not crashed into her room shortly after midday and jumped on her bed.

"Hi, Moonglow, are you awake?"

"No," grunted Moonglow.

Vex bounced around a few times. "Are you awake now? Do you want some tea?"

"All right, I'll have some tea."

"I didn't bring any tea," admitted Vex. "But I've got big news! I have a boyfriend!"

"I have a hangover."

"Not as bad as Daniel's," chortled Vex. "He threw a shoe at me!"

Moonglow sat up in bed. "You're not going to go away, are you?"

Vex grinned. "I have a boyfriend!"

"OK," said Moonglow, through dry lips. "Tell me about it."

"It's Pete. The guitarist from Yum Yum Sugary Snacks."

Moonglow felt some stirrings of interest, despite her dry mouth and slight nausea. "How did this happen?"

"Well, we were talking and dancing and stuff and then we were drinking and then everyone else seemed to be falling asleep so we were drinking some more and then I asked him if he'd liked to see my collection of Hello Kitty T-shirts and then we just sort of ended up in my bed." Vex grinned, very broadly. Her hair was a chaotic mess of jagged blonde spikes, point-ing in all directions. "So now he's my boyfriend!"

"You mean you slept together?"

Vex nodded and looked pleased. Moonglow did her best to look pleased too, though she was far from certain that a drunken encounter with a guitarist really counted as having a boyfriend.

"When he left this morning he said he'd call me."

"That's nice," said Moonglow.

Vex rose from Moonglow's bed, threw open the curtains and danced around the room.

"I really think it's time I had a boyfriend. And he likes everything I like! He's a big fan of *Tokyo Top Pop Boom Boom Girl*." Vex paused and frowned. "Well, I think he is. My memory's a bit hazy."

To Moonglow's distress, Vex sat on her bed again.

"He's really nice looking. And he plays guitar in my favorite band! I can't wait to see him play onstage again now that he's my boyfriend."

"When's he going to call you?" asked Moonglow.

"He didn't say. Soon, probably. Any minute, I expect. I wonder if Daniel's feeling any better? I really want to tell him about my boyfriend!"

Vex hurried out of Moonglow's bedroom. Moonglow shook her head, then struggled to rise. She wrapped herself in her black dressing gown and made her way carefully downstairs. Beauty and Delicious were sleeping on the living room floor, on a bed made from cushions and spare duvets that Moonglow had made up for them. The twins had crawled into it only a few hours ago, very unsteadily. Now, having changed back to human while they slept, as the dawn arrived, they looked peaceful, with their pink and blue hair splayed out over their cushions and onto the carpet. The cat had settled down with them but woke as Moonglow crept by and followed her to the kitchen.

"You love sleeping with werewolves, don't you?" said Moonglow. She opened a tin of cat food and filled the cat's bowl before putting the kettle on. As she waited for it to boil, Moonglow reflected on their party. It had gone well, as far as she could remember. Kalix had seemed to en-joy herself, apart from the brief hostility between her and Decembrius. That had passed quickly, though Decembrius had spent the rest of the night sulking. So had Daniel. But Beauty, Delicious and Vex had created enough of a party atmosphere for anyone. As a celebration for Kalix's birthday, it had been a success.

There were some heavy, stumbling footsteps outside the kitchen.

Daniel appeared, wearing an ancient T-shirt and a crumpled pair of dark khaki shorts. His hair, which he'd grown longer in recent months, was plastered to his forehead.

"I'm going to kill Vex," he mumbled.

"Maybe you should have tea first?" said Moonglow.

"OK. But then I'm really going to kill her." Daniel sat on the kitchen floor, resting his back against a cabinet. "I feel terrible. Vex woke me up and started babbling about her boyfriend. I hate him already and I don't even know who he is."

"It's Pete."

"The guitarist? Isn't he meant to be in love with Dominil or something?"

Moonglow shrugged.

"I think I'm going to be sick," said Daniel. "Is the tea ready?"

Moonglow poured boiling water from the kettle into the teapot, but by the time she'd hunted out two clean mugs, Daniel had left the kitchen in a hurry, looking unwell.

At least that wasn't too uncomfortable, thought Moonglow. She hadn't been looking forward to her first encounter with Daniel after rejecting his advances in the cinema. Perhaps it was fortunate that the encounter had occurred while Daniel was feeling so poorly.

But he won't have a hangover forever, Moonglow realized. It's still going to be awkward later.

Moonglow felt dissatisfied. Now she was going to feel uncomfortable in her own house. What had Daniel been thinking about, trying to kiss her unexpectedly like that? No wonder she'd pushed him off. It was lucky the film had been entertaining and occupied everyone's attention. Otherwise Moonglow and Daniel might have found themselves with a large audience for their uncomfortable love scene.

"No doubt everyone's heard about it by now." Moonglow knew there was no chance of the incident being politely ignored. Vex would have inevitably learned all about it and told everyone.

"They're probably discussing it in Malveria's palace at this moment." Moonglow sighed. She took her tea and headed swiftly upstairs to her room, hoping to avoid Vex. Moonglow didn't feel like enduring another long description from the young Fire Elemental about how good it was to have a boyfriend.

I bet he never calls her anyway, she thought, and then felt a little ashamed for thinking mean thoughts.

CHAPTER 17

Old Minerva MacRinnalch's mountain stood at one end of Glen Marbauch, a deep, glacial valley in a very remote part of the Scottish Highlands. At the other end of the glen was the tiny village of Marbauch, containing only a few cottages and a single shop. Dominil had booked two rooms in a tiny bed-and-breakfast. After successfully negotiating the long drive from Inverness, she halted the car before reaching the village.

The two werewolves looked along the valley. It was raining and, in the distance, under the gray sky, Mount Marbauch looked steep, dark and not welcoming.

"Maybe we should have gone to a clinic," said Kalix.

"Too late now," replied Dominil. "Anyway, we can't. The standard treatments for addiction don't agree with werewolf physiology."

"I know," sighed Kalix. "I was really sick after I took methadone."

"Who gave you that?"

"No one. One time when I couldn't afford laudanum I broke into a chemist and stole it."

Kalix gazed at the mountain, and her heart sank even further. The gray slopes were impressive in their way. Inspiring even, as scenery. But as a place to undergo treatment for addiction, Kalix couldn't help thinking they'd made a terrible mistake.

"Do we have to climb it?"

"Minerva will meet us at the foot. I understand there's a pathway to the top."

"Is it a steep path? Can you fall off?" Kalix's was feeling more and more depressed. She was at least relieved to hear there was a path. She'd had a vision of herself struggling up the mountain with ropes and didn't think she could manage it.

They parked outside the small bed-and-breakfast. There were a few other houses in the distance; hardly enough to qualify as even a village. A few hours ago in London, it had been warm and sunny, but here the rain fell steadily and there was a cold wind. Kalix shivered. She had poor resistance to the elements, much less than would have been expected from a werewolf. It was part of the effect that the drug had on her system.

Dominil wondered if the locals knew that a powerful werewolf sorcerer lived at the far end of the glen. If they did, might they also suspect that she and Kalix were werewolves too? If the landlady did suspect anything, she didn't show it. While she couldn't hide her surprise at the sight of Dominil's icy white hair, she greeted the pair convivially.

"We get a lot of walkers around these parts in the summer," she said. "Are you here for the scenery?"

"Yes," said Dominil. "We like to get back to Scotland when we can."

Dominil didn't sound Scottish. She'd abandoned her accent at Oxford. Kalix still had a strong accent, undiluted by her time in London.

Their rooms were clean and comfortable, as Minerva had assured Dominil they would be. Minerva had seemed very knowledgeable about the local area, and Dominil wondered again if the people here knew about her unusual nature.

Kalix was tired after the flight. "What time are we meant to meet Minerva?"

"At dawn," said Dominil. "We'll have to set off early."

Kalix yawned. "I'm not used to these early mornings."

"Students never are."

Kalix was surprised to hear herself described as a student. She supposed she was. She'd be going back to college soon. But her college was a remedial establishment, helping people with poor learning skills. Dominil had two first-class degrees from Oxford. Kalix didn't feel like a student in her company.

"Did you like the Runaways film?"

"It was interesting," said Dominil noncommittally. "I wondered if it might give me any hints on how to manage a band. At least it gave me some idea how not to."

Kalix asked her cousin what she planned to do next for Yum Yum Sugary Snacks.

"I'm thinking about trying to get them a place on a tour, supporting some band with a reasonable fan base. That would do them good. We've played three gigs in London since that debacle in Edinburgh, and they've gone much better. I think they could cope with a support slot. I'm told that if I could persuade a well-known producer to work on their demo, that would help too. Though I'm not sure any producer would work with the twins, given their bad reputation."

Kalix went off early to her room, leaving Dominil sitting next to her window with her laptop computer open in front of her. As night fell and the moon appeared, Dominil took on her werewolf shape quite smoothly and remained at her computer. It was an accepted fact of life among the

MacRinnalchs that as a werewolf, you couldn't work a keyboard, but Dominil, through determined practice, had almost mastered the art. It meant picking out one key at a time, slowly, with her werewolf claws, but she could do it.

Dominil sat in front of her computer for a long time. She didn't feel like sleeping. She felt uneasy about tomorrow. During the great werewolf feud, Dominil had faced death quite calmly, but the prospect of giving up laudanum troubled her. She knew it would be difficult. She was aware of the changes the opiate would already have made to her brain and body. She was both physically and psychologically dependent on the drug. Dominil had researched the matter quite thoroughly. Unless, as Kalix hoped, Minerva had some magic solution, which was highly unlikely, they were in for an uncomfortable time.

Dominil took her bottle of laudanum from her bag and measured out what would be her last dose, as instructed by Minerva. She drank it swiftly and replaced the top on the bottle. Then she undressed, lay on the bed, calmly cleared her mind of all negative thoughts and went to sleep.

CHAPTER 18

Daniel emerged from the bathroom feeling very unwell. He was not a great drinker and had indulged far too freely at Kalix's party. His head ached and he still felt nauseous. Making matters worse, a great depression had settled in. His plan had completely failed. Moonglow had rejected him. He was now faced with the prospect of living in the same house as a girl with whom he was in love, but didn't want him. Daniel despaired. It was bad enough being a rejected lover without bumping into the person you were in love with every day. He had vague thoughts of somehow avoiding Moonglow, but that, he immediately realized, wasn't practical. He'd already met her in the kitchen, which would have been dreadfully embarrassing had he not been too ill to notice his emotions.

I can't be ill all the time, he reasoned. Sooner or later I have to meet her healthy.

He wondered if he should move. That would create difficulties. He'd only just got his finances in order after the recent crisis. Moving would be expensive. He'd need a deposit for another flat, and he didn't have the money. Perhaps he could take a room in someone else's apartment? Daniel felt even gloomier. He didn't want to move. He didn't really want to not see Moonglow again either. Suddenly he was gripped by another wave of nausea and hurried back into the bathroom.

This is an all time low, thought Daniel. Nothing could be worse.

Vex burst into the bathroom. "Hi, Daniel! I've got a boyfriend!"

"I was wrong," muttered Daniel. "It can get worse."

"Will you be sick for long?"

Daniel shook his head, indicating that he wasn't really in control of the matter.

"OK," said Vex, cheerfully. "When you get better I want to have a house meeting."

"What?"

"A house meeting. I can call one, right?"

Daniel shrugged. Moonglow was the only person who ever convened house meetings, but he supposed anyone was free to call one. By the time he made it to his feet, Vex was gone, running noisily downstairs. Daniel heard some protests from Beauty and Delicious, who were not pleased to be roused from their sleep.

I'm never having a party again in any house where Vex is present, thought Daniel, slowly making his way back to his room. Or Moonglow. Also, I'm never drinking alcohol again.

Downstairs, Moonglow, while not at her brightest, was suffering less. She had a greater tolerance to alcohol than Daniel and had not indulged so freely. With so many werewolves in the house, Moonglow had felt a nagging sense of responsibility, fearing that things might get out of hand. She'd restrained her own celebrations just in case.

"Moonglow," called Delicious from the living room floor. "Please bring us tea and also get rid of this noisy Fire Elemental."

Moonglow put the kettle on again to make tea for the twins. Vex reappeared in the kitchen.

"I want to have a house meeting," she said.

"A meeting? Why, what's wrong?"

"Nothing. But I need help. I'll tell you when Daniel's stopped being sick. Is he being sick because you broke his heart?"

Moonglow was trying not to think about Daniel and didn't reply.

"It's bound to be upsetting, really," said Vex. "What with him being in love with you and you rejecting him. Wouldn't surprise me if he just jumped out the window or something. You know, in despair."

Vex peered out of the kitchen window, in case Daniel might be flying past at that moment.

"Stop being ridiculous," said Moonglow. "Daniel is not going to jump out of the window."

Moonglow refused to discuss it any further. To distract Vex, she asked about Pete. Vex happily returned to the subject of her new boyfriend, carrying on a one-sided conversation while Moonglow made tea and took it on a tray to the twins. By this time they had roused themselves and were sitting on the couch, yawning.

"What's this about Pete?" asked Beauty, whose pink hair was strewn across her forehead. She shoved it back with her fingers, creating a sort of hair mountain on top of her head.

Vex related her story again. The twins were interested to hear that their guitarist had spent the night with Vex. Moonglow noticed them exchanging glances at Vex's description of Pete as her new boyfriend. Obviously, they shared Moonglow's doubts.

It was early in the afternoon before the twins left. They thanked Moonglow for her hospitality and even helped clear the living room. Moonglow was surprised, having not expected them to be so well mannered. She realized she'd never before encountered Beauty and Delicious when they were sober. They departed in a cab. It was an expensive journey, all the way north to Camden, but the twins had plenty of money and never minded paying for a taxi.

"Can we have our house meeting now?" Vex asked Moonglow.

"I'm not sure that Daniel will be ready for a meeting."

"I'll get him," said Vex, and hurried upstairs.

CHAPTER 19

"It is a terrible thing to happen," said Queen Malveria, pacing up and down Thrix's office. Her heels were extremely high, even by Malveria's standards, but the Queen had been pacing relentlessly since arriving in the office. "How could this happen?"

"Calm down, Malveria," said Thrix. "It's not that bad."

"Enchantress, you amaze and distress me. Not that bad?"

The Fire Queen grabbed a magazine from Thrix's desk and glared at it with such loathing that it burst into flames. Thrix muttered a sorcerous word to put out the fire. Malveria scowled at the charred magazine then threw it down in disgust.

"Espionage must be involved! It has happened before and I won't stand for it! I will rain down fire on this designer and his cheap strumpet who is now wearing a surprisingly similar outfit to the one which you have designed for me!"

In ten days' time, the King and Queen of the Mayusta Earth Elementals were paying Malveria a state visit. Malveria had been looking forward to wearing her new line of formal wear. Thrix's designs were so elegant and becoming. Since engaging Thrix as her designer, the Fire Queen had been much happier while performing her official duties. It was so satisfying to be able to turn up at a grand event in a really special coat, with a beautiful hat and handbag to match.

The Fire Queen glared at the charred magazine cover. "Who is this cheap whore anyway?"

"Britain's top Olympic athlete," said Thrix.

"Why is she at Buckingham Palace?"

"She's receiving an MBE for services to the country."

"Pah!" snorted Malveria, who had little time for athletics.

Thrix glanced at the scorched magazine cover, on which the female athlete was pictured wearing a sober but stylish ensemble in dark gray. It was true that it was very similar to the outfit Thrix had designed for Malveria, but Thrix was sure it was just a coincidence.

"There are limited varieties in these formal coats and dresses, Malveria. And everyone's wearing that shade of gray this season."

"But what am I to do?" cried Malveria. "How can I look my guests in the face knowing that my ensemble has already been worn by some woman with no other talent than running around a track? The Mayusta Queen is very gossipy for an Earth Giant and is sure to spread it around."

"Would they even know? Do the Earth Giants read British celebrity magazines?"

"Someone will tell them. Kabachetka's intelligence services scan them regularly. That cheap Empress will steal from anywhere."

The Fire Queen, still pacing, almost lost her footing. She looked down at her shoes.

"I must say, these new, higher heels are a challenge. Since they appeared on the catwalks I've found myself tottering on several occasions. And one simply dreads the humiliation of falling over."

"I'm having difficulty too," admitted Thrix. Like Malveria, Thrix had gleefully embraced the fashion for extremely high heels, but while they looked wonderful on models posing in magazines, they were difficult to wear in real life. "I almost broke my ankle coming out of the lift."

"Perhaps a spell might help?" suggested Malveria.

Thrix was immediately interested. "For helping us to walk in them? That's a good idea."

"I will give the matter my attention as soon as I return to the palace," said the Fire Queen. "If you also work on it, we may make some progress before the designers' reception."

Thrix nodded. The reception was only two weeks away. It was an important event. Each year, a group of the best designers was invited by the British Fashion Institute to a celebration at the Tate Gallery. This year, for the first time, Thrix had received an invitation. The event would be full of journalists, celebrities, buyers, editors and wealthy patrons: everyone that Thrix wanted to meet. It was an excellent opportunity to expand her business. The Fire Queen was looking forward to it just as much, though for different reasons.

"Photographers from *Vogue* will be there," exclaimed the Fire Queen.

Thrix smiled. Her friend's desire to secure a place in *Vogue*'s "fashionable party people" page was stronger than ever.

"With our exceedingly high heels held in place by our new sorcery, we will be quite unstoppable," enthused the Queen. "We shall sweep all before us. You shall be rewarded for your fashion genius by many valuable orders for your beautiful clothes. I will finally get my picture in *Vogue*, thereby grinding the poorly dressed Empress Kabachetka into the dust where she belongs." The Queen smiled happily at the prospect. "My new dress will be ready?"

"It will," said Thrix. "It would have been ready already if . . . " Thrix's voice trailed off.

The Fire Queen looked distressed. "I know I erred in insisting on the lighter blue material. You were right, it does not suit me."

Dealing with fashion crises was something Thrix had become used to during her friendship with the Fire Queen. This time she had matters well in hand.

"I'll have the new frock ready in good time. And don't worry about your formal coat, I'll have something even better for you."

"Really?" Malveria dabbed her eyes. "Forgive me for crying. I am sometimes overwhelmed to have such a good friend to take care of my attire."

The Fire Queen checked her appearance in the large wall mirror. "I should depart, but . . . "

"What's the matter?"

"I had intended to visit Agrivex before returning home. Not that the wretched niece will be pleased to receive a visit from me, but I should check that she hasn't wrecked the house during their party."

"Wrecked the house? Is that likely?"

"There is no telling. Though Agrivex has very little power, she is still a Fire Elemental. As she is too stupid to control her power properly, it's a constant worry that one day she may simply explode, taking all with her in a hideous fireball."

Thrix laughed. She couldn't imagine the skinny and inoffensive Agrivex exploding in a fireball.

"I admit it is unlikely," said Malveria. "Most probably the foolish girl has simply drunk too much and made herself ill." The Fire Queen sighed.

"Malveria, are you still feeling old?"

"A little. And the thought of my niece celebrating her eighteenth birthday is still not helping. What of yourself, Enchantress? Your sister is also eighteen. Does this make you feel old?"

"It didn't till you mentioned it. I've got enough reasons to dislike Kalix already without you giving me new ones."

"You have not forgiven her for killing Easterly?"

The Enchantress looked grim. "I haven't. And I don't care if the rest of the clan thinks she did the right thing. So what if Easterly turned out to be a werewolf hunter? He was still my boyfriend till Kalix assassinated him."

The Fire Queen nodded. "You must be sure to keep her away from your next romantic interest."

Thrix scowled. "If I ever do have a new romance—which I probably won't—Kalix had better stay well away. I'll burn the little brat to a cinder if she annoys me again."

The Fire Queen smiled. "I will be sure to give her your best regards."

Malveria had never found Kalix to be particularly objectionable, but she was well aware of the Enchantress's antipathy toward her. She made a final check on her appearance, then dematerialized with a gentle wave, leaving behind her the characteristic aroma of jasmine.

CHAPTER 20

Dominil woke before her alarm sounded. She washed and dressed quickly and was ready to leave in a few minutes. Outside it was still raining. She could see the mountain from her window, and in the dull morning light it looked even less welcoming. Dominil pursed her lips.

"Time to go," she said.

The corridor outside was silent. Kalix was sleeping in the next room. Dominil knocked gently on the door. There was no reply. Dominil knocked again, then called to her.

"Kalix, are you awake?"

Again there was no reply. Dominil felt uneasy and knocked harder. She tried the door. It was locked. Dominil took a firm grasp of the handle, placed her shoulder against the door and pushed. Even in their human shape, the MacRinnalchs were abnormally strong, and the lock immediately gave way. Dominil stepped inside. She found Kalix lying on the floor. Her bottle of laudanum stood on the bedside table, empty. Kalix had apparently decided to finish off her supply before going to Minerva's retreat.

"Damn it, Kalix," muttered Dominil. "Did you have to do this now?"

She knelt beside her cousin, fearing that she might be dead. She placed her fingers on Kalix's neck. There was a pulse, though it was very weak. Kalix's breathing was very shallow. Dominil pulled back her eyelid. There was no reaction to the light, and her pupil was tiny. Dominil thought that there was a slight bluish tinge to her lips, though it was hard to be certain in the weak electric light in the bedroom.

Kalix had taken an overdose. Dominil wasn't quite certain how serious it was, but had she found a human in this condition, after taking too much heroin, she would now be phoning for an ambulance. Unfortunately, medical care for werewolves was always a problem. There were some werewolf doctors in Scotland, but none close by. Dominil hauled Kalix into a sitting position. She checked her pulse again. It remained weak, but seemed constant.

"As far as I can tell," said Dominil out loud, "you're not about to die just yet. So let's see if Minerva can help."

Having made her decision, Dominil acted swiftly. She gathered up Kalix's belongings, collected her own from next door, then made a swift trip to her car outside, throwing everything in the back seat. She hurried back indoors, passing the landlady on the way. Dominil returned to Kalix's bedroom, picked up Kalix, threw her over her shoulder, then headed back outside. The landlady looked at her in alarm.

"I broke a lock," said Dominil. "I left some money to cover it."

Dominil placed Kalix in the passenger seat, secured her with the seat belt, then pulled away quickly. There were no other cars in sight and it took only a few minutes to reach the turning that led into Glen Marbauch. The road down the valley was narrow, too narrow in places for two cars to pass. Dominil's view was hindered by the intensifying rain. She was a naturally cautious driver, but her concern for Kalix made her drive faster. The rented car jolted over potholes, and after the fourth or fifth time this happened Kalix groaned. Without opening her eyes, she suddenly vomited, quite heavily, over herself and the dashboard.

Dominil edged onto the rough grass verge and quickly helped Kalix from the car. The young werewolf moaned again. Dominil took this as a good sign. She held Kalix while she vomited again. Kalix showed signs of coming back to consciousness. Dominil tried to walk her a few steps. The rain was cold, increasing all the time, and Kalix blinked as it struck her face, reviving her. She was sick for a third time. Dominil let her sink to her knees, keeping a close eye on her to check that her breathing was unaffected by her vomiting. She reached down to feel the pulse at her neck. It was notably stronger.

"It looks like you'll live," muttered Dominil. She took Kalix's hand and tried to lead her back to the car but Kalix resisted, pulling away so she could sink back to her knees and be sick again. Dominil let her go. The crisis seemed to be passing. Kalix was in a poor state, but she wasn't about to die. It took a lot to fatally overwhelm the constitution of a MacRinnalch werewolf. They remained outside the car, in the rain, for some time.

"We'll be late for Minerva," said Dominil. "We should have been there by now."

Kalix was sick again, then flopped onto the wet grass, worn out. Dominil picked her up and took her back to the car. Kalix's eyes briefly opened, closed again, but Dominil was reasonably sure she was no longer in danger.

"Let's hope Minerva doesn't mind waiting," said Dominil, and set off again. Now that the crisis had passed, she felt angry. It was foolish of Kalix to have taken so much laudanum. She had enough experience of the drug to have known the risks. Not only had Kalix endangered herself, she'd made them late, and Dominil hated to be late. The rain was now coming down too heavily to drive fast, so there was nothing to do but approach the mountain slowly and hope Minerva was still waiting for them.

At its nearest point to Mount Marbauch, the road took a sharp turn to the right. Immediately after this turning there was a tiny dirt track that ran behind a large clump of tall bushes. Dominil drove onto the dirt track and parked behind the bushes, leaving the car out of sight of the road. She turned to Kalix.

"Can you walk?"

Kalix was asleep and didn't reply. Dominil gave a small, frustrated sigh. She helped Kalix out of the car, then locked the doors. By the time she'd done that, Kalix had sunk to the ground. Dominil attempted to help her walk by putting her arm around her shoulder, but Kalix hung limply, her feet dragging on the ground, and they made no progress. By now thoroughly annoyed, Dominil picked Kalix up and marched on. They were going to make a fine sight for Minerva. Late, wet through, and Kalix covered in vomit and unable to stand.

The lower slopes of Mount Marbauch were covered with heather, which grew all the way up to an area where the grass petered out, and the mountain rose above in bare black stone. The track they walked on was barely discernible through the heather, but above and ahead of them Dominil could see an isolated pine tree. Minerva had arranged to meet them at this tree, though there was no sign of her.

A familiar scent came to Dominil through the rain and the smell of damp heather. A werewolf scent. But not, realized Dominil, quite the scent she might have been expecting. Dominil looked around suspiciously. Then she laid Kalix on her side and took a few steps forward.

"Minerva?" she called.

There was no reply. Dominil walked on toward the pine tree. By this time, her werewolf senses were screaming in alarm. Behind the tree she found the elderly werewolf, face down on the ground with a great stain on the back of her coat. Dominil turned her over. There was a small hole in her chest. Minerva was dead, shot through the heart by a silver bullet.

CHAPTER 21

Moonglow was surprised that Vex wanted to call a house meeting.

"Kalix isn't here. Shouldn't we wait for her to get back?"

"I have something I need to talk about. Kalix can join in later. Can't we have a meeting without her?"

Moonglow supposed that they could. There was no particular set of rules they had to follow. There was, in fact, no difference between a house meeting and their normal informal gatherings that happened almost every day in the living room. The only reason Moonglow had ever introduced the concept was as a way of forcing everyone to talk about their crippling debts. Now that their finances were in some sort of order, they had no reason for any sort of meeting. Vex, however, wouldn't let it go. Under normal circumstances, Moonglow would have had no objection, but she'd been hoping to avoid close contact with Daniel, at least for a day or two.

Daniel lay on his bed and didn't answer when Vex knocked on his door. Vex came in anyway, and beamed at him.

"Feeling better? It's time for our meeting."

"Go away," said Daniel.

Vex peered at him, trying to interpret his aura. "You're not so ill now," she said. "Come and talk."

"Is this about *Nagasaki Night Fight Boom Boom Girl*? Because I told you, it doesn't start till next week!"

"I can't wait for *Nagasaki Night Fight Boom Boom Girl*!" cried Vex. "But that's not what I want to talk about. Come on, Moonglow's waiting!"

"I'll bet she is," grunted Daniel, and followed Vex downstairs.

Moonglow was sitting with her hair wrapped in a large black towel, still damp from the shower. A few strands escaped onto her shoulders. "Will this take long?" said Moonglow. "I need to dry my hair."

"I don't know," replied Vex. "It's a complex matter. The thing is, I'm in danger of being made Queen and we need to do something about it."

Daniel and Moonglow looked bewildered.

Vex carried on. "I was strolling through the garden of small blue flames the other day, just minding my own business, when Xakthan grabbed me. He's chief minister to Aunt Malvie. He looks about a thousand years old. Maybe more. He's not a lot of fun, to be honest. Though he did give me my fluffy dragon, so he can't be all bad. No other government minister ever gave me a fluffy toy. Which is quite mean, now that I think about it. You'd think the minister for defense might have given me a fluffy elephant. It's not like it would be that expensive, and he knows I need one."

The general bewilderment increased.

"Do you really need a fluffy elephant?" said Moonglow.

"Well, not *need*, exactly," admitted Vex. "But I'd like one. Who wouldn't?"

"Fair point," said Daniel. "Most people would enjoy having a fluffy elephant toy."

"That's what I say!" exclaimed Vex.

"Is that what this house meeting is about?" ventured Moonglow. "Fluffy elephants?"

"Not really," admitted Vex.

Moonglow drummed her fingers lightly on the table. "I would like to dry my hair, Vex. If you could get to the point."

"Of course!" Vex beamed. "The point is Xakthan started giving me a lecture about how I had to start behaving better and dressing better and being responsible, and not causing outrage at banquets, for instance by appearing topless—did I mention my topless banquet experience?—no? It was sort of accidental—I'll tell you about it later—but anyway, the outcome of all this was people expect me to start behaving better because I'm now the official heir to the throne."

Vex paused and drank from her beer bottle. "So what are we going to do?" she asked.

"Do?" said Moonglow. "About what?"

"About stopping me being Queen of course. I can't be heir to the throne; it's ridiculous. Imagine I was Queen. I'd have to spend all my time with government ministers. I can hardly bear to think about it." Vex looked sternly at Daniel and Moonglow. "Steps must be taken," she announced.

"Does Malveria really want you to be Queen?" asked Moonglow.

Vex shook her head. "I don't think so. But now I'm officially adopted, I'm her heir." Vex shuddered. "So what's to be done about it?"

Daniel and Kalix looked blankly at each other.

"Suggest something," said Vex. "I can't be Queen. I had enough of that on the volcano when everyone was shooting fire at me."

Agrivex shuddered, as she was entitled to do. Her recent mission to the volcano, during which Malveria had made her temporary ruler of the Hiyasta, had ended with her foot being blown off. Though the Fire Queen had healed her, restoring her foot, it had been a painful and traumatic experience.

"Is it really likely you'll ever be Queen?" asked Daniel. "Surely Malveria will produce an heir sometime? If she had a child, it would become first in line, wouldn't it?"

Vex frowned. "Yes, but how is she going to do that? She'd need to marry someone and have children, and there's no chance of that happening."

"Why not?" asked Moonglow.

"She never does anything except go to fashion shows. And the only people she could marry, like Hiyasta dukes and earls, don't go to fashion shows."

Moonglow nodded. "Well, that's the crux of the problem, Vex. You'll be Malveria's heir until she produces another one, so you'll have to encourage her. You should match her up with some duke or earl."

Vex slammed her palm on the table, startling the cat, who woke up, meowed and went back to sleep.

"Of course! I can do that. Definitely. Maybe. Can I do that?"

"I'm sure you can," said Moonglow encouragingly.

Vex screwed up her face. "It sounds difficult. If I got a list of all the suitable dukes and earls, maybe you could help me make some plans?"

Neither Daniel nor Moonglow really thought they were qualified for the task of helping the Queen of the Hiyasta find a partner, but they didn't want to discourage their friend.

"We could try," said Daniel.

"Excellent!" Vex's face glowed. "This has been much better than our other house meetings. I'll get more beer to celebrate." Vex stood up, then paused. "You know, I'd really like a fluffy elephant."

"One thing at a time," said Moonglow. "Your fluffy toy problems can wait."

CHAPTER 22

As soon as Vex headed for the kitchen, Daniel and Moonglow rose from the table. Moonglow headed for her room upstairs, so Daniel went in the opposite direction, following Vex into the kitchen. The young Fire Elemental was drinking another bottle of beer and eating chocolate.

Daniel and Moonglow had wondered in the past how she managed to remain as thin as a twig.

"Remember to keep what we were saying a big secret," said Vex. "If Aunt Malvie arrives, don't say we were talking about her."

They walked back into the living room, and at that moment Queen Malveria materialized in front of the fireplace.

"We weren't talking about you," said Vex.

"I beg your pardon, niece?" said Malveria.

"Nothing. I just said we weren't talking about you. We never do. Do we, Daniel?"

"Eh, no," muttered Daniel, and looked guilty.

"Thanks for the computer," said Vex, to change the subject. The Fire Queen, after asking Moonglow what Vex required for college, had given Moonglow money to buy her a laptop of her own, as a birthday present. She looked around with distaste at the bottles and cans that littered the room.

"I presume the party was a success."

"I got a boyfriend," said Vex.

"I have come to talk to Moonglow on an important matter," said the Fire Queen, ignoring her niece.

"I have a boyfriend!" repeated Vex.

The Queen frowned. "Daniel. You look rather downcast. Is something the matter?"

"Moonglow rejected him," said Vex.

"Ah." The Fire Queen nodded sagely. "Crushing his spirit?"

"Completely devastated," said Vex. "But I'm trying not to mention it. You know, in case it upsets him. Daniel, have you noticed how I've hardly mentioned it?"

Daniel nodded glumly.

"Do not worry, Daniel," said Malveria. "The unbearable humiliation of Moonglow's rejection will lessen over time. Moonglow will probably never mention it to anyone, apart from a few of her intimate friends."

She looked encouragingly at Daniel, but by this time he'd left the room.

"Odd," said the Fire Queen. "Does he not wish to talk of the matter?"

"Human boys are funny like that," said Vex, then seized the opportunity to tell her aunt, once more, that she now had a boyfriend.

The Fire Queen regarded her niece with some distaste. "I don't like this overeagerness. While liaison with men is acceptable, you should not bounce around like a little girl, squealing about it. The female Hiyasta royalty are independent women."

The Fire Queen took a step away from the fireplace, but swayed slightly.

Vex looked at her aunt quizzically. "Are you having problems walking in these heels?"

"Certainly not."

"They're really high, maybe you should—"

"Enough, dismal niece. The Queen of the Hiyasta does not have problems with heels, no matter how high." It was Malveria's turn to change the topic. "Tell me about this boyfriend."

"He's a guitarist!"

"You amaze me," said the Queen. "I take it all the doctors and lawyers were unavailable?"

Vex proceeded to tell her aunt all about Pete. Malveria, despite her doubts about the affair, was interested to learn that this was the same young man with whom Dominil had once had a brief liaison. The Fire Queen was always entertained by the romantic entanglements of others, and would have enjoyed nothing better than a furiously jealous Dominil to burst into the room, accusing Vex of stealing her man.

Though that is unlikely, from my knowledge of Dominil's character.

"She was horrible to Pete," said Vex with the instant loyalty of a new girlfriend. "It's really put me off her."

The Fire Queen sat down at the table. "When you say 'boyfriend,' Agrivex, am I to assume that you actually mean one intoxicated encounter which will never be repeated?"

Vex shook her head. "Definitely not! He's going to call me!"

Malveria shook her head. "I anticipate you may have a long wait. But enough of your grubby affairs. I came hear to consult Moonglow over an important matter. I take it she is hiding in her room upstairs, sensitive to encountering the wretched Daniel?"

"Why would she be sensitive?" asked Vex.

"Because Moonglow is a sensitive young woman. No doubt she feels some regret after trampling over Daniel's dreams, and will attempt to stay out of sight for a while. I can empathize. As a young queen, I shattered Lord Stratov's heart, and I avoided him for months afterward."

Agrivex looked interested. "Who's Lord Stratov?"

"Do you pay no attention to anything around you? Lord Stratov is one of our most illustrious noblemen. You met him last month at a banquet."

"Did I? Is he married?"

"Married? No, his wife passed away some time ago. Why do you ask?"

"No reason," replied Vex. "Just wondering."

Malveria felt the strength returning to her ankles. She rose from the table and ascended the stairs, very slowly, leaving a thoughtful Vex behind her.

CHAPTER 23

Dominil hurried back down the hill toward Kalix.

"Now we're in for a troublesome time," she muttered. Dominil could quite clearly foresee the consequences of Minerva's murder. Her cousin Thrix revered her old teacher in a way she didn't revere anyone else. Thrix was going to explode when she learned what had happened. So would the MacRinnalch Clan. That a hunter should penetrate so far into the Scottish Highlands and actually kill Minerva was extremely shocking.

Kalix didn't wake as Dominil picked her up and headed for the car. She knew she'd have to explain what they were doing on the mountain. That was going to be awkward. Dominil didn't look forward to telling the Great Council of the MacRinnalchs that she'd gone there to receive treatment for her laudanum addiction. She could imagine the reaction of her father, the Mistress of the Werewolves, and the barons.

Dominil threw Kalix into the car, no longer bothering to be gentle. She took out her phone, hesitated for only a second, then called Thrix in London.

"Thrix? This is Dominil. I'm on the mountainside below Minerva's retreat. Minerva is nearby. She's been shot and killed. A silver bullet, I'm sure."

Thrix gasped, and then fell silent. A few seconds later, Dominil heard voices on the other end of the line as Thrix talked to her assistant Ann. Thrix came back on the line.

"I'll be there soon."

Thrix rang off. Dominil knew that the Enchantress could use her sorcery to travel through space, though she wasn't sure how long it would take her to reach Scotland. The white-haired werewolf made another phone call, this time to the castle. The Mistress of the Werewolves was shocked at the news.

"Minerva is dead? How could anyone kill Minerva?"

Dominil couldn't say. Minerva's powers of sorcery were legendary. It seemed unlikely that anyone could simply have sneaked up on her. But they had, and she was dead.

"Thrix is coming," Dominil told her. "I'll be at the castle as soon as possible."

The rain poured down. Dominil remained by the car. It took a half-hour or so for Thrix to arrive. She materialized with a wild expression on her face.

"Where's Minerva?"

"Behind that tree." Dominil pointed. Thrix ran up the hill. After a few steps she halted, kicked off her shoes, then carried on running. Dominil walked slowly up the hill after her. By the time she reached the pine tree, Thrix was on her knees beside Minerva's body, crying. Her tears mingled with the rain as she leaned over her old teacher's body. It seemed to Dominil that Thrix was going to examine Minerva's wound, but instead she part collapsed, part embraced Minerva, and broke down in sobs.

Dominil watched impassively. The rain swept down, running through her white hair onto her long leather coat. The heather was sodden under her boots. Eventually, Thrix looked up. It took her several attempts before she could speak.

"What happened?"

"I found her here, like this. I called you immediately. I saw no one else in the vicinity."

The Enchantress levered herself to her feet, slowly and awkwardly. "What were you doing here?"

"We had arranged to meet Minerva. I regret to say we arrived late."

Thrix stared at Dominil, and then past her, down the hill to the car, and Kalix. "Why were you meeting Minerva?"

"For treatment for laudanum addiction. For both of us."

Thrix's tears were drying. The expression on her face changed from agitation to bewilderment. "Laudanum addiction? You?"

"Yes."

It took Thrix a few seconds to digest the news. "So Minerva was waiting here on her own? Why were you late?"

Dominil hesitated to answer. At that moment the front door of Dominil's car opened and Kalix spilled out. She sank to her knees and was sick on the grass.

"Is that why?" demanded Thrix, gesturing toward Kalix. Dominil didn't answer. Suddenly, Thrix rushed past her and ran toward the car. Dominil pursued her, but by the time Dominil caught up Thrix had grabbed Kalix and dragged her to her feet.

"You got Minerva killed!" screamed Thrix.

Kalix was still drowsy. Her eyes were unfocused and she didn't reply. Thrix drew back her right hand and dealt Kalix a brutal slap in the face. The young werewolf slammed into the side of the car then slumped once more to the ground where she lay in the wet heather.

Before Dominil could say anything, Thrix had run off again, back up the mountain toward Minerva. She picked Minerva up and struggled for a few moments to carry her up the hill. Then she put Minerva down, and shouted some words that were incomprehensible to the watching Dominil. To Dominil's great surprise, Thrix transformed into her golden werewolf shape, though it was daytime. Thrix, now stronger, picked up Minerva with ease and marched away up the hill.

Dominil watched her go. She hadn't known that Thrix's sorcery allowed her to make the change in daylight.

Kalix still lay on the ground, wet and dirty. An ugly bruise was forming on her cheek where Thrix had slapped her. Dominil shook her head, helped Kalix back into the car, then drove toward the main road.

CHAPTER 24

Distikka met Mr. Carmichael by arrangement at the Courtauld Gallery in the Strand in London. They had decided that it was best for her not to visit the Guild's headquarters again, lest she give some clue as to their whereabouts. Distikka wore a large brown coat, covering her chain mail. It made her small figure look bulky.

"Minerva is dead," said Mr. Carmichael.

"I know. I watched her die."

"You are quite certain she was a werewolf sorcerer?" said Mr. Carmichael. "We had no records of her."

"She was too cunning for you to have any records, but, believe me, Minerva was an important werewolf."

"I hope so," said Mr. Carmichael. "Otherwise we've just assassinated a harmless old woman on a mountain."

The Hainusta Elementals had many powerful spells for spying. These were difficult to use on Earth, but the Empress, with her newly increased strength, had managed to spy on Minerva. Not directly on her retreat, but the area around it. Following her directions, the Guild had secreted a sniper in the valley.

"It was a good shot," said Distikka.

Mr. Carmichael nodded. "It's not so easy, using a silver bullet in a sniper's rifle, but we have some excellent new hunters these days. I'm expecting great things from them."

Distikka found herself wondering if killing werewolves counted as *great things*, but didn't mention it. They paused beside a sculpture of a dancer by Degas.

"Minerva's death will infuriate the MacRinnalchs," said Distikka. "I'm confident they'll do something rash, thereby exposing themselves to further action."

Distikka examined the sculpture, one of a number of pieces by Degas in the gallery. "I like this," she said.

Mr. Carmichael didn't care for it, but he had never had much interest in sculpture.

"So what next?" asked the chairman.

"The Empress and I will attempt to locate more targets. London is full of werewolves."

"What about Kalix?"

"Kalix is very well hidden," said Distikka. "She carries a pendant of Tamol, given to her by Queen Malveria. It makes her impossible to locate by any known means. But other werewolves may lead us to her."

Mr. Carmichael nodded. He was quite determined that the Guild would kill Kalix.

"And the other one you mentioned . . . what was her name again?"

"Thrix," said Distikka. It was frustrating that Thrix's sorcery was so effective in blocking all knowledge of her. Mr. Carmichael could never re-member anything about her, no matter how often Distikka explained who she was. "She's the most powerful werewolf in London. I hope Minerva's death will madden her and bring her into the open."

Mr. Carmichael looked at his watch. "I'm due back at the Red House."

"The Red House?"

"It's our code name for the Guild's headquarters. No one could ever find it anyway, but you can't be too careful."

Mr. Carmichael left, with an arrangement to meet Distikka again in a week's time. Distikka was not sorry to see him go. She was enjoying the gallery and he had been a poor companion.

"How is the head of the Guild?" asked Empress Kabachetka, stepping out unexpectedly from behind a display cabinet.

"Empress? I didn't expect to see you here."

"I have business in London. My dress is not yet perfect."

For the past week the Empress had been obsessed by the dress she was wearing to the fashion designers' reception.

"It is of the utmost importance," said Kabachetka, not for the first time. "Malveria will be in attendance, and if she eclipses me again I may declare war. Or have harsh words, at the very least." The Empress found herself staring at the back of Distikka's head. "Distikka, are you ignoring me?"

"I was looking at this sculpture."

The Empress frowned. "How did it go with Mr. Carmichael?"

"Quite well," replied Distikka. "He's pleased to have killed an important werewolf."

"I'm glad Minerva is dead," said the Empress. "She was a nuisance, like all these MacRinnalchs. But she wasn't that important. You told me she'd retired from clan affairs."

Distikka nodded. "True. She had retired. But she was very important to Thrix. It's the perfect start to my plan."

They walked on. Distikka studied the sculptures while Empress Kabachetka looked at her own reflection in the glass cases. She too was finding her new extra-high heels a challenge, and was obliged to walk slowly. She frowned as they reached the end of the room and she saw that the next room also contained sculptures.

"Are these horrid statues everywhere?"

"There are paintings upstairs."

"I have no wish to see paintings," said Kabachetka. "I don't like this gallery. One can tell that the people who visit do not care for clothes. You should not spend too long here, Distikka. You don't have the sorcery to survive for long in this dimension."

The Empress left, eager to see her London fashion adviser. Distikka remained behind, calculating that she had enough time left to see some of the works by Matisse and Henry Moore before she had to leave. Distikka liked the gallery. Before departing she picked up a leaflet giving details of their future exhibitions. She was disappointed to find that the leaflet didn't survive the journey back to her own dimension. It took a lot of sorcery to carry any item undamaged from one dimension to another.

However, she'd already memorized most of it, and resolved to visit more exhibitions in the coming weeks.

CHAPTER 25

The Fire Queen knocked politely on Moonglow's bedroom door. Moonglow answered it hesitantly and looked relieved to find Malveria there. The Queen slipped inside.

"I take it you are hiding from Daniel?"

"Sort of," admitted Moonglow. "Everything has become very difficult."

The Fire Queen nodded. "Vex informed me that you had crushed his aspirations, dealing him a savage blow."

"I'm hoping it's not that bad."

The Fire Queen waved her arm dismissively. "It cannot be helped. If he is damaged by his passion, so be it. My realm is full of elementals whose hearts have been sundered by their hopeless passion for me. One does not like to brag, of course." The Fire Queen smiled, but it quickly faded. "These days I seem to have little time for breaking hearts. I'm busy with government all the time, with hardly a moment to attend to my wardrobe. I wouldn't be here had I not sneaked away from my advisory council."

"But you're the Queen. Doesn't everyone have to obey you?"

"One would think so." The Queen lowered her voice. "But I do not mind telling you, Moonglow, that the recent ructions in my country, involving an attempted coup by the dreadful Distikka, were, in a very small measure, encouraged by some distractions I may have suffered."

"Like your shoes and dresses?"

"Exactly. And while I am ruler, it does make life tedious if my government is always angry at me. I have assured them that I will spend less time on fashion and more on government, at least till things settle down."

The Queen sat on the edge of Moonglow's bed. She always felt comfortable in Moonglow's room. It was small and rather dark, with the walls painted black and hung with Gothic posters and some of Moonglow's favorite dark dresses. It reminded the Fire Queen of the caves she'd hidden in so often in her youth, as a fugitive.

"If I do get a spare moment, there is always some trouble with Agrivex.

Really, Moonglow, I sometimes become tired of looking after a whole nation, and Agrivex as well."

"I know what you mean," said Moonglow. "Sometimes I feel that way too."

"How can you feel this?" asked the Queen.

"Well, I don't have a country to look after, but I have got Daniel, Kalix and Vex. None of them are exactly competent. You know, at paying bills. Or washing up, or buying food, or tidying the house. I have to keep making these schedules for everyone and then they get annoyed with me. But if I don't do it, everything just gets in a mess. I really get tired of acting like their mother."

"I know just what you mean!" exclaimed the Fire Queen. "Ministers of state ask me the most ridiculous questions, and I am continually thinking, *Can you not work it out for yourself?* And as for Agrivex . . . "

Moonglow nodded. Agrivex could be a burden.

"I presume this so-called boyfriend will never call her again?" said the Queen.

"That's what I'm guessing. She'll probably be upset."

"She will get over it." The Fire Queen fished in her handbag and produced a small, glossy leaflet. "This is what I wished to consult you about. You will be aware that for a very long time I have been dissatisfied with my lip coloring?"

Moonglow nodded, having heard this complaint before.

"Sometimes it seems as if the universe is conspiring to make my lipstick fade," said the Queen. "No matter what I do, it will neither go on in a satisfactory glossy manner nor retain its luster through the evening. And this is becoming a matter of great importance because, at a fashion show next week, photographers from *Vogue* will be in attendance. And if I tell you that the evil Kabachetka will also be at this party, you will see how important it is that my makeup is flawless, and remains so all evening."

Malveria handed the leaflet to Moonglow. It read "Six Steps to Perfect Lips," and there were six pictures, each with a lengthy caption underneath.

"What do you think?" said the Fire Queen. "Is their six-step procedure worth implementing?"

"It's quite a long procedure," said Moonglow. "I don't know if I'd want to do it every time I went out, but it does look good. Do you want to try it?"

"Yes! Unless you are busy with other important matters . . . "

"My only plans for today were avoiding Daniel," said Moonglow.

She studied the leaflet: *Step one—Prepare and prime the lips by applying a lip conditioner.*

The Fire Queen had come prepared, and produced her lip conditioner from her bag.

"Let's get to work," said Moonglow.

CHAPTER 26

Thrix MacRinnalch was generally regarded as a glamorous young woman. She appeared to be no more than thirty years old. But werewolves lived long and aged slowly. Really, she was much older. She'd first met Minerva MacRinnalch shortly after the end of the Second World War.

A few of the young werewolves at the castle had been planning to attend a dance in the nearest town. They were looking forward to the event. There had not been much in the way of enjoyment to be had during the war. In the two years since, life had been easier, but hardly more enjoyable. Britain was in debt and few people had money. Everything was rationed, including food and clothing. Thrix had become very adept at altering clothes, taking an old dress and making something new for a special occasion. It was satisfying when it worked out well, but she was weary of it. Thrix would have loved to buy a beautiful new dress but she couldn't. Even if the Mistress of the Werewolves had allowed her daughter to spend so much money, which she probably wouldn't have, there weren't any beautiful new dresses to be had in this part of Scotland. As far as Thrix could tell, there was not a fashionable frock to be had anywhere in the north of Scotland.

Thrix was walking down a dark stone corridor, deep in thought, and had almost bumped into her mother.

"My daughter Thrix," announced Verasa to her companion. "Not looking where she's going."

"These corridors are so dark," said Thrix.

Her mother nodded. "I know. It's gloomy. But the Thane won't sanction any more lights. Have you met Minerva MacRinnalch?"

Thrix had been taken aback. Minerva was a famous, or infamous, figure in the clan, and not a werewolf she'd ever expected to meet in the castle. Minerva was a sorcerer, and that was a very odd thing for a werewolf to be. It wasn't respectable. The MacRinnalchs were suspicious of the art. As far as Thrix knew, Minerva had never visited the castle before, and wouldn't be welcomed by the Thane. He set great store by respectability. *The MacRinnalch werewolves are a civilized clan*, he said on many occasions. The clan mostly agreed with him, though some of the younger members were coming to resent the Thane's rather harsh domestic discipline.

"Are you really Minerva the sorceress?" said Thrix.

"I am." Minerva looked around fifty, in human terms, though she could have been any age. Verasa herself was several hundred years old. Minerva was a sorceress and might have lived for far longer than that. Thrix had never heard an exact account of her origins.

"You seem preoccupied," said Minerva.

"Most probably she was wondering about a new dress," said Verasa.

"Ah," said Minerva. "The dance?"

Thrix nodded. "I'm so fed up with wearing old clothes."

Minerva smiled. Thrix felt more uncomfortable. She had the feeling Minerva had quickly summed her up, and wasn't that impressed.

"Why don't you come with us?" said Minerva. "We're off for a small glass of whisky before the Thane returns. Perhaps I can give you some help."

Even now, many years later, Thrix could still visualize the dress that Minerva had created for the dance. Casting a spell on an old garment, she'd produced the most beautiful dress Thrix had ever seen. She just conjured it out of a ragged old frock. Thrix had been staggered. Her mother had seemed puzzled that Minerva would waste her power on what seemed like a trivial matter. But Minerva had done it, and the dress was beautiful, and fashionable. Thrix wore it to the dance, where it caused a sensation. No one could imagine how Thrix had managed to appear wearing such a fine new garment.

Halfway up the mountainside, Thrix came to a halt. She laid Minerva's body at her feet. Thrix's face was anguished as she looked down at her old teacher.

"It was cunning of you to make me that dress. You knew I'd be interested in sorcery after that."

What Minerva had seen in the Thane's daughter to make her select her as a pupil, Thrix had never really understood, but soon afterward she became her student. The MacRinnalchs had been shocked. Her father had raged against it. Her mother, while less angry, had not approved. Nor had her brothers. Thrix had been obliged to ignore her family and the clan to become a pupil of Minerva MacRinnalch.

"You really sucked me in with that dress."

Thrix began to cry. She wanted to take Minerva to the top of her mountain, but she couldn't go on. Horror and misery were engulfing her, freezing her body, making it impossible to act. Thrix knew she should have studied the area where Minerva had been slain. Her sorcerous powers might have picked up some hint as to the killer's identity. But Thrix couldn't go back down the mountain either. She was frozen in misery, halfway up, with her old teacher's body lying in the rain at her feet. Thrix wept bitterly, changing from her werewolf form to her human form and then back again, not knowing which was preferable, and not knowing what to do.

CHAPTER 27

Kalix slept in the back of the car and didn't revive until they were almost at the airport. At first her memory was unclear.

"Where are we?"

"Near the airport," said Dominil.

"Why? What's happening?"

Dominil pulled up at a red light and turned to look at Kalix. "Don't you remember?"

"Everything's hazy," said Kalix.

"You overdosed. You're fortunate not to be dead."

Kalix's memory started to clear. She remembered taking some laudanum the previous night, then taking a little more.

"Did we see Minerva? Why aren't we on the mountain?"

"Minerva is dead," said Dominil.

The lights changed to green and they pulled away. They'd reached the edge of Inverness and were slowly funneling through the one-way system that led to the airport. Kalix still felt confused. Her face was aching. She put her hand to her bruised cheek.

"I remember Thrix hit me!" cried Kalix. "What for?" Kalix was gripped by rage at the thought of her sister hitting her.

The car stopped. Dominil turned again. "She hit you because she blamed you for Minerva's death."

"Me? Why?"

"Your overdose meant we were late arriving. Presumably, Thrix thinks Minerva may not have died had we been on time."

Kalix's outrage drained away, to be replaced by a crushing feeling of guilt and shame. She'd taken an overdose. It had made them late. Old Minerva had been left alone and exposed on the mountainside and now she was dead. Kalix moaned and tried to make herself disappear by shrinking into her seat. She sat in unhappy silence as Dominil drove to the outskirts of the airport.

"I have to leave you here. I've booked your ticket. Are you well enough for the journey home?"

"Why am I going home?" said Kalix. "Where are you going?"

"I have to go to the castle. There will be a lot to discuss now that Minerva's been killed."

Kalix felt her face burning with shame. She, of course, could not go to the castle. She was being sent home like a misbehaving child. Although "misbehaving child" didn't seem adequate in the circumstances. Kalix could picture the scene at the castle, with every werewolf discussing Minerva's death and blaming Kalix for it.

"I don't want to go home," she muttered.

"I don't have time to discuss it," said Dominil brusquely. "I've got a long drive and I have to get there before night."

It was the third of the werewolf nights. They'd all turn into werewolves when the moon rose.

"You'll be back in London in the afternoon," continued Dominil. "I've already called Daniel, and he'll meet you at the airport and make sure you get home."

Dominil opened the doors. Kalix stared hopelessly at the world outside.

"Was it really my fault?" she asked, hoping for some reassurance from Dominil.

"It could have been," said Dominil. "We don't know for sure."

As Kalix emerged from the car she was gripped by a disturbing sense of unreality. She stood outside the departure lounge with her bag in her hand, hardly knowing how she'd got here. Her face hurt and her ribs ached from vomiting. She felt nauseous. Her inherent werewolf strength had revived her a little, but no one could take that much laudanum without feeling the effects afterward.

Why did I take so much? she wondered. She walked slowly into the departure lounge, head bowed, wishing that she might become invisible, or, better yet, cease to exist.

I'll never be able to talk to any MacRinnalch again, she thought. Even the thought of talking to Daniel and Moonglow was troubling. Had Dominil told them about her overdose? Would they know about Minerva's death?

Kalix reached inside her coat and turned off her phone, scared in case any of her family might call to abuse her. She felt her tread growing heavier, and for a moment she felt she couldn't make it to the plane. Her head swam with nausea and unhappiness. She had to hurry to the restroom, where she was once again sick.

In the cubicle, Kalix rested her head on the toilet bowl and felt her eyes fill with tears. She sighed loudly and hauled herself to her feet. She washed her hands and face. When she looked in the mirror over the sink, her skin was deathly pale and her eyes seemed shrunken, with prominent dark lines below them. Her hair was lank and dirty, and there were stains on the front of her coat.

Another journey where I'm the crazy person everyone wants to avoid, she thought, making her way slowly from the restroom to the lounge outside. She looked up at the travel indicators. There weren't that many flights, but, even so, she had difficulty making them out. She found them confusing and difficult to read, and when some of the letters flickered and changed she began to feel a familiar sense of helplessness and panic. Fortunately, her flight was announced via the public address, quite clearly. Kalix made her way toward the departure gate with her eyes fixed on the ground in front of her.

On the plane, she drank some water and then slept again. She wished that Dominil hadn't called Daniel, as she'd rather have slunk home unnoticed, but he was waiting for her at the exit gate at Heathrow, and there was nothing for it but to accompany him to his car. Daniel greeted her heartily. Kalix couldn't raise a smile in reply.

"Dominil said you were unwell."

Kalix didn't feel like lying. "I took an overdose," she said wearily.

"Oh. Are you OK now?"

Kalix nodded. "I'm fine. I'm tired."

She used this as an excuse not to talk, and closed her eyes on the drive home. This didn't prevent Daniel from talking.

"Dominil sounded grim on the phone. She always sounds grim, but this was even grimmer. Did something bad happen?"

Kalix didn't reply.

"I didn't mind driving to the airport anyway," continued Daniel. "Gets me away from Moonglow for a while. Things are a bit awkward just now. We had a discussion at the cinema. It was agreed we should never have a relationship. Agreed by Moonglow, mainly. So that's that."

Daniel noticed that he was exceeding the speed limit and slowed down. He looked over at Kalix, whose eyes were still closed. "That's a bad bruise."

Kalix turned her face away. She didn't want to talk about it. The anxiety to which she was always prone had started creeping up on her. By now, everyone at the castle would be saying it was her fault that Minerva had been killed.

It occurred to her that her sister Thrix wouldn't let the death pass unavenged. Kalix was momentarily heartened by the prospect of revenge, but it faded as she realized she wouldn't be involved. *Thrix won't let me join in. She'll keep me out of it.*

Kalix felt her anxiety growing. She wished that Daniel would stop talking, but didn't want to tell him to be quiet for fear of snapping at him. She kept her eyes shut and pretended to be asleep, though her anxiety and misery were growing stronger all the time.

CHAPTER 28

The Fire Queen's suspicions were immediately aroused by Agrivex's enthusiasm for attending the official reception for the Great Keeper of the Minor Volcano.

"You wish to attend? Why?"

"I'm officially your niece now," said Vex brightly. "I should go to these things. Like a member of the royal family."

Malveria studied her niece, attempting to interpret her aura. "You are quite clearly lying, dismal niece, and had you not recently learned how to partially conceal your aura from me, I would know why. Tell me your motivations for this upcoming outrage."

"What outrage? You'd make me attend anyway."

"True. But normally you would protest."

Agrivex had arrived for her weekly visit to the Fire Queen's palace at the foot of the Great Volcano. Though she could now spend four or five days a week in London, she still had to return regularly to her own realm to replenish her fire.

"I enjoy an official reception every now and then," she said.

The Fire Queen shook her head. Her niece's willingness to become involved in official life at court should have been a welcome development, but Malveria had her reservations. Things tended to go wrong when the young Hiyasta was around.

"Well, Agrivex, I will welcome you at the event. Be aware that even by the standards of the court, this will be a rather tedious affair. The Great Keeper of the Minor Volcano is not one of our most interesting dignitaries, though I admit he does do a splendid job."

"Why does he need a reception?" asked Agrivex.

"It is wise to keep these officials happy. The Minor Volcano does provide power for part of the nation. And the Keeper comes from a very ancient family."

"Will there be dukes and earls there?" asked Vex.

"The full array of our aristocracy will be in attendance. Why do you ask?"

"No reason. Just wondering."

The Fire Queen again glared at her niece suspiciously, certain that she was up to something.

"Is there something different about your lips?" asked Agrivex, cunningly diverting her aunt's attention.

"There is! I have a new lip program entitled 'Six Steps to Perfect Lips.' Yesterday I went through it with Moonglow. Unfortunately, we could not complete the process as we were lacking ingredients, but we will carry on next week."

"They're looking good," said Agrivex.

"Thank you." Malveria frowned. "I do not recall you ever complimenting my makeup before. Are you trying to get me to buy you something?"

Agrivex looked extremely pained. "Can't I do anything? I volunteer to come to this dull reception, and I tell you your lips are on the right track, and all you do is look suspicious."

The Fire Queen's features softened. "I apologize, Agrivex. You are right. I appreciate your efforts. Do you have a suitable dress?"

"Absolutely."

Vex picked a dress up and held it to her frame. To the Fire Queen's surprise, it was almost suitable for the occasion. Agrivex had actually found something respectable. As her niece departed to make herself ready, Malveria was left wondering if she might have turned a corner.

"Perhaps the appalling girl is finally learning some sense. She might even become an asset to the royal household. That would be a great surprise, but one supposes stranger things have occurred."

Vex hurried off to meet her new friend the Honorable Gloria in the Garden of Small Blue Flames. Gloria was some years older than Vex, though still very young by the standards of the Hiyasta. As the daughter of Lord Stratov, she was a well-known figure. She was not especially popular, but was very eligible. Vex didn't really like her, but had purposely made her acquaintance after introducing herself politely.

"It must get lonely in that castle," said Vex. "With your father being a duke and not having a wife any more."

"The castle is always busy," Gloria told her. "We have a lot of functions."

"Of course. But still, not having a wife must get him down a bit?"

"I suppose so," said Gloria dubiously. She couldn't ever remember her father saying he was lonely.

"What he needs to do is marry again."

The Honorable Gloria frowned genteelly. She didn't much care for Agrivex, with her odd clothes and bleached, spiky hair. Had Agrivex remained in her proper station, the Honorable Gloria would have been content never to exchange a word with her. But the Fire Queen, for whatever reason, had adopted her as her niece, and that made Vex an important figure. Gloria was not the only young aristocrat who now found herself obliged to be polite to her.

"I'm sure my father has never expressed any desire to marry again."

"Probably just keeps it to himself," said Vex. "You can see it would be difficult. There aren't that many high-class women available. Although they do say the Queen is on the lookout for a husband."

The Honorable Gloria came to an abrupt halt, crushing a small blue flame flower in the process. She was quite a large young woman, and the flame shriveled beneath her feet.

"The Fire Queen? Are you suggesting my father . . . "

Vex feigned surprise. "I never thought of that. But now you mention it, why not? Didn't they used to uh . . . know each other quite closely?"

"I'd no idea," said Gloria.

"Well, that's what's rumored in court," said Agrivex. "Probably wouldn't take much to stir up the old fires again."

The Honorable Gloria's eyes shone. She liked the idea of her father marrying the Fire Queen. She would be a princess.

"I take it you're both coming to the reception tonight?" asked Agrivex.

"We'll be there," said Gloria emphatically. "Excuse me, I must go and talk to my father."

The Honorable Gloria hurried off, leaving Vex looking pleased with herself.

Easy, she thought. Now if Lord Stratov can just get together with Aunt Malvie, there'd be no more talk about me being Queen.

She looked down at the flower that Gloria had crushed. "Sorry about that," said Vex, who liked the small blue flaming plants. She wished it wasn't damaged, and leaned over it, wishing she could do something to help. To her surprise, a flickering yellow flame flowed from the tip of her finger into the flower. The flower immediately revived, reigniting as it came back to life.

"Hey!" said Vex. "I never knew I could do that." She grinned at the small flower, now engulfed in a healthy blue flame.

"I wonder if I could be a singer in a band like Yum Yum Sugary Snacks?" she said, speaking to the flower. "That would be good. And *Nagasaki Night Fight Boom Boom Girl* starts next week! I can hardly wait!"

Vex wandered back toward her chambers, still carrying her dress. She loathed the garment and could hardly believe she was about to wear it. As she entered the Imperial Palace through the Discretely Flaming Portico, she was surprised to run into the Duchess Gargamond. The Duchess had once been a familiar figure at court but had been absent for several months.

"Duchess Gargamond!" cried Vex. "You're back."

The Duchess greeted her politely, doing her utmost not to react to Vex's shock of bleached hair. She'd forgotten just how bright it was.

"So you've made up your argument with Aunt Malvie?"

"Yes indeed, Agrivex. It was but a trifling disagreement."

"I heard you were cursing each other after Aunt Malvie accused you of being the worst card player in the Hiyasta nation."

The Duchess pursed her lips and didn't comment.

"But I wouldn't worry about it," continued Vex, "Aunt Malvie is often cranky for no reason. You wouldn't believe how she talks to me sometimes. It's scandalous. Did you hear I was officially adopted?"

The Duchess intimated that the happy news had indeed reached her during her self-imposed exile.

"That's a nice-looking dress you have, Agrivex."

Agrivex scowled at the garment. "It's for the reception tonight, for the minor dragon keeper or something like that." A cunning look came into her eyes. "Is your brother Duke Garfire going to the reception?"

"He will be," said the Duchess.

"Didn't he once try and cozy up to the Queen? When he was younger? I'm sure I heard some handmaidens talking about it some time."

The Duchess looked rather embarrassed, as if it were an episode of which she'd rather not be reminded.

"There may have been a fleeting moment when he . . . Why do you ask?"

"No reason," said Vex airily. "No reason at all. Except I did hear Aunt Malvie mention just the other day how much she missed good old Duke Garfire and wished he was around. It was right after First Minister Xakthan was telling her she should get married."

"The Queen really said that?"

"She did. Well, I must get myself into this dress."

Agrivex departed, satisfied with a job well done. Behind her the Duchess looked thoughtful, then abandoned her stroll to hurry off and talk to her brother the Duke.

CHAPTER 29

Dominil noticed an air of unease as she entered the dark stone edifice of Castle MacRinnalch. The werewolves who opened the gate were watchful and alert, more so than normal. Here, at the castle, the very center of the MacRinnalch's world, there had been little need for tight security in recent years. It was more than two hundred years since the castle had been attacked by outsiders. The Avenaris Guild had never dared trouble them here. Yet it was only a few months ago that the hunters made their presence felt in Scotland. They'd attacked an event in Edinburgh that had been hosted by the Mistress of the Werewolves. Edinburgh was far to the south, but close enough to make the werewolves mindful of danger. Now Minerva had been killed in the Highlands. It was a shocking occurrence, and one that suggested that the hunters were becoming bolder.

Thane Markus was waiting for Dominil. He greeted her in the courtyard.

"Is Thrix here?" asked Dominil. "How is she?"

"Barely sane," replied Markus.

Dominil nodded. She hadn't expected the Enchantress to have calmed down. They walked through the central courtyard together.

"Thrix thinks we should go to war," said Markus. "She might be right."

"I doubt the Mistress of the Werewolves will agree," said Dominil.

"You might be surprised. She was furious after her charity event was attacked."

As they left the courtyard the moon came up. Everyone in the castle took on their werewolf shape. Dominil and Markus continued their conversation without a break.

"I called an emergency council meeting," said Markus.

"Are there enough of us?"

"Just about. Marwanis isn't here, of course. She's still not forgiven us for the death of Sarapen. Beauty and Delicious aren't here, but they wouldn't come anyway. And Kalix . . . "

"The makeup of the council really isn't suitable any more," said Dominil. "It's a hangover from the old days when every relative of the Thane was automatically appointed. But in those days young werewolves didn't disappear off to London to be rock stars."

Markus nodded. He knew that the council hadn't been functioning properly. There were meant to be seventeen members, but Dulupina was becoming too old to attend, and the twins never did. Decembrius had shown no interest in appearing since his elevation. Marwanis refused all attempts at reconciliation. As for Kalix, it seemed almost comical that she'd ever been appointed to the council. She'd gained her place automatically as a child of the old Thane, but had been banished before attending a meeting.

"So six of the seventeen won't be there," said Dominil. "The others?"

"I got word to the barons," said Markus. "And the others are here. Eleven is enough for a meeting."

"A meeting containing all our most conservative members," Dominil pointed out. "The barons always want a quiet life. So does my father."

Dominil's father Tupan was brother to the old Thane. He was a respectable werewolf, and not the sort to encourage the clan to make war on the Guild. They carried on through the dark stone corridors of the castle.

"Do you need long to get ready?"

"Five minutes," said Dominil, who carried her small bag of belongings over her shoulder.

"How was Kalix?"

"Healthy enough, last time I saw her. She'll be back in London by now."

Markus paused. "Thrix wasn't very clear about things, but I gather she blames Kalix for Minerva's death."

Dominil made no reply.

"Was it her fault?" urged Markus.

"Let's talk about it at the meeting."

CHAPTER 30

"How can you possibly have lost Kalix?" demanded Moonglow.

Daniel was both shamefaced and exasperated, having already answered this question three times.

"I had to stop for gas. I went to pay for it, and when I got back to the car she wasn't there."

"Didn't you see where she went?"

"No. I drove around looking but she'd vanished."

Moonglow could hardly believe that Daniel, having successfully picked up Kalix at the airport, had lost her on the way home. She stared out the window. "It's getting dark. This is the third wolf night. Kalix will change."

"She's changed hundreds of times. She'll be all right."

"Was she wearing her pendant?" asked Moonglow.

Kalix's pendant, a mystic item given to her by the Fire Queen, kept her safe from prying eyes, hiding her werewolf nature from the hunters.

"I never notice jewelry. She was probably wearing it."

Moonglow was not reassured. "It won't hide her if she runs around the streets as a werewolf. Why did she get out of the car? What did you do?"

"I didn't do anything," protested Daniel. "I went and picked her up at the airport. At short notice, which was helpful of me. I can't help it if she did a runner on the way home."

"Did you insult her? You know how sensitive Kalix is."

Daniel insisted that he hadn't insulted Kalix, but Moonglow was no longer listening. She was putting on her shoes and picking up her keys. "I'm going to look for her."

"How?" asked Daniel. "When she's a werewolf, she can climb over buildings and hide in parks. We'll never find her."

"I'm going to try." Moonglow frowned quite deeply. "I knew something bad would happen. Every time Kalix goes away on werewolf business, something bad happens."

"She had a bruise on her face," said Daniel.

"What?" Moonglow paused while buttoning her coat. "A bruise? Why didn't you say that before?"

"I just remembered."

"How big was it?"

"Quite big."

"I have a very bad feeing about all this," said Moonglow.

Daniel sighed. He had a bad feeling about it too. They'd known Kalix long enough to know that she tended to attract trouble.

"Dominil probably bullied her for no reason then sent her home," said Moonglow. "Now Kalix is upset. She always takes everything so badly. She might have had a big panic attack in the car and run away; she's done that before."

Daniel followed Moonglow to the door. "You know we have no chance of finding her?"

"She can't have gone that far. Kalix won't run around the streets as a werewolf; she must be hiding somewhere."

Daniel remembered a previous occasion when they'd hunted the streets for Kalix. They'd only found her thanks to Malveria's supernatural powers of perception. Kalix had been very badly injured, and had it not been for the Fire Queen's exceptional healing powers she would have died. Malveria wasn't around to help them now.

"She sometimes hides in the park," said Moonglow. "She has a favorite clump of bushes. We can start looking there. Wait while I make tea."

Daniel looked puzzled. "Do we have time for tea?"

"It's not for us, it's for Kalix. I'll take it in a flask."

"Why?"

"Kalix likes tea. It's soothing. I have a feeling we're going to find her in a very agitated state."

Daniel waited in the kitchen as Moonglow boiled the kettle. "I wonder what everyone else is doing tonight?" he mused out loud. "Going to gigs, or clubs, I suppose. Not like us. We get to hunt in dangerous parks for a crazy werewolf. With a flask of tea for protection."

Moonglow smiled. It was the first moment of good humor they'd managed between them since the disastrous events at the cinema. By the time she'd made tea and poured it into a thermos flask, Daniel was ready with his coat and shoes on. They trooped downstairs together, groping their way in the darkness.

"We really should get a light bulb for the hallway sometime," said Daniel.

It took only a few minutes to drive to Kennington Park, but as Daniel pulled up at the curb he felt nervous. "I don't like parks at night. They lock the gates and you're not meant to be there. What if it's full of criminals?"

Moonglow looked at the dark expanse of grass and shrubs and the locked iron gate in front of them. It was quite intimidating. "I brought a torch," she said.

"Won't that just warn the muggers we're coming?"

There were a few pedestrians on the pavement opposite, but no one paid them any attention as they scrambled over the fence.

"Kalix's favorite bushes are this way," said Moonglow, leading the way.

The light from the street didn't extend very far into the park and they soon found themselves enveloped in gloom, following the narrow beam of Moonglow's torch. When they reached the bushes, Moonglow shined her torch into them and called out softly. "Kalix?"

There was no reply.

Daniel called louder. There was no reply.

"Well, I'm not standing here calling out for a werewolf all night," said Daniel. "Let's get it over with."

He plunged into the bushes, struggling toward the center of the large patch of vegetation, which was just as sharp, thorny and uncomfortable as he imagined it would be.

CHAPTER 31

Thrix had never before found herself unable to brush her hair, but as she sat in front of her dressing table she was overwhelmed by a wave of grief and anger so intense that she flung her brush at her reflection and leaped to her feet, crying out with rage. "I'll kill them all!"

The Enchantress slammed two clenched fists on the dresser and then raised her hand to blast it with a spell, just for the satisfaction of destroying something. She halted herself just in time.

"Breaking things won't make things better." She leaned on the dressing table and felt pain and stiffness in her arms. Her muscles ached from climbing the mountain, and each aching muscle was being pulled tighter by stress and anger.

"They're all going to die," she said, though there was no one there to hear her. "Everyone in the Avenaris Guild is going to die."

In her werewolf shape, Thrix's golden hair hung long around her head, shoulder and arms. Normally, she'd brush her coat before making any sort of appearance. Now it was almost time for the council meeting, but she didn't care that she was unkempt.

The clan can agree to go to war with the Guild or not, she thought. I don't care. I'm going to war, on my own if necessary.

Since arriving at the castle she'd been gripped with bursts of extreme emotion that she was finding difficult to control. One had been so powerful that a little magic had inadvertently leaked from her hand, destroying her bedside chair. The grief was so powerful it felt as if it might overwhelm her and cause her to become irrational. Minerva wouldn't have approved. The thought of what Minerva might have approved of brought on another wave of rage. Thrix shuddered, clenched her fists to control herself, then hurried from the room. She headed toward the council chamber with the thought that she'd be doing well if she made it through the meeting without screaming at everyone. Not every member of the clan had held Minerva in the same regard as the Enchantress.

As always, for their nighttime meetings the council chamber was warmed by a great log fire and torches burned on the walls. The room was hung with tapestries and banners in the dark green MacRinnalch tartan. There were pitchers of water on the circular oak table and a large decanter of the clan whisky. Already at the table were Clan Secretary Rainal, Dominil and her father Tupan. They rose as the Thane and the Mistress of the Werewolves entered. The three barons, talking together in a corner, bowed their heads slightly in greeting and waited for them to be seated before taking their own places. Moments later, Kurian and his son Kertal entered the chamber.

As Rainal was about to start the meeting, Lucia, Verasa's sister, hurried in, looking apologetic. She took her seat swiftly.

"I believe that's everyone," began the secretary. "Thane Markus, the Mistress of the Werewolves, Baron MacAllister, Baron MacGregor, Baron MacPhee, Thrix MacRinnalch, Lucia MacRinnalch, Tupan MacRinnalch, Dominil MacRinnalch, Kurian MacRinnalch and Kertal MacRinnalch. Council members not present are Marwanis, Butix, Delix, Dulupina, Decembrius and Kalix. Clan statutes allow for a meeting of the Great Council comprising eleven members."

"It's not good though," said Kurian, a brother of the late Thane who was just starting to turn gray with age. "We never have a full turnout these days."

"In my day, it was an honor to be on the council," said Tupan, who was only a few years younger than his brother Kurian. "No one failed to attend."

"Things are rather different these days," said Verasa. "Not all werewolves live close to the castle."

Beside Verasa, her sister Lucia was looking shamefaced. It was a continual embarrassment to her that her son Decembrius didn't attend meetings. She'd been proud when he'd been elected to the council, but he'd let her down. Thrix clenched her fists under the table. A MacRinnalch as a werewolf, while quite rational, did tend to have a shorter temper than a MacRinnalch as a human. She reached out and poured herself a glass of whisky.

"Perhaps it's time we looked at the membership?" said Baron MacPhee. The Baron was a huge werewolf. While loyal to the MacRinnalchs, he was senior enough to make such a suggestion. "Some of our absent members seem unlikely ever to attend."

"You mean Kalix?" said Kertal.

"And Butix and Delix," added Tupan. Tupan didn't approve of the twins. The only time in recent memory that the twins had shown up for a council meeting, they'd been bribed to attend by the Mistress of the Werewolves. Verasa had needed their votes to ensure Markus's election as Thane. Those werewolves who'd supported Sarapen still resented it. Though Verasa had worked assiduously since the end of the feud to bring the clan back into harmony, some annoyance lingered on.

"I'm sure Butix and Delix will take up their positions in due course," said Verasa smoothly. "Perhaps when they're a little older."

"Decembrius will be here next month, I'm certain," said Lucia.

No one believed her, though no one was rude enough to say it.

"Perhaps Marwanis . . . " began the Mistress of the Werewolves.

Young Baron MacAllister laughed. He'd seen his father and his brother killed in the deadly feud. "Marwanis isn't coming back. And, incidentally, she tells you all to go to hell."

Marwanis had been a strong supporter of Sarapen. She'd left the castle in fury after his defeat, and now resided at Baron MacGregor's keep. Verasa had made several peaceful overtures to her, none of which had brought any response.

"As for Kalix—" began Tupan.

"Enough of this!" roared Thrix, and slammed her palm into the table, causing it to vibrate. "Minerva was murdered and I want to talk about it!"

There was a surprised silence.

"We'll get to it—" said the Mistress of the Werewolves.

"I want to talk about it now!"

Verasa looked toward Rainal.

"We could alter our agenda—"

"Good!" Thrix rose to her feet and leaned forward so that the long blonde hair around her shoulders hung on the table.

"The Avenaris Guild killed Minerva. I want revenge. We've backed off for too long and now this has happened. We should have moved against them long ago."

Thrix turned to look accusingly at her mother and her brother. "The clan thought it was safe because the Guild was far away in London. So we let them get away with the occasional werewolf killing for the sake of not getting ourselves involved in a war. For a quiet life. Because you're all so worried about the outside world intruding into your cozy little castle. Well, now they're almost here. If the hunters can kill Minerva on her mountain then they can strike anywhere. We have to take action."

Thrix slammed her paw on the table again. "I'll be taking action anyway. But I'd prefer if the clan helped."

Baron MacPhee spoke. He was a huge, rotund figure, with a deep voice to match. "Before discussing action, could we have a report? All I know is that Minerva's been killed. I haven't heard how it happened."

"She was shot," said Thrix. "A rifle, I think, which is unusual."

"Didn't she have spells protecting her?" asked Tupan.

Thrix looked at him suspiciously, wondering if he was hinting at disapproval for Minerva's sorcery.

"Minerva had retired. She rarely used magic for anything. She'd gone beyond it. She was living out her life peacefully."

"What did you find when you examined the area?" asked Markus. Thrix's forensic skills were well known. The Enchantress could learn a lot about any werewolf death by studying the surroundings.

Thrix sat down. "I didn't really examine the area. I was too upset. I took Minerva back to the top of the mountain and then I . . . " She fell silent.

"So you didn't see any trace of her attackers?" asked Markus.

"It wasn't Thrix who discovered the body," said Dominil. "It was me."

There was some surprise at this. Tupan turned to his daughter. "You found Minerva? What were you doing there?"

Dominil didn't answer. There was a long pause.

"What were you doing there?" asked Tupan again.

"I'd rather not say."

"This is unsatisfactory," said the elderly Baron MacGregor. "How can we discuss it if we don't know the circumstances?"

Thrix's temper welled up again. "Dominil took Kalix to see Minerva because Minerva was going to help her get off laudanum," she said. "But Kalix took an overdose on the way so they were late arriving. Minerva was left on her own, waiting for them. An old woman without any protection. That's when she was killed."

"Ah," said Tupan. "Kalix."

There was muttering around the table. No one was surprised to learn that Kalix had been involved. She was outlawed and known to be insane. The Mistress of the Werewolves sat stony-faced, not wishing to hear ill of her youngest daughter, but Thrix's eyes blazed with anger.

"Yes, Kalix! Kalix and her laudanum addiction caused further destruction!" Thrix raised her paw and there were several swift moves by werewolves to steady their glasses of whisky before she crashed it on the table again.

"She's always been a disgrace," said Baron Douglas MacAllister. As the youngest baron, with strong reason to resent Markus and Verasa, he was more willing than most to voice his feelings, and not sorry to have an opportunity to criticize Verasa's family.

"My daughter is not a disgrace," said Verasa quietly. "She's had troubles, but she is not a disgrace. And she is not insane."

"But she is banished," said Douglas. "She shouldn't have been visiting a clan member in Scotland."

"Kalix was with me," said Dominil. "As a member of the council, I'm entitled to take a werewolf anywhere, even one who's banished. I judged the journey worthwhile."

"It seems to have gotten Minerva killed," said Douglas. "She'd never have come down from her mountaintop if she hadn't had to treat her for laudanum."

"That's not entirely fair," said Dominil. "Kalix wasn't the only one needing treatment."

There was a long silence while the assembled werewolf council digested this.

"What exactly do you mean?" asked the Mistress of the Werewolves eventually.

"I'm also addicted to laudanum. I made the initial approach to Minerva. I asked her if she could help me. Then I asked Kalix if she would like to accompany me. So the responsibility for bringing Minerva from her mountain rests with me."

In the long, astonished silence that followed, the only sound was the crackling of the great log fire. Everyone stared at Dominil with disbelief.

Markus eventually spoke. "Dominil, you're telling us you're addicted to laudanum? Is this just some way of protecting Kalix?"

"No. I am addicted."

"But you're not. You can't be."

"I assure you I have been for some years now. I've controlled it to the extent where I've kept functioning. But I am an addict, and take the substance every day."

Dominil had not looked forward to confessing her addiction to the council. She was aware of the shock it would cause. The barons looked aghast. The Mistress of the Werewolves, who had the highest regard for Dominil, looked like she'd been struck a blow. Markus's werewolf jaws were parted, as if he wanted to speak but couldn't think of anything to say. As for her father Tupan, he was leaning away from her in his chair, as if trying to distance himself from his own daughter. That Dominil, known as the most intelligent, least passionate and most self-controlled werewolf in the clan, should share a substance addiction with Kalix was unbelievable. Kalix's addiction was shameful enough but had been rationalized by the clan as part of her madness. Dominil had no such excuse.

"So how much laudanum had you taken when you opposed Sarapen's nomination as Thane?" said young Baron Douglas mockingly. The young baron seemed amused.

"There's no need to drag the election up again," said the Mistress of the Werewolves sharply.

The shock may have lasted longer, and the accusations may have fallen harder on Dominil, had Thrix's temper not been so violent. Thrix was not about to let the meeting be sidetracked into a discussion of Dominil's problems. She growled, loudly enough to gain everyone's attention.

"Did you also overdose in the morning?"

"No," said Dominil.

"So you would have arrived on time?"

"Yes."

"Then your addiction doesn't change anything," said Thrix. "Right now we're talking about Minerva being murdered."

Thrix stared at Markus. "I want the clan to declare war on the Avenaris Guild. I want us to find their headquarters and wipe them out. And I want you to ensure that the clan will devote whatever resources are necessary. So let's discuss it."

CHAPTER 32

After failing to find Kalix in the park, Daniel and Moonglow retreated to the car. Daniel had several deep scratches in his hand.

"It was mad to plunge into those bushes," he said. "You shouldn't have encouraged me."

"I didn't encourage you!" protested Moonglow. "You just dived right in!"

Daniel examined his bleeding hand. "I'll probably get some disease. Parks are full of diseases."

"Stop being such a baby," said Moonglow. "You won't get a disease. What should we do now?"

Daniel shook his head. He had no idea. They'd rushed out of the house to find Kalix, but having failed to locate her in the park, they weren't sure where else to look.

"She's probably on a rooftop somewhere," said Daniel. "Looking down malevolently at the world after some werewolf crisis, which she won't want to tell us about anyway. We must be insane, rushing around after her and getting cuts that will almost certainly lead to blood poisoning. Why do we waste so much time and effort on her?"

"Because we love her, of course," said Moonglow, which took Daniel by surprise. He thought about it for a moment.

"I suppose we do," he said.

They sat in silence for a few moments. The werewolf crisis had caused them to forget the awkwardness between them, at least for the moment.

"I just can't think where else to look," said Moonglow.

"I know!" cried Daniel. "The first time I met Kalix, she was hiding in a warehouse. I think she lived there for a while. She might have gone back."

"Good idea. Where is it?"

"Not far away, it's beside the big sorting office."

Daniel set off toward the warehouse. They drove past a series of railway arches and turned into a side road that led into a large industrial estate which was surrounded by a tall wire fence. Daniel drove slowly along the side of the estate while Moonglow scanned the fence, looking for an opening.

"There's a gap; we can get in there."

They came to a halt.

"I'm actually quite scared of going into a dark warehouse in the middle of the night," said Daniel.

Moonglow was already half out of the car and didn't reply. Daniel hurried after her. They slipped through the gap in the fence and approached the warehouse. It looked like it hadn't been used for many years. The whole industrial estate was dilapidated, with old wooden pallets strewn around and rusting oil drums lying on their sides.

"The door's open," said Moonglow, lowering her voice to a whisper.

"Good," whispered Daniel. "It might be Kalix. Or a gang of violent criminals."

"Criminals would have better places to go," said Moonglow. She took her torch from her bag and stepped inside. Daniel mustered his courage and followed her. The moment they stepped through the door they heard a frightful growling.

"Kalix?" said Moonglow, raising her voice.

There was another growl, and the sound of padding feet. Moonglow shone her torch into the darkness. Two red eyes appeared to shine back at them.

"Oh no," said Daniel. "Kalix is a full wolf."

"That's OK," said Moonglow. "At least we've found her."

"It's not OK," said Daniel urgently. "When she's a wolf it's not like when she's a werewolf. She forgets everything about being human. We should go."

"Don't be silly," said Moonglow. "It'll be fine. Hi, Kalix, we've come to take you home."

At that moment the wolf-Kalix let out a terrifying howl and charged at them. Daniel, demonstrating speed and athleticism that he didn't know he possessed, grabbed Moonglow and dragged her toward a gigantic wooden container. He leaped upward to grasp the edge and hauled himself up, dragging Moonglow after him. Moonglow's pointy boots barely avoided the snapping of Kalix's great wolf jaws. The two students had scrambled to safety just in time. Kalix was growling and snapping her jaws, leaping up at them. Fortunately for Daniel and Moonglow, the wolf was unable to mount the tall wooden crate. Her claws made a terrible ripping sound as she pawed at it, trying to climb toward them. She let out a howl even more terrifying than before, then padded up and down, growling savagely, turning this way and that, all the while staring up at Daniel and Moonglow with a crazed look in her eyes.

"Well, we found Kalix," said Daniel. "And now we're trapped on top of a crate. Any suggestions?"

"She just needs to calm down," said Moonglow. "I'll talk to her."

Moonglow, standing on top of the large crate, leaned forward slightly and caught Kalix's eye.

"Kalix, it's us, Daniel and Moonglow. There's no need to be upset, we're here to help."

Kalix immediately made another furious attack on the crate, howling and snarling. Moonglow took a hasty step back.

"That went well," said Daniel. "Maybe you should offer her a cup of tea."

"There's no need to be sarcastic. I'm sure the tea will come in useful. At least I tried to think of something helpful."

"So did I," said Daniel. He was wearing a rather oversized coat. From his deep pockets he took a small music player and then, surprisingly, two small speakers.

"You see?" said Daniel. "I came prepared too. I knew Kalix was probably going to be in some savage, bestial state."

"How could you know that?"

"Since meeting Kalix I've learned to expect the worst." Daniel plugged the small speakers into his music player. "I think this will calm her down," he said.

Moonglow was immediately alarmed. "If you start playing some horrible doom metal Kalix will probably eat the crate."

"My doom-metal collection is not horrible," responded Daniel. "You just don't understand it. But anyway, that's not what I'm going to play. You know"—he turned to look at Moonglow—"it sometimes strikes me you don't give me enough credit for my intelligence. I knew the day would come when Kalix went completely crazy, and I've prepared for it."

Daniel pressed the play button. A gentle sound emerged from the speakers, an acoustic guitar that played quite softly and two female voices.

"What's this?" asked Moonglow.

"Marine Girls. I chose it scientifically as the best music to calm our angry werewolf."

Moonglow looked doubtful. "You chose it scientifically? How?"

"Because when I was making CDs for Kalix, I noticed she usually likes music with female singers. And she likes things from the seventies and eighties. Probably the result of growing up with only the Runaways to comfort her. This is the most soothing music that fits the bill."

Moonglow was still skeptical and half expected the music to drive Kalix into an even worse frenzy. She looked down at the wolf, which was still prowling. But Kalix had stopped howling and was no longer trying to bite the crate.

"I think it's working," said Daniel. At the sound of his voice, Kalix started howling again. With a look between them, Daniel and Moonglow agreed to be silent for a while. Kalix quieted down again. The music played out gently through the warehouse. Kalix stopped howling. She walked around in a circle a few times. As the first song ended and the next began, she lay down and began licking her paws.

"I think it's working," Moonglow whispered in Daniel's ear. She'd been standing rigidly in alarm since arriving on top of the crate, but now relaxed a little. Moving carefully so as not to disturb Kalix, she sat down. Daniel did the same. They sat and watched as the shaggy-coated wolf stretched out on the ground and yawned. Kalix's wolf-mouth was huge, and her teeth were extremely long and sharp, but when she stopped yawning she looked quite peaceful.

For a long interval there was no movement in the warehouse, and no sound save for the gentle songs of Marine Girls. Kalix lay motionless on the ground, occasionally twitching her tail.

"She's so beautiful as a wolf," whispered Moonglow.

Daniel made a face. Kalix was beautiful as a wolf, but she was also abnormally powerful. It didn't take long for her to forget she was human and lose her intellect. It was mainly because of this that she very rarely made the full change. Few of the MacRinnalchs did, preferring to spend their nights as werewolves, the half-human half-wolf state that came to them quite naturally. As werewolves, their intelligence didn't desert them.

"Dominil can be a full wolf and still be rational," whispered Moonglow.

"How do you know that?"

"The twins told me. They never dare go completely wolf because they'd immediately turn crazy."

"I can believe that," whispered Daniel. "So, do you think we'll be here all night?"

Moonglow shrugged. Unless Kalix made the change back to her werewolf form, it seemed likely. Though the day had been warm, the temperature had dropped and it was chilly in the warehouse. Daniel gallantly took off his large coat and draped it over both of their shoulders.

"Do you want some tea?" asked Moonglow, still taking care to keep her voice down.

Daniel nodded. Moonglow carefully drew her flask from her bag and some paper cups. She filled one for each of them, and they sat in silence, listening to the music and gazing down at the slumbering wolf.

"Of all the strange situations we've been in since we met Kalix," whispered Daniel, "this is probably the strangest. Trapped on top of a crate, drinking tea and listening to the Marine Girls."

Despite the strangeness of the situation, Daniel didn't really mind the position he was in, next to Moonglow, snuggled up under his coat. Moonglow giggled.

"What's funny?"

"This. Our situation."

"I suppose so," said Daniel.

Suddenly, Kalix woke. She lifted her snout and started sniffing the air. Then she stood up and looked up at them.

"Is she about to go crazy again?" said Daniel.

"I don't think so. Look, she's wagging her tail."

Kalix was indeed wagging her tail. Though still staring upward at them, her eyes were no longer blazing.

"She's scented the tea. I think she wants some."

"Are you sure?" said Daniel.

"Kalix likes tea. Her family used to drink a lot at the castle."

They wondered how to get the tea to Kalix. Neither was keen to leave the safety of the crate just yet. Daniel and Moonglow did love Kalix, but they'd also seen her kill a hunter.

Daniel fumbled in one of his many pockets. He produced a length of string, and tied it around one of Moonglow's paper cups. Moonglow filled the cup. Daniel leaned over the crate and started lowering the paper cup.

"Nice wolf," he said. "Here's a nice cup of tea. Don't go crazy."

Daniel lowered the tea gently to the ground. Kalix sniffed at it for a few moments, then stuck her long tongue in the cup. The cup quickly spilled over but Kalix didn't seem to mind, and lapped the tea up from the floor. When she'd finished she lay down again, and once more there was peace in the warehouse, broken only by the gentle music. Daniel and Moonglow leaned on each other for warmth and support, while down below Kalix nodded off to sleep, apparently pacified.

CHAPTER 33

Vex had never liked the Red Reception Chamber. It had been decorated centuries ago in a palette of black, crimson and maroon, and was to her mind one of the most unpleasant rooms in the palace. She did her best to ignore the speeches that were droning on endlessly, as dignitaries paid tribute to the sterling career of the Keeper of the Minor Volcano. The general consensus was that he had kept the Minor Volcano in splendid condition.

Vex chafed in her dress and glared at her smart court slippers.

I hate these more than anything in the whole world, she thought, and wondered glumly how much longer the speeches would go on for. *Another five minutes and I'm making a run for it.*

Eventually the speeches ended. There was a gentle movement in the chamber as the assembled Fire Elementals rose gracefully, a movement which was interrupted by Vex sprinting toward the back of the room where refreshments were laid out. The Fire Queen observed her niece's rush to the wine table and could not entirely condemn her. It had been a tedious ceremony. Throughout it the Queen had mainly been worrying about her upcoming engagements. It was all very well for Thrix to blithely tell her she'd have her new frock ready for the fashion designers' reception, but what if she didn't? The event was only a week away, and she simply had to look perfect.

And once I negotiate that, thought the Fire Queen, there's my meeting with the Earth Giants. What if my new formal coat isn't ready?

Malveria began to fret and wondered if she could leave the reception early to pop back to earth and talk to Thrix.

"I will just partake of a glass of wine first."

The Fire Queen smiled blandly at the aristocrats who bowed their heads as she made her way through chamber. She was almost within touching distance of a wine decanter when she was intercepted by Duchess Gargamond. The Fire Queen had been pleased by the return of the Duchess, but there was something about her manner that seemed unusual.

"Such a pleasure to be here," the Duchess said, beaming. "And look, my brother, Duke Garfire, is with me."

The Duchess shoved her younger brother into the Queen's path. The Duke, quite a heavy elemental, bowed politely to the Queen, telling her how honored he was to encounter her again. Gargamond's brother was not often at court, though he was an important member of the nobility. As such, the Queen was obliged to talk to him. She soon found herself listening to a long description of a hunt the Duke had recently organized. She had never been keen on hunting, and struggled to appear interested. Out of the corner of her eye, she could see Agrivex partaking heartily from a large crystal decanter. Making it worse, Iskiline and Gruselvere, the Fire Queen's two most trusted servants, were with her.

How is it that my servants are getting themselves a hearty helping of wine while I'm trapped here with the Duke? thought the Queen, and she chaffed at the unfairness of it.

"Are there no waiters at these events?" she burst out suddenly. "One would have thought waiters would be on hand to bring refreshments to the crowd."

"Pardon, Your Majesty?" said the Duke.

"Nothing, nothing," said the Queen, by now very distracted.

"So you will come?" continued the Duke.

The Fire Queen, by now desperate to escape, nodded, smiled and excused herself from the Duke and Duchess with as much grace as she could muster.

"At last," muttered Malveria. "Next stop, the wine decanter."

To the Queen's distress, she had taken no more than a few steps when her way was blocked by Lord Stratov and his daughter, the Honorable Gloria. They bowed in greeting. The Queen mustered a week smile. Lord Stratov was another important member of the aristocracy, of which, Malveria reflected, the nation had rather a lot.

"Stratov," said the Queen. "I haven't seen you at court for some time."

The Duke nodded but seemed lost for words, perhaps even a little embarrassed. If that was the case, his daughter made up for it.

"I've been telling Father he really must mingle more with his peers," she cried, in a trumpeting voice that the Queen found irritating. "Instead of hanging around in that massive castle of his. One of the largest castles in the land, of course, as befits a man of my father's importance, with his vast wealth and impeccable record of service to the nation."

"Uh . . . of course," said the Queen.

"After all, what is the point of being the most eligible man in the nation if you never meet anyone?" continued Gloria.

The Fire Queen was startled to hear Lord Stratov, who was no longer young, and had never been particularly good-looking, described as the nation's most eligible man. She supposed it was forgivable on the grounds of daughterly pride.

"I was just on my way to—" began the Fire Queen.

"We hold the most fabulous balls and parties at our enormous castle," said Gloria.

"Do we?" said the Duke.

"Our next will be the most tremendous affair." Gloria was enthusiastic. "If the Queen would honor us with her presence I'm sure my father, the Duke, would be so full of delight he would be unable to put it fully into words."

Malveria, with one eye on the refreshment tables, struggled to follow this tortuous sentence.

"Really, there will be no wine left if my handmaidens and Agrivex keep guzzling it in that fashion," she snapped.

"Pardon?" said Gloria, quite puzzled.

"Eh, where were we?" said the Fire Queen.

"Our fabulous ball at the enormous castle," said the Honorable Gloria.

The Fire Queen suppressed a sigh and mentally cursed the Duke, his daughter, the Keeper of the Minor Volcano and anyone else connected with this dreadful event, which was turning out to be far more tedious than she had anticipated.

CHAPTER 34

Sarapen stood alone on the rampart of the small desert fort, staring out over the red sand and brooding about his future. He was pleased to have left the Empress's palace, at least for a few days. The endless parade of courtiers, officials, supplicants and servants was distracting. Here in the vast wilderness of the desert, at least he had peace to think.

Sarapen had originally asked to visit the front lines where there were sporadic clashes between the Hainusta and Hiyasta over the disputed border. The Empress would not agree to that. She'd reluctantly agreed to let him visit some of her nearer military outposts but insisted that he return in a few days. She claimed that the spells that protected him from the hostile environment might not work if he remained in the desert. Sarapen suspected she just wanted him back in the palace as quickly as possible. Quite why she wanted him there, he wasn't sure. As far as Sarapen could see, an association with an alien werewolf was not something Empress Kabachetka's subjects would like.

Not that the Empress seems to care that much what her subjects think.

The Empress was an absolute monarch. She controlled the power of the Eternal Volcano. It rendered her untouchable. There had never been a successful rebellion in the land of the Hainusta.

Sarapen gazed over the hot sands. The Fire Elementals were not as frivolous or unpleasant as he'd once believed. He could tolerate their company. He did not, however, wish to spend the rest of his life among them. The great werewolf would have much preferred to return home to Scotland, or anywhere in his own dimension. According to the Empress, that was still not possible. The effects of the terrible wound inflicted by the Begravar knife would kill him. Sarapen had no way of knowing if that was true. Even if it wasn't, he had no way of returning. As a werewolf, he didn't have the power to travel through dimensions. No werewolf did.

Apart from my sister, thought Sarapen, and scowled. Sarapen despised Thrix almost as much as he despised Markus. It was bad enough that she'd learned sorcery. It was unforgivable that she'd used that sorcery against him. Without Thrix's assistance, his mother and his brother would never have succeeded in cheating him out of his rightful position as Thane.

Sarapen's thoughts turned to Kalix, whom he also hated. He shook his head. What a family. It did strike him that he didn't actually hate Kalix as much as the others, even though she'd struck the blow that all but killed him. Kalix might be mad, addicted to laudanum and a disgrace to the clan, but she was fierce and brave. She wasn't scared of him, though she should be. Sarapen admired that.

"I'll meet you again, sister, and then we'll see who wins, without sorcery and a magic knife to help you."

Below him a troop of Hainusta began to assemble, on their way to the disputed region. The conflict remained at a low level and no one had gained much advantage. Neither side wanted the dispute to escalate into a full-scale war, but neither of them was prepared to back down. Sarapen wished he could join in. He felt ready to throw himself into battle. He had no concern about losing his life. There was nothing he would regret leaving behind.

Apart from Dominil, maybe. Sarapen wondered what his old lover was up to. Was she still in London, taking care of the degenerate twins? Sarapen swiftly dismissed them as not worth thinking about, but the image of Dominil lingered on for a long time.

CHAPTER 35

Verasa MacRinnalch poured two glasses of red wine, one for her and one for Markus. The Great Council meeting had lasted for many hours, and the first faint streaks of dawn were visible through the large windows in Verasa's chambers.

"I just cannot believe that Dominil is a drug addict." The revelation had come as a terrible blow. Verasa had held Dominil in very high regard. Her success in dealing with the twins in London, and her intelligence and bravery during the great feud, had been admired by everyone. It was difficult to get close enough to Dominil to actually like her, but her reputation among the clan had certainly risen.

"How could she let the clan down like that? Poor Tupan, he must be mortified. To learn in the middle of a council meeting that his daughter has been taking laudanum!"

Markus professed to be less shocked and upset than his mother. "She might have become addicted, but she's never gone off the rails. No one even realized she was taking laudanum."

"I appreciate that," said Verasa. "She hasn't been stealing and begging. But still . . . I know you think I should be more sympathetic, Markus, but I just can't be."

Verasa was not the only werewolf who'd been appalled by the revelation. The three werewolf barons had plainly been disgusted, as had Dominil's father. It was a shameful thing among the MacRinnalchs to be an addict. Dominil could expect little sympathy. Her manner laid her open to resentment. Dominil had never attempted to deny that she was the most intelligent werewolf in the clan. Nor had she ever made any effort to indulge in the social niceties that bound the MacRinnalchs together. Now that she'd been shown to be not as self-controlled as she'd led people to believe, she could expect to be on the receiving end of a lot of harsh criticism.

"I expect she's been buying it from that scoundrel Merchant MacDoig," exclaimed the Mistress of the Werewolves. "I know he supplies Kalix. I'm never letting him in the castle again. Really, Markus, I feel so let down. I trusted Dominil."

"Has she ever betrayed your trust?" asked Markus.

"Up till now, no. Or so I thought. But who knows what might have been going on? I've often sent Dominil money for clan business. Has she been using it to buy drugs?"

"I'm sure she hasn't," said Markus.

The Mistress of the Werewolves scowled and wrapped her paw around her wine glass, emptying it in one long swallow.

"You might sympathize with your cousin, but I assure you the clan won't. And I don't either."

"She did try to stop," Markus pointed out. "That's why she went to see Minerva."

"And look how that's turned out!" cried Verasa. "More misfortune."

Markus knew it was no good pursuing the subject. His mother wasn't going to change her mind in a hurry. He sipped a little wine, then changed the subject.

"We seem to have agreed to go to war."

Verasa made a face, an expression that would not have been intelligible to an outsider. To another werewolf, it was clear that she was unsure of her opinion.

"Thrix is right, I suppose," said Verasa. "If the hunters can kill Minerva, they can strike anywhere. We have to do something. But I can't see the barons hurrying to send their young wolves to London to join the fight."

After long discussion, it had been agreed that they should make plans for a campaign against the Avenaris Guild. The council had not gone as far as Thrix wanted. They'd stopped short of immediately mobilizing the clan for war. This was partly because many of the council members were conservative by nature and refused to rush into a violent campaign. But there was sound reasoning behind it too. No one knew where the Guild was located. Their headquarters was hidden. The MacRinnalchs didn't even know if their army of hunters was gathered in one place or dispersed around the country. Until they learned more, the council was not prepared to fully commit itself.

Thrix had been frustrated. She'd brusquely informed the meeting that she would take it upon herself to find the Guild's headquarters as soon as possible, using her powers of sorcery.

"And Dominil's computer expertise," added Thrix, ignoring the cynicism around the table about Dominil's ability to do anything. Between them, Dominil and Thrix would find the Guild's headquarters.

"As soon as we do that," Thrix had said, "I'll expect the clan to be ready to annihilate them."

Verasa had gone along with the general feeling. She knew that something had to be done, but she was uncomfortable with the prospect of an all-out war. She didn't like that her son Markus was so keen on the idea. Markus seemed to think that as Thane he should be leading the troops. Verasa didn't want that to happen. She'd lost one son last year and didn't intend to lose another. She worried about Thrix too. The Enchantress was so powerful that she'd rarely had to worry about her before. But if she went up in direct opposition to the Guild, who knew what might happen? The Guild had access to sorcery too. They had a strong ally in the Fire Elemental Kabachetka. Verasa feared for Thrix's life, and Markus's too, and, as dawn broke and she changed back into human shape, she lay down in her bed very uneasily.

Am I to lose all my children? wondered the Mistress of the Werewolves. Kalix was always in trouble, and although Verasa continued to support her, she couldn't help feeling that her youngest daughter was destined for an early grave. In the course of her very long life, Verasa had learned to take misfortune stoically, but as the sun rose she lay in her bed feeling depressed and very troubled about the future.

CHAPTER 36

Kalix woke in her human form on the warehouse floor. Daniel and Moonglow were asleep on top of a large crate. Kalix was perplexed. She didn't remember what had happened but realized it couldn't have been good. She considered sneaking out quietly, but at that moment Moonglow woke.

"Kalix, are you all right?"

"I'm fine," mumbled Kalix.

"We should go home," said Moonglow and nudged Daniel awake.

They trudged out to the car, stiff from their uncomfortable night's sleep. Daniel opened the car doors.

"C'mon, Wolfy," he said and grinned.

Kalix knew she'd taken on her wolf form last night. She knew she could be irresponsible in that state. She wondered if she'd actually attacked her flatmates, but didn't like to ask. Before she had time to process this, a more profound gloom settled on her. Old Minerva was dead and it was Kalix's fault. She'd been sent home in disgrace. The young werewolf sat in the back seat and tried to make herself as small as possible. She remained silent on the journey home, refusing to respond to Moonglow's anxious questions about what had happened to upset her.

Kalix felt herself becoming anxious as they neared their home. She didn't want to answer questions from Daniel and Moonglow. Last night, she'd felt so anxious about everything she'd fled to the warehouse so as not to have to encounter anyone. Kalix found it very difficult to cope with company when her anxiety came on badly. Now it was a heavy weight on her, fueled by her guilt over Minerva. She was certain the werewolves at the castle would be discussing her. Thrix and Dominil would have told everyone it was her fault that Minerva was killed.

Kalix's shoulders were hunched as she emerged from the car, and she was silent as they made their way inside.

"Are you all right?" asked Moonglow for the tenth time.

"Stop asking me that," said Kalix wearily. She headed straight for her room and closed the door noisily behind her, signaling that she didn't want to be disturbed.

Downstairs, Daniel watched her disappear. "It's fine," he muttered. "Don't bother thanking us for coming to look for you. It was no trouble."

"I wonder what happened?" said Moonglow.

"Kalix isn't about to tell us."

They went to the kitchen to make tea and pour some cereal for breakfast.

"Do you think I should call Dominil?" asked Moonglow. "Maybe she'd tell us."

"She probably won't. They're always secretive about clan business."

Daniel ate his cereal then put bread in the toaster. "They were probably involved in some terrible werewolf fight and half the clan's dead and Kalix killed most of them."

Moonglow was troubled. From their past experiences with Kalix, that might not be too far from the truth. "She was determined not to get involved in any more violence," she said.

"Maybe that's difficult when you're a werewolf. Especially a crazy one like Kalix."

"Kalix isn't crazy."

"I know," said Daniel. "But she's not exactly stable either. As we discovered last night."

Unexpectedly, Moonglow laughed.

"What's funny?"

"Us. Going to the park and you getting cut by the bushes and then us getting chased by a wolf and having to sleep on a crate. Our life is much more exciting than our friends'."

"True. None of them have even met a werewolf, and we've met loads."

They took a plate of toast into the living room. Moonglow carried the teapot and cups and they sat in front of the fire, warming themselves after their cold night in the warehouse.

"What do you think Kalix is doing now?" said Daniel.

"She's probably hiding under her duvet, having dosed herself with laudanum and cut her arm to make herself feel better. Unless she's cut her thigh, which she does prefer sometimes."

Daniel winced. "You're probably right. Should we do anything?"

Moonglow looked hopeless. "I don't have the energy. And we can't be rescuing her all the time. She'll just get more angry if we barge in. Maybe if we just leave her a while she'll calm down."

They were interrupted by an unexpected crashing noise from the kitchen. The cat, which had been idly nosing its food bowl, fled into the living room. Daniel and Moonglow remained calm. Strange crashing noises in the kitchen were something they had grown used to.

"Vex is back," said Daniel while comforting the cat.

Vex emerged from the kitchen, rubbing her arm and looking glum. "I didn't land very well. But I didn't hurt myself. Well, not much. My elbow's a bit sore."

Vex looked hopefully at Moonglow, who obligingly rubbed it better. Vex made a swift recovery and grinned at them.

"Are you having breakfast in front of the fire with tea and toast? Can I join in?"

Daniel went off to put the kettle on again and put more bread in the toaster. Vex studied Moonglow.

"Your aura looks a bit strange. So did Daniel's. Something unusual's been happening, I can tell. Have you been out on a date?"

"Eh, no," said Moonglow.

"Are you sure? I can tell you've been doing something together. Should I leave? Just say and I'll make myself scarce."

"You don't have to leave," said Moonglow darkly. "There was no date."

"OK, I give up, I'm still useless at reading auras. What's been happening?"

Moonglow told Vex about their adventures the previous night.

Vex nodded sagely. "So Kalix has gone mad again. I was expecting it. Do you know what brought it on?"

Vex accepted some toast from Daniel and plastered it with jam, gleefully loading on as much as the bread could take. Vex had a sweet tooth and an enormous appetite. "It's good to be back. You can't get toast at the palace, it's hopeless. You know how we all agreed I should set up Aunt Malvie with some man so they could produce an heir and get me off the hook? Well, I've done it already."

Vex proudly described how she'd encouraged both Duke Garfire and Lord Stratov to woo the Queen. "I was cunning about it. I just dropped a few subtle hints to family members."

"So did it work?" asked Daniel.

"I think so. The last I saw, Aunt Malvie was having this great conversation with them; she looked really fascinated. But then I got into a wine-drinking contest with Gruselvere and Iskiline, so I don't really remember much after that. But I think I've made a good start."

The cat settled down on Vex's lap and purred when she stroked its ear.

"So it's been a good few days and now it's time for *Nagasaki Night Fight Boom Boom Girl*! The first episode is this afternoon!"

"We saw your note on the fridge," said Daniel.

"And the alert you put on my computer," added Moonglow. "Thanks for that."

"I didn't want you to miss it!"

Vex glanced at the clock and frowned. "Another six hours. I can't wait. Do you think Kalix will like it? I'm not sure if she's as keen on *Tokyo Top Pop Boom Boom Girl* as me."

"No one is as keen on *Tokyo Top Pop Boom Boom Girl* as you."

Vex laughed. "She'll like it. It'll cheer her up. Did she really chase you around the warehouse?"

"Just about."

Vex laughed again. "I wish I'd seen that. Kalix is so funny when she's a wolf. She's all shaggy and excitable."

Vex stroked the cat under its chin and it rolled over on its back, enjoying the attention. Moonglow picked up the empty plates and took them to the kitchen. When she returned, she stood for a while, looking thoughtful.

"Don't do it," said Daniel.

"Don't do what?"

"Check on Kalix."

"I wasn't going to."

"Yes, you were. I recognize your expression. It's best just to leave her alone for a while."

"I know." Moonglow fidgeted for a few minutes. "I'd better just see if she's all right," she muttered and hurried upstairs.

Vex watched her go, then turned to Daniel. "At least the two of you aren't so awkward now. I guess all the Kalix adventures got you over the humiliation."

"Thanks," said Daniel, and looked unhappy. He rose slowly, stiff and sore from his night on the crate.

"I'm going upstairs to lie on my bed and listen to music for a few days."

"What about Nagasaki Night Fight Boom Boom Girl?"

"She'll have to do without me."

Daniel trudged off up the stairs. Behind him, Vex grinned.

"They're all in a bad way," she said. "Not like me. I've got a boyfriend. I wonder when he'll call?"

CHAPTER 37

The repercussions of events in Scotland were already beginning to affect other members of the werewolf clan. While Kalix was hiding from the world, Beauty and Delicious were puzzling over what had gone wrong.

"Something's not right," said Beauty

"I know," replied Delicious. "Ever since I got up this afternoon I've felt that something isn't right."

"What is it?"

Beauty shuffled around in her seat. "Maybe it's the couch. The springs are going or something. We need a new one."

In keeping with the rest of the furnishings, the couch was a very expensive piece of furniture, but it was now showing the effects of years of ill treatment.

Delicious agreed. "It's not the couch it once was."

"It's boring buying furniture," said Delicious.

"Dominil will do it for us."

The twins sat vacantly in front of the television, which was new and very large. Dominil had ordered it for them online, after the twins had finally managed to annoy her sufficiently by continually complaining about their old one. Each twin had a glass of the MacRinnalch malt in their hand. In front of them on the coffee table was a large bowl of a pickled onion Monster Munch, which counted as breakfast. The twins had steadfastly resisted all encouragement to change their habits.

"What's wrong with crisps and whisky for breakfast?" Beauty had said to Dominil only last week. "We get healthy again when we're werewolves anyway."

It was true. No matter how much the twins abused their bodies, they were always revitalized by their regular werewolf change.

"I don't think it's just the couch," said Beauty after a while. "Something else is wrong."

Delicious flicked between music channels. "Are we meant to be doing something?"

"How would I know? I never know what we're meant to be doing. I just wait for Dominil to tell us."

The twins had never been good at remembering engagements. Since Dominil had taken over as manager of Yum Yum Sugary Snacks, they'd abandoned any attempt to remember anything. If they were due to play or rehearse, Dominil would tell them.

A dim thought struggled to emerge in Delicious's mind. "Where is Dominil anyway?"

Beauty looked at her sister. "Of course. That's what's wrong. Where's Dominil?"

The twins were mystified. Dominil should be around, telling them what to do, but she wasn't. She had been trying to get them a spot on a tour, supporting some well-known band. The twins had been rehearsing to make sure they were ready, but they had no idea when the next rehearsal was.

"Is it today?"

The twins had an uneasy feeling that it might be. The rest of the band could be waiting for them in the studio. Beauty became angry at Dominil.

"What's the idea of not being here to tell us if we've got to rehearse? She knows we can't remember things like that."

The twins looked hopelessly at each other. "The boys get really mad when we don't turn up," said Beauty.

They sat on the couch feeling annoyed at Dominil, and wondered what could possibly account for her absence.

"And we've run out of Monster Munch," said Beauty, her voice full of sadness. "Everything is going badly. Dominil is the worst manager ever."

CHAPTER 38

Dominil hadn't forgotten about the twins but she'd put their affairs to one side, as a lesser priority. She and Thrix were busy plotting the destruction of the Avenaris Guild. Each had tacitly agreed to ignore, for the meantime, all outside distractions. They sat now in Dominil's stark room, the same room she'd occupied as a child. The walls were bare stone, undecorated save for two posters, one a reproduction of a painting by Mondrian and the other a chart showing programming commands. Though Dominil's room was barely decorated, it was very tidy, with piles of old computer magazines Dominil had read as a child stacked neatly on shelves. The bed was covered in a blanket of green MacRinnalch tartan, very neatly arranged.

"Explain to me the difficulties of locating the Guild's headquarters with sorcery," said Dominil.

Thrix raised her palms. "I just get nowhere when I try. It's hard to explain exactly why, because I don't know precisely what I'm up against. There are a lot of hiding spells. If you don't know which one has been used, it's difficult to penetrate. I've been consulting Minerva's books, and when I get back to London I'll ask Malveria for help too."

Thrix frowned. "It's strange, because the Guild doesn't use much sorcery. I don't think they have access to a strong sorcerer."

"They have been around for a very long time," said Dominil. "It's possible that some time in their history they learned a spell, or picked up a magical artifact, that hides them well."

"True. If they have a pendant of Tamol, it'll make our life difficult. That's what Malveria gave Kalix, and now she's completely hidden from any inquisitive eyes."

"Is it likely they might have one?" asked Dominil.

"I'd say not. They're very hard to come by. But they've certainly got something powerful." Thrix paused to sip whisky from a tumbler. The castle was full of fine crystal, but Dominil seemed to prefer the plainest type of glass.

"I'll find them eventually." Thrix sounded confident, but she was frustrated. She didn't want to spend weeks searching for the Guild's headquarters. She wanted to attack them now.

"I'm also facing difficulties," admitted Dominil. "I used to be able to hack into the Guild's files, but I can't now. I worked my way past several upgrades, but they've finally employed someone who knows what they're doing and I can't crack their security."

Dominil indicated her computer screen. "I've been looking at the old messages I intercepted, trying to find out where their headquarters might be, without success. None of my geolocation is working. But there have been advances in that recently that I'm investigating. I've tried everything else I can think of, from examining the records at Companies House to the files of the Charity Association. But the Avenaris Guild isn't listed as a company or a charity anywhere, or as anything else. I'm not giving up either. I'll have revenge for Minerva too."

Dominil and Thrix both planned to return to London that night.

"I won't be sorry to leave the castle," said Dominil.

"Yes, you're in disgrace," said the Enchantress.

Whether those regarding Dominil as a disgrace included Thrix was not entirely clear. Thrix hadn't accused Dominil of being responsible for Minerva's death. She hadn't even referred to Dominil's revelation about laudanum. But the Enchantress was so furious at the Guild that it was hard to tell if she was angry at Dominil or not.

"My father and the Mistress of the Werewolves insisted I remain in the castle and receive treatment for my addiction from Doctor Angus," said Dominil. "They are not pleased that I've refused."

"I've never seen Tupan so shocked."

"My father is very shocked, I acknowledge. But I need to get back to

London. My laudanum problem will have to wait for a while, as will the affairs of the twins. My priority is to find the Guild."

"Mine too. Though I'm not sure that everyone else agrees. I sometimes get the feeling that nothing would rouse these barons."

"Markus will support us," said Dominil. "When we find the Guild, we'll need a large force to attack them. The Thane will authorize it."

"Let's hope so. Or else it will just be you and me charging into the Guild's headquarters on our own."

"Possibly. And Kalix, I imagine."

Thrix scowled fiercely. "Kalix can stay out of it."

"Kalix hates the Guild as much as anyone. If there's an attack, she'll want to be involved."

"I can't stand Kalix," said Thrix. "And she's too unreliable."

"She's also a savage and experienced fighter who's probably killed more hunters than anyone else in the clan."

Thrix shook her head and refused to talk any further about her sister, who she still blamed for Minerva's death. "I'm giving up my fashion business for a while."

"Can you do that?"

"I'll ask my assistant and my chief designer to keep things moving. It should be OK for a week or two. I can't be worrying about making clothes when I need to find the Guild."

Thrix raised her glass. "To the destruction of the Avenaris Guild."

"To their destruction," agreed Dominil, and drank.

CHAPTER 39

Malveria was cheerful at the prospect of picking up her new dress. She materialized at Thrix's office in Soho to find Ann sitting in front of the computer. The Fire Queen greeted her warmly.

"Hello, esteemed assistant of my dearest friend Thrix. It is good to see you on this fine day when I am picking up a new dress!"

Malveria had always liked Ann who, she knew, was a vital part of Thrix's business. As well as being an excellent assistant, Ann was also one of the very few people who knew that Thrix was a werewolf.

"So, valued assistant, where is Thrix? And where is my dress? I'm really trembling with excitement."

During Malveria's expansive greeting, Ann had been regarding her rather sourly.

"Thrix isn't here. And your dress isn't ready."

Malveria blinked and shook her head. "I fear that travel through the dimensions has affected my hearing. This can happen on occasion. What did you say?"

"Thrix isn't here and your dress isn't ready."

"But how can Thrix not be here and my dress not be ready? These things are not possible."

"There's been some werewolf crisis in Scotland. Thrix went there in a hurry and she hasn't come back. She sent me a message telling me to run the company for a while."

From Ann's expression, she wasn't pleased to have the responsibility of running the business thrust on her so abruptly. Malveria felt her ankles start to give. Her high-heel spell was not yet perfect, and that, coupled with the shock of Thrix's non-appearance, was enough to make her sit down quickly.

"What about my dress?"

"As far as I know it's not ready."

"But it must be ready," protested the Fire Queen. "The fashion event is in two days time and I must be there, wearing it."

Ann raised her palms hopelessly in the air. "I'm sorry, Malveria. I don't really know what's going on. Thrix hasn't explained it to me. All I got was an email and that was vague."

"What did it say about my dress?"

"Nothing."

The Fire Queen struggled to take this in. What manner of crisis could have overwhelmed the Enchantress so completely?

"This makes no sense. If Thrix is well enough to compose an email, surely she is well enough to make a frock?"

Ann knew that Malveria was Thrix's most important customer and couldn't be palmed off, but at this moment she was more concerned about the difficult task of canceling all of Thrix's upcoming appointments without damaging the business. She'd been on the phone with fashion editors, buyers and journalists all morning, making excuses for her employer's absence. Once she'd done that, there was a missing consignment of cloth from Korea to be sorted out, and later in the day Thrix was meant to be interviewing models. Ann didn't know what she was going to do about that.

The rest of the staff was already uneasy, sensing something was wrong.

"Probably worried about their bonuses," muttered Ann, "which all need calculation and authorization. By me, apparently."

Malveria ignored this and looked toward the full rack of clothes at the side of the office.

"Might my dress be there?"

"I'm afraid not."

"Is it in the designers' room?"

"No."

"Are you sure? Could it be at the warehouse? Have you checked?"

"Malveria," said Ann wearily, "I'm really sorry, but your dress isn't ready, and Thrix hasn't given me any idea when it will be."

A flicker of flame appeared around the fingers of the Fire Queen's right hand. Ann was aware of Malveria's nature as a Fire Elemental.

"Please don't get upset and incinerate the room, I can't do anything about it."

"But this is not tolerable! If I have not got my new dress, what am I to wear to the designers' reception in two days time? Some aging creation from last year? The very notion terrifies me."

"Thrix isn't going to the designers' reception," said Ann. "She's canceled."

The Fire Queen reeled in her chair. Flames erupted from both hands and for a few moments she struggled to speak. Ann silently poured a glass of wine and passed it over the desk. Malveria gulped it down.

"Canceled? Without telling me? How can this be? It is the most splendid event and we have both been looking forward to it for the longest time!"

A tear escaped from Malveria's eye, sizzling on her burning cheek. Thrix's absence was so unexpected, and the prospect of not obtaining her new dress so terrifying, that the Fire Queen did not know what to think. She sat rigidly in her chair, completely bemused. It took her some time to compose herself, and by the time she could speak, Ann had returned her attention to Thrix's computer.

"Has Thrix really abandoned me?"

"I think she might have meant for Jason to finish the dress."

"Jason? Your senior designer? Really, Ann, his clothes might do for others, but for me? You must know this is impossible."

Ann was too polite to actually shrug, but she had nothing to add. Thrix had gone to Scotland, she hadn't returned, and she'd sent only the briefest of messages about what to do in her absence. Another flaming tear trickled from the Fire Queen's eye, running down her cheek and disappearing into her long dark hair. She rose to her feet very slowly, as if her joints were stiff. She stood for a moment looking wistfully at the clothes rack and then, without another word, dematerialized.

CHAPTER 40

Eight hundred years in the past.

Though the fairy wedding was a colorful event, the eight-year-old Malveria was dressed severely for the occasion, as was her grandmother Malgravane. Malveria had been excited to receive an invitation—her first visit to another dimension—but she'd had to put up with lots of lecturing from her grandmother about behaving appropriately and not bringing disgrace on the Hiyastas.

"The fairies are old friends," her grandmother had told her, "and have been since before the humans crawled out of their caves. But they are not quite respectable. There will be many elemental dignitaries at the wedding, so be sure not to do anything untoward. Speak only if you're spoken to, stay close to me, and whatever you do"—Malgravane leaned over her granddaughter—"don't play with the fairy children."

"Why not?" asked Malveria.

"Because I say so," barked Malgravane.

Malveria shrank backward. Her grandmother was an intimidating elemental. Far more intimidating than her mother, even though her mother was Queen. But Queen Malgrasin had never been in very good health. She would not be coming to the wedding. She was poorly again, and lay in her chambers in the palace. Queen Malgrasin was a popular ruler, but there was a general worry about how long her reign would last, given her ill health.

Malveria was extremely excited on the day of the wedding, even though she'd been fitted into a heavy black dress that was even more uncomfortable than the dark-red fire wrap she normally wore. Malveria chaffed under the weight. Her grandmother was similarly dressed, in formal black, as were their attendants. Malveria visited her mother before she left. The Queen lay propped up in bed, and though she kissed her daughter affectionately, she was too tired to talk for long.

"Be good," she said. "And do what your grandmother tells you."

Malveria promised she would. On her way out of the chamber she caught a glimpse of herself in one of the great mirrors on the wall, illuminated by the bright yellow torches, and she felt quite important in her formal dress. She wondered for a moment if she might impress the fairies at the wedding. She was the daughter of the Queen, after all. Although, she reflected, her older brothers and sisters would all be there too, and there were many of them.

Malveria had questions to ask her grandmother about the fairies, but her grandmother shushed her impatiently.

"Take my hand," she ordered, which Malveria did. There was a brief darkness accompanied by an unpleasant cold, a coldness that as a Fire Elemental Malveria had never felt before. She hung on to her grandmother and was relieved when they emerged from the darkness into a beautiful green glade, full of flowers and surrounded by trees. Malveria found herself at the tail end of a procession of dark-clad Hiyasta who made their way solemnly through the glade toward a series of tables that seemed to have been formed from the trees and still to be part of them.

Malveria craned her neck to see around the crowd of relatives. A gap opened in front of her and her eyes widened in astonishment. There, clustered around the living furniture, were the fairies. Malveria had seen fairies before, at her mother's court, where their ambassadors would visit, but the fairies she'd seen there had been rather somber. They wore dark robes, with their wings folded neatly behind their back. They were the same size as the Hiyasta. Here, in their own forest, the fairies were different. There were hundreds of them and they were not acting at all somberly. They were brightly dressed, and they seemed to change size at will. Malveria saw one tiny creature, no more than two inches tall, flutter toward some Earth Elementals, then instantly grow to human size before landing and bowing politely. He was immediately joined by another tiny fairy, who perched on his shoulder. She grew in size too, but remained on his shoulders, laughing. As the dignitaries of the Fire and Earth Elementals made their formal greetings to the green-clad fairy, he returned their greetings cheerfully, while the young fairy perched on his shoulders as if it was the most natural thing in the world.

Malveria frowned. She understood what her grandmother had meant when she'd said that the fairies were not quite respectable. Malveria dreaded to think what would have happened if she'd tried to perch on her mother's shoulders while she was greeting royal guests.

As Malveria moved slowly forward, the young fairy, who seemed about Malveria's age, hopped off her father's shoulders and shrank again before floating off. Malveria looked at her departing figure with some disapproval. Clearly, these young fairies did not know how to behave properly. And what was she wearing? wondered Malveria. Her dress seemed to be made of gold. I've never seen anything like it.

Malveria was grabbed rather roughly by her grandmother and dragged forward to be introduced to the fairy in green.

"Princess Malveria, youngest daughter of Queen Malgrasin," announced her grandmother.

Malveria bowed.

"Duke Foxglove Rinnalch Wallace," said Malgravane, formally introducing him to her granddaughter.

Malveria bowed politely again, though she was still straining her neck to see more of the fairies who were fluttering around the tables. Now she could hear strains of music floating over the glade.

"Stay here," said her grandmother. "And don't touch anything."

Malveria did as she was told and stood quietly at the back of the group, while her older brothers and sisters were introduced to the fairy duke. He welcomed them all to his daughter's wedding with extravagant politeness.

"Hello," came a voice behind her.

Malveria turned around. There stood the young fairy in the golden dress. She was now around the same height as Malveria. Whether that was her true height, or she'd just made herself the same height as Malveria so they could talk, Malveria didn't know. The fairy had golden hair and large blue eyes, and her wings were decorated with colors that Malveria would have struggled even to put a name to. More colors than the fire rainbows in the lands of the Hiyasta, it seemed. Her golden dress shone like metal, but it appeared to be made of some substance so light that it floated around the girl's body, lying perfectly on her shoulders no matter which way she turned.

"I'm Dithean NicRinnalch," said the young fairy. "Who are you?"

"Princess Malveria."

The fairy giggled. "That's a funny name."

"No it isn't," said Malveria, and might have said something sharp in return were she not so entranced by the fairy's clothes.

"I like your dress," she said.

"Thank you," said Dithean. "I have hundreds of them. Yours is funny."

"What do you mean 'funny'?" asked Malveria.

"It's so dark and heavy. You look like you might melt."

Malveria bristled. She had the uncomfortable feeling that her dress was indeed very inferior to the fairy's. It was a new feeling for the eight-year-old Fire Elemental, and she didn't like it.

"It's the proper dress for a wedding," said Malveria defensively.

"It's ugly," said Dithean NicRinnalch.

Malveria was aware of the need to be on her best behavior but even so, she felt she couldn't let herself be insulted like this. After all, she was here as a representative of the Hiyasta royal family.

"You're rude," she ventured.

The fairy seemed to find this very funny and laughed loudly. "Poor Fire Elemental in a big black heavy dress. And those big clumpy shoes! How are you going to dance in those?"

Malveria hadn't been aware that she might be required to dance. She tried to conceal her surprise. "I'll manage perfectly well," she said stiffly.

This seemed to amuse the fairy even more. Her wings shook as she laughed. Malveria decided that she didn't like Dithean NicRinnalch at all. Her grandmother had been right to warn her about fairy children. They were obviously rude and uncivilized. She resolved to leave with dignity.

"Would you like me to lend you a nice pretty dress?" said Dithean. "Golden like mine?"

The eight-year-old Malveria forgot all about leaving as she felt a strange elation wash over her. "Oh yes!" she said eagerly. "I'd like that more than anything!"

"Follow me," said Dithean, and ran toward the trees. Malveria ran after her eagerly, catching up the hem of her heavy dress. By the time she reached the trees the fairy had produced another dress—just conjured it out of the air as far as Malveria could see—and was holding it out to her. Malveria tore off her own dress and slipped smoothly into the new one. It fitted her perfectly. Feeling the lightness of the fabric, and the way it hung perfectly, Malveria felt giddy with liberation.

"You can see your reflection in the stream," said the young fairy.

Malveria hurried to do just that, and stood over the stream looking at herself, transfixed and elated by the beauty of her new golden dress. She had never felt as happy as she did at that moment.

"Would you like some fairy shoes?" asked Dithean.

"You have shoes as well?" said Malveria, and felt slightly weak from anticipation.

The Fire Queen sat on her own in her private chambers in her beautiful palace. Though she was deeply upset, she still managed a faint smile at the memory of her first pretty dress.

How I loved that golden frock, she thought. The memory was still crystal clear, even after eight hundred years. "And Dithean NicRinnalch was a rude young fairy!" They'd been friends ever since.

Malveria's transgressions at the wedding cost her dearly. The fairy duke had laughed with pleasure to see his daughter and her new friend in their matching dresses, but Malgravane had been rendered speechless by the sight of Princess Malveria in a golden frock and silver slippers. As it was not possible for Malgravane to discipline Malveria while the duke was there, the repercussions took a little while to arrive. But they did arrive soon enough. When the Hiyasta returned home, young Malveria's serious transgressions were fully reported to her mother. Malveria was duly summoned to her mother's chamber where she was spoken to extremely sharply. The Queen lectured her on the inappropriateness of discarding one's respectable clothing in exchange for a few bits of wispy cloth from a flighty young fairy.

Princess Malveria apologized, but Queen Malgrasin knew the apology wasn't sincere. Malveria didn't really regret wearing the dress, or the shoes. Her aura positively glowed at the memory. Malveria was banished to kitchen duty, which was a great disgrace for a Hiyasta princess. Her many older brothers and sisters regarded her with contempt and her grandmother never really forgave her. Letting down the dignity of the Hiyasta royal family was a serious matter.

Working in the kitchens, Malveria wilted. At the age of eight, she found it difficult to stand up to her entire family. There seemed to be disapproving brothers and sisters everywhere. Her grandmother told her that she would continue to be punished until she was truly sorry for her misdeeds. Weeks later, as Malveria was wearily bringing food from the kitchens and helping serve it to her family—another disgrace—she finally reached the end of her tether. Under the contemptuous gaze of her brothers, Malveria's temper snapped. She angrily smashed a plate on the floor.

"You can glare at me all you like!" she stormed. "I'm not sorry I wore the fairy dress and I'm never going to be sorry! It was a beautiful dress and I liked it much better than this horrible one I'm wearing now! And

I'm never going to apologize."

"How dare you speak like that to us!" cried Malgravane.

Malveria glared at her grandmother. "When I grow up I'm going to be friends with Dithean the fairy and I'm going to wear nice dresses all the time!"

Servants looked on in embarrassment as Malveria was summarily ejected from the dining hall, and after this her punishment carried on for a very long time. Her own servants were withdrawn, leaving her to take care of herself. Malveria became the only princess who had ever been obliged to cook her own meals. Her position in the family became that of a rebellious upstart who was treated with hostility and suspicion.

Malveria was friendless in the palace, apart from Xakthan, a young trooper in the Palace Guard, who still gave her a friendly greeting every day and sometimes let her play with his sword and shield. Life was hard, and Malveria never really made things up with her family. She never apologized, though she did eventually learn to disguise her aura better.

The Fire Queen shuddered, suddenly recalling with too much clarity the beating her grandmother had given her on returning to the palace after the wedding. She sipped from a goblet of wine and stared gloomily at the floor.

"I can't believe Thrix has deserted me," she sighed. "And I want my new dress."

CHAPTER 41

Kalix had been depressed and anxious for the past two days, and her unhappiness increased when she remembered her werewolf improvement plan. It had all gone wrong so quickly. The entries seemed to be mocking her. *Stop taking laudanum* was particularly painful to read, in light of her recent disastrous overdose. Kalix drew a heavy black cross beside this item, denoting her failure. Deciding that wasn't enough, she drew another cross, and then a third.

Get on better with people. Kalix sighed heavily. She'd tried to attack Daniel and Moonglow in the warehouse. The whole MacRinnalch Clan despised her more than ever. Kalix drew four black crosses next to the entry, another three beside *Stop being anxious*, and another three at *Stop being depressed*.

Stop cutting myself. Kalix glanced at the blood trickling from her left arm.

"You'd have to say that was another failure," she muttered.

Eat better. Kalix, having decided never to eat again, drew four black crosses beside this.

"This is the worst self-improvement plan ever. I've failed at everything."

She was gripped by a desire never to see or talk to anyone again. She hid under her duvet. It didn't feel like she was well enough concealed. She considered crawling under the bed, but remembered that as a child, she'd hidden under her bed at the castle and her mother had found her easily. The only other possible alternative was the cupboard. Kalix was briefly tempted. Hiding in the cupboard seemed like an attractive idea.

But someone would find out, she thought. And then they'd make a big fuss about it. Why is everyone always bothering me and interfering in my business?

Kalix noticed a loose leaf at the end of her journal. She opened it. It was a poorly executed sketch of her father.

"I forgot that was there."

Finding the drawing didn't improve Kalix's mood. She didn't like to be reminded of her father. She'd made the drawing a long time ago, at the suggestion of one of her therapists, who'd suggested that drawing her fears might make them easier to deal with. Kalix stared at the drawing.

"What a stupid suggestion. It didn't help at all. And I'm a hopeless artist."

She crumpled up the drawing and dropped it in the bin. Now she felt worse. She wished she hadn't been reminded of her father.

"He's dead. Good. I wish it didn't still bother me."

Kalix felt her anxiety begin to grow. She heard Vex coming up the stairs, recognizing the heavy tread of her boots on the threadbare carpet. Vex yelled out for Daniel.

"Daniel? Are you there? It's an emergency."

Kalix heard Daniel's door open.

"What's the emergency?"

"I've been badly let down by *Nagasaki Night Fight Boom Boom Girl.*"

"What?"

"I hated it. It just wasn't a good anime," said Vex. "Nothing like as good as *Tokyo Top Pop Boom Boom Girl.*"

"What's wrong with it?" shouted Daniel from the top of the stairs.

"A stupid plot and really annoying characters!" cried Vex. "Nagasaki

Night Fight Boom Boom Girl isn't too bad, but she has this young side-kick who is just terrible!"

"Ah," said Daniel. "Bad sidekick. That's a common problem. It happens all the time."

"Does it?"

"Producers have a good show and they get greedy and put out a spin-off, and usually it's not nearly as good as the original."

Kalix wished that Daniel and Vex would go somewhere else to shout about cartoons. At least they weren't attempting to involve her.

"I'm going to tell Kalix about it," announced Vex. Vex knocked on the door. Knowing that not answering the door rarely discouraged Vex, Kalix nimbly slipped into her cupboard and shut the door.

CHAPTER 42

The ancient lift descended very slowly as Mr. Carmichael accompanied Mr. Eggers to the training area in the basement of the Guild's headquarters.

"I do wish Mr. Emerson would stop sending me memos criticizing our management structure."

Mr. Eggers managed a faint smile. "I suppose that's why we employ new blood. Keep us on our toes."

"I know," agreed Mr. Carmichael. "But really, is his obsession with modernizing everything really helping? 'Chairman' is old-fashioned, according to Mr. Emerson. I should be 'MD.' Or even 'CEO.'" Mr. Carmichael shuddered. He had a great aversion to the term "CEO." "I don't think changing our job titles is going to make us better werewolf hunters."

"I don't suppose it will," said Mr. Eggers. "But he might be right about our board of directors. Some of them do belong in the last century. Or the one before."

There was a divide in the board of directors, which could be rough-ly described as traditionalists against modernizers. Mr. Carmichael was firmly on the side of the traditionalists. Had he had his way, most of the Guild's new executives would never have been appointed. His hand had been forced by events. Mr. Carmichael had come under pressure because of the setbacks they'd suffered. They'd lost a great many hunters, including their best operative, Captain Easterly, who'd been killed in Scotland. Also dead was Albermarle, who'd been their best computer specialist. He was sorely missed, although, as Mr. Carmichael grudgingly acknowledged, the new information technology team recruited by Mr. Emerson did seem very competent. Security had improved.

The lift doors opened and they stepped out into the dark corridor that led to the training area.

"I admit Emerson's hired some good people," said Mr. Carmichael. "That doesn't mean he can go around changing people's job titles. And I still don't like the way he tightened up on our expenses. When I became chairman there was no need to record every penny you spent at lunch."

They halted outside a solid metal door, incongruous in the old wood-paneled hallway. Mr. Carmichael inserted his electronic pass and it slid open. They entered the small, glass-fronted room that looked out onto the training area. He greeted his eldest son, who oversaw the Guild's training department.

"Hello, John. How are they doing?"

"Very well," said John Carmichael. "No one has ever gone through the advanced course as quickly as Group Sixteen." John was tall and much stockier than his father.

Group Sixteen was made up of four of their new hunters. They all had military experience, and they'd completed their basic werewolf-hunting training in record time. On their first mission they'd killed Minerva MacRinnalch. It was an auspicious start.

Mr. Carmichael turned to Mr. Eggers. "I'm still in charge of hiring field operatives. Which is the main thing, of course. You need experience for that, no matter what Mr. Emerson and his modern business practices might think."

"Send them through again, John. I want to see how they perform. We have another target for Group Sixteen and I'd like to get them back into action as soon as possible."

CHAPTER 43

"Empress," said Distikka, approaching the throne, "I have a plan."

Empress Kabachetka regarded her adviser coldly. "Distikka. Have I not instructed you to approach my throne in a more deferential manner?"

Distikka drew herself up and eyed the Empress in return. "If Your Majesty prefers, I can come back later with my plan for you to eclipse Queen Malveria in the field of fashion."

"Stop this endless prevarication," said the Empress, "and get to the point."

The Empress had been in a bad mood all day. She'd taken delivery of a beautiful pair of high heels from Milan, but so far she had failed to master them. They were simply too high to walk in. The Empress had counted on her new heels giving her an advantage over Malveria when they encountered each other, as they would in only a few days at the designers' reception in London.

"You're going to a reception in London this week?"

"I am aware of that," said the young Empress. "The event is already causing me some stress."

"Queen Malveria will be there, I understand. And journalists from that magazine you value so highly . . . " Distikka paused, as if searching her memory.

"It is called *Vogue*, as you are perfectly well aware," snapped Kabachetka. "What of it?"

"I have discovered a way in which you might impress these journalists."

The Empress leaned forward. She was interested enough to forget her customary irritation at Distikka's chain mail. Distikka produced a sheet of paper, the cheapness of which caused the Empress to wrinkle her nose.

"What is that?"

"A newspaper from London."

Distikka opened the paper and pointed to a block of text. The Empress was displeased.

"I do not read that language."

"It's a story about St. Amelia's Ball," said Distikka. "Are you familiar with this? No? St. Amelia's Ball is an annual event, targeted toward debutantes."

"Debutantes? Like the wealthy young women who are presented at my court at the Spring Volcano Festival?"

"Much the same," replied Distikka.

The Empress looked suspiciously at her adviser. "As I understood matters, the aristocracy in England has fallen from power."

"They have, Empress. But they remain influential in sections of society. St. Amelia's Ball is an important event in their social season."

"What does this have to do with me?"

"Their sponsor's just gone bankrupt," said Distikka, pointing at the page. "Allied West Securities. It was wiped out in the recession."

The Empress was bewildered by this.

"Allied West was a financial institution," explained Distikka patiently. "They provided money for the ball as a means of garnering publicity and goodwill among the families of the debutantes, who are rich and worth cultivating for their business."

Empress Kabachetka frowned. "For a plan, Distikka, this seems to require a great deal of explanation. Please proceed more briskly to the heart of the matter."

"The heart of the matter is that St. Amelia's Ball now urgently needs a new sponsor, but it's not so easy to find a new sponsor in the space of a few weeks. All of the financial institutions in London are still struggling. I suggest you step in."

Kabachetka was doing her best to follow Distikka's words, knowing her adviser was quite likely to have something clever in mind. "I have heard this word 'sponsor' before," she said. "Connected to the Mistress of the Werewolves, I believe."

"Exactly," said Distikka. "She sponsors events in the arts. She gives them money and gets prestige and influence in return."

"But what influence will I gain from sponsoring this ball? I have no desire to impress these debutantes."

Distikka read from the report in the paper. "St. Amelia's Ball traditionally begins in the afternoon with a charity fashion show, featuring appearances from the debutantes as models. This year's show will be presided over by Emily St. Claire, newly promoted editor of British *Vogue*."

The Empress's eyes opened wide. Her languor vanished. "I can sponsor an event at which Emily St. Claire will be adjudicating? The editor of *Vogue*?"

"Quite possibly. I suggest that at the reception next week, you seek her out and offer to sponsor the ball. She will no doubt be both grateful and impressed. She'll put you in touch with whomever you need to speak to."

The Empress was beginning to like Distikka's plan, and congratulated herself for hanging on through the difficult explanation. "If I am the sponsor, will I be important?"

"Very important," said Distikka. "Though the fashion show isn't a major date in the calendar, it is a well-known charity event, and generally features several well-regarded young British designers." Distikka paused, and looked thoughtful. "Perhaps you could even choose your favorite designer and sponsor them too."

"Yes!" cried the Empress. "Then I could be dressed by the designer who was most successful in the show!"

The Empress levitated several inches in the air. It was a breach of court protocol, and the guards at the door were rather shocked, but the Empress was too carried away to notice.

"Distikka, this is the most marvelous idea! But what if some cunning wretch steps in before me?"

"There is little danger of that," said the Empress's adviser. "The financial markets are still struggling. Even those people who have money don't want to be seen to be flaunting it."

"More fool them!" cried the Empress. "I have money, and I will flaunt it. Distikka, I simply cannot wait till the fashion designers' reception. It can be hard, you know, to approach the editor of *Vogue*. She is always surrounded by dreadful toadying creatures. But armed with your sponsorship idea, I will march straight up to her and announce my intention."

The torches on the walls of the throne room burned brighter, energized by the Empress's enthusiasm. They dimmed slightly as she noticed a possible flaw in Distikka's plan.

"As I understand it, a ball and fashion show in London would not normally be sponsored by beings from another dimension. Might it not cause some comment?"

Distikka smiled. "I have already taken care of the matter, Empress. While last on Earth I took the opportunity of setting up a business in your name. You will adopt the persona of Señorita Kabachetka, heir to a vast gold-mining fortune in South America."

"A gold-mining fortune?" The Empress nodded. "I like that. Is Señorita Kabachetka a famous beauty?"

"Eh . . ."

"You must spread it around that I am a famous beauty. And have broken many hearts. Now I come to London to sponsor debutantes, break more hearts and be photographed in a series of exquisite clothes." The Empress glowed with excitement. "You say the ball goes on all night? Think of the fabulous outfits I will need! And only three weeks to prepare! I must get busy, Distikka, there is much work to do. And I am still having terrible difficulties with my new heels! Have you a plan for that?"

"I would suggest wearing more practical shoes."

"Do not be ridiculous. Even as we speak, the dreadful Queen Malveria is no doubt tottering around in her own extra-high heels, attempting to make her spindly ankles accommodate them. I will not be defeated in this matter. The pride of the Hainusta nation depends on it."

CHAPTER 44

Kalix waited till she heard Vex and Daniel go upstairs, still shouting about anime, before slipping out from the safety of her cupboard. She took her coat, picked up the old canvas satchel she used as a bag and quietly left the flat without being noticed. Kalix's anxiety was growing and she hoped that some activity might prevent it from turning into a full-blown panic attack. Her palms felt moist as she hurried along the narrow streets of Kennington, and her chest felt tight.

Why does this always happen?

In her short life the young werewolf had been through therapy, psychiatry and medication. Some of it had been helpful, in a general sort of way, but none of it had enabled her to overcome the panic that a bad attack of anxiety could bring on.

Kalix found herself near the railway arches. She'd once fought some hunters here. She wished that would happen again. It would calm her down. Kalix felt her heart beating rapidly. She halted on a corner.

"Look at the panic rationally," she muttered. "It will start to fade."

The panic didn't fade. It felt worse. Kalix cursed all therapists with their useless advice. She felt nauseous, and the muscles around her neck and jaw were clamped so tightly her face hurt. She dragged her sunglasses out of her bag and put them on, not wanting to catch anyone's eye. Then she scrabbled around in her bag and took out an old-fashioned brown bottle. Her bottle of laudanum was almost empty. Kalix turned it upside down. A tiny drop appeared on the rim. She licked it.

I need more, she thought.

She'd have to make the long journey over to Merchant MacDoig's shop in East London. At least it would give her something to do. She set off north toward the river. When she reached the Thames she walked northeast along the Albert Embankment, mostly on the paved walkway but occasionally vaulting a fence into one of the small parks that had been landscaped into the area around the South Bank Center. Ahead of her she could see the London Eye, the huge Ferris wheel for tourists that revolved slowly, day and night. It was now close to midnight, and though the concrete walkways around the South Bank Center had emptied of theatergoers, there were still a few people around. Kalix ignored them.

Heading east, Kalix came to an area between the Olivier Theatre and the river. She was paying little attention to her surroundings and was surprised when she suddenly found herself confronted by three youths, all male, blocking her path. Kalix stopped. In the background, she noticed two young women.

"What you doing?" demanded one of the young men.

Kalix frowned. She wished she'd been paying attention to where she was going. If she had, she'd have skirted the group and gone along the other side of the theater. It had happened to her occasionally in the past that she'd found herself in trouble with groups of young men, who sometimes seemed unable to resist focusing on such a small skinny girl out on her own.

Kalix took a step to the side and walked on. One youth, only sixteen or so, grabbed her long coat as she passed. Kalix noticed the two young women striding closer. Her mind cleared, as it always did when trouble arose.

"Don't pick on me," said Kalix. "Or you'll regret it."

That produced a howl of laughter from all five members of the group. The largest, a tall youth wearing a baseball cap under a hooded sweatshirt, moved swiftly to stand directly in front of her. He leaned toward Kalix so that the brim of his baseball cap pressed against her forehead.

Had Kalix felt threatened, she could have transformed into her werewolf shape and savaged her tormentors, but she knew she wouldn't need to do that. She was far stronger and fiercer than all of them, even as a human. She felt the first stirrings of her battle madness, but made an effort to keep it at bay. If a full-scale fight developed, she was liable to kill her attackers.

"Really, you should leave me alone," she said.

Unexpectedly, one of the girls leaned forward and slapped Kalix's face. Kalix was very shocked. It seemed like a strange and unnecessary act of violence. Kalix found it difficult to comprehend how this group of youths could simply pick on a random stranger. She stared at the girl.

"You think it's OK to just slap me?"

The girl raised her hand again. Kalix was unable to keep herself in check any longer. She punched the girl full in the face, smashing her nose and producing an explosion of blood that splattered over all of them.

The tall youth barely had time to cry in surprise before Kalix kicked him in the groin and he collapsed, writhing in pain. Kalix leaped toward the next member of the gang and used her forehead to butt him in the face. There was a sickening noise of crunching bone as the bridge of his nose collapsed inward.

Faced with Kalix's unexpected strength and brutality, the two remaining youths lost their nerve and fled. Unfortunately for them, Kalix was no longer completely in control of her actions. She pursued them, catching the girl first. Kalix flung her to the ground and stamped hard on her ribs, breaking them. Her last attacker was a fast runner, but not as fast as Kalix. Kalix descended on him, grabbing his collar and hauling him back. As he turned to face her, she savagely kicked his legs from under him. She kicked him again as he fell and felt her boots snapping a bone in his chest. He cried out in pain and sprawled on the ground. Kalix raised her boot to stamp on his neck. He screamed in fear. Abruptly, and unusually in the circumstances, Kalix's senses began to return. She had the dim idea that perhaps she shouldn't kill him. She hesitated for a few seconds, her boot poised over her defenseless foe's neck. With some effort, she diverted her boot and stamped on his shoulder instead, breaking his collarbone. She nodded and looked around in satisfaction. All five of her attackers were lying on the ground, moaning in pain. Kalix had dealt them heavy injuries.

She skipped off lightly into the darkness. Her anxiety had vanished, as it always did when she was involved in fighting. She felt refreshed, and quite pleased with herself for not killing anyone. They could all be put back together in hospital.

Kalix ran along the riverbank and felt sufficiently enthused to take on her werewolf shape for a few moments as she leaped another fence around an area of grass which was hidden from public view. As she emerged back onto the road, she changed back into her human shape and marched on briskly, feeling much better about everything.

Kalix continued walking east, staying close to the river. She passed the Tate Modern gallery and Southwark Cathedral before turning left onto London Bridge and crossing the Thames. A police car went past very quickly with its lights blazing. It was soon followed by another speeding car. Kalix wondered if they might be on their way to investigate the youths she'd beaten up outside the theater. She knew from experience that she wouldn't normally be suspected of violent crime, as she looked so frail, but she supposed it was possible that one of the youths might give a description of her. She put her head down and picked up her pace, crossing the bridge quickly and turning into the streets north of the river.

It was now the early hours of the morning. She still had a long way to go before she reached Merchant MacDoig's shop, but she was used to walking around London and didn't mind. There was no point arriving too early. The Merchant's shop in London was usually staffed by MacDoig's son, and he tended not to open the premises till ten or eleven in the morning. More than once, Kalix had spent an uncomfortable morning in the alleyway outside the shop, waiting for it to open so she could buy laudanum.

Kalix wasn't feeling too desperate. The near-euphoria she felt after fighting had mellowed her mood sufficiently for her not to mind waiting. It would mean sleeping out of doors, but the young werewolf had done that many times. She took the main road past Tower Hill and yawned. Kalix wondered where she might sleep. She remembered seeing a park somewhere between here and Limehouse.

Kalix was now alone in the dimly illuminated streets. She liked the feeling. She arrived at the park. There was a sign outside though Kalix couldn't make it out properly. She hopped over a wire fence, padded over some gray tennis courts and disappeared beneath the trees. There she found a large clump of bushes. Glancing around quickly to see that no one observed her, she changed into her werewolf shape, pushed her way into the bushes and lay down comfortably on the ground. She wasn't far from Merchant MacDoig's shop. She'd go there in the morning, buy laudanum and then decide what to do with herself. Though no longer anxious, Kalix could still remember her annoyance at the way everyone in the house had interfered with her business and refused to leave her alone.

Maybe I should move out, thought Kalix. I'm fed up with them all.

With that, she went to sleep.

CHAPTER 45

Kalix woke in better spirits. Spending the night outdoors made her feel less connected with her flatmates and, by extension, with her family and the MacRinnalch Clan. Her mother sent her allowance each month via Moonglow, and Kalix had never liked it that her friends should be linked to her family in this way. Now, in the early morning sunlight, she felt remote from them all. The burden of guilt she'd been feeling since the death of Minerva MacRinnalch felt less oppressive.

Kalix emerged from the bushes looking disheveled but healthy. She set off, hoping that the Merchant's son might open early. She had enough money for a bottle of laudanum. Working in the supermarket during her vacation had allowed her to save a little as well as pay the bills. She passed a small branch of the same supermarket on her way toward Limehouse, and she remembered how strange it had seemed, pushing trolleys around and stacking shelves. Kalix hadn't much enjoyed the enforced discipline of turning up for work, though Daniel's good nature and Vex's indestructible good humor had made the days pass quicker.

Kalix found herself among a dense crowd of smartly dressed pedestrians, employees of the banks and financial institutions in the area. She ignored them, though there were some curious glances directed toward her, with her long coat, extremely long, tousled hair, her old boots and her ancient jeans. She thought about the fight she'd been involved in. She still felt pleased she'd managed to be slightly less violent. Even though she'd been attacked, she hadn't killed anyone. That was surely a step in the right direction. She stopped, took her journal from her bag and placed a tick on the list in the appropriate place.

At least the whole plan isn't going wrong, she thought. She noticed all the crosses denoting her failures and quickly put her journal away.

Kalix strolled along Narrow Street with the river on her right and a great facade of concrete and glass on her left. Here, in this street of modern commerce, was the tiny alleyway that led to the Merchant's shop. The alley was long and dark, and belonged to a former age, as did the shop at the end. Merchant MacDoig's ancient premises still seemed to exist in the time of Dickens, with tiny panes of glass in leaded windows and a tinkling bell on a chain you rang for admittance.

Kalix hoped the shop might be open, but the old door with its flaked black paint was firmly closed and there was no response when she rang the bell. Kalix growled, very faintly. Her need for laudanum was growing slightly. She wasn't desperate yet, but she would be if the MacDoigs didn't appear. Kalix wondered if they ever went on holiday. She'd never known the shop to be closed, but the thought troubled her and brought on a twinge of anxiety. She looked at the door, wondering if she could batter it open. Probably, she thought, unless it was protected by some spell. That was possible. It was notable that neither of the MacDoigs ever showed the slightest sign of nervousness when conversing with werewolves, even angry werewolves. Among the MacRinnalchs, it was commonly supposed that they both carried some sort of sorcerous protection.

Kalix went back up the alley, far less enthusiastically than she'd approached the shop. She didn't want to sit around and be found there by the Merchant, waiting for laudanum. It would be humiliating. Nor did she want to loiter in the main street, where she felt conspicuous. She turned into the first side street she came to and paused idly outside a wine bar, gazing at what seemed to her a very modern decor of mirrors and low-backed chairs. Despite the relatively upmarket nature of the wine bar, there was a cheap-looking sign in the window advertising "Mojito madness." Kalix didn't know what that meant.

"Fancy a mojito?"

Kalix spun around, alarmed to be addressed by a stranger. She found herself facing a young man perhaps twenty years old. He was about an inch shorter than her, with long wavy blonde hair and large blue eyes. Kalix's first thought was that he looked like a girl. She glared at him suspiciously.

"What?" she demanded.

The young man grinned. He was wearing a short blue coat, which was also, Kalix thought, rather girly.

"Mojito madness," said the young man, pointing at the sign. "I'll buy you one."

Kalix was still alarmed, and now she felt annoyed too. "I don't know what a mojito is," she said in a very unfriendly tone. "And why would you buy me one anyway?"

The young man, apparently not put off by her tone, grinned at her again. He had nice teeth, Kalix noticed.

"It's a cocktail," he said. "Made with rum. Sorry, did I offend you by asking if I could buy you one? I just noticed you looking pretty and lonely in the street and thought I'd talk to you."

"Oh." Kalix was nonplussed at this, though she felt a little less angry. It was difficult to remain all that annoyed at the young man who'd just complimented her. He certainly wasn't threatening. Kalix noticed a faint trace of eyeliner around his eyes.

"I like your coat," he continued. "And your nose ring, it's pretty. Would you like a mojito?"

Kalix looked at the wine bar. "It's not open yet," she said.

"It'll be open soon."

Kalix was so shy that she found it puzzling to meet anyone who was confident about talking to strangers. She could never have done it herself. She had a feeling that she wouldn't mind having a mojito with this young man, but she suppressed it. She was here to buy laudanum. She shook her head and took a step away.

"No thanks," she said.

The young man looked disappointed. "I'm Manny," he said. "What's your name?"

Kalix didn't answer but hurried away, back into the main road by the river. She felt a little cheered by the encounter. She supposed it wasn't such a bad thing for a nice young stranger to call her pretty. At least it had passed a little time. She headed back toward the alley, hoping that the MacDoigs might now have opened their shop.

CHAPTER 46

This time, when Kalix rang the bell, she sensed herself being examined through the dusty peephole. The door swung open and Merchant MacDoig's son greeted her with the same hearty smile that his father had directed toward his customers for more than a century. The Merchant had lived an unnaturally long life, though no one knew how.

Young MacDoig ushered Kalix quickly inside. The interior was a treasure house of strange, arcane items, many of them rare, and some of them unrecognizable. Scattered here and there were a few pieces of antique furniture, though the finest pieces were kept upstairs, where the Merchant had made a very cozy nest full of valuable old furnishings and tableware. He'd even managed to maintain his coal fire, though it was no longer legal to burn coal in London. Merchant MacDoig was determinedly old-fashioned, and his son was taking after him. He was stout like his father, he wore the same Victorian clothes and while his shock of hair was red rather than gray, he was developing the same florid face.

"It's fine to see you again, Kalix. Still enjoying yourself in the big city, aye? Pleased to hear it."

MacDoig disappeared behind the counter and almost from view at the back of the shop. He half opened a door and leaned through. The MacDoigs were careful never to display their supply of laudanum in public. Where they obtained it from was unknown. As far as Kalix understood, the opium tincture was not manufactured and sold as an illegal drug in the same way that other substances were. It was produced for medical use only, and its supply was tightly controlled. The MacDoigs had found a supplier, somewhere.

"Finest quality," said Young MacDoig proudly, producing an unlabeled brown glass bottle.

The first time Kalix had bought laudanum from Merchant MacDoig, he'd let her have it cheaply. As a favor, he'd said. It hadn't taken long for the price to increase. Kalix counted out her money and handed it over.

"A terrible business up in Scotland," said the Merchant's son. "Old Minerva, I mean. Poor soul. We did a lot of business with her."

Kalix wondered if he knew about her part in Minerva's death. The MacDoigs always knew a lot of gossip. They might easily have learned of Kalix's shameful part in the affair. Kalix fixed her gaze on the counter as she handed over her money.

"There will be trouble now, I'm sure," MacDoig said. "The clan won't let it go easily."

He looked to Kalix for agreement, but the young werewolf had no desire to stay and trade gossip. Buying laudanum was shameful enough at the best of times. It felt worse now, after Minerva's death. Kalix muttered a barely audible "goodbye" before racing off up the alley, relieved to have escaped. She turned back into the main road then halted abruptly. The overwhelming odors of the city could blunt the sharp senses of a werewolf, but there was no mistaking the scent that Kalix picked up. Decembrius was nearby. Kalix wasn't keen for Decembrius to catch her visiting the MacDoigs. He'd know what she was there for. She ducked her head and hurried on, but halted again after only a few paces. The only times she'd known Decembrius to visit the Merchant had been when he was on some errand for the Douglas-MacPhees. Could he possibly be working with them again?

Kalix unconsciously touched her necklace, a plain metal chain holding an unusual dark jewel. It looked unremarkable, but the powerful talisman meant that she could not be found by sorcery, nor could her scent be noticed. Unless Decembrius actually saw her, he wouldn't know she was there. Kalix slunk into a doorway, then peeped around the corner. Almost immediately Decembrius appeared, heading for the alley. Kalix caught the scent of the Douglas-MacPhees, somewhere nearby.

So, she thought, he is working with them again. Even though he knows they tried to kill me.

Kalix was outraged. She was on the point of storming after Decembrius when her way was blocked by the sudden reappearance of the young man who'd approached her outside the wine bar. He was riding a bike on the pavement.

"Hello again," he said, and smiled.

"Are you following me?" demanded Kalix.

"No! I'm just making a delivery. I'm a courier."

Kalix glared at him. On his bike, with a large bag slung over his shoulder, he did indeed appear to be a bicycle courier, but that was no excuse for bothering her.

"I'm busy," she said. "Go away."

"Your hair is so pretty," he said. "It's so long. I love your hair."

Kalix was taken aback. She almost thanked him before she remembered that she was busy spying on Decembrius. "Go away," she said again, this time more forcibly.

The young man shrugged, and for the first time since they'd met, he looked discouraged.

"OK." He pulled a leaflet from his jacket pocket. "I just work as a courier to pay the bills. Really I'm an artist. You should look at my website. I'm having an exhibition."

He handed Kalix the leaflet and then cycled off. Kalix put the leaflet in her pocket, feeling quite puzzled by the encounter. Was it normal to approach someone twice in the street? She wasn't sure. She'd think about it later. Decembrius had disappeared from view and must now be in the Merchant's shop. Kalix peeped out from the doorway again but withdrew rapidly as she recognized the Douglas-MacPhees' old van parked along the street. Now she felt very angry. How dare Decembrius be working with them again? The three of them had tried to kill her, more than once. Markus, as Thane, had ordered them to leave her alone, but she didn't suppose they would. She felt tempted to pre-empt matters and go and attack them right now. She could charge into their van and beat them all up. Kalix was pleased with this idea, until she remembered that she was trying to be less violent. She felt disappointed, and wondered if being less violent had to include the Douglas-MacPhees.

"Here you are," came a voice.

Kalix looked around. A middle-aged businessman in a suit dropped some coins into her hand, smiled politely and walked off. Kalix flushed red with embarrassment at being mistaken for a beggar in a doorway. It wasn't the first time it had happened. She crammed the coins into her pocket without counting them and attempted to look less poor.

She peered around the doorway again, waiting for Decembrius to appear. A young woman in a formal black business outfit stopped in front of her, and opened her purse.

"No, I'm not—" began Kalix.

"Here," said the woman, and forced some coins into Kalix's hand.

"Thank you," said Kalix glumly. The woman smiled and departed.

"I can't believe you're begging in the street!" cried Decembrius, appearing suddenly at her side. "How could you sink so low?"

Kalix flushed an even deeper shade of red. "I wasn't begging! I was just—"

"And right outside the Merchant's shop! You should be ashamed."

"I wasn't begging!" shouted Kalix. "They just kept forcing money into my hands!"

"Yes," said Decembrius. "Because that always happens in London. People just force money into your hands."

"I can't help it if they were generous," said Kalix rather weakly. She scowled. "What are you doing here with the Douglas-MacPhees? Are you selling stolen goods for them again?"

Decembrius clamped his jaws.

"Well?" demanded Kalix.

"I have to make a living, don't I? It's better than begging."

"I wasn't begging! How could you work with the Douglas-MacPhees when they tried to kill me?"

Decembrius shrugged. "They're not trying to kill you any more, are they? So I visited the Merchant for them. They're not welcome in his shop, after some misunderstandings . . . "

They glared at each other.

"I'm so glad we broke up!" said Kalix.

"Me too," said Decembrius. "Best thing that could have happened."

Kalix suddenly grabbed Decembrius and pulled him toward her.

"What's this?" said Decembrius. "I thought you were annoyed at me?"

Kalix, holding tightly on to Decembrius, dragged him into the doorway.

"I'm not getting back together with you," said Decembrius. "You're too much trouble."

"I don't want to get back together," hissed Kalix. "There are hunters in the street!"

Decembrius understood immediately. He put his arms around Kalix and stood with her as if in a lovers' embrace.

"Are you sure they're hunters?" he whispered in Kalix's ear.

"Yes. I recognize one of them, I've met him before."

"How many of them?"

"Three, I think."

Decembrius resisted the urge to turn and look, though he was tensed, ready to fight.

"What are they doing?"

Kalix, still embracing Decembrius, risked a quick glance over his shoulder.

"They're going toward the Douglas-MacPhees' van. You can look around now. Be careful."

Decembrius looked around. Three men were walking away from them, in the direction of the Douglas-MacPhees' van. Decembrius didn't recognize any of them, but trusted Kalix's assertion that they were hunters. He eased himself from her grasp, and they both watched as the hunters got into a car. Moments later, the Douglas-MacPhees van pulled away from the curb. After a few seconds, the car followed them.

"Were the Douglas-MacPhees meant to wait for you?" asked Kalix.

"No, I came here in my own car. We're meeting at their flat."

"We'd better do something," said Kalix. No MacRinnalch could abandon a fellow werewolf to the hunters, even enemies like the Douglas-MacPhees.

"I'm parked around the corner," said Decembrius. "Let's go."

Kalix and Decembrius hurried around to his car, parked at a meter in the next side road. They had to wait at traffic lights, and by they time they drove back onto Narrow Street neither the Douglas-MacPhees nor their pursuers were in sight.

"They'll be heading home," said Decembrius. They set off in pursuit. Kalix had forgotten her recent embarrassment. She was focused and excited and leaned forward in her seat, scanning the road ahead for any sign of their enemies.

CHAPTER 47

Imperial Adviser Bakmer was always uneasy around Sarapen. Sarapen was so large and grim. As an alien in the land of the Hainusta he shouldn't have been able to maintain his strength, but the Empress regarded him as important enough to grant him a permanent spell of maintenance. It allowed him to survive, and flourish. Bakmer doubted than any of the imperial guards could have defeated Sarapen in combat.

Why the Empress was so keen on an alien werewolf wasn't clear. It was very irregular and wouldn't go down well with the population were they to learn of it. Bakmer wasn't sure whether the two were romantically linked. If so, it was even more irregular. Scandalous really, though as reigning Empress of the Hainusta, Kabachetka was not subject to the same rules as the rest of the population. She could do much as she liked, just as her mother Asaratanti had done.

Bakmer greeted Sarapen politely when he returned to the palace. "Back from the desert so soon? I'm afraid the Empress isn't here."

"Where is she?"

"I don't know."

Sarapen looked suspiciously at Bakmer, whom he didn't like at all. "I thought you kept her engagement diary."

"I keep a copy," Bakmer corrected him. "The main diary resides with Lady Gezinka, who is, of course, Official Diary Keeper."

Sarapen growled. There were many court officials. It was hard to keep track of them all.

"So where is Gezinka?"

"I'm afraid I don't know. Probably with the Empress. Unless she's with Distikka."

Adviser Bakmer pronounced Distikka's name as if he had a sour taste in his mouth. Distikka was another person who surely didn't belong in the Empress's court. She was a foreigner, a Hiyasta. She was notably uncivil, and hardly paid any attention to the normal formalities of court behavior. Bakmer was continually jealous of her good standing with Kabachetka.

"If the Empress appears, inform her I'm looking for her," said Sarapen.

"I will," said Bakmer, forcing more warmth into his voice than he felt. Sarapen departed, leaving Bakmer dissatisfied. He didn't know where the Empress was, which already made him uncomfortable. Might he be falling out of favor? It wouldn't surprise him if Gezinka was using the opportunity to criticize him behind his back. He didn't trust her at all. She was as bad as Alchet, the Empress's chief handmaiden. As for Lady Tecton, who'd recently risen to prominence as the Empress's card partner, she was as bad as the rest: scheming, devious and ambitious. Bakmer sighed. Life had been easier when Kabachetka was only a princess. Then his advisory duties had mainly related to clothes, hair and fashion. He was good at that. Now she was Empress, there seemed a lot more to worry about, and the young adviser wasn't sure he was up to the task.

CHAPTER 48

Thrix, inspired by Minerva, had absorbed her teaching and practiced her art till her skill reached a level few others could match. There were no werewolf sorcerers to equal her, and not many humans. At this moment, she was sitting alone in her flat in Knightsbridge, feeling depressed.

"I've wasted my skill," she said out loud to no one. "I've spent the last twenty years developing fashion-related magic and now I can't do anything else."

She looked down at her ankles with an expression of distaste.

I must have spent weeks trying to perfect the extra-high-heels spell, she thought. Why didn't I realize I should be concentrating on the Guild?

Thrix's spacious living room was cluttered with sorcerous talismans she'd dragged out of cupboards and wardrobes. She'd assembled every magical item she'd ever used in an effort to concoct some sort of spell that might find the Guild's headquarters. The living room table, previously home to stacks of fashion magazines, was now piled high with magical herbs she'd bought or collected in the past week. The room smelled strongly of them, though not as strongly as the kitchen, which had been the scene of several attempts to brew potions, none of them successful.

"I've used every locating spell ever written, including Minerva's secret ones, and none of them has worked. Whatever sorcery the Avenaris Guild is using to hide itself, it's stronger than I am."

Thrix made an effort to force herself into a more positive frame of mind. It was difficult. She'd spent many years trying to boost her self-confidence after an uncomfortable childhood. At the castle, the daughters of the Thane had not been greatly encouraged to develop their talents.

Thrix clenched her firsts. "Don't start thinking about your child-hood," she said out loud again. "That's not going to help."

She was about to snap her fingers to summon a bottle of wine but checked her actions. "No more summoning wine. That's another way I've been wasting magic. Just pour it like everyone else."

Thrix fetched a bottle of wine from the kitchen and applied a corkscrew. She twisted it in then tried to extract the cork. Nothing happened. She pulled harder. The cork sliced in two, leaving the bottle still sealed and virtually impossible to open by normal means.

"Oh damn it," raged Thrix. "Stupid bottle."

She growled the words of an opening spell and the remaining portion of the cork flew from the bottle, ricocheting off the wall.

Thrix filled her glass. She tasted the wine and made a face. "Why did I buy this?"

It struck her she'd hardly had a decent bottle of wine since Captain Easterly had been killed. Her ex-boyfriend had been something of a wine connoisseur.

"Something else to dislike Kalix for. No, don't think about Kalix, that won't help either."

She looked around the room at all her magical artifacts. She was stuck for inspiration. The red light on her answering machine was blinking, as it had been for the past week. Messages from work, no doubt. Thrix ignored them. As she sipped her wine, she thought of the day she'd found Minerva dead. Thrix shuddered. It had been a terrible experience. She could still remember vividly the feel of her dead teacher in her arms as she struggled to take her back up the mountain, to lay her to rest.

"Trust Kalix to get Minerva killed!"

It was easy for Dominil to say that the Guild was responsible, not Kalix, but if Kalix hadn't been so weak-minded and inconsiderate as to take all her laudanum that morning, Minerva wouldn't have been left alone and defenseless on the mountain side, an easy target for the Guild's sniper.

Thrix wasn't feeling too kindly toward Dominil either. What was she doing getting addicted to laudanum anyway? And then bothering Minerva with her problems? Didn't Minerva deserve a peaceful retirement without interference from drug-addled werewolves?

If Kalix and Dominil had just learned to control themselves properly instead of getting addicted to laudanum, none of this would have happened, thought Thrix, and she felt even angrier.

Dominil was meant to be looking for the Avenaris Guild via the internet, land registries, company records and so on, but Thrix didn't believe that would get them anywhere. If the Guild possessed sorcery powerful enough to completely hide it from her spells, it had most probably taken care of everything else too.

She made a sound that was half sigh, half growl, and picked up a manuscript. It was one of Minerva's late writings, details of a spell she'd made but never fully described. As far as Thrix could make out, it was a spell for finding a lover anywhere in the world. That wasn't exactly what Thrix needed, but it contained some unusual and powerful features, and she wondered if she might somehow adapt it. She picked up a notebook from the floor and started to make some notes. A strand of hair fell over her face. She pushed it back impatiently. Thrix's golden hair was tied back and had been unwashed for several days. She wore a very old pair of jeans and she couldn't even have said what color the T-shirt she wore was without checking in a mirror. For the first time in her adult life, the Enchantress had abandoned all traces of vanity.

"I'm going to find them," she muttered. "And then I'm going to kill them all."

Another strand of hair fell over her face. Annoyed at her hair, and everything else, Thrix picked up a pair of dressmakers scissors from the floor and hacked off the loose strand.

I've got too much hair, she thought. It's getting in the way.

She cut off another strand and felt some satisfaction as she watched it fall to the floor.

CHAPTER 49

The Fire Queen was sulking in her palace. Her mood had not improved. There was no word about her new dress for the fashion reception. Apparently Thrix was not going to make her a new dress. Malveria took it very badly. At meetings with her government ministers, she snapped at them for imagined failures and rudely dismissed plans that she herself had originally suggested. She told them she was disappointed in them all, and suggested it was no wonder the nation was in such a poor state if her government ministers were all so inefficient. Even the eternally loyal Xakthan was not immune from criticism. He was deeply wounded by the Queen's sudden decision not to attend his son's military graduation next week.

"But why," raged the Fire Queen later, to Gruselvere and Iskiline, "should I attend the wretched ceremony? I've seen ten thousand young elementals graduate from military academy and this will be no different.

Besides"—Malveria shuddered—"one cannot go anywhere these days without the dreadful Lord Stratov inviting me to his castle. Why does he keep bothering me?"

The Queen looked around at her chief dresser and her wardrobe mistress, but they were unable to supply an answer. It was undoubtedly true that Lord Stratov had been pursuing the Queen in recent weeks. He was never away from court.

"And Garfire is just as bad!" cried the Queen. "Yesterday he absolutely insisted I attend some foul hunt on his wretched estates. He was most persistent. Had a young handmaiden not provided a distraction by dropping a plate of hors d'oeuvre and then bursting into tears, I would have been hard pressed to make an escape. What is wrong with my lords and dukes these days? They are infuriating me. One longs to pick up Garfire and dip him in the Great Volcano, but he is of course Duchess Gargamond's brother and cannot be dipped in the Volcano, at least not just for being tedious."

The Fire Queen drank very deeply from a bottle of red wine and sent a young courier hurrying to the cellars to make sure her personal supply was not running low.

"And when I escaped from the Duke, what do you think happened?"

Iskiline and Gruselvere looked inquisitively toward the Queen, though they had already heard the story. "The Earl of Flamineau practically leaped on me to invite me to a masked ball he's holding in his chateau. Since when does Earl Flamineau hold masked balls? The man is so decrepit I'm surprised he can still dance. What is the matter with them all?"

Gruselvere giggled.

"Are you giggling?" said the Fire Queen. "What is the source of this hilarity?"

"They're trying to woo you," said Gruselvere.

The Fire Queen scowled. "I had worked this out for myself, Gruselvere. But why are they trying to woo me at this moment? I remain the same Fire Queen I have been for . . . uh . . . several years. Why this sudden upsurge of interest?"

Neither Iskiline nor Gruselvere could suggest a reason.

"I suspect First Minister Xakthan," declared Malveria. "He's been trying to marry me off for years. One simply winces at his lack of subtlety. I will produce an heir when I'm ready and not before, and I will not produce it with Garfire, Stratov or Flamineau!" Malveria sat erect in her chair and slapped a palm noisily on the armrest. "None of them are at all suitable!"

"Who would be suitable?" wondered Iskiline, who, like her companion, was taking the opportunity to drink deeply from the contents of the Fire Queen's cellars.

"How can I think about that when I am in the midst of the most severe fashion crisis ever to hit these lands?" cried the Fire Queen. "With Thrix MacRinnalch shunning me and no dress for the fashion designers' reception? Now I cannot attend for fear of inferior frock shame. And yet I'm expected to attend ceremonies, run my government, get married and produce children as if nothing was wrong?"

Fire dripped from the Queen's fingers. "I always knew Thrix MacRinnalch would let me down in the end. No doubt she has been planning this outrage for years. It was simply foolish to trust a werewolf, and a MacRinnalch at that." Malveria scowled mightily, and more fire emerged from her fingers. "Did I tell you I called in to her wretched office in Soho last week? Me, the Fire Queen, reigning sovereign of the Hiyasta nation, appearing cap in hand like a beggar, pleading for a new dress. And she was not there! And her assistant claims not to know where she is! I won't have it!"

The Queen's rage abruptly deflated. She sighed and sank in her chair. "Now I cannot attend the event. When the fashionable people assemble tonight, I will not be there." The Queen drank heavily from her glass. "It is all very trying."

A young attendant in a flawlessly embroidered red costume entered the room and bowed deeply. "Mighty Queen, Duke Garfire is without, asking permission to see you."

"Garfire? Did I not instruct you to tell him I had left the palace?"

"Uh . . . no, mighty Queen."

"Well, you should have guessed. Tell him I'm indisposed. The Fire Queen is not at home to anyone. Now begone, and apart from bringing wine at regular intervals, do not appear again."

CHAPTER 50

"This is where the Douglas-MacPhees live?" said Kalix, looking up at the very ordinary flat above a health-food shop in Hoxton.

"Yes," said Decembrius.

"It looks just like a normal flat."

"What were you expecting, a pirates' lair?"

"No," said Kalix sharply. Really, she had been expecting something like that, and wouldn't have been surprised to find a skull and crossbones hanging out of the window.

The Douglas-MacPhees' van was parked along the street in a resident's parking space. Kalix got out of Decembrius's car. She noticed that he was arranging his hair in the rear-view mirror.

"Do you have to do that now?"

"Why not?" sad Decembrius, unabashed. "Nothing wrong with looking good."

"It doesn't look that good."

"That's not what you said before."

"I've never said anything about your hair."

"Yes, you did, you said you liked it now it was longer."

"I don't remember saying that."

Decembrius had changed in the past year. When he was an associate of Sarapen's, he'd worn a suit. Now he had a leather jacket and his hair was long, swept back and a brighter shade of red than it used to be. It did look good, but Kalix wasn't about to tell him that. They walked toward the door beside the health food shop.

Kalix hesitated. "What are we going to do? Just ring the doorbell?"

"Why not?" asked Decembrius.

"It's going to look strange, me ringing their doorbell."

Kalix felt silly at the prospect of ringing the bell. Duncan Douglas-MacPhee would laugh at her, if he didn't just attack her first.

"Probably the hunters just followed them and now they've gone," said Kalix. "We should leave. You can call them and tell them you saw hunters following them."

Decembrius was no longer listening. He'd walked up to the door and was staring at it fixedly.

Kalix caught up with him. "What is it—" she began, but didn't finish the sentence. She picked up the same scent as Decembrius. The smell of blood was coming from behind the door, unnoticeable to the people who walked by on the pavement, but distinctive to Kalix and Decembrius.

Decembrius looked around. "Give me some cover."

Kalix leaned against him, spreading her coat a little, as if putting her arms around him. When there were no pedestrians nearby, Decembrius slammed his elbow into the door. There was a loud noise as the lock broke, but with the traffic in the street, no one seemed to notice. Decembrius backed quickly inside, followed by Kalix. They found themselves in a dark stairway. The smell of blood was overwhelming. Decembrius pushed the light switch then ran up the stairs.

The door to the flat was open. Kalix and Decembrius rushed in. In the hallway, Duncan Douglas-MacPhee was lying face down in a puddle of blood. His sister Rhona lay beside him, on her side, with a wound in her heart. Their huge cousin William was slumped in the doorway to the next room. Decembrius swiftly felt for a pulse on each body.

"They're all dead," he muttered. "And still warm."

He turned Duncan over. "One bullet in the heart. They've all been killed with one bullet."

Kalix ran through the flat, hoping to find the hunters, but they were gone. She arrived back in the hallway with a wild look in her eyes. "We have to find them and kill them!"

Decembrius shook his head. "Find them? They've gone. They followed the Douglas-MacPhees here, killed them and left, all before we got here."

Decembrius saw the maddened look in Kalix's eyes. "There's no point going crazy. We can't do anything now."

Kalix knew it was true. She tried to calm herself. Decembrius was using his phone, calling someone. He waited while it rang.

"Thrix isn't answering." He looked uncertain. "Who should I call now?"

Kalix didn't know. Previously, when werewolves had been killed in London, Thrix had come and used her skills to investigate the scene. If Thrix wasn't around she wasn't sure what to do.

"Maybe you should call the castle?"

Decembrius nodded. He dialed quickly. "This is Decembrius MacRinnalch. I need to speak to the Mistress of the Werewolves. It's urgent."

Kalix looked around at the hallway. It wasn't dark or dingy, as she'd imagined the abode of the Douglas-MacPhees would be. It was large and bright, as was the rest of the apartment. The decorations and furnishings were much better than those in the flat Kalix shared in Kennington. Someone among the Douglas-MacPhees had obviously had some taste, and their criminal lifestyle must have made them a reasonable income. Kalix looked down at Duncan's body and felt confused. This was a werewolf who'd pursued her, and tried to kill her. She'd fought him and his siblings more than once. She'd happily have killed him during any of these fights. But now he was dead, murdered by werewolf hunters. Kalix felt her customary hatred and loathing toward the hunters, but about Duncan himself, she didn't know what to think.

The Mistress of the Werewolves was extremely alarmed to hear the news, particularly as they were still at the scene of the murder.

"You both have to get out of there immediately," she said. "What if the hunters come back?"

"I don't think that's likely," said Decembrius.

The Mistress of the Werewolves was insistent. The murders were another blow for the clan, but her immediate concern was for her daughter.

"Make the front door secure, then leave. I won't have you risking your lives. Thrix can't be far away, we can ask her to visit later, if it's safe."

"Do you want to speak to Kalix?" asked Decembrius.

"Just get out of the flat!" said Verasa urgently.

Decembrius rang off. "Your mother is worried about us. She wants us to leave. Probably that's the best idea. I'll see if I can fix the door before we go."

Kalix nodded. She took a final look around the hallway. She'd seen a lot of dead werewolves in her short life, and now there were three more.

"I'm going to destroy the Guild," she said.

Decembrius bent down and felt in Duncan's pockets. He took out a set of keys. They left, closing the flat door behind them. Downstairs at the street door, Decembrius did his best to reposition the lock he'd dislodged while breaking in.

"It'll hold for a little while anyway," he said, jamming it back into place. "I hope no one's filming us leaving the scene. There are cameras everywhere these days."

Kalix had a brief, alarming image of seeing herself on a crime program on TV, caught on film as a suspect in a triple murder. They kept their heads down as they headed for the car.

"Thrix and Dominil said they'd find the Guild," said Kalix. "What's taking them so long?"

"Maybe they've already found them. Maybe they're not telling us."

Kalix wondered if that could be true. Might Thrix and Dominil regard her as so untrustworthy that they wouldn't even tell her when they'd found the Avenaris Guild's headquarters? Could the MacRinnalch Clan execute an attack without her? It was a distressing thought, but the more Kalix pondered it, the more likely it seemed. Everyone regarded her as unreliable. Not only that, she was still in exile. It might be against clan rules to let her join in the attack.

"They're not leaving me out," said Kalix. "When they attack the Guild I'm going too." She looked at Decembrius. "You're on the Great Council. Why don't you find out about it?"

"I don't like to get involved with the council."

"Stop being so useless," said Kalix. "Find out what's happening. Take responsibility."

Decembrius laughed. "That's funny coming from you."

Kalix scowled at him, but didn't answer. Nor did she respond to Decembrius's broad hint that she might like to visit North London with him, rather than going back to her own flat. Finding his hint ignored, Decembrius made the direct suggestion that they go to a bar somewhere, have a few drinks and then go home together.

"We just found three dead werewolves and now you want to sleep with me?"

"Good a way as any of getting over a bad experience," said Decembrius.

"You really disgust me sometimes," said Kalix.

Decembrius was offended by her blank refusal and by the time he dropped her off in Kennington they were, as usual, no longer speaking to each other.

CHAPTER 51

It was a surprise to everyone when Pete called Vex and asked if he could take her out on a date.

"He actually called?" Daniel was amazed. "I thought it was just a one-night thing."

"Me too," admitted Moonglow. "I never thought she'd hear from him again."

Since Pete had called, two days ago, Vex had spent her time tripping around the flat, humming cheerfully to herself and carrying the current edition of Absolute Boyfriend, a manga which she regarded as an authoritative text on the subject.

"We're going on a date," she said many times. "I'm so happy to have a boyfriend! Isn't it great?"

This had been endearing for a short while, but for Vex's loveless flat-mates it had now started to grate. Daniel, still stricken over Moonglow, could muster no enthusiasm for anyone else's happy love life. Nor could Kalix. Moonglow was pleased to see Vex happy but was starting to have doubts about her new fixation.

"I'm not sure that manga is good for her," she confided to Daniel. "Suddenly it's like having a boyfriend is the only thing that matters. Maybe I should have a word with her."

"Yes, do that," said Daniel. "Vex would enjoy a long lecture about girls not defining themselves in terms of their boyfriends. Maybe you could throw in a brief history of feminism too? Serve her right for being happy."

"Very funny," said Moonglow. She resolved to say no more on the subject. Her resolve lasted for only a few minutes. "I just don't like the way she's tripping around the place. Can't she walk normally?"

It was true that Vex's gait did seem to have changed. She'd adopted a slightly skipping motion, like a young child.

"So she's skipping around a little," said Daniel. "She's happy."

"She doesn't need to be so girly all the time."

"Vex is always girly," Daniel said. "You know, with the Hello Kitty T-shirts and multi-colored nail varnish."

"Well, now she's being extra girly," said Moonglow.

"And you find this annoying?"

"No, I don't," said Moonglow. "I'm just pointing it out."

Something about Vex's behavior seemed to have touched a nerve, irritating Moonglow. Daniel, whose hopeless, defeated love for Moonglow had naturally made him rather annoyed at her, might have pressed the point further, just to be annoying in turn, had they not been interrupted by the sudden arrival of the Fire Queen. Malveria materialized in their front room with an orange flash which was bright enough to inform them that she was not in the best of moods, but not bright enough to mean that she was furious.

"Daniel, Moonglow," said the Fire Queen, politely. "I apologize for my unexpected arrival, but circumstances force me to flee the palace."

"Oh dear," said Moonglow, and looked concerned. "Not more fighting?"

"Not yet," said Malveria. "Though if Duke Garfire persists with his unwanted advances, there may be violence. I am troubled by amorous advances from my nobles that are quite unwelcome."

The Fire Queen took a seat on the couch. Daniel, fearing that he might have to listen to more about amorous advances than he cared to, hurried to the kitchen to put the kettle on. The Fire Queen valued good manners, and always appreciated the way that Daniel and Moonglow would make tea for her.

"Also," continued the Queen to Moonglow, "I need to talk to my dismal niece. Has she committed any outrages recently?"

Moonglow shook her head. "No outrages at all. Everything is going well."

"Has she made use of the computer that I purchased for her?"

Moonglow hesitated. Vex had learned how to look at fashion websites and read manga online, but whether or not she'd done anything educational, as the Fire Queen had specified, she wasn't sure.

"I think she's been using it quite a lot."

"No doubt for unsuitable purposes," said the Fire Queen. "Rather than learning anything."

"I'm sure she'll be ready for next term at college," said Moonglow encouragingly.

"I hope so," said the Queen. "Though at the moment, other matters occupy my mind. But they are personal, and I can't tell you about them."

"OK," said Moonglow.

"It would involve criticizing my good friend Thrix, which I would not like to do."

"All right."

"But she has deserted me in a most scandalous manner! Really, Moonglow, it is a terrible affair! Two nights ago I should have been at a fashion show in London and I could not go because Thrix had not made me the dress she promised! She has attempted to fob me off with her designers who are not up to the task. Can you imagine the humiliation? I, Malveria, shamefully reduced to the level of an inferior client?" The Fire Queen shook her head. "I never thought she would abandon me this way."

Moonglow was aware of the strong relationship between Thrix and Malveria, and wondered what could have happened. "Did you have some sort of argument?"

"Argument? Why do you say that?"

"Well," said Moonglow, "you have had arguments before."

"True. Tempers have flared at times. It is inevitable in the heady and competitive world of fashion. But there has been no argument. Thrix has simply abandoned me."

The Fire Queen took out a tiny lace handkerchief and dabbed her eyes. Daniel arrived back with a large tray on which were three of Moonglow's best china cups and a teapot.

"Thank you, Daniel. I so appreciate your good manners. It is such a strong contrast with the despicable behavior of Thrix MacRinnalch."

Malveria turned to Moonglow. "As life has been so trying recently, I hoped that we might make another attempt at the six-stage lip process?"

Before Moonglow could reply, there was a noisy clattering on the stairs as Vex appeared wearing the largest pair of boots yet seen on her, along with the shortest skirt.

"Aunt Malvie!" she cried. "I'm getting ready for a date. With my boyfriend!"

Daniel and Moonglow tensed slightly, sensing that Queen Malveria was not in the right mood to listen to Vex enthusing about her boyfriend.

"Boyfriend?" said Malveria. "You mean this guitarist?"

"Yes."

"He actually called you?"

"Of course!" Vex grinned. It struck Moonglow that she'd never seen anyone so completely happy as Vex at that moment. Malveria did not seem so impressed.

"Agrivex, is this a suitable relationship? I did not send you to Earth to gallivant with guitarists." The Queen paused. "What are you wearing on your feet?"

"Sorel boots! They're made for walking over glaciers. Whatever a glacier is. Some sort of big animal, I think."

Vex beamed. Her boots really were large, even by her standards. The Queen barely suppressed a shudder.

"Did the excitement of your boots cause you to forget your other garments?" said the Fire Queen, eyeing the small strip of material that barely qualified as a skirt.

"New from Camden," said Vex happily, and looked at her legs, which were slender and pretty, as she knew.

"Lengthen it immediately," said the Queen. "Exhibiting one's underwear is not done in the best circles."

Vex laughed and then managed to say exactly the wrong thing. "You must be close to getting a boyfriend too, Aunty. With all these dukes and lords wooing you?"

Vex turned to Moonglow and Daniel. "Aunt Malvie's really popular these days! Every day there's some duke or lord asking her to a ball."

"Agrivex," said Malveria, "this is not a suitable subject. Drop it immediately!"

"Must make you feel good to have so many men chasing you, Aunty. Who do you like best? Lord Stratov's a bit old, I suppose, but I hear he's really keen on you. I hear a lot of good things about Duke Garfire too, he's a bit of a favorite at the palace, what with his daughter Honorable Gloria that everyone likes."

"No one likes the Honorable Gloria."

Vex looked at her aunt, and for the first time noticed that something might be amiss. There was a hint of flame around the Queen's left eye.

"I came here to escape from this foolishness, not to hear you prattle about it. It seems to me, Agrivex, that you are not spending your time wisely. I have given you various tasks to complete while in this dimension. How are they progressing?"

Vex looked confused as she struggled to remember what tasks her aunt might have given her. "Was it something to do with shopping?"

"It was not to do with shopping, dismal niece."

"I'm good at shopping."

"Stop saying 'shopping.' It did not enter into your tasks. I instructed you to learn how to use the computer I was informed you required for college. I also instructed you to work on your elemental powers."

The Fire Queen shifted in her seat to speak to Moonglow.

"Agrivex's total lack of control of her elemental powers is a source of continual embarrassment. The four-year-old daughter of my idiot kitchen maid has better control of her flames than Agrivex."

"That's not fair!" protested Vex.

"Really? Can you do this?"

The Fire Queen pointed her finger. A long tongue of yellow flame shot out, which she held in the air quite steadily, not letting it touch anything in the room.

"Well? Can you?"

"Maybe," said Vex.

"Then let us see."

Agrivex held out her hand and screwed up her face. Nothing happened.

"Pah," cried the Queen. "A complete failure."

"I think her finger's going a little bit pink," said Daniel encouragingly.

"Only where she has poorly applied her nail varnish," said the Queen. "Agrivex, this is most unsatisfactory. You must make an effort. You are my officially adopted niece and you cannot disgrace the royal family like this."

Agrivex strained some more, with no result. The Fire Queen was clearly annoyed at her niece, and Daniel and Moonglow began to feel uncomfortable.

"So, abominable girl. You have ignored my instructions again, preferring to spend your time obtaining preposterous boots and ridiculous skirts in an effort to ensnare some unfortunate guitarist. It is not good enough." She glared at her niece. "And what about your computer? Have you learned how to use that?"

Vex looked uncertain. "Well, sort of. It's quite difficult—"

"Your flatmates manage it. Take me to this piece of equipment and let me see your progress."

The Fire Queen marched toward the stairs. Agrivex, looking quite deflated, followed her toward her room in the attic.

"Poor Vex," said Daniel after they'd gone. "Obviously it was a bad time to announce her boyfriend."

Moonglow nodded. "Malveria's in a really bad mood. Something's happened between her and Thrix."

Daniel sat on the couch and refilled both of their teacups. He took a biscuit from the tray.

"It'll probably be OK in the end," said Moonglow. "Malveria usually calms down fairly quickly."

Daniel nodded. At that moment there was a terrible explosion upstairs and the whole house shook. Plaster from the ceiling rained down on their heads. The cat wailed and darted under the table. There was another explosion, this time sending dust and smoke into the living room. Kalix came running out of her bedroom and leaped to the foot of the stairs.

"What's happening?" she cried, but her voice was lost in the sound of another explosion. Moonglow was frozen with terror. Daniel grabbed her and bundled her out of the living room into the hallway. Kalix picked up the cat and followed them. Daniel opened their front door and hauled Moonglow down the stairs. Behind them the flat shook as another explosion ripped through the building. Daniel and Moonglow threw themselves down and lay huddling on the stairs. Kalix and the cat fell on top of them. They heard another terrific explosion. This one seemed further away, but it was strong enough to bring down more plaster from the ceiling.

"Are we under attack?" cried Moonglow.

"I think it's the Fire Queen," said Daniel. "She's gone mad."

"Why? Vex can't have been that bad on the computer."

Another explosion tore through the air above them, almost deafening them with its ferocity. Kalix flinched as the cat dug its claws into her; Moonglow moaned. Daniel put his arm around her and tried to shield her as debris rained down. They lay huddled together in the hallway, waiting for the terrible experience to pass, and hoping they might survive it.

CHAPTER 52

There was a brief, stunned silence after the final explosion.

"Has it stopped?" gasped Moonglow.

"Help, help!" came a voice.

"It's Vex!" said Daniel. He hurried back upstairs into the flat, followed by Kalix and Moonglow. Vex was standing in the living room, apparently unharmed but distressed.

"Aunt Malvie's gone mad! She started exploding all over the place!" Vex paused. "Don't look at me like that. It wasn't my fault."

"What did you do to drive her mad?" demanded Daniel, voicing what the others were thinking.

"I didn't do anything! I was just telling her about my boyfriend and then she wanted me to try producing flames, which I couldn't, and then she just started exploding!"

"It doesn't seem enough to make Malveria lose her reason," said Moonglow.

"I don't know," said Daniel. "Vex can be very irritating."

"Was there anything else?" asked Moonglow.

Vex's bright yellow hair was a dull gray from plaster that had descended from the ceilings. She tried to remember what else had been said.

"Aunt Malvie wanted to see if I could use my computer, so I was showing her how great I am using it, and we looked at some manga, and then some Japanese fashion, and then she wanted to see if there was anything about *Vogue*, so I went to the *Vogue* webpage . . . "

Vex looked thoughtful. "And you know, it was right then that Aunt Malvie exploded."

The flatmates were mystified. Moonglow crossed over to the table where her own laptop had fortunately been closed at the time of the explosions. She blew off the dust then searched for the website of British *Vogue*.

"'On set with Chanel—new street chic,'" she said, reading from the page. "'Our pick of the best summer shoes'—what's this?"

Moonglow clicked on a link while Daniel, Vex and Kalix craned to read over her shoulder.

"Fashionable party people," said Moonglow. "Who's been out and about this week in London. Famous society beauty Señorita Kabachetka, seen here at Tuesday's reception with editor Emily St. Claire. Señorita Kabachetka, heir to a huge gold-mining fortune in Brazil, will be sponsoring this year's St. Amelia's Ball."

Moonglow looked up. "Well, that explains it."

"What?" asked Daniel.

"Kabachetka's beaten her into the 'fashionable party people' page."

"Is that serious?"

"Serious? Have you never heard Malveria talk about it? It's her one ambition to get herself into that page."

"It's true," said Vex. "I've always thought it was a bit frivolous really."

Everyone stared at the screen, where the Empress Kabachetka, in the guise of a South American heiress, looked blonde, happy and fashionable.

"Where's your aunt now?" asked Kalix.

Vex shrugged. "I'm not sure. I was hiding under the bed. I think she went outside and exploded some more."

"Will she be all right?" asked Moonglow.

At that moment there came a sound like thunder: the fiercest, most earth-splitting thunder ever heard in the city. The whole street vibrated. There was another terrible crash as the Fire Queen materialized at the top of the room, hurtling downward. She smashed into the couch, which collapsed in flames, then lay motionless among the wreckage.

"Well, I've seen her better," said Vex.

Moonglow, Daniel, Kalix and Vex gathered around in concern.

"Wake up, Aunty!" said Vex.

There was no response. Moonglow became very worried. "I think we should get a doctor," she said.

"How?" asked Daniel. "We can't call nine nine nine and say we've got an injured Fire Elemental in the house."

"I didn't mean a human doctor," said Moonglow. "An elemental doctor. Vex, you have doctors, right?"

Vex nodded. "Aunt Malvie's got her own doctor. He's famous. He lives in the palace."

"Could you bring him here?"

The young Fire Elemental frowned. "I'm not sure. Most Hiyastas don't like to come to Earth. They don't like the journey."

But Vex, who up till now had been expecting her aunt to suddenly sit up and be normal again, became worried. The Fire Queen, lying among the ruins of the couch, showed no signs of movement.

"I'll get the doctor," said Vex, and disappeared into thin air.

"I'll get a blanket," said Moonglow.

"Is that a good idea?" wondered Daniel. "Isn't the Queen made of fire? What if she overheats?"

"I don't like to just leave her lying there," said Moonglow. "We have to do something."

Moonglow hurried off upstairs to bring a blanket for the Fire Queen. Daniel surveyed the room, which was in a poor state. Apart from the shattered couch, everything was covered in fine dust, and there were cracks and scorch marks on the ceiling. Kalix wondered what she could do to help. Though she had never felt much affinity with the Fire Queen, she knew she owed her life to Malveria's powers of healing.

"Maybe she'd like a glass of water," she said, and went to the kitchen to run the tap.

Daniel sat down beside the Queen and placed his hand gently on her arm, in what he hoped was a comforting way. Soon the Queen lay under a blanket, with a glass of water beside her, and three anxious flatmates watching over her, waiting for Vex to arrive with an elemental doctor from another dimension.

CHAPTER 53

The mood at the Avenaris Guild was brighter than it had been for many months. The gloom caused by the death of Captain Easterly had pervaded the whole organization, but now there was optimism in every part of the building. First there had been the good news about the legacy from the Countess of Nottingham. Using that money, Mr. Carmichael had moved quickly to replace the hunters they'd lost. The Guild was reinvigorated. The assassination of Minerva MacRinnalch had been a fine start. Even if she had not been a well-known werewolf, any success in the Scottish Highlands, where the MacRinnalchs were so strong, was regarded as a triumph. And now the same squadron, Group Sixteen, had scored a great coup by killing all three Douglas-MacPhees. The operation had gone as smoothly as anyone could have hoped for. The four hunters had tracked the Douglas-MacPhees in London and then swiftly eliminated them. There was celebration at their headquarters. Mr. Carmichael had silenced his detractors.

The chairman of the board personally congratulated his four new recruits on their successful mission. He met Stone, Marshall, Braid and Axelsen in his son's office, and told him how proud the Guild was of their achievement.

"The Douglas-MacPhees were three of the strongest werewolves ever to infest London. You've eliminated them in a brilliant operation without sustaining a single casualty. It's one of our greatest moments."

The four members of Group Sixteen accepted Mr. Carmichael's praise without exhibiting any great degree of emotion. They knew there were stronger werewolves than the Douglas-MacPhees. Royston, who was responsible for most of their intelligence, had immersed himself in the Guild's records. He'd briefed his companions on some of the werewolves they were likely to meet.

John Carmichael's office contained the same mixture of furnishings that characterized the Guild's headquarters: a Georgian mahogany bookcase in the corner, a metal filing cabinet from the '60s next to the door and a brand-new computer on his desk. On the screen was a file with pictures of each of the Douglas-MacPhees. Below each picture, the word "eliminated" had been added.

"When will our next mission be?" asked Marshall.

"Soon," Mr. Carmichael told him. "We're still gathering intelligence."

"I don't like waiting," said Braid.

Mr. Carmichael nodded. He knew Braid to be a fine hunter. He also knew he was a very violent man—more violent, probably, than most of their hunters. He'd been dishonorably discharged from the army. Mr. Carmichael had read the report.

"Don't worry, you'll be in action again soon. I warned you that some of these werewolves have extra protection. Sorcery, so it's said. But we've got people on our side now who can deal with that. We'll find them."

Mr. Carmichael leaned over the desk and tapped some keys on the computer. A blurry photograph, taken in the street at a distance, came up on-screen. A young woman, her face partially hidden, with a long coat and very long hair.

"The werewolf princess," said Royston, who'd read all that the Guild had on Kalix MacRinnalch.

Mr. Carmichael nodded. "She's been very hard to find. But we're getting closer."

Braid leaned closer to the screen. "I'd like to meet her," he said.

CHAPTER 54

Many MacRinnalchs had never regarded Markus as a suitable candidate for Thane. The same was true among the smaller clans associated with the MacRinnalchs—the MacAllisters, MacPhees, MacGregors and MacAndrises. After Markus's victory in the election, the animosity toward him gradually ebbed away. This was largely due to the astute politicking of his mother Verasa. The Mistress of the Werewolves had many years' experience in placating dissatisfied werewolves. It helped that Markus had defeated the huge Wallace MacGregor in single combat. The fight had been witnessed by many werewolves, and it had proved that Markus did not lack either strength or spirit.

Markus was now secure in his position. Only some terrible blunder on his part could lead to anyone questioning his authority.

"Markus, is that webcam on?" asked Beatrice.

"Uh . . . I'm not sure," said Markus.

Beatrice slammed the laptop shut. "You have to be more careful!" she said. "Your mother was on the other end of that webcam not five minutes ago!"

Beatrice was angry. "If you don't care about being run out of the castle, I do. I need my job."

Beatrice MacRinnalch was assistant keeper of the archives at Castle MacRinnalch, and in line for promotion to chief curator. She was also one of Markus's two girlfriends, the other of whom was standing next to them, partially dressed, with a safety pin in her mouth as she made adjustments to Markus's long blue dress.

Heather MacAllister took the safety pin out of her mouth. "Beatrice is right. If the clan catches you wearing a dress with two half-naked girlfriends beside you, you'll be the shortest-reigning Thane in history."

Markus was grinning. "Maybe they'd be impressed."

"They won't be. Baron MacAllister would chase me out of Scotland. I'm his grand-niece and he has standards."

Markus was standing in front of a long mirror in the living room of his Edinburgh flat. His two girlfriends were adjusting his dress.

"We've got an openly gay gardener at the castle," said Markus. "Maybe cross-dressing might be the next thing to get past the standards committee of the werewolf clan."

Beatrice laughed. The werewolves didn't actually have a standards committee, but if they had, Markus wouldn't have made it past them, of that she was quite certain. Two separate girlfriends would have been bad enough, though possibly acceptable, if handled discreetly. Two girlfriends that he saw at the same time wouldn't have been. As for his liking for cross-dressing, the uproar that would cause could hardly be imagined.

"You wouldn't be grinning, that's for sure," said Beatrice.

Markus acknowledged the truth of that. "But we're far away from the clan now, and the webcam's off, so let's get this dress sorted."

"I think we should put it to one side for the moment," said Beatrice.

Markus looked at her in surprise. Since confessing his liking for cross-dressing to Beatrice, she'd proved to be rather fond of the whole thing. He looked toward Heather for support.

"Beatrice is right," said Heather. "We should get back to work."

The Thane looked disappointed. "When did you both become so responsible?"

Heather MacAllister picked up her blouse from the floor and put it on. She was a little taller than Beatrice, though in other ways they were similar. Beatrice had lighter hair, but recently Heather had lightened hers, making them both dark blonde. Heather had plucked her eyebrows, making them resemble Beatrice's, which were very finely shaped. They both had brown eyes, as was most common among Scottish werewolves, and both were rather slender, also common.

Beatrice reopened the laptop, carefully pointing it away from anything incriminating while she checked that their webcam connection was indeed off. Satisfied that it was, she opened a folder and started laying out files on the desktop. Markus sighed and joined them at the table.

"I'm not sure we're going to find anything," he said.

"We might," said Beatrice. "Anyway, Dominil said it was worth doing."

For the past week, Markus, Beatrice and Heather had been engaged in collating information about the Avenaris Guild. While the MacRinnalchs had had many encounters with the hunters over the years, no one had thought to classify these encounters in any meaningful sort of way. Dominil had pointed out that it was ridiculous for the clan not to possess some sort of database on their enemies. Markus had taken on responsibility for the task. He recruited Beatrice, who, as an archivist at the castle, was used to recording things. The two of them, with the assistance of Heather, were now engaged on the important though tedious task. Every recorded encounter with the Guild was being classified and filed.

They sat in the front room of the solid Georgian apartment Markus owned on George Street in Edinburgh, making entries in the computer. Beatrice had brought several large boxes from the castle archives, filled with tales of old fights with the hunters, some of them handwritten notes on parchment dating back hundreds of years. There were entries in old diaries, some scraps from newspapers about mysterious fights, faded photographs and a lot of miscellaneous notes, recorded over the years but never organized. For more recent attacks, Markus was contacting those werewolves who'd been involved. It was a large task. Markus was taking it seriously, but would never have put in so many hours had it not been for Heather and Beatrice.

"Who are you going to talk to about the Douglas-MacPhees?" asked Heather.

Markus scowled. Happening so soon after Minerva's death, the murder of the Douglas-MacPhees had come as a serious blow to the clan. Never mind that they were outcasts. They were still werewolves, and they'd been killed in cold blood. It was a clear sign that the Avenaris Guild was again in the ascendency.

"Decembrius found them. And Kalix."

Heather looked up. "Kalix? Are you talking to her?"

"If I can. Though Kalix doesn't like speaking to me."

They worked in silence for a few minutes.

"What's she like?" asked Heather.

"Kalix?" Markus wasn't quite sure how to reply. A year or so ago he'd have replied that Kalix was terrible in every way. Since becoming Thane he'd developed a little more sympathy for her.

"When she was a child at the castle she was awful. Insane, violent, angry. I hated her. She used to smash things and get in fights. Not just with other children, with adults too. It didn't bother her that she'd get beaten. She was so crazy that eventually even werewolves who were much bigger and stronger would avoid her, because if they got into a fight, Kalix would never stop. It didn't matter what they did, she'd just keep fighting. They had to knock her out to make her stop. And that was awkward, with her being the Thane's daughter." Markus shook his head. "Hardly a day passed when there wasn't some Kalix outrage."

"When did it start?"

"She was always like that," said Markus. "She was in trouble as soon as she could walk." He frowned. "Or I think she was. I didn't pay much attention to her when she was an infant. But I remember her well when she got to about eight or nine. None of the other werewolf kids in the castle would go near her; they were terrified.

"A few years after that, she broke into the Thane's study and emptied the whisky cabinet. Drank everything that was there. Young werewolves are always keen to try the MacRinnalch malt, but she took that to ridiculous levels as well. Once she had to get her stomach pumped when she emptied the medicine cabinet." Markus shook his head and frowned. "I suppose it wasn't far from that to laudanum. But by then she was so mad I wasn't surprised by anything she did. She actually fought with my father. No other werewolf would have done that. I wouldn't have dared."

Markus and Kalix's father, the old Thane, had been a famously strong werewolf.

"Did she really kill him?" asked Heather.

"More or less. Fastened her teeth to his throat and flung him downstairs. He lasted a while afterward, but he died of the injuries. He was getting old by then. I suppose that had something to do with it."

Markus was troubled by the conversation. He wasn't used to talking about Kalix with anyone except his mother. "Maybe it wasn't all her fault. Thrix says girls in the family didn't have a good time when they were young. I don't know if that's true."

"What does she do in London?" asked Beatrice.

"She lives with some humans. I've met them; they're all right. They look after her."

Markus abandoned his work and ran a hand through his hair in a pensive gesture.

"This is making me depressed. I don't know what to think about my mad little sister. Perhaps I should have done more for her."

"You helped her out when she came to Edinburgh," said Beatrice.

It was true. On her last visit to Scotland, Kalix had found herself in a difficult situation, surrounded by her enemies. Markus had rescued her and managed to smuggle her back to England without the clan becoming aware of her presence.

"She can't even read," said Markus. "How did that happen? How did we manage to have a little sister who can't even read?"

Heather put a comforting hand on Markus's arm. "I'm sure it's not your fault."

Markus sighed. He picked up an old diary and looked at it with distaste. "Could we carry on with this later? I'm not much feeling like transcribing entries any more."

The phone rang. It was Dominil, asking if they had finished the task.

"Finished? Are you joking? Do you know how many encounters there are to track down?"

"Not precisely," said Dominil. "That's why I asked the clan to make a database."

Markus rolled his eyes and only just resisted the temptation to tell Dominil that he was Thane and no one could tell him how hard he had to work.

"We're doing the best we can," he said instead. "We should have most of the old notes transcribed in a day or two. But there are still a lot of werewolves we have to talk to."

"Try to speed up the process," said Dominil. "I need some results."

Dominil rang off. Markus put the phone down.

"She really is the rudest werewolf in the clan," he muttered.

"Are we taking a break now?" asked Heather.

Markus shook his head. "Not unless we want Dominil on the phone again. We better keep working."

Markus picked up the diary, meanwhile thinking that he'd expected his visit to Edinburgh, with both of his girlfriends and a new dress, to be much more enjoyable than it was turning out to be.

CHAPTER 55

Daniel surveyed the wreckage of the living room. The couch was destroyed, the carpet was scorched, there were cracks in the ceiling and everything was covered with dust.

"Why did we have to make friends with a Fire Elemental? It's so dangerous. Couldn't Malveria be a water queen instead?"

"Then we'd probably get drowned," said Moonglow.

"What about Queen of the Wind?"

"I expect a giant hurricane would blow the house away."

"I never realized the elements were all so annoying."

There was a banging noise in the kitchen, followed by a yelp. Vex had crash-landed again. They found her clambering out of the sink, rubbing her arm ruefully.

"I bumped my elbow," she said. "But it's OK, there's a doctor coming."

There was a gentle flash of light and an elderly Fire Elemental with a dark red beard, dressed in a long dark robe, appeared beside Vex. The small kitchen immediately seemed crowded.

"I bumped my elbow," said Vex, and held her arm toward the doctor.

The doctor, a tall elemental with dark skin and a very stern expression, ignored the proffered limb.

"Take me to the Queen," he said.

Moonglow led him through to the living room, where the Fire Queen was lying under Moonglow's blanket. She was breathing steadily but showed no signs of reviving. The palace doctor, who had not spoken a word of greeting to either Daniel or Moonglow, bent over her then turned to the flatmates.

"Leave me while I examine the Queen."

Moonglow and Daniel trooped upstairs. They didn't much like being ordered out of their own living room by a stranger, but could understand that the examination should be private.

"You also must leave," the doctor told Vex.

"But I'm the Queen's niece. I brought you here."

"Leave."

Vex skipped up the stairs after Daniel and Moonglow. "He'd never have got here without me," she said. "He hasn't even been to this planet for hundreds of years."

Moonglow heard the Runaways coming from Kalix's room and knocked on the door to tell her that a doctor had arrived to attend to the Fire Queen.

"What's he like?"

"Tall and intimidating."

"He wouldn't look at my elbow," said Vex.

Moonglow rubbed Vex's elbow better and they all sat on Kalix's small bed in her room while the Runaways played on her portable CD player.

"Who is this doctor anyway?" asked Daniel.

"Grand Physician and Master of Herbs Idrigal," said Vex. "He's the Queen's doctor. He only attends to her. Maybe a few other important people if he's not busy."

"Is he a good doctor?"

Vex didn't really know. "He's never killed Aunt Malvie, so I suppose he must be all right. But she doesn't get sick very often."

★

Downstairs, Doctor Idrigal drew a black leather case from his long red cloak. He took a small pouch from the case and from that withdrew two red petals. He placed them on the Queen's forehead and then waited. The doctor did not look overly concerned at the Queen's condition. After a few moments, each of the red petals caught fire, quite fiercely. The Fire Queen opened her eyes and some flames emerged, mingling with that of the petals. She raised her head.

"What happened?"

"You were rendered unconscious by fire shock," said the Doctor.

The Fire Queen sniffed. "Impossible. The Great Queen of the Hiyasta does not suffer from fire shock. I am beyond such childish diseases."

"It can happen to anyone," said the doctor, who, unusually among Malveria's subjects, did not address her as "mighty Queen." He had attended to Malveria since she was a child and knew her very well.

"A great shock to the system can temporarily shut off our fire. It's not serious if attended to promptly. I presume you received a very severe shock?"

"Very severe," agreed the Fire Queen.

"What was it?"

"Important matters of state, which I'm not at liberty to discuss."

Doctor Idrigal looked around the room, which seemed tiny to him. "I didn't realize that Agrivex had been sent to live with peasants."

"They are not peasants, dear Doctor. But living space is at a premium in this city, and people are crammed in any old way. Is there any other unnecessary treatment you wish to force on me for this so-called fire shock? I am now feeling quite healthy."

Doctor Idrigal shook his head. "A little rest is all that's needed. I will assist you back to the palace."

The Fire Queen sat up. "I can travel unaided, Doctor. I am quite healthy."

"Very well. In that case, would you permit me to leave? I'm ill at ease in this city. I haven't been here since examining the effects of the Black Death as part of my student studies."

"Ah, the Black Death," said the Fire Queen. "Now that was a plague. Around thirteen fifty in their years, yes?"

"I believe so."

Malveria examined her surroundings. "I seem to have created something of a mess. I must arrange for repairs."

The Fire Queen suddenly pursed her lips and was obliged to control her aura, not wishing her doctor to read what was on her mind. Empress

Kabachetka's unexpected appearance in *Vogue* as a "fashionable party person" had been a shattering blow, and not one that the Queen could get over easily. No news could have been more distressing.

A further troubling thought crossed the Queen's mind. At the palace there would be business waiting for her. First Minister Xakthan and the accursed council of advisers were always wanting to enact some measure or other. Even worse, Count Garfire and various other buffoons from her aristocracy were no doubt waiting on a chance to continue her wooing. The Fire Queen lay back down and pulled the blanket over her.

"Doctor Idrigal. As you say, I require a little rest. I have decided to rest here."

"Really?" The doctor was troubled. "This hardly seems a suitable place."

"There are reasons for it. Important reasons of state, which again I cannot divulge. Please inform First Minister Xakthan that the Fire Queen will be resting in London for a few days and is not to be disturbed."

Doctor Idrigal nodded. It was a strange decision by the Queen, but as he was satisfied her health was in no danger, his work was finished. He departed. Malveria snapped her fingers, using a minor spell to bring Vex tumbling into the room.

"I hate when you do that," said Vex.

"Silence, niece. The doctor has ordered me to rest. I will be remaining here for some days. Kindly clear some space in your attic, emptying it of all excess boots, T-shirts and whatever else is cluttering up the place."

Vex was incredulous. "You want to share my room?"

"Share your room? The Queen of the Hiyasta does not share a room. You will go somewhere else while I recover."

"This is so unfair!" cried Vex.

"Unfair? Who do you think pays the rent for that room? Now depart, ungrateful wretch, and tidy your foul living space to make it suitable for a queen. Then inform your flatmates that I am obliged to remain here on medical grounds for a short while. Moonglow is a hospitable woman and will not object, I'm sure."

CHAPTER 56

There was a day of upheaval in the household as Agrivex was ejected from her room, decamping under protest to share with Moonglow. Daniel went about the task of buying a new couch and organizing delivery. The Fire Queen was paying for this, having graciously apologized for the damage and offered restitution. As Malveria made herself comfortable in Vex's room, the flatmates were busy downstairs cleaning the layer of dust that covered everything.

"It's a complete outrage," said Vex, who had tied a bandana around her face to protect her from the dust. "First my aunt nearly kills us all, and now she's thrown me out of the attic!"

"It's only for a day or two," said Moonglow. "She needs to rest."

"Hah," said Vex. "I think she just wants to spy on me."

Daniel was awaiting the arrival of the new couch with a mixture of anticipation and anxiety. He rather liked the responsibility of selecting a piece of furniture, which he regarded as quite a manly thing to do, particularly as there was measuring involved. He hoped he'd got it right. No one would be impressed if he'd ordered a couch that wouldn't fit their not-very-spacious living room.

"Our lives just get stranger and stranger," said Daniel. "One Fire Elemental was bad enough, now we've got the Queen here too."

"Hey!" said Vex. "What do you mean one was bad enough?"

"It was weird enough when we just had werewolves to worry about," continued Daniel.

"I'm not weird," said Kalix.

"If only that were true," said Daniel.

Kalix began to sulk before realizing that Daniel was only teasing her. She sulked a little anyway, in protest. The cat sat on the table, cleaning its fur, as it had done since the series of explosions. It had survived the experience well and showed no signs of distress, but it was doing a lot of grooming.

"Do you think the neighbors know all these explosions came from this flat?" wondered Daniel. They had never met any of their neighbors, and had no idea what they were like.

"The worst explosions were outside," Moonglow said. "People probably just thought it was thunder."

"I hope so."

When the room was mostly free of dust, Moonglow went to make tea.

She didn't mind sharing her room with Vex for a day or two. Moonglow was relieved that the Fire Queen was not seriously ill.

But she really shouldn't get so upset about her fashion rivals, thought Moonglow while filling a tray to take upstairs to the Queen. It was awkward climbing the short ladder to the attic, and Moonglow balanced the tray rather precariously as she tapped on the door.

"Come in," said the Fire Queen.

Moonglow pushed up the trapdoor and struggled to maneuver herself and the tray into the attic. The attic had been improved and enlarged by Malveria and Thrix, originally as a place to store clothes for Malveria and later as a room for Vex to live in. It was protected by sorcery, and was now quite a suitable environment for a Fire Elemental. The Queen was reclining quite comfortably under Vex's huge pink duvet, propped up on pillows with a magazine on her lap.

"Tea?" said Malveria. "Splendid. And now, Moonglow, let me confess something immediately."

"Confess?"

"I am afraid so. The truth is, I'm not sick, I'm hiding."

"Hiding?"

"Indeed. It was a terrible shock to discover that the appalling Kabachetka has outwitted me. Sponsoring the ball was a shrewd move. It brought her immediately into contact with the editor of *Vogue* and showed her in a very good light. Good enough for the editor of *Vogue* to publish her repellent features as a "fashionable party person." It is a blow. It was widely known that this was an ambition of mine, but the Empress has beaten me to it.

"And I am not blaming anyone," continued the Queen. "For instance, Thrix MacRinnalch, whose callous indifference led to me not attending this fashion event. If I had been there I would have outshone the sordid Kabachetka, easily preventing her from being photographed. But that was not to be. Thrix simply abandoned me, coldly refusing to make my dress. No doubt the duplicitous Enchantress planned this all along, probably in alliance with Kabachetka, whose gold is probably flowing into Thrix's coffers at this moment. Yes, I have been stabbed in the back by both of them. But I will not blame anyone." The Queen dabbed her eyes.

"I'm sure Thrix wouldn't—" began Moonglow, but the Queen held up her hand.

"Do not attempt to exonerate her. I know your kind nature has led to reconciliation in the past, making me forgive the Enchantress for her numerous crimes against me, but this time there is no excusing her."

The Queen sipped tea from her delicate china cup.

"As you can see, I have much to think about, and events at the palace make it difficult for me to think. For reasons which elude me, a considerable portion of the nation's aristocracy has chosen this moment to seek my hand in marriage. It is very wearing. One knows I should produce an heir at some point, but the queue that has now formed is an affront to civilized behavior."

Moonglow fidgeted. Remembering the house meeting with Agrivex, she had an idea of who might be responsible for the Queen's discomfiture.

"So there you have my confession, Moonglow. I require a few days' peace in which to think. I trust you will allow me to remain."

"Of course," said Moonglow.

"We must take the opportunity to make progress with the six-stage perfect lip coloring plan. Tell me, Moonglow, have you ever tried to walk in these extra-high heels? I mean, eight or nine inches?"

It wasn't the question Moonglow was expecting and she couldn't help smiling. "No, I've never tried."

"It is most difficult. But I am determined to succeed, and will work on my spell further while here."

There was a light tapping on the trapdoor. Kalix's head appeared.

"Dominil's coming to visit you."

"Dominil?" The Fire Queen was surprised.

"She called up to check on me and I mentioned you were here, and she said she wants to see you. I don't know why," said Kalix. "I'm leaving anyway, I don't want to see Dominil."

With that Kalix disappeared.

"Do you want me to call Dominil and put her off?" asked Moonglow.

"I do not think Dominil can be put off. But I have no objection to seeing her. She is cold and frigid, and not sympathetic to heels, makeup and frocks, but she has aided me in the past."

CHAPTER 57

In her search for the headquarters of the Avenaris Guild, Dominil had pushed geolocation to the limits of current technology. She had an IP address for the Guild, obtained some months ago when she'd managed to access their system. Though that access had now been closed off by the Guild, she'd still been able to use the IP address to ping the target from multiple servers. She obtained measurements for the time taken by the ping, made adjustments for the speed of light and online delays, and created a map of overlapping circles, eventually finding a postal code for the crossover area she was looking for. She sent trace-route requests to her target and refined her circles until she believed she knew the location of the Guild to within eight hundred meters.

It had been a lot of work. While Dominil was moderately pleased at her progress, it wasn't enough. She was now certain that the Guild's headquarters was in central London, somewhere just north of Oxford Street, and not too far from Marble Arch, but that was a very congested area. It contained thousands of addresses.

Even knocking on every door wouldn't help, reasoned Dominil. Their headquarters could be buried away underground, or hidden behind some respectable facade.

It was frustrating, and Dominil was further frustrated by Thrix. She claimed to be working on some great location spell but seemed to be no nearer finishing it. She was vague about her efforts and not as forthcoming as she should be. Dominil wasn't sure why. She wasn't that impressed by Markus's efforts either. Frustrated by the amount of time it was taking him to complete the database, she called his number again and let it ring. Finally, Markus answered.

"Who is it?"

"It's Dominil—"

Dominil broke off as a great peal of laughter sounded from the other end of the line. There was some amused shouting, from Beatrice, then more laughter from Heather.

"Hello?" said Markus. "Who is it?"

"It's Dominil. Have you—"

"Wait a minute."

There was more laughter at the other end of the line. Dominil fumed.

"Dominil, could you call back later, I'm busy."

"No, I can't call back later," said Dominil. "We need to talk now."

"It's not a very good time."

"Not a very good time? When would be a good time to stop werewolves being murdered?"

"I know," said Markus. "But I'm just, uh . . ."

"You're just having fun with your girlfriends," said Dominil icily. "No doubt drinking the clan whisky and trying on your latest dress, both of which you could do on another occasion."

There was a long silence. When Markus managed to speak, he sounded much more sober. "What did you say?"

"I'm quite sure you heard me," said Dominil. "You can drink, party and try on dresses later, when you've finished the database."

"What do you mean, 'try on dresses'?" demanded Markus. "Has Thrix been talking to you?"

"No. Thrix has said nothing."

"Then how did you know?"

"I saw you wearing women's clothes when I was eight years old," said Dominil. "At the castle. The night after Hogmanay when you thought everyone was asleep. And no, I've never mentioned it to anyone."

There was another silence.

"You never mentioned it to me either," said Markus.

"Because I wasn't interested. I'm still not interested. What I am interested in is finding the Avenaris Guild. I need you to complete the database."

There was more laughter behind Markus, but this time he asked his girlfriends to be quiet. Conversing with Dominil had sobered him. "All right. We'll get back to work."

"Good," said Dominil, and rang off.

She called Kalix. Their conversation was brief. Though Dominil no longer felt irritated at Kalix's behavior in Scotland, Kalix assumed that she was still angry at her. Consequently, she was even less communicative than usual. Dominil ascertained that she was healthy and had not encountered any hunters. She was interested to learn that Queen Malveria was resting in her flat.

"I want to talk to the Fire Queen," said Dominil. "Tell her I'll be there soon."

Dominil brushed her hair, took a measured dose of laudanum, cleaned her teeth and put on her coat. Her car was parked in the small, fenced-off space reserved for tenants next to a large green recycling bin in which Dominil regularly deposited glass and paper, making sure she put nothing in the bin which might identify her. Dominil's car was leased, paid for by the clan, at Verasa's suggestion. That had been before the revelation about Dominil's laudanum addiction. She wondered if the Mistress of the Werewolves would still be so eager to help her financially. It was unlikely. Verasa had been very shocked by the news.

The roads were busy and it took Dominil a long time to make her way south of the river. When she arrived, Daniel welcomed her inside and led her to the attic. He did this as politely as he could, though he was intimidated by Dominil and never enjoyed her company. Fortunately, Dominil made no attempt at conversation, allowing him to take her upstairs in silence. Dominil climbed into the attic, greeted the Fire Queen and nodded to Moonglow.

"Dominil!" said the Fire Queen in her most welcoming voice. "I understand you wish to see me on some matter? I was just discussing lip coloring with Moonglow here, who is very knowledgeable on the subject. Would you care to join us?"

"I don't use lipstick," said Dominil.

"You should. Your lips are rather pale, though you have a fine, wide mouth, as do all the MacRinnalch women."

"I need to ask you some questions about Empress Kabachetka," said Dominil brusquely.

The Fire Queen was surprised. "Kabachetka? What could you wish to know about her?"

"Everything you can tell me," said Dominil.

"She pretends to be natural blonde," said Malveria. "But everyone knows she's not."

Moonglow glanced at Dominil, expecting her to show some sign of irritation. She doubted that Dominil had come here to learn about Kabachetka's hair dye. Dominil didn't show any irritation. She simply nodded.

"Interesting. I'd like to know everything about her, and her staff, if possible."

"Is this in connection with her assisting the werewolf hunters?" asked Malveria.

"Yes. But don't confine yourself to that. I want to know more about her and her surroundings."

Moonglow excused herself, feeling that Dominil would probably rather have privacy for her conversation. After descending the ladder, Moonglow paused. She could hear music coming from Daniel's room. She wondered if she should go and talk to him. She decided against it. The drama of the last few days had made it easier for them to be together. When the house was rocked by explosions, a mistimed kiss in the cinema didn't seem all that important. Now that the drama was over, things felt uncomfortable again. She went back to her own room and started reading, in preparation for next year at university.

CHAPTER 58

"This is stupid," said Kalix, upstairs on the 37 bus. "I don't want to go."

"It's not stupid," said Vex "It's a great idea. That's why I'm coming."

"I didn't want you to come," said Kalix. "I didn't even want to go anywhere. I just didn't want to see Dominil."

"What were you going to do instead? Wander around all miserable and depressed? This is a much better idea."

Against her better judgment, Kalix was on her way to the art exhibition in Brixton, as advertised on the flier given to her by the young man she'd encountered while visiting Merchant MacDoig's.

"I can't just turn up," she said. "I'll look stupid."

"Why will you look stupid? It's an art exhibition. He gave you a flier. You're meant to turn up, that's the whole point."

Kalix looked anxious. "He'll think I'm trying to go out with him."

Vex laughed. "Well, he's certainly trying to go out with you, what with stopping you in the street and telling you how pretty you are and giving you a flier. Maybe you should go out with him."

"I don't want to."

"Why not?" asked Vex. "Because you already have a terrible boyfriend you always argue with and never really see because you fight too much?"

Kalix looked glum. It was true that her relationship with Decembrius had ground to a halt. She wasn't sure how she felt about that.

"A new boyfriend is just what you need," said Vex as the bus approached Brixton.

"No, it's not."

"You said he was pretty, right? Maybe you should try some pretty boy instead of these angry werewolves. Have you noticed how angry werewolves get?"

"I'm a werewolf," said Kalix.

Vex laughed. "You get more angry than anybody."

"I know what's going to happen," said Kalix. "I'll introduce myself and he'll be embarrassed to see me again. Probably his girlfriend will be standing right next to him and she'll hate me because she'll think I've come to steal her boyfriend. There'll be a big scene. The whole gallery will be standing there watching as his girlfriend screams at me and calls me names."

Vex stared at her friend. "You've really given this a lot of thought, haven't you?"

"Yes," said Kalix miserably.

"Don't worry, you'll be fine."

"I don't know anything about art," said Kalix. "What if someone asks me about it? I'll look stupid."

"If anyone asks you anything, just make something up. No one's going to ask you anyway. Who talks about art?"

"People at an art exhibition, I suppose," said Kalix.

"I doubt it," said Vex. "Probably they just go there to meet girls. Look, the only thing you have to do is tell this boy you like his paintings or sculptures or whatever he does. Cosmo Junior says that's really important. If you like some boy and he's an artist you have to say you like his art. Once you've done that you're home and dry."

Kalix stared gloomily at the flier. There were some long words on it she couldn't read and she was convinced they were complicated art terms. Someone was bound to ask her questions about them. Kalix had never been to an art exhibition before and wouldn't have been surprised to learn that she'd be expected to give a talk to the entire gallery.

The bus arrived in Brixton. Vex bounded off, followed by the reluctant Kalix.

"I can't even remember his name," said Kalix, now becoming really anxious.

"Don't worry, I'll find out," said Vex. "And then I'll shove you together."

"Don't shove us together!"

"I'll do it tactfully. Hey, I'm currently arranging for the Queen of the Hiyasta to get married. I'm sure I can help you as well."

"Why are we going in here?" asked Kalix as Vex led them into a pub.

"To get a drink, of course. You can't go around getting boyfriends without a little alcohol inside you. I mean, I can, but you can't. You'll freeze up."

"Does it say that in Cosmo Junior?"

"No," said Vex. "I learned it from my aunt. You never see her talking to a duke or a lord without at least a bottle of wine inside her. She seems to be drinking a lot more these days, I don't know why."

Vex beamed at Kalix. "Was it really true when you said it's illegal to buy a drink before you're eighteen?"

"Yes," said Kalix.

They'd bought drinks in pubs often before, but never legally.

THE ANXIETY OF KALIX THE WEREWOLF

"What a strange law," said Vex, who'd found it almost impossible to understand. "Well, now we can legally drink! Is there any sort of prize when you reach eighteen? Like a free drink?"

"I'm afraid not," said Kalix.

They ordered two pints of lager, which were delivered quickly and looked large in Kalix's and Vex's small hands.

"To boyfriends," said Vex, raising her pint glass.

Kalix mumbled something inaudible in reply, not thinking that was a toast she was ever really going to feel like making. The pub Vex had led them into was busy, mostly with young people dressed in a way that made Kalix wonder if they might be artists themselves, or perhaps people who were going to the exhibition. She felt intimidated and stared fixedly at her drink.

"Stop feeling intimidated," said Vex.

"Stop reading my aura," said Kalix. She'd have liked to have dallied over her drink so as to delay going to the exhibition for as long as possible, but unfortunately she found that in her nervous state, she gulped it down quickly.

"Time to go," said Vex. "Let's see what this art is all about."

Kalix trailed behind Vex as they walked along the pavement. Vex had the flier in her hand. "Here it is!"

The gallery was nothing more than a converted shop.

Kalix looked in dubiously. "I thought it would be bigger. I don't want to go in. There's hardly anyone inside."

It was much emptier than Kalix had anticipated. Previously worried about being surrounded by a throng of art experts, she now became concerned about being the only person there.

"Come on," said Vex, and she hurried them inside. She looked around. "Are these the paintings? I like them."

The walls were covered with paintings of animals, very bright and quite childlike in their application.

"Hey, a funny pink tiger!" called Vex, unconcerned that the few people in the gallery could hear every word she said. "This is much better than I expected." She turned to Kalix, continuing in an even louder voice. "Didn't you think the art would be bad really? I thought it would be rubbish."

Vex's words, echoing off the bare walls of the small gallery, caused everyone to look at her.

"I mean, what are the chances it would be any good?" Vex looked around her. "Shame there's no one here. Everyone else must have thought it would be rubbish too."

Kalix stared at her boots and wished she might just disappear. She didn't see the young man approach, but was made aware of his presence by a violent prod in the ribs from Vex.

"Hi," said Vex. "Are you the artist?"

The young man nodded.

"What's your name?" demanded Vex immediately, for which Kalix was grateful.

"Manny," he replied.

"We've come to see your art. I like the pink tiger and the pink giraffe. I like pink. Why's there nobody here?"

"It's still early," replied Manny. "I hope some more people will turn up in a while."

"Well," said Vex, pushing Kalix toward the young artist. "I expect you'd like to talk about art and things. There's my boyfriend now, so I'm off. Bye."

Vex started to walk toward the front door, where Pete had suddenly appeared. Kalix bolted after her.

"Where are you going?" demanded Kalix.

"Out with Pete. Look, he's waiting at the door."

"You mean you're just going to abandon me?"

"Of course."

"But I wouldn't have come here if I'd known you were going to leave right away!" protested Kalix.

Vex looked puzzled, as if she didn't really understand what the problem was. She'd brought Kalix to the gallery, found out the artist's name and pushed Kalix into conversation with him. To Vex it seemed like a job well done.

"I have to go with Pete," she said. "He's my boyfriend."

"I don't want to stay here alone!"

"You know Manny," said Vex. "You'll be fine."

During the conversation, Vex had been edging her way toward the door. As she reached it she flung herself at Pete and kissed him.

"Hi, Pete!" she cried.

With a wave to Kalix, they departed. Kalix stared hopelessly after them, unable to believe Vex's treachery. To bring her here and then abandon her seemed unbelievably rude. To make it worse, Kalix knew that the few people in the gallery would all have heard the conversation. Knowing there was no way to make this better, she resolved to just put her head down and hurry out of the building.

I'll never have to see any of these people again, thought Kalix. Maybe I could move to North London, to make sure.

She was about to make her exit when she found her way blocked by Manny. He smiled at her.

"Some friend," he said. "Abandoning you like that. But don't leave now. I'll show you my paintings, there's more in the next room."

Kalix couldn't help noticing how pretty Manny was. He had long, curly blond hair, blue eyes, a small nose and quite a feminine face. And he was thin, skinny enough that Kalix thought she could push him over with one finger.

He held out a plastic cup. "And we've got wine."

Kalix accepted the proffered cup. "OK. Show me your paintings. But I don't know anything about art."

"Doesn't matter," said Manny.

He had a soft voice, with a noticeable London accent. Kalix rather liked his voice. She allowed herself to be led back into the gallery, to look at the rest of his paintings.

CHAPTER 59

Beauty and Delicious had sunk into an intoxicated gloom in which they hated everyone. Yum Yum Sugary Snacks were no longer playing, recording or rehearsing.

"That stupid Dominil," said Beauty, sitting in a busy pub near the tube station in Camden. "She just abandoned us."

"Remember how she used to say we were all talk?" asked Delicious. "She's just as bad. All these things she was going to do and now she's disappeared."

"She's ruined our careers," said Delicious.

"Just when these useless boys got a record deal."

Beauty and Delicious scowled. Among the many hopeful bands in Camden, there was one comprising four boys they particularly disliked. They had been rivals for a long time. Last week the boys had been bragging about their new record deal. Though it was only a small deal with a tiny independent label, the twins were eaten up with jealousy.

It was a warm evening. The pub was crowded, as was the garden at the back where smokers congregated at wooden tables.

"Decembrius is here."

"Buy us a drink, Decembrius."

Decembrius had called the twins, asking to meet, which was unusual. They'd never been on particularly good terms. He went to the bar and arrived back with three bottles of lager. As he sat down beside the twins there were some jealous looks from young men standing nearby, who'd been eyeing them with interest.

"How's life?" asked Decembrius.

"Really bad," said Beauty. "What about you?"

"Quite bad as well," said Decembrius.

Delicious laughed. "Three unhappy werewolves."

"So what are you depressed about?" asked Delicious.

"Nothing in particular," answered Decembrius, which wasn't true.

"He's depressed about Kalix," said Beauty.

"I know," said Delicious. "I was just helping to introduce the subject. So it's all gone wrong?"

"We fell out again," admitted Decembrius.

"You were always fighting anyway," said Beauty. "You should just find someone else."

Decembrius looked at her coldly. "That's your solution?"

"It works for everyone else."

"Even Pete," said Delicious. "Though he's only pretending."

"I don't know what you're talking about," said Decembrius.

"Pete, our guitarist. He never got anywhere with Dominil so he went and found someone else, but he's not serious about it. He's been seeing Vex, but really he's only hoping it will make Dominil jealous."

Beauty nodded. "Which is never going to happen. Dominil doesn't have enough emotions to get jealous."

"It's a shame about Vex," said Delicious. "I like her. She should have found a better boyfriend."

"Maybe you should warn her Pete is just using her?" suggested Decembrius.

The twins were incredulous at their cousin's naivety.

"That's the most stupid suggestion ever. She wouldn't believe us and she'd be angry. It would be a waste of time. Don't you know anything? No wonder Kalix gave up on you."

"Kalix is unreasonable," said Decembrius. "You can't suggest anything to her, she always thinks you're criticizing her, she's so defensive. No one could go out with her, it's impossible."

"So how was the sex?" said Beauty brightly.

"It hardly ever happened."

Beauty and Delicious leaned closer, interested in this.

"Why not?"

"I don't know. It just always seemed like a big problem. And no, it wasn't my fault." Decembrius looked defiant, and then abruptly he sagged. "She'll be going out with someone else soon."

"How do you know that?"

"I can tell."

Beauty and Delicious looked at Decembrius suspiciously. He was once said to have powers of foresight, giving him glimpses into the future. That wasn't completely unknown among the MacRinnalchs, though it was rare. They'd never thought that Decembrius showed any particular talent for it. Decembrius saw they were doubtful.

"I can tell," he insisted. "I can feel it."

"Whose turn is it to go to the bar?" said Beauty.

"I shouldn't drink any more," said Decembrius. "I'm making an early start tomorrow. I'm supposed to go to the castle and then on to the Douglas-MacPhees' funeral."

Beauty and Delicious scoffed at this. "The Douglas-MacPhees? Who wants to go to their funeral?"

"I didn't like them any more than you. But they were werewolves still, and they were killed by hunters. They'll get a proper burial from the Baron. If I don't turn up for the funeral my mother will probably disown me."

"Have a nice time," said Beauty, mocking him. "If you see Dominil, tell her we hate her."

"Sometimes I hate Dominil," said Markus. He'd traveled from the castle to the capital expecting to have an enjoyable weekend with Beatrice and Heather. Thanks to Dominil, there hadn't been much enjoyment. They'd spent the whole weekend working. "Who could enjoy themselves when she's always on the phone, nagging and complaining?"

"I suppose she was right," said Beatrice, who was with him in the car as they returned to Castle MacRinnalch.

"I know. But couldn't she have just waited a day before phoning up and ruining our weekend?"

Beatrice looked rueful. "Two girls, one boy and a lot of lingerie. Who'd have thought we'd end up feeling guilty?"

Heather had gone off to work in Glasgow and they wouldn't see her again for weeks. It might be a similar amount of time before Markus was free to try on a dress. He rarely felt comfortable doing it at the castle.

"I'll make the Guild pay," said Markus.

Beatrice looked worried. "When you find the Guild's headquarters, you're not going to go there are you?"

"Of course," said Markus. "I'm going to lead the attack."

"I don't think that's a good idea."

"Why not?" said Markus.

"You're the Thane. What if you get killed? The clan needs you."

"The Thane should be a leader in war," said Markus

Beatrice didn't agree. "The Mistress of the Werewolves won't want you to go fighting in London."

Markus bridled. He hated any implication that his mother influenced his actions.

"I'm going," he said angrily. "If Sarapen was still here, no one would expect him not to go. I'm fed up with people thinking I'm weak."

"No one thinks you're weak," said Beatrice.

They drove on in silence for a long time, the atmosphere now quite strained.

"Damn that Dominil," muttered Markus. "She really knows how to ruin things."

Perhaps the only MacRinnalch thinking fondly of Dominil that moment was Sarapen. They'd been lovers once, though they'd ended up as enemies. He remembered her now as he stood, a huge brooding figure, on the balcony overlooking the fire that poured from the Eternal Volcano.

"She's a proper werewolf," mused Sarapen. "Fierce and determined. Not degenerate like the rest of the family."

Sarapen wondered what Dominil might be doing. Still helping the twins, he supposed. That was a waste of her talents, though he had no doubt she'd be good at it.

I'd like to see her again, he thought. Not that it would go well. He smiled grimly. As part of the feud, Sarapen had kidnapped Dominil. He doubted she'd ever forgive him for that, even if she did have her revenge later.

Dominil, and the rest of the clan, believed him to be dead, according to the Empress.

"I might as well be, while I'm trapped here."

Last night Sarapen had shared the Empress's bedchamber. Given the choice, he'd have preferred not to, but he had a strong suspicion that if he didn't, the Empress might decide to do away with him. Sarapen felt no fear at the prospect of death, but looked forward to meeting it in combat, rather than at the hand of some nameless palace assassin.

Which is my most likely fate, as far as I can see.

Sarapen had grown up in a castle among the ruling family of the MacRinnalchs, and he could interpret the motivations of those who circulated around power. He'd noticed influential courtiers looking at him in a way that suggested that without the Empress's patronage, he'd be gotten rid of soon enough. A position so close to the Empress was valuable in the palace, too valuable to be granted to a stranger like him.

So I stay here as the Empress's lover, and eventually get assassinated by some jealous courtier, thought Sarapen. Or I tell the Empress I've had enough of her, and she gets rid of me even quicker. It seems like a poor choice.

Sarapen put his hand close to his heart, feeling the scar. He wondered again if it were really true that he'd die if he returned to his own dimension. If he found a way to do it, he knew he'd risk it.

CHAPTER 60

"Who's in charge of Empress Kabachetka's social engagements?"

The Fire Queen looked uncertain. "What do you mean 'in charge,' Dominil? The Empress herself is in charge, I'm sure. She's not a woman to listen to advice."

"But who records her engagements? Who keeps her diary?"

"Her secretary, Gezinka."

"Does the Empress trust her? Would she have a full record of her movements?"

"I'm not certain. Who knows what Kabachetka thinks or whom she trusts?"

Under interrogation from Dominil, the Fire Queen was beginning to wilt. "I really can't imagine why you wish to know so much about the court life of the detestable Kabachetka. It is a painful subject, Dominil, as she has so recently cheated and bribed her way into *Vogue*."

Dominil was taking occasional notes, though mostly committing the Queen's answers to memory. It was frustrating trying to get information from the Fire Queen, as she had a habit of straying off topic, but Dominil persevered.

"Does she have a bodyguard who always travels with her?"

"At home, yes. But on Earth, not necessarily. I have known her to come here with only her handmaiden Alchet."

"Who else would know where she was when she visits London? Surely she must inform her government?"

The Queen shook her head. "Again, not necessarily. After all, I sometimes do not. But if anyone else were to know the Empress's movements, I imagine it would be her adviser Bakmer. My intelligence services report that he now has the Empress's ear."

The Fire Queen fidgeted. "Dominil, I am suffering from this relentless interrogation. Would you mind if I were to ask Moonglow to bring us tea? Have you noticed how much care she takes over her tea?"

"Yes," said Dominil. "She brews it properly, in a pot. So do I. I'll make us tea."

Dominil was tall, and stooped slightly as she walked beneath the light shade on the ceiling from which Moonglow had hung a dark, patterned headscarf. As she descended the stairs she heard Moonglow talking angrily on the phone.

"I just pressed these numbers!" Moonglow pressed some more buttons, listened briefly, then gave up and ended the call. "I hate these automated payment things! You have to press so many buttons." She had a council tax bill in her hand. "I must have entered some numbers wrong."

Dominil didn't comment. She used automated payment systems without any trouble. "The Fire Queen asks for tea. If you like, I'll make it."

"That's all right," said Moonglow. "I'll do it. I need a break from these bills. It's always me that has to sort them out."

Dominil accompanied Moonglow to the kitchen and helped her make tea, placing a small milk jug and a sugar bowl on the tray while Moonglow boiled the kettle and warmed the teapot.

"Are you seeing Malveria about werewolf business?" asked Moonglow.

"Yes."

"Is Kalix in trouble?"

"No."

"Is she going to be?"

"I can't say," said Dominil.

Moonglow abandoned efforts at conversation. After sending Dominil on her way with tea for the Fire Queen, she called the council's automated payment line again, with the council tax bill in front of her and her credit card in her hand, ready to make another attempt.

In the expanded attic, the Fire Queen was grateful for the tea and the plate of biscuits Moonglow had thoughtfully provided.

"I do like Moonglow," she said. "She is so welcoming, and so good-mannered."

Dominil nodded. It was true.

"Daniel is rather good-mannered too," continued the Queen. "Even Kalix is, when not afflicted with her fears and worries." The Fire Queen sighed. "I had hoped their good manners would rub off on Agrivex, but have seen no sign of it so far."

"About the Empress's military command," said Dominil. "To whom does she give direct orders?"

The Fire Queen raised her hand. "Please, Dominil. I'm sure that this is all of the greatest importance to the MacRinnalchs, but my throat is simply parched. I have been ordered to rest, you must remember, after suffering a most serious illness."

The Queen nibbled at a ginger biscuit and sipped her tea. "Has it ever happened to you that you have been absolutely overwhelmed with suitors?"

"No," said Dominil.

"I cannot tell you how wearisome it is. There hardly seems to be a duke, lord or earl in the land who has not decided to pay court to me. One struggles to understand it. It is not as if I am a recent addition to the nation. I have been there for some time."

"Presumably it would be a great step up the social ladder to be your consort?"

"Of course. There would be no greater honor. But the normal procedure would be to wait until given a hint by my council of ministers. Once that hint was received, a cautious advance may be permissible. But now they are simply stampeding toward me in a great herd. My first minister swears that the council is not responsible and has not been giving any hints."

"Perhaps someone else has," said Dominil, who hoped to end this part of the conversation quickly so she could return to her questions. "Who else might want to see you married?"

"No one that I can think of."

"How about your niece Agrivex?"

"Why would she want to see me married?"

"So as you could produce an heir, thereby ensuring that she never had to be Queen and take on responsibilities?"

The Fire Queen went rigid. "Why do you suggest that?"

"It seems a reasonable conjecture, given what I know of her character," said Dominil. "Could we return to discussing the Empress?"

Dominil stopped. The Fire Queen had compressed her ginger biscuit in her hand, turning it into a pile of flaming crumbs which fell onto the bedspread. A flame flickered in her left eye.

"Agrivex," muttered the Fire Queen. Heat from her hand caused the tea to start boiling in her cup. "Why did I not see this before? Who else could inflict such misery on me? Wait till I get my hands on this most dismal of nieces. There will be great suffering!"

CHAPTER 61

In the small gallery in Brixton, Kalix was surprised when Manny broke off from describing one of his pictures to whisper in her ear. "You're feeling anxious, aren't you?"

"No. Yes. How did you know that?"

"I suffer a lot from anxiety," said Manny, still keeping his voice low. "I'm getting therapy for it. Never does much good. Do you want to go and sit on your own in the storeroom at the back? Or do you want to talk, would that help more?"

Kalix looked at him. She was interested to meet a young man who knew about anxiety. That had never happened before.

"I'm all right. More wine would help."

Manny smiled. "Anxiety is a big problem, isn't it? People generally don't understand."

They moved away from the paintings to stand by the table where there were a few bottles of wine provided for guests. The gallery was still very quiet.

"How long have you suffered?" asked Manny.

"Always."

"Me too."

Kalix stared at Manny and thought how much she liked this young artist, who suffered from anxiety like she did, and was so pretty with his long blond hair. Her anxiety lessened.

"My therapy was hopeless too," said Kalix. "I stopped going because it just got annoying. Stupid therapists. But I liked the diazepam."

"You got diazepam?" said Manny admiringly. "I wish I'd got that. Do you ever feel like the walls are closing in and you're going to faint?"

"Yes. I hate it when I get a panic attack and there are people around and you know they won't understand about it. I just want to run away."

Manny nodded. "I know the feeling. It takes me ages to get over it."

Kalix nodded enthusiastically. "If I get a bad panic attack, I'm still anxious for days afterward. People say, 'What are you anxious about, there's nothing to worry about.' They don't understand."

They smiled at each other.

"Do you write about it?" asked Manny.

"Yes, in my journal," replied Kalix immediately, though her journal was something she very rarely talked about.

"I thought you'd be a writer," said Manny. "As soon as I saw you I knew you were artistic."

Kalix felt pleased. She'd never been called artistic before. Manny swept his arm around, pointing at all his pictures.

"I like your paintings," said Kalix. It was true. She did like his colorful and childish animals. "Does it make you calm?"

"Sometimes. When you get involved in a painting, you sort of forget your problems for a while. It's good. But it doesn't always work."

Kalix nodded. She understood this. "When it gets really bad, nothing works."

She noticed that she was standing close enough to Manny for their arms to touch. She let it continue and didn't move away. "I'm glad I came now." She looked around at the empty gallery. "I'm sorry other people didn't come."

"It doesn't matter really," said Manny, though he did look disappointed.

"People are stupid," said Kalix by way of encouragement.

Manny poured more white wine. A friend of Manny's approached him to talk, and Manny engaged in a conversation, but he remained close to Kalix. She noticed that her anxiety had almost vanished. Even when a few more visitors did turn up, Manny stayed close to her.

"Do you do your paintings here?" asked Kalix later, and then worried in case that was a stupid question.

"No, I paint at home. I can't afford a studio. But the light is quite good. I live at the top of the block."

Kalix thought she'd like to see the place where he painted, but she suddenly felt tired, which sometimes happened to her after an episode of anxiety.

"I have to go home now."

"Can I call you?" asked Manny.

Kalix gave him her phone number before she left. She'd told Manny her name was Alex, as she always did on the rare occasions she was obliged to introduce herself. Kalix was too distinctive a name to use in public. The pavements outside were busy as people emptied out of two pubs near the gallery. Kalix brushed past pedestrians as she made her way back to the bus stop, her hands in her pockets and her eyes on the ground. She smiled to herself and thought that she liked Manny more than anyone she'd met for a long time.

But it was still bad of Vex just to abandon me!

CHAPTER 62

Kalix slept well. It was past midday when she entered the kitchen to find Moonglow heating a Pop-Tart in the toaster.

"For Malveria," said Moonglow. "How was the exhibition?"

"It was good," said Kalix. "Vex just abandoned me because her boyfriend turned up and they left me on my own, which wasn't very nice, and I felt nervous, but then it was OK because I met Manny who's the painter and he's really nice and we talked a lot and I liked his paintings and he's going to call me."

Moonglow was startled by what was, by Kalix's standards, a long and enthusiastic speech.

"He's going to call you?"

Kalix nodded and looked happy.

"Is this a romance?"

"Maybe," said Kalix.

Moonglow had a fleeting, uncomfortable feeling that romance was breaking out all around but missing her. She suppressed the feeling because it was good to see Kalix looking happy.

"He paints all these funny animals. Like pink tigers and blue elephants. They're good. There weren't that many people at the exhibition, but he's got a better one coming up. He goes to art school and he's a cycle courier to make money till he starts selling paintings."

They heard the sound of the front door, followed by heavy boots on the stairs. Vex had returned. She was humming the theme tune to *Tokyo Top Pop Boom Boom Girl* and arrived in the kitchen looking cheerfully disheveled.

"Hi, Kalix, did you have a good time at the exhibition?"

"You went away and left me!"

"Of course," said Vex with no trace of shame. "My boyfriend arrived."

Kalix looked toward Moonglow. "Aren't girls meant to stay with each other even if their boyfriend arrives? Isn't there some sort of code?"

"Uh . . . it's flexible," said Moonglow.

Vex laughed. "It was for your own good. I knew you'd get on well with him." She peered at Kalix. "And you did, I can tell."

"Stop reading my aura, you stupid Hiyasta," said Kalix.

"Though you didn't sleep with him. Why not?"

"I said stop reading my aura."

"No point hanging around now you've finally met someone you like, after all these loser werewolves you've been dating."

Vex ran her hand through her hair, trying to resurrect some of the flattened spikes. The makeup around her eyes was smudged and there was a stain on her Hello Kitty T-shirt. Moonglow had noticed that when Vex arrived home in this sort of state, she never looked like someone suffering from the excesses of too many late nights. She looked more like a young model who'd been deliberately dressed in an untidy manner for a photo shoot, and was pretty, and pleased about it.

Vex took a bowl from the cupboard and began filling it with two kinds of cereal.

"Who'd have thought I was so good at matching people up? Here's Kalix got a new boyfriend right away and me and Pete getting on really well and"—her voice dropped to a theatrical whisper—"even Aunt Malvie's making some progress."

Vex poured milk on her cereal and covered it with sugar. "Maybe I should take on a difficult challenge. Like finding a girlfriend for Daniel."

Vex stopped. She noticed that both Kalix and Moonglow were looking uncomfortable.

"Why are you looking weird? OK, Daniel would be difficult, but—"

"Good morning, Agrivex."

Vex turned around. The Fire Queen was standing in the kitchen doorway. Both Moonglow and Kalix sensed that she was not in the best of moods.

"Morning, Aunt Malvie. I've just been helping Kalix get a boyfriend."

Vex dug her spoon into the cereal bowl and didn't notice a tiny flicker of flame emerging from her aunt's eye. Kalix and Moonglow began edging their way out of the kitchen.

"You've been helping Kalix find a boyfriend, have you, most adorable niece?" purred Malveria.

Vex nodded.

"Something you have a talent for?"

"It looks like it."

"How splendid. Do you have enough cereal in that bowl?"

"I think so, Aunty."

"More sugar?"

"Maybe a little," said Vex, who liked a lot of sugar on her cereal.

The Fire Queen graciously picked up the sugar bowl and sprinkled some on Vex's cereal.

"Thanks, Aunty."

Kalix and Moonglow had by now managed to wriggle their way out of the tiny kitchen and stood hesitantly at the door to the living room, not quite certain whether to stay or flee.

"Is there anything else I can do for you?" the Fire Queen asked her niece. "I have been thinking I owe you a favor, Agrivex."

"Have you?" Vex looked pleased. "I've been thinking the same, now that you mention it. What with me doing so well at college and then helping Kalix and generally making a big success of everything."

"Yes," said Malveria. "You have made a great success of everything. You have managed to do what seven armies, four hostile nations, several dragons and an invasion of Stone Dwarves failed to do."

Vex looked puzzled. "Uh . . . what was that?"

"You have managed to drive me out of my palace, you imbecile!" roared the Fire Queen. She slammed her fist on the counter, breaking it in two.

"Not again," sighed Moonglow from the safety of the hallway.

"Thanks to you, dismal, abominable, dreadful niece, whom I should have sacrificed at birth, I have been put to flight by a horde of slavering suitors comprising every unmarried duke, earl and lord in the country. What were you thinking? Answer at once, Agrivex, or face a swift trip to the Great Volcano, which is primed and ready to receive you."

"Hey!" protested Agrivex. "I don't know what you're talking about."

"You most certainly do! For weeks I have been beset with suitors on all sides and I have finally realized that you are responsible."

Agrivex looked defiant. "It had nothing to do with me."

"I know you are lying!"

"I am not! I might have mentioned to the Honorable Gloria that you used to be keen on Lord Stratov, but that's all."

"You said that to the Honorable Gloria?" yelled the Fire Queen. "How dare you! I was never keen on the man, he is a profound bore! What did you say to the family of Duke Garfire?"

"Absolutely nothing. If he thinks you called him handsome and attractive it didn't come from me."

"I have never called Duke Garfire handsome and attractive!"

"I'm sure I heard you mention it one time," said Vex. "But I didn't say it anyway."

"Stop making up this nonsense!" The Fire Queen glared at her niece with loathing. "And the Earl of Flamineau? Can you account for his sudden interest in the Royal Personage?"

"I completely deny everything," said Vex.

"Do I have to keep reminding you that I can read your aura, dismal niece? Guilt is written all over you. Do you realize the damage you have inflicted on my status as ruler? The entire country is awash with gossip that the Fire Queen is begging for a date!"

"Really, I'm sure you're overreacting."

Kalix and Moonglow winced as they heard another piece of kitchen furniture disintegrate under the Queen's fury.

"We'll have no furniture left," said Moonglow mournfully.

Vex looked at the kitchen cabinet lying in splinters at her feet. "This isn't very polite to Moonglow and Daniel, you know. You've really got to control yourself when you visit."

The Fire Queen gasped, temporarily rendered speechless by the effrontery of this.

"Anyway," said Vex. "Isn't it time you got married? Xakthan's always saying it."

The Fire Queen held up her hand. "Enough, vile niece. I will hear no more stupidity from you. Have you made progress with your fire, as I instructed?"

Vex looked uncomfortable.

"Have you been preparing for your next year at college?" demanded Malveria.

"Well . . . "

"No, you have not!" roared the Queen. "Instead you have been wasting time with your so-called boyfriend."

"He's so nice," said Vex. "Would you like to meet him?"

"No, I would not. I am not a great admirer of itinerant musicians."

Agrivex looked annoyed. "He's a great guitarist!"

"Highly unlikely," said the Queen witheringly. "Given the intoxicated incompetence of his band. No doubt his conversation is of an equally low standard."

"You're being really mean!" cried Vex.

"There is nothing mean about the Queen of the Hiyasta requiring her niece to gain a basic competence in the ways of the Hiyasta," thundered Malveria. "Your inability to produce flames is the talk of the servants' quarters. My reputation is currently being destroyed by your ineptitude." The Fire Queen leaned forward. "When I was your age I was already laying waste to my enemies with my fire. I am losing patience with you, wretched girl. You are to spend less time with your boyfriend and more time practicing."

"I won't."

Malveria's face began to glow. "Agrivex. You will do as I say."

"No, I won't."

The Fire Queen and her niece glared at each other.

"I will give you till the end of the month to improve your fire powers," said the Queen. "If by then you cannot produce a steady stream of flames from your fingers, I shall send you to a fire tutor."

Vex's eyes widened. "What?"

"You heard me. You will go for tutoring on the slopes of the Great Volcano with Arch-wizard Krathrank."

Agrivex was aghast. "Arch-wizard Krabby? He's ten thousand years old!"

"Do not exaggerate. He is three thousand at most. And do not call him Arch-wizard Krabby, it's disrespectful. He runs a harsh and disciplined school; it will do you good."

Vex stamped her foot on the ground, making the floorboards vibrate. "I'm not going to study with old Krabby. I won't be able to see Pete."

Malveria smiled, rather cruelly. "So it would appear."

"You're destroying my relationship!"

"Again, so it would appear."

"I hate you!" cried Agrivex.

"Nonetheless, that is my decision. Learn to control your fire, if you wish to avoid an extended period under the stern regime of Arch-wizard Krathrank."

The Fire Queen swept through to the living room, her expression still thunderous. Seeing Moonglow and Kalix, she made an effort to rein in her temper.

"Moonglow. You may possibly have heard a slight altercation. I apologize for some unfortunate breakages." Malveria produced a soft leather purse, apparently plucking it from thin air. She handed it to Moonglow. "This gold should cover the damage."

With that the Fire Queen vanished, dematerializing in an angry orange swirl.

Moonglow loosened the drawstring and peered into the purse. "Do kitchen repairers take gold as payment?"

Vex appeared in the living room. "I'm not going to study at old Krabby's place," she declared loudly. "It's a like a prison camp."

"Maybe you should just learn to make fire like your aunt wants," suggested Moonglow. "Is it difficult?"

Vex pointed her index finger toward the fireplace. Her face took on a strained expression. Nothing happened. "Quite difficult," she said.

"I think your finger's gone a little orange," said Kalix.

"That's a start," said Moonglow encouragingly.

Vex shrugged. "I don't care. Who wants to make fire anyway?"

Vex disappeared upstairs, humming loudly, apparently unconcerned. Neither Moonglow nor Kalix were quite as relaxed.

"I can see this ending badly," said Kalix.

Moonglow nodded. "I'll start phoning up people about the kitchen."

CHAPTER 63

Employees at the Avenaris Guild often worked irregular hours. On those days their hours coincided, Mr. Carmichael and his son John would usually visit the wine bar at the end of the street after work, sharing a bottle of wine before going their separate ways. Mr. Carmichael lived in the center of the city and could walk home. His son John lived farther out, in Primrose Hill, and commuted by tube.

At forty-one, John was the eldest of Mr. Carmichael's four sons. He'd been a good hunter. Though Mr. Carmichael had been proud of him for that, he'd been relieved when John retired from hunting to take an administrative job. Fighting werewolves had a high mortality rate. None of his other sons was involved with the Guild, though the two closest to John's age were aware of the nature of their father's business.

Sitting in the wine bar, they kept their voices low as they discussed Guild affairs. John thought that Group Sixteen might be the best team of hunters they'd ever had. Mr. Carmichael was cautious.

"We'll have to wait and see. A lot of hunters start off well."

"They've disposed of Minerva MacRinnalch and three Douglas-MacPhees," said his son. "That's quite a start. They're looking for a new target."

"Not yet," said Mr. Carmichael. "They need more training."

"They think they've done enough."

Mr. Carmichael smiled rather coldly. "They don't realize what some of these MacRinnalchs are like. They think they know it all just because they shot an elderly woman and three outcasts?"

Mr. Carmichael sipped from his glass. The wine bar was full of city workers in suits, talking business and sending emails on their phones.

"Wait till they meet someone like Kalix."

John nodded. He knew as well as his father what Kalix MacRinnalch was capable of. "Still no sign of her. We've had scouts all around Kennington where she was last reported, but there's never any trace."

"What about Merchant MacDoig?"

"He claims not to have seen her. But he says whatever's convenient for him to say, you know that."

Mr. Carmichael nodded. He'd been acquainted with Merchant MacDoig for a long time. He was aware of his untrustworthy nature.

"I was up there last week," continued John. "Perhaps we should keep watch on his shop. There's bound to be werewolf activity there at some point."

"It's difficult," replied his father. "It takes up a lot of man-hours, watching somewhere twenty-four hours a day. We still don't have the staff."

"I saw Manny when I was there."

Mr. Carmichael looked alarmed. "What do you mean you saw

Manny? At the Merchant's?"

"Of course not. He was just in the area, doing his bike courier work, so I asked him to bring me a sandwich."

Mr. Carmichael still looked troubled. "Don't do that. You shouldn't have any contact with Manny while you're on duty."

"Relax, it was only a sandwich, I didn't ask him to start hunting."

"Don't even joke about it, John, it makes me uncomfortable."

Mr. Carmichael's son Manny was the baby of the family. He knew nothing of the Avenaris Guild, or werewolves. Mr. Carmichael hoped he never did. "I dread to think of Manny ever becoming involved."

"I know," said John.

"I was pleased when he turned out to be the artist in the family. It will keep him out of trouble."

Mr. Carmichael's eldest son almost laughed. At one time, his father wouldn't have admitted he was pleased to have an artist for a son. But Manny was indulged in a way his three elder brothers had never been. He was much younger than his siblings, and his mother had died soon after he was born.

"Are you going to his show at college next week?" asked John.

Mr. Carmichael sighed. His pleasure at his son's line of work didn't extend to visiting his art shows more often than he had to. "I might. I missed the last one. But the sort of places he exhibits his paintings . . . "

"This one's at his college. A proper gallery. I promised I'd go."

"Well, I may show up," said Mr. Carmichael. "But really, does any twenty-year-old student actually want his father turning up? I'd probably just embarrass him in front of his friends."

Their conversation turned back to the MacRinnalchs, Group Sixteen, the state of the Guild and whether anything might come of Princess Kabachetka's grand promises to assist them.

CHAPTER 64

The Fire Queen was in a thoroughly bad temper as she hovered between dimensions. She had been abandoned by Thrix, oppressed by suitors, humiliated by Kabachetka and insulted by Agrivex.

How did my once-splendid life come to this sorry ruin? she thought.

I am forced to hide in shame in a small room in London, and even there I have no peace while Agrivex is around. Meanwhile, Empress Kabachetka is bragging about her photograph in *Vogue* to anyone who will listen. It is all so unfair I could simply cry.

The Fire Queen drifted slowly through space.

"Who is responsible?" she said out loud, though her words sounded twisted and eerie in the void between the dimensions. "Thrix MacRinnalch, of course. Without the new outfit she promised me, I was unable to attend the fashion reception. If I had, Kabachetka would never have got her picture in *Vogue*. I would have outshone her, and they would have photographed me. Devastated by this, I have been unable to resist these dreadful dukes. It is no wonder I became ill and was forced to seek refuge with Moonglow."

The Fire Queen's lips compressed tightly together. I have been too lenient in this matter, she told herself. Simply breaking contact with the Enchantress was not enough. There must be a reckoning.

The Fire Queen slipped back into the earthly dimension and headed down a familiar path. Remembering that Thrix had recently increased her sorcerous security, Malveria did not attempt to materialize inside her flat. Instead, she entered the block and approached her door from the outside. The Fire Queen halted, examining the space around her.

"Thrix is home. I can feel her. And I can feel her new spells, protecting the apartment. But I am not just a sorcerer like you, Enchantress. I am the all-powerful Queen of the Hiyasta!"

The Fire Queen struck the door a great, flaming blow with her forearm and it buckled inwards. Malveria marched in triumphantly.

"Enchantress!" she cried. "I am here to make you account for your treachery, perfidious behavior and failure to provide me with a summer frock as promised. What do you have to say for yourself, cursèd werewolf?"

Malveria stood in the smoldering doorway, arms raised to cast spells and deal destruction. Thrix was in the room, lying on her couch.

"Well?" demanded Malveria.

Thrix didn't look up. She lay with her head half hidden by a fashionable jacket, which, rather shockingly, she was using as a pillow. Malveria felt a little foolish, waving her arms in the air. She lowered them and marched over to the couch in a fury.

"I demand you look at me, wretched Enchantress, and prepare to pay for your numerous crimes!"

Thrix raised her head and gazed blankly at the Fire Queen. Malveria yelled and took a step back. "Thrix, what have you done?"

Thrix had cropped off her hair, very roughly. It was short and jagged, clipped hurriedly and carelessly with scissors. The Fire Queen was horrified. Adding to her horror was the sight of Thrix's long golden tresses stuffed into a plastic carrier bag on the floor. Nothing could have affected the Fire Queen more. Thrix had obviously gone insane. Malveria's anger instantly disappeared, to be replaced with distress for her friend.

"Thrix, what has happened?" she cried, and knelt down beside her friend. "Speak to me."

There was a vacant expression on Thrix's face. "I can't do it," she mumbled.

"Can't do it? Do what? What has happened? Have you been attacked with spells of madness?"

Malveria studied Thrix's aura. She had been drinking wine, but that didn't account for the poor state she was in. She was weak, both physically and mentally, and her spirit, usually bright, was flickering unsteadily.

"I will revive you," cried the Fire Queen. "You must not worry about the frock outrage, you could not help it, having lost your senses!"

Malveria placed a hand on Thrix's forehead and another on the back of her neck, and let some of her fire flow into the Enchantress. Thrix's cold body began to heat up. After a few minutes, she began to stir and dragged herself into a sitting position. Her physical strength was returning, but the Fire Queen still didn't like the look of her aura. It was deranged.

"I will bring my strongest potions. They can restore sanity even in the worst cases."

Thrix managed to focus her eyes on the Fire Queen. "I don't need potions, Malveria. I haven't gone mad. I'm just defeated."

"What?"

"I'm defeated. The Guild killed my teacher and I can't find them. I've tried everything I know and it's no use. I can't find the Guild. They've beaten me."

The Fire Queen was perplexed. She realized she might have overreacted by assuming Thrix had completely lost her senses, but when she looked at her aura, there did seem to be a touch of madness there.

"Don't admit defeat. There is always a way to come back from adversity." Malveria glanced around the room. "And I'm sorry about your door."

"That's all right," said Thrix.

"Could one of these helpful men who carry tools fix it?" said Malveria. "My repairing magic has never been very good."

Thrix stood up. Normally her powers of repairing were good, but she had no sorcery in her at the moment. She picked up the door and propped it back in place.

"I'll call for someone later," she said. "Why did you burst in anyway? What were you saying about perfidious behavior?"

"Nothing, nothing." The Fire Queen waved it away. "I will explain another time. First we must get you back to good health. You need coffee, food and, most importantly, some urgent attention from a hairdresser. The gamine look is quite fashionable at the moment. With competent repair work by a top professional, you may get away with it. Otherwise, my salon does excellent work with hair extensions."

Thrix put her hand to her head. "Right. I chopped my hair off. I forgot about that."

"Why did you do such a thing?"

Thrix shrugged. "It was getting in the way." She sat down heavily. "Could you possibly make me coffee, Malveria? I don't even have the power to do that."

Malveria rose gracefully. "I will bring coffee. Not for nothing have I learned the ways of your kitchen appliances."

The Fire Queen hurried to the kitchen, leaving Thrix on the couch. After Malveria's healing, she felt physically restored, but she was still mentally drained. Her last attempt at a spell had gone hopelessly wrong, producing no result other than to drain her strength and send her into a state of despair that a bottle of wine had not lessened.

Thrix reached into her handbag and pulled out a small mirror. It was some time since she'd seen her own reflection. She winced. Studying her jagged, poorly cropped hair and the makeup smeared over her face, she wondered if the Fire Queen had been right. Perhaps she had gone mad. Thrix growled, once more feeling the anger and despair that had tormented her since Minerva's death.

"Do not worry," said Malveria, arriving in the room with two cups of coffee. "I will soon have you back to health. And I have seen some very chic hats in Paris. We will get you through this crisis somehow."

CHAPTER 65

"How are you feeling?" asked the Fire Queen some time later. Thrix had drunk her coffee and managed to eat.

"A little better," said Thrix. "I can't believe you made me a meal."

Malveria smiled. "I learned to cook as a child, though it is not something I like people to know."

The buzzer rang. Thrix had a visitor. She got off the couch unsteadily and stood by the intercom beside the broken front door.

"Hello?"

"It's Dominil."

Thrix made a face. "I'm not feeling that much better," she muttered. She pressed the button to let Dominil into the building.

"This place is a mess," said Thrix. "So am I." She didn't much mind her close friend Malveria finding her in such a state, but would rather not have encountered Dominil. Thrix felt a flicker of the sort of guilt she might have felt as a child when her mother scolded her for having an untidy room.

"Do you have a spell for tidying everything up really quickly?" she asked Malveria.

"Unfortunately, no. I have people who do that for me."

Dominil knocked on the door and it fell inward with a crash, leaving her looking surprised.

"That was quite funny in a way," said Thrix.

Dominil wasn't amused. "Why is your door broken?"

"I am responsible," said Malveria.

"Why don't you fix it?" asked Dominil.

"I don't know how," said Thrix. "I'll call someone."

Dominil studied the door. "It's only been pulled from its hinges. Screwing it back would effect a reasonable temporary repair. Do you have a screwdriver?"

"I think there might be one under the sink," said Thrix.

While Thrix hunted for a screwdriver, Dominil took her laptop out of its bag and cleared a space on the table.

"I hope you have not come to interrogate Thrix as rigorously as you interrogated me," said the Fire Queen. "She is suffering from some weakness brought on by overwork."

"And wine," said Dominil, clearing bottles from the table.

"That too. But she has strained every resource to find the Guild."

Dominil didn't comment. The Fire Queen had the impression that Dominil did not entirely believe that her cousin had been working as hard as she might have been. This Dominil is a terrible creature in some ways, she thought. Never satisfied with anything.

Thrix returned with a screwdriver. "I don't know if it works."

"Are you being willfully facetious?" Without waiting for a reply, Dominil picked up the door, put it in place, then began replacing the screws. Each one was replaced easily enough, though they fitted loosely into the damaged frame. Dominil carefully closed the door, having effected the repair in only a few minutes. The Fire Queen and the Enchantress were both impressed.

"I really could not have done that," said the Fire Queen. "You are so clever and practical."

"Let's sit at the table and talk," said Dominil. "I have an idea for finding the Guild. It's not a very great idea, but it's the best I've been able to come up with."

"One moment," said Thrix.

Dominil waited while Thrix took a bottle of the clan whisky from her cabinet and poured measures into three small glasses. They sat at the table and drank.

"What's your idea?" asked Thrix.

"So far, everything we've tried has failed," began Dominil. "Sorcery, computer espionage, physically searching and the collective intelligence gathering of the MacRinnalchs and the Hiyasta have brought us no nearer to learning their location. Apparently, their defensive sorcery is too powerful, and their cyber security now unbreakable. Is there any prospect of you devising some new locating spell that might actually work?"

"No," said Thrix flatly.

"Very well," said Dominil. "That leaves us only one option."

Thrix and Malveria leaned forward.

"We find someone who already knows where the headquarters is, and ask them."

Thrix, momentarily enthusiastic, was deflated. "That's your idea?"

"Yes."

"I don't think much of it."

The Fire Queen was not so dismissive. "Do you mean capture a werewolf hunter and torture the information out of him? That could be done."

"That's not what I meant," interrupted Dominil. "We couldn't depend on capturing a werewolf hunter. They seem to be the ones surprising us these days."

"Then what is you idea?" asked Malveria.

Dominil sipped from her glass. "Apart from the hunters, who else would know their location? I can think of two, and possibly three or four. Firstly, Empress Kabachetka."

The Fire Queen frowned. "You cannot simply ask the Empress. She will laugh at you."

"I'm coming to that," said Dominil. "The second person who probably knows where the Avenaris Guild's headquarters is, is Distikka. Your intelligence services say she's advising the Empress, so she might even have been there. Then there's Lady Gezinka. She controls the Empress's diary. She may have written a detailed entry there some time. Also there's Alchet, Kabachetka's handmaiden. You told me she sometimes accompanies Kabachetka on her visits to London. She might have visited the Guild with her. Finally, there's Adviser Bakmer. If he's become as trusted an adviser as your intelligence services believe, he might have learned of the Guild's location."

The Fire Queen looked puzzled. "It is true that Kabachetka will know the Guild's location. Distikka may also know. As for her secretary and handmaiden and adviser, it's possible, I suppose, if unlikely. But how does this help?"

Dominil glanced toward her glass, which was now empty. The Enchantress poured a little more whisky into it.

"They wouldn't intentionally tell us. But we might be able to solicit the information somehow. By trickery, perhaps. Maybe the secretary keeps a diary with the address entered somewhere, and we could steal it. Perhaps Distikka's tongue starts to wag when she drinks wine. The handmaiden might be open to bribery."

Thrix shook her head. "This is all sounding very tenuous, Dominil."

"I did admit it wasn't the greatest of ideas. But it gives us a chance. There are three or four Fire Elementals who might know the Guild's address. If we can place some suitable agents in close proximity to them, who knows what might happen?"

"How are we going to get in close proximity with the Empress of the Hainusta?" asked Thrix.

"At St. Amelia's Ball," replied Dominil. "In two week's time. The Empress is sponsoring the event. Surely she'll take her handmaiden there, and quite probably her secretary. As for Distikka and Bakmer, I don't know, but it's possible they'll be there."

"Perhaps I'm being dense," said Thrix, "but I still don't understand what you're suggesting. Isn't St. Amelia's Ball some upper-class charity event? Are you suggesting we gate-crash it?"

"That would be an option," said Dominil. "But it would be better if there was some legitimate reason for attendance. Gate-crashing might be difficult. Security is probably more extensive than one might expect."

"Probably," agreed Thrix. "No one wants their young heiresses being bombed or kidnapped."

"Indeed. The event takes place in the evening, but is preceded in the late afternoon by a charity fashion show. Various designers show their new clothes, often using the young attendees at the ball as their models. This, I imagine, satisfies various needs: publicity for the designers, and pictures in magazines of rich young people who wouldn't normally get the chance to model. No doubt egos are gratified by it."

Dominil finished her whisky and turned to Thrix. "If you were one of the designers at the fashion show, you would have license to take several people with you, in the role of assistant, perhaps, and models."

The Fire Queen leaned far over the table, suddenly enthusiastic. "Yes! I like this idea! Subterfuge at the ball! It is very suitable. I have known many stratagems to be worked on these occasions!"

Thrix shook her head, still not convinced. "Dominil, I don't see this working. Kabachetka's not going to be stupid enough to hand over important information to either me or Malveria. I doubt her secretary will either."

"It might be difficult for either yourself or the Queen to approach any of them," conceded Dominil. "But there are a few other people that could attend. Agrivex, for instance."

The Fire Queen, who was now examining herself in the large mirror, imagining herself in a fabulous ball gown, spying furiously, turned back in alarm. "My idiot niece? The chances of Agrivex successfully performing a spying mission are very slight."

"She did well for you on the mountain. Agrivex could easily pass as one of Thrix's models. She's certainly skinny and attractive enough."

"I suppose so," said Thrix. "Bit short for a model though."

"The other designers won't be using professional models either," said Dominil. "So her height wouldn't be a problem. I thought you could also ask Kalix."

This brought Thrix fully back to life. "Definitely not. Kalix can't model my clothes."

"Why not?" said Dominil. "She looks the part."

"She does," agreed Malveria. "She is waiflike and beautiful. More waiflike and beautiful than models you have used, even when you have specifically called for models who are waiflike and beautiful."

"Fine," said Thrix, her voice rising. "My sister is waiflike and beautiful. She's also unstable, a laudanum addict and I detest her. Have you forgotten her part in Minerva's murder?"

"A part which you have overstated," said Dominil firmly. "Kalix is a Mac-Rinnalch werewolf, and she's as keen as any of us to find the Guild. If she and Vex were to pose as models, they might be able to come up with something."

Thrix fumed at the prospect of employing her young sister. She raised her eyes toward her cousin. "And what about you, Dominil? I take it you'll be coming along?"

"I thought I could pose as your assistant."

Thrix narrowed her eyes. "Malveria can pose as my assistant. I'll need more than two models. You can be the third."

"I'm too old to model," said Dominil.

"Nonsense," replied Thrix. "What are you, twenty-seven? Models go on a lot longer these days. You'll be fine. Tall, good bone structure, exotic white hair. You're in."

Dominil stared at the Enchantress, suspecting that her enthusiasm for including her as a model was mostly in revenge for forcing Kalix on her. After a few moments, she nodded. "Very well, I will model too."

"At least your ridiculous idea has got my energy levels back up," muttered Thrix. She snapped her fingers, turning on the coffee maker in the kitchen. "Have you considered how I'm meant to be selected as one of the fashion designers? The ball is only two weeks away; they must all have been chosen by now."

"I was hoping that you and the Fire Queen could arrange that. Either through your contacts in the fashion world, or by sorcery."

"I not sure—" began Thrix.

"I'm certain we can arrange it!" said Malveria. The Fire Queen was thrilled of the prospect of espionage at a ball and didn't intend to let anything spoil it.

"What is this ball like, Dominil? Is it large?"

"Very large. They rent out an entire hotel in the Strand, including the ballroom on the ground floor. They also use the gardens at the back, which stretch down to the river and include part of the ancient Prince Henry's Tower."

"An entire hotel? A ballroom? Gardens and a river? And an ancient tower?" cried Malveria. This is sounding more splendid by the moment. The Fire Queen halted and frowned. "I have spotted a flaw in the plan. Our targets, as you describe them, are the Empress, her secretary, her handmaiden and Distikka. All female. How are we to seduce them? We have no man in our party."

The Queen spread her arms. "Our seduction is going to falter badly unless Kabachetka happens to bring along some male attendants."

"There is Adviser Bakmer," said Dominil. "He might be there. But really, I'd assumed we had more chance of success by theft, bribery or deceit. I wasn't actually counting on seduction."

The Fire Queen wasn't satisfied. "We cannot ignore seduction. Is there no suitable male we could take? Someone who could perhaps play the part of a model as well?"

Dominil, Thrix and the Fire Queen considered this, as Thrix's recovering powers of sorcery brought three mugs of coffee floating through from the kitchen.

CHAPTER 66

The funeral of the Douglas-MacPhees was well attended, given their poor reputation. In life they'd been unwelcome on Baron MacPhee's estates, but now they had fallen victim to the common enemies of all werewolves, it was time for the clans to show solidarity. Werewolves from the MacRinnalchs, the MacPhees, the MacAllisters and the MacGregors all attended, along with representatives from the lesser clans such as the MacAndrises. Even some MacPhees who'd emigrated in the past sent representatives back to Scotland for the ceremony.

It was an unusually warm day in the Highlands as the Mistress of the Werewolves and the Thane headed toward the funeral at Baron MacPhee's keep, north of Castle MacRinnalch in the Rinnalch Hills. They sat in the back of Verasa's Mercedes, driven by Eskandor, head of the castle guard. Verasa was elegantly attired in black. Her dress, hat and shoes had all been selected for her by Thrix.

"Thrix has excellent taste in ceremonial attire," said Verasa. "It's such a shame she couldn't make it to the funeral."

Markus, himself very elegantly attired in his dark suit, didn't reply. His relationship with his sister was better these days, but not to the extent that he'd miss her presence.

"She tells me she's spending all her time looking for the Guild's headquarters," said Verasa. "Using sorcery, I suppose."

The Mistress of the Werewolves had never entirely approved of Thrix's use of sorcery. It was not respectable. "Have you been to Baron MacPhee's keep since you became Thane?"

"No," said Markus. "I'm not much looking forward to it."

"I'm not surprised, dear, we're going to a funeral. There's not much to look forward to."

Markus smiled. "You know that's not what I meant. Baron MacPhee never wanted me to be Thane. He was one of Sarapen's strongest supporters."

"Only because he was such a friend of your father," said Verasa. "But that's all finished with now. Everyone respects you as head of the clan."

Markus wasn't so sure. His mother had smoothed out the difficulties that had wracked the clan after the leadership feud. That didn't mean Markus was well liked by everyone. Baron MacPhee had attended council meetings since the feud ended and he'd been generally respectful. But the barons were always respectful. Markus didn't believe they really supported him.

"Wallace MacGregor will be there. That's another werewolf I'm not all that keen to see."

"Why ever not?" said his mother. "You defeated him, after all."

There was a note of pride in Verasa's voice. Her son had beaten the huge Wallace MacGregor in single combat, right in front of the castle gates. The whole clan had witnessed it. His triumph had been instrumental in bringing the feud to an end.

"It just seems strange, that's all," said Markus. "Not so long ago I was fighting Wallace, and now we're going to be standing together listening to a service for three departed werewolves whom no one actually liked."

"It will be fine," his mother assured him. They were sitting close to each other in the back of the car. Verasa put her hand on her son's shoulder. "I was very proud of the way you fought," she said. "The whole clan was."

Markus was grateful for his mother's words. "If we find the Guild in London—" he began.

"That's quite different," said Verasa, interrupting him. "You have responsibilities as Thane. It's not your job to travel to England and fight."

"I think it is."

"It's not," said the Mistress of the Werewolves firmly.

In the car behind, Decembrius was being consoled by his mother Lucia.

"Kalix was never a suitable girlfriend, Decembrius. You know she's unstable."

Decembrius had arrived in Scotland depressed, and the depression hadn't lessened. He was surprised to find himself talking with his mother about relationships, but Decembrius's disappointed love seemed to need an audience. Only the night before he'd been through his whole sorry tale with Beauty and Delicious, yet here he was again, talking about Kalix, this time with his mother.

"She's not unstable," said Decembrius. "She just has some problems. With anxiety, mainly. And eating. And a bit of self-harming when she gets depressed. And she's quite prone to violence, I suppose." He sighed. "I suppose you could call her unstable."

"Don't forget the laudanum," said Lucia. She had been horrified to learn her son was going out with Kalix and was delighted it was over. They sat in silence as the car drove up the long winding incline that led through the hills. Decembrius stared morosely out of the window. His mother didn't like to see him so unhappy.

"You'll get over her soon enough. Don't you meet a lot of girls in London?"

Decembrius felt embarrassed. "Not really," he said.

His mother laughed good-naturedly. "Don't lie. I know you've always had plenty of girlfriends. There's nothing wrong with that. You should enjoy yourself. Just meet some nice girls, you'll forget Kalix soon enough."

Decembrius was surprised that his mother knew he met a lot of girls. He'd thought his life away from the castle was sufficiently private for his habits not to be known. Apparently he was wrong. He was more surprised to learn that his mother didn't object. At least she wasn't nagging him to meet a respectable werewolf girl and settle down, as mothers from the castle were prone to do. While he appreciated his mother's support, it didn't cheer him. He thought of Kalix constantly and was tormented by the thought of her with another boyfriend. Decembrius was quite sure she'd started seeing someone else; whether this was because of his powers of seeing, or just because of his jealous imagination, he couldn't tell.

CHAPTER 67

When Moonglow arrived home to find Kalix, Vex and Daniel all looking pleased with themselves, yet strangely guilty at the same time, her first thought was that they might have raided the household kitty and used the money to buy beer.

"Why is everybody smiling?"

"It's nothing, really," said Daniel.

"And why are you looking embarrassed?"

"Embarrassed?" said Daniel. "I'm not looking embarrassed. Kalix, am I looking embarrassed?"

"No," said Kalix. "Neither am I."

Kalix buried her face in a book that Moonglow was certain she couldn't read. She put her shiny vinyl bag on the table.

"What's going on?" she demanded. "Why is everyone smiling? What have you done?"

"We're all going to a ball!" said Vex, almost exploding with excitement. "Kalix and me are going to be models for Thrix and then we've got to seduce people and find secrets! We're going to be spies!"

Moonglow could make nothing of this. She turned to Kalix. "You're going to model for Thrix?"

Kalix made a face. "I have to. Dominil talked me into it. It's important werewolf stuff."

"Is it dangerous? Should I worry?"

"I don't think Dominil would have asked Daniel to go if it was dangerous."

Moonglow froze. "Daniel's going too?"

Daniel nodded and flushed quite a bright shade of red.

"So what about me?" said Moonglow.

There was no reply. Moonglow's flatmates all stared at their shoes. They'd known this was going to be awkward. When Dominil had outlined her plan to them on the phone, Vex was immediately enthusiastic. Kalix had been more reluctant, not wanting anything to do with her sister. On further explanation from Dominil, she'd agreed. She couldn't turn down a request to take action against the Avenaris Guild.

As for Daniel, Dominil told him plainly that while he wasn't perfect for the part, they'd decided he was the best male available. He knew all about werewolves and Fire Elementals already, and none of the elementals they were hoping to spy on would know who he was. Thrix had reluctantly admitted that while Daniel was not ideal model material, she could probably dress him in some outfit that wouldn't completely destroy her reputation. Daniel was so gratified by the prospect of being a model that he barely noticed the insult and agreed immediately.

"You mean everyone is going except me?" cried Moonglow, wounded by her flatmates' disloyalty. "Whose idea was that?"

"It just worked out that way," said Daniel. "You weren't deliberately excluded."

Vex beamed with pleasure. Kalix still looked embarrassed. Daniel struggled to make himself stop blushing by dint of willpower.

"So you're a model now?" said Moonglow, staring at him.

"Stop looking at me like it's the most ridiculous idea in the world. They need a man who knows about werewolves and elementals. I fit the bill." Daniel sneaked a look at himself in the mirror. "Probably I should get in shape."

Moonglow was irate. "I could model as well as you." She glared at everyone. "Is this because I'm not as skinny as Vex and Kalix? Did you all decide I was too fat?"

"Of course not," said Daniel, and tried to sound more placatory, knowing that they were now straying into dangerous territory. "It's just that St. Amelia's Ball has limited numbers and strict security. Thrix can only use four models, that's their limit. No one else can even get in. Kalix and Vex were natural choices. This is all to do with werewolves and Fire Elementals, remember. That's why Dominil's the other model."

"You're not a werewolf or a Fire Elemental," said Moonglow.

"But I am male."

"Why do they need a man?"

"For seducing the women, of course," said Vex. "You know, duchesses and people like that."

"You're meant to seduce duchesses?" Moonglow only just managed to avoid saying something very cutting about Daniel's powers of seduction.

"It's going to be great!" said Vex, tactlessly. "Just like *Dangerous something or other*."

"*Dangerous Liaisons*?" Moonglow was incredulous and even more annoyed. *Dangerous Liaisons* was one of her favorite books, and she was quite sure none of the others had read it. "Is Dominil meant to seduce someone? That doesn't seem very likely."

Moonglow swept an angry gaze over her three flatmates. "Doesn't seem very likely for any of you. It's not fair that I can't go!"

"I'm sorry Moonglow," said Daniel. "But we didn't make the plan, it was Dominil and Thrix." Daniel sneaked a look at himself and fingered his long fringe.

"Will you stop looking in the mirror," said Moonglow crossly. "Your hair looks exactly the same as it always does. I'm really annoyed at being left out. Well, if I can't come with you I'll just buy my own ticket."

Daniel looked uncomfortable. "You can't. There are no tickets for sale. Apparently it's quite exclusive. Invitation only."

Moonglow gave an exasperated grunt. She grabbed her bag from the table and marched up the stairs in a very bad mood.

"Well, that was uncomfortable," said Kalix eventually.

"I knew she'd be jealous," said Daniel. "But it's not our fault. Do you think I should get a haircut? I want to look my best." He flexed his arm muscle and looked disappointed. "I really have to do some exercise."

"Why's Moonglow so angry?" asked Kalix. "It's not that great a thing to go to."

Daniel shrugged. "Maybe she thinks I left her out to spite her. You know, after . . . " His voice tailed off.

"When I'm a model, do I get to keep the clothes?" asked Vex.

"I think they get auctioned off for charity," said Daniel.

"Oh. Can I keep them after that?"

"No, Vex, all the clothes get sold at an auction."

"But after that, can I keep them?"

"No, they . . . " Daniel sighed. "Yes, you get to keep them."

"Brilliant!" cried Vex. "I love being a model. Hey, Kalix, we can keep the clothes."

"No, we can't," said Kalix. "They get auctioned off."

"Why does everyone keep saying that?" demanded Vex. "I clearly heard Daniel say we can keep them."

Kalix was weary of company and loud voices. She stood up to leave but halted at the foot of the stairs and turned to Daniel.

"Maybe if Moonglow is this upset about you going off somewhere without her, it means she likes you more than she admits."

Kalix went upstairs, leaving Daniel looking thoughtful.

"I better get bleaching my hair," said Vex. "It's got to be looking just right. I'm going to be a great spy. And seduc—seduc—what was that word again?"

"Seductress."

"I'll be a great seductress!"

Upstairs in her room, Moonglow was angry. Rather than brood, she decided to take action.

I am a woman of resources, she told herself. We'll see if they can all go without me. She sat down at her computer and started searching for everything she could find about St. Amelia's Ball, quite determined that her flatmates were not going to leave her out.

"I'm not playing Cinderella. If they're all going to the ball, I'm going too."

CHAPTER 68

The next day Kalix sat quietly in the back of Daniel's car as he drove toward Thrix's offices in Soho. The prospect of working closely with her older sister made her both depressed and anxious. Kalix knew Thrix hated her for killing Captain Easterly. Kalix herself had never truly forgiven Thrix for sleeping with Gawain, the great love of Kalix's youthful life. It was bound to make for an uncomfortable experience.

Traffic moved slowly as always. It was a very hot day and Daniel had opened all the windows. Kalix stared glumly at her legs. She was wearing a pair of jeans, once black, now colorless. She also wore a dark gray T-shirt and carried a dark jacket, shapeless and faded. Kalix didn't like the idea of being put into colorful clothes. Too much color made her uncomfortable.

Kalix rubbed her thigh absentmindedly. She could feel the faint remnants of long scars where she'd cut herself. She'd had the urge to do it before leaving, but she could hardly turn up at Thrix's office with blood seeping from her leg. Even if it was hidden from view, her werewolf sister would smell it.

Vex turned around in her seat and shouted, "This is so exciting! We're going to be models!"

The young Fire Elemental's enthusiasm had reached unprecedented levels. "And then we get to be spies and secret agents! Just like Tokyo Top Pop Boom Boom Girl."

She began waving her hands in the air, pretending to do kung fu. "Bam! Pow! Take that!"

"I'm sure we're not meant to fight anyone," said Kalix.

"You never know!" said Vex. "Sometimes spies get discovered and have to fight their way out. Bam! Pow!"

Kalix almost smiled. Agrivex was the least violent person she'd ever encountered.

"Almost there," said Daniel as they neared the underground car park in Soho. He was almost as excited as Vex but did realize Kalix was nervous. As they left the car, he took her arm in a gesture of support.

"Don't worry, it'll be fine. I know you don't get on well with Thrix, but it's like there's a truce while we do this. She won't say anything nasty to you."

"She'd better not," said Kalix.

"And you'll be pleased when we find the hunters' headquarters."

Kalix didn't reply. She wasn't used to discussing private werewolf business with humans, even Daniel and Moonglow. She wasn't sure if they realized what would follow if the MacRinnalchs did find the Guild's headquarters. There would be a battle in which many hunters and werewolves would die. Kalix didn't intend to explain it in detail.

The pavement of Wardour Street was busy, crowded in places with drinkers standing outside pubs. A few diners sat outside small Italian restaurants, crammed into the tiny space available between the front of the restaurant and the pavement. Thrix's fashion house was situated on the upper floors of a rather anonymous gray commercial block between a wine shop and a Thai restaurant. The ground floor was occupied by an insurance company. Beside their main door was another door with a neat list of tenants and a series of buzzers.

"I remember the first time I came here," said Daniel. "Moonglow had to drag me." He looked at Kalix. "She was worried about you, after we first met you. It was smart of her to work out that Thrix was your sister." He looked thoughtful. "I wish Moonglow could have come with us."

He pressed the buzzer and they made their way up to the first floor.

"I forgot how glamorous the receptionists were," he whispered as they walked along the corridor. "Makes me feel shabby."

"You are shabby," said Vex cheerfully. "Don't worry, they'll sort you out here. Probably give you some clothes that attract girls. Hey, Kalix, maybe they'll dress you up in something colorful."

The door at the end of the corridor opened. Thrix was waiting for them; behind her were Malveria and Dominil.

Kalix and Thrix stared at each other. Neither of them seemed able to manage a civilized greeting. The Fire Queen banished the slight awkwardness by crossing to Daniel and embracing him warmly.

"You see, Thrix? Daniel is not so unsuitable as you claimed. Dominil was quite wrong to call him flabby."

Daniel blushed as soon as Malveria embraced him, as she knew he would.

"I've been doing some exercise," he mumbled.

"Excellent, Daniel. I believe you can manage the role of model and even seducer, should it come to that. It will be dark in the ballroom, and the ladies will all have been drinking."

"Are you modeling too?" Vex asked Dominil.

"I am," said Dominil.

"You'll be a good model. Very glowery."

"Glowery?"

"You know. Glaring at the audience like you hate them. Just like you normally look, really."

Thrix and her assistant Ann began to take measurements of their prospective models. It was normally a task that would have been delegated to junior staff, but Thrix had decided it was wiser to do it herself. There was no chance of Agrivex being discreet, and she didn't want her designers to be on the end of some alarming story about werewolves and Fire Elementals.

Kalix hadn't spoken since entering the building. "I don't want anything too colorful," she said suddenly.

"Pardon?" said Thrix.

"I don't want anything too colorful. I don't like bright clothes."

"Models don't get to choose," said Thrix.

Kalix and Thrix glared at each other again.

"Just don't give me anything too bright," said Kalix.

CHAPTER 69

Moonglow was determined to go to the ball. She had waved her flatmates away cheerfully, faking good humor, but the moment they were gone she began to put her plan into action. She'd spent the previous evening researching St. Amelia's Ball and now had a good idea of what kind of event it was. She'd looked at pictures on websites and seen a lot of wealthy-looking young men and women enjoying themselves, both at the ball and the fashion show. Moonglow saw that the young women modeling the clothes were not professionals. Vex and Kalix would look just as good, and probably better.

But so would I, thought Moonglow, and once more felt annoyed about being excluded.

One thing she had been unable to find out was how tickets were obtained. They didn't seem to be on sale anywhere. As far as she could judge, tickets were simply given out to people who had the right contacts.

They don't want people like me barging in uninvited. So how can I barge in uninvited?

King's College had its fair share of wealthy students. Moonglow considered all the people she'd met, and wondered who might be suitable. One name stood out—Eleanor, with whom she shared several classes.

She's always away on expensive holidays. I remember giving her my notes on Sumerian law when she was late back from a skiing trip.

Moonglow knew her well enough for it not to be strange for her to call, but she hesitated. *Might it be insulting to call her up unexpectedly and start asking about St. Amelia's Ball?*

She might think I'm making assumptions about her being rich, thought Moonglow. Some people are sensitive about that sort of thing. She might think I'm accusing her of being posh.

Deciding that it would be all right providing she didn't actually use the word "posh," Moonglow made the call. Eleanor answered right away.

"Hello, Eleanor, am I disturbing you, are you on a skiing trip or anything?"

Moonglow winced. She hadn't meant to say that. Eleanor assured Moonglow she wasn't on a skiing trip. She was at home, and sounded friendly enough. Still fearing that it might sound insulting, Moonglow launched into her request.

"I really want to go to St. Amelia's Ball, but I don't know how to get a ticket. Can you help me?"

Eleanor laughed. "St. Amelia's Ball? Why on earth do you want to go to that?"

"I'm trying to meet this guy who's probably going to be there," said Moonglow, who knew this was an acceptable excuse for almost anything.

"I see," said Eleanor. "Why did you decide to ask me?"

"Uh . . . "

"Is it because you think I'm posh?"

"Definitely not," said Moonglow.

Eleanor laughed. "I am quite posh really. I went to the ball last year. I drank too much and fell over and ruined my dress."

"Are you going this year?"

"I'm not sure," said Eleanor. "I do have a ticket but I haven't decided yet. I'd give it to you but it wouldn't do any good. They're all numbered and they have a lot of security. It would be a scandal if you pretended to be me and you were found out."

"Is there anything you can do to get me in?" asked Moonglow.

"I'm not sure. I get my tickets because my brother was at Eton with one of the organizer's sons. I tell you what, Moonglow, let me think for a little while. I might be able to come up with something."

After the phone call, Moonglow was reasonably encouraged. She started going through her list of contacts again, in case Eleanor couldn't help, but she'd hardly started when the phone rang.

"I can get you into the ball," said Eleanor.

"That's so good of you! How?"

"You know William, in our history class? He needs a date."

"But he's gay," said Moonglow. "I've seen him wearing a badge."

"Exactly. But he's only gay at college, as it were. His parents don't know. He doesn't feel like telling them yet. His mother has something to do with organizing the ball so he has to attend. Turning up with you would probably be a weight off his mind."

"That's a great idea!" enthused Moonglow. "William's nice."

"He is. But he's been through most of the female friends he can use as pretend dates. I just talked to him about you and he seemed keen."

"Thank you so much, Eleanor!"

"Incidentally, did you know he's a viscount?" said Eleanor.

"What?"

"That's his title. He doesn't use it around college, but he's entitled to be called Viscount Ainsley."

"Why?"

"Because he's the son of the Earl of Bathgate."

Moonglow couldn't follow the logic in this, but took Eleanor's word for it.

"You never know, you might end up a duchess," said Eleanor. She gave Moonglow William's phone number.

As she put the phone down, Moonglow felt extremely pleased with herself.

So you're all going to be spies, are you? she thought. Well, who's the spy now? It only took me one day and I've already infiltrated the ball.

Moonglow looked at the pictures of the young women dancing. It struck her that she didn't have a suitable dress, and buying one would probably cost more than she could afford.

I'll deal with that later, she thought. First I have to make a date with a viscount. I'm still not sure what a viscount is. I'd better look it up before I call him.

CHAPTER 70

"This, valued adviser Distikka, is for you."

The Empress Kabachetka indicated a small chest at the foot of her throne.

Distikka opened the chest. Inside were piles of gleaming coins.

"The purest gold, from my personal treasury. I wondered what to get you as a reward. Fine weapons, perhaps? But you have so many weapons already. Beautiful clothes? I knew you would not wear them. And you have shown no sign of being interested in handsome courtiers. So I decided on gold. Do you like it?"

"Yes, Empress," said Distikka, quite sincerely. Money was not Distikka's main motivation, but she had been born poor and never been wealthy. She was pleased to be given a chest full of gold.

"Good," said Empress Kabachetka. "Because I have never had greater pleasure than that afforded me by my picture in *Vogue*. The ladies of the court cannot stop talking about it."

The Empress glowed with pleasure, as did her throne room. The entire city outside was lit up by the splendor of the palace illuminations, and Fire Elementals throughout the land rejoiced, knowing that the young Empress was in a good mood. Distikka's plan of sponsoring the ball had proved to be a brilliant stroke. The Empress, in the guise of a South American heiress, had been constantly in the company of the most fashionable people during her visits to London.

"I would not be at all surprised to find myself photographed in many more magazines," said the Empress. "Each one a dagger to the heart of the aging Queen of the Hiyasta.

"There is one small wrinkle in my happiness, Distikka. I have promised to assist the Avenaris Guild in their werewolf hunting. The werewolf hunters claim some recent success, which is to be admired. But Mr. Carmichael seems to expect something more from me." The Empress looked questioningly at Distikka. "Is there something more to come? I admit I have lost track of our plans with regard to werewolves."

"Everything is in order, Empress. But for now, we have to await the werewolves' next move."

"What will their next move be?"

"I'm not quite certain, Empress, but it will be one that plays into our hands."

"Are you sure of this?"

"Quite sure."

"Very well." The Empress nodded. "In that case, please make an arrangement to talk to Mr. Carmichael, and assure him that everything is well. I have too much to do before the ball to be worrying myself about it."

An attendant advanced and bowed respectfully. "Sarapen is here, great Empress, seeking an audience."

The Empress looked pleased. "Send him in."

The attendant withdrew.

"Sarapen has been in quite the bad mood, Distikka. I hope it has improved."

Distikka said nothing. She had no advice to give the Empress about Sarapen, and did not understand exactly what the Empress wanted from him.

"It's a shame he cannot come to the ball," said the Empress.

"Why can't he go?"

"Sarapen is under the impression he can't return to Earth without dying, Distikka. One can hardly take him dancing in London in the circumstances."

"Perhaps you should just let him go," said Distikka.

The Empress laughed. "You are amusing on occasions. Where would an Empress be if she simply dismissed a lover who has not yet fallen in love with her?"

A lot better off, probably, thought Distikka.

"No, I would not be a lot better off," said the Empress, reading her adviser's thoughts. "I would have failed. The Empress of the Hainusta does not fail in matters of love or clothes."

"You can't make someone love you."

"Yes, you can." The Empress was emphatic. "And I will."

Distikka left the throne room, carrying her chest of gold. She nodded to Sarapen as she passed him in the doorway and thought that he was never going to fall in love with the Empress, no matter how much she wished it. She returned to her private chambers and made a determined effort to improve her powers of concealing her aura. It annoyed Distikka that the Empress could so easily read hers.

The Empress is a great fool, thought Distikka. But I mustn't let anyone know I think that. Adviser Bakmer would like nothing better than to see me executed, and I'm not going give him the opportunity.

CHAPTER 71

Kalix lay on her bed, examining her self-improvement list. She had some doubts about the tick she'd put beside be less violent. Initially she'd been pleased that she hadn't killed any of the gang she fought with beside the river.

But I did beat them up quite badly, she reflected, remembering the sound of breaking bones. It was still quite violent by other people's standards. But I wouldn't have had to be violent at all if they hadn't attacked me.

Kalix couldn't make up her mind if the encounter qualified as being less violent or not, and felt frustrated at the difficulty.

Stop taking laudanum was still definitely marked as a failure. And get on better with people was hovering in the balance after her experiences in Thrix's office. It had been a very uncomfortable day. Dominil was as unfriendly as ever. Thrix was annoyed at being forced to work with Kalix. Even Vex's normally unquenchable good humor had been dented by Malveria's continuing displeasure with her niece. The enthusiastic trio of prospective models who'd left the flat earlier in the day had arrived home feeling tired and stressed. Kalix had fled to her room, leaving Daniel and Vex to complain to each other and Moonglow in the living room.

Kalix looked at her list. *Eat better.* "I don't even want to do that. Why did I put it on the list?"

Improve reading and writing and maths. Maybe she could do something about that. Kalix opened her new laptop and hunted for the lessons she was meant to complete before returning to college. She'd been avoiding them, feeling unable to work when distracted by anxiety.

I can do these, she told herself. They're not that difficult.

Downstairs, Vex's complaints were in full flow. "That was awful."

"It wasn't as much fun as I thought it was going to be," agreed Daniel.

Moonglow was surprised that they'd arrived home in such poor tempers, and wondered what had happened to spoil their day.

"Aunt Malvie was cranky because she's a horrible person and hates me for no reason. Dominil was unfriendly. Thrix was angry because she hates Kalix. Kalix was rude to everyone. Daniel feels bad because the office was full of glamorous people and now he feels shabby," explained Vex.

"That would just about cover it," said Daniel. His fragile confidence had wilted under the glamour of Thrix's co-workers.

"I should never have agreed to do it," he told Moonglow. "I'll look ridiculous modeling clothes."

Vex sat on the floor with her back resting on the couch, and picked up the remote control to flick through their cable channels.

"Aunt Malvie can't wait to send me to Old Krabby," she said. The Fire Queen's continuing disapproval had finally convinced Vex of the seriousness of the situation. "She's so mean. Only a really mean person would send their niece to Old Krabby. Everyone says he's terrible. I'll be lucky to survive." Vex sighed heavily. "I should run away."

"You are absolutely, definitely not going to run away," said Moonglow. "We have enough trouble with Kalix."

"If I try modeling I'll trip and fall and everyone will laugh," said Daniel. "I can feel it coming."

Moonglow poured tea for everyone. "Well, I have some good news." She paused for effect. "I'm going to the ball."

"What? How?" asked Daniel.

"A rich young man is taking me. So I can help with the spying. Isn't it great?"

Daniel didn't look like someone who'd just received great news. "What rich young man? How did this happen?"

"I just asked around. I'm going with William."

"Who's William?" demanded Daniel

"He's in my history class, and tutorial. He's rich and well connected."

"This has all happened very quickly," said Daniel. "I leave the house for five minutes and now you've got a date for the ball? I thought it was hard to get into."

"Not when you're as rich as William, apparently," said Moonglow. "He's a viscount."

"What?"

"That's his title: Viscount Ainsley."

"Why?" asked Daniel.

"He's the son of a duke."

Daniel put down his mug of tea quite forcefully. "I don't like the sound of this. Should you be swanning off to a ball with a viscount you hardly know?"

"I knew him fairly well at college," said Moonglow. She might have mentioned to Daniel that William was gay, but chose not to. She was still annoyed that he'd arranged to go to St. Amelia's Ball without her. "I need to start looking at some dresses. You're all getting free clothes for the ball, but I'll have to buy something."

Moonglow left the room.

"That was quick work," said Vex. "Got a date for the ball just like that. You have to admire her."

"I don't think you have to admire her!" said Daniel. "The whole thing sounds very suspicious to me! Who is this Viscount William? Why's he suddenly taking Moonglow to the ball? Why doesn't he have a girlfriend already if he's so rich and good-looking?"

"Who said he was good-looking?"

"I'm assuming the worst."

Vex told Daniel he was reading too much into it. "So she has a date with the son of a duke and he's really rich and probably handsome as well. What's bad about that?"

"Everything."

"Maybe you're right," said Vex. "You shouldn't have let it happen."

"What does 'viscount' mean, anyway? It's ridiculous we still have an aristocracy in this day and age. All titles should be abolished. As a first step, we should get rid of viscounts."

Daniel groaned with frustration. He reached out for the last biscuit but was beaten by the nimble fingers of Vex. Kalix arrived downstairs. She was plainly dressed as always, but she'd brushed her hair till it shone.

"Off to see Manny?" asked Vex.

Kalix nodded.

"It's so nice having boyfriends," said Vex. She turned to Daniel. "You should get a girlfriend."

Daniel stared at Vex. Then, without a word, he headed upstairs to his room to listen to music and contemplate the unfairness of life.

"I don't know if Manny is really my boyfriend," said Kalix.

"Why not?" said Vex.

"I don't know. Maybe he is. He's nice anyway. He understood when I got anxious. He didn't think it was weird."

"Isn't it nice when boyfriends don't think it's weird when you do weird things?" said Vex. "Pete is good at that. But of course he's met werewolves, so anything's more normal after that."

CHAPTER 72

Thrix had gone along with Dominil's plan, weak though it was, for lack of anything better. She was already regretting it. She hated being in Kalix's company and, after spending time with Daniel and Vex, she'd come to the conclusion that they were completely unsuitable for the mission.

"If they're the best spies we can muster we're doomed."

It wasn't just their incompetence that irked the Enchantress. Involving outsiders in werewolf business was taboo. It didn't seem so long ago that Moonglow and Daniel had first appeared in her office looking for Kalix. Thrix had refused to even communicate with them. Werewolf affairs were not the business of outsiders.

"And now they're helping us find the Avenaris Guild. How did that happen?"

Thrix felt it was Kalix's fault. Everything went wrong when she was involved. She frowned, and then winced. She had a headache, and thinking about Kalix was making it worse. Malveria had advised her to rest, but Thrix didn't feel like resting. The tangled knot of misery, guilt and bloodlust that had formed inside her wouldn't be cured by resting.

Thrix wondered if a representative from the Guild might appear at the ball. She hoped so. She'd kill him on the spot. The Enchantress longed to kill hunters.

"First I have to get myself into the ball."

That wouldn't be easy, and there wasn't much time. The designated designers were all in place. Replacing one of them would require bribery or sorcery on a grand scale. She gathered her thoughts and began laying plans.

"I can insert my name into programs even after they've been printed. I've done that before. And I can make one of the designers withdraw. But making the organizers think they've chosen me as a replacement is going to be tricky. That's a difficult piece of sorcery."

Thrix was sitting at her computer with a cup of coffee on the mouse mat. She opened up a file to start recording the names of all the people she'd have to enchant, but her attention was diverted by another file that Dominil had once managed to steal from the Guild. It was a list of temporary accommodations they'd been using for their new hunters. Dominil had visited one of the addresses and killed a hunter.

I'd like to do that, thought Thrix.

Dominil believed the addresses would now be out of date and no longer used by the Guild.

Thrix studied the file. Some of the addresses might still be current. There might be hunters there.

I'd really like to meet a werewolf hunter right now.

Thrix's headache was becoming worse. She could feel the muscles in her neck tightening. Almost without realizing she was doing it, she changed into her werewolf shape and snarled at the computer screen.

CHAPTER 73

Official business finally dragged the Fire Queen back to her own realm. The Mayusta had appointed a new ambassador to her court and there was a reception to attend. The Mayusta were one of two races of Earth Elementals. Large and physically imposing, they were colloquially known as "stone giants," though this was considered rude and never said in polite society.

"And they are not really so clumsy," said Malveria as she made ready for the reception. "The last ambassador caused very few breakages. Less than Agrivex, to be fair."

Gruselvere and Iskiline had been relieved by the Fire Queen's return, as had her council of ministers. The news that the Queen had suffered a mild fire shock had come as a blow, given her previously robust health.

"Please do not fuss," she'd told First Minister Xakthan. "It was nothing. Were it not for my idiot nice and my ridiculous aristocrats, it would never have happened."

The Fire Queen gave strict instructions to Iskiline and Gruselvere that she was to be protected from all unwelcome attention at the reception.

"Keep all ambitious noblemen away from me. Fling yourselves in front of them if necessary. I intend to make polite conversation with the new ambassador and no one else." The Fire Queen paused. "With the exception of Beau DeMortalis, I suppose. The Duke of the Black Castle is good company, and will not try to marry me."

"He might," said Iskiline, who was busy applying some finishing touches to the Queen's makeup. "He's no longer in disgrace."

It was some time since the notoriously rakish DeMortalis had actually been in disgrace, but it was true that until recently he had not been respectable. The Duke had fought against the Queen in the Great War. She had spared his life only because of his immaculate dress and ready wit. That was many hundreds of years ago, and recent events on the Great Volcano, where DeMortalis had fought quite heroically at the Queen's side against the attempted coup, had raised the Duke high in the public's estimation.

The Fire Queen smiled. "I suppose he is not. But he still has a notable weakness for pretty kitchen maids."

The Fire Queen suddenly sagged in her chair, causing Iskiline to smudge her eyeliner.

"He also retains his cruel wit. One dreads to think what he may say about the 'fashionable party people' debacle. Even now he may be fashioning hurtful barbs."

Despite her fears, Malveria arrived at the reception as if she had not a care in the world. She was perfectly attired and perfectly in control of her aura. She greeted the new ambassador with overwhelming court politeness, and was relieved to see that while he did tower over her, he was not so tall as to force her to crane her neck at an unbecoming angle. She had a pleasant conversation with him and thought, once again, that the stone giants were a much more civilized race than their neighbors, the stone dwarves. The dwarves, or Maynista, as they were properly called, were not on good terms with the Fire Queen, and their ambassador rarely attended her receptions.

"Mighty Queen, you are looking more splendid than ever." Beau DeMortalis presented himself with an elegant bow. He was dressed in an

THE ANXIETY OF KALIX THE WEREWOLF

immaculate dark-blue frock coat, customary formalwear for a Hiyasta duke. Around his collar he wore a piece of white lace, knotted to perfection.

"DeMortalis. How pleasant to see you. Was your visit to your distant estates a pleasant one?"

"The distant estates are never pleasant. It's a relief to return to civilization." The Duke smiled winningly. "And always a pleasure to see the Queen again."

Beau DeMortalis looked around the room. "I'm surprised at the turnout. I didn't expect to see Garfire and Stratov here . . . When did they start attending official court functions?"

The Fire Queen felt herself tensing, wondering if the Duke was about to unleash some wounding comment about her suitors. The moment passed, but before she could relax the Honorable Gloria blundered up and stood right in front of DeMortalis.

"DeMortalis, Duke of the Black Castle? What a pleasure to meet you!"

The Fire Queen frowned, and was almost moved to shake her head in disapproval. It was so like the Honorable Gloria to ignore court protocol and simply barge into a conversation and introduce herself.

And really, thought the Queen. There is no need to look so longingly at the Duke. He already knows he is the most handsome man in the room.

CHAPTER 74

Manny lived in an old block of flats in Clerkenwell, north of the river. His block was part of a red-brick estate, built at the end of the nineteenth century, originally owned by the local council but now mostly private. He had a small flat at the top of the block on the fourth floor. The living room was crowded with his paintings and the hall was mostly occupied by his bike. Fortunately, Manny had few other possessions. There was a TV in the corner, several large cushions to sit on and almost nothing else. His bedroom, also full of paintings, had bare floorboards, a rug and an old futon next to a radiator, which made gurgling noises in the night and never heated up properly. Kalix felt quite comfortable in his small flat.

"I would have tidied up," said Manny, "but . . . " He raised his arms hopelessly. With so many paintings everywhere, and paint, and brushes and an easel, there was no way of making the place look tidy.

Kalix didn't mind. She thought it must be difficult to paint in such a small space, though the light was quite good.

"I paint at college; I've a lot of work there. But I can't afford a studio yet."

Kalix understood; Manny was still a student. Daniel and Moonglow were always short of money too, and Kalix herself wouldn't have survived without money from her family.

Ascending the narrow staircase up to the fourth floor, Kalix had noticed that she wasn't feeling anxious at all. That was unusual. Visiting someone she didn't know very well would normally have brought on anxiety, and even panic. There was something about Manny that seemed quite calming.

Maybe it's because he's so girly, she thought, and then wondered if that was a bad thing to think. I'd better not say he looks girly. It might be an insult.

With his wavy blond hair, soft features and blue eyes, he was certainly different from any MacRinnalch Kalix had ever been involved with. Gawain and Decembrius had both been prone to scowling and looking moody. Manny seemed quite the opposite.

"I forgot to buy any food," he announced cheerfully after Kalix arrived.

"I don't mind," said Kalix. "I don't want to eat."

"I should get something. I'll feel guilty if I don't offer you anything. I always get carried away painting and forget to do anything else."

Kalix didn't care if he had any food or not, but Manny did seem quite guilty about not having anything in the fridge, so she agreed to accompany him to the small supermarket on the main road.

"We can get beer anyway," she said.

Manny peered in the small mirror in the hallway. "Do you like these earrings?" He had a lot of earrings, two in one ear and four in the other.

Kalix nodded.

"Good. I wasn't sure about them."

Manny opened the front door. Kalix walked out and was profoundly shocked to meet Thrix. They stared at each other in astonishment.

"What are you doing here?" demanded Kalix. "Are you following me?"

"Of course I'm not following you," said her sister.

"Then what are you doing here?"

Thrix struggled for an explanation. She was obviously as surprised as Kalix.

"I'm visiting someone," she said.

Kalix, enraged at this intrusion into her private life, knew that wasn't true. Manny's flat was right at the end of the corridor. Thrix couldn't have been going anywhere else.

"Who are you visiting?"

"I must have the wrong address," said Thrix.

"Uh . . . hello," said Manny hesitantly.

Kalix's mind whirled. She had no idea what to say to Manny. How could she possibly explain that her sister had mysteriously followed her there?

"Don't follow me!" she shouted at Thrix, for want of anything better to say.

"I wasn't following you!" shouted Thrix.

Kalix and Thrix glared at each other with loathing. Thrix turned on her heel and marched away as quickly as she could. Kalix and Manny watched her go.

"Who was that?" asked Manny.

"My sister."

"What was she doing here?"

"I've no idea," said Kalix.

"Does she often follow you around?"

"No. I don't know why she came here."

Kalix felt as embarrassed as she'd ever felt in her life. She was at a complete loss as to why Thrix had suddenly appeared. *Now Manny thinks I've got a mad older sister who follows me around. It's so humiliating.*

Manny put his arm through hers and smiled. "Never mind. These things happen. There are a lot of flats here and the blocks all look the same. She might just have gotten the wrong address."

Kalix was grateful to Manny for making light of it, even though it seemed obvious that her sister wouldn't have turned up at his flat by coincidence.

"Let's go get some beer. And food, if we see anything we like."

Kalix allowed herself to be led gently along to the stairs, but Thrix's unexpected appearance had upset her and brought on some anxiety. She cursed her sister for apparently trying to spoil her date, and made up her mind to confront her about it when they next met.

I'll teach her to spy on me, thought Kalix, and she felt very angry.

CHAPTER 75

Thrix hurried downstairs. She drove off in a state of confusion and parked a few streets away, to call Dominil.

"Dominil? Something very strange just happened. You know that list of addresses you gave me?"

"I told you it was out of date."

"Well, I thought I'd check some of them anyway."

"Why?"

"Because I want to kill a werewolf hunter, that's why."

Dominil waited for Thrix to continue.

"I checked out a few of them. Either they were empty, or the tenants were obviously not hunters. But I just drove to an address in Clerkenwell. The last address on the list. It's an old block of flats." Thrix paused.

"What happened?" asked Dominil.

"Kalix was there."

"Kalix? You mean she'd gone there looking for werewolf hunters too?"

"No," said Thrix. "I mean she was there making a social call."

"That's odd."

"I'd say it was more than odd. I'd say it was so strange that it can't just be a coincidence."

"Is Kalix all right?"

"She was fine. She was with some young man. I didn't recognize him. I'm sure he wasn't a hunter though, I can usually tell."

There was a long pause.

"So what do you think?" asked Thrix.

"I really don't know. It is strange that Kalix should be at an address previously used by the Avenaris Guild. Coincidences between werewolves and werewolf hunters tend to not be coincidences at all."

"I know," said Thrix.

"Did Kalix actually see you there?"

"Yes," said Thrix. "Which is going to be hard to explain. Now she thinks I'm spying on her."

"We'll need to investigate further. Meanwhile, you shouldn't be driving around randomly looking for hunters. It's much more important that you make progress with our plan."

"Don't tell me what I should be doing," snapped Thrix. "I'm the one who has to do all this complicated sorcery to get us into the ball. If I want to look for werewolf hunters too, that's my affair."

Thrix rang off. Talking to Dominil hadn't enlightened her and it had made her bad mood worse. Her headache was returning. She fumbled in the glove compartment for painkillers.

How on earth did Kalix end up in a flat that used to be used by the Avenaris Guild? she wondered again, but could see no explanation. And who was that boy?

Thrix drove home, puzzled and concerned. She felt frustrated that she hadn't managed to meet any members of the Guild. She had a yearning to kill hunters that was getting stronger all the time. When she arrived home she changed immediately into her werewolf shape. She let out a low growl and paced around her living room, frustrated and annoyed.

"I'm going to kill them all," she said, again.

Thrix knew she should be working on her sorcery. It took her a long time before she felt capable of making a start. As she sat at her desk, writing out the list of spells she'd need, she could feel the ever-present knot inside her, constantly irritating her and breaking her concentration.

If I don't kill a werewolf hunter soon I'm going to explode, she thought, and was then distracted by images of what she was going to do to the Avenaris Guild when she finally managed to invade their headquarters.

CHAPTER 76

Two days before St. Amelia's Ball, excitement was growing in the small flat in Kennington. It increased when Moonglow appeared downstairs in a strapless black ball gown that rendered Daniel completely speechless.

"Moonglow!" cried Vex. "You look fantastic!"

Moonglow had been concerned that attending the charity ball might entail wearing something summery or floaty, which she knew she'd hate. On perusing the photos she'd found of past events, white seemed to be the main color of choice. However, there were some colorful dresses as well: girls in red and blue. She decided that she'd risk wearing something dark, and hope it wasn't too out of place. Moonglow had proceeded to scour the local charity shops. It had been a long search, and she'd been forced to travel further afield, visiting a charity shop in Chelsea where she paid a lot more than she'd intended to for a dress. She was pleased with the result.

Agrivex was impressed enough to shout up the stairs, "Kalix, come and see Moonglow looking really great in a dress."

"You look wonderful," said Daniel, recovering his power of speech. He had a sudden urge to ask how the dress stayed up, given that it was strapless, but refrained in case it was a foolish question.

"What are you screaming about?" said Kalix, appearing from her room. She stopped when she saw Moonglow. "Moonglow, you look great!"

Moonglow was gratified. She couldn't ever remember Kalix saying any clothing was great before.

"You're all set for your date with the viscount," said Vex. "It's so romantic! I read a story just like it in Total Boyfriend. Poor girl goes to ball, rich prince falls in love with her and they get married. You'll probably end up Queen or something."

Moonglow laughed. Daniel didn't. He'd been trying to forget about Moonglow's date. He looked at Moonglow's bare shoulders, very pale against the black fabric of her dress, and wondered if he might be able to spend the whole evening at the ball getting in between Moonglow and her date.

"When are you getting your clothes?" asked Moonglow.

"Tomorrow," said Vex. "Then we have to practice."

Kalix, Daniel and Vex, as models at the afternoon event, were required to rehearse their appearance. Thrix had assured them that nothing complicated was expected. They just had walk down the catwalk.

"It won't even be a proper catwalk," she'd told them. "From what I can gather, the models just walk down a small platform."

Vex had regained her enthusiasm for their enterprise. Daniel was still convinced he was going to make a fool of himself. Kalix had hardly spoken about it. The bad feelings between her and Thrix had made all their meetings uncomfortable for Daniel and Vex. Last time they'd been at Thrix's office, Kalix and Thrix had ended up screaming at each other. It took an intervention by Dominil to produce an uneasy truce for the rest of the day.

Daniel checked the time. "Dominil will be here soon."

"We're getting spying instructions!" said Vex. "It's so exciting!"

At exactly the arranged time, the doorbell rang. Vex charged downstairs. She led Dominil upstairs under a barrage of questions.

"Who's the chief spy? Is it you? Do you have ninja powers? Do we have secret identities? Do we need weapons? Do we have a secret code? What if there's a bomb?"

Dominil was doing her best to ignore Vex's questions but was moved to react to the last one. "A bomb? Why would there be a bomb?"

"You often see bombs in spy stories," said Vex. "Hidden under a table, maybe. Or even strapped to the hero's leg by the villains. What do we do if someone straps a bomb to our legs? Do we have a plan for that?"

"There will be no bombs," said Dominil. She looked at Moonglow.

"From the dress you're wearing I assume you have somehow acquired an invitation to the ball and are now determined to join in with the activities of your flatmates?"

Moonglow was impressed by the white-haired werewolf's powers of deduction. "Uh . . . yes. Is that OK?"

"I see no harm in it," said Dominil. "I was expecting you to force yourself in somehow. Kalix, Daniel, Vex—are you clear on our aims at the ball?"

"Not really."

"Not entirely."

"No."

"Did you read my notes?"

"What notes?"

Dominil pursed her lips. "I will refresh your memory. We're trying to find the location of the Avenaris Guild's headquarters. Very few people know this. We hope that some attendees at the ball will. If they do, we hope to obtain it."

"What attendees?" asked Moonglow.

"Kabachetka, principally," said Dominil. "Why do you grimace at her name? Have you encountered her?"

"We once knocked her out with a bottle," said Daniel. "Well, Moonglow did. I lent moral support."

Daniel and Moonglow had found themselves involved in the great werewolf feud, when Kabachetka had used her sorcery against the MacRinnalchs. As Daniel accurately reported, Moonglow had knocked her out in an alleyway in Camden. It was the single act of violence he'd ever known her to commit.

"She's not going to be very pleased to see you again," said Vex.

"I don't think she knew it was me. I sneaked up behind her." Moonglow asked Dominil the same question she'd been asked before. "Surely Kabachetka isn't going to just tell us where the Guild is?"

"She won't, but she may have companions there. Her secretary and her adviser, possibly. Some opportunity may present itself for finding the information. A representative from the Guild may even attend. If you're about to say it sounds like a tentative plan, spare yourself the trouble."

Moonglow did think it was a tentative plan, but she was as keen as the others were to spy, so she didn't mind. Feeling that she might not have been hospitable enough to Dominil, she went to the kitchen to make tea. Daniel followed her.

"Kalix," said Dominil. "Thrix assures me it was a coincidence that she encountered you at your friend's flat. She was not following you."

"It seems like a strange coincidence," said Kalix.

"I agree. However, it was not deliberate. I admit I'm troubled by it. Thrix was checking on addresses that had once been used by the werewolf hunters."

"That's stupid," said Kalix. "There weren't any hunters there."

"Are you absolutely sure you saw no sign of anything that could suggest the Guild may have had an interest in your friend's flat?"

Kalix became annoyed. "Of course I'm sure. The whole thing is stupid. Thrix probably just made it up about the address."

Dominil dropped the subject.

"Kalix has a new boyfriend," said Vex.

"Is that relevant to our endeavors?"

"Probably not."

"Then don't tell me about it."

CHAPTER 77

"Dearest Thrix, you are so tense." Malveria still didn't like the look of her friend's aura. She could see the tangled knot of grief and violent emotion inside her.

It will not disappear until she has revenge, thought Malveria. Let us hope it does not carry her off with it.

"You have been working too hard."

"I had to," said Thrix. "Getting us into the ball took a lot of sorcery."

Thrix had now completed the process. She was booked as one of the designers at the afternoon fashion event. Malveria would be there as her assistant. Both of them, and their models, could attend the ball afterward.

"It was a mighty effort, and worthy of a great sorceress," said Malveria.

"And now, if you would step into that impractical pair of heels you have secreted under your desk, I will show you the fruits of my own labors."

"Pardon?"

"The high-heel spell. I completed it in a splendid manner. Observe, Enchantress."

The Fire Queen's hand disappeared as she reached back into her own dimension. She plucked a pair of shoes from out of the air, itself an impressive feat of sorcery, given the difficulty of transmitting anything between dimensions.

"You observe these heels? Eight inches at least. Outstandingly beautiful, but, as we have learned to our cost, very difficult to walk in."

The Queen slipped on the shoes. With a small movement of her hand, she cast a spell. "Watch as I now walk the room with great elegance."

Malveria proceeded to do just that.

"Good spell!" said Thrix. "Try it on me."

Thrix took her heels from under the desk. The Fire Queen cast her spell and Thrix, too, walked elegantly. "I can't believe how easy this is."

"It is splendid, is it not?" said Malveria.

The door to Thrix's office opened and Ann appeared. She was surprised to see both Thrix and Malveria walking round the room for no apparent reason. "What are you doing?"

"Testing out our new very high heels," said Thrix.

Ann was impressed. "You've really got the hang of that. How did you manage it?"

"Continual practice," said the Fire Queen. "Both myself and Thrix are very dedicated."

"Good," said Ann. She looked at her employer. "Are you dedicated enough to start running the business again?"

Thrix was aware of the burden she'd placed on her assistant and her employees recently. "Not quite. But I'll be back in a few days, I promise."

"The buyer at Eldriges isn't pleased he can't see you."

"Just hold him off for a little while. Once this fashion show is out of the way I'll have more time."

"No one understands why you're doing this show," said Ann. Thrix's staff had been puzzled to learn that Thrix was participating in the small fashion event, which wasn't that prestigious.

"Didn't I ask you to make something up?" said Thrix.

"Yes. But I'm not very good at lying. Anyway, the clothes are all ready. Your sister and her friends are going to look good."

Thrix sat down, her good humor dissipating at the thought of Kalix modeling her clothes. "It's bound to be terrible," she said. "Kalix will do something stupid and humiliate me."

"I don't know," said the Fire Queen. "My feeling is that Agrivex is the more likely to disgrace you. I'll be surprised if her appearance at the ball does not lead to outrage."

"What about Daniel?" said Ann. "He keeps tripping over. Is he normally that clumsy? He looks terrified every time he takes a step."

"This is going to be a disaster," said Thrix. "We should never have listened to Dominil."

At least there was no concern over Dominil's performance. She looked elegant in her clothes, had rehearsed perfectly and would undoubtedly manage well. She looked bored with the whole process, but that wasn't really a problem for a model.

"We won't know how big a disaster it's going to be till we actually get there," said Thrix. "The proof of the pudding is in the eating, as my mother used to say."

"What?" Malveria looked alarmed. "I did not know pudding was involved."

"It's just an expression—"

"Are you implying that I have been secretly eating pudding?" She glanced at her waistline. "It is true that I may have indulged in a very small portion, but that was only to please the new ambassador from the stone giants. Afterward I exercised most assiduously." Malveria looked cross. "Really, there is no need to torment me with your continual references to pudding. It is most unkind."

Thrix was by now drumming an irritated finger on the desk. "Malveria, it's only an expression. It means you don't know how something really is until you try it."

The Fire Queen considered this. "Very well, Enchantress. I understand your meaning, and will excuse your poor choice of words."

Thrix stretched her arms above her head, trying to remove some of her stiffness. "Malveria, there's something I need to ask you. Dominil called me last night. She's been burrowing about in libraries again."

"She is keen on that."

"She is. She found some old book in the castle archives written by Sèitheach MacRinnalch. He was an adventurer in his time. He lived about three hundred years ago, so Dominil tells me." Thrix wrinkled her nose. "She told me a lot more about Sèitheach MacRinnalch than I'd ever want to know, but there was one thing that was interesting. When he was coming back from a trip to Italy, he passed through London and there he recorded that he met an elemental, a stone dwarf."

"A stone dwarf? One of the Maynista? That seems most unlikely. They do not like to visit this planet."

"I know. But that's what he wrote. He met him in a tavern in Cheapside."

"The stone dwarves are keen drinkers. But what of it?"

"According to Sèitheach MacRinnalch, this stone dwarf was a renegade prince who was hiding from his enemies. Which is why he'd come to London. Isn't it true that the stone dwarves are the greatest builders of all the elementals?"

"So they claim," said Malveria.

"What if he built a 'House That Can't Be Found' while he was in London? That's a specialty of the Maynista, isn't it?"

"Yes," said Malveria. "But what of it?"

"It might explain why we can't find the Avenaris Guild. A stone dwarf's 'House That Can't Be Found' means just that. It can't be found by any means."

"Indeed," said Malveria. "But does it not seem very unlikely?"

"Perhaps. But how else do you explain our complete inability to find the Guild? With all the sorcery we can use? And all Dominil's tracking skills? Maybe this renegade prince did build a 'House That Can't Be Found' in London. And maybe the Guild moved in after he left."

Malveria shook her head. "It would be the oddest of coincidences."

"Would it? Three hundred years ago, London was a much smaller place. The Avenaris Guild was in existence then. They knew about werewolves and elementals. It's not so strange that they might have come into contact with a stone dwarf who visited the city."

Malveria seemed uninterested in the conversation, and took to studying her heels.

"Do you think you could find out more?" asked Thrix.

"I wonder if I could even elevate these heels a further inch?"

"Malveria, why aren't you paying attention?"

"I am sorry, dear friend. But in truth, the stone dwarves are enemies of the Hiyasta, and I do not like to talk of them."

"Why? Are they dangerous?"

"Not to me. But they are unpleasant."

"Please see if you could find out anything."

Malveria sighed. She looked very unwilling. "I suppose I could. There is a new ambassador at my court from the stone giants, or Mayusta, as they are properly called. They are not really giants, of course, although rather on the large side. 'Stone giants' is not a polite thing to say in their company. I will ask him if he knows anything of this renegade prince from the stone dwarves. 'Stone dwarves' is also an impolite term, though as we have never been friends, I do not mind using it."

"Are they actually dwarves?"

"No, but one needs some way of distinguishing the Stone Elementals. I really am on very poor terms with them. It pains me to concern myself with them in any way. But I will ask the Mayusta ambassador if he can find out anything. And now, Enchantress, I must depart. I am in a state of indecision regarding perfume. Which, one wonders, will be most suitable for seduction?"

"Are you really planning on seducing someone?"

"If it is called for, absolutely. As should you be."

"If I'm called on to seduce anyone it'll go badly. Unless my target happens to be a man who doesn't mind listening to my problems. I wouldn't mind that."

"Who knows, Enchantress. You may find exactly that, and have sex and a sympathetic ear all in one night."

CHAPTER 78

Two targets had been set up at the far end of the training room in the Avenaris Guild's basement. One depicted a life-size werewolf, the other a teenage girl with very long hair. Some yards away there was a brick wall. Braid from Group Sixteen suddenly vaulted over the wall, landing in a crouch with his gun in his hand. Two shots rang out. He stood up, still pointing his gun.

Axelsen appeared from behind the wall. He looked at the targets. There was a neat bullet hole in the heart of the werewolf, and another hole in the young girl's forehead.

"Nice shot on the werewolf."

The silver bullet through the heart would have killed the werewolf instantly. Axelsen wasn't so sure about the bullet through the girl's forehead.

"We're meant to aim for the heart at all times."

"Force of habit," grunted Braid. "I reckon it would kill her anyway."

It was a moot point. The Guild was not certain of the effect of a silver bullet to the head of a werewolf in human form. The result of such an attack had never been recorded because at one time hunters were forbidden to attack werewolves before they'd transformed. Attitudes had changed recently. Now, in certain circumstances, their most trusted hunters were authorized to shoot at werewolves before they transformed.

"The Guild say a silver bullet won't penetrate a werewolf's skull," said Axelsen. "But the human variety . . . "

"It wouldn't do them any good, that's for sure," said Braid, and laughed. "When I meet this girl I'll put a bullet through her heart and another through her head, no matter what form she's in."

John Carmichael left his station at the back of the training room. He congratulated the two hunters on their work on the training course.

"These are good scores. Marshall and Stone did well too."

"So when are we getting another mission?" asked Axelsen. "Have you found this werewolf princess yet?"

"No. The werewolves in London are keeping themselves well hidden. Most of them aren't reckless like the Douglas-MacPhees. But we're drawing them out. We'll soon have some targets for you."

CHAPTER 79

On the day of St. Amelia's Ball, Kalix, Daniel and Vex left the flat before midday. Vex shepherded an unenthusiastic Daniel downstairs and into his car. Kalix followed on, scowling. Moonglow noticed that she was wearing her oldest clothes, and her hair was messy, and wondered if the young werewolf had made herself look as shabby as possible to antagonize Thrix.

After they'd left, Moonglow spent some time tidying the living room. William was coming here to pick her up. Pretend date or not, she didn't want him thinking she lived in a messy flat. William hadn't protested about Moonglow's desire to arrive in time to see the early evening fashion show. His mother had something to do with the organizing committee, so it gave him an opportunity to show support. His relationship with his mother was slightly uncomfortable, and he'd be pleased of the opportunity to improve it.

Moonglow dressed and did her makeup. She studied herself in the mirror and wondered if she looked like the sort of girl who'd impress a wealthy young man's parents.

"Maybe I shouldn't have gone with the black dress."

She turned her back on the mirror then craned her neck to get a view of herself, and couldn't help thinking she looked good.

"I'm sure it will be fine. It's not like I've got a tattoo on my neck or anything. Anyway, I'll charm his mother. And make her think he's not gay." Moonglow felt a small pang of guilt. Was making someone's mother think he wasn't gay really a good thing to do? Maybe she should have encouraged him to tell her instead.

"Well, it's his decision. I'm just following instructions, so to speak."

The doorbell rang. Moonglow walked elegantly downstairs and welcomed William into her home. She led him up the dark stairs, apologizing for the absence of a light bulb. William emerged from the gloom of the stairway looking, Moonglow thought, exceptionally attractive in his evening dress, complete with bow tie. She was about to compliment him, but he got there first.

"I love that dress, you look beautiful."

That got them off to a good start. Though Moonglow still didn't know William all that well, she felt comfortable in his presence.

"Do you think the dress is all right? I wasn't sure about it."

"It's perfect."

"I'm still worried about the curtsey."

William laughed. "It's all right, no one will be studying you."

"Someone might be."

Moonglow had been surprised, and alarmed, to learn that the ball was presided over by Princess Morozov, a descendant of the Russian royal family. On entering the room, all the women were meant to curtsey toward her. Moonglow had never curtseyed before and wasn't certain she could manage it.

"I looked up curtseying up on the internet. That wasn't much use."

"Well, let's see it," said William.

Moonglow curtsied.

"Perfect."

"Good. If we meet your mother, do you want me to hold your hand? Or kiss you? Is that going too far?"

"You don't need to do that," said William. "Just being there is good enough."

William had a car with a driver downstairs, ready to take them to the hotel in the Strand.

"I'm suddenly nervous," said Moonglow. "I'm not a debutante, people will know."

William dismissed this lightly. "There will be all sorts of people there. You're a perfect date, really."

Unlike Moonglow, Kalix, Daniel and Vex were not currently engaging in light or pleasant conversation.

"I hate this," said Kalix, studying her outfit with loathing.

"You hate everything," said Thrix. "Just shut up and wear it. Did you consider washing your hair any time this week?"

"I like it messy," muttered Kalix.

"Can I put some Hello Kitty badges on this vest?" said Vex.

"If you do I'll kill you," said Thrix

"And I will assist her," said the Fire Queen. "Thrix's beautiful clothes are not to be spoiled with foolish badges."

Vex didn't really mind. To her surprise, Thrix had dressed her for the show in an outfit she liked. She wore a red tank top under a sleeveless, brightly colored, tie-dyed crochet vest, and tiny black shorts. She had a wide, red plastic belt, and black clumpy ankle boots with tartan side panels. It was bright and colorful, it showed off her slender legs, and Vex was pleased with the effect.

"Do I get to keep the clothes afterward?"

"No," said Thrix.

"When do I get them then?"

"You don't get them."

"Oh. So can I keep them?"

"I just said you can't," said Thrix.

"OK."

Vex looked at her colorful reflection again. "This is such a great outfit. Can I keep it?"

"Stop tormenting Thrix, miserable niece," said the Fire Queen. She was attending the ball in the guise of Thrix's assistant, though she had shown little inclination to actually assist. Malveria had secured an extremely satisfactory outfit from the Enchantress, and was content to wear it, which, she reasoned, was assistance enough, given how fabulous she looked.

"I can't wait to model!" said Vex. She rushed over the room and hugged Thrix, taking her completely by surprise. "I love my clothes!" she cried. "Thank you."

Thrix was taken aback. She wasn't used to models being so expressive, or grateful. "Uh . . . all right." The Enchantress waited for the embrace to end but Vex clung on tenaciously. "I'm glad you like the clothes. You can let go now."

"I love my outfit," said Vex, and maintained the hug.

Thrix looked perplexed. There seemed no obvious way to release herself. She looked toward Malveria. "Could you remove your niece?"

Malveria shrugged, rather mischievously. "Should one discourage a display of sincere gratitude?"

Everyone else seemed amused. Thrix felt very uncomfortable. She was used to a great deal of perfunctory embracing and kissing of cheeks at fashion events, but as a werewolf who grew up at Castle MacRinnalch, hugging did not come naturally. It had never been done in her family. Thrix suddenly became alarmed by the forced intimacy.

"If you let go you can keep the clothes."

"Really?" cried Vex.

"I mean let go right now."

Agrivex whooped with joy and leaped away from Thrix.

"Really, Enchantress," said the Fire Queen, "I did not expect you to give up so easily."

"She caught me on my weak point."

The Fire Queen smiled. "I have noticed that the MacRinnalchs are not great huggers." She turned to her niece. "Agrivex, control your violent emotions before you break something. Kalix and Dominil, you are both looking very fine."

Kalix was slouched on a chair, looking bored. Her outfit was almost identical to Vex's but was completely without color. Her tank top, vest, tiny shorts, wide plastic belt and clumpy ankle boots were all either black or dark gray. The contrast between the colorful Vex and the monochrome Kalix was startling, as Thrix had intended. Vex's dark skin was surrounded by the brightest hues, and Kalix's very pale frame was sheathed in darkness.

Though Kalix had informed Thrix that she loathed the clothes, really she didn't hate them quite as much as she'd expected. At least they weren't bright. But she didn't like displaying her legs or her arms. There were various scars on view, and she was sensitive about them.

Knowing that Dominil would refuse to appear in public dressed as a messy urchin, Thrix had taken the opportunity to show her expertise in evening gowns. Dominil was dressed in a dark-blue, full-length dress, which contrasted quite startlingly with her long white hair. She wore pearls at her neck and stood very tall in her matching high heels.

"Dominil, you look most splendid," enthused Malveria. "I have met real ice queens who looked less like ice queens than you."

Thrix thought to herself that if it turned out that any seducing did need to be done, Dominil might be the one to do it. She doubted that many people could withstand her beauty, provided they weren't too intimidated to talk to her.

"For someone not used to high heels, you seem to have mastered them easily," said the Fire Queen.

"I practiced."

"Of course you did," muttered the Queen a little testily.

Daniel, looking slightly lost, wandered into the middle of the room. He studied his reflection in the mirror. "Do I look all right?"

Thrix didn't normally design clothes for men. That didn't mean she wasn't aware of current and upcoming trends. Perhaps fortunately for Daniel, who had feared being dressed in anything too outlandish, she had dressed him in a sober, stylishly cut gray suit and, unusually, a gray shirt, a garment that was just about to come into fashion. The only flash of color came from a dark-blue tie, which Daniel thought was acceptable.

"You look nice," said Kalix.

"Is it suitable for seducing duchesses?" Daniel looked troubled. "'Duchess' sounds quite old. Do you get young duchesses?"

"It depends on whether the old duchess fell into the volcano or just burned up naturally," said Vex.

"Agrivex," said Malveria. "Try not to talk to anyone at the ball."

Dominil raised her voice to address them all. "I doubt there will be any need to seduce duchesses. We're more likely to find ourselves trying to steal a wallet, or look at an address book."

"But we might have to seduce people!" cried Vex. "You never know!"

"I admit it's possible," said Dominil.

"I'm not going to be doing any seducing," said Thrix.

"But surely it is a thrilling prospect?" said the Fire Queen. "To outwit the enemy by luring them with sex?"

"I really don't think I'll be doing that, Malveria."

The Fire Queen looked disappointed. "Really, Enchantress, what possible objection could you have? And remember, you have access to the most potent means of increasing passion."

"You mean a love spell?"

"No, I mean alcohol."

"Returning to the subject," said Dominil coldly. "We won't know till we get there who we'll be targeting. I'll try to assess the situation during the fashion show and then give you your assignments."

Dominil seemed to have assumed command of the operation. Thrix might have objected, but knew she'd be too busy to give much thought to anything other than her fashion show. It might be only a minor event, but Thrix was always serious when it came to showing her clothes.

"Queen Malveria," continued Dominil, "the Empress Kabachetka does not know we're attending. I imagine she will be shocked."

"I hope she is," said the Fire Queen.

"It occurs to me that there may be some sort of confrontation."

The Fire Queen's eyes lit up. "I hope so. I will put her in her place very swiftly, I assure you."

"I'd rather you didn't," said Dominil. "It won't help. It will put her on guard. It will be better if we can all remain calm."

The Fire Queen pouted. "You may be right, Dominil. I will try to avoid an immediate confrontation. But I was looking forward to abusing the Empress."

"Is everyone ready?" asked Dominil. "Then we should go."

CHAPTER 80

The Empress and her entourage materialized smoothly in the hotel. Kabachetka, Distikka, Adviser Bakmer, Secretary Gezinka and Handmaiden Alchet appeared one after the other, completing the journey from the realm of the Hainusta. The Empress wrinkled her nose.

"This is their best suite? It is hardly satisfactory. Bakmer, complain to the manger."

Adviser Bakmer appeared not to understand. "The manager?"

"Yes, the manager," snapped the Empress. "Please do not be tiring, Bakmer. I know you have never been in this realm before, but if you go around wondering what everything is, it will be very tedious."

The Empress turned to her handmaiden. "Alchet, stop whimpering."

"I don't like it here," said the unfortunate Alchet. She hated when the

Empress brought her to Earth, and spent the whole time terrified in case she got wet.

"Must you always be like this?"

"I'm scared of the rain."

"There is no rain in a hotel. Pull yourself together. I will need you to travel back and forth from the palace to bring me clothes and other items as necessary."

The young handmaiden looked miserable. "I might get lost on the way."

"Alchet, it is a curse that you have such a great talent for dressing me. Were it not so, I swear I would have replaced you long ago. Forget your foolish fears of being rained on or getting lost. Observe."

The Empress took a jewel from her handbag and laid it on a dressing table. She touched the jewel and a large oval portal of light opened up in the room.

"You see? I have brought this jewel to make a passage. Using it, you may travel from here to the palace without fear of losing your way."

The Empress surveyed her companions. "This is a great day for me and I do not want it spoiled. Bakmer, have you complained to the manager yet?"

"There's no point," said Distikka. "This is the best the hotel has to offer. I made sure they gave us their three finest suites."

The Empress looked round at her rooms, which were, by any normal standards, very luxurious.

"This is the best they have? Really? It is most unsatisfactory." She strode into the main bedroom and frowned as she saw the full-length mirror on the wall.

"Very poor quality," she muttered. She uttered a spell, causing a new mirror to materialize, bigger and clearer than the other. "That is a little better. Alchet, prepare to help me dress. Distikka, what is first on the agenda?"

"The afternoon fashion show and clothes auction."

"Excellent. No doubt there will be some worthy young designers showing us their wares. Fill my purse with gold coinage. We must bid enthusiastically for some items, to show our generosity."

The Empress smiled for the first time since her arrival. "Bakmer, inform the relevant people that I am here. The fabulous heiress from South America has arrived, to sponsor events, break hearts and have her picture taken. This is going to be the most glorious day."

CHAPTER 81

The Mistress of the Werewolves had tramped a long way through Colburn Woods and was beginning to feel frustrated.

Where is she? She should have appeared by now.

Verasa walked along paths that were not as familiar as they once had been. She swore as she caught her skirt in some thorns, and struggled to release it.

"I knew I should have come at night," muttered Verasa. At night she'd have been able to change into her werewolf shape, leaving her untroubled by thorns. She'd realized some time ago that her clothes were unsuitable for walking through the thick woods. Her skirt kept getting caught up in the vegetation. The Mistress of the Werewolves disliked wearing trousers. She'd grown up in an era when that was seldom done, and it had never come naturally.

Am I even going in the right direction?

It was so long since Verasa had visited Colburn Woods that she'd almost forgotten the way to the dell where the Fairy Queen held court. She was sure the pathways had been different back then. Verasa carried on, but was brought to a halt almost immediately by another thorn bush.

This is infuriating! And why hasn't the Queen appeared? She must know I'm here. Does she expect me to walk all the way through her woods just for an audience?

There was a sudden peal of laughter behind her. Verasa turned round to find a very small fairy hovering in the air.

"Is that really Verasa MacRinnalch, Mistress of the Werewolves, blundering through Colburn Woods in her Sunday best?"

"Nice of you to put in an appearance, Dithean NicRinnalch," said Verasa. "I thought I was going to have to walk all the way to your dell."

"You'd never have made it," said the fairy. "Not in that skirt."

Verasa looked down at her skirt, which was torn in several places. "It was a poor choice," she admitted. "Though I wasn't expecting to have to walk so far."

"Why not? Did you expect the Fairy Queen to just pop out the moment you arrived, when you haven't visited me for hundreds of years?"

It was an awkward moment, as Verasa had known it would be. The Mistress of the Werewolves had not visited Colburn Woods for a long time. She knew the Fairy Queen would be offended.

"You exaggerate, Dithean. It's not *hundreds* of years."

"It's a very long time."

"It is. I apologize." The Mistress of the Werewolves was finding the conversation with the small fairy difficult. "Could you make us the same size?"

"Of course," said Dithean. "Big or small?"

"Big, if you don't mind. I don't think I could cope with small any more."

Queen Dithean laughed again, quite mockingly. "What happened to you, Verasa MacRinnalch? You used to love coming here and playing as a fairy."

The Fairy Queen made a slight movement with her hand and immediately became the same size as Verasa. They stood facing each other on the path. The Fairy Queen's long golden hair swayed gently in the breeze.

"So," said Dithean. "Here we are. One human-sized fairy and one werewolf in human shape. And what does the werewolf want from the fairies, after neglecting us for so long?"

"Could we go somewhere a bit less thorny? With somewhere to sit?"

"Are you tired?"

"Yes. I'm not the same young werewolf that used to play with the fairies, Dithean."

"I'd say you were still quite vigorous," said Queen Dithean, leading Verasa along the path. "Vigorous enough not to have ignored me for so long."

Verasa realized that the Fairy Queen was not going to drop the subject easily. She understood why. The MacRinnalch werewolves were friends and allies of the fairies of Colburn Woods. They had a shared history, and their roots extended far back in time. They had many connections. It was from the pure water of the burn running through the wood that the MacRinnalchs obtained the water to distil their whisky. The fairies had assisted the MacRinnalchs in difficult times. Their Queen did not like to be taken for granted.

"Not all the MacRinnalchs ignore us, of course," said Dithean. "Why, not long ago we were honored by a visit from many of your clan, and the MacAllisters too."

The Fairy Queen halted and turned to look accusingly at the Mistress of the Werewolves. "They fought, and there was death and bloodshed in my forest."

"Yes . . . we're very sorry about that. The feud, you know. Many regrettable incidents occurred."

"I do not expect the MacRinnalchs to spread fear and destruction in my land."

"I'm sorry. I understood Clan Secretary Rainal sent you reparations."

"MacRinnalch gold is not as welcome as MacRinnalch respect. Why has the new Thane not been to visit me?"

Again, it was a difficult topic. Verasa knew that Markus should have visited Queen Dithean. Markus was aware of it too. But somehow, other things kept getting in the way.

"I'm sorry, Dithean, it's remiss of us. But life outside, it's different these days. There's so much to take care of."

The Fairy Queen sniffed. "I am aware of life outside the woods. And I know more about Markus than you might suppose. He could have made time to visit me."

"I promise he'll come soon."

The Fairy Queen did not look assuaged. She tossed her long blonde hair as she turned and led Verasa on. They emerged into a clearing. Whether it was the Queen's Dell or another space, Verasa couldn't tell. A young fox was drinking from a small pond, and glanced up as they arrived. Verasa and Dithean sat on a natural shelf on the grass. The fox ignored them and carried on drinking. The glade was sheltered from the wind, and warm in the sun. Verasa caught glimpses of a few other fairies in the trees. She wondered if she might know any of them. She had once been a frequent visitor.

"That was a long time ago," said the Fairy Queen, reading her thoughts.

The Mistress of the Werewolves felt a tinge of annoyance. "Dithean, are you going to spend my whole visit lecturing me? I'm sorry I've ignored you. I can't do anything to change that now. And if I haven't visited, I haven't let the clan forget you either. We keep up our payments for your water."

"True. Though you are not the only ones willing to pay for the pure water that flows through my woods."

Verasa felt herself bridling, though she controlled it. In recent times the Hiyasta Fire Queen had also paid in gold for the water from the woods, using it in her potions of youth and regeneration. The Fire Queen regarded it as the purest liquid in any dimension. The Mistress of the Werewolves did not like the arrangement, though she knew it was entirely up to the Fairy Queen whom she did business with.

"The Hiyasta take only tiny amounts," said Dithean. "It doesn't interfere with the flow of the stream. Or your whisky production."

The fox trotted off into the trees. The glade was silent.

"I'm worried about Markus," said Verasa abruptly.

"Markus? Why? I understood that he was now secure as Thane."

"He is. But . . . " Verasa paused, and an expression of unbearable sadness settled on her features. She stared into the pool and shook her head.

"He's going to go and fight in London. He'll be killed, I know it. I
can't bear to lose him."

CHAPTER 82

The Empress Kabachetka was leading her entourage along the corridor toward the west reception room when she was intercepted by Adviser Bakmer.

"Empress! Queen Malveria is here!"

"Malveria? Ridiculous. Have you been drinking already?"

"She is here, Great Empress. I saw her, in the company of a blonde-
haired woman with a strange aura."

"How strange?"

"Very strange. Not human."

"Thrix MacRinnalch!" cried the Empress. "Thrix and Malveria have
dared to invade my ball! I will soon put a stop to this."

A flame shot from the Empress's hand as she prepared to confront
her enemies. She found herself halted by Distikka, who dragged her back.

"What is this, Distikka? You put your hand on the Empress?"

"We're in a hotel in London where people don't normally shoot flames
at each other. Your new friends at *Vogue* are going to find it strange if
they see it, which they will."

The Empress considered this. "You are right. I must control my mighty
flame. But what is the meaning of this, Distikka? Why have these people
come? Are they here to sabotage my event?"

"I doubt it," said Distikka. "I'd say it was more likely they're here to
spy on us."

"To spy? Yes, sneaking and spying is quite in character for the appalling Fire Queen and her unspeakable werewolf companion. Well, they
shall get no information from me."

The young Empress addressed her followers. "Everyone is to remain calm. Do not shoot flames in public." She composed herself, and continued along the corridor. "But I will kill them in private if they do try any sabotage," she muttered to Distikka. "I'm more powerful now than the last time I encountered Malveria. I have my mother's spells, and the power of the volcano. Malveria may find herself burned to a cinder, and the world would thank me for getting rid of her."

In a small dressing room beside the west reception room, Kalix sat quite passively while Thrix applied the finishing touches to her makeup. It was an unwelcome experience, but Kalix had made up her mind to accept the inevitable indignities of the evening as calmly as she could. Aiding her in this was a large dose of laudanum.

I really hate my sister, she thought. But I don't care at the moment.

Kalix was extremely pale. There were traces of dark shadows beneath her eyes; less than before, though still noticeable. The scars on her arms and legs were also noticeable. Thrix was aware of this. Rather to her shame, she didn't mind.

"So I'm sending out a model who's underweight, scarred and probably drugged. It's not like it's the first time. And she does look good."

Thrix's professional interest had begun to outweigh her personal feelings. Kalix looked quite special. With her wild beauty, her wide mouth, her perfect cheekbones, her scars, her scrawny frame, her deathly pallor, her long hair tousled like a river in flood, she was certainly going to stand out from the crowd. Most of the other models, amateurs helping out for the night, had the wholesome look of well-fed and wealthy young women. Kalix was nothing like them. And while St. Amelia's Ball, as a friendly charity function, was not really the place for causing outrage, Thrix never minded drawing attention to her clothes.

If I get lucky, some rich sponsor will object to Kalix and make a fuss. There's nothing like a bit of scandal for getting your clothes in magazines.

Daniel stood at the door, peering out of the dressing room into the main hall outside.

"What are you looking at?" asked Vex.

"The other male models. I'm checking how good-looking they are. There's one over there who's quite good-looking. I don't like him."

Vex squeezed herself into the doorway. "He's not that good-looking. His nose is funny."

"Is it? You're right. What a weird nose. I feel better now. And look, that guy next to him is fat. I've got a much better body than him."

Vex grinned. "You'll be fine."

Daniel stared at her. "Right about now you'd normally say something tactless and make me feel bad."

"That's so unfair! I'm never tactless. You look fine, Daniel; you'll be a good model."

The Fire Queen, resplendent in her evening dress, approached the doorway.

"What are you whispering about, dismal niece?"

"Daniel's worried in case the other models are more handsome than him. But they're not. Apart from the boy in the black jacket, he's really handsome."

Malveria peered out the door. "He is, isn't he? Very striking. And his companion is rather good-looking too."

"You're right," agreed Agrivex. "He's really attractive. But if Daniel just stays away from them he'll be fine."

Vex turned to Daniel. "Try to stand next to the fat one."

But Daniel had gone, retreating to the back of the room. He was already intimidated by the opulence of his surroundings, and had been since walking in through the entrance of the Lancaster Hotel, with its liveried doormen and rows of carefully cultivated bushes sheltering it from the main road. The room assigned to them for their preparations was more luxurious than anything Daniel had ever encountered, though it was a very minor room in the hotel. It had a gray marble floor, paintings on the walls, some highly polished furniture and elegant flower arrangements. Daniel feared that he might break something, and attempted not to look intimidated. No one else seemed to be affected. The Fire Queen was used to luxury, and Vex had been raised in a palace. As for Thrix, she'd been to this hotel in the Strand before. Dominil wasn't used to luxurious surroundings, he supposed, though she might have frequented some wealthy establishments as a student at Oxford. But he didn't suppose she would be intimidated by anything anyway. She was sitting quietly, reading a book. She looked up as Thrix spoke to her.

"It's time for your makeup."

Dominil remained silent as Thrix descended on her with her extensive array of cosmetics. Thrix seemed enlivened by the task. "I've been wanting to do this for a long time."

"As have I!" cried the Fire Queen, rushing to join them. "Dominil's lack of makeup is quite terrifying. It is high time it was rectified."

"I'm glad you've decided to assist with something," said Dominil dryly.

"Empress Kabachetka is here," said Vex. "She just came in."

Dominil looked up. "Please hurry, Thrix. I want to examine our enemies."

"Plenty of time for that," said Thrix. "We've got a whole fashion show and a ball to get through. Just keep still while I do your eyes."

There was a sudden crash as a jar of flowers fell from a table onto the floor.

"I didn't do it!" said Daniel immediately.

"Agrivex!" cried the Fire Queen. "Control yourself!"

"Sorry, Aunty."

"You are not in my palace now, vile girl. Sit down and attempt not to break things. Really, it will be a miracle if we escape this establishment before my niece burns it to the ground."

Far too quickly for Daniel's liking, they were ready for the fashion show. Daniel didn't feel ready. "I can't do it. I feel sick. It's this hotel, it's too rich. Everything's all . . . " Daniel struggled for the word.

"Opulent," said Dominil. "It's an interesting mix of Edwardian and art deco. But I see no reason to be intimidated."

"Isn't it a bit intimidating when you know you're surrounded by people who're all rich and you're not?"

"Not unless you allow it to be," said Dominil.

Daniel wasn't reassured. "I can't help it. I've got this feeling the minute I walk out there everyone will point and laugh."

"There were many wealthy students at Oxford. I didn't find them to be rude, as a general rule."

"Well, they probably wouldn't be rude to you," said Daniel. "For one thing you're too intimidating, and for another you're a beautiful woman. It's different for me."

Dominil looked at Daniel, faintly surprised. It was unusual for him to talk to her. Presumably, she now realized, because he was intimidated. She began to reply but was silenced by the arrival of Malveria.

"Did I just hear Daniel call Dominil beautiful? Why, he is a sly rogue. The first time I encountered him he quite won me over with his outrageous flattery. One would not suspect he had such a silver tongue. Daniel, I expect you to have great success with your seductions tonight. No lady can resist such lavish praise from a handsome young man."

Daniel had flushed bright red at the start of Malveria's speech. He was rescued from his embarrassment by Dominil.

"Is everyone ready?" she asked. "Then it's time to go."

CHAPTER 83

Moonglow had also suffered some qualms on arriving at the hotel. Like Daniel, she felt out of place. William had put her at ease, strolling into the foyer as if it were the most natural thing in the world. Which, Moonglow supposed, it was for him. His family was extremely wealthy, and he'd stayed at this hotel before moving to London as a student. He guided her to the room where the fashion show was being held, ordered drinks for them both and then complimented her dress again. Moonglow thought that was a good start to the evening. She asked him if his mother was there.

"She'll be around somewhere, organizing things. She loves the ball." William looked guilty. "My mother can be a bit more intimidating than I admitted when we made this date."

"Don't worry," said Moonglow. "I'm good with mothers."

The west reception room was very grand, with an impressive marble doorway, marble pillars and a classical frieze running around the walls. As the afternoon turned into early evening, it began to fill with guests. The reserved seats in the front row remained empty, but the tables farther back were occupied by young debutantes already dressed for their ball, and their escorts. Studying them objectively, Moonglow decided that her date was really the most attractive man on view, and told him so.

"I haven't been feeling attractive recently," he confessed.

"Why not?"

"I got my heart broken. Or damaged, anyway."

William told Moonglow about a relationship he'd been in that had ended recently. "He went back to his old boyfriend. And he'd sworn he wasn't going to do that."

"He probably regrets it already. You can find someone better."

William ordered them more drinks and they gossiped about recent relationships, people they knew at college and how bad their new history professor was.

"There's the editor of *Vogue*," said William, indicating a woman taking her seat right next to the catwalk. Moonglow felt a tinge of worry about her friends. She knew Daniel would find it stressful to walk out in front of an audience. So would Kalix. Moonglow hoped she wouldn't do anything crazy. Having had recent experience of Kalix's craziness in the warehouse, there was no telling what she might do if things became too much for her. Vex would be fine, of course. She'd come bounding down the runway with a large grin on her face, no matter what.

A few minutes later, Moonglow noticed a familiar face, also heading for the front row. Empress Kabachetka. Moonglow turned her face so as not to be seen. The appearance of the Empress reminded Moonglow why she was here. She'd been having such a good time with William that she'd almost forgotten the mission. She was still determined not to be left out. Kalix, Daniel and Vex were all meant to be spying, and she was going to spy too.

I wonder who we're meant to spy on? wondered Moonglow. Kabachetka, I suppose. Well, Daniel will tell me after he's finished modeling. Unless he's frozen with fear.

"I hope he doesn't fall off the catwalk," she said out loud.

"Pardon?" said William.

"Daniel. My flatmate. He's not used to modeling."

"But surely he wouldn't fall off the catwalk?"

"I don't know. He can be clumsy when he gets stressed. Vex is really clumsy as well. I can see some sort of accident happening."

"Why is it that they're all modeling tonight?"

Moonglow had explained that she was slightly acquainted with one of the designers in the fashion show.

"The designer wanted to use her sister as a model, and she lives with us. The others were just suitable, I suppose. It's for charity; they didn't want to waste money hiring professional models."

"Are you planning to bid for any of the clothes?"

"I doubt I'll be able to afford any of them," said Moonglow.

"I'll bid for you," said William.

"You can't do that!" said Moonglow, who certainly didn't intend letting William buy her anything. Still, she appreciated the offer and, as she sat with William, she thought that she'd have enjoyed being there with him anyway, whether or not there was a mission to take part in.

CHAPTER 84

"I don't want Markus to go and fight in London," said the Mistress of the Werewolves. "I'll lose all my children. I lost Sarapen last year. Kalix is doomed, some way or other."

"Doomed? That's a strong judgment. Do you have foreknowledge of some event?"

"No," admitted Verasa. "But you can't run around in the same city as the Avenaris Guild and get away with it forever. Not when you act like Kalix anyway." She sighed. "I've tried to think of some way of getting her back to the castle, but it just can't be done. The clan won't allow it. Every day I expect to hear that she's dead."

The Fairy Queen stared into the pool beside her. "You haven't mentioned your other daughter."

"Thrix? She's too powerful for her enemies. Though . . . " Verasa paused. "Since Minerva was killed there's been something wrong with her. I hope she doesn't do anything too foolish. Really, Dithean, can you help me with Markus?"

"Can't you persuade your council to order Markus to remain at the castle?"

"The Thane always fights. Markus would be furious if anyone tried to stop him. He probably wouldn't pay any attention anyway." Verasa shook her head. "It's my fault. I tried to protect him too much and now he's trying to break away."

A fish appeared on the surface of the pool. It gazed at the Fairy Queen. A sparrow flew from the trees to perch beside her. The Queen smiled at the fish before it retreated back into the depths. The sparrow chirped merrily.

"I'm glad your chicks are doing well," said Dithean. "Here." She opened her hand, and the sparrow took a dark red berry from her palm. It flew off with its food, back into the shelter of the woods.

"What would you like me to do about Markus?" asked the Fairy Queen.

"Stop him from going."

"How?"

"When the time comes, make him ill."

Queen Dithean gazed at her old friend, surprised by the request. "Make him ill?"

"You have the power to do that."

"It's not a power I use often. It's never been the easiest of powers to control."

"I'm sure you could do it," insisted the Mistress of the Werewolves.

"Verasa, I don't think it would be a good idea. Better to let matters take their course."

"I'm not asking you to unleash the full powers of the Unseelie Court on Markus," said Verasa, referring to those fairies who had the power to bring the worst sort of misfortune. "Just a little sickness he'll recover from."

The Fairy Queen frowned. She turned her head toward the edge of the clearing, and called out a sentence in a language Verasa didn't know. A dark shadow appeared in the trees. "Come forward," said the Fairy Queen.

A fairy appeared. She was very small, with a lot of dark hair. Her skin was deathly white, her eyes were large and black and there was more shadow around her than there should have been. She wore a short black dress, was barefooted and, rather eerily, there were bandages on her arms.

"This is Teinn," said the Fairy Queen. "She has power over health. But she's unpredictable. Aren't you, Teinn?"

The fairy laughed. It was a harsh sound, and seemed to chill the glade.

"Do you really want me to set her on Markus?"

"Yes, if he wants to go and fight."

"Once she's sent on a task, there's no stopping her. And there's little controlling her either. The sickness would probably be minor, but . . . " The Fairy Queen's voice tailed off.

"But what?"

"Misfortune may follow."

"I've dealt with plenty of misfortune in my life, Dithean. As long as Markus is alive and well, I don't mind."

CHAPTER 85

Shortly before the fashion show was due to begin, there were chaotic scenes backstage. Instructions were given, models struggled in and out of clothes, last-minute adjustments were made and makeup was reapplied.

Vex's manic jumping and shouting no longer seemed unusual; plenty of others were doing the same.

Dominil cast an unsympathetic eye over the scene. "This all seems very disorganized. Is it normal?"

"Very normal," said Thrix. "This isn't too bad. Things can really get out of hand at a big event."

"It's inefficient. Why doesn't everyone simply get ready on time, without making a fuss?"

"It never seems to work out that way."

The Fire Queen, who for some time had been deep in conversation with a young man modeling evening wear, hurried up to them. "Did you notice how attractive that young man is? What's wrong with Dominil's dress? I must say, for one so young, he has a splendid physique."

"Dominil's dress?" snapped Thrix. "There's nothing wrong with it."

"I assure you there is. Look at the hem."

Thrix looked down. "Dominil! What did you do to the hem?"

"I didn't do anything."

"It's coming down. Did you tread on it?"

"Certainly not," said Dominil. "The workmanship must have been defective."

"You're due on in a few minutes. Sit down while I fix it."

Vex bounced up toward them. "Whoa! Problems with Dominil's dress? Why didn't you get ready early like me? Why are you staring at me like that?"

Daniel and Kalix did their best to ignore the uproar around them. Both were so tense they couldn't cope with anything else. Daniel wondered how he'd ever thought he could model clothes in front of an audience.

"I know I'm going to fall off the runway. If I even make it that far. I had a dream once where my trousers fell down in public. What if it was an omen?"

Kalix was wrapped up in her own anxiety but did manage to emerge long enough to tell Daniel that she was sure his trousers wouldn't fall down. She even managed a smile. "I'd probably be less anxious if it did happen. At least it would be funny."

"Not for me," wailed Daniel. He prodded his midriff. "Do I look flabby? Why didn't you encourage me to exercise more?"

Kalix rubbed her arm. She had several fresh scars that were itchy. So far, the laudanum she'd taken, and her determination not to fail in their mission, was keeping her anxiety at bay, but only just. If she could just make it down the catwalk and back, she could leave and get away from the crowd. When the show was over, Kalix and the others were meant to mingle with the audience, but Kalix was planning on escaping, at least for a while. There were gardens between the hotel and the river, and she hoped she might find a quiet spot where she could transform, to renew her strength. She was concentrating on controlling her anxiety when Daniel suddenly asked her if she ever had the urge to become a werewolf in public.

"What do you mean?"

"You know, sometimes people get urges to do stupid things. Like shouting 'fire' in a crowded room. I wondered if you ever got an urge to just let go in public, and turn into a werewolf."

Kalix was immediately alarmed. "I didn't up till now! Not before you suggested it anyway. Why did you say that?"

"I didn't mean anything . . . " said Daniel.

"Now I'm going to turn into a werewolf in public!"

"No, really you won't."

"I can feel it happening!" cried Kalix. "Why did you have to go and say that?"

"I'm sorry," said Daniel. "I was just making conversation."

Kalix started to look desperate. "What if I do? What if I'm in front of the audience and I get this mad urge to become a werewolf?" She moaned. "I can feel it coming on. I won't be able to stop myself. Why did you have to go and suggest it?" Kalix felt the first tinges of perspiration on her palms and forehead. She rubbed her arm vigorously. "I can't do this, I have to go home." She looked around desperately, wondering which direction was best to flee, but she was too late.

Thrix appeared in front of her. "You're on," said Thrix.

"I can't do it!" cried Kalix.

"Why not?"

"I'm going to change into a werewolf!"

"Don't be ridiculous. Why would you do that?"

"It's Daniel's fault! Don't send me out!" cried Kalix.

"Get out there and model these clothes!" said Thrix, and pushed Kalix through the curtain.

Kalix emerged into the spotlight, still cursing Daniel for his foolish chatter. If he hadn't suggested she might get the urge to transform it would never have occurred to her. Now she couldn't think of anything else.

I can't stop myself, she thought. It's going to happen.

Now she was on the runway, there was nothing to do but carry on. Kalix clenched her fists. Her face froze into her fiercest scowl as she tried to hold the panic at bay. She could barely see the spot she was heading for, and marched toward it with her head bowed. The audience looked on with amazement. So far they'd been treated to a rather anodyne collection of wholesome young debutantes in light summer outfits. Kalix took them by surprise. She stormed down the runway with her black clothes and pale face, her abnormally long hair streaming down her back in a tangled mess. Her slender legs, bare from ankle to thigh, looked as if they'd never seen sunlight, or even daylight. Her expression was murderous. Most dramatic of all, blood was now seeping from one of the scars on her arm where she'd rubbed too vigorously.

Kalix arrived at the end of the runway and realized she didn't know what to do next. She glared through the spotlights at the people in the front row with loathing, and looked for a moment as if she might leap from the catwalk and attack them. Her wide red mouth twisted into an ugly snarl, accentuated by her heavy dark lip gloss. She growled, loudly enough to be heard over the music, then turned on her heel and stormed back up the runway. The audience, previously silent, began to show their appreciation. By the time Kalix stumbled back through the curtain, she was being loudly applauded.

"I must say, the crowd liked you," said the Fire Queen.

"I thought they would," said Thrix. "Nice job, Kalix, you really sold that outfit."

"I can't go out again," said Kalix urgently.

"Yes, you can. Get these clothes off and get into the new outfit."

"I'm going to turn into a werewolf!"

Thrix brushed this off. "No, you won't. Now hurry, there's not much time for the turnaround. Malveria, help me get these boots off."

Kalix stood rigidly as she was undressed and dressed again. Though she was suffering, her sister seemed to think that everything was going well.

"This time, pause a little longer in front of the editors at the end of the runway."

"Should someone wipe the blood from her arm?" asked the Fire Queen.

"Just leave it," said Thrix.

"I'm going to have a panic attack!" yelled Kalix.

"You can do that later. Right now, get out there and model."

"I hate you all," said Kalix as they prepared to push her through the curtain again.

Kalix was thrust onto the catwalk, to the sound of more applause.

"You know, dearest friend," said the Fire Queen to Thrix. "All the things that people have written in disapproval of models, you seem to have rolled up into one package and sent down the catwalk."

"I know. If I'm lucky someone will complain."

"That would be splendid publicity," agreed the Fire Queen. "I must say, Enchantress, it has been a novel experience for me, acting as your assistant."

"I appreciate it," said Thrix with a straight face, though Malveria had lent almost no help. "Dominil, you're on."

Dominil, bored by the proceedings, was now listening to music on her iPod. Thrix tapped her shoulder. Dominil removed the headphones.

"What are you listening to?"

"Schoenberg's orchestration of Brahms."

"Of course. What else? It's time for you to make your debut."

Dominil placed her iPhone carefully in her bag and stood up just as Kalix crashed back through the curtain. The young werewolf stumbled toward a chair and sat down heavily.

"Modeling is terrible," she moaned.

"It's my turn again!" cried Vex, and sprinted through the curtain. Vex had also proved popular with the audience, being slender, beautiful, well dressed and, unlike Kalix, showing no sign of psychopathic rage. She completely ignored the instructions Thrix had given her, and walked down the runway smiling and waving at people, turning back occasionally to wave some more. She halted at the end of the catwalk and peered over at the front row.

"Are you the editor of *Vogue*? Really? My aunt loves you! You'll probably meet her later. Bye!"

Vex tripped back up the runway, leaving the front row laughing. Only the Empress was unamused.

"I still cannot believe that Thrix MacRinnalch has invaded my event," she hissed in Distikka's ear. "And sent out the loathsome Kalix and the appalling Agrivex as models. The effrontery is incredible!"

The Empress controlled herself, sat up straight and looked dignified. "I will have my revenge," she muttered.

CHAPTER 86

Dominil strode coolly down the runway with a look of disdain on her face. When she reached the far end of the catwalk she paused for a few seconds, as if studying someone in the audience. After this brief hesitation, she retreated elegantly up the runway, to great applause. There was by this time a certain buzz in the audience about Thrix MacRinnalch. Her designs had been well received, but it was her models that had really drawn attention. She'd certainly sent some unusual young women down the catwalk. Kalix and Vex had both been extremely notable, and Dominil's long, snow-white white hair and frozen beauty would have captivated any crowd. Thrix thanked them all sincerely, even Kalix. When Daniel arrived back from his trip down the runway with a look of fear still etched on his face, she thanked him too.

"You did well."

"It was so scary walking in front of all these people!"

"You were good. Thanks for being a model."

Daniel hadn't expected any gratitude from Thrix, and felt his spirits revive.

"I did do all right didn't I?"

"You were great!" enthused Vex. "You didn't look like you were going to fall off at all, hardly anyway."

The fashion show was coming to an end. Soon it would be time to auction the clothes. The room backstage was still crowded and noisy, though the air of panic had now passed. Dominil drew the party close to talk to them privately.

"I've identified our targets. Listen carefully. Queen Malveria, please take care of the Empress Kabachetka, at least for the early part of the evening. We need freedom to operate, and I don't want her to interfere by way of sorcery. Can you do that?"

"Block her sorcery? Yes. But it will be tedious, remaining in her company. There are several men here whose acquaintance I was hoping to cultivate."

"There will be time for that later. Thrix—a representative from the Avenaris Guild will be turning up soon. Deal with him. By which I mean see what you can learn, not kill him. Your sorcerous protection will make sure he doesn't know you're a werewolf."

"How do you know he's coming?" asked Thrix.

Dominil tapped her iPad. "I've accessed the hotel's system. I know all the rooms the Empress has hired. Distikka has booked a meeting with a Mr. Eggers. I recognize the name."

Thrix smiled, quite grimly. She seemed satisfied with her task.

Dominil turned to Daniel. "I saw several Fire Elementals in the audience. One of those was, I believe, Lady Gezinka, her secretary. Gezinka may know the location of the Guild. She is your target."

"My target?" said Daniel. "What am I meant to do?"

"Use your initiative."

"I'm not really that good with my initiative."

"Engage her in conversation and do what you can. That is, after all, why you are here. Kalix and Vex, I want you to target the Empress's other adviser, Bakmer. From the few seconds I saw him, I judge him to be young and insecure. He may be susceptible to the attentions of two young models."

Dominil looked around at her companions. "I will engage with Distikka. I doubt she'll give anything away. But I will at least keep her occupied, giving the others a chance."

She looked down at her feet. "These high heels are uncomfortable and impractical. Now, is everyone clear on their mission?"

CHAPTER 87

The Fire Queen made her first foray into the room outside, where she immediately encountered her rival.

"Kabachetka! How splendid to see you here. I had no idea you would be attending."

"Really?" replied the Empress very civilly. "I am the sponsor, you know."

"I had not noticed."

"Perhaps the Queen is tired these days, and does not notice things so well."

Malveria kept smiling. "I do notice that my former adviser is lurking behind you, Empress, though I hardly recognize her in a dress. How fare you, Distikka? Have you been busy since you tried to overthrow me?"

Distikka bowed to the Fire Queen. "Greetings, Fire Queen. The attempted coup was terrible, was it not? An insane idea by General Agripath. I tried my best to dissuade him."

"Very likely, I'm sure. Despite having no involvement, you felt the need to flee to Kabachetka?"

"No doubt because I am more generous," said the Empress.

"The Fire Queen is famous for her lavish generosity," said Malveria. "Generosity of her hips, perhaps."

"What did you say? Why, I'll . . . " The Fire Queen stepped forward angrily. She felt herself delicately restrained by a hand on her shoulder. Dominil stepped forward, not wanting a fight to erupt that would interfere with her plans for espionage.

"Ah," said the Empress. "One of Thrix's singular models."

"Thrix's show was a great triumph, was it not?" said the Queen.

"I favored another designer," said the Empress sniffily.

"But the audience did not."

"The audience may have been swayed by the collection of strange and freakish models. The clothes were very ordinary."

"Thrix's clothes are most superior, as you have learned to your cost."

"I believe I've seen you before," said Dominil to Distikka, interrupting the Fire Queen and the Empress.

"That is unlikely," replied Distikka.

"In the Courtauld Gallery."

"Ah. That would be possible. And you are?"

"Dominil MacRinnalch."

Distikka nodded, as if recognizing the name.

Dominil indicated a vacant table. "Would you care to discuss the gallery?"

Distikka looked carefully at Dominil for a moment or two. "Why not?" she replied. They sat down together, leaving the Fire Queen and the Empress to insult each other in their politest voices.

"So you are Dominil MacRinnalch," said Distikka. "I've heard several things about you. I understand you're not the most popular of werewolves."

"That's true."

"And you're intelligent and scientific."

"Yes."

They paused while a waiter arrived. Distikka accepted two glasses of champagne from his tray and gave one to Dominil. Around there was a bustle of activity as preparations were made to auction the clothes that had been on display.

"Isn't it strange, being scientific and also being a werewolf?" asked Distikka.

"What do you mean?"

"As I understand science on your planet, it doesn't believe in werewolves."

"It does not," agreed Dominil. "But no doubt there is a scientific explanation. We just haven't found it yet."

"And Fire Elementals?"

"Likewise."

Distikka laughed. "I doubt that the scientists at CERN are ever going to find an explanation for the Empress Kabachetka and Queen Malveria."

"No doubt all these beings can eventually be explained," said Dominil.

"Perhaps as part of a grand unification theory," said Distikka.

"I didn't expect to meet a Fire Elemental with a knowledge of particle physics."

"I like to read. I have wide interests. But so do you, Dominil. From computers to Latin poetry."

Dominil looked at her companion carefully. "You seem to know a great deal about me."

"Our intelligence services are very efficient. You're quite a talented artist too."

"What of it?"

"It's unusual for one person to have all these attributes. And here you are as a model. Another talent."

"I wouldn't say being a model was much of a talent," said Dominil.

"Neither would I. But people make a living from it. You made quite an impression." Distikka looked down at herself. "I don't like wearing this dress."

"Then we have something in common," said Dominil. "I don't like my high heels."

"Are you any closer to finding the Guild's headquarters?"

It was an abrupt change of subject. Dominil didn't react, but Distikka knew she'd surprised her.

"It's obvious to me that you came here to learn the whereabouts of the Avenaris Guild."

"Is it?"

"Yes. It seems like a hopeless endeavor, but I can see why you attempted it. The Guild has gained the upper hand. You can't fight back if you can't find them." Distikka looked around her coolly. "Who are you targeting? Kabachetka? Gezinka?"

"I'm targeting you," said Dominil.

"Ah. Well, that would make sense. I do know the address of the Guild's headquarters. But I'm not going to tell you."

"Why not?"

"Why would I?"

"They mean nothing to you."

Distikka considered this. "True. But the Empress is keen for them to succeed and, for the moment, I'm reliant on the Empress's goodwill."

"How unfortunate for you," said Dominil. "Lackey to a foolish creature like Kabachetka? Don't you think you should be doing something more worthwhile?"

It was Distikka's turn to fall silent. She rallied quickly. "Having burned my bridges with the Hiyasta, rather spectacularly, I must live with the Hainusta. As the Empress's guest, I need to remain on her good side."

There was a faint trace of a sneer on Dominil's face. "I wouldn't do it."

"Really? And what would you do?"

"I'd live quietly in poverty rather than be a servant to some idiotic Empress."

"I had quite enough poverty in my youth. But we seem to be straying from the point."

"If the point is the location of the Avenaris Guild," said Dominil, "you already insisted you weren't going to tell me."

"I presume I'm not your main target. No doubt your companions are also trying to learn the address. They won't succeed."

They sat in silence for a while, sipping champagne. The auction had begun, and there was some excitement in the room as bids were made.

"The Courtauld Gallery is a fine place," said Distikka. "I was entranced by Degas's sculptures."

"I like them too."

"It's a pleasure to meet someone so intelligent and civilized." Distikka leaned over the table. "You should abandon this. All the werewolves will end up dead, including you."

Dominil leaned forward. "Perhaps all the werewolf hunters will end up dead instead. And their helpers."

Distikka smiled. When she smiled, which was rarely, she looked very young, with her short hair and small stature. "I like you, Dominil. But I'll kill you if you get in my way."

"I'll kill you if you get in my way."

"I'm disappointed."

"That I'll kill you?" asked Dominil.

"No. That you didn't also say you liked me."

"I like very few people, Distikka."

CHAPTER 88

Moonglow was pleased that all of her friends had managed to model successfully. No one had plummeted from the runway or attacked the audience. She counted that as a success. William was less impressed. He'd looked on askance as Kalix marched angrily down the catwalk.

"Is that blood on her arm?"

"Probably just scratched herself on a zipper," said Moonglow.

"She looks like she's about to kill someone."

"She can be a bit temperamental," admitted Moonglow.

"What's she like to live with?"

"Fine. Always has a good word for everyone. And she's very helpful around the house."

William had looked dubious.

"She's a good model," said Moonglow. "She looks really beautiful."

"Maybe."

"*Maybe?* She is."

"I suppose so," said William. "But when I'm on a date I've never found it wise to describe anyone else as beautiful."

Moonglow laughed. "I think it's OK on this sort of pretend date."

"All right," said William. "She is really beautiful. But I'm not sure I'd like to share a flat with her."

They watched as Vex appeared, careering cheerfully down the runway. She'd made a lot of effort with her hair, bleaching, spiking and teasing it out. Under the spotlights her dark features appeared to be surrounded by a halo of light.

"It's like a bleached afro," said William. "You don't often see that."

Next Dominil strode down the runway.

"Your designer friend certainly knows how to pick models that stand out from the crowd," said William. "How long does it take her to make herself look like that?"

"No time at all," said Moonglow. "Dominil looks like that naturally."

"Even the white hair?"

"Yes."

"Do they all come from some family of beautiful vampires or something?"

"I like Thrix's clothes designs," said Moonglow, hastily changing the subject.

William had liked them too, and they were in a quite animated discussion about current fashion when William suddenly paused and looked around.

"My mother's bound to appear soon. She'll pretend she has some reason, but really she'll be wanting to check you out."

"I'm sure your mother isn't as bad as you make out," said Moonglow.

"Wait till you meet her. She can be intimidating."

"Is she worried I might get my claws into the family fortune?" asked Moonglow. She meant it in good humor, but William looked embarrassed.

"Among other things. She never seems to approve of any girlfriend I pretend to have."

"It will be fine," said Moonglow confidently.

"I hope so. Meeting my mother on a first date is a lot to ask. Especially as you've come here for a different reason."

"What?" said Moonglow.

"The man you were trying to meet?"

Moonglow had been having such an enjoyable time with William that she'd forgotten she'd pretended her reason for coming to the ball was to meet someone she thought would be here.

"Right. I don't think he's here yet. Probably he'll just turn up for the ball. He's a keen dancer." Moonglow bit her lip and wondered why she'd said that.

"William, there you are." William's mother arrived at the table having successfully maneuvered her way toward them without being observed. She was younger looking and more glamorous than Moonglow had expected. She was slender, her hair was very blonde, and she wore an elegant white evening gown and a diamond necklace.

"Are you going to introduce me?" she asked.

"This is Moonglow," said William, standing up.

"Moonglow?" said William's mother. "Such an unusual name. William, could you please pop backstage for me? I forgot to bring my bag, you'll find it at the table with my name on it."

"Uh . . . Do I . . . " William hesitated to leave Moonglow, but could find no reason not to go. "I'll be as quick as I can," he said.

"No rush," said his mother. "I always enjoy having a little chat with your girlfriends."

CHAPTER 89

As Dominil had predicted, there was tight security around the ball. The hotel entrance was a narrow space, easily guarded, but the extensive gardens at the back leading down to the River Thames required more protection. The organizers had hired a large group of uniformed security guards who had already turned back several uninvited guests and kept a watchful eye on all river traffic.

Decembrius waited till dusk, then slunk into the bushes at the edge of Victoria Embankment. He emerged as a werewolf, in the shadows of the ancient Prince Henry's Tower. The tower was solid, black and smooth, and appeared unscalable. Decembrius studied the edifice.

I might make it to the top, he thought. He was a skillful climber. As a werewolf he'd scaled many tall buildings. But I might not.

He took a coin from his pocket and turned it over in his fingers. *I'm sure this isn't going to work.*

Decembrius pressed the coin to the wall and spoke the words the Enchantress had told him to say: "Minerva's silver ladder."

Tiny tendrils of wispy gray smoke emerged from the coin, forming themselves into a ropelike ladder which quickly grew until it reached the top of the tower.

How about that, thought Decembrius. Thrix's sorcery is actually useful for something besides designing clothes.

The strands of the ladder were thin and translucent, almost invisible in the darkness. Decembrius began to climb. The sorcerous ladder felt wispy and insecure, but he reached the top without incident.

"Ladder disappear," he said. The ladder vanished. Decembrius turned his attention to the gardens below. As yet there was no one there apart from the security men, most of whom were concentrating on the river. Beneath him, the inner face of the tower sloped gently to the ground. There were many ridges and ledges, making it an easy descent. He dropped into the gardens.

"Time to prowl."

Decembrius disappeared into a thick clump of bushes, protected by his dark red werewolf pelt, and made his way toward a tree. With an athletic leap, he pulled himself into the lower branches, climbed higher, then settled down to watch. He looked over toward the rear of the hotel. The thought of Kalix modeling clothes made him smile. He knew she'd hate it. His smile disappeared quickly. The depression over Kalix hadn't lifted. One reason he'd agreed to stand guard was simply the opportunity of seeing her. Decembrius wasn't happy to acknowledge this to himself but he knew it was true.

As if it wasn't bad enough that I've been whining to everyone, including my mother, about Kalix, now I seem to have moved on to actually stalking her. It's pathetic.

Decembrius shook his head. He really couldn't believe he'd talked to his mother about Kalix. He gazed at the hotel, imagining the ball.

She's probably in there with her boyfriend. She'll come into the gardens, she'll know I'm here and she'll think I'm following her. I should have told Dominil I didn't want to do this.

Not, Decembrius reflected, that he had much else to do. His life seemed to be empty these days. Like certain other MacRinnalchs, Decembrius wasn't clear how to move forward. He lay on a branch, hidden in the shadows, safe from observation, and waited for something to happen. He wasn't really expecting the werewolf hunters to turn up, but if they did he wouldn't mind. Decembrius did not go looking for fights, but he had no hesitation in joining one if necessary.

And after that I'd still be unhappy about Kalix, he thought, and growled softly to himself.

CHAPTER 90

"Wasn't it great being models?" Vex had enjoyed the whole experience.

Kalix shuddered. "I'm never doing it again. I need some fresh air. I'm going out to the gardens."

"You can't. We have to seduce Bakmer."

Kalix scowled. "Stop saying 'seduce.' We don't have to seduce anyone. We just have to spy."

"OK, we've got to spy on Bakmer."

"I'm too stressed. I need to escape for a while."

"I thought this mission was really important for werewolves?"

"It is. But . . . " Kalix suddenly felt hopeless. Everything was feeling too difficult, and her anxiety was still at a high level.

"Come on," said Vex. "It's not that bad."

The young Fire Elemental placed her hand on the back of Kalix's neck. Kalix felt a very small amount of heat spread into her body.

"What was that?"

"Hiyasta healing power," said Vex. She looked pleased with herself. "I've been practicing on flowers. Do you feel better?"

"Uh . . . " Kalix had hardly felt anything, but she appreciated Vex's effort and didn't want to be rude. "A bit better. All right, let's go and look at this Bakmer," she said. "But I don't know how we're meant to learn anything. Everyone we're spying on seems to know we're spying on them."

"I thought that might be a problem too," said Vex. "But every time anyone said anything Dominil just said we were to use our initiative. How's your initiative?"

"Useless."

They passed through the curtain, out into the busy room where the auction was in progress. Vex spotted Adviser Bakmer immediately. He was younger than Kalix had expected, appearing to be no more than thirty. His evening dress suited him well, but as he sat on his own, he looked ill at ease.

"Have you met him before?" asked Kalix.

"No. But I've seen him at some events. Let's go."

"Wait," Kalix said urgently. "We don't have a plan yet!"

"Is there any chance of us thinking of a good plan?" asked Vex.

"No."

"Then let's go."

"I feel conspicuous," said Kalix. She was abruptly conscious of her clothes. Her tiny shorts left her legs bare. Her arms were uncovered too, and though she'd stopped the bleeding by putting a plaster over her latest cut, she was keenly aware that it must look conspicuous.

"Everyone else is in ball gowns and we're wearing shorts and tie-dyed vests."

"Well, that's good," said Vex. "We look like models. Everyone likes models."

"Do they?"

"Of course, if they're young and pretty like us."

Kalix suddenly felt ashamed that she was hanging back while Vex was urging them on. She should be doing her best, even if she was quite certain they wouldn't succeed.

"OK," she said. "Let's go."

They hurried across the room, dodging waiters and trying not to interfere with the clothes auction. Without waiting to be invited, Vex sat down next to the adviser.

"Hi," she said. "You look a bit miserable. We've come to cheer you up."

"I know you. I've seen you before. You're a Hiyasta."

"That's right," said Vex. "Is there anything you want to talk about?"

"I don't think I should be talking to you," said Bakmer. "The Empress wouldn't like it."

Vex grinned at him. "She wouldn't mind. Just pretend we're ambassadors at court. Ambassadors are always telling each other stuff, right?"

Bakmer eyed Vex suspiciously. "Are you spying on me?"

"Absolutely not. We're not looking for any sort of information. Unless there's something you really want to tell us."

Vex pressed herself close to Bakmer. Kalix cringed. The ball hadn't even started yet and already they were the worst spies in history.

CHAPTER 91

William retrieved his mother's handbag as swiftly as he could. He was quite certain that she'd sent him to fetch it merely as a way of interviewing his date in private. He was worried she might already have scared Moonglow away, but arrived back to find them talking quite happily together.

"Here's your bag."

"Thanks, William. It was so careless of me to forget it. I've been having an interesting chat with Moonglow. You didn't tell me she was such a good student."

"Right . . . I didn't think you'd be interested."

"Of course I'm interested. You never talk about your degree course." William's mother rose gracefully. "I'll leave you alone. The ball will start any minute and I have to make sure the Princess is in position. William, you must invite Moonglow for lunch. I insist you bring her over to meet the family."

William's mother departed. William looked at Moonglow.

"How did you do that?"

"What?"

"Make her like you so quickly? She's never insisted I invite anyone for lunch before."

"I talked about exams and studying," said Moonglow. "I told her about the good marks I'd been getting."

William looked puzzled. "And she was impressed by that?"

"Of course. Mothers always like anyone who's studying hard and working for a good degree. Didn't you know that?"

"No."

"What did you think she was worried about? Family connections?"

"Yes."

Moonglow put her hand over William's. "She just wants you to end up with someone with some ambition."

"That might explain why she never liked any of my other dates," said William. He was cheered by Moonglow's success with his mother, and ordered a bottle of champagne from a waiter.

"Are you sure I can't buy you any clothes? The auction's almost finished. Look, these are great shoes."

"They are nice," agreed Moonglow. "But no, you can't buy me them. Why are you suddenly looking sad? I can manage without new shoes."

"It's not that," said William. "I just realized that my mother liking you doesn't really get me any further forward. With her not knowing I'm gay, I mean."

"Yes, that's still a problem."

The waiter appeared with their bottle of champagne. After depositing it on the table, he leaned over to speak discreetly in Moonglow's ear.

"A lady with white hair asked me to give you this."

Moonglow accepted a folded napkin. She glanced inside. It contained an electronic room pass and a note from Dominil. "Distikka's room— 438. Search it while I keep her busy."

"I have to leave for a few minutes. I'll be right back." Moonglow left swiftly and was almost out the room before she considered what she was doing. *I'm about to break into a hotel room. Is that illegal? Am I going to be arrested?* Well, thought Moonglow, she had insisted on coming and joining in with the espionage mission. She wasn't going to back out of it now. Excited and slightly fearful, Moonglow headed for the corridor, where she asked an employee for directions before taking the lift to the fourth floor.

The Fire Queen approached Thrix at the end of the clothes auction. "Enchantress, it has gone splendidly so far, yes? I saw your clothes sell for great amounts. Once more, your designs have triumphed." Malveria studied her features in one of the mirrors that had not yet been cleared from the backstage area. "I am looking fabulous in every way, am I not?"

It was true. The Fire Queen was looking fabulous. Her pale blue evening gown set off her bare shoulders quite perfectly. Her long hair displayed subtle hints of a warm dark red, an effect the Fire Queen had been practicing for a long time, in which she allowed the merest hint of her internal fire to flow into her tresses.

"One expects to turn heads, of course. But tonight I have the advantage of this supreme gown, my extra-high heels and lip coloring that cannot be faulted."

The Fire Queen frowned. Thrix seemed to be lacking in enthusiasm. "Despite the success of your clothes, and my fabulous appearance, you seem dissatisfied. Why is this?"

"I'm frustrated because I'm not doing anything."

Thrix pointed discreetly to the far side of the room, where Dominil still sat with Distikka. "Dominil's already matching intellects with Distikka. Daniel's gone off looking for Lady Gezinka. Even Vex and Kalix are . . . uh . . . "

They looked over to another table where Vex was wiping champagne off Adviser Bakmer after spilling it on his shirt, while Kalix attempted to mop the table with a napkin.

"Well, I'm sure they're doing their best."

"I also am busy," declared the Fire Queen. "Even now I am monitoring Kabachetka, and have prevented her from likewise monitoring our progress. Our sorcery is struggling for supremacy, and I will not falter."

"I don't seem to be doing anything," said Thrix.

"And that is just what I have come to talk to you about. Your target, the werewolf hunter Mr. Eggers, will shortly be arriving. I overheard Kabachetka mention it."

Thrix's eyes flashed. "Now I'm feeling better. Mr. Eggers? He's a senior member of the Guild."

"The timing is splendid. The ball is about to start. You may dance with Mr. Eggers, and learn his secrets."

"I was thinking more of just killing him."

"Dearest Thrix, you know that will not do," said the Fire Queen sternly. "You need information from this man. And you are golden and splendid. How can he resist?"

Thrix checked her own appearance in the mirror. "I'm not all that confident about these hair extensions."

The Fire Queen assured her they looked natural, and also splendid. "As they should, given the amount of sorcery we worked over them."

"Yes," said Thrix. "Don't mention that to Dominil. She'll accuse me of being frivolous. Again."

They turned toward the crowd in the room, many of whom were now rising from their tables.

"Moonglow is searching Distikka's room," said the Fire Queen. "Dominil sent her, which I enabled her to do by briefly distracting Distikka. The espionage is all underway, Enchantress."

They walked elegantly toward the marble pillars at the door.

"Nothing will distract me from this mission," said the Fire Queen. "The foul Empress Kabachetka will not succeed in seducing the handsome Mr. Dewar."

"Pardon?"

"Mr. Dewar. Did I not mention him? He is the features editor at *Vogue*, and part of the Empress's party. Kabachetka has her eye on him, but I fancy he would do better with me."

"I thought you were focused on our mission?"

"My task is mainly to distract the attention of the Empress, is it not? Rescuing Mr. Dewar from her dreaded clutches will certainly divert her attention. Really, Enchantress, I can see this night being a memorable one, for many reasons."

CHAPTER 92

Daniel changed into evening dress, which he'd hired. Dominil had provided him with the money. He examined himself in the mirror, mentally checking off everything—black jacket, black trousers, black silk bow tie, black waistcoat, white dress shirt, black socks and black patent leather shoes.

"I look strange." He wished that Moonglow were there to encourage him, but she was busy elsewhere. Daniel felt a familiar chill at the thought of Moonglow on a date. He hoped it was going badly.

Daniel had been given the task of approaching Lady Gezinka, Kabachetka's secretary. He had a sense of impending doom, which had not been helped by Vex informing him that Gezinka was regarded as stern and unfriendly.

How am I meant to seduce a stern, unfriendly Fire Elemental? Dominil has a lot more confidence in my initiative than me.

Through the huge marble door he could see that the ballroom was filling up. All the men wore evening dress. At least he wouldn't stand out.

Except they're all used to it, he thought. Probably I look like someone wearing it for the first time.

Kalix emerged from the ballroom, head down and moving rapidly. Daniel intercepted her. "Kalix, do I look all right?"

"Can't stop."

"Have you seen this Gezinka woman?"

"She just sat down with Vex and Bakmer. I have to go."

"Where?"

"Gardens," said Kalix. "Nervous. Feeling sick."

With that, Kalix departed quickly. Daniel walked past several liveried attendants as confidently as he could and entered the ballroom. He was struck by the size of the room and the magnificence of the decor. It was brighter than he'd expected, with pale blue walls and white marble columns, a light gray floor and tables round the walls with white covers and white candles in silver candelabras. Everything seemed to be gilded, from the edges of the chairs to the frieze high up on the walls, illuminated by series of golden chandeliers.

No one was dancing yet, but there were clusters of people everywhere and it took Daniel a while to spot his target. Vex was sitting with two people who he presumed were Bakmer and Gezinka. He advanced hesitantly.

Now this feels even weirder. There are three Fire Elementals at the table. What if they're all talking about Fire Elemental stuff? I'll be left out.

Although, as Daniel studied his target, it didn't seem as if Lady Gezinka was talking about anything. She was indeed stern-faced. She looked around thirty years old, though Daniel knew that looks were no real indication of an elemental's age. When Daniel first met the Fire

Queen, he'd thought she was in her twenties, but she was hundreds of years old, possibly thousands.

I don't like the way she's sitting rigidly in that chair, thought Daniel. Nothing good ever comes from sitting as rigidly as that.

Gezinka was not unattractive, though she had neither the youthful beauty of Agrivex nor the overwhelming glamour of the Fire Queen. There was nothing otherworldly about her. Here in the ballroom she appeared to be simply a thirty-year-old woman, Indian perhaps, or North African, who'd dressed properly for a formal dance but was rather bored with the proceedings.

Daniel realized he'd come to a halt. He reprimanded himself. *It's time to stop dithering. I have a mission.*

He took a step forward. *I'm not very good at talking to women I don't know. And this is even worse. What am I meant to say?*

His nerve deserted him. He turned and walked rapidly in the opposite direction.

"Is there a bar near here?" he asked one of the liveried attendants.

"Waiters will come to your table, sir."

"I know. But is there a bar near anyway?"

The attendant directed Daniel toward the nearest bar, of which there were several in the hotel. Close to the entrance, he almost bumped into Moonglow. He was relieved to see she wasn't with her date.

"Moonglow, I need help! I don't know what to say to Gezinka."

"I'm in a hurry, I've got a mission. Just talk to her normally."

"What about?"

"Anything."

"Like what? She won't have seen any of my favorite TV programs, will she? And she's probably never heard any death metal bands."

"Well, that's never really been a good subject anyway," said Moonglow. "Tell her you like her dress, that'll get you started."

With that, Moonglow hurried off. Watching her go, Daniel was struck by how much he liked her dress. He wished he'd told her.

This is hopeless. I can't talk to Lady Gezinka. Dominil should have thought of that before sending me on such a difficult mission. Her planning is useless. Daniel gratefully ordered a bottle of beer, but winced when he learned the price. It seemed like a staggering sum for a small bottle. He drank it down quickly, and ordered another.

CHAPTER 93

Moonglow kept her head down as she approached Distikka's room, hiding her face from the security cameras that, she feared, were recording her movements.

I never had to hide from security cameras before I met werewolves.

Moonglow knocked on the door of room 438. There was no reply. She produced the passkey but hesitated. *Am I really about to burgle a hotel room? I've never committed a crime before.*

Moonglow steeled herself, then opened the door to Distikka's hotel room. To her great relief, there was no one there.

"Search the room and get out quickly," she said to herself. Moonglow had no idea what she'd do if Distikka were to return while she was still in her hotel room. It didn't bear thinking about.

Dominil and Distikka were the last remaining couple in the west reception room.

"Everyone has gone through to the ball," said Distikka. "Perhaps you should join your companions?"

"I'm content to remain here."

"Really? You find me such good company?" Distikka laughed. "I think you're trying to detain me, Dominil. Probably because the Fire Queen is trying to study the contents of my room. You're wasting your time. The Empress has protected all our rooms. They can't be penetrated by sorcery."

"I do find you reasonable company," said Dominil. "It's a long time since I had a tolerable conversation about sculptures."

Distikka stood up. "Perhaps we can continue it later. But now I have a pressing engagement."

They bade each other a polite farewell. Dominil watched impassively as Distikka left the reception room. As soon as she was gone, Dominil took out her phone and composed a rapid text message to Moonglow, warning her that Distikka was coming. The Empress Kabachetka might have protected their rooms from sorcery but, as Dominil had anticipated, neither she nor her advisers were up to date with Earth's technology. It had not occurred to them that Dominil might be able to duplicate hotel passkeys.

✻

On the fourth floor of the hotel, Moonglow was methodically searching Distikka's room. Dominil had told her to look out for written material, any sort of note, diary and anything else of interest. Moonglow hurried through the small suite, checking cupboards, shelves and cabinets. She hadn't found anything of interest, apart from some chain mail hanging in a wardrobe.

Nothing so far, she thought. Where else might a diary be? What sort of secret place?

Moonglow decided to check under the mattress. She was just bending down to search when she heard a passkey being inserted in the door. The door swung open. Moonglow did the only thing possible under the circumstances and dived under the bed. She held her breath. Could a Fire Elemental like Distikka sense the presence of a human being? Moonglow didn't know. If she was discovered hiding under the bed, it was going to be the most embarrassing experience of her life.

Distikka and a man, whose voice Moonglow didn't recognize, were engaged in conversation as they entered the room. Beneath the bed, Moonglow could hear them quite clearly.

"So I'm not going to be able to talk to the Empress?"

"I'm afraid not. The Empress will not allow anything to distract her from the ball."

"Hardly worth me coming in that case."

"I wouldn't say that, Mr. Eggers. I have full authority in all matters relating to the MacRinnalch werewolves. I can bring you up to date, and I can give you some information you weren't expecting."

"What's that?"

"There are werewolves here tonight."

"What? Are you serious?"

Moonglow was startled by the vehemence in the man's voice.

"I am. Queen Malveria decided to infiltrate the ball, for her own reasons. She came in the company of Thrix, Dominil and Kalix MacRinnalch."

"What's the Empress doing about it?"

"The Empress won't risk causing trouble at her ball. Not with the editor of *Vogue* sitting beside her."

"So you're just planning on doing nothing?"

"The Empress has no obligation to do anything," said Distikka. "Werewolves are your business, not hers. The Empress has agreed to help you if she can. That's doesn't mean she's obliged to act every time a were-wolf shows its face."

"So are you telling me the Guild can't do anything either?"

There was a pause. Moonglow held her breath.

"Not exactly," said Distikka. "But the Empress won't appreciate any-thing happening that might cast her in a bad light. Violence in the hotel is out of the question."

"What about outside the hotel?

"That would be up to you," said Distikka.

"I should talk to Mr. Carmichael."

"Again, that is up to you. Would you mind accompanying me to the next suite? I have to send a message to Alchet, the Empress's handmaiden."

Moonglow heard them leaving. The moment they'd gone she rolled out from under the bed, intent on making a swift escape. She had a brief, rather irrelevant moment of worry about her evening gown.

I hope I haven't ruined it. But it seemed clean under the bed, she thought. Good cleaning staff.

Moonglow peeped out of the door. Seeing no one in the corridor, she fled toward the elevator. Realizing that waiting for it to arrive might be too risky, she hurried past and flung herself through the door that led to the stairs. Moonglow felt a sense of elation. Not only had she been spy-ing, she'd encountered the enemy, evaded them and escaped with valuable information

I knew I'd be a good spy, she thought, and hurried as quickly as she could to report her findings to Dominil.

CHAPTER 94

Kalix hurried into the gardens. They were empty, apart from two security men at the door and one young couple on a bench who were engaged in an embrace. Kalix avoided them. The grounds sloped down toward the river. Noticing that there were more security men at the perimeter, Kalix turned into the nearest clump of bushes. There she was sick, quite violently.

She wiped her mouth and stood up. Kalix was often sick. Sometimes stress brought it on. Sometimes the feeling that she'd eaten too much, though that was less frequent these days. Now that it had happened, she felt better. She wondered if she might slip further into the darkness and change into her werewolf shape for a few minutes, to regain her strength.

"You can never just act normally, can you?" came a voice, very unexpectedly.

"Decembrius! What are you doing here? Are you following me?"

"I knew you'd say that," said Decembrius. Still as a werewolf, he remained in the shelter of the bushes. Kalix thrust herself into the bushes, changing into her own werewolf shape.

"How dare you follow me?! Don't spy on me!"

"I wasn't spying on you. Dominil asked me to keep guard out here."

Kalix looked at him suspiciously. "She didn't tell us that."

"I can't help that. What's your problem? Too much wine already?"

"No," said Kalix angrily. "I just got nervous with so many people around."

"So you thought you'd be sick?"

"What if I did? It's none of your business."

"You really ought to sort yourself out," said Decembrius. "Is that blood on your arm?"

"Yes."

"You must have been a great model."

"I did all right."

They looked at each other quite hostilely.

"So how's the new boyfriend?" said Decembrius. "Good dancer?"

"What do you mean 'new boyfriend'?"

"The pretty boy."

"He's not here and it's none of your business anyway. I knew you'd been following me."

"I wouldn't waste my time," said Decembrius. "If you want to go out with a painter who looks like a little girl, that's your affair."

Kalix's eyes flashed. "He doesn't look like a little girl."

"Yes, he does."

"So what? Better than some stupid werewolf who just wants to fight all the time."

Decembrius laughed. "That's rich, coming from you, Violent Werewolf of the Year."

"Leave me alone," said Kalix. "And stop following me."

With that, Kalix retreated from the bushes, changing smoothly back to human. She felt refreshed from the brief change.

I wish Manny was here, she thought as she made her way back toward the hotel. That would show that idiot Decembrius.

They had an arrangement to meet tomorrow night. Kalix smiled. She still liked Manny a lot. She wanted this whole night to be over so she could forget about the MacRinnalchs and visit Manny in his small flat and watch television together. She already felt comfortable doing that.

Kalix noticed some odd looks from the security guards at the door as she went back inside. Because of her outfit, she supposed. She did stand out from all the other women in ball gowns. While Kalix wasn't all that keen on wandering round in her skimpy clothes, she was relieved that she hadn't been obliged to wear a long dress. She'd probably have tripped over it, or ripped it somehow. She made her way back through the west reception room, arriving at the door to the ballroom at the same time as Moonglow.

"Where's Dominil?" said Moonglow.

Kalix didn't know. At that moment Daniel arrived.

"Daniel, aren't you meant to be being nice to Gezinka?" said Moonglow.

"It took a short break to compose myself," said Daniel.

"And drink a few beers?"

"That as well."

The three of them entered the ballroom. At that moment the lights went up and there was a loud public announcement.

"The Princess Morozov."

Princess Morozov swept into the room, followed by several attendants. Younger and blonder than she had anticipated, she reminded Moonglow of William's mother. Everyone in the ballroom stood up.

"Time for the curtsey," whispered Moonglow. She did the required motion, quite well. Kalix's attempt was so hopeless that Daniel burst out laughing.

"That was the worst curtsey ever."

"You can't really do it wearing shorts," Kalix defended herself.

"Yours was good," said Daniel to Moonglow. "Now where's this Gezinka? I've got a handle on it now. It's like she's some lonely middle-aged lady and I'm just the sort of young man she needs to cheer her up. Why wouldn't she be pleased to meet me? I'm a model. I expect I'll just sweep her right off her feet."

"How many beers did you have?" asked Moonglow.

"Five. You wouldn't believe how expensive they were. Do you think

Dominil will reimburse me?"

"There's Dominil," said Moonglow, who'd spotted her white hair in the middle of the room. "I need to talk to her."

Daniel, Dominil and Moonglow advanced through the ballroom, ready to engage on the next part of their mission.

CHAPTER 95

Vex, by dint of her refusal to believe that anyone would be unwilling to talk to her, had succeeded in winning over Adviser Bakmer. Aided by liberal doses of champagne, they were now engaged in animated conversation, having bonded over the dullness of traditional Fire Elemental clothing.

"Can you believe how terrible the fire wrap is?" said Vex. "I had to wear one for my adoption ceremony. What a stupid uncomfortable garment!"

Bakmer, who had started his diplomatic career as a fashion adviser to Kabachetka, was sympathetic.

"They're so ugly! And what about the fire cloak? Terrible. I watched thirty young Hainusta receive their military commissions last week and all I could think was how ridiculous their cloaks were."

"I hate fire cloaks," agreed Vex. "Malveria might be all fashionable here, but when it comes to palace officials, ladies-in-waiting and beloved nieces, she's a real stick in the mud."

"The Empress is no better!" agreed Bakmer with feeling. "The antiquated outfits of her attendants are simply disgraceful."

Vex and Bakmer finished off the bottle of champagne and ordered another.

"I do love your boots," said Bakmer.

"Thrix designed them. So when does this dance get started?"

"Any moment," said Bakmer. "Here comes the Princess now."

"It's curtsey time," cried Vex, and stood up to curtsey enthusiastically, though not very well. Beside them, Lady Gezinka performed the move perfectly. Since joining them at the table, Gezinka had hardly spoken a word. She plainly did not approve of Vex, or, by the look on her face, of anything else. As the Princess took her seat, the orchestra began to play. Couples stood up to dance.

"There's Daniel!" screamed Vex. "Daniel, over here!"

Daniel was caught in the middle of the dance floor. He barged into several dancers as he made his way over, and sat down looking quite flustered.

"Hi, Daniel," cried Vex. "Gezinka, this is Daniel. He lives with me. He knows we're elementals. Daniel, see if you can cheer Gezinka up, she's looking a bit miserable."

Vex turned back to Bakmer. Daniel blushed. Lady Gezinka looked down her nose at him.

"I have not seen a man blush for a long time. In my land, it is not done."

"It happens to me quite a lot," admitted Daniel.

Unexpectedly, Lady Gezinka smiled. "You live with Agrivex?"

Daniel nodded. "We're flatmates. There are four of us."

"That must be . . . trying."

"It is, sometimes. And crowded. But it's quite cheerful as well."

Lady Gezinka turned to examine Vex for a moment, then spoke again to Daniel. "I cannot imagine what your life is like. You say it is crowded?"

"It's quite a small flat."

"What is 'flat'?"

"Like a house. But smaller. We live above a shop."

"How strange. What does it sell?"

"Nothing, it's been boarded up since we got there. Where do you live?"

"In the palace of the Empress Kabachetka."

"That sounds nice."

"It is," said Lady Gezinka. "Although . . . " She paused. "It can be . . . Never mind. I saw you modeling clothes, is that something you normally do?"

"No, I was just doing it as a favor. I'm a student."

Daniel wasn't finding it nearly as difficult to talk to Lady Gezinka as he'd imagined. He seemed to have broken the ice by blushing. Which, he remembered without much pride, had also served him well the first time he'd encountered Queen Malveria. Elemental ladies seemed to find it amusing.

Dominil and Thrix listened closely as Moonglow described the events in Distikka's room.

"So, Mr. Eggers is here," said Dominil. "Thrix, it's time for you to go into action. I wonder if he will indeed call for assistance?"

Thrix and Dominil had both thought it unlikely that they'd encounter other hunters, knowing that the Empress wouldn't want the ball to become a battleground. In the light of Moonglow's report, they were no longer quite so sure.

"I'll find out if any more are on the way," said Thrix. "And I'll warn Decembrius to be alert."

"I wonder how Distikka intended to transmit a message to the handmaiden Alchet, given that she's in the Empress's palace?"

"Perhaps she's just traveling back there," said Thrix.

"From Moonglow's report, it sounded more like there was some sort of communicating device. Is that possible?"

"Maybe, given how powerful the Empress is."

They were standing at the side of the ballroom, which had now come alive with dancers. The level of music and conversation had increased. Dominil leaned closer to talk to Thrix, but was interrupted by a gentle tap on her shoulder. She turned round to find a young man in evening dress looking at her admiringly.

"Would you like to dance?"

"Not at this moment."

"I saw you model. I thought you were terrific."

"Thank you."

"You were the best model. Would you like to dance?"

"No."

Dominil turned back to Thrix.

"Maybe later," said the young man, before going away disappointed.

"Perhaps you should have accepted the invitation," said Thrix. "He looked rich."

"I didn't come here to meet a rich man. Or to dance." Dominil pursed her lips, considering her next move. "I think it's time to visit the Empress's suite."

"Do you want me to come with you?" asked Thrix.

"No. You should look for Mr. Eggers and any potential threat from hunters. Provided Queen Malveria continues to occupy the attention of the Empress, I believe I can visit her rooms safely."

Kalix appeared. "Decembrius is here! Is he following me?"

"No," said Dominil. "I asked him to stand guard."

"Well, I don't like it."

"Have you made any progress with Adviser Bakmer?"

"No. I had to go outside." Kalix noticed her sister sneering at her. "What's the matter with you?"

"It never takes long for you to mess things up, does it? You overdosed in Scotland and got Minerva killed. And you've hardly been here five minutes and you're outside throwing up."

Kalix was stunned by the unexpected attack. Since the beginning of Dominil's plan there had been an uneasy truce between them. Apparently, with the modeling now over, Thrix had reopened hostilities.

"Stop saying I got Minerva killed!" she shouted, raising her voice above the music.

"Why? You did."

"No, I didn't!"

"Stop arguing," said Dominil brusquely. "Thrix, you should look for Mr. Eggers. Kalix, come with me. I need your help."

Dominil led a fuming Kalix away from Thrix.

"Where are we going?"

"To break into the Empress's rooms."

"What about Bakmer?"

"Vex is doing well with him at the moment. Meanwhile—"

They were interrupted by two young men who accosted Dominil, wondering if she might like to dance. At the same instant another younger man, possibly a student, attempted to talk to Kalix, though he seemed rather tongue-tied and only managed to blurt out how much he'd liked her when she walked down the catwalk. Dominil brushed them aside and dragged Kalix on.

St. Amelia's Ball had now come to life. The dance floor was full and the corridors outside the ballroom were busy. There was a constant coming and going of guests between the dance, the rooms upstairs and the gardens outside. Girls laughed, men attempted to look gallant in their evening clothes, waiters carried trays of champagne, a few older heads discussed business in corners and, somewhere in the middle of it all, Queen Malveria vied with the Empress Kabachetka for supremacy.

"Did I really get Minerva killed?" asked Kalix as she followed Dominil up the stairs.

"No. But it might be said you made a contribution."

"Oh," said Kalix.

The fourth floor was quieter but there were still people around, mainly women hurrying back to their rooms to make adjustments to their dress.

Two fair-haired girls of no more than nineteen went past them, searching in their handbags and laughing about something.

"I'm going into the Empress's suite," said Dominil. "If the Empress or Distikka appears, delay them."

"How? OK, I know, use my initiative."

Dominil took out a plastic passkey and slipped into the Empress's room. Kalix stood for a moment, then walked slowly down the corridor.

It was rare for Kalix to think about being a werewolf. Having been born that way, it was completely natural, and not a topic for introspection. But she did think, as she wandered down the corridor, that this was a very unusual situation for anyone to be in. Here she was, at the debutantes' ball, surrounded by rich young women in ball gowns, wearing a tiny little outfit designed by her sister, whom she hated, strolling down a corridor in the most expensive hotel in London, pretending to be nonchalant while actually standing guard for her cousin, who was at that moment burgling the room of a powerful Fire Elemental from another dimension.

And we're all werewolves, thought Kalix, suddenly contrasting her life to that of everyone else at the ball. This has to be one of the strangest things that's ever happened anywhere to anyone.

"Oh, it's the model!" boomed a voice behind her.

Kalix whirled round to find herself confronted by a man of around forty who'd accessorized his evening dress with quite an extravagant aquamarine scarf.

"I've been hoping to meet you!"

"You have?"

The man's hair was rather longer than normal for a man of his age. It was turning gray prematurely, but stylishly. He whipped out a business card and thrust it at Kalix.

"You were so fantastic on the catwalk! You must come and model for me!"

Quite puzzled by this development, Kalix looked blankly at the business card, and thought that everything had just become stranger.

CHAPTER 96

Dominil closed the door behind her. She found herself in a marble foyer. A door led to an office on her right. Straight ahead was the sitting room. Empress Kabachetka was staying in the Queen Victoria Suite, which the hotel claimed to be among the finest accommodations in the country. Dominil had studied pictures of the rooms on the hotel's website and knew what to expect. She knew there were eight windows with views of the Thames and the Houses of Parliament. There was a dining room, a kitchen and several bedrooms, all recently refurbished back to their original Edwardian style.

Dominil advanced into the huge sitting room. She took a moment to glance at a painting by George Clausen, but was otherwise unmoved by the luxuriance of her surroundings. There was no time to thoroughly search the suite. It was unlikely that the Empress would leave the ballroom, but she might send her staff to her rooms. Dominil didn't really expect that she'd find any useful documents there. The Empress wouldn't carry documents. The possibility of a portal to her own dimension was another matter. Dominil quickly examined the office, looked round the sitting room and living room, and glanced into the kitchen. Everything seemed normal. Outside she could see the dark gothic shape of the Houses of Parliament and the Thames below. She walked into the master bedroom, switching on the light.

This hotel is keen on chandeliers, she thought. There were clothes strewn untidily on the bed, and the dressing room door was open. Inside she found more clothes hanging neatly and a dresser covered with cosmetics. She noticed a small marble-topped table next to the dresser. On top of it was a flower arrangement and an object she couldn't put a name to. Some sort of jewel, which seemed to pulse with an internal light. Dominil studied it.

It doesn't come from this world, she decided quickly. Is this the communication device?

Dominil reached out her hand, but hesitated. For all she knew the jewel might suck her into some nether void. Or a volcano, perhaps.

Dominil shrugged. *It would be an interesting way to die.* She touched the jewel. Pale yellow streamed from the gem into the room, forming itself into a large oval disc, tall enough to step into. Through the pale disc she could see what appeared to be another room. It was opulent too, but dark red, with a black marble floor. From the otherworldly designs on the red tapestries, Dominil surmised that she was looking into a room somewhere in the Empress Kabachetka's realm. She heard footsteps. The sound was coming through the oval light.

Interesting, thought Dominil. The portal allows both light and sound to pass through. I wonder who's there?

A large, dark figure came into view. The figure turned toward the portal. A huge man, with long dark hair and a distinctive scar on his jaw. As he saw Dominil, his eyes opened wide with surprise. There was a long pause.

"Hello, Sarapen," said Dominil.

CHAPTER 97

Mr. Eggers contacted the Guild as quickly as he could. Reception for mobile phones in the hotel was unstable, so he used the line in Distikka's room to call Mr. Carmichael at home. Carmichael was as agitated as Eggers to learn there were werewolves at the ball.

"Kalix MacRinnalch is there?"

It was an astonishing piece of news. The Avenaris Guild had invested a huge amount of time and manpower searching for Kalix, without success. Now she'd turned up at an event organized by their ally, the Empress.

"What's Kabachetka doing, letting werewolves in?"

Mr. Eggers found it difficult to answer. Distikka had explained it to him but, as always, anything concerning Thrix was confusing for the hunters. Her spells of concealment were so strong that it was hard for an enemy even to remember her name.

"I don't know why Kalix is here, but she is. And another werewolf, the one with white hair." Mr. Eggers had some concerns for his own safety. He was a senior member of the Guild but had given up hunting many years ago. It was years since he'd shot a silver bullet. He didn't even have his gun with him.

"You said the Empress doesn't want trouble at her ball. Is she going to refuse entry to our men?" asked Mr. Carmichael.

Mr. Eggers wasn't certain. "Distikka insisted there couldn't be any trouble inside. But there are a lot of gardens between the hotel and the river. That's a possible entry point."

Mr. Carmichael rang off and began the process of deploying hunters. At short notice, this wasn't so easy. The Guild did maintain a round-the-clock presence at its headquarters, but the night commander told Mr. Carmichael that Group Sixteen wasn't in London, having gone off for a weekend of training in the countryside. Group Twelve, containing several senior hunters, wasn't available either.

"They're in Serbia for International Werewolf-Hunter Cooperation Week."

"Well, who is available?"

"Group Fifteen is on duty. But two of them have never been in action before."

Mr. Carmichael hesitated. Group Fifteen contained two newcomers and another hunter with limited experience. They did have an experienced leader, and he'd expressed optimism about his charges.

"We can't miss this opportunity. Send them to the hotel. Perhaps they can find an opening to attack. But emphasize it's a dangerous mission. They're not to take any chances."

The night commander acknowledged Mr. Carmichael's orders, and alerted Group Fifteen. There was a very hurried visit to the storerooms to stock up on silver bullets, while a logistics officer studied maps and looked for the best way to get the hunters close to their targets.

Mr. Eggers was reassured as he left Distikka's hotel room. Hunters were on their way. He wondered what he could do to help. Could he somehow lure Kalix outside? If he could isolate her in the gardens, Group Fifteen would have a good chance of killing her. He hurried along to the lift. There he met a blonde-haired woman in a red evening gown. He was surprised to find that she was weeping. Mr. Eggers stood uncomfortably beside her as they waited for the lift. She turned toward him. Tears ran down her face from her beautiful blue eyes.

"My husband's gone off with that woman again!" she sobbed. Then, as if all her strength had gone, she leaned against Mr. Eggers, taking his arm for support. Mr. Eggers was nonplussed. Though he was busy with other matters, he felt a gallant desire to comfort her.

"I'm sure it will be all right," he said.

The woman cried even more. The lift arrived and she stumbled in. "I'm going to throw myself in the river," she wailed.

"You really mustn't do that," said Mr. Eggers anxiously. "These things generally sort themselves out, you know."

The blonde-haired woman sobbed and leaned against Mr. Eggers for support. She cried all the way to the ground floor, so that as the lift doors opened, Mr. Eggers wondered what he could possibly do to prevent her from throwing herself in the river, something he feared that she might really do, so upset did she seem.

CHAPTER 98

Moonglow had not been expecting to dance. She only faintly remembered the basic steps of the waltz, which, for some reason, mysterious to her at the time, she'd learned at school. William, however, was in high spirits, partly because he liked being in the grand hotel, and partly because he was having such an enjoyable time with Moonglow.

"You're a really great date," he told her. "Let's dance."

"I'm not sure I can."

"Look, it's crowded on the dance floor. Half these people are just shuffling round. We can do that."

It was true that many couples were not exhibiting a great deal of skill. Some of the young debutantes and their partners moved gracefully in time with the music, but there were others who seemed fairly inept. Young lovers, content just to hold on to each other, did no more than slowly rotate while resting their heads on each other's shoulder. While not exactly chaotic, it was all less formal than Moonglow had expected, and more cheerful. There were a lot of happy-looking people in evening dress on the dance floor.

"All right," said Moonglow. "Let's dance."

She followed William into the throng and put an arm round his waist and the other on his shoulder. She noticed that the muscles on his arms felt hard and strong. They danced easily together. Though they didn't know it, William's prediction that no one would notice them wasn't quite accurate. William was the son of a duke and heir to a large fortune, and several young women in the room wondered who the young woman in the black dress might be, because they'd never seen her before at any of their events. A few of their mothers asked William's mother about her. She told them truthfully that she didn't know the girl well, but had spoken to her, and liked her very much, and wouldn't mind at all if the romance was to flourish.

✴

The area around the Princess was a little less congested than the rest of the room. There the editor of *Vogue* and several other fashion luminaries sat with Empress Kabachetka. As sponsor of the ball, she was as important as she'd hoped she'd be. It would have been a great triumph, had the Fire Queen not been doing her best to ruin it. Not that Malveria was doing anything untoward. Her manners were perfect. She'd congratulated the Empress warmly on the success of the ball. She'd been a little pushy in introducing herself to the organizers as Thrix's assistant for the evening, but Thrix's clothes had been very well received, and it wasn't strange that one of her staff might want to introduce herself.

"Assistant indeed," hissed Kabachetka, turning to Distikka, who sat quietly at her side. "The Fire Queen could not assist in anything. Look at how ridiculous she appears on the dance floor."

Distikka didn't reply. The Fire Queen danced beautifully, even in her very high heels. Her evening gown clung to her lithe figure, and her long hair seemed to somehow glow under the chandeliers. Several men, previously arrested by the site of Kabachetka, now seemed more interested in observing Malveria.

"Have you noticed how she is flinging herself at poor Mr. Dewar?" said the Empress. "One trembles at the thought of her stepping on his foot and crippling him. Distikka, prepare to distract the Fire Queen."

"Pardon?" said Distikka.

"I must rescue Mr. Dewar from her clutches. There is no time to lose."

"I really don't think I know how to distract her," said Distikka.

"You will just have to do your best!" said the Empress sharply. "As no one else seems to be around. Where is the rest of my staff? I shall have harsh words for Bakmer and Gezinka."

The music ended with a flourish.

"Now is your chance," said the Empress. "Distract Malveria and be quick about it."

Distikka shook her head, but rose to her feet. She had not expected to enjoy the ball, and her expectations had proved accurate. She hated her ball gown, the ballroom and everyone in it. Apart from Dominil, whom she had rather liked.

I wonder what Dominil is doing now? she thought as she approached the Fire Queen.

CHAPTER 99

"Dominil!" Sarapen cried out in surprise. He walked toward the portal, but it wouldn't let him through. He took a step back. "Where are you?"

"I'm in a hotel in London," sad Dominil. "Where are you?"

"At the Empress Kabachetka's palace."

"Ah." Dominil nodded. "So the Empress took you there and revived you. I never considered that possibility."

"Why not?" demanded Sarapen.

"I believed you were dead."

"Why?"

"Because I went to your funeral."

Sarapen found this difficult to take in. He was already shocked by the sudden encounter with Dominil. The last time he'd seen her she was passing the Begravar knife to Kalix, just before his sister stabbed him.

"How could there be a funeral?"

"The Empress handed back your body. Which, I now perceive, was a fake. The Empress's sorcery has grown stronger since she ascended to the throne."

Sarapen growled. "It has." He tried to pass through the portal again but again it resisted him. "Is the Empress there?"

"She is," said Dominil. "But I don't have time to talk. I'm here on a mission."

"You don't have time to talk!" roared Sarapen. "If I could get through this portal I'd have some things to say to you! Like thanking you for the mortal wound!"

Sarapen abruptly changed into his werewolf form: huge, dark and terrifying.

"We were engaged in combat," said Dominil. "One of us was going to get a mortal wound. It happened to be you."

"If I could get back I'd repay the favor." Sarapen paused and suddenly changed back into his human form. He lowered his voice. "Would it be too much to expect you to express some emotion at finding me alive?"

"I admit to some surprise."

"That's it?"

"I'm really in too much of a hurry for anything else."

"Damn you, Dominil, I need your help."

"Why?"

"I'm trapped here. The Empress says I'll die if I return to Earth. I don't believe her, but I can't get back. There's no way for me to travel through dimensions."

"Why would I help you?"

"Because we used to be lovers. And I'm a MacRinnalch."

Dominil nodded. "That's a reasonable point. At least about you being a MacRinnalch. I would help you return if I could. When I'm finished here, I'll ask Thrix if she knows how it might be done."

"No!" roared Sarapen. "I refuse to take help from her. I'd rather die here. Let her think I'm still dead."

"I could consult the Fire Queen, though it may take longer. If I succeed in returning you, do you still plan on attacking me?"

Sarapen smiled grimly. "That would hardly be reasonable. I won't."

"You'll need to promise to leave Kalix alone too."

"What? She stabbed me. I'll kill her like she deserves."

"You'll leave her alone or I won't help you."

"You mean you'd leave me here, stuck in another dimension?"

"Yes."

Sarapen laughed. His mood seemed to have improved since encountering Dominil. "Very well. I'll leave Kalix alone too. But that's the last promise I'll make."

Dominil leaned toward the portal, testing it. She was unable to pass through. "How are your relations with the Empress?"

"Not good," said Sarapen. "I think she plans to get rid of me."

"I'm sure you can improve matters, at least for a while."

"You don't know what that would entail," said Sarapen.

"I can imagine exactly what it would entail. And I'd advise you to do it until I can find a way of rescuing you. Meanwhile, I wonder if you might be able to help me."

Dominil succinctly explained her current situation to her old adversary.

"The Empress is helping the Avenaris Guild?" Sarapen looked furious. "I didn't know that."

"Don't tell her you know. I don't want her learning anything of our plans. It would be more useful if you could find some information. This portal was left here for her handmaiden Alchet. Alchet must be somewhere close to you, and it's possible she may have knowledge of the Guild's location."

"How long do you have?" asked Sarapen.

"I might be discovered at any moment."

"I'll be as quick as I can." Sarapen disappeared from view, leaving Dominil thoughtful, though still apparently impassive.

CHAPTER 100

Mr. Eggers was comfortably married. He didn't have any notions of embarking on a romance with the blonde-haired woman he helped into the gardens, but he did feel a strong desire to assist her. He'd been completely taken in by a subtle spell of attraction and Thrix's acting abilities.

"Here we are," he said as they emerged from the hotel. He eyed the river in the background uneasily, remembering the woman's talk of suicide.

"Thank you," said Thrix. "I'm sorry I've been such a bother. Could you help me over to that bench beside the bushes? It's so embarrassing to be crying like this in front of all these people."

The gardens were now busy. Groups of friends emerged from the hotel, talking and laughing, a few of them quite raucously. Here and there people lit up cigarettes in the open air. Mr. Eggers led Thrix over to a vacant bench at the side of the grounds, well away from the crowds. She sat down.

"Thank you," she said. "You've been so helpful."

"It's nothing," said Mr. Eggers. "Are you feeling better? You're not still thinking of doing away with yourself are you?"

Thrix managed a small smile. "No. I'm sorry I said that. It was silly to get in such a state."

She dabbed her eyes with a lace handkerchief. Mr. Eggers was pleased to have helped a woman in distress, but he had his own business to attend to. He hovered awkwardly, unsure of what to say.

"I should . . . "

"Of course," said Thrix. "You have to get back inside. I'm so sorry to have dragged you away."

Thrix glanced around to check that they were unobserved. Then she rose, as if to bid Mr. Eggers farewell. Instead her hand shot out, fastening on to his collar. With strength that Mr. Eggers could not have predicted, she threw him into the bushes. Thrix leaped after him, and by the time she landed she'd changed into her werewolf form. She placed her golden paw on Mr. Eggers's throat and dragged him upright.

Mr. Egger's eyes widened in fear. "You're—"

"A werewolf. And you killed Minerva MacRinnalch."

Thrix slashed with the back of her hand. Her vicious claws tore the man's throat. Blood spurted from his neck and he fell down dead without a sound. Thrix was pleased, but not quite satisfied. She hauled his body upright, and then slashed again, almost decapitating the corpse. She let it drop to the ground. Thrix smiled, displaying her werewolf fangs.

"You're the first," she said.

Thrix looked through the bushes, toward the river. She imagined a target, floating in the air, just above the water. She looked down at Mr. Eggers's body, then spoke a few words. The body disappeared, reappearing over the river in the place Thrix had imagined her target. She released it over the water, and it sank from view.

Thrix changed back to human and emerged from the bushes with a smile on her face. A group of men, smoking cigarettes, looked at her admiringly as she walked past. She strode toward the river, halting as she sensed Decembrius, still in the shadows.

"It's a beautiful evening," said Thrix.

"Is it?"

"Yes. I just killed a hunter." Thrix laughed, rather unsettlingly. "I'm enjoying the ball much more than I expected."

"I'd wipe the blood off your hand if I were you," said Decembrius.

"I like it."

"Maybe. But if Daniel and Moonglow like playing at being spies, they won't like you killing people."

Thrix shrugged. "I suppose not. But it was their choice to get involved with werewolves."

"Who was the hunter?"

"Mr. Eggers. Senior member of the Guild."

"What did you learn from him?" asked Decembrius.

"Learn?"

"You're supposed to be spying, aren't you? What did you learn before you killed him?"

"He wouldn't say anything," said Thrix, sharply.

"Did he have any documents on him?"

"I don't think so."

Decembrius raised his eyebrows. "It sounds like you were in such a hurry to kill him you forgot to do anything else."

"I did the most important thing," said Thrix. She laughed.

"Why are you laughing?"

"Because I just killed a hunter. That always puts me in a good mood. Don't you feel the same?"

"Not really."

"Well, if you're looking for a miserable werewolf, my little sister is inside. Except you seem to have missed your chance with her."

"You're becoming less likeable all the time," said Decembrius.

"Gawain and Decembrius. Two stupid werewolves who thought they loved Kalix. And look what happened to Gawain. You should be pleased she ditched you while you were still alive."

Decembrius scowled. "Maybe you should just mind your own business."

"Kalix always becomes my business. And always in some bad way. Keep a good look out for hunters, there are probably more on the way."

Thrix departed. Decembrius slunk back into the bushes, retaking his werewolf form and climbing his lookout tree.

I'll keep a good lookout for you as well, Thrix MacRinnalch, he thought. As you seem to be getting less sane every day.

Thrix was still smiling as she made her way through the west reception room. She had barely advanced into the ballroom when she was accosted by the Fire Queen.

"Dearest friend, conceal your aura," said Malveria urgently.

"Pardon?"

"Your aura. It is most obvious to me that you have recently killed someone. It will be obvious to the Empress too."

"Right. I forgot." Thrix muttered a few words to herself, part of the process of concealing her aura.

"I presume it was a hunter, and not just a waiter who insulted you?"

"Malveria, my temper isn't that bad."

"It has been very bad recently."

"Well, I haven't been killing waiters. A senior member of the Avenaris Guild arrived to talk to Distikka. I disposed of him. Are you looking disapproving?"

"Not exactly. But I do not like to see you so savage on this occasion, which is full of glamour and excitement. Do not forget, your clothes were a great success. The editor of *Vogue* herself would tell you so were you to approach her, thanks to the excellent boost I've already given you. Mr. Dewar also liked them, though at this moment he has been cornered by the detestable Kabachetka. I am about to rescue him. Observe, Enchantress, as I lay waste to my rival's foolish hopes."

The Fire Queen quickly checked her appearance in a mirror. She adjusted the strap of her ball gown a fraction. "I thought it may be a risk, exposing so much of the regal shoulders. And indeed, several men have been overwhelmed and flung themselves at me, only to be disappointed. But it was worthwhile. There is seduction to be done, and all advantages must be brought into play."

CHAPTER 101

Kalix desperately hoped that no one appeared while she was on guard outside the Empress's hotel room.

What if Kabachetka or Distikka show up? she thought. How would I stop them going inside?

She could hardly change into a werewolf and fight them off. Guests could still be seen entering and leaving their rooms, and there were security cameras mounted discreetly on the walls.

Maybe I could fight them off without turning into a werewolf? But that's not going to look good anyway, struggling with the Empress in the middle of the corridor. I'm sure Dominil expects me to do something more clever. With my initiative.

Kalix was very worried about her initiative. *I'm going to mess everything up. I can feel it happening.*

Kalix was feeling very negative. She wished she had her journal with her so she could give herself bad marks in her self-improvement program.

I've failed in every category. I'm the worst self-improver ever. And now I don't have any initiative either.

Initiative hadn't been on Kalix's list of self-improvements, but she realized now that it should have been. *I'll have to add it so I can give myself bad marks.*

Kalix's gloomy introspection was interrupted by the electronic beep announcing the arrival of the lift. She looked on anxiously as the doors opened. There, about to step out into the corridor, was Distikka.

I can't let Distikka find Dominil in the Empress's room.

Kalix frantically searched for inspiration. None came. She could not think of any clever way of delaying Distikka. Cursing her lack of initiative, Kalix flung herself at the elemental. She tackled her round the waist and they both flew into the lift. Kalix pinned her to the floor. The doors closed, and the lift moved.

"What is this?" demanded Distikka. She was very strong, and Kalix struggled to keep her down. "Is this some ridiculous plot to keep me from our suites?"

"No," said Kalix.

"Are you planning on lying on top of me as we ascend from floor to floor?"

"Maybe."

"Other people will enter the lift."

Kalix frowned. She supposed they would. That was going to look strange. She released Distikka. Distikka leaped to her feet and looked furiously at the young werewolf.

"What's this about?"

"Nothing," muttered Kalix.

"Nothing? I wouldn't say it was nothing. I'd say you were violently trying to keep me from entering my room."

"No, I wasn't."

"Well, what were you trying to do?"

"Nothing," said Kalix. "I just slipped."

The lift halted at another floor. There was no one there. The doors closed and they carried on.

"I suppose Dominil put you up to this?" demanded Distikka.

"No."

"I can read your aura, you know."

"No, you can't," said Kalix.

"It's no use simply saying no to everything," said Distikka. "I can plainly tell that Dominil asked you to stand guard. No doubt as part of some plan."

"I don't know what you're talking about."

If Kalix lacked initiative, she did have a lot of experience in denying things, a talent she'd learned as a child at Castle MacRinnalch. As a very young werewolf, Kalix had flatly denied raiding both her father's whisky cabinet and her mother's medicine chest, though the evidence against her had been overwhelming. Even on the notorious occasion when she'd been rushed to hospital to have her stomach pumped, Kalix had never fully admitted she'd been guilty of anything.

The lift reached the top floor. A couple in evening dress entered. The lift began to descend.

"You can't keep me out of my room forever," whispered Distikka.

"I don't know what you're talking about," said Kalix, and attempted to look innocent. The lift halted at the next floor. The couple got out, leaving Distikka and Kalix alone.

Distikka studied Kalix for a few seconds. "The Empress greatly dislikes werewolves," she said. "You'll regret it if she catches you breaking into her suite."

"The Empress isn't here," said Kalix, just to keep Distikka talking.

"I can fetch her easily enough," replied Distikka. With that, she disappeared.

Kalix was alarmed. "I forgot elementals could do that." She began frantically pushing the buttons in the lift. "I have to warn Dominil before Kabachetka gets there."

Dominil still stood impassively in front of the portal of light. Sarapen had been gone for some minutes. She knew she was risking death by remaining there. She would have given herself a fair chance in a fight with any of the Empress's servants, but if the Empress herself returned, she would probably kill her. The ruling monarch of a Fire Elemental nation could call upon vast amounts of power, enough to burn Dominil to a cinder.

Dominil glanced at the clock on the mantelpiece. It was an original Edwardian piece, in keeping with the rest of the decor. She felt a vague sense of approval at the consistency of the furnishings. Nothing was out of place. Only a few minutes had passed since Sarapen departed. It felt like much longer.

Dominil's skin prickled. She had none of the powers of future-seeing claimed by certain werewolves, but she had a strong feeling that the Empress was on her way. She resisted the urge to look at the window again, and stood quite still, waiting for Sarapen to reappear.

Empress Kabachetka had warned her servants not to use their powers of teleportation in the hotel. None of them were used to being on the Planet Earth. It was quite likely that if they tried to teleport, they'd get lost, or end up transporting themselves into the middle of a concrete wall.

Nonetheless, Distikka took the risk and teleported out of the lift. She knew she couldn't reappear directly in the ballroom, but Distikka was wise enough to have prepared for such an emergency. Before the ball started, she'd found a small cupboard in an employees' washroom in the basement that looked as if it had not been used for some time.

She materialized silently in the cupboard, then emerged into the corridor. She hurried up the stairs in the direction of the ballroom. Once there, she made her way around the edges of the crowd. It took her a while to reach the Empress. Kabachetka had been waltzing with Mr. Dewar and was now leading him off the dance floor while keeping a watchful eye out for the Fire Queen. Malveria was no doubt lurking nearby, waiting for an opportunity.

Distikka appeared. "Empress, I need to talk to you."

"Did she just call you Empress?" asked Mr. Dewar.

"A family nickname," said Distikka smoothly, realizing her mistake.

"This is not a good time—" began the Empress.

Distikka whispered in the Empress's ear, for which she had to stand on tiptoe.

Empress Kabachetka frowned. "I see." She turned to her partner. "Mr. Dewar, I must attend to something. Please excuse me. I will be back as soon as I can."

With that, Empress Kabachetka and Distikka hurried off.

"How rude to just leave you like that," said Malveria, appearing as if by magic. She slipped her arm through Mr. Dewar's. "I expect her feet are troubling her. Poor Señorita Kabachetka does suffer from an unfortunate malformation of the feet, and cannot dance for long. A side effect of all that mining for gold, I believe. Shall we share a bottle of champagne?"

Sarapen finally appeared. "Sorry I took so long," he said.

"Did you learn anything?"

"Handmaiden Alchet is warming herself in the sunroom. She has a morbid fear of rain. She left her engagement diary in the changing room. I could only glance at it quickly before the servants became suspicious. Most of the entries were for court events, but about two weeks ago there was an entry saying 'Gloucester Place.'"

"Gloucester Place? What about it?"

"Nothing. Just these words. There's no Gloucester Place in this realm, so it might relate to somewhere in London."

Dominil's attention was suddenly alerted by a frantic banging on the outside door, loud enough to permeate the whole suite.

"Thank you, Sarapen. That may be very useful. I must go."

"I could try talking to Alchet if you like."

"I must leave now, before the Empress returns."

"Then goodbye, Dominil."

They looked into each other's eyes for a brief moment.

"I'll find some way to bring you back to this world," said Dominil. Then she touched the jewel, turning off the portal, and hurried from the room. The banging on the door was becoming louder. Dominil ran through the sitting room and the reception room. She unlocked the front door to find Kalix outside.

"I chased off Distikka but she's gone to get Kabachetka!"

Dominil and Kalix ran along the corridor, avoiding the lift and heading for the stairs. They rushed through the door at the top of the stairwell and came face to face with the Empress. Empress Kabachetka's face twitched with anger at the sight of Kalix, but she quickly regained her composure.

"What are you doing on this floor?"

"Visiting acquaintances," said Dominil.

"Were you trying to burgle my room, vile werewolves?"

Kalix growled. Dominil remained calm.

"Certainly not."

"You are wasting your time. My sorcery protects my rooms. You cannot pass through it."

Dominil looked the Empress in the eye. "Then you have nothing to worry about."

"You will have something to worry about if you bother me in any way," said the Empress. She held out her hand and a terrible heat permeated the stairwell, choking Dominil and Kalix.

"I'll burn your little werewolf claws off if you oppose me."

Kalix could not tolerate being insulted and choked with heat. She began to transform into a werewolf, preparing to attack. Dominil placed her arm across her, preventing her. She still looked the Empress in the eye.

"Enjoy the rest of the ball," she said evenly. "Kalix, let's go."

Dominil led Kalix down the next flight of stairs, wondering if they were about to be blasted by a bolt of flame. They were perspiring with the heat and gasping for breath by the time they were out of the Empress's sight.

"Thank you for the warning," said Dominil. "And for chasing off Distikka."

Kalix was pleased. She hadn't done so badly after all. "Did you learn anything?"

"Possibly," said Dominil. "We may be nearer to finding the Guild's headquarters."

They made their way down the stairs.

"A man wanted me to be a model," said Kalix. "And you and Vex as well."

"What?"

Kalix took a business card from her pocket and showed it to her cousin. "He said he wanted to hire us."

"Was he a werewolf hunter? Or some other spy, enemy or conman?"

"I don't think so," said Kalix. "Why would he be?"

"I'm suspicious of everyone tonight."

"I think he just thought we were good models. Which is strange, I suppose. I was a terrible model. But you were good."

"Nothing would induce me to model again," said Dominil.

As they made their way through the crowds gathered round the entrance to the ballroom, they encountered Moonglow.

"I'm having such a good time!" she enthused.

"You are?" Kalix had been stressed since she arrived at the hotel and couldn't imagine why anyone would be enjoying the evening.

"Definitely! You know how in a film or TV when a straight girl goes out with a gay man and she's pretending to be his girlfriend, she always has a really good time? Because he's like a perfect date so she has the best time ever and wishes he could really be her boyfriend?"

"Uh . . . " said Kalix and Dominil simultaneously.

"Well, it's exactly like that!" enthused Moonglow. "William is the best date ever. I so wish he wasn't gay!" She beamed at them.

"We're here to spy," said Dominil.

"Right," said Moonglow, and looked deflated. "Of course. Well, what's next?"

"Where is Daniel?"

Moonglow hadn't seen him for some time.

"We should find him," said Dominil. "And check on Vex. Moonglow, come with me. Kalix, I'd like you to check on Decembrius in the gardens."

"I don't want to do that!"

"We're here to work," said Dominil.

"Fine," muttered Kalix, and walked heavily back through the reception room toward the gardens. She was interrupted twice in the space of a few yards by young men who wanted to talk to her.

"I saw you on the catwalk . . . I like your clothes . . . Your hair is so long . . . You're really beautiful, do you model all the time?"

Kalix ignored them, pushing her way past.

"Decembrius better not say anything stupid when I get outside. I've had enough of him and his stupid comments. I'm starting to hate him."

CHAPTER 102

Dominil and Moonglow made their way toward the corner of the room where Vex and Daniel had last been seen. A young woman in a white ball gown lurched drunkenly into their path, tottering on her high heels. Just before she toppled over, her date came to her rescue. He steadied her, and they stumbled off together.

"Some of these debutantes are really drinking too much," said Moonglow, moving sharply to avoid another unsteady figure in evening dress. "Look, there's Vex."

Moonglow and Dominil paused, unsure of whether to approach or not. Vex was tangled up in an embrace with Adviser Bakmer.

"She did say she'd be a good seductress," said Moonglow. "Should we interrupt?"

"I'm unable to read intimate body language," said Dominil. "Is Vex attracted to him, or is this part of her spying?"

"I don't know."

They were joined by the Fire Queen, who raised her eyebrows at the sight of Vex and Adviser Bakmer. Though manners at the ball had relaxed as the evening progressed, most couples who wanted to become physical had headed for the privacy of the gardens. Enquiring glances were being directed at the passionately embracing couple from those nearby.

"My niece would have to make an exhibition of herself," muttered the Fire Queen. "Really, those shorts may have been acceptable on a catwalk, but they're not at all suitable for wrapping one's legs round one's companion while the Crown Prince of Denmark sits at the next table."

They were still unsure whether to interrupt, or let Vex carry on. The matter was solved by the imperious arrival of Empress Kabachetka.

"So this is where my staff has got to! Adviser Bakmer, disentangle yourself from that disreputable Hiyasta immediately!"

The Fire Queen bridled. "What do you mean disreputable? You're talking about my niece."

"A low-born temple prostitute whom you have invited into your palace!" sneered Kabachetka.

"One would not want to examine the Empress's own parentage too closely with regard to temple prostitutes," retorted Malveria.

"How dare you!" cried the Empress, outraged. "I will have security eject you from the premises and rain down fire on your realm as well!"

"The Empress could not rain down fire on a children's picnic," said the Fire Queen. She looked toward her niece. "Agrivex. Remove yourself from the uncivilized Hainusta who has so grievously taken advantage of your good nature."

"Do not call my adviser uncivilized! Adviser Bakmer, for the last time, free yourself from the clutches of that harlot and come with me."

Adviser Bakmer had drunk a good deal more champagne than he was used to. It took some time for him to realize that the Empress was talking to him. When he finally noticed, he pulled away from Vex very sharply.

"Of course Empress. I was just . . . " He halted, unable to provide any sort of explanation. He stood up unsteadily. People looked on with interest at the scene, the volume of which had temporarily drowned out the orchestra. The Crown Prince of Denmark seemed particularly entertained. Adviser Bakmer sheepishly followed Empress Kabachetka away from the table. Agrivex waved them a cheery goodbye, and then smiled broadly at everyone.

"I told you I'd be a great seductress."

"Really, Agrivex," said the Fire Queen. "There are standards of behavior in public."

Dominil, Moonglow and Malveria sat down at the table.

"Isn't this dance great?" said Vex. "We should come here every week."

"We're meant to be spying," said Dominil. "Did you learn anything?"

Agrivex grinned. "Of course. You don't think I was kissing old Bakmer for fun, do you? Look." She fumbled in her pockets and pulled out several crumpled sheets of paper. "I stole these. Maybe it's secret information!" Vex looked extremely pleased with herself as she handed the papers to Dominil.

"How did you manage to steal them?" asked Moonglow. "You seemed very, uh, occupied."

"I have a talent for pickpocketing. I learned in the palace."

"What?" said Malveria.

"I mean I've never done it before," said Vex.

"Where's Daniel?" asked Moonglow.

No one knew. He'd been sitting at the same table, but Vex had been too occupied to notice him leaving. Moonglow was worried that Gezinka might have kidnapped him, though the Fire Queen did point out that Gezinka was an aristocratic Hainusta, and not known to indulge in kidnapping.

"Maybe they've gone for a walk in the gardens," said Moonglow. "Were they getting on well?"

Vex didn't know. "I didn't pay much attention. Gezinka was all hostile so I just ignored her."

"How hostile?" said Moonglow, alarmed. "What if she's done something terrible to Daniel?"

"That is unlikely," said Dominil. "Nonetheless, we should find him. Vex, these papers look interesting. You did well. Everyone has done well. We may even have learned what we came here to learn. Once we locate Daniel our night will be over."

CHAPTER 103

It was past midnight when Kalix re-entered the gardens. She could feel the moon, though it was hidden by clouds, and she paused for a second, gathering her strength. With so many people around it took her a few moments to locate Decembrius's scent. As she turned into the shadows and walked through the bushes she trod on something soft.

"Hey!" came an irate voice.

Kalix looked down. She'd stepped on a young couple who appeared to have mislaid some of their clothes.

"Sorry," said Kalix, and hurried on, embarrassed. At the edge of the gardens, beside Prince Henry's Tower, she climbed quickly into a tree. Decembrius was sitting in the upper branches.

"Dominil sent me here," said Kalix. "So don't make any stupid comments about me trying to stalk you."

"Why did she send you?"

"Probably she doesn't trust you to guard properly."

"And she thinks you'll do better?"

They settled down into an unfriendly silence. It was broken by Kalix giggling.

"What's funny?"

"I stood on a couple having sex in the bushes. They weren't very pleased."

"Lucky you weren't a werewolf. They'd never have got over it."

The atmosphere thawed a little.

"When we were going out . . . " said Decembrius.

"Yes?"

"I'm sorry we kept arguing."

Kalix didn't know how to reply.

"I've never been that good at keeping relationships going," continued Decembrius.

"That's all right," muttered Kalix.

"What do you mean 'that's all right'? Is that it?"

"What did you expect me to say?"

"I expected you to admit it was your fault too."

"You mean you just apologized so I'd apologize too?"

"Why not?" said Decembrius. "We only kept arguing because you were crazy all the time."

"I was not crazy," cried Kalix.

"Well, you weren't exactly calm."

"Bad things kept happening. It's not that easy being a werewolf in London."

"But they don't all go crazy."

"They don't all get stupidly depressed and lie around feeling sorry for themselves either," said Kalix pointedly.

Decembrius was stung by this. "I think you'd win any contest for mental problems."

"Probably. So what?"

"So don't say everything was my fault. You've got no idea how to be anyone's girlfriend."

"That's not true."

"It is," said Decembrius. "You were always upset about something. And if it wasn't that, I was having to calm you down from some panic attack, or listen to you complain about your family. And then there was the laudanum."

"I really sound like a nightmare," said Kalix. "Why did you ever go out with me?"

"I thought you were pretty for a while. Though if I'd known you were allergic to sex, I'd never have bothered."

"I am not allergic to sex!"

"Really? I don't remember you ever wanting to do it."

"You're talking rubbish."

Decembrius looked round at the gardens. "Hey, I'm jealous of the couple in the bushes. They're having more than we generally did."

"We might have had more if you hadn't wanted to watch football all the time," said Kalix.

"Not that again," said Decembrius. "It was one time. So I wanted to watch a football match. That's not so strange. Plenty of people like football."

"Werewolves don't."

"Yes, they do. I used to play football with other werewolf kids at the castle."

Kalix sniffed. She'd never been friends with any other werewolf children, and didn't really know if they liked football or not.

"I hate you," said Kalix.

"At least I made an effort to apologize," said Decembrius.

"You spent one second apologizing and then launched into a long description of everything that's wrong with me! If we weren't on a mission I'd punch you right off the tree."

"Violence is another one of your problems," said Decembrius. "I feel sorry for your new pretty boy."

"Stop calling him a pretty boy! He's a painter. A good painter."

Decembrius sneered. "A pretty boy who paints. And now he's going out with Britain's most notorious crazy werewolf. I can see that ending well."

Kalix growled.

Decembrius suddenly held up his hand and looked down. "What was that? Did some hunters just go past?"

"I can't see anyone."

"I can feel something," said Decembrius.

It was Kalix's turn to sneer. "Feel something? You mean with your pretend, made-up powers?"

"Shut up, you idiot," snarled Decembrius, and began to climb down the tree.

"You shut up," replied Kalix, following him down.

Decembrius landed heavily on the ground. "Three hunters," he said. "They went right past. We'd have seen them if you hadn't been arguing about everything."

Kalix landed more nimbly. They set off through the bushes. There were unfamiliar scents in the air, but with so many people around it was impossible to know if they were hunters or just guests at the ball. Decembrius seemed convinced, and was agitated about letting them past.

"We have to stop them getting inside the hotel," he said.

There was an anguished cry from under a bush. Kalix looked down.

"Sorry again," she cried, and hurried on. The prospect of fighting had calmed her and focused her attention. She was ready to hurl herself into the fray.

"They're right ahead," hissed Decembrius.

Kalix transformed into her werewolf shape and threw herself forward, jaws wide open, her long sharp teeth ready to bite and tear. Decembrius did the same and the two werewolves flew into a clearing between the bushes. They pulled up immediately, surprised at the sight that confronted them. Thrix was standing over three bodies, each of them facedown on the grass. Fiery energy still crackled around her werewolf claws and over the bodies. She was smiling in triumph. She looked up at Decembrius and Kalix and laughed.

"Nice work guarding the perimeter."

Decembrius looked down at the bodies. Two young men, one older, all struck down instantly by Thrix's sorcery.

Thrix's smile vanished and her expression turned ugly. She bent down and grasped the collar of one of the bodies, dragging him from the ground. Then she took a swipe with her claws, making a great gash in his chest.

"You don't need to do that," said Decembrius. "They're all dead."

Thrix snarled. So did Kalix. The young werewolf's tongue lolled from her mouth. Having changed into her werewolf shape, ready to fight, she'd been on the verge of her battle madness, and was now confused. She looked around for someone to fight, then looked down at the bodies. She growled, and began to paw at one of them.

Decembrius changed back to human and quickly searched the hunters' pockets. As he did so a young couple arrived in the clearing. They looked with horror at the sight of the three bodies and two snarling werewolves, and opened their mouths to scream. The Enchantress pointed one long werewolf talon at them.

"*Fear-faol Dìochuimhnich*, forget werewolf," she said. "And go away."

The couple turned round and left the clearing quite calmly.

"The hunters don't have any documents," said Decembrius. "Kalix, stop snarling. Thrix, get rid of the bodies."

Thrix didn't seem to hear. "I love this ball," she said.

"Yes, we're all having fun," said Decembrius. "Now can you do something about the corpses?"

Thrix turned to leave. Decembrius grabbed her, holding on to the long blonde hair that hung from her werewolf shoulders.

"What's the matter with you? You can't leave."

"Why not?"

"You're still a werewolf. And there are still bodies here."

Thrix looked down at herself, and then at the bodies. She looked momentarily puzzled. "Right. I should move them."

Thrix changed back into human and raised her arm. Nothing happened. She frowned. "I can't. I don't have any power left."

Kalix finally got over her confusion and changed back too. "What's happening?"

"Thrix doesn't have enough power left to move these bodies. Which is a problem. We can't leave them here."

They could hear happy voices, not far away, debutantes laughing in the gardens. Kalix had a sudden inspiration.

"Hide them under the bushes. I'll get Malveria."

CHAPTER 104

Kalix made her way through the gardens into the hotel. For a few moments, as she stood over the bodies, Thrix had looked completely insane. Kalix wondered if that was how she looked when her battle madness came on.

At least I'm not the only mad one in the family any more.

She made her way into the ballroom. By now she was sick of crowds, evening dresses and chandeliers. She hadn't forgotten how unpleasant Decembrius had been.

He couldn't wait to insult me. I'm never going to speak to him again.

Taking less care than before, Kalix plowed through the crowded dance floor. She finally arrived at the back of the ballroom where she found Dominil, Vex, Moonglow and Malveria. Kalix whispered in the Fire Queen's ear. The Fire Queen nodded and hurried off.

"What happened?" asked Dominil.

"Just some fashion stuff with Thrix," said Kalix, who didn't want to let Moonglow know there were dead hunters in the gardens. "Are we still spying?"

"We're done," Dominil told her. "But we have to find Daniel."

"Someone asked Dominil and Vex to be models," said Moonglow as they worked their way through the room.

"He asked Kalix too!" said Vex.

Kalix felt embarrassed and didn't respond. When Moonglow was a few paces ahead of them, Kalix caught Dominil's arm and whispered in her ear, telling her what had happened in the gardens. Dominil nodded, and carried on. She led them out into the corridor, seeking a quiet spot.

"So how do we find Daniel?" asked Kalix when they could hear themselves.

"We should split up and search everywhere," said Dominil.

"That sounds tedious," said Vex. "And things always go wrong when you split up. Monsters pick you off, one by one."

"That's more when you're in a lonely mansion or something like that," said Moonglow. "I don't think monsters will pick us off here."

"I still don't like it," said Vex. "Anyway, why not just look in Lady Gezinka's room? They're probably in bed together."

There was general surprise at the suggestion.

"Why would they be in bed together?" asked Dominil.

"I thought you said Gezinka was unfriendly?" said Kalix.

"She was," admitted Vex. "But you know, lonely middle-aged lady, handsome young guy—or Daniel in this case, but he did look better in that suit—plus champagne, glamorous ballroom and stuff. They've probably gone to her room."

Dominil was baffled. She turned to Moonglow. "Is this credible?"

Moonglow hesitated. "I suppose it might be."

"We've already had several narrow escapes while visiting the rooms of the Hainusta elementals. I don't want to go there again unless it's absolutely necessary."

"We could just leave them to it," said Vex. "They probably don't want to be interrupted. Humans are funny like that."

"We can't leave anyone behind," said Dominil firmly. "I doubt that Daniel is in Lady Gezinka's room, but I'll check. Wait here."

"If you're going to burst in on Daniel I want to come!" protested Vex.

"Stay here." Dominil was firm. They'd been fortunate so far and she didn't want to risk a further confrontation with the Empress.

"How are we going to get home without Daniel?" wondered Vex.

"I suppose we'll have to find a cab," said Kalix.

Vex screwed up her face. She'd been in London long enough to know that it could be difficult to find a taxi willing to go south of the river in the early hours of the morning.

"We could get the night bus."

"I'm not getting on a bus dressed like this," said Kalix. "It's bad enough being half-naked in here."

In the early hours of the morning, the ball was still going strong, though a few people had started to leave. William appeared, escorting his mother to the front of the hotel, where a car was waiting for her.

"So nice to meet you, Moonglow," she said. "Remember, you must come for lunch."

"I'll be back soon," said William.

They walked off toward the foyer.

"You really impressed his mother," said Kalix.

"I know! I was such a good date!"

The lift door opened. Dominil emerged. Moonglow noticed that even at this late hour, in her unfamiliar heels, she walked very upright. *And her stomach is really flat too. I wonder if she works out.*

"Well?" said Vex.

"You were correct. Daniel is currently in Lady Gezinka's room. In her bed, to be precise."

Vex laughed. "I told you. Did you walk right in on them?"

"I did."

"What happened?"

"They weren't pleased."

"What were they doing when you went in?"

"There is no need to explain that exactly," said Dominil. "I asked Daniel if he wanted to leave with us." Dominil pursed her lips. "He didn't. He made the point more strongly than was strictly necessary."

Vex laughed uproariously at the image of Dominil marching into Gezinka's bedroom and asking Daniel if he wanted to leave. Even Kalix smiled. Moonglow didn't seem to find it funny.

"Is he safe? What if the Empress decides she's annoyed with him?"

"I'm also concerned about that," said Dominil. "Nonetheless, Daniel was quite vehement that he did not wish to leave."

"The Empress won't care," said Vex. "She's busy with *Vogue* journalists and some man she keeps dragging onto the dance floor."

"Perhaps you're right. We have some work to do before we leave. Thrix's clothes and materials need packing."

"Doesn't she have teams of people to do that?"

"Not tonight. We deemed it unsafe to involve anyone else."

Vex and Kalix groaned at the prospect of working so deep into the night, but at that moment William appeared and cheerfully offered to help.

"Vex," said Dominil. "Locate your aunt and find out what's happening with Thrix."

"OK," said Vex, and hurried off, pleased to have an excuse for not packing up and loading with the others.

CHAPTER 105

After St. Amelia's Ball Kalix slept better than she had done for months. She woke up slowly, drifting in and out of a funny dream about the animals drawn by Manny. A blue furry elephant smiled at her and asked her if she'd like to ride on its back.

"You should visit Vex," said Kalix. "She likes elephants. Especially furry ones."

"I'm very furry," said the blue elephant.

Kalix felt comfortable in her bed. She was warm and cozy. The late-morning light barely penetrated the thick curtains. She remembered the ball last night, and all the adventures they'd had. Dominil said she might have gathered enough information to locate the Guild. If that was true, they could count it as a great success. Kalix was pleased to have participated. For once, she hadn't messed everything up.

She rolled over and bumped into someone. That was unexpected. Kalix sat up.

"Decembrius!" she yelled. "What are you doing here?"

There was no reply. She hit him on the shoulder. "Wake up!"

Decembrius opened his eyes. He saw Kalix leaning over him and grinned. "Morning."

Kalix's first impression on finding Decembrius lying beside her was that he must have somehow sneaked into her bed. But as her mind cleared her memory returned. She covered her face with her hands and moaned. "I can't believe we slept together!"

Decembrius sat up, still grinning.

"Stop smiling!" said Kalix.

"Why? I'm feeling OK."

"We can't have slept together. I have a boyfriend. How did it happen?"

Decembrius shrugged.

"You tricked me!" cried Kalix.

"How did I trick you?"

Kalix fumbled for an answer. She was so furious she felt that Decembrius must have tricked her somehow but she couldn't see how.

"I must have been drunk!"

"No, you weren't. We'd all sobered up by the time we'd got home."

It was true. It had taken some time to pack up Thrix's belongings. By the time Decembrius had given Kalix and Vex a lift home, the effect of the champagne she'd consumed had worn off.

"You took advantage when I'd been a werewolf," said Kalix. "That makes me think funny."

Decembrius raised his eyebrows. "You really think that's true?"

Kalix sighed. It was true that turning into a werewolf could cause some sense of arousal, but the MacRinnalchs were all so used to it, it couldn't be blamed for flinging Kalix unwittingly into bed with Decembrius. Besides, she'd made the change back to human some time before arriving home.

"You just felt like . . . you know," said Decembrius, and moved a little closer.

"Stop trying to snuggle up!" said Kalix angrily. She glared at Decembrius with loathing. "I'm sure you tricked me somehow."

"Do we have to go through this every time?" asked Decembrius. "Just admit you like sleeping with me."

"I do not! This is a disaster. I've got a boyfriend."

"You mean your—"

"If you insult him I'll bite you," said Kalix angrily.

Decembrius laughed. He used a hand to brush back his long red hair. Kalix looked at his lean muscular frame and felt even more annoyed at herself. She just didn't understand how she'd managed to end up in bed with Decembrius, whom she was quite sure she didn't like at all. She got out of bed quickly, intending to jump into her clothes, but was frustrated to find that the only clothes lying around were from the outfit she'd modeled last night, which she didn't intend on wearing again. She hurried to the cupboard and dragged out a T-shirt and jeans, dressing as quickly as she could.

"Don't just sit there," she said. "You have to leave."

"I'm in no real hurry."

"I don't want anyone to know you stayed the night!"

There was a gentle knocking at the door. "Hey, Kalix and Decembrius," came Vex's voice. "Moonglow wants to know if you want some tea."

"Ooohhh!" wailed Kalix.

"I think maybe they're still doing it," yelled Vex. "I can hear moaning."

Kalix hung her head in misery. "This is a disaster," she muttered.

Decembrius swung his legs from the bed. He was still smiling good-naturedly. "It's lucky I'm easy-going," he said. "Otherwise I might be insulted at all this talk of disaster. Hey, we slept together. I had a good time. So did you, though you don't want to admit it."

"Get your clothes on and get out!" yelled Kalix. "Right now!"

Decembrius shrugged, pretending indifference. He'd have liked to stay but he had too much pride to beg Kalix for anything. He dressed, far too slowly for Kalix's liking.

"I'll call you," he said, putting on his smart black boots.

"Don't bother."

"Then you can call me when you change your mind again."

"I won't."

"I've heard that before."

Decembrius put on his leather coat and walked toward the door. He paused, and turned round. "Do you ever feel bad when hunters get killed?"

Kalix was taken aback. It was the last thing she was expecting to hear. "What do you mean?"

"All these deaths. Does it ever make you feel bad?"

"Of course not," said Kalix. "Why would it? They're the enemy."

"I know. But it's still a lot of death. I've never seen Thrix so happy as she was last night. I don't see there's a lot to be happy about."

Decembrius's point of view seemed so strange to Kalix that she was even moved to defend her sister. "Why shouldn't she be happy? She killed hunters. That's what we do. They'd kill us if they could."

Decembrius shrugged, and didn't pursue it further. He left Kalix's bedroom without another word. Kalix heard him politely refusing the offer of tea downstairs, and then the sound of the front door as he departed. She locked her own door and flung herself fully clothed on her bed, dragging the quilt over her head to hide from the world.

"Why did I sleep with Decembrius?" she moaned. "What's the matter with me?"

CHAPTER 106

In the aftermath of St. Amelia's Ball, Empress Kabachetka was satisfied with herself, if not her staff. She had socialized with important people in the fashion industry, and been introduced to several eminent figures. She'd been on the receiving end of many compliments for her generosity in sponsoring the event, and her evening dress and shoes had gone down well, even if the editor of *Vogue* had not been quite as enthusiastic as she'd have liked. It was annoying that the Fire Queen had gate-crashed the event, but the Empress was satisfied that she hadn't managed to spoil anything.

Poor Malveria, she mused. *Thinking she could upstage me. Why did she bother? It shows her desperation. I'm sure the staff from* Vogue *hardly noticed her. And as for Mr. Dewar, he was no more likely to fall for her than he was for the young man serving drinks at the late-night bar.*

She frowned. Mr. Dewar hadn't actually fallen for either of them. He'd seemed more keen on the young man serving drinks.

But that is beside the point. At least Malveria did not get her claws into him. It was all a waste of time on her part. And as for her dreadful werewolf friends, what did they hope to achieve?

The Empress had not enjoyed having Kalix MacRinnalch turn up at her ball, particularly as she was modeling Thrix's clothes.

I should have killed her on the spot. But that may have caused trouble. Fashion journalists are very sensitive about death at their events.

The Empress's thoughts turned to her servants. Their behavior had been far from glorious. Adviser Bakmer was quickly summoned and lectured at length.

"To be publicly kissing a young Hiyasta woman? What were you thinking?"

Bakmer struggled for an explanation. "The wine . . . it was strange and fizzy . . . I wasn't used to it."

"If you were not used to champagne you should have taken care not to indulge so freely. I am shocked, Bakmer, shocked. You have provided me with much good advice relating to frocks, and some helpful hints on handbags, but this has cast a deep shadow over your reputation. You are henceforth demoted."

"Demoted?"

"Report to the kitchens to begin your new career."

Young Adviser Bakmer left the throne room in a daze, hardly able to contemplate the depth of the disaster that had overwhelmed him. Distikka saw him leave, and entered without being summoned.

"What are you doing here?" demanded the Empress. "I asked for Lady Gezinka."

"I told her to wait," said Distikka. "I have important news."

The Empress sniffed. "I see you have wasted no time in donning that aged chain-mail shirt. What was wrong with your dress?"

"I disliked it," said Distikka. "Now about my news—"

"I cannot quite make up my mind about Lady Gezinka's dalliance in her hotel room last night," said the Empress. "On the one hand, I am shocked. Gezinka was there to assist me. She was not meant to retire early with an unknown young man for a night of pleasure. So one is annoyed at her for abandoning her duties. However . . . " The Empress laughed lightly. "On the other hand, she is no longer in her youth. And as I have rarely observed Lady Gezinka to so much as smile, perhaps she deserves some enjoyment from life. I confess, Distikka, the thought of my staid and reserved diary keeper suddenly flinging off her garments in the company of a young stranger does amuse me. Is this not amusing?"

Distikka looked blank.

"Remind me to hire some advisers with a modicum of humor," said the Empress. "What was it you wished to see me about?"

"The werewolves. It's time for the next part of my plan."

"I have never understood any part of your plans, Distikka. But tell me the next part anyway."

"We have to let the Avenaris Guild know that the werewolves have learned the location of their headquarters and will soon attack."

"But how can we tell the Guild this?" asked the Empress. "How do we know the werewolves have learned their address?"

"That's why they came to the ball," said Distikka.

The Empress leaned forward in her throne. "I do not follow you, Distikka. How do you know that's why they came?"

"Why else would they?"

"To annoy me?"

"No. To learn about the Guild."

"Even if that is true, I don't see how they could have learned anything. We are always most careful never to give away the address. Did someone inform them?"

"No, Empress. No one informed them."

"Then how do they know?"

"I don't know, exactly," admitted Distikka. "But I'm sure they do. I talked to Dominil. She's a very intelligent werewolf. I don't know what she did, but I'm confident that if she came to St. Amelia's Ball to learn the location of the Avenaris Guild, then she will have succeeded somehow."

The Empress frowned, strongly enough for a ripple of heat to emanate through the throne room. "You seem to place a lot of confidence in this werewolf's intelligence."

"I do."

"I do not like the idea of being spied on. And you say they were successful? Distikka, this sounds bad."

"It isn't bad, Empress."

"Distikka, you are making me frown, and I deplore this, as it is harmful for the skin. If we wanted the werewolves to discover the hunters' address, why did we not simply give it to them?"

"We couldn't give them the address because they'd have been suspicious if they learned it too easily. They would have known it was a trap. You must not underestimate the MacRinnalchs, Empress."

"I will underestimate them if I choose," said the Empress. "Continue describing your unnecessarily complicated plan."

"The MacRinnalchs would not easily walk into a trap. But now they don't know they've been trapped. They had to work hard to find the Guild's address, and they think they've outsmarted us. They will attack the Guild, quite certainly. But instead of catching the Guild by surprise, they'll find them ready and waiting. Thrix and Kalix will both take part in the attack and will be killed. That, I believe, is what you desire."

"Well . . . I suppose it may be a tolerable plan. But the Avenaris Guild will not be pleased that we have allowed the werewolves to learn their address."

"That's true," acknowledged Distikka. "But they can't do anything about it now. All they can do is make sure they're ready for the attack."

Distikka took a step forward, making her chain mail rattle, which always irritated the Empress.

"It may mean the loss of a few hunters, but do you care about that?"

"Not at all," said the Empress. She rose from her jeweled throne. "Now that you have finally explained it properly, your plan does not seem so complicated. Foolish werewolves believe they have cunningly obtained the location of their enemies. We inform the Guild what has happened. Werewolves attack, the Guild is ready, and all the werewolves get killed. I like this." Kabachetka smiled. "When will it happen?"

Distikka could not say for certain. "We'll need to monitor them. It shouldn't be too hard to tell when the attack is imminent."

"Excellent," said the Empress. "This has put me in a good mood. I will forgive Lady Gezinka for her lapse. I depart for a manicure, in very good spirits."

The Empress Kabachetka swept out of the throne room. The guards at the door noticed how happy their Empress looked, which pleased them. On the rare occasions when the Empress was truly happy, her aura was very expansive, and it warmed the hearts of her subjects.

CHAPTER 107

Kalix lay face down on her bed. She could barely comprehend the enormity of the mistake she'd made.

Why did I sleep with Decembrius? she asked herself, over and over.

Kalix couldn't account for it. She tried making excuses but none of them worked. She'd arrived home quite sober, thinking clearly. She'd had every opportunity to wish Decembrius a polite goodnight before retiring alone. And yet somehow she'd ended up inviting him to stay.

"How did that happen?" she moaned. "I have a new boyfriend. I don't even like Decembrius."

Kalix dragged a pillow over her head. It didn't help.

I must be insane, she thought. Everyone was right about me. I really am clinically insane.

She rolled over and stared at the ceiling. She felt the weight of the atmosphere pressing down. In recent times Kalix had been more prone to anxiety than depression but now she felt a huge depression settling in.

How could I do that? What would Manny think?

Unable to bear the thought of what Manny would think, Kalix tried the pillow again, this time dragging it over her face.

I'm the worst person in the world. No one else would sleep with an ex-boyfriend for no reason.

The day was now well advanced, but little sunlight penetrated the thick curtains of Kalix's room. The unhappy young werewolf lay in silence for a long time. Eventually, she heard the front door opening and closing, and Daniel's footsteps on the stairs.

I'll have to run away, thought Kalix. I can't face anyone ever again.

Her phone rang. She ignored it. It rang again but she didn't answer. A few minutes later Moonglow knocked on the door.

"Kalix? Dominil called. She needs to talk to you."

Kalix didn't answer.

"Kalix? Speak to me or I'm coming in."

"Go away."

"Dominil says she needs to talk to you. She's on the phone downstairs."

Kalix groaned. She stood up and walked slowly toward the door. Her hair was matted over her face. She ignored it. Moonglow smiled as she emerged from her room. Kalix ignored her too. She walked downstairs with a heavy tread. She picked up the phone.

"What is it?"

"You didn't answer your own phone," said Dominil. "Is everything all right?"

"Yes. What is it?"

"I'm calling to thank you for your efforts last night. Please thank your flatmates as well. Everyone did well, and I believe I have the information we need."

"OK," said Kalix.

Dominil, either not noticing or not caring that Kalix sounded less than enthusiastic, asked if Vex was there. Kalix mutely handed the phone to her flatmate.

"Vex," said Dominil. "I need to speak to Queen Malveria. Will you be in touch with her soon?"

"I have to go back to the palace tonight."

"Please ask her to contact me on a matter of urgency."

"OK."

Vex ended the phone call. Then she joined Daniel and Moonglow in staring at Kalix.

"Why are you looking at me like that?" asked Kalix.

"No reason," said Moonglow.

"Apart from you slept with Decembrius," said Daniel.

Kalix looked accusingly at Vex. "Daniel just got back! Did you have to tell him right away?"

"It wasn't me!" protested Vex. "Moonglow beat me to it."

Moonglow looked guilty.

"Be fair," said Daniel. "It's a juicy piece of gossip. Anyone would have shared it. It's probably all over your werewolf castle by now."

Kalix moaned. She lay on the couch and curled up in a ball.

"So, not the greatest idea in retrospect?" said Daniel.

"I'll make a pot of tea," said Moonglow. "And you can tell us all about it."

"I'm not telling you anything," muttered Kalix.

"Too late for that," said Daniel, moving Kalix's feet so he could sit on the couch. "The days when you could clam up about these things have long gone. You've got friends now, and friends have the right to know all about your relationship disasters."

"It's none of your business!"

"Of course it's our business. Aren't I about to tell you about my night in a hotel room with Lady Gezinka?"

"I want to hear about that too!" said Vex.

"I'm ready with a full account," said Daniel. "Right after Kalix opens up about Decembrius."

Even in her miserable state, Kalix could tell that Daniel had arrived home feeling rather pleased with himself.

Daniel lowered his voice. "William isn't here, is he?"

"No," said Vex.

"Good," said Daniel. "I was worried he might be."

Moonglow arrived back with a tray on which were a teapot, four mugs and a carton of milk. The cat joined them. Moonglow was ready for this, and had brought an old saucer. She poured some milk into the saucer and set it down on the carpet.

"Well," she said. "That was an interesting night at the ball."

There was an expectant silence. Moonglow poured a little milk into each mug. Due to the breakages in the kitchen by Vex, they were currently using a set of Beatles mugs given to Daniel by his aunt. Daniel picked up the Ringo Starr mug and handed it to Kalix.

"So," he said. "Tell us how you ended up sleeping with Decembrius."

"No," said Kalix.

"Come on," said Vex. "You don't have to be explicit."

"Though explicit details are fine if you want to include them," added Daniel.

"Definitely," said Vex. "Whatever you're comfortable with, really. I heard some quite interesting noises when I walked past your room in the middle of the night."

"Have you been spying on me?" demanded Kalix.

"Of course not. I was just going downstairs for a bowl of cereal and by coincidence I had to stop outside your room to tie my shoelace. So, who made the first move? You or Decembrius?"

Kalix appealed to Moonglow for relief. "Make them stop asking me questions."

"Sorry, Kalix," said Moonglow. "Daniel is right. Some events are so momentous that flatmates have a right to demand information."

"The broad outline will do to get us started," said Vex. "You can fill in the details later."

CHAPTER 108

Kalix gave a very brief description of the previous night's events. It wasn't enough to satisfy her flatmates but she was reluctant to offer more.

"I can't believe you're all so nosy. I made a mistake sleeping with Decembrius. That's all. I don't want to talk about it."

"You should get your side of the story out quickly," said Vex. "After all, Decembrius will. He's probably talking about it already."

"What do you mean 'my side of the story'?" said Kalix. "It's not a court case."

"Well, Decembrius will be bragging anyway. Like Daniel."

"I haven't bragged about anything," protested Daniel.

"How did you end up in Gezinka's hotel room?" asked Vex.

"She asked me. We were just sitting at the table and she wasn't saying much. But she got a bit more animated after some more champagne and then she told me how bored she was with life at the Empress's court and one thing led to another. I suppose she was quite impressed with me being a model, you know, as soon as you appear on a catwalk women are flinging themselves at you."

"Well, at least you're not bragging about it," said Moonglow.

"The basic outline is not bragging," said Daniel. "Just a factual report on me spending the night with an aristocratic Fire Elemental who really had a good body under that evening dress."

"At least she got to hide her body under a dress," moaned Kalix. "I had to walk around all night practically naked. I knew no good would come of it. That's probably why I ended up sleeping with Decembrius."

Moonglow didn't think that made much sense, but was sympathetic to Kalix's misery. "It's all right. These things happen. Don't get anxious about it."

"I'm not anxious about it. Now you've mentioned anxiety I'm starting to get anxious. Now I'm more anxious."

Moonglow, perched on the end of the sofa, patted Kalix's head.

Kalix was surprised. "Did you just pat my head?"

"Yes."

"Why?"

"To stop you getting anxious."

"I wouldn't be anxious if everyone didn't keep mentioning it. Don't pat my head. It's a big insult for a werewolf."

"I like being patted on the head," said Vex, and leaned toward Moonglow. Moonglow obligingly patted her head, or rather her hair, which still formed a stiff, spiky, protective sphere.

Kalix sipped some tea, awkwardly, as she was still lying down. It dribbled down the side of her mouth. She wiped it off and sat up on the couch.

"Now my relationship with Manny is ruined."

"Why?" asked Daniel.

"Because I slept with Decembrius! Manny won't want to see me any more."

"How will Manny find out?"

"I'll have to tell him, of course."

Vex burst out laughing. "Are you mad? You don't have to tell him. Moonglow, tell Kalix she doesn't have to tell Manny."

"Well . . . " Moonglow hesitated.

"I don't think you should tell him," said Daniel. "What's the point?"

"I don't want to lie," said Kalix. "Aren't you meant to tell people about things like that?"

"Only on TV," said Daniel. "Television is full of people confessing things. But that's just for dramatic effect. In real life, don't do it."

"Definitely don't do it," agreed Vex.

Kalix looked toward Moonglow. Moonglow seemed uncomfortable.

"I'm not sure . . . I think perhaps you should tell him. It's always better to be honest."

"No it isn't!" cried Daniel. "If Kalix is honest it'll just ruin everything."

"Honesty would be a terrible mistake," said Vex.

Moonglow glared at her flatmates. "I don't like the way you're both advising Kalix to lie like it's the most natural thing in the world. Lying isn't good, you know. If Manny slept with someone else, wouldn't you want Kalix to know?"

"That's different," said Daniel. "Kalix is our friend. We'd want her to know stuff about Manny. That doesn't mean we want Manny to know stuff about her."

They were interrupted by a small electronic bleep. Kalix took her phone from her pocket. She looked at it and sighed.

"Message from Manny?"

"He says he's looking forward to seeing me."

Kalix curled up on the couch again. Vex got to her feet and stood in front of the mirror, pushing her hair into shape with her fingers.

"Well, I'd love to stay here and watch Kalix falling apart with guilt and Daniel bragging about his nights of passion, but I'm due at the palace tonight, so I've just got time for a quick visit to Pete before I go."

"Is your aunt still making you visit that arch-wizard?" asked Moonglow.

Agrivex scowled. "Yes. Unless I learn to control my fire."

"How's that going?"

"Hopeless. I can't do it. But I'm not going to some prison camp with Old Krabby. Aunt Malvie will cheer up and forget all about it when the next part of my super-cunning plan gets underway."

Vex was immediately cheerful again. "I'll see you all in a few days. Kalix, don't do anything stupid like tell your boyfriend the truth. Bye!"

With that, Vex hurried from the house, heading for the tube station and a trip to North London to see Pete.

"They seem to be getting on well," said Moonglow. She absent-mindedly placed her hand on Kalix's head, and almost patted her. "Sorry," she said immediately, withdrawing her hand.

"It's all right," muttered Kalix. "It's not really a big insult for werewolves. I just made that up. I must be one of these people that tells lies all the time. What's the word for that?"

"Pathological," said Moonglow. "But you're really not like that."

Daniel poured more tea into his John Lennon mug. He yawned. "I didn't get any sleep last night. Gezinka was quite energetic—"

"Maybe you should start lying about a few things," said Moonglow. "Or at least concealing the truth." She picked up the tray and took it to the kitchen.

"I knew she'd be jealous," said Daniel, and sounded pleased about it.

Kalix wasn't listening. She was staring at the text message from Manny, leaving Daniel to lapse into his fantasy of Moonglow being eaten up with jealousy over his night with Gezinka and confessing her love for him, something which he half expected to happen as soon as Moonglow returned from the kitchen.

CHAPTER 109

Two days after the ball, Dominil arranged to meet Thrix in Marylebone Library. She was waiting in the reference section when her cousin arrived. Thrix was unsettled by her surroundings.

"Did we have to meet in a library?"

"Why shouldn't we?" asked Dominil.

"Aren't there any bars or restaurants around here?"

"There are plenty. But we're not here to eat or drink."

Thrix lowered her voice in response to several hostile glances from other occupants of the reference section. "I feel uncomfortable," she whispered. "Can we go somewhere I don't have to whisper?"

They walked past a series of posters encouraging children to read and arrived at the glass doors that led out onto the main street.

"So why are we here?" asked Thrix.

"We're at the top of Gloucester Place. I believe the Guild's headquarters is on this road."

Thrix forgot her discomfort. "You do? Why?"

"While in the Empress's suite I read her handmaiden Alchet's diary." Dominil lied quite smoothly to her cousin. She would have preferred to tell her that the information had come from Sarapen, but felt obliged to keep her promise not to let Thrix know he was still alive.

"There were several entries mentioning Gloucester Place. I believe these entries relate to visits to the Guild."

"The Empress just left that lying around?"

"She thought her sorcery would keep out any intruder."

"Then let's find them," said Thrix, and stepped through the glass doors into Gloucester Place.

"That may not be easy," said Dominil. "It's a long road. It runs all the way down to Oxford Street. I've walked its length before and never noticed anything that made me think of the Guild. Have you learned any more about the Maynista's 'House That Can't Be Found'?"

"Not much. Do you really think the Guild's headquarters was built by a stone dwarf?"

"It's possible," said Dominil. "It would explain our inability to locate it. It would be good to learn more about the subject."

"I've asked Malveria to look into it but for some reason she's not keen. As far as I can gather, it would exist the same as any other building. You can see it, and walk into it. You just can't find it by sorcery. Or on the internet, apparently." Thrix gazed down the long street. It was mostly Georgian, large terraced houses, the ground floor faced with white marble and the three upper floors all of brown stone. "Most of these houses look the same."

"They do. But I have more information." Dominil drew a sheet of paper from her leather satchel.

"Why do you have such a fashionable item?" asked Thrix.

"Pardon?"

"Your leather satchel. It's been all over the magazines this summer."

Dominil looked at her plain, functional satchel. "I had no idea it was fashionable. I bought it because it was practical."

She showed Thrix the sheet of paper. "Vex stole this from Adviser Bakmer. It appears to be some notes he's made, perhaps prior to writing them in his own diary. Look here." Dominil indicated a scrawled line in the notes. "Distikka off to red house again. Always worming her way in with the Empress."

"Red house?"

"The entry appears on the same day as Alchet's entry about Gloucester Road. 'Red house' may be a code word for the Guild's headquarters."

Thrix didn't look convinced, but shrugged. "OK, it's good enough for me. Let's find a red house in Gloucester Place." She paused. "The ball was two days ago. Did you just learn all this?"

"No, I knew as soon as I saw the documents."

"Then why didn't you call me right away?"

They were interrupted by a siren as an ambulance made its way through the dense traffic. Dominil waited for the noise to subside.

"I thought I'd give you a day to recover."

"What do you mean?" said Thrix. "I didn't need time to recover."

"Malveria had to take you home after the ball."

"I briefly used too much power. I was fine the next morning."

Dominil examined Thrix. Her cousin seemed healthy enough, but Dominil wasn't sure. There was a certain look in her eyes that Dominil didn't like. She turned her attention back to the long road in front of them.

"I examined Gloucester Place as carefully as I could with satellite maps and I couldn't see anything that looked like a red house. But perhaps we'll find something. Red curtains, or a red door."

"Enough talking," said Thrix. "Let's go."

"If we find their headquarters we're not charging in to attack them. We'll notify the Great Council, and take it from there."

Thrix's frown deepened. "I'm not liking this so much."

"I knew you wouldn't. But it's time for you to start acting responsibly."

"What do you mean by that?"

"I mean you've been acting irresponsibly."

"I've been acting irresponsibly?"

"Yes. You killed those hunters with little thought for the consequences. Had Kalix not quickly brought Queen Malveria to the scene to dispose of the bodies, they might well have been found. That would have led to police, publicity and everything the MacRinnalch Clan strives to avoid. Besides which, there's no telling what the Empress may have done had she learned of it."

"I can't believe this," said Thrix angrily. "You're actually criticizing me for killing hunters?"

"With some forethought you could have baffled the hunters and led them away to some quiet spot. Killing them in the middle of the gardens was highly irresponsible."

"We were in the bushes. No one could see. I admit my power dropped after that and I couldn't get rid of the bodies. But the Guild don't bother about leaving bodies when they target werewolves."

They walked on down the pavement. The afternoon was warm, much warmer than usual for the last days of summer.

"I'm not the one who takes laudanum," muttered Thrix. "How irresponsible is that?"

"I've heard more than enough about that," said Dominil. She began to study the houses around them, but Thrix seemed unwilling to let the disagreement drop.

"What would you expect me to do if hunters appeared right now? Just let them shoot you?"

"I've managed to take care of myself quite satisfactorily so far," said Dominil.

"Really? How's your laudanum intake these days?"

"Carefully measured, as ever." Dominil halted, and looked Thrix in the eye. "Is there any particular reason for this hostility?"

Thrix glared back at her. She seemed on the verge of an angry retort, but controlled herself. "I'm sorry. I haven't felt right since Minerva was killed. I've been getting these terrible moods. Anything can set me off."

Dominil nodded. "Let's search."

The Scottish werewolf cousins walked on in the sunshine along Gloucester Place, looking for their enemies' headquarters.

CHAPTER 110

Dominil and Thrix walked south, all the way down Gloucester Place. They didn't pass any red houses and they didn't find the Guild's headquarters. Dominil was thoughtful as she looked back along the street.

"I saw nothing that gave any hint of the Guild. Thrix, will you pay attention?"

Thrix was studying her reflection in the window of a shop selling expensive Chinese antiques.

"Are these extensions still looking natural? I can feel something at the back. Can you see where it joins?"

"This is not the time for worrying about your hair."

"Any time is fine for worrying about your hair. Is there something wrong at the back?"

"The extensions are fine. There is no sign of artificiality."

"Good. You need to take a lot of care with extensions."

"Are you seeking to infuriate me?"

Thrix turned to her cousin. "No, I'm just being vain about my hair. That's not a crime. You're vain about your hair too."

"I am not."

"Oh really?" Thrix was amused. "You walk around with that huge white main and you claim you're not vain about it? I've never seen it anything other than perfectly brushed and conditioned."

"I take normal steps to maintain it."

"Dominil, if you weren't vain about it you'd have cut it short years ago. Much more practical, and you love being practical. You'd have dyed it some normal color too. Make you much less identifiable to the hunters."

"I refuse to change my appearance for the sake of werewolf hunters."

"So you won't admit to even the tiniest bit of vanity?"

Dominil considered this. "Perhaps a little. Having settled this matter, could we get back to looking for the Guild? We should walk back up the opposite pavement."

Thrix shrugged. "All right. Though it's a fairly boring road, for the center of London."

"I noticed some blue plaques," said Dominil. "I always like them."

"Blue plaques?"

"Signs placed by English Heritage commemorating notable people who lived in these houses. You are aware of them?

"Vaguely," said Thrix.

"There were four. For Sir Gerald Kelly, Rupert Edward Dawson, William Wilkie Collins and Elizabeth Barrett Browning."

They crossed the road at a zebra crossing and began to walk back up the other side.

"Are they famous?" asked Thrix.

"Famous? Sir Gerard Kelly was quite a well-known painter in his day. I wouldn't say he was famous. I don't care for his portraits. Rupert Edward Dawson was once a renowned political essayist but I don't think his renown has lingered."

"Good," said Thrix. "I've never heard of them."

"But the other two are well known. Wilkie Collins was a Victorian novelist, often cited as one of the originators of the detective genre. Elizabeth Barrett Browning you will of course be familiar with."

"I've never heard of her," said Thrix.

Dominil halted. "You've never heard of Elizabeth Barrett Browning?"

"No."

"How can you not have heard of her?"

Thrix shrugged. "I wouldn't know. What did she do?"

"She was a poet."

"Was she any good?"

"Sometimes," said Dominil. "I wouldn't class her in the top rank of poets, but some of her work is worthwhile. Generally I admire her. She had an interesting life. You might even describe her as a feminist icon."

They walked on, studying the houses as they passed.

"Do you have many feminist icons?" asked Thrix.

"Icon may have been putting it too strongly. But I admire women who made their mark in history."

"Plenty of women made their mark in the fashion industry," said Thrix. "Why don't you admire them?"

"Who said I didn't?" replied Dominil.

"You know you regard it as a waste of time."

Dominil halted again. "It's true that it's too frivolous for my tastes. That doesn't mean I regard it as a waste of time. I admire women who've been successful in the industry. I admire you for your efforts."

"Do you?"

"Yes."

"Oh."

They walked on. Thrix was surprised to hear Dominil say she admired her. She tried to think of something complimentary she could say about Dominil in return. She couldn't immediately think of anything, and was on the verge of praising her satchel again, when Dominil came to an abrupt halt. She was staring back across the busy street at one of the large houses they'd passed earlier.

"What is it?" asked Thrix.

"That blue plaque."

"Rupert Edward Dawson? I've still never heard of him."

"The initials," said Dominil. "R-E-D. Perhaps that's the red house."

They stared at the house. It looked the same as many others in Gloucester Place: four stories, brown stone above with a white marble facing at ground level.

"I'm not picking up anything," said Thrix. "I need more time to study it."

"We should walk on for now," said Dominil. "It would be unfortunate if a hunter were to look out a window and recognize me."

They walked on.

"So how are we going to . . . " began Thrix.

"It was right next door to a hotel," said Dominil. She took out her phone, then changed her mind, and walked up the next side street till she came to a phone box. Dominil found the number of the hotel and immediately called to book a room.

"Quick work," said Thrix. "You don't hang around."

"If we visit the hotel you should be close enough to study the building next door with your sorcery," said Dominil. "Perhaps you can positively identify it."

"I hope so. I still need to know more about this 'House That Can't Be Found' magic. I'll talk to Malveria again."

"I'd also like to speak to her."

"What about?"

"An unconnected matter."

They returned to the main street. Thrix glanced back at the building though Dominil resisted the urge.

"If they weren't getting help from Kabachetka I'd destroy them right now," said Thrix.

"It is unfortunate that the Empress has become involved," said Dominil.

"Why does she hate us so much, I wonder? Just because Kalix killed Sarapen, and she liked Sarapen?"

"You also infuriated her by dressing her rival Queen Malveria in superior clothes. Which should not be enough reason for a murderous feud, but I regard the Empress as an unstable character. In her struggle with Queen Malveria, we seem to have become stuck in the middle."

"I need a glass of wine," said Thrix. "And there's a nice-looking wine bar right over there."

They crossed the road, weaving their way between a long line of stationary traffic. It was hot in the city and a few drivers sounded their horns in frustration at the delay. They found a table inside and ordered two glasses of wine. As always, the beauty of the MacRinnalch women drew attention. Customers at nearby tables stared; some discreetly, some openly.

"Dominil, I'm a little ashamed of this, but I wasn't paying full attention to everything that went on at the ball. When you learned all this information, did Kabachetka know what you were up to? Is she going to warn the Guild we're on to them?"

"No," said Dominil. "Distikka knew we were looking for something, but there is no way they can know we've located the Guild, if we have indeed located it. In terms of surprise, we now hold the upper hand."

CHAPTER III

As Dominil and Thrix walked the length of Gloucester Place, an emergency board meeting was taking place inside the Guild's headquarters. Three members of Group Fifteen had not returned from their mission, and nor had Mr. Eggers. All were now presumed to be dead. It was a very serious blow. Mr. Carmichael found himself facing hostile questioning.

"Whose decision was it to send Group Fifteen into action before they were ready?"

Mr. Carmichael admitted it had been his decision, but defended himself. "They were the only hunters available. We had to do something, we couldn't just let the opportunity vanish."

"Why not?" demanded Mr. Evans, head of the Intelligence Department. "It was obviously too dangerous to send three inexperienced hunters up against a werewolf like Kalix MacRinnalch."

"They were not all inexperienced. Jefferson was in charge and he's been a hunter for a long time. The others had completed their training."

"But they'd never encountered anything like the ruling family of the MacRinnalchs. You made a mistake sending them."

"Is the Avenaris Guild just to ignore a confirmed werewolf sighting right in the middle of London?" said Mr. Carmichael. "If we don't pursue werewolves then what are we here for?"

Mr. Evans was not satisfied, and he wasn't the only one.

"We couldn't afford to lose these men. Group Fifteen wasn't ready. I think you got carried away because of Group Sixteen's success."

"You're forgetting that Mr. Eggers was already in the hotel," said Mr. Carmichael. "What was I meant to do, just leave him there on his own?"

"Now Eggers is dead and so are our hunters."

"It would have been better to tell Mr. Eggers to get out of there as quickly as he could."

"With a savage beast like Kalix MacRinnalch on his tail? She might just have torn him to pieces anyway. And don't forget, Kabachetka was at the hotel. I thought she'd assist our men." Mr. Carmichael paused. "Apparently that didn't happen."

"Why didn't it happen?" asked Mr. Evans.

Mr. Carmichael didn't know. "I'll be able to give you a fuller account after I've talked with her adviser Distikka."

Mr. Dale, head of Northern Operations, made a dismissive gesture.

"You place a lot of faith in these Fire Elementals. I've never thought they were suitable allies."

"They've helped us in the past."

"It's never turned out well though, has it?"

The meeting ended without any agreement. Mr. Carmichael received support from his son John, who was also a member of the board, but most others were critical. After the meeting broke up, Mr. Carmichael had a brief word with his son.

"Distikka had better have something good to tell me or I'm liable to lose my job."

"The board won't get rid of you," said John. "They need you. They're just angry because we lost four men."

"I'm not so sure about that. Evans has been after my job for years."

"Where are you meeting Distikka?"

"The Courtauld Gallery again. She likes the place, for some reason."

CHAPTER 112

Vex was still obliged to return to her own realm for two days every week to recharge her fire. She arrived at Malveria's palace in good spirits.

"Here I am!" she announced, walking uninvited into the Fire Queen's private chambers. "The hero of the ball."

The Fire Queen, engaged in some quiet reading, welcomed her adopted niece without much enthusiasm.

"Have I not told you to announce yourself properly? And what do you mean 'hero of the ball'?"

"Master spy and seductress," said Vex. "I expect the papers I cunningly got from Bakmer were just what Dominil needed. Probably the vital clue."

"It was not all that cunning to get him drunk and stick your hand in his pocket," said the Fire Queen. "And as for your behavior at the ball, it left a great deal to be desired."

Agrivex looked exasperated. "You see, Aunt Malvie, this is why I don't like coming to the palace. It's just criticism all the time. What did I do wrong now?"

The Fire Queen laid down her scroll. "You became hopelessly intoxicated and made an exhibition of yourself."

"I did not. I was just pretending."

"I can tell when you are intoxicated, dismal niece. Your aura turns a particularly unpleasant shade of purple. But your public grappling with Adviser Bakmer is not the only reason I was displeased. I expected you to formally greet the Empress of the Hainusta."

"Why would I do that?"

"Because you are her equal. As my heir, you now carry heavy responsibility for the dignity of the Hiyasta."

"Well, I didn't want to be your heir in the first place," protested Agrivex. "You only adopted me in a hurry so I could use the powers of the volcano."

"Nonetheless it was done," said Malveria. "And I expect you to act accordingly. As a first step, start wearing appropriate clothing while in the palace."

Agrivex looked down at her clothes. She had on the same tiny shorts she'd worn to the ball, now accompanied by a very chunky pair of glacier boots, a colorful *Tokyo Top Pop Boom Boom Girl* T-shirt, accessorized with some yellow plastic beads.

"What's wrong with my clothes?"

"Everything that is possible. Retire to your chambers and put on a dress."

"Absolutely not."

"I insist."

"I'm not doing it."

The Fire Queen's eyes blazed. "You dare to speak to me in that tone?"

"Yes. You're really the worst aunt ever. I come here after doing my best at the ball and what happens? You start moaning about my clothes. What are you in such a bad mood about anyway?"

"I am not in a bad mood," said the Fire Queen, who quite obviously was.

There was a discreet knock at the door.

"Enter," said the Fire Queen testily. A young attendant put his head into the room, rather nervously.

"Duke Garfire is without, mighty Queen."

The attendant withdrew swiftly. The Fire Queen glared at her niece. "Garfire! How I loathe this man. And now I have agreed to spend the afternoon with him in the Royal Galleries. This is all your fault, vile niece."

"Have you been sitting here in a bad mood just because you made a date with Garfire?"

"Garfire would put any right-thinking woman in a bad mood."

"Well, just cancel the date."

"It is not as simple as that, idiotic niece. It was easy for you to plunge me into this whirlwind of ambitious noblemen. It is not so easy for me to extricate myself. One cannot insult Garfire without insulting the Duchess Gargamond. Palace politics are complex, and you would do well to learn about it."

"Pfff," said Agrivex.

"What does 'pfff' mean?"

"I'll get you out of it," said Agrivex, and headed for the door.

The Fire Queen rose hurriedly. "Agrivex, do not meddle—"

By this time Agrivex was in the outer chamber. Garfire stood there, in his best formal fire cloak.

"Duke Garfire!" said Vex. "Nice to see you. I'm sorry the Queen can't see you today. She's got another engagement. All my fault, I double-booked, you know how scatty I am."

"Another engagement?"

"I promised she'd receive Beau DeMortalis."

"Agrivex," came the Queen's voice as she rushed from the chamber.

"I just forgot all about it," continued Agrivex. "But we can't disappoint DeMortalis, he'd be crushed. Anyway, understandable error, all my fault."

The Duke looked from Agrivex to the Fire Queen, and back again.

"Well, I am most sorry to hear this. I suppose the error is . . . understandable." He bowed. "I trust we can make the arrangement another time, mighty Queen." The Duke left the chamber.

"See?" said Agrivex. "That wasn't so difficult."

"Why did you say I would receive Duke DeMortalis?"

"Well, he's in the palace, isn't he?"

"In the visitor's guest wing. I cannot officially receive him in my chambers."

"Why not?" said Agrivex. "Aren't you always saying he's the only aristocrat you actually like?"

"Yes, but he is not a suitable person for me to receive."

"I don't see why not. You can't be carrying on ancient prejudices forever. If anyone objects, just say your idiot niece organized it. Well, Aunty, I'm tired. I'm off for a sleep."

The Fire Queen glared at her niece. "One moment, dismal niece. I take it your powers of fire have not improved?"

"I'm working on them."

"Would you care to demonstrate your progress?"

"I really need to sleep," said Vex, who had made no progress at all. "Traveling between dimensions really wears me out."

"I think your unsuitable boyfriend is more likely to have worn you out."

"Do you have to read my aura all the time?" said Vex.

"One does not need to read your aura. Your annoying grin gives you away."

"I'd better get some sleep," said Agrivex, and departed as quickly as she could.

Behind her the Queen was thoughtful. She sent for Gruselvere and Iskiline. "My niece has just announced that I am to receive Beau DeMortalis."

Her chief dresser and her wardrobe mistress were astonished.

"Here in your own chambers?" said Iskiline. "Officially?"

"Yes. Can I allow the Duke to visit me?"

"I don't think so," said Gruselvere. "He fought against you in the war."

"He did. But the Duke has surely restored his reputation. More recently he fought at my side during Distikka's rebellion. It's true that he stumbled upon the battle by accident after leaving the bedchamber of a kitchen maid, but at least he came."

Gruselvere picked up a heavy crystal decanter and poured three glasses of port.

"The Duke still has a bad reputation," she said. "There's the gambling. And drinking. And the succession of kitchen maids."

"But he is such a wit," said Iskiline. "And he has beautiful clothes."

The Fire Queen sipped from her crystal goblet. "Xakthan would no doubt be unhappy were I to receive DeMortalis. But I believe the population would not be outraged."

In her bedchamber, Vex noticed that one of her small blue flowers was wilting. She put her hand over it and a tiny blue flame flowed into the flower. It responded immediately, raising its face healthily toward the ceiling. The ceiling was still covered in streaks of silver, spray-painted by Vex, to the Fire Queen's great disgust.

"My super-cunning plan for marrying off Aunt Malvie is going well," she told the flower.

✱

Beau DeMortalis, Duke of the Black Castle, was surprised to be summoned to the throne room.

"DeMortalis," said the Queen, quite imperiously, "I will receive a visit from you in my own wing of the palace."

"This is a great honor—"

"You will make sure your attendants are respectable. I want none of your dubious entourage of harlots and so-called kitchen maids. Nor will you bring any of your disreputable gambling associates, particularly the Dead Prince of Garamlock, who I am quite certain cheats at cards by summoning information from beyond the grave."

The Duke of the Black Castle bowed. "I'll do as you say, mighty Queen."

CHAPTER 113

After finishing her glass of wine, Dominil was ready to visit the hotel room.

"Have you considered the Guild might use that hotel?" said Thrix. "It could be full of hunters."

"I've considered it. I'll take the risk."

Thrix was struck by Dominil's courage. Thrix was untroubled by the prospect of meeting hunters. Due to the spells of bafflement she'd woven around herself there was little chance of her being recognized. Even if she were, she had power enough to either kill her enemies or simply disappear into thin air. Dominil had no such power, and she was very recognizable. By now there must be many members of the Guild who'd heard of the tall werewolf with white hair.

"I'll come with you," said Thrix. "But I think I need to talk to Malveria first. When I looked at that house I really sensed nothing. I don't know if that's because there was nothing to sense or because of the stone dwarves' powers."

Dominil nodded. "I took the room for a week. We could wait till we've talked to Queen Malveria. How do you normally communicate?"

"I can summon her. We could drive back to my apartment and I'll do it there."

They both tried to pay the bill.

"I've got it," said Thrix.

"Has your income not suffered recently?"

"You mean since I started neglecting my business? Yes, a lot. I can still afford to buy you a glass of wine."

Thrix drove them toward her flat in Knightsbridge. Another driver cut them off as they went round the roundabout at Hyde Park. Thrix swore so loudly and violently that Dominil looked at her with an expression of surprise.

"Sorry," muttered Thrix. "Still a bit on edge."

The traffic lights were at red. When they changed to green, there was a very slight delay as the car in front of them took a few seconds to move. Thrix again gave forth a torrent of abuse.

"Sorry," she muttered again.

"I don't recall you being quite this unpleasant when driving," said Dominil.

Thrix made an effort to control herself. Dominil noticed that Thrix's knuckles were white as she gripped the steering wheel. Driving her Mercedes seemed to have brought all her anger back to the surface. Dominil was displeased as they drove into the car park beneath Thrix's apartment block.

"You'll need to control yourself better when we attack the Guild," she said quite curtly.

"What do you mean?" said the Enchantress. "And who says you'll be in charge anyway?"

"Whoever is in charge will need you to control yourself better."

Thrix glared at her cousin. "Let's call Malveria," she said, and marched toward the lift.

Having seen fresh evidence of Thrix's abrupt mood swings, Dominil was concerned. When they did make their attack on the Guild, Thrix really would have to control herself better. If she didn't, Dominil felt sure that something would go wrong. Thrix's apartment was now very untidy, though she had managed to get the front door repaired. She made a quick visit to her storeroom, returning with a handful of dried herbs that she dumped unceremoniously into a bronze jar. She spoke a few words and the herbs began to smolder. An aroma of jasmine filled the air.

"Well, this is a surprise," said the Fire Queen, appearing in the middle of the room. "It is a long time since you summoned me."

"That's because you visit every day."

"And it is always so nice to see you." The Fire Queen raised her eyebrows as she caught sight of the jar. "I notice you didn't perform the full ceremony."

"Sorry, Malveria, I was in a hurry."

"I am the Fire Queen, you know. Great ruler of the Hiyasta elementals. To be summoned only in time of dire need, at great personal effort, with due ceremony."

"The new shoes have arrived from Milan," said Thrix.

"Really?" Malveria skipped with joy. "I must see them."

"They're at my office. But first I need help. We think we've found the Guild's headquarters but we're not sure."

Thrix and Dominil looked expectantly at the Fire Queen.

"Did the pink peep-toe platform court shoe arrive?" asked Malveria.

"Yes," said Thrix. "But we were rather hoping for some information about the stone dwarves' 'House That Can't Be Found.'"

"I am much keener to talk about shoes."

"Malveria, every time I've mentioned the stone dwarves' house you've been unresponsive. Why?"

"No reason. I just do not like stone dwarves. Do we have to keep talking of them?"

"It is important," said Dominil. "We need information."

Malveria was looking quite unhappy as they pressed her on the subject. "I have little knowledge of stone dwarves' lore."

"That's hard to believe," said Thrix. "You know everything about elementals."

"Well, I don't know about the stone dwarves!" snapped Malveria. "Were I not keen to see my new shoes, I would depart in a temper."

"The yellow sandals arrived too," said Thrix.

"Enchantress, are you attempting to blackmail me with shoes?"

"Yes."

"It will not work."

"The pink platforms have ruched rosettes, delicately draped across the ankle and spilling down to the open toe."

"I must have them immediately!" The Fire Queen looked momentarily anguished. "If you really wish to know more about the stone dwarves, ask Queen Dithean NicRinnalch. She has encountered them in the past. More than that, I won't say. Now take me to the shoes."

"I have something else to discuss," said Dominil. "But it has to be in private."

The Fire Queen looked at Dominil with some surprise. "You mean without Thrix knowing?"

"Yes."

"Is this something about your laudanum addiction?" asked Thrix. "Because I already know about that."

"It's a personal matter."

Thrix shrugged, apparently unconcerned. "Fine. Talk in private. Malveria, I'll head over to my office. You can follow me there when you've finished with Dominil."

"But I want the shoes now!" The Fire Queen, faced with a delay in obtaining her new shoes, seemed about to deny Dominil her request. She relented, not very gracefully.

"Very well. I will talk in private. But really, this has been a poor visit. First I am summoned without proper ceremony and then I am cruelly interrogated and now I am prevented from having my new shoes. It is all very trying."

Thrix put a few things in her bag, and left her apartment.

"Well?" said the Fire Queen.

"I need a favor and you can't tell Thrix about it."

"Realistically, that is not likely to happen," said the Fire Queen. "I end up telling Thrix everything."

"Then perhaps you could promise not to tell her this."

"Tell me what it is and I will see if I will promise."

Dominil had known that it would be a problem keeping the matter of Sarapen from Thrix. Malveria was not discreet, but Dominil could think of no one else who might help her.

"A werewolf I know is stranded in the land of the Hainusta, at the Empress's palace. I want to rescue him."

The Fire Queen blinked. This was stranger than she had expected. For a moment she forgot about her shoes. "Which werewolf?"

"I can't tell you his name."

"Really. And how did he become stranded?"

"The Empress is not willing to send him back, and he has no means of transporting himself here."

"How did he get there in the first place?"

"The Empress took him."

By now Dominil had the Fire Queen's full attention. "What you are asking, Dominil, does not sound easy. The mere act of transportation would not be difficult. Were I standing beside this werewolf, I could simply carry him with me. But I am not standing beside him, and nor am I likely to be if he is a prisoner in the Empress's palace."

"Are you the only one who could transport him?"

"No. Any reasonably powerful elemental could bring him back. But again, how is this elemental to get there? The Empress does not allow free access to her palace."

"I wondered if your espionage services might be able to help."

The Fire Queen fell silent. She looked at her reflection in one of Thrix's large mirrors, and appeared satisfied. "You are asking for a very large favor. One which there seems no reason for me to grant."

"So you won't help?"

"I did not say that. What did you have in mind as a payment?"

"Whatever it costs."

The Fire Queen laughed. "That is not a payment you should offer lightly to the Fire Queen. You encounter me here, a friend of Thrix, and you forget what I really am."

A halo of golden flame appeared round Malveria's head. "I am the ruler of the Hiyasta, Wielder of Flame, Guardian of the Great Volcano. And for favors to mortals, I charge very highly."

"Well?" said Dominil. "What do you want?"

The Fire Queen let the flames around her head dispel.

"My new shoes, at this moment. But I will consider your request. I will be in touch to tell you if I can help and what it will cost."

Dominil nodded. The Fire Queen snapped her fingers and disappeared. Dominil let herself out of the flat and walked toward the lift, wondering just what sort of payment the Fire Queen might expect for her services. Whatever it was, Dominil knew she would feel an obligation to pay it. Sarapen was an enemy, but he was also a MacRinnalch werewolf. She couldn't leave him trapped in a hostile dimension.

CHAPTER 114

Thrix took the Fire Queen's advice, and traveled to Scotland the next day to consult the Fairy Queen. She approached Colburn Woods with some anxiety. Thrix knew she'd neglected the Fairy Queen in recent years. She hadn't paid her respects nearly as often as she should.

"I hope she's in a good mood."

Thrix arrived in the Queen's private glade just as the Fairy Queen was scolding one of her subjects. Thrix halted at a respectful distance. She recognized the fairy with the slight bluish tinge to her skin, the great mass of thick black hair and delicate black wings. Teinn, bringer of ill health.

Queen Dithean raised her voice in anger. Teinn responded by giggling before somersaulting into the air. Her black wings flickered, too quickly to follow, and she darted into the cover of the trees. Queen Dithean shouted after her but there was no response. Thrix felt embarrassed, as if she'd arrived in the middle of a family argument.

"Have I come at a bad time?"

Queen Dithean flew over and floated in front of Thrix's face. "Not really. It's just Teinn misbehaving again."

"That was a stern lecture. I am sure she won't do it again."

The Fairy Queen laughed. "She will take no notice at all." She changed her size, becoming human. "I keep Teinn mostly under control but she will break out occasionally."

"Has she caused deaths among the local population?"

"No, though she started a terrible outbreak of flu in the village. As humans are so weak, that may carry some of them off. But flu will come to humans anyway, with or without Teinn. Unfortunately, she wasn't content with that. She will insist on spreading the most harmful gossip."

Thrix walked with Dithean to the top of the mound. In the late summer the grass was thick and green. So were the surrounding trees. Everything in Queen Dithean's wood was lush and healthy.

"What did Teinn do?"

"She whispered in the postmistress's ear that her husband was having an affair with the wife of the man who owns the local garage. It's created a terrible scandal."

"Was it true?"

"Yes, unfortunately." The Fairy Queen frowned. "But while it remained private there was no great harm done. Now the village is in uproar. And I like that postmistress. She leaves whisky out for us. If she moves away, I'll be furious with Teinn."

"But you have plenty of whisky."

"True. But it is always nice to be treated with respect."

"I brought you this scarf from London," said Thrix immediately.

"Thank you! That is a lovely gift."

Queen Dithean turned her face to the edge of the glade and clapped her hands. Two fairies in bright yellow costumes flew forward and handed her tiny thimbles full of whisky and dew. The Fairy Queen thanked them, enlarged the thimbles and handed one to Thrix.

"*Slàinte mhath*," said the Fairy Queen, wishing her guest good health.

"*Slàinte mhath*," responded Thrix. They drained their glasses.

"It is some time since you last visited me." The Fairy Queen looked pointedly at Thrix.

"Is it?"

"Yes."

"I'm in London most of the time. I don't get much opportunity—"

"It's not flattering to be ignored, and visited only when you need something."

Thrix felt a flash of temper but managed to suppress it. It would not pay to upset the Fairy Queen. "I'm sorry."

"Not very, I'd say."

There was a silence during which Thrix felt increasingly uncomfortable, like a child about to be lectured by an angry adult. She couldn't think of anything to say to smooth things over.

"Well," said the Fairy Queen eventually. "What is it you need?"

"I'm looking for information about the stone dwarves' 'House That Can't Be Found.' I asked Malveria but she seems reluctant to help."

"Malveria does not like to talk of the stone dwarves. She has her reasons. Did she suggest that I could help?"

"Yes."

"I might be able to." Queen Dithean looked at Thrix as if trying to make up her mind whether to be helpful or not. "What did you want to know?"

"How to identify the house, principally. And I'd like to find out who inhabits it, if possible."

"Is there such a house in this land?"

"So it would seem. Constructed in London by a renegade stone dwarf."

The Fairy Queen turned her head to the south. Her eyes, unusually large and unusually blue, stared off into the far distance, as if she might be gazing all the way to London.

"I think it might be the headquarters of the Avenaris Guild," said Thrix.

There was another silence, during which they could hear rustling in the nearby bushes. Animals always gravitated toward Queen Dithean and would rest nearby, basking in her aura.

"If this house does turn out to be the headquarters of the hunters, what will happen?" asked the Fairy Queen. "Violence and death?"

"Most probably," said Thrix.

"I am not fond of assisting death. Though I am an ally of the MacRinnalchs, or I was, when they paid me proper attention."

Thrix sighed. "I haven't just been ignoring you, Dithean. I've ignored my business too. It's going to ruin. Everything is, since Minerva was killed. Won't you help me take revenge?"

Old Minerva, the werewolf sorceress, had been a good friend of the Fairy Queen, and her name struck a chord. The Fairy Queen's voice lost a little of its frostiness.

"The Maynista were clever builders. When they wanted something not to be found, it could not be found. No spell you have will penetrate or identify such a house. Nothing could be learned of it. By humans, anyway. Or werewolves."

"What about fairies?"

The Fairy Queen chuckled. "We have magic that is older than the race of stone dwarves." She summoned her attendants to refill their thimbles. "I noticed you drank with some alacrity."

"I've been feeling the strain."

The Fairy Queen could see the strain within Thrix. It seemed to her more than normal stress. There was great violence lurking inside her, waiting to come out.

The Fairy Queen folded her wings, quite somberly. "For me to let any of my sorcery be used outside my woods is no small matter. It weakens me, and lessens the protection I can give my people."

"I appreciate that."

"And if I were to help you, and weaken my lands, it's possible that the result will be your death. I'm not sure this would be a sensible use of my power."

"I need to take revenge for Minerva," insisted Thrix.

It seemed to Queen Dithean, as she studied Thrix, that the werewolf was expecting death, and was untroubled by it, provided she could take her enemies with her. That bothered the Fairy Queen, and she found it difficult to decide whether she should help or not.

CHAPTER 115

Kalix sat upstairs on a bus on her way to visit Manny. Her eyes were fixed firmly on the floor. When the bus suddenly filled up with schoolchildren, screaming, shouting and brandishing their phones, she didn't notice. She didn't even notice the delay caused by an extended argument between the driver and two children who'd forgotten their bus passes. Kalix was too preoccupied with her own thoughts. She was dreading meeting Manny. She didn't know what to tell him about Decembrius. She wasn't satisfied with Daniel and Vex's advice not to mention it. Nor was she happy with Moonglow's advice that she should tell him. Kalix tried peering in-between the two options to see if there might be a third, but there didn't seem to be.

Kalix's journal had seen a lot of activity in the last twenty-four hours. She'd marked herself very badly in every one of her self-help categories, and added some new ones that were all extremely self-critical.

She felt her phone vibrate in her pocket. She quailed when she saw it was a message from Manny. *He's found out I slept with Decembrius,* she thought. Kalix reluctantly opened the message, knowing she would be unable to withstand the hatred and malevolence it undoubtedly contained.

"Still in art shop meet me in café," it said.

Kalix looked at the message, studying it closely for signs of hatred or malevolence. There didn't seem to be any. Really, there was no way that Manny could possibly know what Kalix had done, but for some reason she imagined he'd guess.

I'll never be able to lie about it. He'll know. I shouldn't lie anyway, I should just admit it.

But then, reasoned Kalix, Manny would hate her and never want to see her again. Her head began to swim. It was all too difficult. She cursed Decembrius, and tried to put all the blame on him. Somehow that didn't work.

Kalix got off the bus at the stop nearest Manny's small flat and pointed herself toward the café. She stood there, unwilling to take another step. It was another warm afternoon, warmer than normal for the time of year. Kalix felt too hot in her coat. She'd known she didn't really need it, but felt in need of the protection it gave her from the outside world.

I'll just go and admit it, she told herself. *Then it'll be over. I won't eat* any more afterward and I won't talk to anyone. Maybe Dominil will have found the Guild's headquarters and I can just charge in and get killed.

Heartened by the thought of never eating again, never talking to anyone and then dying in battle, Kalix forced herself to walk toward the café.

Manny was on the phone outside the café. His brother John had called him as he left the art shop.

"We've had some trouble at work. I don't think I'll be able to make it to your art show. Probably Dad won't either."

Manny was disappointed. It was unusual for his brother and family to tell him they were having problems at work, though Manny remembered it had happened once or twice before. Some problems with financial markets, he supposed.

"I'm sorry we can't come."

"That's OK." Manny was disappointed. He'd have liked his family to see his new art.

"I'm doing some courier work next week," he told his brother. "Delivering parcels. Maybe I'll see you up at Limehouse again."

"Don't go near there!" said John, immediately, which was strange.

"What do you mean?"

"Don't go near these streets in Limehouse. It's not safe."

"What do you mean it's not safe?"

"Just don't go there. I won't be able to meet you anyway. I have to go now, Dad's waiting on me."

After the call Manny was puzzled. He wondered why his brother was so stressed. And what was he thinking, warning him not to go to Limehouse? He often delivered parcels around there on his bike. He stopped thinking about it when Kalix appeared. He smiled at her, then hugged her.

"Are you ready to eat?"

"OK," said Kalix.

She didn't say anything else as they entered the café, but that was quite normal. Manny filled in the gaps in the conversation with some enthusiastic talk of his new paintings and his art show.

"You're still coming, right? I hoped my brother would be there, but he canceled. Some work crisis. It's a shame; I wanted you to meet him. He'd like you."

CHAPTER 116

Distikka read the sign in the foyer: The exhibition presents highlights from the Courtauld Gallery's collection of Spanish drawings, and features examples by many of Spain's greatest artists, including Ribera, Murillo, Goya and Picasso. Distikka was interested. She liked Goya and Picasso and was keen to see the others. She was due to meet Mr. Carmichael but had purposely arrived early, allowing herself time to look at the exhibits.

She was prepared for an uncomfortable encounter. Mr. Carmichael was not going to be pleased to learn that the werewolves had discovered the location of their headquarters. But now it was done, there was nothing for the Guild to do but prepare themselves properly for the inevitable assault.

"And get rid of these annoying werewolves once and for all," as the Empress had said.

Distikka didn't find werewolves that annoying. She'd rather liked Dominil. But the Empress wanted them all dead, and it suited Distikka's ambitions to assist the Empress. She was examining a drawing by Murillo when she sensed the arrival of Mr. Carmichael. Distikka was not as highly skilled in the interpretation of auras as the Empress, but she could tell he was far more agitated than she'd anticipated. She greeted him with her customary lack of warmth, and waited to hear what was bothering him.

"St. Amelia's Ball," began Mr. Carmichael. He looked round to check that no one was listening. "That turned out very badly."

"Badly? Why?"

"Are you mocking us?"

"I really don't know what you mean," said Distikka.

"The deaths of my hunters," hissed Mr. Carmichael.

Distikka was baffled. "What deaths?"

"We lost four men at the ball."

"This is news to me."

"Really? You didn't know?" Mr. Carmichael raised his voice sufficiently for him to be shushed by a uniformed attendant.

"I had no idea," whispered Distikka. "There was no disturbance that I was aware of."

"Well, there were killings nonetheless. Mr. Eggers and three hunters."

"What were the hunters doing there?"

"I sent them, after Mr. Eggers reported there were werewolves at the hotel."

"And they were killed? I wasn't aware of this. Nor was the Empress. It must have been done very discreetly."

"Very discreetly. We haven't found the bodies. But I'm sure they're not coming back."

An influx of Italian tourists forced them away from the Murillo drawings.

"I'm sorry you lost hunters," whispered Distikka. "But perhaps it was unwise to send them to the ball?"

"Unwise? We thought the Empress was in charge of the event. We didn't know it would be a playground for the MacRinnalchs."

"We weren't expecting them either. But really, the Empress was occupied with other matters. You couldn't have expected her to assist your men."

"I might have expected her to save Mr. Eggers, given that she'd asked him to meet her."

It was an uncomfortable moment. The Empress had agreed to meet Mr. Eggers at the ball. The Guild might reasonably have expected that she'd keep him safe.

"This does make my news a little more difficult to transmit," said Distikka.

"What news?"

"The MacRinnalchs have learned the address of your headquarters."

Mr. Carmichael came to a dead stop. "What?"

"They know where you are."

"They can't. It's impossible."

"I believe it to be so."

"They can't," insisted Mr. Carmichael. "No one can find us."

"Dominil MacRinnalch has learned your address. Or perhaps I should say, if she has not quite learned it yet, she very soon will."

Mr. Carmichael was appalled. "How can you possibly know this?"

"I've extrapolated on past events."

"You mean you're guessing?"

"I wouldn't put it that way. We may stand here discussing it for any length of time, Mr. Carmichael, but the outcome will still be that the MacRinnalchs know your location. Soon they'll muster their forces and attack you."

"I can't believe I'm hearing this. There's no way they could find us. Have you given us away?"

"The Empress would never betray you. Even now she's thinking of ways to assist you. When the attack comes, Mr. Carmichael, you must be ready for it."

Distikka glanced at a charcoal drawing by Picasso, and nodded appreciatively.

"And really, is it so bad? You've spent months, or years, unable to find all these important werewolves. Now they're all going to arrive on your doorstep. I'd say that's a good thing, as long as you're prepared."

Mr. Carmichael didn't see it that way. He was aghast to learn that their headquarters might have been found. It was ingrained into the culture of the Avenaris Guild that they were untraceable. The news that they might not be was profoundly shocking.

"Nothing remains the same for ever," said Distikka, reading his thoughts. "I repeat, it's not such a bad thing. When Kalix, Dominil, Thrix and their companions are all lying dead inside your building, you won't regard it as such a disaster."

CHAPTER 117

Decembrius sat in his shabby armchair in his small rented flat in Camden, watching football on TV. He hadn't moved all day. Since the charity ball he'd spent all his waking hours in front of the television, before slouching off into his small bedroom where he slept badly, and woke up depressed.

Decembrius knew he suffered from depression. He sometimes had the uncomfortable feeling that, knowing this, he should be able to shake it off. Unfortunately, he couldn't. He'd never been able to. He could suffer the most serious depression for no reason. When something happened that was worth being depressed about—Kalix for instance—the extra pressure it added became almost unbearable.

The football provided some diversion. Decembrius liked football. But even as the match was in progress, he'd get a sudden unwelcome jolt, and he'd think about Kalix, off enjoying herself somewhere with her new boyfriend.

When the match finished Decembrius took the unusual step of phoning Dominil. He wanted to know how the hunt for the Guild was progressing.

"Quite well," she told him. "I think we've found the building."

"So we can attack?"

"Not yet. We have to receive clearance from the Great Council."

For the first time Decembrius felt keen to attend a meeting of the council. "I'll be there. I'll vote we attack."

Decembrius felt a little better after the conversation. At least something was happening. He looked forward to a confrontation with the Guild. He planned to rush suicidally into the Guild's headquarters and kill as many hunters as possible before they shot him down. As he sat on his own in front of the TV, he found that quite an attractive prospect.

When the moon rose he transformed into his werewolf shape without thinking about it, and remained seated, wondering how many werewolf hunters he might kill before they put a silver bullet through his heart.

"What did Decembrius want?" asked Thrix.

"He wanted to know if we've found the Avenaris Guild. He's eager for action. Eager enough to go to Castle MacRinnalch and vote at a council meeting."

Thrix scowled. "Do we really have to bother with that?"

"Yes," said Dominil.

"If the council doesn't want to attack, I'll do it anyway," said Thrix.

"So will I," said Dominil.

"Really?"

"Yes."

They sat at the large table in Thrix's living room. Thrix had a scroll open in front of her, and there were piles of very old books scattered around.

"This is difficult," she said. "These spells of destruction are all ancient. None of them was designed to erase computer files."

Thrix's idea of destroying the Guild had been vague, amounting to little more than entering their headquarters and killing everyone they encountered. It had fallen to Dominil to point out that this would not be enough.

"What does destroying the Avenaris Guild really mean?" she'd asked. "I'd say it means destroying not only people, but their records as well. There's no chance of us killing every single person associated with the Guild. Someone will survive. So we have to make sure they can never be effective again. We need to erase all of their knowledge of werewolves."

Thrix had seen the wisdom of this, though it would be difficult. No doubt the Guild had a library which could be destroyed, but who knew what they had in their computers files? Dominil regarded it as a very difficult task to completely destroy all of the Guild's computer records. They could be located anywhere, on computers in the building, on laptops in hunters' homes, or on a server somewhere, or in a computer cloud. She'd turned her thoughts to the task of erasing them all.

"Do you think you'll survive this?" asked Thrix.

"Survive the attack? Why do you ask?"

"I just wondered. We've been in some bad situations in the past few years. There was the feud with Sarapen. I thought we'd all die in that pub in Kentish Town. And then there was the opera in Edinburgh. I thought we'd die there too." Thrix sipped from her glass of wine. "But we got lucky. We might not get lucky this time."

"Our survival on these occasions does not influence our chances of survival on this," said Dominil.

"Doesn't it? I'd say if you get lucky twice, the third time you probably won't."

"Statistically, I would disagree," said Dominil. She sipped her wine. "But even so . . . No, I'm not really expecting to survive. If we penetrate the heart of the Guild, there will be deaths. I hope we can do enough damage to make the sacrifice worthwhile."

"Are you scared?"

"No."

"Neither am I," said Thrix. "But I'm probably going to die as well."

"We're getting ahead of ourselves," said Dominil. "We still haven't confirmed we've found the Guild."

"We'll know tomorrow, when I work the Fairy Queen's spell. For a while I thought she wasn't going to help me."

"Why not?" asked Dominil. "You've known her a long time."

"I haven't paid her enough attention. She doesn't like that."

Thrix picked up her glass. "To the Forests of the Werewolf Dead."

"To the Forests of the Werewolf Dead," echoed Dominil. They drank their wine, and carried on with their planning.

Kalix looked down at her small salad. She knew she couldn't eat it. Manny was eating a vegetable lasagna, one of the specials on the café's menu. Manny was cheerful, pleased with his new paint and pleased to see Kalix.

"I wish I'd seen you modeling!" he enthused. "You must have been a great model."

"I was probably no good," mumbled Kalix.

Manny leaned over and touched her hand. "Of course you were good. You'll probably get more offers."

Kalix managed a weak smile. "Someone else did ask me to model for them."

"You see?" Manny looked delighted. "You're so pretty. Who wouldn't want you modeling for them?"

Kalix came to a sudden decision. She had to tell Manny the truth. With Manny touching her hand, and smiling, and being funny and encouraging, she thought she sensed a faint ray of optimism. It would be unpleasant, but perhaps it wouldn't completely ruin everything. Manny might understand.

"So what else happened at the ball?" he asked.

"A clothes auction, and then a lot of people dancing."

"What were the debutantes like?"

Kalix admitted she didn't really know. She hadn't talked to any of them. She leaned forward. "I have to tell you something."

Manny grinned. "Yes?"

"After the ball I slept with my old boyfriend. I wish I hadn't done it. I'm sorry."

Kalix had never seen anyone's expression change so quickly. Manny's grin disappeared to be replaced by an expression of anguish. Tears appeared in his eyes. "What?"

"I didn't mean it to happen. I thought I should tell you. I'm sorry."

The tears began rolling down Manny's cheeks. He looked young and vulnerable, more like a schoolboy than a student. He stood up. "I can't believe you did that," he said.

A few other diners looked round with interest.

"Don't ever talk to me again!" said Manny, and then ran out of the café.

Kalix sat where she was, staring at the table. She could sense everyone looking at her. She looked at her uneaten salad and Manny's vegetable lasagna. She felt frozen, incapable of movement. She couldn't even lift her head. She sat quite still for a long time. Manny's reaction had been worse than she'd feared. She'd thought he'd abuse her, and she'd take the abuse, and maybe manage to make it all right afterward. She hadn't thought he'd just burst into tears and run out the café.

Kalix wanted to leave but didn't think she had the strength. She was still frozen. Her mind went blank for a moment or two, then an image of Dominil came to her.

I wonder if she's found the Guild's headquarters? Kalix imagined herself running into the building as a werewolf, tearing and rending hunters, killing them in droves before they finally shot her. She looked down at her chest, and imagined a silver bullet piercing her heart.

That's what's going to happen, she thought. She was quite certain of it. That's what my whole life's been about. I kill the hunters and they kill me.

Kalix nodded. She found herself looking forward to the attack, and hoping it would be soon.

CHAPTER 118

"I'm sure this will cause a terrible scandal," said the Fire Queen. "Whatever induced my abominable niece to invite Beau DeMortalis to my private wing? Iskiline, has there been much talk among the servants?"

"They talk of nothing else," said Iskiline.

"We must make sure we give them no more to gossip about. The visit is merely an indication that the Duke is now in good standing in the nation. There shall be none of the drunken revelry, gambling, wenching or dueling with which the Duke is regrettably associated. I've instructed my chief steward to lay on a very simple repast. We will dine lightly, in a civilized manner, with polite conversation."

The Duke of the Black Castle arrived exactly on time, which pleased the Queen, though she made him wait for half an hour while she finalized her makeup.

"You're looking well, DeMortalis."

It was true. The Duke *was* looking well. He'd put on his best dark-blue topcoat, the cut and color of which had been copied by aristocrats all over the realm. Beau DeMortalis was a leader of fashion. Less flamboyant than the Queen, but elegant, and precise in his attention to detail. He was handsome too, with thick dark hair and warm brown eyes.

"How is the Black Castle," asked the Queen, referring to the Duke's ancestral home.

"Ugly as ever."

The Fire Queen laughed. "It is a remarkably ugly building. But functional of course, as a castle."

The Fire Queen spoke to her chief steward. "Is Gargamond here? Excellent."

Malveria had invited the Duchess to join them. The Queen, while prepared to receive the Duke in her private wing, was not prepared to dine alone with him. That really would have caused a scandal.

"I hope you are in good form tonight, DeMortalis," said the Fire Queen, "With wit and pleasantries. I could do with relief from weighty matters."

"Affairs of state?"

"No, werewolves."

"Ah."

"From your aura, Duke, you do not approve of werewolves."

"The MacRinnalchs are historical enemies, mighty Queen."

"Please, you sound like Xakthan. You know perfectly well you were enamored of Thrix MacRinnalch when she visited. One wondered if the compliments on her blonde hair would ever end."

"The werewolf Enchantress has a certain allure. And she has dressed Your Majesty beautifully. But the others . . . "

"The others are engaged in a war. I have become involved in this war because Kabachetka is supporting their enemies. I cannot let her kill my clothes designer. Tell me DeMortalis, have you encountered Dominil MacRinnalch?"

"I don't believe so."

"You would remember if you had. I admire her intellect. And her looks, though she takes little enough care of them."

Dominil had been much on the Fire Queen's mind. She had talked to First Minister Xakthan, and to her intelligence minister, ordering them to attempt to contact an unknown werewolf in the Empress Kabachetka's palace.

"But Dominil is cold and superior," continued Malveria to the Duke. "She requires a great favor from me, and I am therefore entitled to ask a price. I may take her down a peg or two."

The Fire Queen smiled. "I will ask for something very troublesome, I assure you. Ah, Gargamond, how pleasant to see you. Without your brother."

Duchess Gargamond's suggestion that she invite her brother, Duke Garfire, to the meal, had been quickly squashed by the Queen.

"We are dining in the Azure Suite," the Fire Queen informed her guests. "One of my smaller chambers. But you may find us boring, DeMortalis,

I have no entertainment planned. I know you favor banqueting to the accompaniment of music and dance, but we have a simpler life here at the palace. If you are expecting your usual fare of raucous debauchery, you will be disappointed."

CHAPTER 119

Thrix visited her office for the first time in a week. "I can't stay long," she told Ann. "Just picking up mail. Any problems?"

"There are problems everywhere," said her assistant. "I've been calling you all week."

"Sorry, I'm still busy."

"Why don't you just sell the place if you don't want to run it any more?" Ann's customary good humor had vanished under the strain of keeping the fashion house going.

"Stop being dramatic," retorted Thrix. "You can cope."

"No, I can't. And I'm not being paid to."

"So I'll pay you more," said Thrix curtly. She swept out of her office, leaving an angry assistant behind her.

Thrix put on her sunglasses as she left her building. The late summer sun wasn't that powerful but Thrix was feeling delicate. Her eyes were red and she looked tired. She glanced at her watch. *Late again. Dominil will complain.*

Thrix had been spending a lot of time with Dominil and it was starting to grate. Dominil was not Thrix's idea of an ideal companion.

It's lucky we're both werewolves or we'd have nothing to talk about.

Thrix had not quite forgiven her for her role in Minerva's death, though she did appreciate that without Dominil they wouldn't now be on the verge of discovering the Guild.

"If she's wearing that same pair of black boots today I think I'll scream. Doesn't she ever change them? I'm fed up with her coat too."

Thrix walked west along Great Marlborough Street, crossing over Regent Street, heading for Hanover Square. Dominil was waiting, her coat draped over her arm.

"Sorry I'm late," said Thrix.

Dominil wore a plain black T-shirt. Thrix noticed how well defined the muscles of her shoulders and arms were and felt jealous. They walked into Hanover Square, a small patch of greenery. There were a few benches under the trees, and one or two pedestrians.

"Why aren't there any flowers?" said Thrix.

"I don't know. I thought there would be."

They had arranged to meet at the park, presuming it would contain a flower bed.

"So much for that," said Thrix.

"Could we buy the flowers?" asked Dominil.

"No. The Fairy Queen says they have to be grown locally. We can try Cavendish Square, that's on the way."

They crossed Oxford Street in silence. To their disappointment Cavendish Square was closed to the public. They stood outside the locked metal gate.

"There are flowers in there," said Thrix. "I can see them."

She looked round to check that she was unobserved, then placed her hand on the padlock. It crackled and glowed, then fell to the ground. They walked in.

"We need twelve petals from twelve different flowers," said Thrix. "And we have to ask politely before we take them.

Dominil pursed her lips. "I am aware of Queen Dithean's power," she said, "but this is straining my credulity."

Dominil and Thrix disappeared from public view under the thick trees, and halted at a small patch of wild purple flowers.

"Do you know what sort of flowers these are?"

"Harebell," said Dominil. "Why?"

"If we're asking permission, it's polite to know their names."

Thrix addressed the flowers. "Pretty harebell flowers, we're here to borrow twelve petals. Queen Dithean NicRinnalch sends her best regards from Scotland and promises to take care of your brethren in her woods."

With that, Thrix plucked twelve petals from twelve different flowers. She placed them carefully in a small plastic bag. They carried on walking west, heading for the hotel in Gloucester Place.

"We're early," said Thrix. "We can't work the spell until after dark."

"We can wait in the hotel."

"Or we can wait in a pub."

Thrix disappeared into the nearest bar before Dominil could protest. By the time she caught up, Thrix was studying a list of wines chalked up on a board.

"What'll you have?" asked Thrix.

Dominil asked for a glass of water.

"Dominil. We're about to walk into a hotel that might be full of hunters. This could be the last thing we ever do. Show some proper Scottish werewolf spirit, and drink something."

Dominil smiled, which surprised Thrix. "Perhaps you're right. Our forefathers would not have gone into battle on spring water."

Dominil took a glass of whisky, refusing the barman's offer of ice. "Why are these people so keen to spoil whisky with ice?"

They drank. Both sensed the moment when the sun dipped below the horizon.

"Time to go."

They left the bar and walked on until they reached the hotel in Gloucester Place. The young receptionist in the foyer greeted them without much interest.

"Miss Theodota," said Dominil. "I have a room booked."

The receptionist produced a passkey, which Dominil signed for. The hotel was fairly small, but from the appearance of the lobby, comfortable and expensive.

"Theodota?" said Thrix as they took the lift to the second floor.

"An ancient Athenian prostitute."

Thrix and Dominil stepped calmly out of the elevator though both were tense inside.

"I didn't sense anything strange when we came in," said Thrix. "Which doesn't mean the clerk isn't phoning his friends at the Guild right now."

"It's possible the Guild avoids this hotel. They might not want to use somewhere so close to their headquarters."

At the far end of the corridor Dominil slipped the passkey into the door. They entered the room. Dominil studied the far wall.

"We're at the end of the building. If we're right, the Guild is on the other side of that wall."

Thrix stood facing the wall, staring at it intently. After a moment she muttered a few words, too softly for Dominil to catch. She shook her head.

"Nothing. As far as my sorcerous investigation is concerned, that's a perfectly ordinary building."

Thrix fished in her handbag for the flower petals. "So let's see what the fairies say."

CHAPTER 120

Kalix took the tube home. At Kennington Station she walked slowly up the staircase. She was jostled by two young men rudely barging past her but she didn't react. The sun was setting as she emerged into the street, next to the cricket ground. She made her way toward her home, keeping her eyes fixed firmly on the pavement.

Kalix opened the front door. Her eyes adjusted automatically to the darkness in the hallway. Her flatmates regularly stumbled as they made their way up the dark stairs, but the lack of light never inconvenienced Kalix. She entered her flat and halted. Now that she'd arrived home she seemed unsure of her next step and stood in the corridor feeling confused. There was a tiny old table close to the door, left there for no real purpose. Kalix looked at it. Then she kicked it as hard as she could. It disintegrated with a loud crash. Kalix burst into tears, and stood in the hallway, crying.

Daniel and Moonglow rushed to see what was happening.

"What's wrong? Did you bump into the table?"

"Don't cry, it's just an old bit of furniture."

Moonglow and Daniel halted. They'd never seen Kalix crying like this before. She stood quite hopelessly, her long coat hanging off her skinny frame, sobbing in the hallway.

Moonglow put her arm round her. "Come into the living room," she said.

Kalix allowed herself to be led into the living groom. Moonglow gently propelled her onto the couch.

"Is this about Manny?" said Daniel.

Kalix wailed and put her head in her hands. Daniel looked at her hopelessly. Confronted by a sobbing female friend, he felt quite useless. Moonglow sat down beside Kalix.

"I'll make tea," said Daniel, thinking that it might help. As he filled the kettle he could picture what had happened. Kalix had told Manny about sleeping with Decembrius, and Manny hadn't taken it well.

I knew she should just have kept quiet. What's the matter with Moonglow and her mania for telling the truth all the time? Now look what's happened.

Daniel remembered the first time he'd ever met Kalix. She'd been under attack, and had fought savagely. When she'd moved in with them she'd still been savage. He wouldn't have imagined then that he'd ever see her sobbing over a boyfriend.

Moonglow's not as smart as she thinks she is about relationships, thought Daniel. A little lying never hurt anyone. It would have been better than this.

As Daniel carried the tea tray into the living room he was worried about what Kalix might do when she stopped crying. Something crazy, perhaps. Moonglow had her arm round her shoulders, comforting her. That was unusual in itself. Kalix was normally not fond of being embraced. Daniel set the tray down. He remembered that he'd had a good idea when Kalix had been demented. He'd calmed her down with music. Unfortunately, this wasn't the same. There was nothing in his huge music collection that was going to make Kalix feel better. So he poured tea for everyone, placed Moonglow and Kalix's cups at their feet, then sat at the table, with no idea of what else he might do to be helpful, but not wanting to desert his friends.

CHAPTER 121

"We only get one shot at this," said Thrix as she prepared the spell. "The Fairy Queen doesn't like giving away magic. It will be a long time before she'll do it again."

Dominil and Thrix turned into werewolves, which was necessary. The Fairy Queen's sorcery could not be worked by humans. Thrix took the twelve petals from the plastic bag. She took another twelve petals from her handbag, these ones from Colburn Woods. Finally, she took out a small sheet of paper containing a diagram. She began to lay out the flower petals according to the diagram. This proved not to be easy. The tiny petals were hard to manipulate with her werewolf paws. Thrix's hands trembled ever so slightly, and she swore as she dropped a petal in the wrong place. When it happened a second and third time Thrix clenched her fist, and seemed almost on the point of sweeping them all away. Dominil noted once more that it didn't take long for Thrix to become upset these days.

"Let me try," she said.

"I can manage!"

"You obviously can't."

"Just back off," snarled Thrix. "I can do it."

She picked up another petal and glanced at the diagram. They had to be arranged in an arrow-like shape, pointing to their target. Thrix placed two petals successfully but then her hand trembled again and the next one went astray, fluttering under the bed. Thrix scrambled to retrieve it.

"Did we bring spares?" inquired Dominil.

Thrix emitted a loud throaty growl, and glared at her cousin. Her temper, never far from the surface, began to make the intricate task almost impossible. Dominil felt her own frustration starting to rise. She was quite sure she could have arranged the petals in the required order quite easily. Thrix struggled on.

"Finished. Does that look like the diagram?"

"It's close. Though not quite perfect. I'll move those two into place."

"Go ahead," said Thrix, in a bad mood.

Finally, the petals were all in position. They snaked toward the wall in a twisted arrow.

"What's next?" asked Dominil.

"I recite the spell."

Now that the petals were in position, Thrix managed to calm herself. She knelt on the floor and closed her eyes. Dominil watched silently.

Thrix opened her eyes, then said a few words in the secret language of the fairies of Colburn Woods. Next she said a sentence in Gaelic, and waved her hand over the petals. They wavered, as if blown by a breeze.

"Are there enemies?" asked Thrix in English.

The petals rose from the floor and, as if they were a real arrow, shot toward the wall, hitting it with some force.

"What does that mean?" asked Dominil.

"It means the Avenaris Guild is on the other side of this wall."

The two werewolves stared intently at the wall, trying to imagine the scene on the other side. What was happening there? Were hunters planning their raids? Practicing with silver bullets?

"You're all going to die," muttered Thrix, and bared her fangs.

Suddenly, the petals rose from the floor, formed themselves back into an arrow, and flew through the room. They hit the door and fluttered to the ground.

"I wasn't expecting that," said Thrix, lowering her voice.

"More enemies?" whispered Dominil.

Thrix nodded. They crept toward the door, muscles tensed, ready to fight. Dominil swept a strand of long white hair from her face and flexed her great werewolf claws. They put their ears to the door and listened with their keen werewolf ears.

"This room will do for a week or so until we find you a more permanent address."

"A lot of hunters have stayed here when they first arrived in London." The voices faded.

"Well, now we know," whispered Thrix. "The Guild does use this hotel."

There were more footsteps in the corridor, and more talking, followed by the sounds of room doors opening and closing.

"It sounds like they're putting a lot of hunters in here," whispered Thrix. "We could kill a lot of them right now."

"It would ruin our plan. We should wait till things are quiet, and leave discreetly."

"I suppose so." Thrix sat on the bed. "Seems comfy," she said. "Do you think we could get room service?"

"I hardly think that's necessary."

"We might be here for a while."

Dominil sat in one of the plush armchairs. They remained there in silence, still alert to danger, wondering if they'd be able to leave the hotel safely and report everything to the clan.

"Are you going to take up that offer of modeling?" asked Thrix.

"That seems like a strange question at this moment. But no, I'm not."

"Why not? I know that agent, it was a serious offer."

"One experience of modeling was enough."

"Didn't you once say you were looking for a career?"

"I am not modeling again. Although it strikes me that Agrivex and Kalix could take up the offer. They'd earn money, and they both have the energy."

"They're too short," said Thrix dismissively.

"I understood that a few models of smaller stature have succeeded, due to their exceptional beauty. Both Kalix and Vex might be said to fit that role."

Thrix didn't want to think about Kalix and she didn't enjoy hearing her described as an exceptional beauty. She dropped the subject, and they sat in silence again. At midnight, having heard no sound outside for some time, Dominil suggested they leave. They picked up the flower petals and slipped quietly out of the room. They encountered no one as they left. The werewolf cousins made their way quickly up Gloucester Place, turning into the first side street they came to.

"I'll see you in Scotland," said Thrix.

Dominil nodded, and they went their separate ways.

CHAPTER 122

At 3 AM Kalix lay on her bed, fully dressed, wide awake and very depressed. She'd cried herself out, eventually. Finally prying herself away from Moonglow's embrace, Kalix had retired, hoping to go to sleep and forget about everything. She felt physically exhausted after sobbing for such a long time. Unfortunately, she couldn't sleep, even with a dose of laudanum.

Stupid werewolf vitality, she thought.

The weight of depression felt like it was crushing her into the mattress. She couldn't believe how badly she'd messed things up.

It's an all-time low. I must have set a new record. Again.

Her arm felt sore. She'd put a long cut on her bicep with the special sharp blade she kept for that purpose. That usually made her feel better. This time it hadn't.

Kalix sat up. *I wish hunters would attack.*

Kalix wondered again if Dominil had found the Guild. She hoped she had, so that there might be a battle. Kalix again imagined herself charging into a large group of hunters, rending and tearing at them. She sighed. Dominil might not find the Guild.

"And they might not even tell me." She became angry at the thought, and resolved to call Dominil the next day, to make sure she wasn't left out of their plans.

Kalix felt the moon outside. She changed into her werewolf shape for comfort. Her cupboard was open, and she could see her reflection in the long mirror attached to the back of the door. Kalix stared at herself. A few of Vex's crayons were lying on the floor. Kalix noticed that the brown crayon was the same color as her fur. For want of anything better to do, she picked it up and drew an outline of herself on a blank page at the back of her journal. It was hard to manipulate the crayon in her werewolf paw so she changed back and forth for a while, becoming human to draw in the details, and changing back to werewolf to make broader strokes. It took her mind off things for a little while.

When she'd finished, she examined her self-portrait.

I'm a hopeless artist, she thought, and ripped the page from her journal, and crumpled it up. She turned to her self-improvement pages.

"Werewolf Improvement Plan—be less violent—be independent—stop taking laudanum—get on better with people—stop being anxious—stop being depressed—stop cutting myself—eat better and don't throw up—improve reading and writing and maths."

She shook her head. *What was I thinking? I can't do any of that.*

Kalix ripped out the pages and went downstairs to the kitchen. She searched in the drawer and found a box of matches. Then she put the pages in the sink and set fire to them. She lit more matches to burn them quicker. Suddenly, and very unexpectedly, there was a great wailing sound as an alarm went off. The noise made Kalix leap backward in surprise. There was not much room in the kitchen and she banged her head painfully on a cabinet.

There was the sound of doors slamming upstairs.

"What's happening?" cried Daniel, appearing in only a pair of tracksuit bottoms. "What's that noise?"

The shrieking alarm was sounding incessantly. Moonglow ran into the kitchen, clutching a black dressing gown around her.

"Where's the fire? What's happening?" Moonglow looked at the burning papers in the sink. "What are you doing?"

Kalix was very embarrassed. She hung her head. "Sorry," she mumbled. "I didn't know we had a smoke alarm."

"Neither did I," said Daniel. "When did we get a smoke alarm?"

Moonglow climbed on a chair, reaching up to switch the alarm off. "It's always been here," she said. "I put a battery in last week."

"Couldn't you have warned us?" said Daniel. "I almost had a heart attack." He looked at the burning embers. "What were you burning?"

"Nothing."

Daniel was going to inquire further, but Moonglow nudged him quiet, thinking that it was probably something Kalix didn't want to talk about. The cat arrived, meowing energetically.

"I'm not surprised you're meowing," said Daniel. "Kalix nearly frightened us to death."

"It was my self-improvement plan," said Kalix.

"What?"

"My self-help plan. For making things better. Like in my therapy book."

"Oh. So you burnt it?"

"It was a stupid plan. Sorry I woke everyone. Goodnight."

Kalix walked out of the kitchen. The cat hurried after her. Moonglow and Daniel looked at each other.

"That's so sad," said Moonglow. "I think I'm going to cry."

"I didn't know Kalix had a self-improvement plan. Did you know?"

"No."

They peered into the sink.

"I don't believe in self-help," said Daniel.

"Maybe you should. You're looking a bit flabby."

"I am not!" Daniel looked down at his naked torso. "Maybe a bit. But I got in shape for modeling."

Moonglow smiled. "True. And it worked. Lady Gezinka just whisked you off to her room."

At the mention of Lady Gezinka, Daniel looked keenly at Moonglow, wondering if there was a hint of jealousy there. But Moonglow had turned toward the kitchen cabinet, and he couldn't see her face.

"What do you think Kalix will do next?" said Daniel.

"Be depressed, I suppose. And crazy, going on past experience."

"Did she really like Manny that much?"

"I don't know. I think she felt happy around him. That would be a change for Kalix."

"Hey look." Daniel fished a crumpled piece of paper out of the sink. Though blackened round the edges, it hadn't suffered much in the fire. He smoothed it out. It was Kalix's self-portrait, drawn in brown crayon.

"Kalix did that?" said Moonglow.

They both stared at the paper, quite surprised.

"That's such a good picture," said Daniel. "It's really like her."

There was something about Kalix's crayon drawing that had caught her spirit exactly. Though roughly drawn, it showed her in a way both Daniel and Moonglow recognized immediately—troubled and unsure of herself.

"This is a really good drawing," said Moonglow. "It can't be easy making a werewolf look vulnerable with a brown crayon. I'd no idea Kalix was such a good artist."

They took their tea into the living room.

"I wish Kalix hadn't burned her self-help plan," said Moonglow. "It wasn't such a bad idea."

"Unlike telling Manny she'd slept with Decembrius. That was a bad idea."

Moonglow sighed. "Maybe it was. I didn't think it would go so badly. But people should be honest."

Daniel remained unconvinced. "Some healthy lying never hurt anyone. I wonder what was in her self-improvement plan."

He looked at the sheet of paper in his hand. "I wish I could draw that well."

CHAPTER 123

The Fire Queen and her dining companions had not yet finished their first course when the Queen summoned her chief steward.

"Steward, what is this wine?"

"The light sun-grape, mighty Queen."

The fire Queen wrinkled her nose. "Light sun-grape? Is that a suitable wine for my table? One can hardly taste it."

"It was served at your instruction—"

"Nonsense," the Queen interrupted him. "One cannot entertain guests with light wine fit only for children. Take it away and give it to any children who may be nearby. Then bring us some proper wine."

"Very good, mighty Queen."

The Queen looked round at her dining companions. "My chief steward. A good man, but sometimes becomes confused."

As the next course was being served the chief steward hurried in with several bottles of volcano grape wine, a thick, dark red liquid.

"Splendid," said the Fire Queen. "You will enjoy this, DeMortalis, unless the advancing years have dulled your tastes."

"I believe I can cope," said the Duke.

The Fire Queen looked at her chief steward. "Steward, is it not customary to have music as an accompaniment to dining with guests?"

The chief steward was alarmed. "I believe the Queen instructed that no music . . . Obviously I have made a mistake. I will summon the royal chamber orchestra."

"Please do," said the Fire Queen. "And bring more volcano grape, one cannot stint when there are guests."

Outside the Queen's dining chamber the corridors were now full of servants running to round up the royal musicians. This was a potentially difficult task: given the day off, most of the orchestra would be now ensconced in the nearest tavern, and might resist any attempt to recall them.

"Are you enjoying your meal, DeMortalis?"

"It is splendid, mighty Queen."

"Excellent. You must excuse the simple fare, Duke. As I said, I am much in need of rest, and can take no excitement. Ah, here are some of the royal musicians now. Excellent. Steward, did I not instruct you to bring more wine? Send to my cellars for the special vintage, the Duke is in need of a pick-me-up."

The Fire Queen looked at the Duke. "Where is Garamlock?"

"I beg your pardon?"

"The Prince. Is he not always in your entourage? How are we to play cards if you have no partner."

The Duke of the Black Castle, not until now looking as if he required a pick-me-up, did look a little puzzled.

"I understood there was to be no card-playing . . . "

"Really, Gargamond," said the Fire Queen. "One might almost be disappointed with the Duke. Here he is, drinking light wine, and unwilling to risk his hand at a game of cards. It is not like you, Duke. I fear age must be catching up."

The Duke sent a servant out hastily to fetch the Dead Prince of Garamlock.

The Queen looked around for her chief steward. "Steward, this dessert is unsatisfactory. When I asked for a light meal I did not mean I should be brushed off with a sandwich. Kindly rectify matters."

"Yes, mighty Queen," said the steward.

Some time later, while studying her cards, the Fire Queen was annoyed to have her concentration broken by a tap on her shoulder.

"What's this?" She looked with displeasure at her young page. "Can you not see I am busy playing cards with the Duke?"

The page bent down to whisper in the Fire Queen's ear. "You asked me to interrupt if the game went on too long."

"So?" said the Queen. "I have hardly sat down to play."

"Dawn is breaking," whispered the page. "You've been playing for six hours."

The Fire Queen waved him away. "Stop talking nonsense. And then bring wine."

She turned to the Duke. "These young pages, always fussing. Your turn to deal, I believe, Garamlock."

The Prince shuffled the cards with a look of intense concentration, the same look he'd worn for the past two hours since the cards had turned in Malveria's favor and she'd starting winning money from him. There was a huge stack of gold coins at her elbow, and a similar sized pile beside her partner Gruselvere. DeMortalis and Garamlock had both suffered heavy losses, and had been obliged to send servants to fetch more gold.

"I trust the Queen is enjoying her rest," said DeMortalis.

"One is tremendously rested," replied the Queen. "Did I tell you how well you are looking, DeMortalis? Your new hairstyle quite disguises your age."

DeMortalis, a man of ready wit, thought immediately of several good replies he could have made to this, but restrained himself. The Queen's age was not something that could be talked about lightly.

"It has met with some appreciation."

"From kitchen maids everywhere, I imagine," said the Fire Queen. Gargamond laughed.

"The stories of my adventures with kitchen maids are greatly exaggerated," said the Duke.

The Fire Queen laughed. "If it wasn't for your dalliance with Gargamond's kitchen maid you'd never have been near the volcano on the day of Distikka's rebellion."

"And fortunate it was that I was there," said the Duke. "Defending the nation while the Queen was absent."

"Absent?"

"As I recall, I held the volcano while the Queen was trapped in limbo."

"Arriving just in time to prevent the Duke from being roasted by a dragon, as I recall," said Malveria, good-naturedly. "But one does appreciate your efforts, DeMortalis. As did my council of ministers, who discussed awarding you a campaign medal."

"A medal?"

"Yes," said the Queen. "A splendid device of flaming gold. It would have looked very fine on your chest."

"What happened to it?"

"I vetoed the idea. As I said to my council, the Duke of the Black Castle thinks well enough of himself without making it worse by awarding him medals."

"I appreciate your thoughts, mighty Queen."

The Fire Queen smiled. "Garamlock, are you ever going to deal the cards? And where is the page with my wine?"

The Duke picked up his cards. "My lead, I believe? Let us see if the Queen's good fortune can continue."

"I feel it can," said the Queen.

She concentrated on her cards, as did her companion Duchess Gargamond, who thought that the Fire Queen was enjoying herself more than she had for a long time, even to the extent of allowing a faint tinge of happiness to be visible in her aura. It was poor etiquette to display one's aura in public, but here, in her private wing, the Fire Queen seemed a little more relaxed.

"Is that another hand to me?" said the Queen. "Excellent. Ah, here is the wine at last. Pay up, DeMortalis, and deal the cards again."

CHAPTER 124

There was anxiety and confusion at the Avenaris Guild as news spread that the werewolves had learned their location. The board of directors went into emergency session. Once more, Mr. Carmichael found himself on the receiving end of some fierce criticism. It was he who'd encouraged the Guild to ally itself with Empress Kabachetka.

"And now she's sold us out!" Mr. Dale was irate. "I knew we couldn't trust these elementals."

"The Empress has not sold us out," retorted Mr. Carmichael.

"Then how else could the werewolves have found us? This building has been completely untraceable for hundreds of years. It's a 'House That Can't Be Found.'"

"We should never have let that elemental Distikka visit the premises," said Mr. Hofmann. "As head of security I advised against it."

Mr. Hofmann, a graying ex-commando, was responsible for protecting the Guild's headquarters, and was livid that their location had been betrayed. There was anger all round the table. The only member of the board not to join in was John, Mr. Carmichael's son.

"We don't know it was anything to do with the Empress," he said. "Perhaps the problem is that we underestimated the MacRinnalchs. Maybe they just found us in some way we can't guess."

"Preposterous." Mr. Dale, head of northern operations, was dismissive. "There must have been treachery somewhere."

Despite the criticism directed toward Mr. Carmichael, there was no attempt to remove him from his position. It was not the right time for an acrimonious change of leadership. Preparations had to be made, and no one else could marshal the resources of the Guild in such an efficient manner as the present chairman. He finally managed to bring the meeting to some sort of order.

"Gentlemen, it's happened, and we have to deal with it. We need to know how the werewolves might attack and when they're going to attack. Then we can make plans."

Mr. Evans, who still had ambitions to be chairman himself, was not quite prepared to let the matter drop. He aimed a few more words of criticism at Mr. Carmichael, but he also admitted that Mr. Peters, his second-in-command in intelligence, hadn't taken the news so badly.

"Peters says he's looking forward to it. He thinks we can annihilate them as they enter the building."

A few other board members reported similar reactions from their staff. Some of the younger hunters didn't think it was such a disaster that the werewolves were going to attack. The Guild would be ready, and would slaughter them.

"We should be able to slaughter them," said John. "If we know when they're coming."

"Distikka assures me they can monitor the MacRinnalchs and give us warning," said Mr. Carmichael.

"How do they plan to enter the building?" asked Mr. Able, who worked in the armaments department. He was something of a historian, and knew a lot about the Guild's history. "The 'House That Can't Be Found' can't be penetrated by sorcery. What are they going to do? Knock on the front door?"

It was a reasonable point. Even if the werewolves knew where they were, it wasn't obvious how they could attack. They couldn't possibly risk gathering outside the building, not as werewolves anyway.

"They'd have to rush in the door, and then transform. We'd kill them all the moment they entered."

"What about the roof? The walls?"

"They can't get in by sorcery. Are they really going to risk using some sort of explosive? It doesn't seem likely."

"I don't see any obvious way of attack either," agreed Mr. Carmichael. "But I think it's certain there will be one. Mr. Hofmann, have your security department assess the building immediately. Check for any possible means of entry. Mr. Able, we'll need extra armaments, and quickly."

"I have an appointment with Merchant MacDoig tomorrow."

"Good. Mr. Dale, we'll need your northern unit to concentrate on gathering intelligence. We need to know when this attack is happening. John, get Group Sixteen back here immediately. From now on they stay in the building, on guard duty. How many new hunters did we put in the hotel?"

"Eight."

"Good. We're almost back up to full strength. Get them into training right away."

By the end of the meeting, much of the confusion and anxiety had dissipated. If the MacRinnalchs had gained a temporary advantage, it was one that would rapidly backfire on them. The Avenaris Guild was an ancient and proud organization and it was not about to surrender. If the werewolves dared to attack its headquarters, the Guild would annihilate them.

John remained behind after the other board members had gone. "That went better than I expected," he said.

"I suppose we can see it as an opportunity, regrettable though it is," said his father. "You're going to be busy in the training rooms."

"I've already started booking everyone in for the afternoon."

"Why not right away?"

"I promised I'd meet Manny for lunch."

Mr. Carmichael was not pleased to hear this. "Manny? You should cancel it."

"I don't want to cancel. He's upset about some girl. He sounded very down."

"Manny's upset over a girl? That's hardly a reason to delay training."

"It's only for an hour. I promised I'd see him."

Mr. Carmichael shook his head. "I know you like to look after Manny, John, but there are priorities. Well, make it quick. And don't bring him close to this building, not at a time like this."

"Don't worry, I won't."

John departed. His father was dissatisfied but didn't dwell on it as there was so much to do. It was a long time since Mr. Carmichael had been in active service. Like several other senior board members, he found himself quite excited by the prospect of seeing action again.

CHAPTER 125

Kalix remained in her room, hoping that Moonglow and Daniel wouldn't force their way in and insist on talking.

They always want to talk about things. I don't want to talk. At least Vex isn't around to say something annoying.

She wished she could be a werewolf again right now, to dull her depression, but it was still hours before the sun went down. Kalix looked out of her window.

"Stupid daylight," she muttered.

She felt at a loss as to what to do. There just didn't seem to be any way of blocking her unhappiness over Manny.

I didn't know him that long! she thought. Why do I feel so bad? I didn't even want a boyfriend in the first place. It's all Vex's fault, she made me get involved.

Kalix growled, a low hostile growl that only a werewolf could produce. She stood up.

I need to do something. I'll go mad sitting in here.

She looked at her supply of laudanum. She had enough to last her for a while but wondered if it might be a good idea to buy more. She put on her boots and coat, and then her headphones. Daniel had digitally transferred her old Runaways tapes into her new music player. Kalix liked the tiny music player. She was surprised to have anything so modern. She sneaked quietly from the flat, careful not to let anyone hear her go. She was scowling as she walked though Kennington but at least it felt better to be doing something.

The late summer weather was still too warm for her coat but Kalix wore it anyway. She liked the feeling of being wrapped up and protected from the world. She put her sunglasses on for more protection, and walked over Vauxhall Bridge. North of the Thames, she turned onto the steps that led down to the walkway along the riverbank. Just then, for some reason, she was overwhelmed by an attack of misery so crushing that she couldn't take another step. She wiped some tears from her eyes and stood there feeling like a tiny, unloved, unlovable speck in a hostile universe.

Kalix, in the depths of her misery, was unexpectedly mowed down by a jogger coming down the stairs. She tumbled onto the pathway and landed in an undignified heap.

"Hey!"

"Sorry, didn't see you there."

The jogger helped Kalix to her feet. Kalix glowered at the woman, who was wearing a sports vest and jogging pants. She looked healthy, lithe and muscular, with short dark hair. Kalix noted that she had an American accent.

"Are you OK?"

Kalix nodded. She stared at the woman, who looked familiar. "Are you Joan Jett?" asked Kalix.

"Yes."

"Joan Jett from the Runaways?"

"Yes."

"I'm listening to the Runaways right now," said Kalix, motioning toward her music player.

"There's a coincidence."

"It's nice to meet you," said Kalix, who immediately wished she could have thought of something better to say.

"Nice to meet you too. Sorry I knocked you over."

"What are you doing?"

"Jogging. Have to keep in shape."

And with that, the jogger departed, running off along the riverbank.

I just got knocked over by Joan Jett. Kalix watched the figure disappear. *She really looks healthy.* Kalix frowned. *I wish I was that healthy.*

She put her music player back on. The Runaways' *Live in Japan* was still playing. She wished she'd thought of something better to say to Joan Jett. She wondered what she was doing in London. Playing a gig, maybe.

The unexpected encounter had driven Manny from her thoughts.

I should get healthy, thought Kalix.

She abandoned her plans to visit Merchant MacDoig's, and turned back across the bridge, heading for home.

CHAPTER 126

Sarapen noticed a change in the Empress's demeanor. She no longer pro-tested at his reluctance to share her sleeping chamber. She didn't mind if he went missing for long periods. She stopped complaining about his lack of interest in her affairs. At the same time he noticed court officials dis-tancing themselves from him. Even those few who'd sought his friendship were now withdrawing.

The Empress is bored with me, and these people know it.

Sarapen was briefly pleased. Perhaps she'd finally send him home. He still didn't know if he'd survive on Earth but he was willing to take the risk. He'd been trapped in this palace for far too long, surrounded by el-ementals he didn't especially like, wooed by an Empress he didn't care for.

Sarapen thought about his old keep in Scotland, the ancient family building he'd carefully renovated. He remembered the pleasure of hunting stags on his land, and prowling the forests at night.

The Empress isn't going to send me back, he realized. Her vanity won't allow it. His failure to respond properly to the Empress's advances was a deadly insult. She wasn't just going to send him on his way. She'd kill him first. Sarapen knew it wouldn't take much for the Empress to get rid of him. All she'd have to do would be withdraw her sorcerous pro-tection. In the harsh, burning environment of the Fire Elementals, he'd shrivel and die in no time.

He thought about Dominil. She'd agreed to help. Sarapen knew she'd keep her word. She'd try to rescue him. But realistically, how could she? Werewolves could not cross dimensions like elementals. Even if they could, how could she reach him here in the palace?

Still . . . if anyone can work it out, it's Dominil, he thought. She might manage it. Though I doubt the Empress is going to wait much longer.

His thoughts turned toward Castle MacRinnalch and, inevitably, his brother Markus. Sarapen still hated him.

Some day the MacRinnalchs will regret they elected him as Thane.

At Castle MacRinnalch, Markus was giving no thought to his depart-ed brother. He'd rarely thought of him since his funeral. Sarapen was still sadly missed by some werewolves, but in the past months Markus's own popularity had been growing. He was friendly and approachable, and he gave the impression of working hard for the clan, an impression that was boosted by the assiduous support of his mother. Not only had Markus shone at several important charitable events, he'd provided work for many local werewolf businesses through his contacts in Edinburgh. He'd persuaded the Great Council finally to release funds for drainage improvements in the marshland that ran between the lands of the MacGregors and the MacAllisters. As if that was not enough, the Mistress of the Werewolves had let it be known that her son had decided it was time the clan's records were organized properly, and was already hard at work on the task.

Markus had been busy with the database, and was consequently a little deflated when Dominil called to tell him she'd tracked down the Avenaris Guild without his help.

"Are you sure?"

"Yes. Thrix has confirmed it."

Markus put his disappointment aside. This was momentous news. "We have to act quickly."

"Thrix will give a report at the next council meeting," said Dominil. "That's only two days away."

"Shouldn't you do it?" asked Markus, who knew that a report from Dominil would be clearer and more concise.

"I'm still in disgrace in certain circles."

Markus couldn't contradict her. Dominil's fall from grace hadn't been forgotten by his mother, or the barons.

"Dominil, you've really done well. I'm grateful. Everyone will be."

"I hope so," said Dominil. "Thrix is uncertain that the council will be keen to attack."

"I'll get it through the council," said Markus.

CHAPTER 127

The next day Dominil consulted her iPad as she ate breakfast. She'd made a list of five people she needed to talk to: the twins, Merchant MacDoig, the Fire Queen and the Fairy Queen. She intended to take care of the first four today. Tomorrow she'd travel to Scotland where she could visit the Fairy Queen. Summer was now turning into autumn but while London remained warm, Dominil noted it was already much colder in the north around Castle MacRinnalch. She had experienced many bitter winters in her youth.

She had arranged to meet the Fire Queen in the National Gallery in Trafalgar Square, refusing the Queen's offer to visit. Dominil guarded her address closely, and received no visitors. She arrived at the gallery early, hoping to have time to look around the Renaissance rooms before the Fire Queen arrived. It turned out that she had plenty of time. The Fire Queen was late, failing to appear at the gallery's restaurant as arranged. Dominil walked round several more exhibition rooms before returning to the restaurant. Again, there was no sign of the Fire Queen. Dominil was irritated by the Queen's poor timekeeping. It wasn't till her fourth visit to the restaurant that Malveria appeared.

"You're late," said Dominil.

"I'm a Queen," said the Fire Queen, deeming that to be a sufficient explanation. She put a hand to her temple. "With something of a headache. Really, one is upset with DeMortalis. The man will insist on music, banquets and wine. And there is no getting him away from the card table. The gambling is quite shocking. Could you order me one of those nice little almond cakes, and some coffee?"

Dominil did as requested.

The Fire Queen looked around her. "This restaurant is rather bland. I had expected better in the National Gallery. I take it we are meeting here because you enjoy the art?"

Dominil nodded.

"I would not claim to be a great art lover," said the Fire Queen. "Though I did donate a painting to this gallery, a long time ago."

"You donated a painting?"

"Yes. By Caravaggio. He gave it to me as a gift, but really, there was nowhere to hang it in my palace, and it would have wilted in the heat."

Dominil stared at the Fire Queen. "You met Caravaggio?"

"There is no need to sound so surprised, Dominil. I have encountered many interesting mortals in the course of my life. He was a handsome young scoundrel, always fighting when he wasn't painting." The Fire Queen smiled. "I could tell you some stories about him. But another time, as I sense you are busy." The Fire Queen nibbled on her almond cake. "So. About Sarapen."

Dominil looked surprised. The Fire Queen was pleased. "Surely you did not think you could tell me some tale of a werewolf in the Empress's palace without me quickly realizing who it must be?" The Queen lowered her voice conspiratorially. "Is this really something you should be keeping from your clan?"

"I made a promise."

"My intelligence services have been making enquiries. Do you know he's been the Empress's lover?"

"I imagined as much."

"It's not thought that he is the most enthusiastic partner. There has been gossip in the servants' quarters."

"Can you bring him back?" asked Dominil.

"Possibly."

"Will he survive?"

"That is difficult to say. The strike from the Begravar knife should have been fatal. The Empress has healed him, but whether the healing is permanent or would fade on his return to Earth, there is no telling."

"He has no real choice than to make the attempt," said Dominil.

"Indeed not. The Empress will get rid of him if she's bored. But does it not worry you, bringing him back? He is your enemy. Letting him die would benefit you."

"I can't abandon a MacRinnalch."

The Fire Queen smiled. "You used to be lovers, yes?"

"That has nothing to do with it."

The Fire Queen was still smiling as she drew a red brooch from her handbag. "Elementals who are poor travelers occasionally use the jeweled pathways. I could provide you with a simple form of this sorcery. This brooch will act as a target. If Sarapen has a similar jewel, he will be able to step through dimensions." The Fire Queen kept hold of the brooch as she spoke to Dominil. "Needless to say, it is a rare piece of sorcery. That brings us to your payment."

"Which is?"

"I'm finding it difficult to decide."

"Really." Dominil looked the Fire Queen in the eyes in a way that few people ever did. The Fire Queen was not troubled by Dominil's intense gaze, though it did nothing to endear the werewolf to her. "Would that be because you're looking for some price which would be humiliating or annoying for me?" asked Dominil.

"It may be."

"Perhaps it's time for you to move past that," said Dominil.

"I do not understand your meaning."

"Instead of treating bargains as things that are amusing but ultimately bring you no benefit, why not ask for something you need?"

The Fire Queen regarded Dominil with suspicion. "That does not sound very amusing."

"But it would be practical. I suggest you give me what I require, and in return I'll tutor Agrivex through her next year at college."

"Tutor Agrivex?"

"Unless someone does, she won't pass. I'll make sure she does."

The Fire Queen pondered Dominil's words for a moment or two, and frowned. "Really, Dominil, you are taking all the enjoyment out of this. A bargain with the Fire Queen is generally meant to lead to a broken heart, or some other misfortune involving unforeseen complications. You seek to reduce it to a simple matter of commerce. Am I a tradesman, to simply sell you what you want?"

"How much do you want Agrivex back in the palace having failed her exams? Besides, tutoring her will no doubt be a frustrating task."

The Fire Queen ate the last of her cake, and seemed disappointed. "Such a small morsel. But I must keep my figure, so perhaps it is as well. Very well, Dominil, I will accept your unsatisfactory bargain. I will attempt to rescue Sarapen and you will tutor Agrivex. I have one additional condition."

"Go ahead."

"At some time in the near future you must inform Agrivex of the true nature of her boyfriend's feelings. I believe the guitarist Pete simply dallies with her in an attempt to make you jealous."

"I'm aware of that," said Dominil. "He never stops sending me messages. But why tell Agrivex?"

"Because she has grossly interfered in my private affairs. And it is time she received a harsh lesson in the ways of the world."

Dominil shrugged. "Very well, I agree. How soon can you get the jewel to Sarapen?"

The Fire Queen wasn't sure. She had spies in the Empress's palace, but they were not able to roam freely. "He will be difficult to reach. But we will endeavor to do it as quickly as we can."

The Queen looked round for a waitress. "I really must have another cake. One needs to build up one's strength to withstand DeMortalis's deprivations. Can you guarantee Agrivex will pass her exams next year?"

"Yes," said Dominil.

"She is not the most intellectual of Hiyastas."

"If I'm tutoring her she'll pass, or die in the attempt."

The Fire Queen smiled. "That is the spirit, Dominil. Perhaps this is not such a bad bargain after all."

After concluding her business with the Fire Queen, Dominil hurried off. She would have liked to examine the Caravaggio painting the Fire Queen had donated to the gallery, but she had no time to spare. As she drove east toward Merchant MacDoig's, she reflected that the Queen must indeed have had an interesting life.

Both Merchant MacDoig and his son were in the shop in East London. They greeted Dominil effusively. Regular customers were welcomed like long-lost friends. Any MacRinnalch was welcome to a glass of whisky and a long conversation about affairs in Scotland. Dominil did not desire anything of the sort, but even so it took her some time to conclude her business and extricate herself from the Merchant's animated conversation.

Dominil knew she was in for a hostile reception at the twins' house. In the eyes of Beauty and Delicious, Dominil had abandoned them, and ruined their careers. She expected to find them intoxicated and belligerent, and she wasn't disappointed.

"What are you doing here?" demanded Beauty as she answered the door. "I thought you had better things to do."

"Is that Dominil?" Delicious stormed out of the living room with her pink hair tangled around her head and a can of beer in her hand. "What do you want?"

Dominil stepped into the twins' house. In the weeks since Dominil had stopped visiting, it had degenerated into chaos. There was clutter everywhere and a strong aroma of alcohol.

"How are you?" asked Dominil.

"Don't ask us how we are!" said Beauty. "You ruined our lives!"

"You are exaggerating."

"Where's our new producer?" cried Delicious. "And our tour? And what's happened to our website?" Yum Yum Sugary Snacks' website had crashed after the twins had attempted to update it. "No one can even hear our songs any more. It's all your fault."

"Assisting you was always a temporary arrangement," said Dominil. "There is a crisis within the clan and I must attend to it."

"To hell with the clan," said Beauty angrily. "You shouldn't have started helping us in the first place if you were just going to abandon us. Now everyone's laughing at us again."

The twins cared deeply about their status among their fellow musicians in Camden. This had soared when Dominil got them back onstage, but had now plummeted again. People who knew the twins were not surprised when everything fell apart. It was exactly what everyone had expected.

"I came to make a brief suggestion, "said Dominil. "Decembrius might be able to help you."

"Decembrius? What good would he do?"

"He has no particular expertise in music or management, but he's intelligent, and he is a fellow werewolf with time on his hands. Perhaps he could help to get your affairs back in order."

Beauty marched up to Dominil and looked her in the eye. "Dominil, that's the worst idea you've ever had. Decembrius would be no help and you know it. You're just trying to fob us off with him because you're feeling guilty."

"I'm not feeling guilty at all. I was simply trying to be helpful."

Beauty thrust her beer can toward Dominil. Lager flew from the can, covering Dominil's face. Dominil stared at her with surprise.

"Ha-ha," cried Delicious. "That was good. Do it again."

Delicious's own can was empty. She threw it at Dominil. It hit her chest and fell to the carpet. Dominil calmly wiped her face. "I'm sorry I can't help you more," she said, and turned to leave.

"Hey, we did write a new song," shouted Delicious. "It's called 'Selfish Inconsiderate Albino Werewolf Bitch.' Do you want to hear it?"

Dominil didn't respond. She walked swiftly from the twins' house and drove off, heading home. With her business concluded for the day, she intended to catch a late train to Scotland. All the way home she could smell the beer that Beauty had thrown in her face, but she drove without expression, and it would have been hard to tell what Dominil thought about the incident.

CHAPTER 128

Vex arrived back in the flat in Kennington feeling pleased with herself. She was grinning as she walked into the living room.

"I'm back! Hi, Kalix. Do you want to hear about my super-brilliant plan for getting Aunt Malvie married?"

"Lend me some running shoes," said Kalix.

Vex looked bewildered. "Did I forget the language? That didn't make sense."

"I need shoes to go running," said Kalix.

"My plan is really extra-super brilliant . . . " Vex saw that Kalix wasn't going to show any interest in her plan. "I've got six pairs of Hello Kitty sneakers. Would they do?"

"Do you have any that aren't Hello Kitty?"

"Why would anyone have sneakers that weren't Hello Kitty? It wouldn't make sense."

"I suppose they'll have to do."

"Wait!" said Agrivex. "I just remembered."

"What?"

"I have seven pairs. No, it's eight."

Kalix followed Vex upstairs to the attic. As Vex opened her wardrobe, Kalix winced at the sight of her Hello Kitty shoes. She'd never imagined that there would be so many different designs. They were predominantly pink. Some featured a large Hello Kitty figure, others were covered in small pictures. To Kalix's dismay, the pair that fitted her best featured Hello Kitty with fairy wings.

"Good choice," enthused Vex. "You like fairies."

"No, I don't."

"Yes, you do. You've still got a children's book with fairy pictures hidden in your room."

"Stop going through my stuff!"

"You can keep the shoes if you like. I've got more than I need."

Kalix was in a determined mood, and eager to get on. "Thanks for these," she said, and disappeared down the ladder. She was dressed in a pair of child's tracksuit bottoms she'd bought for eighty cents at a charity shop, and a shapeless gray vest. The singlet displayed her shoulders, which were bony, and her arms, which were thin and scarred. She hurried downstairs and out of the flat, breaking into a run as soon as she touched the pavement. Inspired by her encounter with Joan Jett, Kalix had decided to get in shape. Any time now the MacRinnalchs would be involved in a violent confrontation, and Kalix had decided to make sure she was ready. It would help her to kill more hunters. She hoped it would also take her mind off Manny.

Kalix ran through the backstreets, going at a fast pace. No one paid her any attention; joggers were a common sight in the city. Her unusually long hair made her stand out a little, but she'd tied it back in a long ponytail, and looked like any other young runner, apart from the Hello Kitty footwear.

Kalix knew she was out of shape. By human standards, she ran quickly for a long way before feeling any fatigue, but as a young werewolf she ought to be able to do better. Her heart pounded as she ran through Vauxhall Park but she didn't slow down. She passed out of the park, back into the streets, and headed toward Clapham Road, intending to make a long circuit back toward Kennington. Her face was damp from perspiration and the recent cuts on her arm began to itch as she continued running. By now she was feeling the pace. Her heart was pounding and she was beginning to pant for breath. Kalix stopped for a moment, annoyed with herself. She remembered how she could run as a child, for hours on end, through the forests, over hills, not stopping for rivers or bushes. Then, her energy had seemed endless. Now, at eighteen, it had diminished.

I shouldn't have let this happen, thought Kalix. She started again, and ran down Clapham Road, sprinting past shoppers and schoolchildren, her ponytail trailing behind her, sweat glistening on her shoulders. She was close to home when her strength gave out and she was forced to stop, leaning on some railings for support. Kalix cursed.

"I'm going to get healthy," she said out loud, and started off again, running as fast as she could toward her house.

Daniel arrived downstairs to find Vex eating cereal and watching cartoons.

"Hi, Daniel, I'm back! Has Kalix gone mad again?"

"I don't think so. Why?"

"She's gone out running. I gave her Hello Kitty sneakers."

Daniel was troubled. "Running? That does sound quite mad. Did she say why?"

"No. She just rushed out." Vex cast a dark look toward the TV. "I'm giving *Nagasaki Night Fight Boom Boom Girl* one last chance. If this episode is as bad as the rest I'm really going to complain. Is Japan far away?"

"Very far."

"I'll go and complain anyway," said Vex.

Daniel sat down beside Vex to watch *Nagasaki Night Fight Boom Boom Girl*. He knew it was a serious matter when your favorite show suffered from a poor spin-off.

"Maybe this episode will be better," he said, encouragingly.

Kalix crashed through the front door and stumbled into the living room. She collapsed onto the floor and lay there face down, panting. Daniel and Vex looked at each other.

"I'm sure no good will come of this," said Daniel.

"Running's hard," gasped Kalix. She rolled over onto her back. "I ran a long way."

Kalix glanced down at her feet. Her Hello Kitty training shoes were stained with dirt from the park. "Sorry I messed up your shoes."

"It's OK," said Vex, who didn't mind at all.

Kalix lay on her back, too stiff and sore to move. The cat appeared and, finding Kalix in such a convenient position, climbed on her chest and went to sleep.

"What brought this on?" asked Daniel, who was very suspicious about physical activity.

"I met Joan Jett."

"What?"

"She knocked me over when she was jogging. Then I noticed how fit she looked. So I thought I'd go jogging."

Daniel was on the point of questioning Kalix further but Vex shushed them as *Nagasaki Night Fight Boom Girl* began.

"I'm giving you one last chance," she said to the television. "You'd better improve or there's going to be trouble."

CHAPTER 129

On the night before the full moon, the first wolf night of the month, clan secretary Rainal politely called the assembled werewolves to order. There were twelve werewolves at this month's council meeting. Decembrius, easily recognizable by his dark-red pelt, had traveled up from London to make a rare appearance. His mother Lucia looked at him with pride as he took his place around the large circular table. As always, a log fire burned in the corner. Torches on the stone walls cast a flickering light over the chamber, illuminating the dark green banners of the MacRinnalch Clan. In front of each werewolf were a crystal decanter of water and another of the clan whisky, and thick crystal tumblers. Rainal turned to the Enchantress, whose golden pelt made her even more distinctive than Decembrius.

"The first business lies with you."

"Thank you, Rainal." Thrix looked round at the assembled were-wolves. "We've located the headquarters of the Avenaris Guild in London. I propose we plan and execute an attack."

"I thought it couldn't be found," said Tupan, Dominil's father. "Are you sure you've got the right place?"

"Dominil and I confirmed it with the help of Queen Dithean."

Werewolf brows were raised in surprise. The Fairy Queen was an important ally but she wasn't known for participating in the war with the Avenaris Guild.

"I'm not sure how much Queen Dithean knows about werewolf hunters," said Baron MacPhee. "Could you tell us some more details?"

"Do you need every detail?" snapped Thrix. "We've found it, and now we should be planning an attack."

Thrix's display of temper seemed unwarranted.

"It's not unreasonable to ask for more details," said Verasa.

"We believe the headquarters is situated in Gloucester Place, north of Oxford Street," said Dominil smoothly. "We believe that because of information we gathered at a ball where the Empress Kabachetka was present. She is, you will recall, an ally of the Guild. Thrix and I examined the scene, and entered a premise next door. We used sorcery provided by the Fairy Queen, which confirmed our suspicions. If you look at the folders in front of you, you'll see I've provided maps and pictures."

Dominil's speech was received in silence. Several council members had already suggested privately that she be removed from the council, though no formal motion had been made.

"It's excellent work," said Markus. "From both Dominil and Thrix. And I agree we should now be planning an attack."

Markus drew out several sheets of paper from his folder. The rest of the council followed his example. For some minutes there was silence save for the rustling of papers as the werewolves coped with the rather difficult task of manipulating papers with their paws.

"So this is their headquarters?" said the youthful Baron MacAllister. "It doesn't look like much."

Dominil had copied pictures from the internet, showing the front and back of the house, along with several aerial views.

"It's a larger building than it might appear from the photos," said Dominil. "There are four stories and it goes back a long way inside. It's also possible there are floors underground. The Guild has had many years to make alterations."

"How are we expected to attack it?" asked Baron MacGregor.

"That's what we're here to discuss." Thrix could feel a lack of enthusiasm in the room, and it angered her.

"We can't just send a group of werewolves openly into a London street, can we?" said the Baron.

"There are only two entrances, as far as I can tell," said Dominil. "A front door and a back door."

"They're bound to be well fortified and defended." Baron MacGregor was an old campaigner, well used to fighting. "How are we to send werewolves against this place?"

"I wondered about entering through the wall," said Dominil. "Thrix and I visited a hotel room next door. If we could penetrate the wall—"

"What, you mean blow it up?" said Baron MacGregor. Though not quite as old as Baron MacPhee, he was a very senior werewolf, and cautious in outlook. "In the middle of London? You'd have the police there in no time."

"Even if you did get through the wall, how would you get enough werewolves into the hotel to mount an attack?" asked Kertal. Kertal, brother of the old Thane, rarely spoke at council meetings, but it was clear he shared the others' doubts.

"Is everyone trying to be as awkward as possible?" said Thrix. "The hunters murdered Minerva MacRinnalch and now we're going to get revenge."

"I'm not sending my wolves on a foolhardy mission to get killed in London," said Baron MacGregor.

"It is not foolhardy!" shouted Thrix.

"What's this I hear about the building being a 'House That Can't Be Found'?" asked Baron MacPhee. "Is that true?"

"Yes," said Dominil.

"Have any of you young werewolves ever met a stone dwarf?" asked the Baron. "No? Well, I have. I remember talking to him when I was out hunting with the old Thane. Clever elementals, the stone dwarves. They build a house to be secure. You can guarantee that place will be almost impossible to get into. You can't get in by sorcery and if you do get in some other way, you won't be able to use sorcery inside." The old Baron looked pointedly at Thrix.

"We've worked our way round that so far," retorted Thrix. "We found the house."

"And now you want to send werewolves to get gunned down by silver bullets," said Baron MacGregor. "I don't think it's a good idea."

From the expressions around the table, the Baron wasn't the only werewolf there who thought it might not be a good idea. Dominil realized that she and Thrix had miscalculated. They hadn't anticipated the level of opposition. They knew that Thane Markus supported the attack, and they'd assumed that his opinion would sway the council. Perhaps that wasn't the case. Dominil mentally reappraised the situation. There were twelve council members in the room. None of the three barons seemed enthusiastic. Nor did her father, Tupan. Kurian was old and conservative and usually against anything that threatened clan tradition. His son Kertal would probably support him.

So there are six werewolves here quite likely to vote against attacking the Guild, she realized. *As for Lucia, who knows? She might be against it too if she thinks her son Decembrius will be in danger.*

"I thought this was already decided?" Decembrius sounded impatient. "Didn't you agree you were going to attack?"

"We agreed to investigate it further," said Baron MacAllister.

"But we did agree that something needed to be done," said Markus. The Thane looked round at every werewolf there. "The Guild has been getting stronger and more daring. Are you all forgetting that they attacked us in Edinburgh? And then came even further north to kill Minerva? Now we have the chance to strike back."

The Thane's word carried a lot of weight but Baron MacGregor seemed determined in his opposition.

"We still haven't heard a credible plan for attacking this place. Baron MacPhee just told us how difficult it will be to get in. We're going to look foolish if we send a group of werewolves down to London and they're stuck outside in the street when the moon comes up."

"And we'll look even worse if they finally do force their way in and get shot down by hunters who've had plenty of time to prepare," said Baron MacPhee. "The old Thane would never have agreed to it."

"The Old Thane isn't here," said Markus. "I'm Thane now and I'm supporting this." He turned toward Thrix. "Have you worked out a plan of entry?"

"Not yet," admitted Thrix. "I plan to visit Queen Dithean tomorrow."

At this Baron MacGregor actually snorted in derision, causing Thrix's eyes to flash with anger.

"So you're asking Dithean NicRinnalch for help again? Since when do the MacRinnalchs depend on the fairies to help them fight?"

"We're not asking for help fighting! We just need help to overcome the defensive power of the stone dwarves' construction."

"I don't know how likely that is," said the Mistress of the Werewolves. "I tend to support the idea of attacking the Guild, but I'm surprised Queen Dithean's helped you even as much as she has. She doesn't like to let her magic out of Colburn Woods. She probably won't agree to do it again."

"I'm not convinced by any of this," said Tupan. "Whether the Fairy Queen helps or not seems irrelevant. If we can't come up with a solid plan of our own then we shouldn't do it."

Dominil turned to her father. It wasn't the first time they'd found themselves on opposite sides in the council chamber.

"We should not prejudge. Let Thrix approach Queen Dithean. Even if she won't help, I haven't abandoned hopes of finding a more conventional way into the headquarters."

"Maybe if you'd just all move back to Scotland instead of living in London we wouldn't have to be thinking about this," said Baron MacGregor.

"Don't start that again!" roared Thrix. "I'll live wherever I want."

"Even if it means putting the whole clan in danger? No wonder we've attracted so much attention with young werewolves running wild around the city."

"I don't think we really need to—" began the Mistress of the Werewolves, but the Baron carried on angrily.

"We all saw what Butix and Delix looked like when they visited the castle! Pink and blue hair! And there's Thrix in fashion magazines, Kalix roaming round like a maniac, and as for Dominil, could anyone be more conspicuous?"

Thrix rose to her feet and smashed her fist on the table. "Don't you criticize me! I've the same right to live my life as anyone else. If you want to spend your time stuck in your drafty old keep in the Highlands that's your affair."

"What do you mean, 'drafty old keep'?" cried the Baron, rising in turn. "Better living in the ancestral home than running off to London like a badly behaved puppy!"

Being referred to as a puppy was guaranteed to antagonize any werewolf. Thrix took a step around the table. It would not have been the first time a council meeting had come to blows, but Markus prevented it by grabbing Thrix and pushing her back toward her chair.

"Stop this! The council meeting will not descend into chaos while I'm Thane."

Markus spoke to his sister. "Thrix, I suggest you continue with your plan of consulting Queen Dithean. Secretary Rainal, please bring this meeting to an end, and announce that we will reconvene tomorrow night, to continue our discussion."

CHAPTER 130

Kalix was frustrated that the wolf nights had arrived, confining her inside during the hours of darkness. She didn't want to stay in her room doing nothing; she knew she'd become depressed about Manny. She wished she could go running again. The young werewolf ached from her earlier exertions, but she was pleased she'd made the effort. She planned to make herself so healthy that she would crash into the Guild's headquarters like a missile.

The moon rose and Kalix changed. It felt good for a moment, but again she wondered what to do with herself, and became anxious. The door burst open. Vex and Daniel marched into the room. For some unfathomable reason, Vex was wearing a paper party hat. Daniel was carrying a bundle of discs.

"Welcome to the first wolf-night party!" announced Daniel.

"What?"

"We're here to entertain you," said Vex. "Because we know you get stressed when you can't go out. Especially now when you've messed everything up with your boyfriend."

"Thanks," said Kalix. "I'm feeling better already."

"We've got all your favorites," said Daniel, brandishing discs.

"So you won't have to go mad and start biting people," added Vex.

"I hardly ever bite people!" protested Kalix.

"And you don't have to hide in a warehouse and try to eat your flatmates!"

"I only did that one time," said Kalix, and started to sulk.

Vex leaped on the bed and sat right beside Kalix. She leaned her head on her shoulder. "Mmm, furry werewolf. You're really comfy when you're a werewolf, you know that?"

"Don't use me as a pillow!"

Daniel was setting up a large screen at the foot of the bed. The cat, hearing activity and not wanting to be left out, raced into the room and jumped straight onto Kalix's lap.

"I know," said Vex to the cat, "she's really comfy. All warm and furry."

"OK," said Daniel. "I've set up the screen. Let's see what we have here." Daniel sat on the other side of Kalix, opened his laptop and showed Kalix his collection of discs. "We've got all your favorites. Like uh . . . *Tokyo Top Pop Boom Boom Girl*? How did this get here?"

"I put in a few of my favorites too," said Vex. She dragged her bag onto her lap. "I've got some beer. I've got a cake too. And crisps. And eight raw lamb chops."

Kalix became more enthusiastic at the sight of the lamb chops. As a werewolf, she had a powerful appetite for raw meat. On the wolf nights, all her inhibitions about eating would disappear.

"And here's your party hat," said Vex. "Look, I made some holes for your ears."

"Thanks. That's really considerate."

"Here we are," said Daniel. "The complete Runaways concert in Japan. And then another bootleg of them playing in Detroit. And then the not-so-popular last series of *Sabrina the Teenage Witch* when Sabrina goes to college."

"I still liked it!" said Kalix, her mouth full of meat.

"And then we've got uh . . . *Shakugan no Shana*. What's this?"

"Flame-haired flaming-eyed swordswoman," said Vex. "It's really great."

Since being given her laptop, Vex had used it almost exclusively for watching Japanese anime online, and had become something of an authority.

Moonglow appeared in the doorway. "What's going on?"

"First wolf-night party," explained Daniel.

"So as Kalix won't have to go out and bite people," added Vex.

"Stop saying that!" said Kalix.

Vex laughed, and put her head on Kalix's shoulder.

"Can I come?" said Moonglow.

"Well . . . " said Daniel.

"Hmm . . . " said Vex.

Moonglow immediately felt cross. "What do you mean 'well' and 'hmm'? Since when am I not invited to a party in my own house?"

"We wanted to keep it entertaining," said Daniel. "You know, favorite music and cartoons. And I've got a whole folder of funny cat pictures. We didn't want anything too serious."

"I'm not too serious!" cried Moonglow. "Kalix, do you think I'm too serious?"

"Mmm, lamb chop," said Kalix with her mouth full.

"I don't go around being serious all the time!"

"What's that book you're carrying?" asked Daniel.

"A Catalogue of Ancient Mesopotamian Temples."

Daniel and Vex laughed.

"I wasn't about to make you read it," said Moonglow. "Shove over and make room."

Moonglow clambered onto the bed and sat beside Daniel, so that the four flatmates were all perched against the headboard.

"Vex," said Kalix. "Why did you just prod me and then prod the cat?"

"I was seeing which one was most soft and fluffy. It's about equal."

Vex produced two more party hats, which she passed along to Daniel and Moonglow.

"I can't believe you were going to ignore me," said Moonglow, and elbowed Daniel in the ribs. "I'm as much fun as anyone else."

As the moon rose high in the night sky, the first Kalix wolf-night party got underway, with the first half of the Runaways' *Live in Japan*, followed by two episodes of *Shakugan no Shana*. The cat went to sleep on Kalix's lap, Vex leaned on her comfortable furry shoulder, and Kalix herself, once full of raw meat, began to enjoy the unexpected event.

CHAPTER 131

The Mistress of the Werewolves' chambers were by far the lightest and airiest in the castle. She'd had them renovated since the old Thane died, enlarging the windows, brightening the decor and bringing in modern furnishings of which her late husband would never have approved. She stood with her son by the main window, gazing in the direction of Colburn Woods, though the wood was too far away for even the sharp-eyed werewolves to make out from the castle.

"I think you're going to have to suspend your disapproval of Dominil, Mother."

Verasa made a face. "I don't want to."

"You used to regard her very highly. She hasn't changed, you know."

"She's changed in my eyes, Markus. She let us down."

"You're being too hard on her. So she takes laudanum. That's bad, but she's still doing a lot for the clan."

"It's more than bad. It's a disgrace. You can't just pretend it's not."

Markus looked at his mother. "Kalix is worse. You haven't started disliking her."

"Kalix is my daughter. And she's troubled. Fighting, running, living with all her fears and worries. I can understand how it happened. None of that applies to Dominil."

"Who knows what goes on in Dominil's mind? Maybe she had her reasons too. Anyway, the clan needs her. We wouldn't have found the Avenaris Guild without her. I doubt we can mount an attack without her either."

"We don't know that yet," said the Mistress of the Werewolves. "Thrix might bring us everything we need."

Thrix had left the castle to visit Queen Dithean, her second visit in the space of a few days.

"I wouldn't put that much faith in Thrix," said Markus. "Haven't you noticed how unstable she is these days?"

"Not really."

Markus shook his head. "Only because you don't like to admit that anything's ever wrong with your children. Take it from me, Thrix is about to go off the deep end."

The Mistress of the Werewolves couldn't deny that Thrix had displayed an unusually sharp temper at the council meeting, but argued there were reasons for it.

"Baron MacGregor was being more obstructive than ever. I blame Marwanis."

Marwanis MacRinnalch, niece of the old Thane and strong supporter of Sarapen, had refused to make peace after the feud. She'd left the castle, moving to the lands of Baron MacGregor.

"She has a lot of influence with the MacGregors."

The Baron's son Wallace, and his chief adviser Lachlan, were both known to be in love with Marwanis. It seemed to be casting a baleful influence over the whole clan, judging by the Baron's opposition last night.

"Can't you at least ask Dominil to come and talk?" asked Markus.

"Wait till we've heard from Thrix."

Thrix returned to the castle earlier than expected. She arrived in her mother's chambers looking cold and downcast.

"Queen Dithean can't help. Or won't help. It comes to the same thing."

"Did she have anything to say about the stone dwarves' 'House That Can't Be Found'?"

"I'm sick of hearing that," said Thrix. "You'd think they could have given it a shorter name. Queen Dithean says she can't help us enter it." She shivered. It was much colder in the Highlands than it had been in London. "She was quite abrupt about it. I don't think she appreciated me asking for a second favor so quickly." Thrix shivered again. "So we have nothing to tell the council tonight."

"We just need a plan of attack," said Markus. "It's a building with doors and windows. We must be able to invade it somehow."

The Mistress of the Werewolves didn't share Markus's optimism. "MacAllister made a fair point when he said we couldn't have a troop of werewolves outside in the street. Our need for secrecy is greater than our need to attack the Guild."

"Why would we have werewolves outside? We can all go in as human and transform inside."

Markus's mother shook her head. "I'm sure you'd all be shot before you got through the front door. And I don't see why you're including yourself, Markus. I still don't think you should lead the attack."

"We've been over this. If there's an attack, I have to lead it."

"Well, whoever leads the attack, we need some sort of plan," said Thrix. "And we need it before tonight. Why isn't Dominil here?"

"Mother doesn't like inviting her to her chambers any more."

"Really, Mother?" Thrix was exasperated.

"There's no need to look at me like that, Thrix. You're the one who's been blaming her for Minerva's death."

"We still need her help."

"Very well, let's visit her."

Still avoiding the need to invite Dominil to her chambers, the Mistress of the Werewolves accompanied her son and daughter through the long stone corridors of the castle to the room Dominil had lived in since she was a child. It had never been refurbished and was as plain now as it had always been. They found Dominil sitting with her laptop open on her desk and an old book in her hand, glancing from one to the other.

"Queen Dithean won't help us," Thrix told her.

"I'd like to talk to her," said Dominil.

"It's no use, she can't help."

"Nonetheless, I intend to talk to her."

Thrix was exasperated again. "Why would that help? Have you ever even met her?"

"No."

"Well, I have, often, and I've already asked."

"Do I have to keep repeating myself?" asked Dominil. "I intend to speak to the Fairy Queen." She closed her laptop, put on her coat, and left her room.

"What good is this going to do?" said Verasa.

"None," said Thrix. "Apart from frightening the young fairies when they get a look at Dominil."

CHAPTER 132

Dominil took the main footpath into Colburn Woods. She had been here often in her youth, though she'd never met Queen Dithean. She noted the slight rise in temperature in the shelter of the trees. Colburn Woods was known for maintaining a climate milder than that outside. The harsh winters of the Scottish Highlands were not quite so harsh here.

Dominil walked along the main path till she reached the burn that flowed through the woods. She crossed the water, briefly consulted a map she'd placed on her iPad, then took a turning to the left, a path so faint as to be almost invisible. The trees became denser and the light dimmer. When she reached a silver birch tree next to a rowan tree, she left the trail and made her way through thick undergrowth, walking carefully round several huge thistles. After a difficult journey, she finally emerged into a small clearing, where the land rose into a mound, covered in grass of a particularly vibrant shade of green. Dominil walked confidently to the top of the mound.

"Queen Dithean NicRinnalch," she announced. "I am Dominil MacRinnalch. I've come to visit you."

Nothing happened. Dominil thought she could hear some faint giggling in the trees around her.

"I will be very honored if the Queen of the Fairies would grant me an audience," said Dominil loudly.

A tall, slender woman stepped out from the trees. Dominil was surprised at the bright blondness of her hair, though not by her diaphanous silver gown, which seemed appropriate for a fairy queen.

Queen Dithean strode up to Dominil. Noting Dominil's height, the Queen had made herself a few inches taller than normal. She looked the werewolf in the eye, and smiled faintly.

"Dominil MacRinnalch. I saw you often when you were young, playing in my woods. Or rather, standing in the snow."

Dominil nodded. "I did come here as a child."

"Yet never to visit me."

"No."

"Did Thrix MacRinnalch tell you the way?"

"No. I learned how to find you from an old book in the castle library."

"Really? I had no idea I was in your books."

"A past caretaker, Fenella MacRinnalch, wrote a short treatise about the fairies of Colburn Woods in the nineteenth century."

"Fenella? I remember her. She was a pleasant werewolf." The Queen was still smiling faintly. Not threatening, but not welcoming either. "I have heard much about you, Dominil."

From the Fairy Queen's tone, Dominil was unable to tell if that was good or not. "I've come to ask for your help."

"Of course. Why else come now, when you've never cared to visit me before?"

"I acknowledge that," said Dominil. "My interests have lain in other directions."

"You're not the first MacRinnalch to visit in recent times, needing help, after neglecting me." The Queen's faint smile disappeared. "It is hardly flattering."

"I apologize for the slight," said Dominil calmly. "But my not visiting you was not out of disrespect, rather it was from having no wish to bother you for no reason."

Again there was some giggling from the trees.

"My young fairies are intrigued by your white hair. It amuses them. So tell me, what help do you require?"

"It concerns the werewolf hunters. I'm sure Thrix has told you of our need."

"I already helped."

"And your help was excellent, Queen Dithean. But we need more. We need a way to enter the Guild's house quickly. Otherwise we'll be defeated and many werewolves will die."

The Queen studied Dominil keenly. "Your own death does not trouble you, does it?"

"No. But I want to defeat the Guild."

"Death didn't seem to trouble Thrix either," said the Queen. "It would have at one time. But she's changed. I can sense another werewolf in your family, far away. Kalix. She's looking forward to dying. Perhaps there's some problem in the MacRinnalchs, Dominil, that you should all be so unconcerned about dying. Perhaps you should deal with that before fighting the Guild."

"I'm sure there are many MacRinnalchs looking forward to long, happy lives. A few may not be. We really need your help."

The Fairy Queen stepped away, and looked toward the trees. A hedgehog peeped out from the undergrowth but, seeing Dominil, withdrew swiftly.

"I can't give you sorcery to be used outside these woods. I've already done it once, and it will cost us. Without my protection, all the creatures of Colburn Woods face a cold winter."

"Would one more spell really cause you great trouble?"

"Sorcery that would enable you to enter a 'House That Can't Be Found' does not count as *just one more spell*. It would be an old piece of magic, treasured from centuries gone by. The stone dwarves were cunning. Overcoming their cunning is not easy."

"But you could do it?"

"Yes. But I won't. Already the cold of winter is approaching. I can't give away any more of my power."

Dominil looked at the Fairy Queen for few moments, then nodded gravely. "Very well. I appreciate your time." She reached inside her coat and drew out a small canvas bag. "I brought you these as a gift."

Dithean looked surprised. She extended her hand, taking the bag. "What is it?"

"Twelve thistle brooches."

The Fairy Queen opened the bag and studied the contents. She drew out a brooch, then another. She smiled broadly, so broadly that the glade seemed to light up. "There are twelve of these?"

"All different."

Dithean drew more out, examining each one with pleasure. "I love thistle brooches. How did you know that?"

"Fenella MacRinnalch recorded it in her book."

The Queen pinned a brooch onto her dress, and another below it. "How did you find twelve?"

"I hunted many shops in London," said Dominil. "I hoped it would be a suitable gift."

The Fairy Queen cried out in pleasure as she took out another brooch, a thistle with a small ruby in the center. "This is lovely."

"I'm pleased you like them," said Dominil. "I'll take my leave now." Dominil turned to go, and began to walk down the incline toward the trees.

"This one is even nicer," said the Fairy Queen, behind her. "Wait, Dominil MacRinnalch. I have more to say."

Dominil retraced her steps till she stood beside the Fairy Queen.

"You do appreciate that you're making a difficult request?" said Queen Dithean.

"I do."

"I hope so. The 'Entrance Spell of the Fairy Traveling From Sky to Earth' would give you access to the house, were I to grant it to you. Unfortunately, I can't. My fairies would shiver for a month."

The Queen went silent. Dominil waited. She noted, objectively, that Dithean's eyes were unusually large, and intensely blue.

"Do you know Queen Malveria?"

"Yes," said Dominil.

"Do you like her?"

"I don't dislike her. We have little in common."

The Fairy Queen smiled. "That is true. Though you're not completely dissimilar. The Fire Queen has a very resolute determination, and great courage, though she attempts to hide it. You also have these qualities, I perceive."

The Fairy Queen put her hand to her necklace, an unusual piece made of red stones, and smiled.

"We met when we were children," she said. "We've been friends ever since. When we were still young we became friends with Gasanda, a princess of the stone dwarves. Her parents discouraged our friendship. They weren't keen on their daughter meeting with strangers. They refused to let her out to play with us, and kept her locked away in their 'House That Could Not Be Found.'"

The Fairy Queen gently rubbed the tips of the fingers of one hand together. Out of nowhere, two tiny blue flowers appeared.

"But it never stopped Gasanda from coming out to play. She was such a funny, bright child. Always laughing. What fun we had, Malveria, Gasanda and I." The Fairy Queen laughed. "I remember we were all playing in the big circle of stones on the Isle of Lewis, and it started to rain, and Malveria almost cried because she thought the rain would extinguish her. We were only young at the time. So Gasanda used her powers to move the stones and make us a shelter. We had a picnic under the stones, looking out at the rain." Queen Dithean smiled. "Malveria was never worried by the rain after that, which is unusual for a Fire Elemental." She looked at the flowers in her hand. "Gasanda's parents trying to keep her inside never bothered her for a moment. She had a spell of her own, you see. The 'Maynista Princess Two Flower Pathway.' As long as Malveria and I had one of these flowers, and she had the other, she could just walk in and out of her house. I'm prepared to let you use this spell. It will cost me power, but the effects will not be so severe."

The Fairy Queen handed the flowers to Dominil. "It's not as convenient as the 'Entrance Spell of the Fairy Traveling From Sky to Earth.'" With that, you could breach their walls from the outside. With this sorcery, you'll need to somehow position one of the flowers inside the house. If you do that, you can create a pathway."

Dominil examined the small blue flowers. "Thank you, Queen Dithean."

An expression of sadness flickered across the Fairy Queen's face. It was very brief, but Dominil noticed.

"What happened to Princess Gasanda?"

"She married a prince. They became King and Queen of the Maynista. But he was a warlike king, and fought many long campaigns. Eventually they invaded the land of the Hiyasta. They were both killed in battle by Queen Malveria." The Fairy Queen fell silent for a moment, remembering. "Afterward the Maynista cursed Malveria for killing their rulers. Malveria is too strong for their curse to trouble her. She can't enter any of their buildings, but is otherwise unaffected." Queen Dithean frowned. "Though the curse does not trouble her, she has always regretted killing Gasanda. We were all such friends as children."

"Thank you for your help," said Dominil. "I'm grateful and honored."

Dominil turned and walked back down the slope toward the trees, leaving behind her the Fairy Queen. As soon as the werewolf disappeared, the Queen shrank to her fairy size and flew to the nearest tree, where she sat for a long time thinking about her old friend the Princess, and the fun they'd all had together, when Dithean, Malveria and Gasanda were young, and had no responsibilities.

CHAPTER 133

The Fire Queen sought out First Minister Xakthan when she returned to the palace.

"Xakthan, I apologize for missing the undoubtedly vital meeting on drainage problems."

As absolute monarch, the Fire Queen had no real need to apologize, but after the unfortunate events surrounding Distikka's attempted coup, she had promised her loyal first minister that she would pay more attention to state affairs, and had endeavored to keep her word.

"The truth is, I had to meet Dominil MacRinnalch, in an art gallery, and that was a stressful experience. One could not help worrying she was on the verge of saying something very clever at any moment, and perhaps even lecturing me on painting."

"I can see that would be stressful, mighty Queen."

"Indeed. So worrying was it that I ate several almond tarts, which were not on my diet, and am now wracked with shame and remorse. And all this on top of a visit from the Duke of the Black Castle, from which I have not yet recovered."

"Did it go quietly, as planned?"

"Far from it, Xakthan! The Duke was his usual dissolute self. The music, gambling and drinking were almost non-stop. One is quite shattered."

"Could you not have discouraged him?"

"Well, one does not like to be too harsh," said the Fire Queen. "Between ourselves, I made quite a dent in the Duke's finances at the card table. You should have seen poor Prince Garamlock settling up at the end, with a face like thunder. He'll be off to complain to his relatives in the netherworlds, no doubt. I must cast the appropriate spells for appeasing the dead, just in case."

They walked together through the enormous golden gates outside the throne room. Ceremonial flames shot from the gates as the Queen passed by.

"Has anything happened that I should be aware of, First Minister?"

"There is report concerning Empress Kabachetka."

"Not more cosmetic surgery, surely? The woman's nose cannot take another operation."

"Uh, no, mighty Queen. It concerns the werewolf in her palace." Xakthan lowered his voice. "So far our agent has been unable to make contact. Time may be running out. The Empress has a new lover, and Sarapen is to be got rid of."

"How do we know this?"

"The information comes from the Empress's keeper of shoes, who's usually well informed."

"We must keep trying, Xakthan. I depend on this scheme working so that Agrivex will be properly tutored next year."

"Very well. Incidentally, Agrivex is here."

"Agrivex? It's not time for her usual visit."

First Minister Xakthan looked embarrassed. "I think she may have deliberately visited while the Queen was absent, in order to address the council of ministers."

"How extraordinary. What did she have to say?"

"A strong demand for an increased allowance, followed by a long denunciation of the Earth nation of Japan."

The Fire Queen blinked. "Pardon?"

"Apparently they have spoiled her favorite cartoon. She wondered if we might cause a volcano to erupt in retaliation."

"How did the council of ministers respond?"

"We did not get the chance. While becoming animated, Agrivex tripped over a small table, bumped her elbow and burst into tears."

"She has had trouble with that table before."

"Indeed. As she was hopping around in pain, she stumbled into the great flaming seal of state and burned her hand."

"Burned her hand?" said the Queen. "Agrivex is a Fire Elemental. She can't burn her hand."

"I'm afraid she did. She is in the infirmary, receiving treatment."

The Fire Queen rolled her eyes in exasperation. "Really, Xakthan, this is greatly humiliating. The foolish creature has no control of her fire whatsoever."

By now they had reached the throne room, but the Fire Queen changed her mind, and turned off into one of the main corridors that ran through the palace.

"I will visit the wretched girl now. Send word to Arch-wizard Krathrank that Agrivex will be arriving for tutoring soon, and may need two months instead of one."

Xakthan bowed, but the Queen noticed he was uncomfortable. "What is the matter?"

"Arch-wizard Krathrank is a harsh taskmaster. I'm not sure he's a suitable tutor for Agrivex."

"A harsh taskmaster is exactly what she needs, Xakthan. When we were her age we had full control of our fire."

"Agrivex is very different to us. Perhaps a gentler approach—"

The Fire Queen held up her hand. "Enough, Xakthan. Your kindness is laudable, but Agrivex is my adopted niece and must do better."

With that the Queen swept off down the corridor, heading for the infirmary where her niece was currently under the care of Grand Physician and Master of Herbs Idrigal. As the Fire Queen arrived he was placing red leaves on Agrivex's hand.

"Not sufficient, Idrigal," said the Fire Queen. "I have treated burns on Earth, among humans. Who, lamentably, my niece seems now to resemble. Bring orange flame stalks, the kind we use to treat fire cows."

"Hey," protested Agrivex. "Who are you calling a fire cow?"

"Silence, dismal niece. Do not make this more humiliating than it already is."

Physician Idrigal fetched the orange flame stalks from his storeroom and handed them to Malveria. She placed two on Agrivex's burned hand, then moved her own hand over them, causing them to melt. The unsightly blemish on Agrivex's hand began to heal.

"Thanks, Aunt Malvie."

"Come with me, embarrassing niece."

Agrivex pouted. "I'm sick. Shouldn't I stay here for a while?"

"You are now perfectly healthy, and wish merely to avoid my wrath."

"Could we just forget the wrath?" said Agrivex, following her aunt out of the infirmary. "It doesn't really serve any purpose."

"How would you expect me to react when my niece has humiliated me in front of the entire palace by burning her hand on the great seal? Is there no end to your stupidity? How dare you ask my council to erupt a volcano in the splendid Japanese nation?"

"They deserve it," cried Agrivex. "Have you seen *Nagasaki Night Fight Boom Boom Girl*? It is so bad!"

The Fire Queen came to a halt. "Agrivex. Putting aside the utter preposterousness of your idea, is it not the case that this country, Japan, makes many of your favorite books, games and cartoons?"

"I suppose so."

"Indeed. Yet you foolishly fly off the handle because of one thing you dislike. This is not statecraft, Agrivex. As my niece, I expect you to have some grasp of statecraft. Along with some grasp of controlling your flame. I am contemplating sending you immediately to Arch-wizard Krathrank."

"That's so unfair!" cried Vex. "You said I had more time."

"Will you make progress?"

"Maybe."

"I doubt it."

"Well I won't make any progress if you're doubting me all the time," said Agrivex. "Cosmo Junior says the number one reason for girls failing to fulfill their potential is their parents not supporting them."

"I have supported you greatly!"

"No, you haven't! You just criticize me all the time. No wonder I can't control my fire. I'm telling Wizard Krabby it's all your fault."

"You will tell him no such thing! And don't call him Wizard Krabby!"

"Really, Aunty, I thought you'd have better things to think about than persecuting your niece. Like producing an heir for instance."

The Fire Queen came to an abrupt halt, and glared at her niece. "That is none of your concern, vile girl. I hear enough on the subject from my ministers without you joining in."

"Fine, I won't mention it again," said Vex. "On a completely unrelated subject, how was dinner with Beau DeMortalis?"

"An uncivilized affair from which I have not entirely recovered."

"So you had a good time?"

"I did not admit that," said the Fire Queen. "And I still have not forgiven you for inviting him to my private wing. What were you thinking?"

"Why not have dinner with him?" said Vex. "He's the only aristocrat you really like. Maybe if you had a few more friendly dinners you might not feel the need to persecute your beloved niece all the time." She looked at her hand. "It's healed. Thanks, Aunty. Well, I'd better get back to

London. I've got a lot of important studying to do."

"I did not give you permission to leave!" shouted Malveria, but her niece was gone, fading quickly from view.

My niece becomes more idiotic by the day, she thought. She wears me out. I need wine, and conversation with Gruselvere and Iskiline.

The Fire Queen hurried toward her chambers, to talk to her closest companions.

CHAPTER 134

Kalix ran through the streets of Kennington, picking up her pace as she entered the park. She could feel the rhythmic tapping on her back from her long, thick ponytail, and a similar sensation on her chest from her pendant. She sprinted through the park, oblivious to mothers with baby buggies, youths playing football under the warm afternoon sun and the small group of alcoholics gathered by the benches, passing round bottles. She could feel the strain as she emerged onto the pavement outside, but kept going. Kalix's fitness was improving, and she was pushing herself hard. She only just made it through her front door before collapsing onto the floor, panting for breath. She lay in darkness for a few minutes, feeling her heart pounding.

Better, she thought, dragging herself to her feet. Her muscles ached as she ascended the stairs. There was no shower in the old flat, so she ran the bath. It gave her an opportunity to do push-ups in the privacy of the bathroom. Kalix had never done push-ups before, and was finding them too easy. Despite the scrawniness of her arms, she was still immensely strong. She remembered, a long time ago, seeing her brother Sarapen exercising in the castle. He'd done push-ups with weights on his back to make it harder. Kalix wondered if she could do something similar.

Outside the sun was going down. Kalix flopped into the bath, and immediately changed into a werewolf. She lay soaking in the hot water, satisfied with her progress.

The moon rose forty minutes later, far north at Castle MacRinnalch, where the members of the Great Council were gathering. Dominil and

Thrix were talking as the changed happened; there was no break in their conversation, though their voices deepened in mid-sentence.

"Perhaps you should start things off," said Thrix. "I'll just lose my temper again."

"I'm not in good standing with the council," said Dominil. "It will be better if you lead. You can control your temper."

"I'll try," said Thrix, without much conviction.

Thrix had been surprised, and jealous, when Dominil had returned from Colburn Woods bearing new sorcery from the Fairy Queen.

"I can't believe she gave you the 'Maynista Princess Two Flower Pathway.' How did you persuade her?"

"I read one of our library books to find out what she liked."

The Enchantress swallowed her annoyance. They now had the means to infiltrate the Guild's headquarters, and that was the most important thing.

"So how do you feel after meeting Queen Dithean?" asked Thrix.

"How exactly do you mean?"

"Are your passions raging? She has that effect, especially when you meet her for the first time. Even more especially on a wolf night. There are plenty of virile young werewolves in the castle if you get an uncontrollable urge."

"I have never had an uncontrollable urge," said Dominil.

As soon as they arrived in the council chamber, Rainal called the meeting to order.

"Our first business lies with Thrix MacRinnalch," he said.

Thrix addressed the assembled werewolves. "We now have a way of entering the Guild's headquarters. Dominil was successful in persuading Quean Dithean to assist us."

"So we're still going with the fairy magic?" said Baron MacGregor. Werewolf eyebrows were very faint, but they could still be noticeably raised, as his were.

"Yes, to get us inside. After that, it's up to us."

"You say Dominil succeeded?" said Baron Douglas MacAllister. "I thought you were going to see Queen Dithean?"

"I did. I failed. Dominil managed to change her mind."

"That doesn't seem to bode very well," said the young Baron MacAllister. "You're the one that can make her sorcery work. Why wouldn't she help you?"

"How do we know she really helped Dominil?" added Baron

MacGregor. "What if it turns out to be something that doesn't work?"

Thrix had been determined to control herself. Unfortunately, at the first sign of opposition, her temper snapped. She leaped to her feet, crashed her fist on the table and launched into a tirade against cowardly barons who wanted to hide away while other werewolves were dying at the hand of the Guild. Once again, her fellow members of the council were startled at the speed with which Thrix lost control. Within seconds, Baron MacGregor was on his feet, roaring back at her. Baron MacPhee remained seated but joined in with the heated argument while others shouted at them to calm down. It was almost impossible for a werewolf under the full moon to remain completely calm while in the company of other werewolves who were so agitated, and in no time the council meeting had descended into chaos again. Howling werewolves rose from their chairs, crashing their fists on the table, shouting and growling. Crystal goblets tumbled to the floor and papers flew in the air. Dominil remained implacable, but none of the others did. Even Lucia, a very mild-mannered werewolf, found herself shouting at Baron MacAllister when he made some slighting reference to werewolves who didn't care about the clan and just came to council meetings to cause trouble, an insult she was sure was aimed at her son Decembrius.

It took Markus, Rainal and the Mistress of the Werewolves some time before they could calm everyone down.

"We will discuss this in a civilized manner!" roared Markus. "Thrix, sit down! Baron MacGregor, you sit down as well."

"I'll not have Thrix MacRinnalch insult me!" yelled the Baron. "I was fighting for the clan before she was born!"

"Everyone sit down!" repeated Markus. "Are we unable to behave properly?"

"I'd say it was mainly Thrix who's unable to behave properly," said Tupan. All eyes turned toward Thrix.

"So it's my fault?" she said, angrily.

"Yes," said Tupan. "The moment you hear something you don't like you're out of your chair, roaring and shouting."

Tupan, brother of the old Thane, would have liked to have been Thane himself. He'd never had the support for that to happen, but his voice was still influential.

"Fine," said Thrix. She sat down heavily. "I'll try and control myself."

There was a silence, broken by the sound of papers being shuffled back into order and glasses being returned to the table. The heavy crystal tumblers were sturdy items, and could take a lot of abuse, which is why they were chosen for council meetings.

"Perhaps Dominil could carry on for the meantime," said Markus.

Dominil nodded. "We've obtained a spell from Queen Dithean. Using it, we believe we can enter the Guild's headquarters. Once there we will dispatch all hunters we find, and erase as many of their records as we can. By that I mean physically destroy their archives, and corrupt or destroy their computer records."

"How many werewolves do you need for this attack?"

"Twenty, we think. We can get them into position in the hotel next door."

"Unseen?" Baron MacGregor was dubious. "That's a lot of werewolves to gather without anyone noticing."

"We'll introduce some of them as guests in the hotel, on the pretext of being a business party."

"Isn't that going to raise suspicion?"

"There's no reason it should. Remember, the Guild has no idea we're coming."

"I'd like to hear more about this help from Queen Dithean," said Baron MacPhee. "What sort of spell is going to get us inside the building?"

"Do you need every detail?" asked Thrix.

"I think it would be helpful," said the Mistress of the Werewolves.

"Very well. It's called the 'Maynista Princess Two Flower Pathway.' Using flowers supplied by Queen Dithean we'll make a pathway from the hotel room to their headquarters."

Baron MacPhee wasn't satisfied. He'd met the stone dwarves during the course of his very long life, and he knew what they were capable of. "So you just point this spell at the building and it cuts right through their defenses?"

"Not exactly," admitted Thrix. "We have to get one of the flowers inside the building."

"Inside? So someone has to go in first?"

"Yes."

Those werewolves who'd been excited by news of the breakthrough were deflated, and those who'd been cynical had their reservations reinforced.

"I thought the whole point of this was that we couldn't get inside the building," said Baron MacGregor.

"It's not impossible to enter in normal circumstances," said Thrix. "Hunters go in and out. We just need one person to get inside, and conceal the flower somewhere."

"You mean send someone in disguised as a postman, or a plumber?" asked Markus.

"Something like that."

"Surely no matter how a werewolf was disguised, they'd know it was a werewolf?" said the Mistress of the Werewolves. "Wouldn't they?"

"I think they probably would," admitted Dominil. "The Avenaris Guild doesn't use much sorcery, but they have sometimes detected werewolves in the past. I feel they must have some sort of alarm that will sound if a werewolf enters through the front door."

"So the whole thing is still hopeless," said Baron MacAllister.

Thrix felt her temper rising again. "Can't you just trust us to work it out? We've managed everything else so far, haven't we?"

Baron Douglas MacAllister laughed. The young baron was not as opposed to the attack as some of the others, but his father and brother had died in the great feud, leaving him with a general dislike for Thane Markus and his family. "I don't think I'd trust Thrix to go five minutes without screaming at everyone. That might be OK when she's designing dresses, but it's not much good for anything serious. As for Dominil, she'll need her regular laudanum breaks, won't she? It's not really the greatest leadership."

Dominil didn't react to the insult. Thrix did. She stood up, banging her fist on the table and shouting at Baron MacAllister, and once more there was uproar.

CHAPTER 135

In the early hours of the morning Dominil was alone in her room. The meeting had come to a disorderly end. No agreement had been reached. Dominil found it extremely frustrating. Tomorrow was the third of the wolf nights and the last night on which a council meeting could be convened. If they couldn't come to an agreement then, further discussions would have to wait till the meeting at the next full moon.

Thrix won't wait, thought Dominil. If the council doesn't authorize an attack, she'll do it anyway.

If Thrix did carry out an attack, Dominil would go with her. She didn't like the thought, but she was intransigent in her own way. Dominil still carried a burden of guilt over the death of Minerva. She wanted revenge. She wouldn't let her cousin attack alone.

Dominil knew that they'd fail. Thrix still hoped to use sorcery inside the building, but everything they'd learned about the stone dwarves' house suggested it would be impossible. There would be no magic, only the strength and ferocity of the MacRinnalchs. Two strong werewolves like Dominil and Thrix might do a lot of damage. They might kill a lot of hunters, but they'd be defeated in the end. They wouldn't be able to deal the Avenaris Guild a fatal blow.

Dominil reflected that if she were killed, she would not be missed much by anyone. The clan still shunned her. The Mistress of the Werewolves showed no sign of warming to her. She might not even be able to attend another council meeting. There was still talk of removing her from the council. She thought briefly of the twins, who had thrown beer in her face. Dominil hadn't reacted when it happened. She wouldn't allow the twins to see they could affect her, but they had. Dominil kept her emotions well hidden, but she felt a private sadness that Beauty and Delicious had ended up disliking her so much.

She looked up, sensing that Thrix was approaching. She opened her door just as her cousin arrived.

"Another useless meeting," said Thrix.

"We still have tomorrow," said Dominil.

Thrix sat on the bed. She smelled faintly of the clan whisky. "I thought with Markus on our side we'd get agreement but the barons seem set against it."

"They don't want to send their werewolves to London."

"They should."

"I know they should, but they don't want to. The clan hasn't settled down as much as we thought. There are still resentments against Markus. Kurian and my father are just as bad as the barons."

"Looks like it's just going to be us," said Thrix. "And Decembrius, maybe."

"I haven't given up hope of persuading the council," said Dominil. "Perhaps we made a mistake, going to them before our plans were complete."

"We don't have a complete plan," said Thrix. "Unless you've thought of one in the past few hours."

"I have."

Thrix looked up sharply. "Really?"

"Yes. We need to get someone inside the building to plant the other end of our pathway. We talked lightly of postmen and so on. I don't see why that couldn't work, provided it's convincing. Merchant MacDoig does business with the Guild. What if we arranged for him to send some legitimate package to them? A courier carrying such a package could gain access to the building."

"Maybe. The Merchant would probably help." Thrix frowned. "And he might just as easily sell us out."

"That would be a risk. But the MacRinnalchs are more valuable clients than the Guild. If the Thane or the Mistress of the Werewolves made the arrangement, I think he'd stick to it."

"Do you have any whisky?" asked Thrix.

"Do you really need more?"

"Don't you start as well."

"As well as who?"

"As well as my mother, who said I'm drinking too much."

Dominil produced her bottle of the clan malt from her cupboard and poured a small glass for Thrix, and one for herself.

"So we send a package to the Guild," said Thrix. "And the courier has the petal in their pocket. Once inside the building they hide it somewhere. That sounds good. But who's going to take it in? You were probably right about them having some sort of warning system. An alarm will sound if a werewolf walks in."

"Kalix could do it."

"Kalix? That's ridiculous."

"I don't see why. She has her pendant. She's the one werewolf who can never be detected."

Thrix considered this. "I suppose you're right. I'd forgotten about Kalix's pendant. It would conceal her from any sort of finding spell. And she's quite resistant to sorcery anyway."

It had been noted in the past that Kalix did not seem to be much affected by sorcery, even by spells that affected other werewolves. No one knew why, though Thrix suspected it was to do with her unusual birth.

"I can see problems," said Thrix. "Even putting aside the fact that Kalix is bound to let us down, remember she's fought with hunters all over London. She's killed enough of them, but there are probably some left who'd recognize her. What if she walks straight into a hunter who's seen her before?"

"That would be a risk," admitted Dominil. "But we don't know what the inside of the Guild's headquarters looks like. The front door probably just leads to a reception area. Whoever is on duty is unlikely to be a werewolf hunter. More likely it will be some civilian employee who's never seen a werewolf before. If Kalix was suitably disguised she might be able to deliver the package without being detected."

"How would she hide the petal?"

"She'd have to use her initiative."

"Kalix doesn't have enough sense to have any initiative."

"You're being too hard on Kalix and I have no desire to discuss your prejudices again," said Dominil. "It's a reasonable idea and we should present it to the council."

Thrix poured herself another drink, uninvited. "You can present it," she muttered. "I'm not recommending Kalix for anything. I can see trouble with the barons. MacGregor and MacPhee still blame her for the old Thane's death, and MacAllister doesn't like any of our family."

"I'll call Kalix tomorrow," said Dominil. "If she agrees to my proposal, I'll talk to Markus."

CHAPTER 136

Moonglow was wrapped in a black dressing gown with a black towel round her hair when Kalix arrived in the living room around midday. Moonglow had washed her hair and was drinking tea while reading a book before engaging in the lengthy drying process.

"Morning, Kalix."

Kalix joined her at the table by the window. Though it was a very old table, badly stained with age, it had taken on a cheerful, almost jaunty air, thanks to the vase of yellow flowers Moonglow had placed there, now illuminated by the sun's rays which streamed in through several holes in the net curtains.

Kalix was dressed in her running vest. "Look," she said, and flexed her bicep. "I've been exercising."

Moonglow thought that Kalix's arms looked just as skinny as they always had, but nodded encouragingly.

"It's really making me feel better. I've been running and doing pushups and I'm much healthier. And I ate loads last night when I was a werewolf and I don't feel like throwing up at all."

"That's really good."

"I should have tried getting healthy before, instead of all that stupid self-improvement stuff," said Kalix. She poured herself a bowl of cereal, something she would not normally have done after a night of eating meat. Moonglow felt quietly pleased, though didn't say anything, for fear of making Kalix think she was monitoring her diet. There was a loud banging upstairs.

"It's OK!" shouted Vex. "I fell out of the attic again but I didn't hurt myself!"

She ran down the stairs, smiling.

"Trouble with your ladder again?" asked Moonglow.

Vex nodded. "My feet got confused. It's these shoes."

Unusually, Vex was wearing one of her many pairs of Hello Kitty running shoes, instead of boots.

"Kalix looks so good in them I thought I'd try them as well." Vex nimbly lifted her leg and planted her foot on the table. "See?"

"Very nice," said Moonglow.

"Hey, Kalix is eating breakfast!" said Vex. "I knew we'd cheer her up with our wolf-night parties."

Kalix immediately felt sensitive about people watching her eat, and put her cereal bowl down.

"I'm going to the pictures with Pete!" said Vex. "We're going to see some romantic comedy. Isn't that funny? Who likes romantic comedies? But it's OK when you go with your boyfriend. It's so great having a boyfriend. I have to rush! Bye!"

Vex hurried out of the living room. They heard her filling up her bag in the kitchen with food to eat on her journey to Camden, then she was gone, running down the stairs and out the front door.

"Kalix?" said Moonglow.

Kalix had slumped forward so her face was resting on the table. "I hate everything," she mumbled.

There was a long pause.

"Still not feeling better about Manny?"

"Apparently not," said Kalix, with her face still pressed to the table.

Moonglow wished that Vex could be more tactful. The young Fire Elemental's bright enthusiasm about her boyfriend was enough to give anyone a relapse.

Kalix sighed. "Everything is hopeless."

"You'll get over it soon," said Moonglow.

"No, I won't."

Moonglow tried another tack. "Have you actually tried speaking to Manny again? Maybe he's not so mad any more."

"He doesn't want to speak to me."

"You don't know that."

"He's got a new voicemail message. It says, 'Go away I don't want to speak to you.'"

"Oh."

There was another silence.

"I'm going upstairs," said Kalix. The good mood brought on by exercise had disappeared, to be replaced with depression. As she closed her bedroom door she had the mean thought that she wished Vex might suffer a disastrous break-up and feel as bad as she did. She immediately regretted it. She was on the point of taking her supply of laudanum from her cabinet when her phone rang.

"Kalix? This is Dominil. Before we can attack the Guild we need something done that may be very dangerous."

"I'll do it," said Kalix.

"Wouldn't you like to hear what it is?"

"I don't care, I'll do it."

"Let me explain anyway."

Dominil told Kalix about the Fairy Queen's spell. "But the pathway will only work if we can get one of her flowers inside the building."

"I'll do it," said Kalix.

"Please let me finish. I plan to arrange for Merchant MacDoig to send the Guild a package. You will deliver the package, disguised as a courier. Your pendant should keep you from being detected. There is of course the risk that you might encounter a hunter who recognizes you."

"Fine," said Kalix. "When can I do it?"

"We still have to seek authority from the council."

Kalix was disappointed. She'd hoped it might be today.

"You do appreciate how dangerous this may be?" said Dominil.

"Just give me the flower and I'll take it in," said Kalix.

As she rang off she found she was a little less depressed. She wasn't going to be left out of the attack as she'd feared. She was going to be involved right from the start, and she was doing something dangerous. Nothing could have suited her more at this moment. She put on her shoes and prepared to go running again.

*

There was incredulity leading to outrage when Dominil suggested the Great Council that Kalix could take the marker into the Guild's Headquarters.

"Kalix?" shouted Baron MacPhee, who on this occasion lost his temper before Thrix. "Kalix is an outlaw! If she dared show her face round here we'd be sentencing her for her crimes."

The elderly Baron MacPhee had always resented that Kalix hadn't paid the penalty for the lethal assault on her father. The old Thane and Baron MacPhee had been friends and companions for hundreds of years.

Baron MacGregor was equally annoyed. "We can't work with a werewolf who's been outlawed."

"Even if she hadn't been," said Tupan, "would we want to? She's known for being extremely unstable."

"I'm not sending my MacPhees down to London to be killed as a result of some madness perpetrated by Kalix MacRinnalch," insisted Baron MacPhee.

"Kalix is the only werewolf who can enter the building with any degree of safety," said Dominil. "She's the obvious choice. And clan history contains other examples of werewolves who were outlawed, working with the clan for the common good."

"Like who?" demanded Baron MacPhee.

"James MacPhee MacRinnalch joined with the forces of Baron Cosgrach MacPhee at the battle of Stirling Bridge in twelve ninety-seven," said Dominil. "Though he was outlawed at the time, after killing MacBeatha MacRinnalch in a dispute over grazing rights."

The council was silenced for a moment or two, disconcerted by Dominil's superior knowledge of clan history. Baron MacGregor was the first to recover.

"That was a war of Scottish independence. All available men were sent to support William Wallace. That's not the same as recruiting the drug-addled Kalix to carry out a mission. And while I'm on the subject of drugs"—the Baron gestured toward Dominil—"how can we be sure we can trust Dominil's judgment on this?"

"My judgment is perfectly fine," said Dominil.

"Are you still taking laudanum?"

"I take a small, measured amount each day."

Several competing voices were raised in opposition to Dominil's plan but they were silenced by a roar from the Thane. Markus had come into the meeting determined not to allow it to degenerate into the same sort of disarray that had blighted the previous two nights. He demanded silence.

"I trust Dominil's judgment," he said. "And I trust this plan. It's true that Kalix is still outlawed but as Thane I'm giving her authorization to be involved. I have the authority to do that. I also have the authority to approve the plan, which I now do." Markus swept his gaze round the table. "This council has previously agreed that something needed to be done about the Guild. They've become bolder and now threaten werewolves everywhere. I won't allow that to continue. We will attack them. I'll lead the attack. Thrix, you said you needed twenty werewolves? From this room, myself, Thrix, Dominil and Decembrius have all volunteered already. Eskandor, captain of the castle guard, is one of our most experienced fighters. He'll go too, along with Feargan MacRinnalch, his deputy, and Barra, the castle sergeant. That makes seven MacRinnalchs. Each baron—MacPhee, MacGregor and MacAllister—will provide four werewolves for the mission. That makes nineteen werewolves. I'll instruct the MacAndris Clan to provide one warrior, making twenty, and another two as back-up in case anyone withdraws. Kalix herself will not take part in the attack. Are there any objections?"

There were sullen faces around the table, but no one voiced an objection. The Thane had a right to exert his authority in time of war.

Lucia, perhaps thinking of her sister Verasa, did have a query. "Are you sure you should lead the mission, Markus? You're the Thane—what if something happens to you?"

Lucia looked to her sister, expecting support, but the Mistress of the Werewolves seemed unconcerned about her son going to London to fight.

"I'll lead the mission," said Markus emphatically. "I'll expect the barons to send their most suitable werewolves to the castle while we make plans. We should be able to leave in a matter of days."

CHAPTER 137

The Empress's jeweled throne room had plunged to a temperature rarely experienced by any Hainusta. Courtiers shivered as they attended their monarch. Guards pulled their cloaks tighter, cursing whatever terrible occurrence had put Kabachetka in such a bad mood. The Empress's internal fire had sunk so low that she was now sucking heat from the atmosphere, rather than spreading it around.

"Where is Distikka?" cried the Empress. "Did I not summon her an hour ago?"

"She approaches the throne room," replied an attendant, and tried not to look cold, for fear of insulting the Empress. The torches on the wall were dimming as if not only the heat but the light too was being sucked out of existence. Distikka walked into the throne room and bowed politely. She did not appear to notice the temperature.

"Where have you been?"

"Attending to your affairs in London."

"Did I ask you to do that?"

"Yes."

The Empress scowled. "Well, I'm sure I asked you to do it more quickly. Do you know what has happened?"

"A handbag crisis?"

"Exactly!" cried the Empress, completely missing Distikka's sarcasm. "How did you know?"

"I—"

"Never mind how you know. I attended the Fashion Show in Aid of Famine in Africa, carrying my favorite quilted handbag, which Lady Gezinka assured me was still in fashion, only to find that it had passed so far out of fashion as to earn me mocking looks and several whispered comments. Imagine the humiliation!" The Empress folded her arms and glared at Distikka. "How could this happen? Why was there no one to advise me?"

For once, Distikka was at a loss. "Who normally advises you about handbags?"

"Bakmer. But he is not here because I banished him to the kitchens for his unsatisfactory behavior at the ball. And look what it has led to!"

The temperature dropped another few degrees. In the far corner Kabachetka's handmaid Alchet began to whimper.

"Then why not just recall Bakmer?" asked Distikka.

"It would be admitting I made a mistake in banishing him. I would lose face. You must sort this out."

"How?"

"How? Is it not obvious? Adviser Bakmer must beg for his position back so I may mercifully reinstate him. Make that happen. Ensure he begs in a suitably pathetic manner. I need him back quickly. There may be another charity fashion event at any time; I am informed that famines in

Africa are not uncommon."

"Very well, Empress," said Distikka. "Would you like to hear about your affairs on Earth?"

"Which affairs?"

"Your investments, for one thing. I made some recent adjustments, and they're doing very well."

The Empress did not seem interested to learn that her investments were doing well. Distikka carried on. "Also, I believe the werewolves will attack very soon. I've arranged for our spying to be stepped up."

"Good. Are the hunters prepared?"

"They are."

The Empress nodded. The temperature rose a fraction. She turned to Alchet. "Leave the throne room," she said.

Alchet hurried out, relieved to be free of the cold. The Empress dismissed her remaining courtiers, leaving her alone with Distikka. The Empress's throne room was impregnable to any sort of sorcerous spying but even so, she waved her hand in the air, placing an extra layer of protection around them.

"It is time to get rid of Sarapen. Please arrange it."

Distikka raised her eyebrows. "Why now?"

"He has resisted falling in love with me for too long. I am now bored with him."

"He only survives because you provide him with protection. Without it he would die in the heat. Why not simply withdraw the protection?"

"Really, Distikka, I am shocked. Do you know nothing of the rules of hospitality?"

"I wasn't aware they applied to a person you wished to see killed."

"That is because you were never properly educated, I regret to say. The rules of hospitality clearly state that sorcerous protection, once granted, cannot be withdrawn."

"But assassination is acceptable?"

"Of course," said the Empress. "Assassinations do not breach our ancient codes."

"Very well," said Distikka. "I'll arrange it."

CHAPTER 138

On instructions from Dominil, Kalix spent an uncomfortable two days in Kennington Park, learning how to ride a bicycle. She'd never owned one as a child. Bicycles were not a common sight at Castle MacRinnalch. She'd borrowed the bike from Moonglow, who never rode it either. Kalix found it humiliating learning to ride the bike, and wheeled it to the furthest part of the park where there were less people to laugh at her for falling off. She stuck to her task, and mastered it well enough for her purposes. She was confident enough to ride back home from the park, though she went slowly, and dismounted at traffic lights to push it across the road on the pedestrian crossing.

"This isn't going to be much good for making a quick escape," she mused, as she trundled home.

Kalix didn't really know if she'd be making an escape. She might be killed in the Guild's headquarters. Or perhaps the werewolves would all flood in when she was still there. Dominil hadn't told her details of her plan. Kalix was due to meet her at Thrix's apartment later in the afternoon. Kalix bridled at the thought of actually visiting Thrix, but accepted it as necessary for the success of their mission.

Moonglow was starting to immerse herself in her coursework for next year at university, now only a few weeks away. She'd been hinting broadly that Daniel, Kalix and Vex do likewise. None of them had responded. As Kalix left the flat, on her way to visit Thrix in Knightsbridge, she reflected that she was very unlikely to be starting a second year at her remedial college. She regretted this. She hadn't exactly enjoyed her time there, but she was pleased her reading and writing had improved. She'd always been shamed by her poor literacy. Given another year's study she thought she might have approached something like a normal standard.

Kalix walked past the shops in Knightsbridge without looking in the windows. They were expensive shops, and when she reached Thrix's block, that seemed expensive too. Kalix felt out of place. She began to feel anxious as she rang the downstairs buzzer.

Thrix better not say anything stupid or annoying.

Inside the apartment block there were plant pots in the corridors. The hallways were carpeted, clean, well lit and well cared for. It struck Kalix that Thrix must have paid a lot of money to live here. She wondered if it had all come from her fashion business, or if the family had helped.

Thrix opened the door. Neither of them spoke as Kalix entered. The awkwardness was alleviated by Dominil's presence, though she wasn't effusive in her greetings either. Kalix was surprised to find the apartment less tidy than she'd expected. Clothes were strewn about, and books and scrolls, and empty wine glasses.

"Did you learn how to ride a bicycle?" asked Dominil.

"Just about. It's difficult. Can you do it?"

"I learned how to at Oxford."

Kalix could imagine Dominil as a student, cycling around with her books in a basket. "So what's the plan?" she asked.

"You're to deliver a package from the Merchant to the Guild. We don't know for certain what sort of alarms they have but we know you can't be detected."

Dominil produced a small purple flower. She'd had it for several days though it showed no sign of wilting. "You need to hide this inside the building."

Kalix took the flower. "OK. I can do that."

"I'm not sure you appreciate how dangerous this might be," said Dominil.

"Stop saying that," said Kalix. "I know it's dangerous. I don't care."

"Very well." Dominil picked up a bundle of clothes from the table. "You'd better try these on."

Kalix was alarmed to see that Dominil had provided her with a pair of black Lycra cycling shorts and a high-visibility yellow jacket.

"This is what cycle couriers wear," said Dominil. "I checked."

"I'll look ridiculous."

"That's hardly important, is it?"

Dominil also handed Kalix a cycling helmet and a pair of cycling goggles. "These will help to disguise you. With your hair tied back and hidden inside your jacket you should be hard to recognize."

Kalix tried on the outfit. "I *do* look ridiculous."

"You do," said Thrix. "I've never seen a cycle courier with such skinny legs."

"They were fine for modeling your stupid shorts," retorted Kalix, who wasn't going to take criticism from her sister, though she also thought that her legs looked far too skinny for a person who made a living cycling.

"The disguise will suffice," said Dominil. "After you've planted the flower, I'll be waiting round the corner in my car. With luck we can depart without anyone knowing we've been there."

"So when do we attack?" asked Kalix.

"You don't," said Thrix.

"What do you mean I don't?"

"You're not in the raiding party. Markus says you're not going."

"I am going," said Kalix hotly.

"The council didn't want to include you at all," said Dominil. "You're still outlawed."

Kalix glared at Dominil then at Thrix. "I'm not staying behind," she said. "When you attack, I'm coming with you. If you try to keep me away I'll just follow you in."

Thrix shrugged. "I told you she'd say that. Personally, I don't care who's there as long as I can get inside the building."

"I tend to agree," said Dominil. "I won't prevent you from participating. It may be necessary for you to join the party at the last minute, to prevent others from objecting."

Kalix was still suspicious. "You'd better not try to exclude me."

"We won't," said Dominil. "Now if you'll take a seat, I'll explain the plan."

They sat at Thrix's dining table. Thrix swept aside a bundle of papers to make space for Dominil's iPad. She poured more whisky for each of them, and listened as Dominil went over their plans with Kalix.

"We're hoping that the 'Maynista Princess Two Flower Pathway' will take us straight in."

Kalix found herself smiling faintly. Unlike certain other werewolves, she was pleased at the thought of using magic from the Fairy Queen to attack the Avenaris Guild. Having the spell was a good omen. It was clever of Dominil to have obtained it. Kalix imagined herself running howling through the fairy pathway into the Guild's headquarters, full of her werewolf power, ready to spread destruction.

CHAPTER 139

Sarapen climbed the long spiral staircase leading to the palace's rooftop yellow flame garden. He often came here at night. Usually it was deserted. It was not a popular place with the Empress or her fashionable friends, being difficult to reach. There was another flame garden lower down, easily accessible from one of the mezzanine floors on the palace's south wing. There the Empress often entertained guests. Sarapen might have gone there tonight, but he'd had his fill of the Empress's friends. He was heartily sick of the palace and everyone in it, including the Empress. Even since gazing through the portal back to his own world, Sarapen had thought about little else. He wondered if Dominil had made any progress in helping him. Sarapen didn't doubt that she'd be trying. Dominil was a werewolf of her word, and wouldn't abandon him.

How did I end up fighting her? he wondered. She's the only MacRinnalch I really like.

Halfway up the spiral staircase, he paused. He thought he'd heard a footfall behind him. He listened for a few moments then continued. He was sure he heard it again, but carried on till he reached the top. Once in the roof garden, he walked out into plain view, standing beside the large bushes that glowed with a gentle yellow flame as they swayed in the hot breeze that blew from the slopes of the Eternal Volcano.

There was no further sound but Sarapen knew he'd been followed. He waited a moment then turned abruptly to find two Fire Elementals in black clothing emerging from the staircase. Each held a long dagger. Seeing that they were discovered, they sprinted toward him. Sarapen changed in an instant into his huge werewolf form. He opened his great jaws and roared. As a werewolf, Sarapen was a terrifying figure. He was well over six feet tall, huge, broad and muscular, with a cruel cast to his face, long sharp fangs and fearsome talons. His pelt was dark and shaggy and his black and yellow eyes blazed with anger.

His assailants paused, as if unprepared for the transformation. Sarapen had rarely changed in public since arriving in the land of the Hainusta. Vey few elementals had seen him in his werewolf shape. They advanced, their knives raised, but by now Sarapen was charging toward them. He was too quick for his opponents. Though he was unarmed, Sarapen had no trouble in grabbing the wrist of the nearest elemental, pulling him toward him then swinging his body with great force into the other assassin. They collided with each other and in the same instant Sarapen was upon the first of them, fastening his jaws to his neck in a terrible bite that almost decapitated him. He fell to the ground. The second assailant lost his nerve and turned to flee. Again, Sarapen was too quick. Before he had gone three steps, Sarapen had caught up with him and slashed at the back of his neck with his talons. The assassin fell down dead in an instant.

The whole affair had lasted for only seconds. Sarapen had killed the two trained assassins with one bite and one swipe of his claws.

Sarapen looked down at the bodies. He wondered who had sent them. The Empress? One of his rivals at court? For a moment Sarapen was undecided as to what he should do next. Remain in the palace? Flee into the desert? He knew he only survived here because of the Empress's sorcerous protection. In the desert he would quickly die.

I'll take my chance with the assassins, he thought. I hope Dominil's making some progress, because I'm not going to be able to survive for long with the palace against me, and the Empress.

CHAPTER 140

Kalix didn't feel comfortable in Thrix's apartment but was determined to stay as long as she could, learning about their plans. When Thrix left the room, Kalix told Dominil that she'd been concentrating on becoming fitter.

"I've been running and exercising. I got inspired after I met Joan Jett."

Dominil knew of Kalix's liking for the Runaways. "You met Joan Jett? How did that happen?"

"She bumped into me. She was jogging on the Embankment. I think it was her. It looked like her. So I was inspired to go running. I feel better already."

It was true. Kalix had been exercising for only a short while but it seemed to have reinvigorated her natural werewolf vitality. She felt stronger than she could remember.

"The rapid improvement is probably psychosomatic," said Dominil.

Kalix didn't know what that meant, so she nodded in agreement.

"And I'm not feeling so bad about Manny." Kalix chewed her lip. "I still feel quite bad. I wish I hadn't ruined everything."

"You will have very little time to hide the flower in the Guild headquarters," said Dominil, showing no interest in Kalix's failed relationship with Manny. Kalix felt embarrassed, and regretted mentioning it. As Thrix returned to the room the buzzer sounded at the door.

"It's Beauty," came a voice.

"And Delicious."

Thrix pressed the button to let them in. "What can they want? Dominil, did you ask them to come here?"

"No."

The twins arrived noisily.

"Hi, Thrix, this is a big place; you must be richer than we thought. Beauty, have we been here before?"

"I can't remember. Hi, Kalix."

The twins saw Dominil, and came to a halt.

"Hello, Dominil," said Beauty. She shuffled her feet uncomfortably. "We were sort of hoping you'd be here. The Mistress of the Werewolves said you might be."

Delicious looked at Dominil and seemed about to say something. She changed her mind, and turned toward her sister. "Shouldn't someone be welcoming us with some whisky?"

"You'd have thought so," agreed Beauty. "It is traditional."

"You'd have thought it would be here by now."

"You've only been here for thirty seconds," said Thrix. She picked up her bottle and poured drinks for the twins.

Beauty looked toward Dominil and again seemed to be on the verge of saying something, before thinking better of it.

"We were at our hairdresser. It's not far from here."

The twins' pink and blue hair was looking very bright, and even more voluminous than usual. They wore shiny black leather biker's jackets and torn jeans.

"We're busy," said Dominil. "From the way you keep looking at me I presume you have something to say. If you want to insult me again kindly get it over with so I can get back to work."

"We didn't come here to insult you!" protested Beauty. "You're always jumping to conclusions."

"Harsh conclusions with no basis in reality," said Delicious.

"It's probably why people keep insulting you. We came here to apologize. I'm sorry we threw beer at you."

"And threw other stuff as well," said Delicious. "Because, you know, you've probably done quite well for us . . . "

"As best as you could anyway . . . "

"Given your hostile nature . . . "

"And other personality problems . . . "

"And we're sorry we wrote a song called 'Selfish Inconsiderate Albino Werewolf Bitch.' We probably shouldn't have done that."

"Although it is a really good song. Do you mind if we add it to the set?"

"Not at all," said Dominil. "Though I'm not an albino. I'm leucistic."

"Is that even a word? Well, anyway, now that's out of the way, we've come to offer our help."

Delicious turned to Thrix. "We'll join in the attack."

Thrix, amused by the twins' attempt at apologizing, raised her eyebrows. "You want to join the attack?"

"Well, we don't exactly want to," admitted Beauty. "But we will. We talked to the Mistress of the Werewolves. She said the council was making a fuss about everything. We know what these people are like. They'll probably just let you down. We'll come along if you need us."

Thrix felt an unusual burst of clan pride, something she hadn't experienced for a while. Noticing that the twins had already finished their drinks, Thrix refilled their glasses.

"I appreciate the offer," she said. "But when we discussed the attack, we didn't include you because we, uh . . . I don't suppose we thought you'd be eager to participate."

"We're not," admitted Delicious. "But we will."

Thrix knew perfectly well that the twins, though strong like any MacRinnalch, were neither keen nor experienced fighters. She smiled at them. "Thank you for offering. I wish all the clan were as ready to help. But we've made a plan of attack for twenty werewolves, and we have all the positions filled. It would be difficult to fit you in now."

"That's OK," said Beauty.

"We'd probably be no help anyway," said Delicious.

"But we'll still come if you need us," said Beauty. She looked at her glass, which was empty again. "Isn't it normal to give visiting clan members some token of hospitality?"

Thrix shook her head, and refilled the sisters' glasses.

"I should have brought some extra bottles down from Scotland. Though it's not easy to get my mother to open the storeroom."

The twins' arrival, their clumsy apology and the clan whisky had all combined to ease the werewolves' mood. Kalix and Thrix managed to forget their mutual antipathy for a little while, and Dominil seemed a degree less frozen. They sat at Thrix's table, sipping their drinks, gossiping about affairs at the castle, the twins' adventures in Camden and whatever else came to mind, and managed to forget for a little while about the upcoming attack on the Guild, from which none of them felt likely to return.

CHAPTER 141

Beauty and Delicious eventually made their way home in a taxi, as did Dominil. Kalix took a night bus. It was well into the early hours of the morning and Thrix was on the point of retiring when the Fire Queen appeared at her door.

"I apologize for the lateness of my visit," she said as she swept into the apartment. "One is simply run off one's feet at the palace. I had to escape. Another minute discussing drainage problems with the ministerial subcommittee and I really would have lost my mind."

Thrix was puzzled. "That doesn't sound like the sort of thing you'd be involved in. Can't the committee sort it out themselves?"

"Drainage is a serious matter around the palace," explained Malveria. "We have so little surface water that any unexpected appearance causes panic among the citizens. A spring has recently burst forth and it must be attended to."

The Fire Queen looked around. Her powers of detecting auras were extremely acute, and she could see traces of Thrix's previous visitors.

"Why Thrix, you have had many guests. Dominil, Kalix and the colorful twins. Have you had a girls' night? Should I be jealous I was not invited? Or was it for werewolves only?"

"It wasn't planned. I was discussing our attack with Dominil and the others just appeared."

"Is your attack imminent?"

"Yes."

"I see."

The Fire Queen moved some clothes from the couch, clearing a space to sit. "Is it as you suspected? The Guild's headquarters is a 'House That Can't Be Found'?"

"Yes."

"It's a bad place to attack," said the Fire Queen. "I advise against it."

"Why?"

"You are unlikely to be able to use your sorcery. The house will prevent it. You should wait for a better opportunity."

"We don't know for sure if I'll be unable to use sorcery. Anyway, I've fought without it before."

"Not in the home of your enemies."

"There will be twenty werewolves. We're going to take them by surprise and slaughter them."

"Do you really believe that?"

Thrix hesitated. "Maybe."

"I don't want you to go to this place!" said the Fire Queen, urgently.

"It's all been decided."

The Fire Queen became agitated. "You should listen to my advice. I have much experience of war and I'm telling you this is a mistake. Do not attack this house."

"Malveria, what's the matter with you? Why are you getting upset about this?"

"I don't want you to go and die in a place I can't help you!" said the Fire Queen. "There are reasons I cannot join you there."

"Ah." Thrix nodded. "The Maynista Curse."

"How did you learn of that?"

"I didn't. Dominil did, from Queen Dithean."

"Dithean should not be telling stories of my past. And why is she telling Dominil?"

"I don't know. But she wouldn't agree to help us at all until Dominil persuaded her. She gave her the 'Maynista Princess Two Flower Pathway.'"

The Fire Queen moaned and a flaming tear appeared at the corner of one eye. "That spell is a very sad memory. I don't want you to use it."

"I have to. It's the only way in."

"Really, Thrix, you should not go and fight in some place that I cannot help you. I'm sure you'll die."

"Malveria, you're not being very encouraging."

"Why should I be encouraging? I do not feel encouraging."

Thrix couldn't persuade the Fire Queen that it wasn't a bad idea, and soon gave up the attempt. She appreciated her friend's concerns, but Thrix had never envisaged the Fire Queen accompanying her on the mission, so wasn't concerned that the Queen couldn't enter the house. It was MacRinnalch business, and though Thrix wouldn't have said as much to Malveria, the rest of the werewolves wouldn't have wanted her there.

"When is this attack?" said the Fire Queen.

"In a few days. The twelfth, if everything goes to plan."

"The twelfth? The night of Takahashi's launch at H&M at which Donatella Versace herself is rumored to be in attendance?" The Fire Queen looked sulky. "We should be going together. But you would not have come anyway, I expect. For weeks you have failed to accompany me to all the most important shows. My clothes have suffered, Enchantress, though I have borne it well."

"I'm sorry, Malveria. When this is all over, I'll design you the best clothes you've ever seen."

"If you are still alive. Who knows what you may meet in their head-quarters? What armaments the hunters may have? It is madness to rush in."

"It won't matter what armaments they have. We're going to take them by surprise. Don't underestimate twenty werewolves. Once we break in we'll be through that building in seconds."

"What if they receive warning?"

"How?"

"I don't know. But what if Kabachetka decides to visit? She might sense you coming."

"I doubt Kabachetka will be there," Thrix said. "I don't think she socializes with the Guild. Anyway, she'll probably be at the H&M launch."

"Wearing her pitiful new outfits from her hopeless new designer," said Malveria, and was temporarily cheered by the thought of Kabachetka and her fashion failures. She quickly became gloomy again. "I don't like any of this. If I meet Donatella Versace I will not be able to concentrate at all, knowing that you are risking your life not far away. It will quite spoil my evening."

CHAPTER 142

On the day Kalix was due to hide the flower in the Guild's headquarters, the weather changed. The temperature dropped, the sky turned gray and heavy rain poured down on London. Kalix pushed her bike to the end of the street. Dominil was waiting there in her car.

"Poor weather for cycling," said Kalix.

Dominil didn't reply. She quickly stashed Kalix's bike in the boot of the car, and handed Kalix a bundle of clothes as they drove off. Kalix struggled into them, dressing herself in the yellow jacket and cycling shorts. She tucked her long ponytail inside the jacket.

"This is the package you're to deliver." Dominil handed a parcel to Kalix. It was the size of a shoebox, and quite heavy. "I picked it up from Merchant MacDoig this morning."

"What's in it?"

"Silver bullets."

They drove on toward the center of town.

"I'd have thought they'd get more silver bullets than this," said Kalix when next they stopped at traffic lights.

"They have plenty," said Dominil. "This is a special batch. They have soft cones, specially adapted to explode inside a werewolf's body."

Kalix looked at the package, and winced. "Maybe we shouldn't deliver them."

"It's the only way to get you inside."

Traffic moved more slowly in the rain. It took them a while to negotiate the bridge over the river. They passed the Houses of Parliament in silence. There were a few protesters on the other side of the road. Kalix gazed at them but she couldn't read their placards. They drove up Regent Street, still moving slowly. There was a very large queue outside the Apple Store.

"What's that for?" asked Kalix.

"They've released a new iPad," Dominil told her. "I picked mine up first thing this morning."

They crossed over Oxford Street, heading for Gloucester Place. Kalix was calm, as she always was facing danger.

"I'll drop you off here," said Dominil in the street parallel to Gloucester Place. "So you can cycle there, as a courier would."

"OK," said Kalix. She put on her goggles and cycling helmet, picked up the package and a clipboard Dominil gave her, and stepped out of the car. Dominil slipped out as well and swiftly took Kalix's bicycle from the boot.

"Thrix is parked on the next corner," said Dominil.

"Why?"

"Because I can't park outside the Guild's building. I'll drive round the block, but if I'm not in sight when you come out, get into Thrix's car and she'll take you away."

"OK."

The rain poured down. It was a very poor day for cycling. Kalix mounted her bike without much confidence. Dominil drove off without a word. Kalix maneuvered the bike toward Gloucester Place. She hadn't ridden in the rain before and the downpour made her nervous. She felt like she was going to fall off. It was a relief when she arrived at the Guild's headquarters and she could step off the bike. She noticed Thrix's car on the corner, but didn't acknowledge it.

Kalix locked her bike to nearby railings, as Dominil had told her to, maintaining the pretense that she was a courier. She glanced briefly at the building then approached it confidently. She held her breath as she pushed the small buzzer on the wall, wondering if an alarm might sound. Her pendant should hide her from anything, but Kalix had gathered from listening to Dominil and Thrix that they didn't quite know what powers might be contained within the stone dwarves' house.

"Yes?" came a voice through the small metal intercom.

"Parcel delivery," said Kalix. She wondered if she should have tried to disguise her Scottish accent. It was something no one had thought about. It was too late now. The door buzzed and Kalix pushed it open: she was the first werewolf ever to enter the headquarters of the Avenaris Guild. Inside she found herself in a small hallway, her progress blocked by a thick glass door. Behind the door a uniformed security guard examined her. Apparently seeing nothing amiss, he pressed another buzzer and the door opened. Kalix walked into a larger foyer than she'd expected. There was dark wooden wainscoting around the foyer, giving it the appearance of an old country house rather than a modern office. There were dark wooden chairs in the foyer too, and a thick brown carpet, worn with age. An elderly man with gray hair sat behind a dark wooden desk. As Kalix advanced toward him she heard the security guard locking the door behind her. She was now locked in the Guild's building, in daytime when she couldn't transform, with two strong doors between her and the street outside, and werewolf hunters all around. Kalix walked up to the man behind the desk and handed him the parcel in silence.

"What's this?" he asked.

Kalix handed over her clipboard so as he could sign for the package. There were already signatures there. Dominil had forged them earlier, making an authentic-looking document.

The man frowned. "Wait here a moment," he said. He stood up and walked from his desk, disappearing through the dark wooden door behind him. Kalix felt a twinge of worry. She glanced around to see if the security guard was watching her. He was. There seemed no opportunity for planting the flower without being seen. Kalix cursed silently to herself. She somehow hadn't anticipated that there would be two people watching her. The gray-haired man came back into the foyer, followed by a younger man. He was wearing a dark gray suit and looked to Kalix like an executive. He studied Kalix's clipboard.

"We weren't expecting this."

Kalix shrugged and attempted to look bored. She didn't suppose a cycle courier would really be that interested in the parcels she was delivering. The man in the suit picked up the parcel and stared at it. He shrugged, then shook his head.

"MacDoig. He should have retired years ago."

With that, he accepted the pen that Kalix was holding out, and signed for the parcel. At that moment the outside buzzer sounded again. Kalix glanced swiftly over her shoulder. Through the glass door she could just make out two figures at the entrance. The security guard was approaching the glass door to study the new visitors. Kalix took her chance. As she took back the clipboard and pen she dropped the pen deliberately and reached down quickly as if to snatch it up. As she did so she tucked the small purple flower under the carpet, managing the operation so smoothly that no suspicions were aroused. Without saying a word she headed back toward the front door. The security man held it open for her and she kept her head down as she passed the two strangers who'd just entered the building.

"I'm due at the training ground," she heard one of them say.

The glass door shut behind her, the front door opened, and Kalix was free. She resisted the urge to run, and walked calmly toward her bike. She fumbled for a moment as she attempted to unlock it, but managed it quickly enough. The rain was coming down even harder, making her goggles almost impossible to see through. Kalix struggled on for only a few yards before coming to a halt. She took off the goggles to wipe them.

"Alex?" said someone, right beside her on the pavement.

Kalix jerked her head around, startled to be recognized. It was Manny. He was standing in the rain, accompanied by an older man with a coat over his suit and a briefcase in his hand. Kalix, previously calm, felt her heart begin to pound. Manny was the last person she had expected to meet and she was at a complete loss as to how to react.

"Alex? What are you doing here? On a bike?"

"I'm a courier," said Kalix.

"Since when?"

"I just started."

Kalix and Manny looked at each other as the rain poured down. Cars drove past, splashing water onto the pavement.

"You picked bad weather," said Manny, who was obviously feeling just as awkward as Kalix. Kalix nodded. She wanted to cycle off, but feared she would fall off the bike in the rain. The strangeness of the situation was bringing on her anxiety, quite strongly.

"Are you going to introduce me?" said the man who accompanied Manny.

"This is Alex," said Manny. "Alex, this is my brother John."

John nodded and smiled. Kalix guessed by his expression that Manny had told his brother about her. He probably knew she'd slept with someone else. She felt humiliated, and her anxiety became worse.

John studied Kalix for a few seconds, then spoke to his young brother.

"I'm almost at the office. I'll leave you here. I'll see you at your show."

With a courteous nod to Kalix, he walked off up the street. There was another moment of silence.

"I tried to call you," said Kalix.

"I know."

Kalix longed to say something profound, or even something sensible, but knew she wouldn't be able to. She wasn't capable of dealing with complex emotions in the street, on a bike, in the rain, without warning. She put her foot on the pedal to cycle off.

"Call me again," said Manny.

"OK," said Kalix, and cycled away. She tried to hold the bike steady as she approached the nearest turn. At the corner she looked round to see if Manny was still watching. He was. Kalix had reached Thrix's car but she cycled past so Manny wouldn't see her dismount. Thrix, who'd been watching events from her car, pulled out from the curb and drove after Kalix. A little way along the side road Kalix halted. Thrix halted too, stopping traffic. There were a few horns sounded as they put Kalix's bike in the boot then drove off.

"How did it go?" asked Thrix.

"I hid the flower."

"Well done. Who was that you met?"

"Manny. My ex-boyfriend."

Thrix didn't comment. She had had an earpiece in her left ear, connected to her mobile phone. She touched a button on the phone, dialing Dominil's number.

"I've picked up Kalix. She planted the flower."

"Good," said Dominil. "I'm not far behind you, I can see your car. I'll meet you at your apartment."

Thrix and Kalix drove in silence toward Knightsbridge. Kalix was lost in thought. She didn't notice how wet she was, and she hardly thought of the dangerous mission she'd just completed. She was thinking about Manny, and how strange it had been to meet him in the street, and how uncomfortable it had felt. Now that she was leaving the scene her anxiety was diminishing. She wished she'd thought of something better to say. *Manny had said she should call him again. Did he really mean that?*

Thrix was also deep in thought. She'd seen Kalix talking to Manny, and she'd seen the man who was with Manny. She'd also seen something that Kalix had not. After he left Kalix and Manny he'd gone straight into the headquarters of the Avenaris Guild. That gave Thrix a lot to think about as she drove home.

CHAPTER 143

Strands of Daniel's hair hung over his eyes. He liked the effect but it did make it difficult to see. It was a complex balancing act between aesthetics and practicality. He was standing in front of the wall mirror in the living room, trying to get it right, when Vex came downstairs, singing a song about her boots.

"Glacier Boots, glacier boots, I like my glacier boots, I can walk right over glaciers in my great big glacier boots."

It was quite a tuneful song. Agrivex had a pleasant singing voice.

"I like my glacier boots," she said.

"So I gathered," said Daniel. "Off to see Pete?"

Vex nodded, and her face lit up.

"Please don't say 'It's so nice to have a boyfriend, you should get a girlfriend,'" said Daniel.

"I'm not that tactless."

Vex joined Daniel in front of the mirror, and began pushing strands of her hair around. Her bleached-blonde afro was now so impressive that people would stop in the street and stare, and draw their friends' attention to the girl whose skinny little body seemed suspended between her huge hair and huge boots. While shopping in Camden she'd been stopped on numerous occasions by tourists wanting to take her picture, and there was a photo of her in the current edition of a hip-hop fanzine in an article on ethnic street fashion.

"Where's Moonglow?" said Vex.

Daniel didn't know.

"Maybe she's gone to see William?"

Daniel was alarmed. "Don't say that!"

"Why not?"

"I don't want her to see him, that's why."

Vex teased her hair into shape. "It's OK, I just remembered where she is."

"Where?"

"She's gone to see William."

Daniel sighed. "This hasn't gone the way I expected. I thought that Moonglow would be more affected after I slept with Gezinka."

"What, and leap into your arms after realizing she always loved you?"

"Yes."

"I have seen that happen in Ultimate Boyfriend," said Vex. "So you never know. But I think you're just meant to let it happen naturally."

"What do you mean?"

"Well, not mention it all the time."

"I didn't mention it all the time."

"Yes, you did," said Vex. "You kept bragging about sleeping with that woman."

"Maybe I should have been more discreet," said Daniel. "Like you are about Pete."

"Exactly. No one likes to hear endless tales about someone's girl-friend, it gets really tedious. Do you think you'll ever see Gezinka again?"

"I doubt it. She probably never thought about me after that night."

Daniel remembered Lady Gezinka fondly. For a brief encounter with an older woman, it had all gone very well. Unfortunately, it hadn't been enough to drive Moonglow into his arms.

"Anyway, what if I did mention it a few times?" said Daniel. "Moonglow keeps going on about William."

"No, she doesn't."

"Yes, she does. William does this. William does that. William has nice clothes."

Vex laughed. "He'd be a good boyfriend if he wasn't gay. Bye." Vex headed for the door.

Daniel sprinted after her. "Wait a minute. What do you mean he's gay?"

Vex looked puzzled. "Well, I thought you'd know what that means."

"I know what it means!" cried Daniel.

"Then why did you ask?"

"I meant . . . " Daniel paused to organize his thoughts, knowing that a conversation with Vex could become hopelessly confused if you didn't approach it properly. "I mean why did no one tell me he was gay?"

"I don't know."

"I wouldn't have been bragging about my night with Gezinka unless I'd thought Moonglow was sleeping with William."

"I have to go or I'll be late," said Vex brightly. "It's so nice having a boyfriend. You should get—"

"I know," sighed Daniel.

Vex rushed out the door, leaving Daniel thoughtful and dissatisfied.

Daniel was wrong about Lady Gezinka. She had thought of him, quite kindly. She didn't regret sleeping with him, though she didn't enjoy the mockery the affair had engendered from the Empress. Kabachetka had amused her friends with her anecdote about the staid and respectable Gezinka and her brief fling with a young man at the ball.

"Poor Gezinka was quite worn out afterward. She could hardly hold her head up in the palace the next day. Though whether that was tiredness or shame, I am not certain."

Gezinka bridled under the mockery, though she smiled as good-naturedly as she could. Unfortunately, her powers of protecting her aura were no match for the Empress's powers of discerning emotions, and Kabachetka could tell she was discomfited.

"Really, Gezinka, one would have hoped you could find a better companion than a poor little student boy. If you had to give in to your passions, could you not have chosen some young man who had two shillings to rub together?"

There was great hilarity among the Empress's friends.

"I swear he was there in a rented suit," continued the Empress. "It fitted him in one or two places, but not in most."

The Empress had invited her closest friends to admire her new bag, with which she was very pleased. It had been produced by her personal sorcerers, made with the specific purpose of carrying clothes from one dimension to another.

"It is always such a problem," declared the Empress. "I lose count of the frocks and shoes I've damaged along the way. And one shrinks from paying Merchant MacDoig's prices for his transportation services. With this bag I can take a spare set of clothes, with no worry of frock injury."

The Letaka sisters, cousins of the Empress, admired the new bag. They had never traveled to London, but knew of their Empress's adventures in the fashion world there.

"I thought they would never finish designing it," said the Empress. "But Bakmer hurried them along. Really, since recalling him, he has been most eager to please. Much like Lady Gezinka in the hotel, one might say."

At this, Lady Tecton laughed so hard she almost choked. One of the Letaka sisters pounded her on the back.

"The pounding and gasping," cried the Empress. "It reminds me of the noises that emerged from Gezinka's hotel room!"

There was more laughter. Lady Gezinka bore it as well as she could, but as she lay in bed that night, on her own, she felt a great deal of resentment toward the Empress and her mockery.

CHAPTER 144

Wallace MacGregor was one of the largest werewolves in Scotland. Possibly the largest, since the death of Sarapen. The eldest son of Baron MacGregor was a fierce werewolf, and extremely strong. He'd never been defeated till the day Markus MacRinnalch surprised everyone by beating him in single combat outside the gates of Castle MacRinnalch. The MacGregors, MacAllisters and MacPhees had been besieging the castle, but all hostilities had come to a halt while the fight took place. The MacRinnalchs cheered him from the battlements, and Markus's victory had been instrumental in securing his position as Thane. Though many werewolves regarded him as unsuitable, there could be no more questions about his courage.

Wallace MacGregor was honorable as well as fierce, and strode into Castle MacRinnalch without any feelings of animosity. Having been defeated in a fair fight, he didn't hold a grudge. When the Thane called for werewolves to travel to London, he'd volunteered for the mission. The Mistress of the Werewolves welcomed him sincerely. It was good to have such a strong ally. Wallace brought three other MacGregors, joining the four MacPhees and four MacAllisters who'd already arrived. The MacAllisters were led by Morag, sister of the young baron. Like her brother, she was not sympathetic to Markus. However, she was a war-like character and liked the idea of going to London to fight. Morag was not tall, but she had a certain stockiness about her, and was known to be strong when she transformed. There were some MacAllisters who could only change into their werewolf form around the time of the full moon, but Morag could do it on any night, as could her companions. That was necessary if the attack was to take place soon.

"In the next day or two, we hope," Verasa told Morag. "We're just waiting for confirmation from Dominil."

The twelve werewolves, plus two more from the MacAndris clan, were making the journey to London in separate vehicles. Though it was regarded as unlikely that the Guild could get close enough to the castle to spy, Dominil insisted on tight security, and wanted no unusual behavior. The attackers were to travel in small groups to London, before assembling at Thrix's apartment.

Markus spoke to all the participants after they arrived. He was calm and authoritative, and confident about their chances of success. His confidence was felt by the whole assault group, and spread around the castle, so that in the days preceding the attack, there was less worry than might have been expected. The feeling grew among the MacRinnalch Clan that their Thane was right. Something had to be done about the Avenaris Guild.

There were a few who remained unenthusiastic. Decembrius for one, though he kept his thoughts mostly to himself. As far as he could see, the clan was rushing into an attack without proper preparation. He did confide to his mother, in a moment of depression, that he believed the attack was being driven more by Thrix's fury and Dominil's wounded pride than by good sense.

"Thrix has been irrational since Minerva was killed. And Dominil just can't stand it that the Guild outsmarted her."

"I don't think Dominil would do anything unless she thought it was right for the clan," said his mother Lucia.

"That's the impression she gives. But if she hadn't been involved that day when Minerva was killed, I don't think she'd be so keen on rushing into this. She thinks the Guild got one over on her. It wounded her pride. Now she's trying to prove she's superior."

If Decembrius had his doubts about the wisdom of the plan, he had no doubts about his own participation. He was still looking forward to flinging himself into battle, so he didn't voice his concerns to anyone else, for fear of damaging the werewolves' morale.

Heather and Beatrice, Markus's girlfriends, didn't support the plan at all. They hated the idea of Markus going off to fight, and were terrified he'd be killed. Even when Heather sneaked in to join Beatrice and Markus after dark, their nights were gloomy, and not enjoyable.

CHAPTER 145

The Fire Queen put down the scroll in front of her, and sighed. "I have lost confidence, First Minister."

"Lost confidence, mighty Queen?"

"Yes, Xakthan. I know you will find it difficult to believe. My splendid rule continues, my frocks are unmatched and my subjects continue to revere me."

"That is true," said the loyal Xakthan. The Fire Queen's reign was continuing in splendid fashion, and her subjects did adore her. As for her frocks, he was prepared to take the Queen's word for it.

"Is there something in the new drainage scheme you're not certain of?"

Malveria scowled. "My knowledge of drainage schemes is slight. If you say it is satisfactory, I'll sign the order. But it is not drainage that troubles me. Ever since the malevolent Kabachetka was photographed for the 'fashionable party people' page in *Vogue*, I have felt matters slipping away from me. What if she were to truly overtake me in matters of fashion?"

"That seems very unlikely."

"Is it? Perhaps *Vogue* is trying to tell me something. Perhaps it is time for me to retire from matters of style, and spend my days wrapped in one of these dreadful old garments my mother used to wear, may she walk peacefully in the warm flames of the afterlife."

First Minister Xakthan had never understood fashion, but did his best to reassure the Queen. "Does not Thrix MacRinnalch keep you ahead of the Empress?"

"She did. But Thrix has been too busy with werewolf affairs. And I fear she may die soon."

"Die soon? Is she ill?"

"In a way. She is ill inside. She is obsessed with revenge, and has used much difficult and harmful sorcery in an effort to attain it. It is burning her up. But that is not what will kill her."

The Fire Queen gave her first minister a short account of recent events on Earth concerning the MacRinnalchs. "It is a very dangerous mission they embark on. I fear for Thrix. I would go with her but I cannot enter a dwelling of the stone dwarves. I have never regretted that before, but I do now. I wish they had not cursed me."

"But the curse was worthwhile," said Xakthan. "It happened because we destroyed their army. How we chased them from the field!"

First Minister Xakthan had fought that day, and he was proud of the memory.

"We did. But I wish I had not killed Gasanda. It has always been a source of regret."

"You had no choice," said Xakthan. "She was an invader."

The Fire Queen sighed, and looked morose. "We had such fun when we were children."

Xakthan was silent, unable to think of anything that might cheer her.

"So now I can't accompany Thrix. The worry has been affecting me. And this, added to the *Vogue* disaster, has quite drained my confidence. It has never struck me before, First Minister, but perhaps the reason I have not produced an heir is because no one would want to produce one with me."

Xakthan was astonished to hear this, and would have rushed to reassure the Queen, had he not always found it both difficult and inappropriate to comment on the Queen's personal life. "I am sure that's not true at all," was all he could manage and, even at that, he felt embarrassed.

"Really? There must be something wrong with me. Do you know that my dismal niece's efforts to find me a partner now extend to the Duke of the Black Castle?"

"I suspected as much."

"You did? How?"

"I'm not quite as unobservant as you think."

The Fire Queen managed a small smile. "I suppose you are not. One is tempted to throw Agrivex in the volcano for her impudence, and yet . . ." The Fire Queen raised her palms. "Is it so ridiculous? I suppose I must have some sort of consort if I am ever to produce an heir."

"How about Duke Garfire?" suggested Xakthan. "He's very respectable."

The Fire Queen shuddered. "Please, First Minister. Were I to marry Garfire, I would soon be obliged to kill him before fleeing from an outraged populace. And the same goes for Stratov and all the rest. What is it about my aristocracy that makes them all so tedious?"

"Is DeMortalis tedious?"

"No. He is witty, handsome, charming and even rather exciting. But he is not respectable, and I just do not see him as a consort. The population would not like it. Or perhaps they would. I can no longer tell. This worry is affecting my judgment. And it is quite ruining my encounter with Donatella."

"Donatella?"

"Versace," explained the Fire Queen. "She is involved in the launch of Mr. Takahashi's new fashion line.

"Mr. Takahashi?"

"A young Japanese designer. I've been keenly looking forward to this event, but now I shrink from the affair. Kabachetka will be there, in the company of those fashion editors she has managed to fool with her charitable pretensions. Worse, it is on the very night that the MacRinnalchs are planning their attack. I cannot be charming and beautiful when I'm worried that Thrix may be on the receiving end of a silver bullet."

"Werewolves are hardy creatures," said Xakthan. "She'll survive a silver bullet, unless it pierces her heart."

"That is not very reassuring, First Minister. I fear there will be many silver bullets, and one of them will find her heart. I also fear that Kabachetka may be involved."

"Why would she be?"

"She still assists the werewolf hunters. Thrix does not fear this. She insists the Empress does not know of the attack. But I am suspicious, Xakthan. I will watch her on the night, and make sure she does not leave to assist the hunters. Which reminds me, is there word from our spies in the Empress's palace?"

"There was an attempt on Sarapen's life. He survived it."

"Have we managed to give him the means of escape?"

"Not yet. The Empress's agents watch him at all times."

"Keep trying. I have made a promise to Dominil MacRinnalch."

"Very good, mighty Queen."

CHAPTER 146

Thrix and Kalix drove home in silence. Dominil followed them, arriving moments later.

"How did it go?" she asked, in the lift.

"Good. I hid it under the carpet," said Kalix.

They walked along the corridor to Thrix's apartment.

"Describe the foyer to me," said Dominil. "We need to know what to expect."

Kalix told Dominil everything she could remember about the interior of the Guild's headquarters.

"There wasn't much space. There was some old furniture."

"Did you see any computers?"

"There was one behind the counter."

"Good. I may be able to get access to their system from there."

"Not if you have hunters shooting at you," said Thrix.

"There might be only a single person at the desk in the middle of the night. We may be able to dispose of him quickly without being observed."

"Are we going to destroy the building as well?" asked Kalix.

"Yes," said Thrix.

"No," said Dominil.

"We should set it on fire." Thrix was insistent. "Why risk leaving anything?"

"We can't burn it down without endangering everyone in the buildings around."

"The fire brigade will arrive, won't they? They can rescue the neighbors."

Dominil took out her phone. "I need to let Markus know that we've planted our marker."

She talked to Markus on the phone for some time. Kalix and Thrix sat in uncomfortable silence. The werewolf sisters had no light conversation to share with each other.

Dominil ended her call. "Everything is in place at the castle. They'll all travel down tomorrow. We attack the night after."

Dominil asked Kalix if she needed a lift home. Kalix was about to accept the offer when Thrix interrupted.

"Could you stay here for a moment? I need to talk to you about something."

Kalix eyed Thrix suspiciously. "About what?"

"A private family matter."

Kalix scowled. She didn't want to be left alone with Thrix. "OK. If I must."

Dominil left them alone.

"Now I won't get a lift home," said Kalix.

"When you met your ex-boyfriend in the street, who was with him?"

"Why?"

"I'm curious."

"It was his brother."

Thrix stared at Kalix. "His brother? Have you met him before?"

"No. Why?"

"Do you know what he does?"

"Stop asking annoying questions!" cried Kalix.

"I've a good idea what he does," said Thrix. "He's a werewolf hunter."

Kalix's eyes opened wide. "What?"

"He's a werewolf hunter. I saw him go into their building."

"You're making it up."

"Of course I'm not making it up. Why would I? When you cycled off your ex-boyfriend walked back down the street and his brother went straight into the Guild's building. I saw him take some sort of identity card from his pocket as he went inside."

"Maybe he was just delivering something."

"Did he look like a delivery boy?" said Thrix. "You've been going out with the brother of a werewolf hunter!"

"Stop talking rubbish," said Kalix, angrily. It was ridiculous. How could Manny be related to a werewolf hunter?

"Have you ever asked him what his family does?" asked Thrix.

"No. Why would I?"

"Did you ever tell Manny you were a werewolf?"

"Of course not."

"Was he ever curious about werewolves?"

"Stop asking stupid questions!" yelled Kalix.

"I wouldn't say they were stupid questions!" Thrix yelled back. "Manny's probably been spying on you all along. How could you be so stupid?"

"I didn't tell him anything! He doesn't know anything about werewolves. It's ridiculous."

"You've put the whole mission in danger," said Thrix. "Do you know why I didn't mention this to Dominil? Because she'd have told the council and the mission would have been cancelled. They'd have said it was too dangerous after you've been spied on."

"I haven't been spied on."

"That's what you think. I think you've been going out with a were-wolf hunter."

The sisters glared at each other with loathing.

"You're the one who goes out with werewolf hunters," said Kalix.

Thrix smiled malevolently. "And look what happened to him."

Thrix's unfortunate affair with the werewolf hunter Captain Easterly had ended when Kalix killed him.

"You'd better hope your boyfriend doesn't show up during the attack," said Thrix.

"Don't you do anything to him!"

"Why not? If he's been spying for the Guild, are you just going to let him off?"

Kalix became confused, and was stuck for an answer. She didn't know what she'd do if it turned out to be true. When the MacRinnalchs confronted a werewolf hunter, they killed him. There were no exceptions.

"I don't believe any of it," said Kalix. "I'm leaving now."

She stormed out of Thrix's apartment, slamming the door. Thrix poured herself a drink. "Young Manny better not have been spying on us," she muttered. She sipped her whisky, then laughed. "Maybe it's not so bad. I owe Kalix a dead boyfriend."

CHAPTER 147

Daniel and Moonglow were shopping in the small supermarket close to their flat.

"Do you think they ever notice our weird shopping patterns when it comes to meat?" asked Moonglow.

"What do you mean?"

"Most of the time we hardly buy any. But around the full moon we always load up with pounds of beef and lamb for Kalix."

"She does have a powerful appetite when she's a werewolf. But they probably don't notice. When we were working in that supermarket I was struggling just to get through the day."

Moonglow put a bottle of bleach in her basket, and a packet of four sponge-scrubbers for the kitchen.

"Do we need milk?" she asked.

"Yes. And what's this I hear about William being gay?" said Daniel.

"He's gay," said Moonglow. "What of it?"

"Aha!" said Daniel, inappropriately loudly. "So you admit it!"

"I was never hiding it."

"Yes, you were! You deliberately pretended he was Mr. Ideal Boyfriend."

"He is Mr. Ideal Boyfriend," said Moonglow.

"Apart from being gay."

"I suppose so. I don't see what the problem is."

"The problem is you've been pretending to go out with him and he's gay!"

"I wasn't 'pretending to go out with him.' I just helped him out at the ball. He hasn't come out to his parents yet."

"But you've seen him loads of times after that!"

"Because we get on well. What's wrong with that?"

Daniel came to a halt. "It's no use putting milk in your basket like nothing's wrong. You know you've been pretending to go out with him and deliberately not telling me he was gay."

"Nonsense," said Moonglow. "I thought you knew."

"How would I know?"

"At college he wears badges saying 'I'm Gay.'"

"Who reads badges?"

Moonglow shook her head, amazed at Daniel's lack of observation. "What about his T-shirt, you know, the pink one with "Queer" on the front?"

"I thought that was ironic."

"How would it be ironic?"

"I don't know. Stop obsessing about T-shirts. The point is you've been pretending to go out with someone who's actually gay."

CHAPTER 148

Mr. Hofmann, head of security at the Avenaris Guild, studied the purple flower suspiciously. He'd been called down to the foyer by Marshall and

Braid from Group Sixteen. While thoroughly examining every inch of the Guild's headquarters, they'd found the flower under the carpet. Mr. Evans from Intelligence arrived a few moments later.

"What is it?"

"A flower. Someone hid it under the carpet."

"Why would anyone do that?" asked Mr. Evans.

"I don't know," replied Mr. Hofmann. "But I don't like it."

They stared at the purple bloom. The lift opened behind them and Mr. Carmichael stepped out.

"I heard there's a security alert. What's happened?"

Mr. Hofmann showed him the flower. "We're wondering if it might be more than just a flower."

Mr. Carmichael nodded. "Who found it?"

"Marshall and Braid."

"Good work."

Mr. Carmichael carefully took the flower from Hofmann and examined it. He was the oldest member of the board, the oldest serving member of the Avenaris Guild. In his lifetime of hunting werewolves, he'd seen things that few of the others had.

"Looks normal. But I doubt that it is. Ask Ms. Leclair to come here at once."

Nicole Leclair, a Frenchwoman, was currently employed as esoteric adviser to the Avenaris Guild. The Guild did not have much recourse to sorcery, but in their business of hunting werewolves, they did encounter it on occasion. Ms. Leclair was not a sorceress herself, but she claimed to have knowledge of the magical arts. Where she had obtained this knowledge was not widely known. Ms. Leclair arrived, dressed in a black business suit, the fashionable cut of which rather emphasized the lack of style exhibited by the senior members of the board. She declined to touch the flower, but had Mr. Carmichael place it back on the floor, then knelt to examine it. The examination went on for quite a long time, leading to some frustration from Mr. Hofmann and Mr. Evans, neither of whom were sympathetic to sorcery, and who both privately suspected that Ms. Leclair made it up as she went along.

"It's a portal," she announced, finally. "A means of opening a pathway."

There were some skeptical looks exchanged among the men around her. Mr. Carmichael, however, was not skeptical.

"A pathway? From where?"

"I can't tell. It could be placed anywhere nearby."

"Can people walk through this pathway?"

"I believe so."

"But that's impossible," protested Mr. Evans. "You can't use sorcery in this building, everyone knows that."

"This is a very unusual piece of sorcery," said Ms. Leclair. "It's different to anything I've encountered before. I think it might penetrate even the walls of this building."

"Ridiculous," said Mr. Hofmann.

"Not ridiculous," said Mr. Carmichael. "This is exactly the sort of thing I was expecting. Gentlemen, this is the point of attack. The MacRinnalch werewolves are going to walk into this foyer."

"When?" said Mr. Hofmann.

"I don't know. At night presumably, when they're strongest. It will be soon, we can be sure of that. Maybe tonight."

Mr. Carmichael noticed the expressions of dismay on his fellow board members' faces.

"I don't see why you're all looking so worried. This is perfect. We already knew the werewolves were going to attack, and now we know exactly where they're going to attack. We'll be ready for them."

Mr. Carmichael eased the flower back under the carpet.

"From now on, no one leaves the building. All other business is cancelled. Mr. Hofmann, maintain security here, while I organize the rest of the Guild members and make sure we're ready."

CHAPTER 149

After the assassins' attack, Sarapen walked around openly, refusing to hide. Though the Empress shunned him, and everyone in the palace avoided him, knowing he was marked for death, Sarapen refused to show fear. If the Empress wanted him dead, he wasn't going to end his days skulking in the shadows.

He walked to the palace kitchens and picked up food from the serving trolleys. Kitchen staff lowered their eyes, and moved to avoid him. Sarapen regarded them with scorn, and filled his plate with no sign of discomfort. There was whispering all around but he ignored that too. He put the silver plate on one of the fine palace trays made from thinly sliced black volcanic rock, and strode back through the palace toward the chamber he'd inhabited since his arrival. The corridor was lined with the distinctive black and red marble that the Hainusta used for their grandest buildings, and the light from the torches on the walls reflected brightly from the polished surface. The Empress's palace was far brighter than Castle MacRinnalch. Sarapen had no difficulty in spotting the three elementals who waited for him outside his chamber. All three were fully armored. Soldiers, rather than assassins, thought Sarapen. Experienced fighters from the looks of them. Each carried a sword and a *meldrava*, the slingshot favored by the Empress's troops. They were loaded with still-burning lava from the Eternal Volcano, sometimes mixed with other deadly substances. Silver, in this case, Sarapen felt certain.

Sarapen changed into his werewolf shape and charged. One of the soldiers swung his *meldrava*, and a ball of white fire the size of a fist hurtled toward him. Sarapen leaped to avoid the attack and the ball of fire exploded violently on the wall behind him, shearing off a great slab of marble, which crashed to the floor. Sarapen felt an intense heat as another flaming sphere flew over his shoulder. Then he crashed into his attackers, biting and slashing with his claws, pulling all three of them to the ground. There was a furious struggle and when Sarapen sprang to his feet, only one of the soldiers did likewise. Two lay still on the floor, badly wounded or dead.

Sarapen snarled savagely, and laughed. "You're no match for me!" He leaped forward, striking the solider and snatching his *meldrava* from him. At that moment the corridor erupted in flames and he was thrown off his feet as a huge explosion engulfed them. Sarapen found himself flat on his back staring up at the sky. The explosion had blown a hole in the palace wall, flinging Sarapen out into space. He twisted in the air as he fell. Fortunately for the werewolf, the corridor had been only one floor up, and it was not far to the courtyard below. He landed on four legs like a cat, then sprinted into the darkness of a recess in the wall. Behind him there was shouting as the soldiers came after him in pursuit.

Sarapen found himself facing a small wooden door. He kicked it open and ran into another courtyard, one he'd never seen before.

"Sarapen MacRinnalch?"

He was shocked to find himself addressed. He whirled to face the person who'd spoken. It was a young woman, a Hainusta wearing the garb of a palace servant.

"What—" he began.

"Don't speak. No time. Queen Malveria sends you this jeweled mirror of travel, at the request of Dominil MacRinnalch. When the last ray of sunlight touches the top of the volcano, you can use it to bridge the dimensions."

The Hainusta woman thrust a small oblong mirror into Sarapen's hand. Without another word, she turned and hurried out of the courtyard. Sarapen stared at the mirror. Behind him the shouting was growing louder as the soldiers poured out of the palace. No longer so keen to sell his life dearly, having a means of escape, Sarapen fled from the courtyard, disappearing into a maze of small passageways that ran through the servants' quarters.

When the last ray of sunlight touches the top of the volcano. How long was that? Sarapen wasn't sure. He hurried on through the servants' corridors, looking for somewhere he could hide from his pursuers, preferably a place where he could observe the Eternal Volcano, and then take his chance at freedom.

CHAPTER 150

In the early hours of the morning, a fairy rose from Colburn Woods. She had unusually pale skin, very dark wings, and she was partially hidden by a shadow that enveloped her tiny form. She drifted on the breeze for a little while, enjoying the feeling of the cold air on her wings. When the wind pushed her toward the west, in the direction of Castle MacRinnalch, she lifted up her head and laughed.

"Werewolves. I've never cared for them much."

Teinn, bringer of ill health, flew toward the castle. It was further away than human eyes could see, but Teinn's vision was sharper than any human. It was sharper than an eagle's; she could already see a few werewolves entering the castle through the postern gate, MacRinnalchs who'd been hunting at night, returning before the sun rose.

Teinn flew rapidly, still chuckling to herself. It was rare that Teinn was allowed to come here. Normally the Fairy Queen kept her well away from Castle MacRinnalch, knowing the harm she might do. Even now, Teinn's mission was strictly limited. She was permitted to make Markus sick, and that was all. Queen Dithean had explicitly forbidden her to do anything else. Teinn smiled. She'd been to Castle MacRinnalch more often than the Fairy Queen knew, and seen things there that the Fairy Queen didn't know about. She was sure she could find something else to do.

She skimmed over the rough, heather-covered moor, thinking back to the time she'd observed a great fight in front of the gates. She'd watched from high above as Markus MacRinnalch heroically struggled against the huge Wallace MacGregor. Teinn remembered the MacRinnalchs on the battlements, cheering Markus as he emerged victorious. She laughed again. Her dark wings beat faster as she approached the castle and she rose in the air before swooping down over the high wall. She hovered above the central courtyard, invisible in the gloom. A few werewolves moved quietly around below her.

Teinn scanned the dark stone internal walls of the castle. She sensed Markus's presence in the east wing. She flew quickly to the window outside and landed on the stone ledge. The fairy peered inside. The glass was old and cloudy but Teinn's vision was such that she could see inside the room quite clearly. Markus was asleep in a great wooden bed. Teinn was surprised to see two women, one on each side of him. The fairy laughed, very amused. That was a sight she hadn't expected.

Teinn put her lips to the window and breathed on it. The lock clicked and she pulled the window open a few inches, enough to let her tiny frame squeeze through. The early dawn light outside had not yet penetrated the stone chamber but Teinn could make out every detail of Markus and his two lovers, entwined together in sleep. Her dark wings flapped as she flew down to perch on Markus's forehead. Markus didn't react, but when the fairy bent over his face and placed her lips on his mouth to kiss him, he moaned quietly, as if troubled in his sleep.

"*Am fiabhras-clèibhe*," whispered the fairy, which was Gaelic for "pneumonia."

She fluttered to the top of the headboard, pleased with herself. "You won't be going anywhere for a while, Thane Markus. But you'll survive the illness, probably."

The fairy looked at Markus's partners. Silly werewolves, she thought. I'd make you sick as well if the Queen allowed me.

She flew back down onto the bed, landing next to Heather MacAllister. She put her lips close to Heather's ear, and whispered, "When Markus MacRinnalch defeated Wallace MacGregor, his mother had secretly poisoned Wallace before the fight."

Teinn hopped over to the other side of the bed and whispered the same into Beatrice MacRinnalch's ear. She smiled with satisfaction, then flew out of the window, not bothering to close it behind her. Next to the great gates of the castle there was a guardroom, and beside that a small barrack room for the guards. Teinn paused as she flew above, then flew into the guardroom where three werewolves were sleeping. She whispered the same thing in the ears of each of them: "When Markus MacRinnalch defeated Wallace MacGregor, his mother had secretly poisoned Wallace before the fight."

Satisfied with her actions, Teinn rose high above the castle. The sun was now rising, sending shafts of light onto the battlements. Teinn looked back across the moors toward the Colburn Woods. She wondered about staying at the castle to do more mischief, but decided against it. The sun would soon be up, and Teinn was not as keen on daylight as the rest of the fairies in the wood. She headed home, pleased with her work. It had been an enjoyable visit to Castle MacRinnalch for the fairy who brought ill health and misfortune, and was always covered in shadow.

CHAPTER 151

On the evening before the attack, Kalix was alone in her room, making herself ready. It didn't take long. She made sure she had some money, her phone and a small plastic container of laudanum secreted in an inside pocket. She put on her coat.

"I'm ready to go."

She had the feeling that perhaps there was something else she should have done. For such a momentous enterprise, it felt like there should be longer preparations. Kalix shrugged. There was nothing else to do. With the battle approaching, she was feeling unusually calm. She sat on her bed and looked around her room. Kalix didn't really expect that she'd be coming back.

It's been good living here.

Kalix had a moment of clarity in which she saw her life before she'd met Daniel and Moonglow, and her life after. Moving into their flat had been a great improvement. Not just in comfort; she'd made friends, which she'd never expected to do.

Daniel and Moonglow have been nice to me, Kalix thought, smiling to herself. So has Vex.

The young werewolf frowned. She had been planning on slipping out of the house without telling anyone where she was going. Now she wondered if that was a bad thing to do.

If I don't come back, they'll think I didn't like them enough to say goodbye.

The thought troubled Kalix. She didn't want to appear ungrateful. She remembered when she'd first moved in, and she'd kept being sick, and violent, and hostile.

I wonder why they even put up with me.

Kalix felt more and more uncomfortable at the thought of leaving without saying anything. But if I tell them it will be worse, she reasoned. What am I going to say? I'm off to attack the Guild, I probably won't be back? Then they'll be even more upset. They'll try and stop me going.

Kalix didn't think she could face the unpleasant scene. She tried not to think about it. There were still some hours left till she was due to leave. All the other werewolves would be at Thrix's flat by now but Kalix wasn't meeting them there. She planned to sit in a pub near Gloucester Place, then arrive at the hotel just before the attack began. That way it would be too late for any of the others to object to her presence.

Kalix picked up Vex's crayons again. She'd been trying to copy one of Manny's pictures from memory but it hadn't worked out well. She abandoned it and picked up another sheet of paper. She remembered the night that Daniel, Vex and Moonglow had appeared in her room to cheer her up. They'd all perched on the bed together, watching anime. Kalix smiled. That had been good. She tried to draw a picture of the four of them, sitting on the bed. She applied herself to the task, just to pass the time. Once more, without really noticing that she was doing it, Kalix slipped between her human form and her werewolf form as she worked, drawing fine details with her hands and vigorous blocks of background shading with her werewolf paws.

Eventually she heard noises downstairs. Her flatmates were all home.

I should have bought them a present, she thought suddenly. Like a going-away present.

Kalix felt bad. They had all given her presents in the past. She wished she'd thought of it earlier. It was too late now; it would soon be time for her to leave. Quite abruptly, she came to a decision.

I shouldn't go off without telling anyone. If it causes a big scene, I'll just have to cope with it. It won't matter in a few hours anyway.

Kalix walked out of her room. She hesitated for a second at the top of the stairs then descended quickly. Her three flatmates were all watching TV.

"I've got something to tell you," said Kalix.

Daniel looked up from the television. "Yes?"

"I'm going out soon to . . . I'm . . ." Kalix struggled to find the right words. "The werewolf clan is going on a mission."

Moonglow swiftly muted the TV. "A mission?"

"Yes. A big mission."

"You mean dangerous?"

"Yes, dangerous. There's going to be fighting. It's something the MacRinnalchs have to do. I know you won't want me to go and you're probably going to argue, but it's no use. It's my duty to the clan. And anyway, I want to go." Kalix felt her mouth going dry. "I just wanted to tell you before I left," she mumbled.

Kalix's announcement caught her friends by surprise. They'd been expecting a peaceful evening.

"Can't you not go?" said Moonglow.

"No. I have to. I want to."

"Is it really dangerous?" asked Daniel.

"Yes. But I'll be OK."

"Don't go," said Vex. "I don't want you to go."

"Neither do I," said Moonglow.

Kalix moved toward the door.

"Where are you going?" asked Daniel. "Where's the mission?"

"I can't tell you that," said Kalix. "And you can't get involved."

"Don't go," said Moonglow.

"I have to go now. It was nice that you let me live here. Thanks." Kalix looked down and found that she was holding a piece of paper in her hand.

"Look, I drew a picture of us sitting on my bed, watching cartoons."

Kalix thrust the paper into Moonglow's hand and then hurried out the front door. She ran down the steps, pleased that it was over. There hadn't been nearly as bad an argument as she'd anticipated, but it had still been excruciating. Moonglow had looked anguished.

In the living room, Moonglow looked at the picture Kalix had drawn with Vex's crayons.

"That's a *really* good picture." She burst into tears.

"Well, this is no good," said Daniel. "Kalix suddenly tells us she's going on a dangerous mission and we're just meant to sit here and let her go?"

"What can we do?" said Vex.

"I've no idea," admitted Daniel.

"Kalix said we couldn't get involved," said Vex.

"We're not letting her go and get killed without doing something about it!" said Moonglow, wiping her tears on her sleeve.

"I agree," said Daniel.

"Me too," added Vex. "What should we do?"

"Where is this mission?" said Moonglow. "Someone must know. Vex, would Malveria know?"

Vex shrugged. "Maybe. Aunt Malvie usually knows what Thrix is doing."

"Then go to the palace and find out everything."

"OK," said Vex. She disappeared from view, dematerializing in a businesslike manner. There was a crash in the kitchen.

"I went the wrong way! But I'm all right! I'm leaving again now!"

Vex departed.

"I can't believe Kalix thinks she can just go and get killed and expect us to do nothing!" said Moonglow.

"Absolutely. It's ridiculous." Daniel paused. "What exactly are you planning?"

"I don't know."

"If it involves a load of werewolf hunters with guns, for instance, there's no point us just charging in and getting shot."

"No one is getting shot!"

Daniel hoped not. He didn't share Moonglow's confidence. It had always been in the back of his mind that living with a werewolf who had enemies was liable to get him into serious trouble at some point.

CHAPTER 152

Kalix sat on the top floor of the 159 bus, making the slow journey from Kennington to the center of town, staring vacantly out the window. It had now turned cold and condensation formed on the inside of the glass. She rubbed the window with her sleeve, clearing a patch to look through. The streets outside looked damp and gray.

Someone sitting nearby was listening to music. Kalix found it vaguely annoying. A rather large person sat down beside her, squashing her up against the window. Kalix might have been annoyed, but instead saw some humor in the situation. Here she was, suffering the common problems of commuting on a bus, while on her way to a deadly battle. She supposed it was probably quite normal to be uncomfortable on your way to battle. She didn't mind. The prospect of fighting had made her calm. Her phone rang. It was Dominil.

"Where are you?"

"On a bus, on the way to the hotel."

"Don't go. There's a problem."

"What problem?"

"Come to Thrix's flat instead."

Dominil rang off, leaving Kalix puzzled. Why would Dominil want her to go to Thrix's flat? Wasn't that where the other attackers were gathering? Surely she wouldn't be welcome? Kalix didn't know what to make of it. She got off the bus as soon as it crossed the river, then walked down into Westminster tube station. Sloane Square was only a few stops along the line. A busker was singing and playing guitar at the entrance as she emerged. Kalix had some loose change in her pocket. She dropped it into the hat he'd placed on the ground, thinking that she probably wouldn't be needing it any more.

When she arrived at the apartment block, Dominil buzzed her in and was waiting for her upstairs at Thrix's front door.

"What's happened?"

"The attack is off," said Dominil.

"No it isn't," said Thrix, behind her.

Dominil closed the door. "We can't do it now."

"We haven't finished discussing it," said Thrix.

Thrix was wearing a pair of trousers that looked like a fashion designer's take on a military style.

"What's happened?" asked Kalix.

"Markus is sick," said Dominil. "Quite badly. He's got pneumonia."

"What? How?"

"I don't know," said Dominil. "Pneumonia usually only affects people in poor health. I've never heard of a healthy werewolf coming down with it before. Doctor Angus says he'll recover but he's going to be in bed for a week or two."

Kalix sat down heavily. It was a strange piece of news. Sickness among the MacRinnalchs was rare.

"Why can't we do the attack? Can't someone come in Markus's place?" she asked.

"Everyone has pulled out," said Thrix, angrily. "The barons have recalled their men. We don't have an attack force any more."

Kalix was puzzled, and annoyed. "I don't understand. We could still have attacked, even without Markus. So what if he's sick?"

"There's more to it than that," Dominil told her. "Apparently the castle has erupted in bad feeling during the past twenty-four hours."

Kalix felt bewildered. "Why?"

"A rumor has spread that when Markus defeated Wallace MacGregor in single combat, Wallace was drugged," said Thrix. "By our mother."

"Drugged? Oh." Kalix nodded. "I wondered why he won."

"That's not the most appropriate response," said Dominil.

"It's no doubt what everyone's thinking," said Thrix.

"Perhaps. But it would be better for the MacRinnalchs to deny it. We don't know it's true."

"You know it's true," said Thrix. "We both knew it was true the moment we heard it."

Previously, there had never been the slightest suspicion that there had been anything untoward in the fight between Markus and Wallace. But now, as soon as the suggestion had been made that Markus had cheated, everyone seemed willing to believe it.

Thrix groaned and shook her head. She had an empty glass in her hand. She poured a little whisky into it then handed the bottle to Dominil. Dominil poured herself a small amount and did the same for Kalix.

"Baron MacGregor is livid," said Thrix. "He's threatening to leave the council and break with the MacRinnalchs entirely. MacPhee and MacAllister are furious too. So are the MacRinnalchs. Everyone's ashamed." Thrix sipped from her glass. "It doesn't help that Markus had to choose this moment to get sick. It doesn't look good."

"Who started this rumor?" asked Kalix.

Neither Dominil nor Thrix knew. It seemed to have come from nowhere.

Kalix drank from her whisky. "I wanted to attack the Guild."

"So did I," said Dominil.

"I'm still going to," declared Thrix.

"Don't be ridiculous," said Dominil. "You can't do it on your own. And the three of us can't do it either. We'll just have to wait for the next council meeting and see if we can come up with another plan."

"If we don't do it now, we'll lose our chance. The Guild won't just let that flower lie there for a month. Either they'll find it or the magic will wear off. We'll never have as good an opportunity to walk into their building again."

"We don't know that," said Dominil.

"I'll still do it," said Kalix to Thrix. "I'll come with you."

"No," said Dominil, firmly. "You won't. All that would achieve is two dead werewolves. The Clan would be weaker and the Guild would be unaffected. I've no objection to facing danger but it's pointless throwing our lives away."

The buzzer sounded. It was Decembrius. He walked in looking cheerful. "Time for the gathering of the clans," he said. "Where is everyone?"

Dominil told Decembrius what had happened. His high spirits dissipated. "So we can't attack?"

"No," said Dominil.

"There's four of us now," said Thrix. "Isn't that enough?"

"No." Dominil was emphatic.

Thrix growled. "What a complete farce. Some plan we made, Dominil."

"We couldn't know that Markus would fall ill."

"How do we know he's really ill?" asked Decembrius. "Maybe he just changed his mind."

"He's ill," said Thrix, and looked at Decembrius angrily. Though Thrix didn't get on that well with Markus, she didn't intend to let her brother be accused of cowardice. "Pneumonia. It happens."

"Really?" said Decembrius. "I've never heard of it happening before. Not to a werewolf anyway."

"Stupid pneumonia," said Kalix. "I wanted to attack the Guild."

"So did I," said Thrix. "And I still think we should, before the opportunity vanishes. The Fairy Queen isn't going to give us another spell, no matter how much Dominil bribes her."

Thrix's phone rang, and she had a very brief conversation. "That was Morag MacAllister, the Baron's sister. She's on her way here."

"Why?" asked Dominil.

"She still wants to take part in the attack. Baron MacGregor called them back from the castle and she just ignored him. She's always been fierce."

"I fought her," said Kalix. "She is fierce. I'm glad she's coming."

"So that makes five of us," said Thrix.

"Any chance of a cup of tea?" asked Decembrius.

"If you make it."

"What happened to MacRinnalch hospitality?" Decembrius headed for the kitchen.

"Is five enough?" asked Kalix.

Dominil hesitated, but shook her head.

"I say it is." Thrix was insistent. "If we get five strong werewolves here, I'm going. You can stay behind if you want."

Dominil glared at her cousin. "You know perfectly well that if you attack the Guild's headquarters, I will accompany you. That doesn't mean you should do it."

Thrix's phone rang once more. "Hello? Eskandor? Really? Good."

Thrix rang off. "That was Eskandor. He's coming as well. And he's bringing Feargan and Barra. From the sound of Eskandor's voice, they weren't about to let the MacRinnalch name be disgraced." Thrix smiled in satisfaction. "Wallace MacGregor is with them."

"Wallace?"

"Apparently. Wallace likes to fight. When he saw the MacRinnalchs were going anyway he didn't want to be left out."

"I wouldn't have expected him to go against his father, the Baron."

"Maybe he feels like it's time to break away from his father. Anyway, that makes nine of us. That must be enough. Their headquarters might even be empty. We'll be able to destroy everything, all their records, everything they've learned. We can't pass up the chance."

The others waited for Dominil to speak.

"Very well, I agree. Nine werewolves may suffice."

Kalix was pleased. She'd started to feel anxious, but now that they were definitely going to fight, calmness descended again.

Decembrius arrived back from the kitchen with a mug of tea. "What's happening?"

"We've got nine werewolves. We're going to attack," said Thrix.

"Good. Did you know you're out of milk?"

"There's another pint on the bottom shelf in the fridge," said Thrix, whose mood had dramatically improved. She snapped her fingers, and a few seconds later the pint of milk floated into the room. It was rare for the Enchantress to use her sorcery for any minor reason in front of other werewolves, perhaps because the clan had a tendency to look down on it. Now she was in too good a mood to worry about such things.

"I hope the building isn't completely empty," she said. "If there aren't at least a couple of hunters there, I'll be disappointed."

CHAPTER 153

The Fire Queen was in a poor temper. She'd felt herself to be on the defensive ever since Kabachetka had ingratiated herself with the editor of *Vogue* by sponsoring the ball. Thrix's designs may have been a success on the night, but the overall effect had still been to boost the Empress's profile. Kabachetka was receiving more invitations to events than she ever had before.

It would not have been so bad had she not appeared in the "fashionable party people" pages, thought the Fire Queen. But it gave her confidence, and boosted what Thrix calls her "credibility." Now the awful woman is everywhere. One simply dreads the Versace event tomorrow. If she is seated more favorably than me, I shall simply die.

Donatella Versace was sponsoring her new partnership with Takahashi, a young Japanese designer who'd been creating waves in the fashion world for some time. His arrival in Europe was an important event.

The Fire Queen's thoughts carried on in the same gloomy train. *One is fortunate to even have a decent frock to wear. I practically had to beg Thrix's assistant Ann to have the designers finish it for me.*

Malveria shook her head, and drank heavily from her wine glass. Thrix had promised to design more for her when she rejoined her business, but Malveria had no confidence that this would ever happen.

"Thrix is more likely to be dead than back in business."

The Fire Queen looked up, sensing that her niece had just arrived in the palace. Vex hurried in to the Fire Queen's chambers.

"Hello, Aunt Malvie."

"Do not call me 'Aunt Malvie,' snapped the Fire Queen. "You may as well bring me a woollen blanket and drape it around my aging shoulders. What do you want?"

"Kalix is going to get killed on some mission."

"I am aware of this."

"Oh." Vex was surprised. "Aren't you going to do something about it?"

"The Queen of the Hiyasta does not spend her time protecting werewolves, no matter what you may think," said Malveria, grandly.

"Come on, Aunty, you can't just let her get killed."

The Fire Queen shook her head. "There is nothing I can do. They are going to a place I cannot enter."

"What do you mean?"

"The Maynista curse, which you would know about had you ever paid the slightest attention in your history class."

"So you really can't help?" Vex was deflated. She'd assumed that her aunt would be able to do something. "I don't like this at all."

"I don't like it either, Agrivex. But such is life."

"Could I do anything to help? Does the curse affect me?"

The Fire Queen shook her head. "No. But you should not get involved. And neither should Daniel or Moonglow."

"Where is this building they're going to?"

"I don't know. Only someone with prior knowledge of its location can find it."

"Well, this is no good," said Vex. "Kalix might get killed."

"Thrix may also die. But we can't help."

"But you always manage to help."

"Usually I do," agreed the Fire Queen. "But we all have our limits, including me. It's time you appreciated that."

"I suppose so," said Vex, gloomily. It had never previously occurred to Vex that her aunt had limits. She was thoughtful for a few moments. "Was it difficult for you to become Queen? What with all the fighting and so on?"

"It was. Did you not realize that?"

"I never thought about it much."

They sat in silence for a few more minutes.

"Agrivex, while we cannot directly help, there is one thing we may do. While the werewolves are fighting, both myself and Kabachetka will be in London. The werewolves attack is secret, and Kabachetka should not know. But I worry about that. If Kabachetka does know, she may assist the Guild, and that would be disastrous. Unlike myself, she can enter their building, and even without sorcery she has great elemental power. So come with me to the event, and keep an eye on Kabachetka. We can at least make sure she does not add her power to that of the hunters."

"OK." Vex brightened a little at the prospect of helping in some way. She looked down at her bag, which resembled a green plastic shopping basket. "Do you like my new bag?"

"It's the vilest thing I have ever seen."

"Isn't it great? I got it on eBay with some manga."

The Fire Queen shuddered. "Kindly keep it well away from Donatella's fashion show."

"I bet it will be a big hit at the show!" enthused Vex.

"Green plastic is rarely a fashion winner, dismal niece."

"How could anyone not like it?" said Vex. "I love my green plastic bag."

CHAPTER 154

While Morag MacAllister, Wallace MacGregor and the three MacRinnalchs were still en route to London, Distikka visited the Guild's headquarters. She was allowed through the front door but no further. She waited as Mr. Carmichael was summoned. He took quite a long time to arrive and when he did he appeared distracted.

"Sorry we can't let you in. We're on high security alert. We're anticipating the attack any day now."

Distikka nodded. "It will be tonight."

"Are you sure?"

"The Empress's spies have observed unusual movement around the castle. We think they have set out. Are you prepared?"

"We are," said Mr. Carmichael.

"Good," said Distikka. "That is all I came to say."

"Do you have any reason to believe the werewolves know we're expecting them?"

"Not as far as I know," said Distikka. "They still think they'll take you by surprise."

Distikka departed.

Mr. Carmichael returned to his task of preparing for the attack. All four members of Group Sixteen were gathered in the foyer, standing behind a makeshift but sturdy barrier that had been erected overnight. Another barrier, similar in size, had been put up on the other side of the foyer.

"We can fit eight hunters in this space," said Braid. "All with guns trained on the werewolves' point of arrival. There's space for another three or four on the stairs. The rest will have to wait on the first floor."

The old building was full of narrow corridors and small rooms. It wasn't the ideal location for fighting a prolonged battle with werewolves. There were too many corners to hide around, and not enough clear space for uninterrupted fire. Mr. Carmichael hoped that the fighting would not extend to other parts of the building. The plan was to cut the werewolves down the moment they arrived. With the firepower at his command he was confident of success.

Distikka returned to the Empress's palace. Though she had become used to the journey between dimensions, the cold, gray voyage still left her fatigued. It would have been hard to tell as she entered the throne room. Distikka walked very erect, with her head high.

"The hunters are ready," she informed the Empress.

Empress Kabachetka was busy with her dressmakers who were making some final adjustments to her gown. Also in attendance were three servants, laying out shoes for her approval. The Empress wasn't satisfied with any of them.

"Bring me more shoes," she commanded. Her servants hurried off to bring more shoes.

"Do you trust the hunters to finish the task?" she asked Distikka.

"They should succeed."

"You sound as if you have some doubts."

"Not really. The werewolves will be surprised. They should all die. But the Avenaris Guild has failed in the past. And they're facing Dominil. I have a high regard for her abilities."

The Empress looked at her adviser with some annoyance. "I deplore your high regard for this werewolf. Just because you share a taste in art does not mean she can defeat a volley of silver bullets. Is the Guild well supplied with silver bullets?"

"I believe so."

"Good. Where is Bakmer? I need advice. This hemline is making my ankles look thick." The Empress turned this way and that in front of a mirror. "Have you news of Sarapen?"

"The army is still in pursuit."

"You certainly failed in this, Distikka. It should have been done by now."

"I didn't appreciate your soldiers were so inefficient," said Distikka. "I have assigned more to the task. They'll find him soon."

The Empress wasn't listening. "Where is Bakmer? I need him immediately. And who is responsible for my nails? Distikka, find whoever is responsible for my nails, admonish them severely, then send them to me."

CHAPTER 155

There were nine werewolves in Thrix's apartment. Eight of them were eating quietly in the seldom-used dining room. Kalix had sneaked off to the bedroom to call Manny. She'd agonized over it, fearing rejection. It would be terrible if she called him and he didn't want to speak to her. Realizing that it might be her last ever opportunity, she gathered up her courage and dialed his number. It was a surprise when he answered.

"It's Alex. I just thought I'd call you . . . You know . . . you said I should . . ."

There was silence at the other end of the line.

"I'm sorry I messed everything up," said Kalix. Her voice faltered. She didn't know what she could add to that. Her eyes became moist, much to her annoyance.

"It's OK," said Manny. "I'm glad you called. Maybe I got too upset about it anyway."

Kalix still had no idea what to say next. Another long silence ensued. She gathered up her courage. "Do you want to meet?" she said, finally.

"OK," said Manny. "When? Tonight?"

"I'm busy tonight," said Kalix. "Maybe tomorrow?"

"OK. You should call me."

"OK."

The phone call ended. Kalix's heart was pounding. It had taken all her effort to make the call. If Manny had been rude to her she wouldn't have been able to bear it. Now it was done, Kalix felt pleased with herself for making the effort. Her pleasure was quickly dispelled by a very hostile growl behind her. She spun round to find Thrix glaring at her.

"Were you just talking to Manny?" cried Thrix. "I can't believe this! I told you he was connected to the Guild and you've just gone and told him you're busy tonight! Why not just send them a message that we're about to attack? You moronic, pathetic excuse for a MacRinnalch."

"He doesn't have anything to do with the hunters!" yelled Kalix.

"His brother works in the building!" yelled Thrix. "I already knew you were selfish and inconsiderate, but I didn't know just how stupid you were. You know what would happen if I told anyone about this? They'd cancel the mission. And the only reason I'm not going to tell is because I'm so crazy for revenge I don't care if the Guild knows I'm coming. I just want to kill hunters. But if everything goes wrong tonight, it will be your fault."

Thrix's eyes blazed as she shouted at her sister. "Never speak to me again. Just forget we're sisters. I'm finished with you, for good."

Thrix wrenched open the bedroom door. Decembrius was outside. "What's going on?"

"Nothing," snapped Thrix. "Just an argument." She stormed off.

"What was that about?" Decembrius asked Kalix.

"Nothing," mumbled Kalix. "Just sisters arguing."

"It's almost time to leave. Are you ready for a fight?"

"Very ready," said Kalix, and looked savage as she spoke.

Kalix followed Decembrius back into the main room where the attackers were assembled. Thrix, Dominil, Kalix, Decembrius, Eskandor, Feargan, Barra, Wallace and Morag looked at each other. Thrix produced an unopened bottle of the MacRinnalch whisky and nine crystal goblets, previously unused.

"Nice glasses," said Decembrius.

"Edinburgh crystal, eighteen seventy-five," said Thrix. "A present from my mother."

Thrix raised her glass. "*Slàinte mhath.*"

"*Slàinte mhath,*" responded each werewolf.

"I'll see you all in the Forests of the Werewolf Dead," said Decembrius. They drained their glasses, and then left Thrix's apartment, on their way to Gloucester Place.

CHAPTER 156

Vex traveled back to her flat to tell Daniel and Moonglow the disappointing news that Malveria didn't know where Kalix had gone.

"But we're going to keep an eye on Kabachetka tonight. If I learn anything else I'll let you know."

Vex hurried off again. She was due to meet her aunt close to the large

Eldridge clothing store on Oxford Street where Donatella Versace was presiding over Takahashi's foray into the European market. As soon as Vex arrived, the Fire Queen snapped her fingers, plucking a sheet of paper from the air. She handed it to her niece.

"I have fabricated an invitation for you. Try not to lose it during our fifty yard walk to the venue."

"OK, Aunty."

They emerged into Oxford Street, which was still busy with evening shoppers. Malveria stood out from the crowd, beautiful and elegant with a long gray coat draped over her new turquoise dress. Even though the outfit had been completed by Thrix's subordinates, rather than Thrix herself, the Fire Queen grudgingly admitted that she was beautifully dressed. She paused to examine herself in a shop window, admiring the way the coat hung from her shoulders, the dress showed off her figure, and both matched her very high turquoise heels to perfection. She felt an added thrill of pleasure at the way her handbag, gray with a turquoise clasp, set off her outfit perfectly.

"If Thrix is to meet bloody death tonight, we may at least remember how fabulously she dressed me."

Agrivex was wearing her huge black glacier boots, a very short red tartan kilt and a Hello Kitty pajama top. She waved her green plastic shopping basket quite merrily as they approached the venue.

"If anyone asks, pretend you are a fashion student," said Malveria. "They are allowed a certain eccentricity."

"What does that mean?"

"It means they can look as atrocious as you without being expelled from polite society."

The Fire Queen walked in with her head high, ready to meet her rivals. "Observe, Agrivex, how a Hiyasta monarch behaves in a crisis. I will not flinch. If Empress Kabachetka has already been introduced to Donatella Versace, I will face it bravely."

She noticed that her niece was fumbling in her pockets. "Why are you hesitating, Agrivex?"

"I've lost my invitation."

The Fire Queen sighed, and wordlessly plucked another one from the air. "Try not to embarrass me inside."

Vex immediately stumbled over a small step and sprawled on the floor.

"Agrivex, is there any chance of us proceeding further without you losing something or tumbling to the ground?"

"I'm fine now. Is there any food here? I'm hungry."

"There will be a buffet. Please be discreet. It's not the done thing to wallow like a pig in a trough."

Agrivex laughed, and didn't dispute the Queen's description of her eating habits. The Fire Queen entered the store with an air of quiet grandeur, aware of the very fashionable nature of her outfit, but also on the lookout for the Empress Kabachetka.

CHAPTER 157

Vex's brief reappearance hadn't done anything to reassure Moonglow and Daniel.

"So the Fire Queen says we shouldn't get involved. That doesn't make me feel any better," said Moonglow. "Obviously it's so dangerous that Kalix is going to be killed. We have to do something."

"What?"

"I don't know."

"Maybe William could help," said Daniel, sourly.

"I can't believe you're still going on about that! Just how immature are you anyway?"

"Very immature," said Daniel. "I'm well known for it." Daniel was still angry over William. It was unfair that everyone had let him think that Moonglow was in a relationship with William when really she wasn't. He sat on the couch, staring at the carpet.

"And I don't like that smell of that candle," he said, wanting something more to complain about.

"What candle?"

"Whatever scented candle you've lit. It smells funny."

Moonglow was puzzled. "I didn't light any candle."

"Something smells like almonds."

Moonglow took a step back as a light began to flicker in the center of the living room. They were used to the sudden appearances of the Fire Queen and Agrivex, but this looked liked someone struggling to materialize. Daniel hurried to Moonglow's side, standing protectively beside her as the light gradually grew stronger. When it finally took form, they were surprised to see Lady Gezinka.

The Hiyasta aristocrat frowned. "I am sorry for my slow materialization. I'm not used to making this journey." She looked at Daniel. "What do you mean 'funny smell'? That's rather insulting."

Daniel blushed. "I just meant it was . . . uh . . ." He looked toward Moonglow to help him out.

"It's a lovely perfume," said Moonglow. "Like almonds. We just weren't expecting it." She looked from Daniel to Gezinka. "Do you want me to leave you alone?"

Lady Gezinka wrinkled her nose. "Please, I have not come here in a fit of passion, unable to survive without seeing Daniel again. I have come to give you a warning about your friend whose name escapes me, but is a werewolf."

"Kalix?"

"Yes, Kalix. Are you aware that she is involved in a dangerous mission?"

"Yes," said Daniel.

"Are you also aware that her enemies know every detail of this mission, and are simply waiting for the werewolves to arrive so they can cut them down?"

"What?" cried Daniel."

"Are you sure?" cried Moonglow.

"I am quite sure. The Empress has known of it for some time. It will be a slaughter." Lady Gezinka paused, and looked around the small room. She raised her eyebrows. "You did tell me you lived in a rather cramped space. I did not quite appreciate what that meant."

"We have to warn Kalix," said Moonglow. "Where is she?"

"That I do not know. The enemies of the werewolves have their headquarters somewhere in the center of the city, but I have never been told the precise location."

Gezinka began to flicker. Without the Empress beside her, she was finding it difficult to sustain her presence on Earth. "I must leave now."

"Thanks for warning us," said Daniel.

Gezinka managed to stabilize herself for a second. She studied Daniel.

"He never stops talking about you," said Moonglow.

Lady Gezinka looked pleased. "Good," she said. And with that, she was gone.

"It's not really true I never stop talking about her," said Daniel.

"You talk about her enough. Anyway, it was the polite thing to say. Now she's happy. So what are we going to do about Kalix? She's not answering her phone."

"We should try Dominil and Thrix, we've got their numbers."

They hurried to call Dominil and Thrix but neither of them was answering their phones either. The situation seemed hopeless, and neither of them had any inspiration.

"We should drive into the center of town," said Moonglow. "Maybe we'll spot them."

"That's not very likely."

"Well, who knows, it might happen. We have to do something. Maybe when we're driving we can think of something better."

They hurried to put on their coats and shoes.

"I really must have made a big impression on Lady Gezinka," said Daniel, as they rushed down the stairs. "She liked me enough to warn me that my friend was in danger."

"Stop looking so pleased with yourself," said Moonglow. "She's probably just annoyed at the Empress for some reason, and wants to pay her back."

"No, I think it's more likely I made a big impression."

Daniel and Moonglow got into the car, and drove off.

CHAPTER 158

Sarapen crouched in the hollow, and squinted upwards toward the summit of the Eternal Volcano. He had worked his way through the palace and its environs, keeping one step ahead of his pursuers, finally ending up in the burning lava fields that surrounded the volcano. He could go no further. Even the Empress's sorcery could not protect him from the intense heat. The palace was swarming with guards. Soldiers were flooding from the east gate, heading in his direction. It wouldn't take them long to find him.

Sarapen looked up at the volcano. The sun was going down. *When the last ray of sunlight touches the top of the volcano.* That's what the agent of the Fire Queen had said. When that happened he could use the jeweled mirror she'd given him to transport himself back home. Or rather, back to wherever Dominil happened to be. Once more, he was impressed at Dominil's resourcefulness. He'd asked her for help, and she'd provided it. He wondered how her plan of attack was progressing. He wished he could be there to join in, even if his help was unwelcome. He was an out-cast from the clan now, or would be, if he were known to be alive. He was as much an outcast as Kalix.

Sarapen looked back toward the palace. The light was dimmer now but he could see figures clambering over the rocks, swarming toward his position with weapons in their hands. He looked up at the volcano. The summit was still wreathed in sunlight. The last rays had not yet arrived.

Sarapen took the jewel in his hand, and crouched down in the hol-low. He'd conceal himself till the last possible moment, but if he were discovered before he could escape, he'd make his pursuers pay dearly. He changed into his werewolf shape, and snarled savagely at the thought of battle. He would not be the first Scot to meet his end in some foreign, lonely spot and, as the greatest of the MacRinnalchs, he didn't intend to let the clan down.

"My death stand will be so bloody and glorious that word of it will one day reach Castle MacRinnalch, even if it is a dimension away."

✳

A dimension away, Dominil was letting herself into a hotel room in Gloucester Place. She was the first to arrive, having calmly announced herself at the foyer downstairs, and taken her room key from the clerk. Dominil closed the door then took out her phone. She called Thrix.

"Everything is fine."

"See you soon," said Thrix.

The Enchantress and the others had arrived together in a Transit van, hired for the evening. It was parked nearby. They had booked several more rooms under false names, and would arrive in small groups before gathering in Dominil's room, at the far end of the hotel. Thrix would work her spell, the pathway would open and they'd attack immediately.

As Dominil ended the conversation, she noticed the light flashing on her phone, indicating another missed call. She checked the number. It was Daniel. Dominil ignored it, not having time to be distracted by Kalix's friends, no matter how worried they might be about her.

Wallace MacGregor and Morag MacAllister joined Dominil almost immediately.

"I asked you to wait a few minutes," said Dominil.

"No sense hanging around," said Wallace, affably. The huge werewolf was in a notably good temper. He had been ever since hearing the rumor that Markus had cheated. Defeat by Markus had damaged his self-esteem.

Now he felt better and had spent the past day bragging good-naturedly about his unmatched strength.

"I'll show these MacRinnalchs what a real werewolf can do," he'd told Morag, on the journey down, many times. Morag had laughed, at Wallace's bravado, and at the MacRinnalchs deceit. She had a very low opinion of Markus and his mother, and wasn't at all surprised to hear of their treachery.

Thrix arrived, her long, blonde hair extensions tied back in a functional ponytail. She carried a soft leather purse, old and embroidered, containing the flower that would open the "Maynista Princess Two Flower Pathway," and let them into the Guild's headquarters.

"Are you sure this is the wall that joins on to the Guild's building?" she asked.

"Quite sure," said Dominil.

Decembrius was next to arrive, tapping discreetly on the door and slipping inside.

"Did you see anything unusual?" asked Dominil.

"Nothing. Just went to my room, waited, and came here. The whole place seems quiet."

"Good."

"Time for your revenge," said Decembrius.

"I'm here on a mission, I'm not looking for revenge," said Dominil.

"I am," said Thrix.

There was another gentle tap on the door. Eskandor, Feargan and Barra strode into the room.

"The MacRinnalchs are here," said Wallace. There was a gentle touch of mockery in his voice, but no one responded. Seconds later there was another knock. It was Kalix. She came in without saying anything and stood awkwardly at the side of the room. With the shortage of attackers, no one had objected to her presence, but it was still odd for her to be in the company of so many werewolves while she was still an outlaw.

"Everyone's here," said Thrix.

"Does everyone remember their instructions?" asked Dominil. Using what little knowledge she had of the layout of the Guild's headquarters, garnered mainly from communications she'd intercepted in the past, Dominil had sketched out a plan of action, giving each attacker a specific target. "You do? Good. Then it's time to begin."

Thrix took the purple flower from the antique purse and laid it on the floor. Outside the night was cold and dark and the moon had been in the sky for some time. Thrix changed into her werewolf shape, and the others followed her.

A phone rang.

Thrix twisted her head and looked at them furiously. "I told you all to switch off your phones."

"I left mine on in case of news from the castle," said Dominil. She glanced at her phone. Her white werewolf brow wrinkled. "That's the fourth time Daniel has called me."

"Don't answer it," said Kalix, who didn't want her friends to make a fuss over her.

"If someone calls four times, perhaps they have something to say that needs listening to," said Dominil.

Thrix paid no attention. She was already moving her hands over the purple bloom on the floor. She spoke several sentences in a language that no one in the room had ever heard before, repeating the spell of the long-dead Maynista princess. Immediately, the flower glowed with a soft light, before projecting a beam onto the wall.

"It's done," said Thrix.

The assembled werewolves gazed at the large oval of purple light on the wall of the hotel room.

"We just step through that and we're in their headquarters," said Thrix.

"Let's go," said Wallace, stepping toward the wall. The others rose to follow.

"One moment," said Dominil.

"What is it?" asked Thrix, frustrated at the delay.

"I've just listened to my messages from Daniel. We have a problem."

CHAPTER 159

"My evening is blighted," complained Empress Kabachetka. "Why does it happen so often that my evenings are blighted?"

"I'm sure you won't need the extra shoes," said Alchet.

"One never knows when one will need extra shoes," said Kabachetka. "These fashion shows are full of ruffians, treading on the feet of their betters."

The Empress's new bag, crafted by her sorcerers to be capable of carrying clothes between dimensions, had mysteriously gone missing from her chambers.

"There will be executions, Alchet. Whoever has that bag will die very swiftly. Where are we?"

"Close to the store, I think," said Alchet. She looked up nervously at the dark sky above. She hated being in this dimension, fearing that at any moment she might be rained on.

"Pick up the pace, Alchet, we must hurry."

The search for the bag had delayed the Empress, much to her frustration. Arriving late was normally not a bad thing to do but the Empress had other affairs to take care of.

"Remember, Alchet, when we locate our seats, you are to guard mine with your life. If any interloper attempts to usurp my place, you are to kill them."

"Kill them?" wailed Alchet.

"Yes. With great violence. Some of these fashion journalists understand nothing else."

They entered the large store, making their way toward the space that had been cleared in the center of the ground floor for Takahashi's show.

"If you see me in conversation with Donatella Versace, don't let anyone interrupt us."

"How will I do that?"

"Kill any who approach."

"I'm really not very good at killing people," protested Alchet. She was a very young Fire Elemental, and had never been to war.

"You are not much good at anything," said the Empress, testily.

"I cannot agree with that," said Malveria, appearing in front of them. "Alchet is renowned for her powers of emergency make-up repair, which is why the Empress so often requires her services. But the Empress cannot help having so many natural blemishes."

The Empress glowered at the Fire Queen. "I have no natural blemishes. And what are you doing here?"

"Performing my duties as a leader of fashion, naturally."

The Empress compressed her lips, wishing she could insult Malveria's outfit, but not being able to find fault with it.

"I am indeed looking splendid," said the Fire Queen, reading her enemy's mind. "It is such a blessing to have Thrix MacRinnalch designing for me."

"You think so? I have never been that impressed. But perhaps Thrix MacRinnalch will not be around forever."

The Fire Queen and the Empress stared at each other, each striving to conceal their aura, while reading the other's.

"I see no prospect of her departure," said the Fire Queen.

"You may be surprised," said the Empress.

Both rulers searched for a crushing put-down, but were interrupted by Alchet.

"I like your boots," she said to Vex.

"Thanks," said Vex. "That's a nice necklace."

"Stop exchanging pleasantries!" roared the Empress.

"My niece will exchange pleasantries if she wishes," said the Fire Queen. "And really, Alchet is looking very youthful and pretty."

Alchet was dressed in a frock plain enough not to draw attention away from the Empress, but she did look young and pretty.

"It's rather a contrast to those making too much effort," continued Malveria.

The Empress drew herself up and only just prevented herself from levitating for extra height. Faced with the infuriating Fire Queen, it was a struggle to keep pretending she was human. The Empress longed to blast her with a stream of flame, something she felt capable of doing, with her increased power.

"Alchet, follow me. It is time for us to take our superior seats. We must not keep Donatella waiting."

With that, the Empress departed, sweeping her handmaiden along with her.

"Poor Alchet," said Vex. "I'd hate to work for the Empress. She's so mean. Probably she's mean enough to send Alchet to some horrible crabby old sorcerer as a punishment. You wouldn't want to be like that, would you?"

"Abandon these futile efforts, scheming niece. You are going to the Arch-wizard as promised. Now accompany me to the restroom. I must check my make-up, and then we will present ourselves as ladies of superior fashion." The Fire Queen looked at her niece. "I mean one lady of superior fashion and her eccentric student niece. Please stop waving that plastic handbag around, it is a terrible embarrassment to people of good taste."

CHAPTER 160

"The Guild know we're coming," said Dominil. "They're waiting for us."

Dominil's revelation caused extreme consternation.

"How do you know that?" cried Thrix. "What was the message?"

"Daniel was contacted by a Fire Elemental called Gezinka whom he met at St. Amelia's Ball. She informed him that the Empress of the Hainusta and the Avenaris Guild know our plans."

"How can they know?" asked Decembrius. "You said it was secret."

"Perhaps I overestimated our discretion." Dominil swept her gaze around the room. "Someone may have talked."

There were cries of anger and outrage at the notion. Who could possibly have been so careless? Thrix took a step toward Kalix.

"Manny," she said.

Kalix looked at the floor, and didn't reply.

"Who's Manny?" asked Eskandor. The Captain of the Castle Guard was not so surprised that their plans had been discovered. In common with his companions Feargan and Barra, he didn't have total faith in the discretion or competence of the werewolves in London.

"An informer, probably," said Thrix. "It doesn't matter now. We need to decide what to do. Dominil, is Daniel reliable?"

"He wouldn't make it up. But he might be misinformed."

There was a silence, and a shared feeling of confusion, bordering on unreality. They were right next door to the Guild. The pathway was open. All they had to do was step through. But now, they didn't know what they would find when they arrived.

"I'm going anyway," said Thrix.

"I'm not certain that's wise," said Dominil.

"I'm going," said Kalix, stepping toward the purple light on the wall. Assuming that Manny had betrayed them, making her responsible, she was now determined to fling herself into battle and die. "I'm sorry if I've given us away."

Dominil caught her by the collar and dragged her back. "Wait," she said. She crossed the crowded room and stood beside the door. "If the Guild really knows we're coming, there might be some sign of them outside."

Dominil opened the door and looked out. A shot rang out, and wood splintered as a bullet slammed into the doorframe.

"I'd say that's a sign," said Decembrius.

Dominil hastily shut the door. Thrix raised one hand and spoke a spell she'd prepared, sealing the entrance.

"That'll keep them out for a while. What now?"

"I knew you'd mess it all up," said Wallace. "MacRinnalchs, you can't get anything right." He looked around the room. "Might as well carry on. We're that close it would be a shame not to attack."

There was a general movement toward the wall.

"This may not be the only alternative," said Dominil. "We could investigate means of escape. There's a window to the courtyard."

"The hunters will be there too," said Thrix.

Dominil nodded. "You're right. Let's go."

Kalix, now slipping into her state of battle madness, was eager to begin. She stepped toward the wall, ready to launch herself through. Once more she was prevented, this time by a most unexpected event. Another large oval of light flickered into existence in the middle of the room. Out of it stepped Sarapen. Even in the midst of such a crisis, it was a startling occurrence. Most of the werewolves in the room had attended his funeral.

"What—?" cried Thrix.

"Sarapen!" Decembrius gasped in amazement. "You're dead!"

Kalix jumped in alarm and began yelping, confused and distressed to see her hated elder brother return.

"What's going on?" demanded Wallace. "Have you come from the Forests of the Werewolf Dead?"

Sarapen, dark and massive in his werewolf form, looked around him. "What's happening?"

Two shots were fired outside the room, and bullets slammed into the door.

"We're about to attack the Guild," said Dominil. "But they've been warned of our coming."

"How are you alive?" demanded Thrix. "And why isn't Dominil surprised?"

"The knife didn't kill me. The Hainusta Empress saved me. I've been trapped in her palace. I asked Dominil to rescue me."

"And no one thought to tell me about this?"

Another shot slammed into the door.

"Explanations can wait," said Morag MacAllister.

"Tell me your situation," said Sarapen, who seemed untroubled to have arrived back in the midst of such desperate circumstances.

"We're about to go through that purple light, directly into the Guild's headquarters," explained Dominil. "We hoped to surprise them but now they've got us surrounded."

"Is this all the werewolves you could muster?"

"There have been problems," said Dominil. "I take responsibility."

"We're still going ahead," said Thrix.

"Good," said Sarapen. "Perhaps we can surprise them anyway."

Sarapen lifted the bag he carried. It was made of soft yellow leather and looked incongruous in his massive grasp.

"I took this from the Empress. I brought something back inside it."

More shots slammed into the door. It creaked. Thrix's spell threatened to give way. Sarapen produced a *meldrava* from the bag, the slingshot used by the palace guards.

"This is loaded with lava from the Empress's own volcano. As I understand, it can't normally travel between dimensions. I'm hoping it might do some damage."

Thrix looked at the smoldering lava. "In this dimension I'd say it might blow up the whole street."

Sarapen laughed. "Then let's hope we survive it."

He stepped toward the pathway. Kalix was still confused. She opened her mouth and growled at him. The huge werewolf grinned, and laid a hand on her shoulder.

"Best save it for the Guild, sister. Is everyone ready?"

Everyone was, apart from Dominil, who was calmly making a phone call. She ended the call quickly. "I'm ready."

"Then let's go."

With that, Sarapen charged into the pathway on the wall, and the rest of the werewolves charged after him.

CHAPTER 161

Daniel and Moonglow drove through the center of the city, anxiously looking for any sign of Kalix. They crossed over Oxford Street numerous times, scanning one side street and then another.

"This is hopeless," said Daniel. "We'll never find her."

"We have to keep trying. Why won't they answer their phones?"

"Maybe the attack's started already," said Daniel.

They drove on. It did seem hopeless. They had no real idea of where to look. All Lady Gezinka had been able to tell them was that the attack was happening somewhere in the center of town.

"That might not even mean around Oxford Street. It could be Knightsbridge, or Regent's Park."

Daniel drove on. "We'll never find Kalix by just driving around."

"We did before," said Moonglow.

Despite his worry, Daniel managed to smile at the memory. Soon after their first encounter with the young werewolf, they'd moved to a new flat, slipping out quietly in the night because they owed their landlord money. They'd found Kalix in the street, and rescued her. Daniel stopped smiling as he remembered what had happened after that.

"That was the first time we saw Markus."

"Don't mention Markus," said Moonglow.

"Why not?"

"You know why not."

"It's not my fault if you fell in love with a cross-dressing werewolf," muttered Daniel, still smarting at the memory.

"Be quiet," said Moonglow, who didn't remember Markus any more fondly, after the way he'd ended their brief relationship.

Daniel's phone rang. It lay on the dashboard. He pressed a key to send it to speakerphone.

"Daniel? This is Dominil."

"Dominil? Where—"

"Don't speak, I have no time. Our van is parked in Montagu Place, close to the Swedish Embassy. It says "MacIntyre Removals" on the side. Find it and bring it close to three hundred and fifty-six Gloucester Place. We may need assistance later. The keys are tucked under the rug between the seats."

Dominil ended the call. Moonglow was already looking up Montagu Place on her map. They had to drive across Gloucester Place to get there. There was no sign of anything unusual, but Daniel and Moonglow both feared the worst. Kalix might be in the middle of another terrible battle. She might be already dead.

"Montagu Place," said Moonglow. Her voice trembled but she forced herself to be calm. "I can see their van."

"I wish Malveria was here," said Moonglow. "I know there are going to be injuries."

★

Malveria was not far away. She was standing elegantly among the crowd at the fashion show, outwardly calm but inwardly seething at the sight of Empress Kabachetka talking familiarly to the accessories editor of *Marie Claire*.

"It is truly scandalous the way that woman has ingratiated herself," muttered the Fire Queen to her niece. "What has she done to deserve it?"

"Given about a million pounds in sponsorship," said Vex. "Why didn't you do that?"

"Because I did not know it was an appropriate thing to do!" hissed the Fire Queen. "The vile Empress would never have dreamed of giving her gold away had not Distikka advised her to. She is a cunning adviser, Distikka. Would that I had one so intelligent." The Fire Queen suddenly tensed. "Be alert, niece. Something is afoot."

Vex giggled. "*Afoot*. That's a funny word."

"Silence, imbecile. Donatella Versace has just entered the room. Kabachetka should already be worming her way toward her, intent on forcing her company on the poor woman. Yet she is not."

As Malveria and Vex looked on, the Empress withdrew from the accessories editor. Instead of making her way toward Ms. Versace, as indeed would have been expected, she was heading in the opposite direction.

"Agrivex, follow me."

"What's happening?" asked Vex, hurrying after her aunt.

"There is only one conceivable reason why the gruesome Empress would not not be throwing herself on Donatella Versace like the craven lickspittle she is. Thrix believed her attack was a secret, but I have always suspected otherwise. I think the Empress is now going to assist the hunters."

"You can't let her do that! Kalix is there."

"As is Thrix. The Empress of the Hainusta will not harm my fashion designer, not while I am alive to prevent it."

Malveria walked swiftly through the crowd, moving quickly and smoothly in the crowded room. Vex barged her way long behind her, upsetting drinks as she passed. They followed Kabachetka to a restroom. Malveria opened the door and marched inside. Kabachetka was just beginning to dematerialize.

"And where might you be going?" demanded the Fire Queen.

"Where I am going is no business of yours," said Kabachetka.

"I think it is."

"Well, it isn't."

Kabachetka disappeared. The Fire Queen did the same. They both materialized in the air outside, several hundred feet above London.

"I know where you're going," said the Fire Queen. "To assist the hunters against Thrix."

The Empress looked down her nose at the Fire Queen. "It has always pained me that a fellow elemental ruler should consort with these vulgar werewolves. It is the talk of the Elemental Rulers Council."

They hovered in the air, invisible from below, half in and half out of this world.

"You will not seek to hinder me if you know what's good for you," said the Empress. "My power has increased since I took charge of the Eternal Volcano."

Malveria drew herself up so that the toes of her high heels pointed almost vertically toward the ground. "It has increased to the point where it is still a fraction of mine."

The Empress laughed. "We'll see about that."

The Empress raised her hand and a great bolt of blue fire shot from her palm toward the Fire Queen. Malveria brushed it aside imperiously and retaliated with a bolt of yellow flame. As Kabachetka deflected that, there was an explosion like the loudest clap of thunder. People on the streets below looked up in alarm, and saw blazing lights in the clouds. They hurried on their way, not wanting to be caught out of doors in such a fierce storm. The thunder and lightning grew louder as the reigning monarchs of two elemental nations joined in combat in the dark, cloudy skies over London.

CHAPTER 162

Kalix was relieved when it was time to attack. Her confusion vanished and her cares disappeared as her battle madness descended. In combat Kalix had no worries. She was overwhelmed by a savage ferocity unmatched by any other werewolf. Once embroiled in fighting, Kalix had no regard for her own safety; she could not be halted by anything except death. She leaped with the others into the oval of purple light on the wall and raced through the sorcerous pathway. Her mouth opened wide, displaying her long werewolf tongue and her sharp teeth. Her claws were extended, ready to tear at the hunters' throats. As she neared the glowing exit, Kalix prepared to leap at the first hunter she saw.

Once more, the young werewolf was thrown into confusion by an unexpected event. The moment she flung herself into the Guild's headquarters there was a terrific explosion, several flashes of blinding light and a billowing cloud of dense smoke. Sarapen had used the *meldrava*, catapulting the fragments of lava from the Empress's volcano right into the midst of the foyer. The lava, already seething and boiling in an alien dimension, exploded with a force that blew the foyer apart, sending the hunters concealed behind their barricades flying in all directions, injured or killed by the blast.

Kalix found herself in a burning, smoke-filled space where she was unable to see anything. Her keen werewolf senses were almost overwhelmed by the acrid smoke that poured from the blazing wood paneling. She roared in annoyance and ran blindly about the foyer, searching for someone to kill. She stepped on something she recognized as a body but to her annoyance the hunter was already dead, killed in the blast. Kalix growled angrily and ran on, blundering into Decembrius who was holding an arm over his snout, protecting it from the smoke.

Decembrius was not as out of control as Kalix. "This way!" he shouted, and dragged Kalix toward the charred remnants of a doorway. She followed him down a flight of stairs. The air was still thick with smoke. Fire alarms sounded and there were screams of men and werewolves in all directions. There was the sound of gunfire too, and then another explosion. Kalix sprinted down the stairs, overtaking Decembrius. The door to the stairwell opened and a hunter appeared with a gun in his hand. Kalix leaped at him, fastening her jaws round his throat before he had time to react. They crashed into the basement corridor. Kalix savagely twisted her neck, biting a huge chunk of flesh from her victim's throat. He fell down dead, his blood gushing out over Kalix's face. She roared in satisfaction then ran down the corridor, looking for another opponent.

As Kalix and Decembrius rushed downstairs, Thrix was heading the opposite way. According to Dominil, the leaders of the Avenaris Guild were most likely to be found in the executive offices on the top floor. Thrix struggled through the smoke and chaos in the lobby before stumbling onto a staircase. She ran up the stairs, her golden werewolf hair streaming behind her. She passed the second and third floor unopposed. As she reached the top a young woman with a sheaf of papers in her hand appeared in front of her. The woman screamed as she saw Thrix, and ran back into the corridor. Thrix sprinted after her and dragged her back.

"Don't kill me!" cried the terrified woman. "I'm just a secretary!"

Thrix slashed her throat with her talons, killing her instantly. Her eyes lit up with the satisfaction. Fire alarms were ringing, and as smoke began to drift upstairs, the sprinklers were set off. Thrix looked round the corridor. At the end was an office with a name of the door: MR. CARMICHAEL.

Thrix tried the door. It was locked. She spoke a spell to open it. Nothing happened. Her magic was ineffective inside the building. Thrix took a step back and hurled herself at the door. It broke under her weight and she flew into the room. She heard a gunshot and felt a sharp pain in her side as a silver bullet penetrated her werewolf pelt. Thrix snarled and kept on going. Two men in suits faced her, each with a gun in their hand. Thrix flew at them. There was another shot but the bullet missed the charging werewolf, who approached at a speed the men couldn't counteract. Thrix hit them simultaneously, knocking them to the ground. She used her talons on one of the men, tearing at his throat. As she turned her attentions to the other she felt another very sharp pain, this time in her thigh. The second Guild executive, on the ground, had managed to fire at her again. Thrix immediately fastened her jaws around his throat, killing him. She stood up, and winced. She had a silver bullet in her side and another in her thigh. The silver burned. She roared in pain and triumph. She had killed the head of the Avenaris Guild. Mr. Carmichael lay dead at her feet. Another fire alarm went off nearby, masking the sound of a hunter in the corridor. He saw Thrix and took aim. A bullet raked her fur before the hunter was brought down by Wallace MacGregor who'd just reached the top floor.

"Are you all right? he asked Thrix.

"I'm fine."

Wallace had killed two hunters in the first moment of the attack, and his snout was still damp with their blood. Temporarily disorientated by the chaos in the foyer, he'd rushed up the stairs looking for more. He grinned at Thrix. "Let's kill more executives."

A door opened at the far end of the corridor. A shot rang out. Wallace gasped as a silver bullet hit him in the shoulder, but it didn't slow him down. He sprinted toward the shooter. Thrix sprinted after him, each werewolf traveling so fast along the corridor that the gunman had time for only one more shot, which missed. Wallace flung himself onto him, breaking his neck as they fell. He roared, then looked at his shoulder.

"Silver bullet."

He shrugged. A strong werewolf like Wallace could take many wounds, even from silver bullets. Thrix, ignoring her own wounds, smashed open the door of the next office, and they leaped inside, looking for victims.

CHAPTER 163

Dominil, Sarapen and Morag MacAllister encountered fierce resistance as they fought their way to the IT department. Dominil was targeting the computers and Sarapen chose to stay at her side. Morag had appeared from the smoke, coughing and snarling.

"Nice job with the bomb, Sarapen. You almost killed us."

Sarapen laughed. "It got us in."

"Where now?"

"This way," said Dominil, leading them onto the second floor.

Not far away, on the same level, experienced hunters from Group Eight had been resting between their shifts on guard duty. Now they advanced toward the fray. The second floor of the old building had never been renovated, and there was no long corridor where they could take cover and fire at distant targets. They were obliged to creep forward slowly, unable to judge much of what was in front of them due to the noise and smoke that now came from all parts of the building. They turned the corner into the stairwell just as Dominil and her companions arrived. The three werewolves leaped to attack and the fury of their werewolf battle cries could be heard even over the fire alarms. Three members of Group Eight fell before them. The last turned and fled.

Dominil stood over the bodies. "Anyone hurt?"

No one was.

"Good start," said Morag. "So where are these computers?"

"At the end of this corridor, I hope," said Dominil. Further along, the smoke was less dense, though the sprinklers drenched them as they hurried along. Dominil was unexpectedly knocked sideways as a door flew open and a very large hunter stepped into the corridor. He was startled to find himself confronted by three werewolves, but he didn't panic. He raised his weapon and squeezed the trigger. Nothing happened. The gun had jammed.

"That's unfortunate," said Sarapen. He swung his right paw at the large hunter and dealt him a crushing blow on the side of the head. The hunter was killed instantly. Dominil bent down and picked up his weapon. It was a small machine gun, similar to an Uzi.

"I've never seen a hunter use a machine gun before." Dominil opened the magazine. Inside was a row of thirty silver bullets.

"I wouldn't have thought silver bullets would work in a gun like this."

"Maybe that's why it jammed," said Sarapen.

A volley of shots sounded from behind them, ending the discussion. They turned to fight but as another shot sounded from somewhere in front of them, they dived for cover in the nearest office.

"Hunters on both sides," said Sarapen. "I'll deal with it."

On the first floor, the three werewolves from Castle MacRinnalch found themselves struggling with the intensity of the fire. The explosion below had brought down part of the flooring, and flames now leaped from the foyer into the level above. Thick dark smoke swirled all around and the sprinklers were having little effect on the flames. The werewolves found themselves facing a door, which was blazing furiously, as were several pieces of old furniture. Eskandor, Captain of the Castle Guard, took in the situation calmly.

"We can't get through here. We need to go back."

"We're meant to find the library and destroy it," said Barra.

"I think the fire will take care of it," said Eskandor. "We should go downstairs and see if there's another way up."

Eskandor, Feargan and Barra turned round, heading back to the main staircase, stepping over the bodies of several werewolf hunters who'd been killed in the original explosion. As they reached the burning foyer, another explosion shook the walls as a fragment of the lava from the land of the Hainusta erupted, sending flaming embers in all directions. Part of the floor gave way, and Barra MacRinnalch fell through the gap. Eskandor and Feargan jumped after him. They tumbled into the basement to find themselves in the midst of a group of hunters who were crouched behind a makeshift barricade of tables and couches. The hunters scrambled to untangle themselves and turn their guns on the unexpected arrivals from above. Several shots were fired, but at that moment the door was kicked open and Kalix and Decembrius burst into the room. Seeing three werewolves in a melee with a large group of hunters, they leaped over the barrier to attack. There was a mixture of screams, roars and gunshots, as werewolves and men tried desperately to see what they were doing, with smoke in their eyes, enemies at their throats and flames leaping into the room from the blazing corridor outside.

CHAPTER 164

"You can't follow me to the Maynista House," cried the Empress. "Because the stone dwarves cursed you for your wickedness."

"I was not wicked," said the Fire Queen. "Just successful in battle. As I will be now."

"Really?" Kabachetka's bleached-blonde hair streamed out on the wind as she rose in the air. "You still have not grasped that I now have more power than you."

The Empress flung a dazzling bolt of white flame at the Fire Queen.

"And I have more important friends!" cried the Empress, flinging another bolt. "You are yesterday's fashionista, Malveria!"

With that the Empress flung the greatest fire bolt yet, dragging power from the Eternal Volcano through the dimensions and sending it against the Fire Queen in a blast that shone brighter than the sun. The Empress yelled in triumph as the Fire Queen was enveloped in flames. She was dismayed as the flames cleared to reveal Queen Malveria floating opposite her, a fire bolt in each hand and one at her feet. She had caught Kabachetka's bolts.

"More power?" said the Fire Queen. "Your power is to mine as your shoes are to mine. That is to say, very inferior."

"You have cheated in the matter of shoes!" yelled the Empress. "There is sorcery on your extra-high heels!"

"Nonsense. I simply learned to walk in them properly. You will never be more fashionable than me, Kabachetka. You lack style."

"You will lack style when Thrix dies!"

"Thrix is not going to die!" yelled the Fire Queen. But she felt a tremor of discomfort because she could sense the battle below. She could feel the fire tearing through the Guild's building and she worried for Thrix's safety.

Empress Kabachetka, now completely enveloped in her Cloak of Protective Flame, raised her arm above her head. "Great Empress's Burning Spear," she cried. A flaming spear appeared in her hand, and she flew toward the Fire Queen.

"Fire Queen's Sword of the Exploding Sun!" cried Malveria. A fiery sword appeared in her hand, and she raced to meet the Empress. As their weapons clashed there was a blinding light and a deafening roar that lit up the night and tore the clouds apart. People on the streets below looked up in awe at the blazing sky. No one one had ever seen a lightning storm like it. They gasped at the fury above, as the Queen of the Hiyasta and the Empress of the Hainusta, who had loathed each other for many years, finally came to grips with each other in combat.

The battle in the clouds couldn't be heard in the Guild's headquarters, but Thrix was aware of it. She could sense the elemental sorcery, and knew that the Empress and the Fire Queen were fighting above. Thrix mentally thanked Malveria for her help.

Thrix and Wallace had killed five members of the Guild on the top floor.

"What now?" yelled Wallace. "These offices are empty."

"The rest must have gone downstairs."

Smoke was billowing up the stairwell. Thrix heard a crashing noise below, as if some part of the structure had given way. She felt a pang of anxiety that she might be crushed by masonry before she'd had a chance to kill more hunters. Thrix's bloodlust was still very strong. She barely noticed her wounds as she ran down the stairs. Wallace ran beside her, but in their eagerness for action they were careless. They hurtled through the door into the second floor to find themselves confronted by two hunters who'd seen them coming and were ready. Their guns were raised. Each of them fired. Thrix felt her chest explode in pain as a silver bullet ploughed into her. The bullet missed her heart but the shock sent her plunging to the floor.

Wallace had also taken a bullet in the chest but his exceptional strength kept him on his feet. He staggered, then roared and charged at the hunters. Both fired again from only a few feet away. Wallace crashed into them, taking them down with a huge taloned paw round each of their throats. There was another shot, and a scream. Thrix dragged herself to her feet. Blood was pouring down her chest. She grimaced in pain, and her werewolf tongue lolled over her teeth like a panting dog. Wallace and the two hunters lay still in a tangle. Thrix bent over them. The hunters were both dead from wounds to their throats. She turned Wallace over. He was dead too. The final bullet had gone straight into his heart. Blood seeped from the chest wound but he was no longer breathing.

CHAPTER 165

Kalix's jaws were fastened around a hunter's throat.

"He's dead," said Decembrius.

Kalix kept hold, biting deeper.

"That won't make him any more dead."

Kalix ignored him. Decembrius growled in frustration. There were four dead hunters in the room, but Barra, Deputy Captain of the Castle Guard, had also been killed in the melee. Eskandor and Feargan were both wounded. Kalix and Decembrius had so far escaped injury but Decembrius thought they might die in the fire anyway.

Suddenly, the door at the far end of the corridor was kicked in and a fusillade of shots rang out. The werewolves ducked down behind the remains of the hunters' barricade. Bullets slammed into the old wooden desks and tables, threatening to rip them apart.

"Retreat," hissed Eskandor. "Keep down."

Decembrius began to follow him but Kalix paid no attention. She leaped over the barricade, running straight toward the hunters.

"Oh for God's sake," muttered Decembrius, and threw himself after her. Kalix sprinted with astonishing speed toward the hunters, leaping at them from a distance. Decembrius expected to see her torn apart by bullets, but she made it to the door and disappeared in a snarling whirlwind of limbs. By the time Decembrius arrived Kalix had killed one hunter and was attacking another while a third tried to fire at the werewolf without hitting his companions. He managed to get off one shot before Decembrius was on him. Decembrius killed him swiftly with his jaws. He turned angrily toward Kalix.

"Do you have to be so crazy all the time?"

Kalix was snuffling about over her two victims. Decembrius saw she was bleeding.

"Are you all right?" he asked.

"I'm fine."

Kalix had two bullet wounds in her arm, though she apparently hadn't noticed. There was a crash as a window shattered in the heat. Decembrius grabbed Kalix. "We have to get out of here, the whole corridor's about to go up in flames."

Kalix looked longingly in the opposite direction. She wanted to run down the burning corridor, looking for more hunters. There was another loud crash as more of the ceiling gave way. Decembrius dragged Kalix back toward the foyer, catching up with Eskandor and Feargan, who were slowed by their wounds.

"More hunters," growled Kalix. "I want more hunters."

"Oh shut up," muttered Decembrius.

Group Sixteen, the Avenaris Guild's most deadly band of hunters, were finding it difficult to join the battle. After finishing their guard duty, they'd withdrawn to temporary quarters in the basement. With so many hunters stationed inside, employees had been temporarily billeted all over the building. The first explosion brought down the roof outside their room. They were unable to reach the foyer and had to make a long detour toward the fire escape at the back of the building. They ran into the yard and halted next to the large gray recycling bins. Another figure appeared from the fire exit at the opposite end of the building.

"Stone!" It was John Carmichael.

"We couldn't get through," said Stone. "We're heading for the hotel. We'll go out into the street and get back into our building through the front door."

"I'll round up the reserves in the hotel," said John Carmichael. He noticed that their headquarters, despite being consumed internally by flames and war, showed no sign of anything wrong on the outside, as if the "House That Could Not be Found" was unwilling to divulge any of its secrets to outsiders. There was a deafening explosion high above as lightning illuminated the sky. It was the most violent thunderstorm any of them had ever seen, but they had no time to contemplate nature. They ran across the yard, vaulted the low wall that separated them from the hotel, and hurried into the kitchens.

"The fire must be getting worse," said Carmichael. "The werewolves won't know where the fire exits are and I doubt they can reach them anyway. If you can block off the foyer, we can trap them inside."

He looked at Axelsen, who carried one of the small machine guns recently modified by the Guild, but not yet fully tested. "Does it work?"

"I'll tell you soon."

Group Sixteen raced through the hotel and into Gloucester Place to retake the foyer from the front. Carmichael sped around the hotel, gathering the hunters he'd positioned there in reserve. The ambush had not gone as planned, but he was still confident they could wipe out every werewolf who'd entered the building.

CHAPTER 166

In their own dimension, a clash between two elemental rulers would have caused such destruction that towns would have burned to the ground, mountains turned to lava and lakes evaporated. It was fortunate for the inhabitants of London that neither the Fire Queen nor the Empress could exert their full power as they fought in an alien dimension. The struggle was still titanic. Each of them reached back through the void, dragging as much energy as they could from their volcanoes to power their weapons. Malveria's grandmother Malgravane had carried the Fire Queen's Sword of the Exploding Sun when she turned back an invasion of the Ice Elementals in a battle that had turned the once fertile Plains of Warmth into a barren wasteland. The Fire Queen wielded it now with all her might. She was a far more experienced warrior than the Empress but as the battle raged on, Malveria was forced to admit to herself something she would never have acknowledged in public: Kabachetka had become an extremely powerful Fire Elemental. Since the death of the old Empress, she'd apparently not spent all of her time at fashionable parties. She'd learned to use the Great Flaming Spear, which was also renowned for its power.

The Empress cursed the Fire Queen, and slashed at her with her spear, sending a great wave of flame toward her. The Fire Queen deflected the flame but the Empress sent another fire bolt directly after it and this one caught Malveria squarely in the chest. The Fire Queen was thrown backwards. Her adversary yelled in triumph and advanced through the air, brandishing her spear. Their weapons met, and locked, and they pressed together in a final trial of strength and will.

Down below, Agrivex looked on. She knew if she came between the Fire Queen and the Empress she would be killed. She also knew her aunt was in trouble, and she had to assist her. Vex wondered exactly how she was going to get there. A really powerful elemental like the Fire Queen could levitate so freely, and drift through dimensions so effectively, as to appear to be flying, but Vex lacked her aunt's skill.

I'll probably plummet to my death, she thought. And just when I have a boyfriend too. It's so unfair.

Vex took off, attempting to project herself up to the clouds where the battle raged. She judged the distance quite well, materializing close to the Fire Queen and the Empress. White flames poured from their weapons, enveloping them in a blazing sphere of light. As Vex arrived, the sphere grew larger, expanding rapidly till there was an explosion more deafening than all the rest, and a flash of light so intense that the clouds became momentarily transparent. Vex had a glimpse of the Empress soaring upwards, screaming in pain and rage before abruptly disappearing from sight.

"Go back to your palace!" yelled Queen Malveria at the departing Empress. "Face me again when you've learned how to fight."

Vex noticed her aunt's aura was imbued with flames of triumph. They lasted only a few seconds before fading to nothingness. The Fire Queen's body went limp, hanging motionless in the air. Vex caught her, and they began to fall from the sky together.

"Are you all right, Aunty?"

"I am triumphant. But my strength has gone."

"I came to rescue you."

"I appreciate it. Do you have a plan for preventing us from plummeting onto the concrete below?"

"Not really," admitted Agrivex.

"Splendid," said the Fire Queen. "We can meet our ancestors together. You'll like my mother."

"I can save us!" said Vex. The ground was approaching alarmingly fast. Vex, who was bad at teleporting herself, had never before tried carrying anyone with her. Needing a point of reference, Vex saw the store they'd been in earlier. She kept a tight grip on her aunt, and desperately attempted to fling herself through the dimensions. There was a second of freezing cold, and then a gentle thud as she and Malveria materialized in a deserted room, just one foot from the ground.

"I did it!" cried Vex, springing to her feet. She looked at her aunt, who lay on the floor, making no attempt to rise. "You're all bleeding and burned. Are you all right?"

"I will be fine. I need to rest, and heal. Where are we?"

"Back in the big store with the fashion show. In a stationery cupboard. Maybe it's not stationery. Some sort of big cupboard anyway. It could be other office supplies."

"We will just accept that it's a cupboard," said Malveria. "Now I must rest before I can heal myself."

"Let me help," said Vex.

"I doubt that you are able, niece."

"I am! I've been practicing. I healed flowers!"

"Well done. I am impressed. But I can heal myself, and I have another task for you. Find Thrix and her companions. If you can really help with healing, they'll appreciate it."

"I don't want to leave you in this cupboard."

"I will be fine. I want you to help Thrix. Kalix too, if you can find her. The building is in Gloucester Place, not far. Travel there and you may sense their presence."

The Fire Queen lay back on the floor to rest. If she could gather a little strength, she could open a tiny portal to her volcano at home, and restore her powers.

"OK, Aunty," said Vex. "Look after my bag." She dematerialized quickly. The Fire Queen gave Agrivex's green plastic handbag a disapproving glance, and then closed her eyes to concentrate on healing.

CHAPTER 167

Thrix knelt in an office on the top floor of the Guild's headquarters, alone, knowing that unless she could overcome the building's dampening field that was suppressing her sorcery, she might soon die. She had four silver bullets inside her. The pain was excruciating. The bullets had missed her heart but they'd fragmented inside her, and now the shards of silver were tearing her insides apart.

"I'm not giving up while there are hunters left alive."

The werewolf Enchantress made the change back to human. She closed her eyes and placed her hands on her lap. If her own sorcery wouldn't work, perhaps she could coax a response from one of Minerva's most powerful spells.

"Minerva's Healing of Last Resort," she said. "*Cneasaich.*"

Thrix felt a disturbance in the sorcerous field that surrounded her, as Minerva's spell struggled to take effect. For a few moments, she felt calm, and then she yelled in pain. Her eyes opened wide and she saw fragments of silver emerging from her skin. Some came from her bullet wounds, but other fragments made new holes in her flesh, tearing their way out of her body. Thrix screamed and collapsed in agony on the carpet. The pain became too much to bear and she passed out for several seconds. When she awoke she'd been sick all over herself and there were shards of silver everywhere. She wiped the tears from her eyes.

"Good spell," muttered Thrix. "Apart from the unbearable agony."

Thrix could still feel damage inside her. Suppressed by the power of the Guild's headquarters, Minerva's spell had not fully worked. But it had helped, partially renewing her strength, and allowing her to carry on.

She left the office and headed for the stairs. The sprinklers were still operating, washing away the blood and vomit from her body. Thrix changed back into her werewolf form. She was about to run down the stairs and rejoin the battle when she paused, and went back. Wallace MacGregor, in death, had changed back to human. Thrix picked him up with ease, with the thought that if she survived the battle, she'd take him back to the castle for a proper burial. Then she hurried on through the smoke, downstairs, toward the sounds of werewolves howling and guns firing.

Dominil had located the Guild's main computer room. Unlike most other parts of the building, this area had been modernized, with several offices converted into one large space, separated by glass partitions.

"I need a few minutes," she said, ignoring the smoke, flames and gunfire.

"Won't everything get burned anyway?" asked Morag.

"Their files won't only all be stored on these computers," said Dominil. She changed into her human shape and sat down at a terminal.

"Protect me while I erase their files."

Morag grinned. "You're an odd werewolf, Dominil. I like you more than I—"

Her words were cut off by a shot. Morag looked surprised, then fell down dead. Dominil swiftly took a terminal from its desk and crouched on the floor. Sarapen joined her, using the desk as cover. He touched Morag's neck, checking for a pulse.

"She's dead," he said.

"Try to keep me alive till I'm finished here."

Dominil sat on the ground, loading software into the computer with a flash drive. Sarapen crawled from the booth, looking for whoever had shot Morag. There was a flurry of gunfire nearby, and some screaming. Dominil kept her eyes on the screen, attempting to locate all of the Guild's files, wherever they were stored. Morag lay beside her, face down, with a gaping wound in her back where the silver bullet had exited from her body. Dominil ignored her. Her fingers flew swiftly over the keyboard. She left a program running and carefully reached up to the next desk, taking hold of another terminal. She began another program, finding and erasing all the locally held files. She barely noticed the gunfire that erupted nearby, though she was obliged to put her sleeve over her mouth to protect her from the smoke, which was now making it difficult to breathe.

Sarapen appeared back in the cubicle with blood on his fur. "I got rid of them," he said.

Dominil remained silent, still working at the keyboard.

"Are you going to be much longer?"

"A few more minutes. I'm erasing their cloud files in Arizona."

"I've been shot," said Sarapen.

"Will you survive?"

"Yes. But the ceiling's about to come down."

Dominil glanced upwards. "We have a few minutes. I'm almost done."

CHAPTER 168

Thrix came across two more hunters as she descended the stairs, falling on them savagely and killing them instantly. A wave of elation swept over her. She'd killed many hunters, and the Guild's headquarters would soon be consumed by flames. It was time to leave. She arrived on the ground floor to meet Eskandor and Feargan, limping toward the foyer. Both were wounded, and they were carrying the body of Barra. The foyer was blackened and charred, with several smoldering holes in the walls and debris from the ceiling scattered around everywhere.

"We have to leave," said Eskandor. The smoke had temporarily cleared from the foyer but it was thickening again as the flames on the floor above intensified.

"We're not all here yet," said Thrix.

Decembrius and Kalix appeared, their faces blackened from smoke. Decembrius looked unharmed but Kalix was bleeding in several places.

"More hunters," she snarled.

"I think we're finished," said Thrix.

Eskandor fell to the ground, more badly wounded than Thrix had realized. Feargan looked at him anxiously. "We need to get him out of here."

"We can't leave without Dominil," said Decembrius.

There was an anxious wait. The werewolves had loosely arranged to meet in the foyer after their attack, but the chaos caused by the ambush, and Sarapen's explosive device, seemed to have wiped out their planning.

"I'll look for her," said Decembrius.

"How? The whole place is on fire," said Eskandor.

Suddenly the wall at the end of the corridor caved in. There stood Sarapen and Dominil. Unable to reach the door because of the heat, they'd smashed down the wall. They were both soaked from the sprinklers, which had helped to protect them from the flames. Sarapen carried Morag MacAllister's body in his arms.

"Well?" said Thrix.

"The Guild's computer records are erased," said Dominil. "We can assume their library has been incinerated too. It's time to leave."

The werewolves took a step toward the inner of the two doors that led to the street outside. At that moment the door burst open and Group Sixteen appeared. The tallest of the hunters was pointing a machine gun. He pulled the trigger and emptied the whole magazine of thirty silver bullets into the werewolves. At the same time the hunters behind him opened fire with their pistols.

Dominil, Decembrius, Thrix and Feargan fell to the ground. Kalix and Sarapen were thrown backwards, slamming into the smoldering wall of the ruined foyer. The hunter with the machine gun rapidly took another magazine from his belt and loaded it while the others kept firing. Kalix, blood pouring from every limb, flung herself toward them. Sarapen, only a fraction of a second slower, did the same. The machine gun was reloaded just as Kalix reached them. She snarled, and leaped upwards, fastening her jaws around the tall hunter's neck. The gun was firing as Kalix dragged him to the ground. Sarapen slammed into the other hunters, and there was a terrible sound of snarling and screaming as the werewolves and hunters fought for their lives.

The fight ended, and there was silence, save for the crackling of flames. Dominil dragged herself to her feet, now badly wounded. She stumbled forward to where Sarapen and Kalix lay in a huge pool of blood. Dominil was close enough to the exit to see the street outside. Another group of hunters was about to rush into the building. She slammed the inner door and bolted it. The Guild's doors had been constructed to keep out intruders and could not be broken down quickly.

Dominil groaned as she fastened the bolts. Her ribs had been smashed by bullets and it was difficult to move. As she turned slowly from the door, she saw Thrix hauling herself upright, blood dripping from her chest and her legs.

"Help me," said Dominil.

Thrix staggered forward. Between them, they managed to pull the limp figures of Sarapen and Kalix back from the door, dragging them behind the remains of one of the hunters' barricades. Dominil thought that Sarapen was still alive. She wasn't sure about Kalix. Thrix's strength gave out and she collapsed behind the barricade. She had an ugly wound on her face, which had torn her lips. Dominil could hear hunters banging on the door and feel the heat of the flames, which were now burning through the nearest wall. She hauled herself toward her fallen companions. Feargan was dead, torn apart by the machine gun. Eskandor was also dead. Decembrius had been shot several times in the chest, and lay on his back in a pool of his own blood. He was still breathing faintly, but Dominil didn't have the strength to move him. She crawled back toward the barricade.

"Eskandor and Feargan are dead."

"We'll be joining them soon enough," said Thrix, who was now too weak to heal herself.

The front door began to give way.

"Bye, Dominil," whispered Thrix. "See you in the Forests."

Dominil took two guns from her pocket. She handed one to Thrix.

"I took these from the hunters," she said. "We're not at the Forests yet."

CHAPTER 169

"What are we meant to do now?" said Moonglow. She felt agitated, sitting in the van the werewolves had hired, waiting for something to happen.

"I don't know," said Daniel. "What can we do?"

"There's Vex!" cried Moonglow. She opened her door to call on the young Fire Elemental, who was running up the pavement.

"Vex, what's happening?"

"Aunt Malvie sent me to help but I can't find anyone!"

Daniel's phone rang. "It's Dominil."

"Daniel?" Dominil's voice sounded weak over the speakerphone. "Are you close?"

"Yes. We can see the building."

"Good. You may be able to help."

"How?"

"We're trapped between hunters and fire. We have many injuries."

"Is Kalix all right?"

"She may be. Ram your van through the front door."

"What?"

"Ram it through the door. It will allow us to escape. I have to go now."

Moonglow and Daniel gaped at each other.

"Ram the van through the door?"

"What did she mean Kalix may be all right?"

Vex clambered into the van. "What are we going to do?"

"Ram it through the door," said Daniel.

"No we're not!" cried Moonglow.

"Dominil says they're trapped."

Moonglow shook her head, resigned to her fate. "Fine. Do it."

In the darkness they could see lights flickering behind some of the upstairs windows, though there was no real sign of the fire that Dominil had mentioned. As they approached the building, a group of men disappeared inside, closing the front door behind them.

"Check your seat belts and hang on tight," said Daniel. He swung the vehicle round so as the rear end faced the building. Between the van and the front door there was a small step up to the pavement, and another small step in front of the door. There was a screech from the gearbox as

Daniel thrust the van into reverse and slammed backwards into the wide front door. Moonglow, arms covering her face, felt a severe jolt followed by a very loud crash. Wood and masonry crumbled under the violence of the impact, and the van filled with dust.

They sat in shocked silence, unsure of what to do next. They heard the back door being wrenched open, and looked round in terror, expecting to find a werewolf hunter pointing a gun at them. It was Thrix. She leaned on the doorframe, supporting herself with difficulty. She seemed to be grinning though it was hard to be sure, with her lips badly cut and blood pouring down her face. Seconds later a werewolf hunter did appear. He was struggling, dazed from the smoke and the impact of the van. When he saw Thrix he started to slowly drag a gun from inside his jacket.

Thrix realized that she was now outside the building, and free of the barrier that prevented her from using sorcery. "Rach ann an laige!" she said. "My enemies collapse in the dust."

As soon as she spoke, the hunter's eyes closed and he fell unconscious to the ground. Thrix looked briefly triumphant. Then her head sagged as the last of her strength disappeared and she toppled forward. Dominil emerged from dust and smoke, her face red with blood. She carried Kalix, who was unmoving, and also covered in blood. Dominil laid her in the back of the van.

"Help me get the others," she said. Dominil turned, but stumbled. She tried to rise, but could go no further. Moonglow and Vex scrambled to help her into the van. Daniel ran past them into the foyer where he almost fell over a huge werewolf who was crawling along the floor, dragging another werewolf behind him. He noticed another werewolf lying prone on the carpet and started to drag him toward the van. Moonglow came to meet him, and between them they lifted the stricken werewolf into the vehicle.

"That's six," said Moonglow. "Is that everyone?"

Dominil opened her eyes. "Three more," she said.

A man, who Daniel took to be hunter, emerged from the shadows, either unaffected by Thrix's spell, or recovering. He paid them no attention, so eager was he to make his escape from the flames. He ran out of the shattered door.

"Come on," said Moonglow. "We can't leave anyone."

Daniel, Moonglow and Vex ran back into the foyer. Moonglow stepped on something soft. She recognized Decembrius. He had been shot in the chest. Moonglow couldn't tell if he was alive or not. She dragged his body away from the flames. As she attempted to hoist him into the van, a huge arm emerged to help.

"Thanks," said Moonglow. She recognized the huge werewolf. "I thought you were—"

"I'm still alive." Sarapen grimaced. He had many wounds, and much silver inside him.

Vex and Daniel appeared, dragging two werewolves, both dead, as far as Moonglow could tell. She helped lift them into the van, and tried to ignore the feelings of nausea brought on by the carnage.

"Time to go," said Daniel. He clambered over the back of the seats, positioned himself in front of the steering wheel and drove off as fast as he dared. "Where am I going?" he yelled.

"Kalix needs help," shouted Moonglow from the back of the van.

Kalix had numerous wounds and several of them were still bleeding badly. Moonglow put her hands over them, trying to stop the flow. She felt a twinge of hysteria. They needed help and there was no one to help them. Moonglow looked toward Thrix for assistance, but Thrix was unconscious. Moonglow could hardly imagine what had happened inside the building.

"I can help," said Vex, squeezing her way to her side. "Maybe."

She put her hands on Kalix's chest. A faint orange glow came from her fingers. She put one hand on Kalix's forehead and a little more light passed between them.

"I didn't know you could do that," said Moonglow.

Vex looked troubled. "I can only heal flowers, really." She kept her hand on Kalix's forehead, trying to send some of her elemental fire into the young werewolf's body.

"I'll go to Thrix's flat," said Daniel. "Maybe she has werewolf medicine."

They weren't far from Knightsbridge. Daniel headed for the car park underneath Thrix's block.

"How are we going to get everyone upstairs?" said Moonglow.

There was no reply. Daniel parked in the car park, and looked round. "What now?"

Moonglow and Vex looked hopelessly at the wounded werewolves. Kalix was still unconscious though her breathing had become more regular since Vex's intervention. Dominil was fading quickly. Her eyes were open, but unseeing. Moonglow leaned over her, and thought for a moment that she was already dead. "Can you help Dominil?" she asked Vex.

"This is all terrible!" cried Vex. "Stupid werewolves, fighting all the time!" She put one hand over Dominil's throat and the other over the wound in her chest. The faintest of blue flames emerged from her fingers, penetrating Dominil's skin. Beads of perspiration appeared on Vex's forehead as she grappled with the unfamiliar and difficult task. The blue fire from her hands grew fainter then disappeared.

"I think you saved her," said Moonglow.

"I need to lie down," said Vex. She lay limply on the floor, her strength completely gone.

Eskandor had reverted to his human form in death. Moonglow couldn't bear to look at the body. One of the werewolves she didn't recognize cried out in pain as he was burned inside by silver. Kalix was so battered as to be hardly recognizable.

"What are we going to do?"

Daniel didn't know. They'd managed to rescue the werewolves from the Guild's headquarters but now it seemed likely that they'd all die in the back of a van in an underground car park in Knightsbridge.

CHAPTER 170

The Fire Queen lay on the floor of the stationery cupboard for a long time. Eventually she gathered enough strength to haul herself upright.

"A tremendous triumph against the vile Kabachetka." She smiled. She looked down at her dress. It was badly scorched. Her smile vanished. "Once more I am obliged to turn up at a fashion event in damaged clothes. It is so trying."

Though the Queen felt weak she was determined to at least make an appearance. "I have vanquished Kabachetka. I will say a polite hello to Donatella Versace if it's the last thing I do."

She could no longer maintain her high-heel spell, and was walking with difficulty as she emerged from the cupboard. "No doubt Agrivex has carried me to some part of the building inhabited only by junior sales clerks. Donatella may be miles away."

The Queen stepped round a corner and found herself facing a large wall mirror. She grimaced. Her hair was tangled and her make-up was in a very poor state. Worse, she was carrying Vex's green plastic bag.

The ultimate disgrace, she thought. She had a strong urge to throw it away but was prevented by an innate sense of honor. Having agreed to look after the handbag belonging to another female, even Agrivex, she could not simply discard it. The chivalrous code of the Hiyasta does not permit one to throw another woman's handbag in the bin, no mater how wretched it may be.

The Fire Queen attempted to make some emergency repairs in the mirror. She touched up her eyeliner, but as she studied her reflection, she felt her spirits sag.

I look terrible. I'm in no fit state to encounter anyone fashionable. I will return to the palace.

The Fire Queen turned round and bumped right into Donatella Versace who emerged from a private room, with the Japanese designer beside her. Next to Versace and Takahashi were the editors of *Vogue* and *Elle*, and behind them a collection of journalists, photographers and models. The Fire Queen looked at them blankly. For once in her life she felt completely lost for words. She smiled weakly as the group moved around her.

Mr. Takahashi stopped. He was a young designer, no more than twenty-five, with very long dark hair. He looked at the Fire Queen. His face lit up. "You have the bag!" he said, excitedly.

"Pardon?"

"The green plastic bag from my first collection! Such a rare item!" He embraced the bag. Then he embraced Malveria. "I'm so happy to see this bag again."

By now the assorted editors, models and designers had come to a halt. The Fire Queen found herself the unexpected center of attraction.

"This bag launched my career in Japan!" enthused Takahashi. "I did not know any of them ever reached Britain! It is so good of you to bring it to my launch!"

The Fire Queen felt some strength returning to her ankles. She drew herself up elegantly. "I thought you may appreciate it, Mr. Takahashi."

"However did you find it?"

The Fire Queen smiled. "I have many sources around the world."

"It's such a splendid piece," said the editor of *Elle*, very appreciatively.

"It's been a favorite of mine for a long time," said Malveria.

Noticing several photographers about to take pictures, the Fire Queen put her hand to her hair as if to straighten it, and then, with her power returning, let a little of her fire flow into it, so it would look good for the cameras.

"One of myself beside Donatella and Mr. Takahashi? Certainly. Have you noticed my heels? I chose them to go with the bag, in an amusing contrast. Another picture? If you really insist."

CHAPTER 171

Daniel was bracing himself for the task of carrying nine werewolves to the lift, when the back door of the van sprung open. There stood the Fire Queen, looking exuberant.

"I have had a most unexpected fashion triumph!" she said. Malveria cast her eyes over the scene of carnage that confronted her. "But I will tell you about it later. Thrix, are you still alive?"

Thrix opened her eyes.

"Excellent," said the Fire Queen. "I would miss you so. I fought Kabachetka, and suffered mightily, but emerged in splendid victory."

"Thank you," whispered Thrix.

"I suppose you will want me to heal your companions?"

"Please," said Thrix.

"For you, dearest friend, anything. Though I must insist in return you give some serious thought to my winter wardrobe, which must be immaculate."

The Fire Queen lifted both hands and uttered a spell. Moonglow felt a sudden freezing chill, and then, astonishingly, found herself in Thrix's apartment. Malveria had transported them all.

"Yes, Moonglow. I am indeed much more powerful than you imagine." The Fire Queen frowned. "But not at this moment powerful enough to cope with so many injuries. Agrivex, go to the palace and bring Grand Physician and Master of Herbs Idrigal.

"I can't move," protested Vex.

"Get up, wretched girl," commanded the Fire Queen. "Performing a little healing does not entitle you to laze around all day."

Vex climbed to her feet, grumbling about the ingratitude of her aunt and departed.

"My goodness, Thrix, you have been shot very badly. Fortunately, I came as quickly as I could. Nothing could delay me, except I had to talk a while with dear Donatella. It would have been rude not to. She has invited me to a little soirée next Wednesday."

The Fire Queen bent over Thrix and put her lips to her mouth, breathing fire directly into her body. Thrix shuddered. The Queen withdrew. "Also, I have a date with a Japanese fashion designer."

The Queen returned to healing her friend. Minutes later, Grand Physician Idrigal appeared in the room. Vex followed, though on arrival she lay on the couch and closed her eyes, exhausted.

"Ah, Idrigal," said the Fire Queen. "I need you to heal werewolves."

The tall physician looked surprised, and slightly offended. "I'm not sure I can do that."

"Of course you can. They are not complicated creatures. You have healed horses at the royal stables, have you not? Think of them in similar terms."

Grand Physician Idrigal attempted to help the other werewolves, while the Fire Queen continued her efforts with Thrix.

"How did you manage to attract so many silver bullets?"

"They had a machine gun."

"Ah. But the attack was a success?"

"Yes."

"Good. Brace yourself, dear friend, it may be painful as I extract this silver from your liver. Did I mention that I had my picture taken by the photographers from *Vogue*?"

The Queen paused, and swayed slightly. The fire that flowed from her fingers halted for several seconds before spluttering reluctantly back to life. She had expended a huge amount of energy in defeating Kabachetka and her power was still greatly depleted.

"Had I realized that half the MacRinnalch Clan would need healing, I would have asked you for a good deal more than a new winter wardrobe. One is quite shattered, I assure you, and cannot keep this up forever."

CHAPTER 172

The Mistress of the Werewolves sat alone in her chambers, brooding. Events had not turned out as she'd expected. She'd been prepared for Markus's illness. Teinn's illnesses were rarely fatal. It was the fairy's additional mischief that was so damaging. The rumor that Verasa had secretly poisoned Wallace MacGregor had rapidly spread beyond the castle. The Mistress of the Werewolves had already found herself on the receiving end of an irate phone call from Baron MacGregor, demanding to know if it were true. Verasa denied it, as strongly and persuasively as she could, but she knew the Baron hadn't believed her.

The Mistress of the Werewolves was privately unrepentant. If she hadn't managed to slip a debilitating potion into Wallace's drink before the fight, he'd have beaten Markus, and quite possibly killed him. She couldn't allow that to happen. She never expected that anyone would learn of it.

Damn that Teinn! she thought. Markus would be beside himself with fury when he learned about it. At least he's alive. Which he wouldn't have been if he'd gone to London.

Verasa's thoughts turned to Thrix. She hadn't expected that the attack would continue once Markus had withdrawn. Unfortunately, Thrix would not be dissuaded. The Mistress of the Werewolves felt a mother's terror that she might lose another child. And there was Kalix. She'd been forbidden to go, but Verasa feared she'd turn up anyway.

I tried to modernize the clan, she thought. I wanted us to manage without all this fighting. Now I'm losing my children in a war.

She sighed, very deeply, and drank more wine. She lit a cigarette, and sat alone in her chambers, very unhappy. Even though her thoughts were mainly for her children, she worried about the other MacRinnalchs who'd gone to London: Eskandor, Feargan and Barra. She hadn't expected that either, but when Thrix and Dominil had carried on anyway, Eskandor and the others had followed. Wallace MacGregor too, apparently. No doubt he was trying to show Markus up by letting everyone know how brave he was.

"Markus has left his bed. He's on his way here."

Verasa nodded. The servant withdrew.

At least I have one healthy child left, thought Verasa. She was not looking forward to the encounter, but was comforted by the thought that no matter what anyone said, her favorite child was still alive, and not lying dead in London.

CHAPTER 173

"Mighty Queen," said Grand Physician Idrigal. "I have stabilized the white werewolf and the young werewolf. The large werewolf is recovering. I can do nothing for the red werewolf, and I can't sustain my existence in this realm any longer."

"I need you to stay," said the Fire Queen. "I'll lend you some power." Malveria extended her arm, pointing at Idrigal. Nothing happened. She had no power to lend. Idrigal faded from sight. The Fire Queen looked round her in frustration.

"Really, Thrix, next time someone points a machine gun at you, I advise you to take cover."

Thrix lay beside a pile of silver fragments. She was breathing heavily and still in pain, but was now out of danger. Kalix and Dominil were safe for a little while, though they would need more attention soon. Both lay with their eyes closed, unlike Sarapen, who was conscious of events around him.

"Do you need assistance?" asked the Fire Queen.

"I'm fine," growled Sarapen.

The blood on Decembrius's chest had now congealed into a thick, ugly stain. The Queen frowned as she knelt down to examine him.

"This one has almost reached the Forests of the Werewolf Dead." She put her hand on his forehead. "Though he has halted his journey." Her frown deepened as she continued her examination.

Moonglow was still anxious about Kalix. She reached over to shake Vex awake.

"Go away I'm sore," muttered Vex.

"Kalix needs more help," said Moonglow.

"I hurt too much."

"You have to do something!"

Vex dragged herself from the couch. "It feels really bad doing this when you can't do it properly."

Vex put her mouth close to Kalix's lips and attempted to breathe some energy into her. Kalix was still deathly pale, but Moonglow thought there was a tiny improvement.

"Thrix," called the Fire Queen. "There is a problem with Decembrius. There is a silver bullet lodged so close to his heart that I fear to move it. If it touches his heart, he will die."

"Can't you magic it away?" asked Daniel.

"If you mean make it disappear, no I can't. It needs to be drawn out. But the bullet may come apart. I really cannot remove it without some fragment touching his heart."

The Fire Queen attempted to stand up, then, realizing how weak she was, thought better of it. "I'm sorry, Thrix. In a little while I may have enough power to help Dominil and Kalix. But I can do nothing for Decembrius."

Dominil, hearing this, opened her eyes. "Doctor Angus," she said. "Perhaps he could take it out with surgery. He has an operating theater in Edinburgh."

Angus MacRinnalch was an experienced surgeon who had often helped his fellow werewolves. In the course of his long career, he'd removed many silver bullets.

"He has a werewolf nurse and an anesthetist. They might be able to save him," said Thrix.

"Someone help me with my phone," said Dominil. Daniel found Dominil's phone and put it in her hand.

"I'll tell the Mistress of the Werewolves to alert Doctor Angus."

"Angus is in Edinburgh," said Thrix. Like Dominil, she was lying on the floor, looking at the ceiling, and the conversation was conducted in whispers. "How is Decembrius going to get there?"

"I hoped the Fire Queen could transport him."

"You may not have noticed that I am also lying on the floor," said the Fire Queen. "I don't have the power to stand, let alone transport an ailing werewolf."

The room fell silent. If the Fire Queen couldn't transport Decembrius to Edinburgh he was going to die.

"Vex, don't you have any power left?" asked Moonglow

Vex was now lying on her side, hugging a cushion and whimpering.

"Apparently not," said Daniel.

"I do have one suggestion," said Malveria, from the floor. "I am drained, but there are two people here with some vitality."

"Do you mean us?" asked Moonglow.

"Indeed, young humans. If you permit me to take power from you, I may have sufficient energy to transport Decembrius to Edinburgh. And may I say, Thrix, that a new winter wardrobe is far from sufficient for this service."

"What do you mean, take power from us?" said Daniel, sounding worried.

"Your life force. Human life force is not remarkably strong, but you are a healthy pair of teenagers. Your energy may take me to Edinburgh."

"Our energy? Will we die?"

"Almost certainly not. But you will feel bad."

"How bad?" asked Daniel.

"Much worse than you have ever felt."

"I don't like the sound of that."

"The MacRinnalchs will be very grateful," said Thrix, quietly.

Moonglow looked at Kalix, who was still unconscious. "We should do it, I suppose. Decembrius is a friend of Kalix."

"Didn't they have a lot of arguments?" said Daniel. "Maybe she'd rather just let him go?"

Moonglow looked at Daniel pointedly.

"All right," he sighed. "Fine. Suck out my life force. It's not doing me that much good anyway."

Malveria raised herself to a sitting position. She pointed one hand at Daniel and one at Moonglow. A blue flame appeared on each of their chests. The flames grew, and fire flowed toward Malveria.

The Fire Queen smiled. "Human energy. And human thoughts and emotions."

"Don't read my thoughts," said Daniel.

Malveria laughed. "Why Daniel, I am one of the universe's great beauties. It would be strange if you had never had any fantasies about me."

"I deny it," said Daniel. Then he went quiet, as a terrible numbing cold entered his body. Both he and Moonglow became paler and paler. They shivered as Malveria took their energy.

"Stop it," cried Daniel, as he slumped to the ground.

"Just a little more," said Malveria.

Moonglow began to cry as she felt her life energy being sucked from her, to be replaced by a freezing cold which felt impossible to bear. Malveria rose to her feet.

"Better than I expected," she said. "You are quite a healthy pair, for students. Thrix, I will now take Decembrius to your werewolf doctor." Malveria paused, and briefly touched both Kalix and Dominil, healing them a little more. Then she snapped her fingers and dematerialized, taking Decembrius with her. After she had gone the room was silent, save for the moaning of Moonglow and Daniel, who were both feeling much worse than they'd ever felt before, as promised by the Fire Queen.

CHAPTER 174

Markus had argued with his mother in the past, but he'd never raged against her the way he did now.

"Everyone is saying I cheated against Wallace! They say you drugged him! Is it true?"

"Of course it's not true, Markus. I'd never do that."

"If it's not true how did the rumor get started?"

"I don't know how," said his mother. "Just one of those foolish things that people say. Just ignore it, people will forget about it."

"No one is going to forget about it because everyone believes it! They don't think I could have beaten Wallace in a fair fight."

"But you did," insisted Verasa. "Everyone saw it."

Markus's face was glistening with perspiration. The fever had not yet left his body, and he should still have been resting. "This is a nightmare! I was supposed to lead the clan into battle and instead fell ill! Did you have something to do with that?"

"Please, dear, don't be ridiculous. How could I make you ill?"

Markus glared at his mother suspiciously. He didn't know how she could have made him ill but he wouldn't put it past her.

"Instead of postponing the attack, they've gone ahead without me! They couldn't even wait a few days till I was better. Why didn't you stop them?"

"I tried to—"

"And Wallace has gone with them!" Markus found this particularly galling. "No doubt he's telling everyone I cheated. Why did you poison him?"

"I didn't," insisted the Mistress of the Werewolves.

"I don't believe you!" said Markus.

"Markus, are you accusing me of lying?"

"Yes! And now I'm disgraced!"

"Really, Markus, you're making far too much of a silly rumor—"

The Mistress of the Werewolves' phone rang. It was Dominil. There was a short conversation during which the Mistress of the Werewolves quickly became agitated. When the call ended, she stared at the phone as if she couldn't believe what she'd heard.

"Sarapen isn't dead," she said.

"If course he is, we buried him."

"Whoever we buried it wasn't Sarapen. Empress Kabachetka kept him alive. He joined in the attack in London."

It was an astonishing piece of news. Nothing could have been more disturbing. Markus and his mother had fought a civil war to defeat Sarapen and now he was back.

"What happened in the attack?" asked Marcus.

"Dominil says they defeated the Guild and destroyed all their records. But Wallace MacGregor is dead, and so are Eskandor and Barra and Feargan, and Morag Macallister. Decembrius is badly hurt. They're taking him to Doctor Angus."

The Mistress of the Werewolves sat down, shaken by the news. Markus did the same. He felt light-headed from his fever, and could hardly grasp what had happened. "Wallace is dead? And Eskandor? And Sarapen is back?"

Verasa could barely imagine how Baron MacGregor would react to the death of his eldest son. Young Baron MacAllister would be equally outraged at the death of his sister.

"They shouldn't have gone ahead," she muttered. "They should have waited."

The Mistress of the Werewolves left Markus in her chambers as she hurried off to tell her sister Lucia the bad news about her son Decembrius.

CHAPTER 175

Distikka looked around her small cell. It was, she reflected, a very poor place to spend the last few hours of her life. The walls were hard black stone, as was the bed. The prison beneath the palace was not a comfortable place. She had been sent there after a summary trial, presided over by the Empress.

"Distikka. Your scheming has ended in disaster. Thrix MacRinnalch still lives, as does her sister Kalix. My agents report that they inflicted a defeat on the werewolf hunters. Furthermore, Sarapen has escaped. Worst of all, my spy in the offices of *Vogue* informs me that the Fire Queen has somehow managed to inveigle her way into the next edition of the magazine, clutching a repulsive plastic handbag. There is even talk of a pleasant little lunch with Donatella Versace. For all this, I hold you responsible."

The Empress looked down at Distikka from her throne. "Do you have anything to say in your defense?"

"Really," began Distikka," I don't think—"

"The court has heard enough!" cried the Empress. "You are guilty of everything and will be executed at noon tomorrow. Adviser Bakmer, please ensure a suitable crowd is gathered to see Distikka thrown into the Eternal Volcano."

"Very good, Your Excellency," said Adviser Bakmer, and bowed very low, to hide his inappropriately broad smile.

Distikka sat in her cell. What a loathsome creature the Empress is, she thought.

She looked up at the sound of footsteps outside her cell. "At last. I wondered when you were going to get here."

Ex-adviser Tarentia appeared very anxious. "I don't like this at all," he whispered. "Do you know how dangerous this is for me?"

"I'm the one who's about to be executed," said Distikka.

"As will I be, most horribly, if the Empress discovers I'm helping you escape."

Distikka smiled, and even in her desperate circumstance, she looked young and boyish, with her short dark hair. "It's your only chance of getting back into the throne room, Tarentia."

"Do you have the documents?"

"When you get me out of here," said Distikka.

Tarentia opened the cell. "Hurry, I couldn't get rid of the guards for long."

Distikka slipped out of the cell, and followed the aging ex-adviser along the corridor. He opened a rarely used door, to which only he had the key. "Once you're above ground you'll be out of range of the prison's dampening field and you'll be able to travel anywhere."

"Good," said Distikka. She drew a small key from her pocket and handed it to Tarentia. "There's a hidden drawer beneath the bottom drawer in the dresser next to my bed. In there you'll find details of every piece of embezzlement carried out by Bakmer. There's a lot of it. More than enough to see him ousted, and you back in favor."

"Are you sure it's accurate?"

"I keep very good records," said Distikka. "Be thankful it's not you I'm turning in."

"Goodbye, Distikka. Never come back."

Distikka slipped out of the underground caverns, and looked up at the Eternal Volcano. "I never really liked the Hainusta," she mused. "I'll be pleased to leave."

CHAPTER 176

It took eighteen hours before Daniel and Moonglow felt well enough to leave Thrix's apartment. Kalix was too weak to walk and had to be helped into the lift. Vex was still unwell after her emergency healing duties. Daniel felt too weak to drive, so they were returning home in a taxi. They made for a sorry sight as they waited on the curb. The Enchantress herself was recovering, though Dominil was still unable to rise. Sarapen was healing quickly. He'd been badly injured, but his enormous strength had flooded back in no time.

Vex's shoulders were drooping as she stood on the pavement in Knightsbridge. "I never realized how difficult healing people was. I thought Aunt Malvie was making a big fuss about nothing. I feel awful."

When the taxi arrived Daniel helped Kalix inside.

"I still can't get warm," said Moonglow. She'd been shivering for eighteen hours. When they reached their flat in Kennington it took an effort to climb the stairs. Daniel switched on the gas fire in the living room, then lay down in front of it.

"I can't go another step," he said.

Malveria taking his energy had left him not only physically frozen, but mentally numbed. For hours he'd been sure that he was either going to die or else be permanently crippled. Only now, having reached his own flat, was he starting to think he might recover.

Vex sprawled in front of the fire. "I can't make it to my room," she mumbled. "Stupid healing."

Kalix tumbled down beside her. The cat, thinking that this bundle of bodies looked inviting, jumped on top of Kalix, purring contentedly. They all lay in front of the fire for a few minutes, then felt themselves being covered by something soft and warm. Moonglow, showing some determination, had made it upstairs, where she'd taken both hers and Kalix's duvets. She covered Kalix, Daniel and Vex, took a cushion for a pillow, then lay down herself.

"We seem to be doing a lot of lying on floors these days," said Daniel. "Are you feeling any better?"

"Not really," said Moonglow. "I'm still freezing."

"Could you change into a werewolf?" Daniel asked Kalix. "Then you'll be warm and furry."

"I'm not a hot-water bottle," said Kalix. "Anyway, it's daylight."

The four flatmates fell asleep in the living room, under their duvets, waiting for their health to recover.

Kalix slept well enough to revitalize her strength, but she was troubled by bad dreams. She woke up thinking about Decembrius, and felt confused, not knowing if he were alive or not. She wondered if she might have done more to prevent him from being so badly hurt. She remembered all the other werewolves who'd died.

"They probably deserved to live more than me. Maybe I could have helped them more."

But from the moment she'd run into the Guild's headquarters till the moment she'd been carried out, Kalix had hardly been aware of anything around her. She'd been completely taken over by her battle madness. All she could do was attack her enemies. She looked down at her fresh scars. It was a miracle she'd survived.

She thought about Sarapen. It was hard to comprehend that he was actually alive. They'd always loathed each other. If they'd encountered each other in any other circumstances, Kalix would have attacked him. Now they'd fought together. Kalix wondered if that made things different. She didn't really know. Any strong emotion could bring on Kalix's anxiety, and the combination of guilt and confusion began to make her feel bad. She rose quietly and headed upstairs to her bedroom. She reached for her laudanum, but paused. She opened the cupboard, where she had several small blades hidden for cutting herself. Again she hesitated. She realized she probably shouldn't be cutting herself, or taking laudanum, so soon after being badly injured.

She wondered if drawing might take her mind off her anxiety, but that made her think of Manny.

Did he really betray us?

Kalix could hardly imagine that Manny would have betrayed them. It didn't seem like the sort of thing he would do.

"But Thrix is sure he did. And he was related to the hunters. I might have said something that gave him a warning. Because I'm stupid like that."

She wondered why Manny had asked her to call him again. It might really have been because he'd forgiven her for sleeping with someone else. That didn't seem likely to Kalix. Perhaps Manny just had wanted to talk to her so he could find out more about werewolves.

"And if he didn't betray us, how did the Guild know we were coming?"

Kalix shook her head. She didn't know what to think. She was more troubled now, and ended up taking some laudanum to ease her mind.

CHAPTER 177

Baron MacGregor was beside himself with grief over the loss of his eldest son, and neither of his other children nor his trusted advisor Lachlan could say anything to comfort him. He cursed the MacRinnalchs for their pride and stupidity in persisting with the attack. It was bad enough that the Mistress of the Werewolves had cheated Wallace out of his reputation. Now the insufferable arrogance of Thrix and Dominil had carried him off to his death.

The next day the Baron traveled to Castle MacRinnalch to confront the Thane and his mother. He arrived in a fury, and the guards who led him to the Thane's reception chamber did so quite nervously, wondering if they'd be called on to restrain and eject the furious werewolf. It was many years since a baron had been forcibly ejected from the castle.

MacGregor wasted no time in letting Markus and his mother know what he thought of them.

"I've come to tell you to your face that I blame you for the death of Wallace. It was your daughter Thrix's arrogance that led to this doomed attack. And Dominil's too."

"The attack happened because the Guild killed Minerva," said Markus.

"And we'd have been revenged in time! There was no need to act rashly. I told you it would end in misery and now my son is dead."

Verasa made sympathetic noises, but Markus, lacking his mother's tact, pointed out that the attack had been a success. The Avenaris Guild had all but been destroyed.

"So what!" roared the Baron. "There will always be more hunters!

But I've lost my son!" He looked at them with furious contempt. "I know you cheated Wallace in single combat."

"The rumors are quite untrue," said the Mistress of the Werewolves, calmly.

"Really? I always wondered how Markus defeated Wallace, and now I know. You drugged my son. And then you sent him off to his death."

The Baron drew out an ancient piece of parchment from his cloak. "This is the original oath of fealty, sworn by my ancestor Baron Murdo MacGregor, pledging his loyalty to the Thane of the MacRinnalchs."

The Baron ripped the parchment in half and threw it contemptuously at Markus's feet. "You're not fit to be Thane, and the MacRinnalchs aren't worthy of my loyalty. You will see us no more at your castle."

With that, he stormed out, vowing never to return.

Thane Markus was upset. "That was worse than I was expecting."

"Let him grieve," said Verasa. "He has four other sons and two daughters to comfort him. He'll get over it."

Markus sat on a chair and stared at the floor. His fever was passing, though he hadn't fully recovered.

"No one forced Wallace to go to London," Verasa pointed out. "It was his own choice."

"He went to London to show me up," said Markus. "Because he knew I'd cheated him."

"I keep telling you, these stories are false."

Markus shook his head. He didn't believe his mother. "And then I got sick when the clan needed me. I'm not much of a Thane."

The Mistress of the Werewolves put her arm on his shoulder. "Nonsense. Haven't you presided over the destruction of the Avenaris Guild? You had the courage and authority to authorize the attack, and we destroyed them."

Markus would not be comforted, and spent the rest of the day alone in his room, turning away the attentions of all who sought him out, including Beatrice and Heather. They were distressed to be turned away. Neither of them believed the rumors about his victory over Wallace, and nor did they mind that Markus hadn't taken part in the attack. Both were so in love with him that they were relieved he was still alive.

There was much grief in the castle over the deaths of Eskandor, Feargan and Barra. Grief was felt throughout all the estates of the werewolves.

The MacAllisters were proud of the warrior spirit shown by the baron's sister Morag, but deeply shocked that she had been killed.

It was a matter of opinion whether it had all been worthwhile. Some werewolves thought it had been, because they'd struck such a blow against the Avenaris Guild. But others thought it had not been, because the Guild was far away, and hadn't had an impact on the lives of most werewolves in Scotland. So why send werewolves to die in London? Some thought that an attack had been justified, but it had all been too rushed, and blamed Thrix and Dominil for not planning it carefully enough.

Preparations for the funerals were made, but they would not be glorious. They would be quiet, sad affairs and, at some of them, the Thane would not be welcome.

CHAPTER 178

Thrix had called her mother, asking about Decembrius. Verasa told her that Doctor Angus had operated on him, but the outcome was still uncertain. Decembrius was still hovering between life and death. The Mistress of the Werewolves had much more to say to her daughter, particularly about Sarapen, but Thrix ended the call abruptly. She was driving through London and had reached her destination. She emerged from her car with a scowl on her face.

"Wallace, Morag, Eskandor, Feargan and Barra," she muttered to herself. "And probably Decembrius."

Thrix climbed the stairs of the old, red-brick council block. On the top flight, she knocked sharply on the last door. Manny answered. He was surprised to see Thrix, though he recognized her as Kalix's sister.

"Alex isn't here. We . . ."

"You broke up. I know. May I come in?"

"I suppose so."

Thrix entered Manny's flat, which smelled strongly of oil paint. She looked around at his pictures of animals. She wasn't that impressed, though there was something cheerful about his bright use of color.

"Kalix told me what happened."

"Who's Kalix?"

"I mean Alex."

Manny pursed his lips. "I wish I hadn't broken up with her."

"I don't think you can blame yourself," said Thrix. "She did sleep with an old boyfriend. A lot of people would break up over that."

"Maybe. But you know . . . I shouldn't have got so mad." Manny suddenly looked hopeful. "Did Alex ask you to come here?"

"No. But I know she misses you a lot. She's been unhappy ever since you broke up."

Manny looked unhappy in turn. "I didn't mean to make her sad. I just . . . I was just so upset, you know."

Thrix nodded sympathetically. "Of course."

"I was quite mean to her. I'm sorry about that. I met her in the street and I asked her to call me, but she hasn't."

"Alex is very shy. She's probably just trying to work up the courage."

"Really?" Manny looked hopeful. "Thanks for telling me. I should call her."

"You're welcome," said Thrix. She smiled at Manny. He was quite a pretty boy, she thought. And pleasant too. She could see why Kalix liked him. Thrix transferred her gaze to a painting of a yellow cat. Or perhaps it was a lion, it was hard to tell.

"Just one more thing. What does your father do?"

Manny was surprised at the question. "Some sort of banking, I think. You know, in the city."

"Banking?"

"Or investments maybe, I've never been sure. Why?"

"Is this a cat or a lion?"

"A lion."

"I like it," said Thrix. "You do have a way with color." She turned back toward Manny. "Your father is head of an organization that hunts werewolves."

"What? Why would you say something like that?"

"Because it's true. As you well know. And you told him the werewolves were coming."

"There's no such thing as werewolves. Is this some sort of joke about my animal paintings?"

Thrix shook her head. "Nothing to do with your paintings. Although now you mention it, Alex would be an excellent subject. When she's a werewolf, I mean."

"Stop saying things like that!" said Manny, now quite alarmed.

"You warned the Guild we were coming. But it didn't work. Don't you know your father's lying dead in the ruins of his headquarters? I killed him!"

"Go away!" cried Manny. "Stop saying all these mad things!"

Thrix laughed. She transformed into her werewolf shape. Manny yelled in terror and stepped back, crashing into his easel and falling to the floor. Thrix picked him up, lifting him into the air with one hand.

"Don't kill me!" screamed Manny.

Thrix drew the terrified young man toward her so that her snout almost touched his nose. "Why not?"

"You said your sister was in love with me!"

"Who cares what she thinks?"

Thrix let go of Manny, then hit him across the face with the back of her taloned claw, a blow powerful enough to break his cheekbone. He crashed into the wall, blood spurting from his nose. Thrix hit him again, deliberately not killing him yet, because she wanted to hurt him. When Manny fell unconscious from the assault, she looked down on him with a mixture of loathing and disappointment.

"I hoped you might last longer," she snarled.

She paused. "I really do owe my sister a dead boyfriend."

Thrix opened her jaws and bent down to kill him.

"I think this is perhaps not the best idea," said the Fire Queen, materializing at Thrix's side.

"Malveria!" yelled Thrix. "This is none of your business."

"Perhaps not. But I care about your welfare, dearest friend, and I do not think killing this young man will be good for you."

"That's for me to decide," said Thrix. But the madness went out of her eyes, and she looked around her, distracted, as if suddenly wondering what she was doing here.

"I hoped that the violence of the attack might have purged the madness from your soul," said the Fire Queen. "I see it has not."

Thrix stared out of the window, and didn't reply.

The Fire Queen looked down at Manny's crumpled frame, unconscious on the floor, still bleeding. "Perhaps there really is a curse on the MacRinnalch women when it comes to love. Their boyfriends certainly do not fare well."

Suddenly, there was a loud banging on the front door.

"What's going on in there?" demanded a woman's voice. "Are you all right? Should I call the police?"

"It's time for us to go," said the Fire Queen. She spoke a spell in one of the ancient languages of the Hiyasta, a spell to hide Thrix's aura and scent, so that no one would ever know she'd been there. "If the young man recovers, which is questionable, he will not remember you."

Malveria placed her hand gently on Thrix's shoulder. "Perhaps the pure air of Minerva's mountaintop will clear your mind." With that, she dematerialized from the flat, taking the unresisting Thrix with her.

CHAPTER 179

A week after the attack, life was returning to normal in the small flat in Kennington. Kalix had been changing into a werewolf every night to accelerate her healing, and she had largely recovered, though she still suffered some pain from her wounds.

"It's lucky I got in better shape by exercising," she said, limping into the living room. "Or I might have been in a really bad state."

Kalix sat down heavily beside Daniel. He'd spent most of the week in front of the fire, thawing himself out.

"You've no idea how bad it felt when Malveria sucked out our energy," he said, for perhaps the fiftieth time.

"It wasn't any fun getting machine-gunned either," said Kalix.

"Hey, you volunteered for that," said Daniel. "Moonglow and I were unwitting victims."

Kalix smiled. Daniel was proud of his part in the rescue. "How did you know we needed rescuing anyway?"

"Lady Gezinka told me," said Daniel. "Obviously I made a big impression on her."

"Is Daniel going on about Lady Gezinka again?" said Moonglow, appearing from the kitchen. Kalix laughed. To hear Daniel tell it, the most beautiful aristocrat in the land of the Hainusta was obsessively in love with him.

Moonglow shivered. "I'm still getting these bouts of feeling really cold."

"Me too," said Daniel. "If I'd known how bad it was going to be I'd have let Decembrius die. How is he anyway?"

"He's getting better," said Kalix, who'd been had been talking to Dominil on the phone.

There was a crash in the kitchen.

"You'd think Vex would be able to navigate to the living room by now," said Daniel.

Vex appeared. "This is the worst outrage ever! Aunt Malvie has requisitioned my bag!"

"What bag?"

"My Japanese green plastic bag! She says it's a matter of national importance." Vex looked down at the bag she was carrying, a new pink Hello Kitty basket. "She gave me this one to replace it."

"It's nice," said Moonglow.

"I know. I like it better, really. But what's the world coming to when your aunty steals your bag?" Vex grinned, and didn't really seem very outraged. "Everyone feeling better?" she asked.

"Just about," said Kalix.

"Me too," said Vex. "And I'm going to see Pete tomorrow. I can't wait."

Vex had been too busy to see her boyfriend for a week, and was feeling his absence. The doorbell rang. Vex bounded downstairs, and soon arrived back in the living room with Dominil. The white-haired werewolf also seemed to have made a full recovery. If she was still feeling pain from her wounds, she wasn't admitting it.

"Please excuse my intrusion," said Dominil. "Are you all well?"

Daniel, Moonglow, Vex and Kalix nodded. There was a moment's awkward silence. No one had ever worked out how to make small talk with Dominil.

"I have come to express thanks, both personally and from the clan. Daniel and Moonglow, thank you for rescuing us from the Guild's building. Had you not arrived with the van, I doubt we would have survived. Agrivex, thank you for your healing. I have a letter from the Mistress of the Werewolves, formally declaring you friends of the MacRinnalch Clan. The Mistress of the Werewolves wished me to add, on a personal note, that if you are ever in the vicinity of Castle MacRinnalch, you are welcome to visit." Dominil handed over the letter.

"Does this include me?" asked Vex.

"It does," said Dominil. "The Mistress of the Werewolves has also written to the Fire Queen, declaring a wish that the long-standing bad feeling between the MacRinnalchs and the Hiyasta might be ended, in view of the assistance rendered to the clan by Queen Malveria and yourself."

Moonglow had risen from the couch, feeling it was the proper thing to do. "Thank you," she said. "We appreciate it."

"We're pleased to be werewolf friends," said Daniel.

"I shall inform the Mistress of the Werewolves when I visit the castle tomorrow," said Dominil, quite formally. "There is one other thing I have to attend to. Agrivex, may I have a word with you in private?"

"Like a secret meeting? Are we spies?"

"No," said Dominil. "Please come with me."

Dominil led Vex to the kitchen, leaving Daniel and Moonglow puzzled.

"I have something unpleasant to tell you," said Dominil.

"What?"

"Your boyfriend Pete. His motivation in pursuing a relationship with you is largely to make me jealous. This is a foolish endeavor. I have no interest in him."

Vex laughed. "Don't be silly, Dominil. Why would you say such a silly thing?"

"I'm under an obligation to inform you. It doesn't matter to me whether you believe it or not. But as proof, if you desire it, I called Pete and made a date with him tomorrow night. He was very eager. I will not be making an appearance."

With that Dominil departed, walking calmly out the front door.

Vex ran back into the living room, laughing. "Dominil's gone mad," she said. "You won't believe what she just said! She thinks Pete is only going out with me to make her jealous! Isn't that the silliest thing you've ever heard?" She looked at Daniel, Kalix and Moonglow, sitting on the couch. "Why aren't you laughing?" she demanded.

There was a long pause, ever more awkward than that generated by Dominil's arrival.

"Well . . ." began Daniel.

There was another silence.

"Don't tell me you believe it?" cried Vex. "It's the most stupid thing ever. Moonglow, you don't think it's true, do you?"

Moonglow looked at the floor.

"Kalix?" said Vex.

Kalix looked at the floor, and also tried to hide behind Daniel.

"I can't believe this!" cried Vex. "What sort of friends are you? Dominil makes some mad accusations against my boyfriend and you all think it's true!" Vex was rapidly becoming very agitated. "I'll show you!" she cried. She took out her phone. "Dominil had some story about making a date with him tomorrow."

Vex called her boyfriend. "Hello, Pete! I've missed you this week!

What are we doing tomorrow?"

There was a pause. A slight wrinkle appeared on Vex's forehead.

"What do you mean you can't see me? We arranged to go to the cinema."

There was a longer pause. Vex's brow became furrowed. "You have to visit your grandmother in hospital? Really? Well, OK." She ended the phone call. "He has to visit his grandmother in hospital."

Daniel, Moonglow and Kalix were still looking at the floor. Vex stared at them for a while, then looked at herself in the mirror above the fireplace. She teased out a few strands of hair. "I need to bleach it again," she said. "I can see some dark roots."

Vex turned swiftly toward her friends. "Would everybody stop staring at the floor?"

"I think I'll make some tea," said Moonglow.

"Don't run away and make tea!" cried Vex. "Is this true? Does Pete really not like me? He said he did." Vex was suddenly filled by a crushing feeling of humiliation which she'd never encountered before. "Does everyone know about this?"

"We suspected," said Daniel. "Because that's what the twins thought."

"Oh." Vex looked bewildered. "Well, this really sucks." She began to glow, a faint trace of orange becoming visible over her dark skin. "I can't believe this. This is the worst thing ever. I get a stupid boyfriend who pretends he likes me and really he's only using me to make someone else jealous!"

The orange glow became more noticeable.

"And this is right after *Nagasaki Night Fight Boom Boom Girl* was such a letdown! I really hate it!" Vex clenched her fists. "I am so angry with everything!"

The young Fire Elemental stretched out her arms to indicate how angry she was, and then, to everyone's astonishment, a bolt of red flame shot out from her hand. It hit the wall like a laser, and pierced the brick, leaving the wallpaper on fire.

Vex froze. She looked at her hand in wonder, amazed at what had happened.

"Congratulations, niece," said the Fire Queen, materializing smoothly in the room. She snapped her fingers, extinguishing the flames. "I am sorry, Moonglow, for yet another piece of household damage. I will pay for repairs."

She turned to Agrivex. "It seems that you have finally learned how to produce fire. I will not send you to Arch-wizard Krathrank."

"Oh," said Vex. She was still stunned. "That's good I suppose." A tear trickled from her eye, sizzling as it made its way down her cheek. "I lost my boyfriend."

"Nothing could have been better for teaching you fire," said Malveria. "A disastrous relationship will benefit you greatly in the end."

"It doesn't feel like a benefit."

The Fire Queen looked toward Moonglow.

"I'll make tea," said Moonglow.

"Excellent," said Malveria. "We shall drink tea, Agrivex, and you may eat biscuits, and tell us of your hatred for Pete. Afterward you will come back to the palace, and share a bottle of wine with myself, Iskiline and Gruselvere. The pain of your boyfriend disaster will soon fade, but your new powers of fire will remain."

CHAPTER 180

"Markus can't resign as Thane," said Verasa. "The Thane is appointed for life."

Clan Secretary Rainal studied the letter, handwritten on the thick, cream-colored stationery used by the clan for official business.

"He says he's resigning."

"He can't."

"He's left the castle."

"I expect he's in Edinburgh," said the Mistress of the Werewolves. Markus's letter of resignation had come as a severe shock, but she was refusing to let it show. "He just needs time to sort out his thoughts."

There was little indication as to what Markus's thoughts may have been in the brief note he'd sent to Rainal, but Verasa knew why Markus had resigned. He'd been humiliated to the point where he no longer felt able to continue as leader of the MacRinnalchs.

"It's preposterous," she said. "I won't see my son driven from the clan by these false rumors."

Rainal didn't reply. He'd heard Verasa's vehement denials and he wasn't going to contradict her. Privately, he believed the rumors. He'd watched the fight from the battlements, and he remembered clearly how

Wallace's strength had suddenly deserted him, just when it seemed he would defeat Markus.

"What are we going to tell the clan?" he asked.

"Nothing. I'll go to Edinburgh and bring Markus back."

"What about the council meeting?"

"Meeting?" said Verasa. "We don't have enough council members for a meeting."

Baron MacGregor had announced his intention of leaving. The MacGregors would take no further part on the confederation of the werewolf clans. The MacAllisters had not yet taken such a drastic step, but Baron MacAllister was in mourning for his sister and would not attend the forthcoming meeting. Whether he would attend any other remained to be seen. Thrix was apparently still too ill to travel. Decembrius was also too unwell to attend. With the habitual absence of Butix, Delix, Marwanis and Kalix, the Great Council no longer had enough members to function.

"Even if we coaxed Great Mother Dulupina from her chambers, we'd still only have eight out of seventeen." The Mistress of the Werewolves couldn't remember the last time a council meeting had been cancelled for lack of attendees. "And now, of all times. With Sarapen back."

Rainal scanned the Mistress of the Werewolves' features for some sign of her thoughts about the unexpected return of her eldest son. They'd never been close and they'd ended up as bitter enemies. But on this, Verasa was guarding her feelings.

"Do you think Sarapen will try for the Thaneship?" he asked.

"There's no *Thaneship* for Sarapen to try for. Markus is Thane." Verasa put Markus's letter in her pocket. "Don't mention this to anyone. Is Dominil here yet?"

"She should be arriving at the castle any minute."

Verasa had informed Dominil that there was unlikely to be a council meeting, but Dominil had expressed her intention of coming to the castle anyway. She wanted to make a report on the attack, which, she felt, was due to the clan.

"There are a lot of relatives waiting to hear what she has to say," said Rainal. The families of Eskandor, Barra and Feargan all wanted to know how they'd died. Dominil might be in for a difficult time.

"She's not one to shirk her duties, I'll give her that," said the Mistress of the Werewolves.

"She seems like the only one who's fully recovered. Where do you want to meet her?"

"Show her here," she said. "There's no point refusing to receive her when she's the only one who can tell us what happened in London. And we need to know everything about Sarapen."

Rainal paused as he was leaving. "Are you going to tell Dominil about the motion to remove her?"

"I'm not sure. I don't suppose I have to, if there isn't going to be a council meeting this month."

Baron MacPhee had tabled a motion proposing that Dominil be removed from the council because of her laudanum addiction. He wasn't the only one who was unhappy with her continued presence. Feelings against her had grown after the deaths in London. There was some antipathy against Thrix as well, but she was the Thane's sister, and too well connected to be assailed. Dominil was a different matter. She'd never been popular.

"It would be best if you told her," advised Rainal. "She'll hear it from someone else anyway. Eskandor's father is furious about his son's death. I've asked the guards on duty to make sure there's no trouble."

CHAPTER 181

Kalix wanted to contact Manny but her nerve failed her.

He asked me to call. It won't be humiliating. I should do it.

Kalix started to dial his number, but gave up halfway through. She couldn't face it. What if she called and he'd changed his mind about wanting to talk to her? She was too fearful of rejection to take the chance.

After much consideration, she'd decided, almost, that she didn't believe that Manny had spied on her for the werewolf hunters.

"I don't think he'd do that. If he really was related to them, it was just a coincidence."

It struck the young werewolf that if she lacked the nerve to call Manny, it might be easier to just knock at his door. Once she actually saw his face, her nervousness might vanish.

Kalix set out almost immediately, hurrying to Kennington tube station, carried on by a wave of enthusiasm for her plan. The enthusiasm lasted almost all the way to Oxford Circus, where it evaporated.

This is stupid, thought Kalix. I'm planning to knock on his door?

He'll just tell me to get lost. He's probably got another girlfriend by now anyway. She'll be there and it will just be humiliating.

Kalix got off the tube train and walked through a tunnel to the platform where she could catch a train back home.

What a waste of time, she thought, and cursed herself for her cowardice. She realized it was no use. She just lacked the nerve to contact Manny.

Maybe he'll call me sometime, she thought, as she sat on the train home, her gaze fixed firmly on the floor.

Kalix arrived home to find Moonglow loading clothes into the washing machine. It was a small machine, fitted snugly beside the sink in their small kitchen.

"Hi, Kalix."

"I was going to call Manny but I lost my nerve," said Kalix.

"Oh. I'm sorry."

"I thought it might be easier to just visit him but I lost my nerve again." Kalix looked depressed.

"Maybe he'll call you," said Moonglow.

"Maybe. Probably not."

"Well, don't give up," said Moonglow. "Sometimes relationships just have to wait until the time is right."

Kalix felt vaguely cheered by Moonglow's words. Perhaps the time would be right in a little while. She might get to see Manny again.

CHAPTER 182

Dominil walked into the park by Ladbroke Grove in the early hours of the morning. She checked to see that she was unobserved then changed into her werewolf shape. Her senses were immediately sharpened. She followed a werewolf scent into a clump of trees in the middle of the park.

"Hello, Sarapen."

The huge werewolf was sitting with his back to a tree. He rose to greet her. "I wasn't expecting you to contact me," he said.

"I guessed you'd be staying in one of the clan properties."

Sarapen nodded. The MacRinnalchs owned property in London. As an exile, Sarapen shouldn't have been using any of it, though Dominil didn't care that he was. They sat down together, with their backs to a tree.

"That was some fight," said Sarapen. "You're still a great fighter."

"Thank you." Dominil didn't feel the need to return the compliment. Sarapen already knew he was a great fighter. They sat in silence, two werewolves in London, in a public park, watching the moon as it faded in the dawn light. When it disappeared they each made a smooth transition back to human form.

"What are they saying at the castle?"

"That it was all unnecessary," said Dominil. "Some of them anyway."

"They're fools."

"No one is much pleased to hear you're back."

Sarapen smiled. "I knew that already."

"Now you are back, what do you intend to do?"

"I haven't decided."

"Were you planning on starting another war with the clan?"

"If I was," said Sarapen, "I wouldn't tell you about it."

They fell silent as a young man passed nearby, walking his dog in the early morning. The dog barked, and strained at its leash, trying to flee.

"We've never been popular with dogs," said Dominil.

"Neither of us have ever been that popular with anyone," said Sarapen.

They lapsed into silence again, though it was not uncomfortable. Even as lovers, Dominil and Sarapen had never been keen conversationalists.

"Markus has resigned as Thane," said Dominil, eventually. "Though it's being kept secret."

"He was never suitable as Thane."

"Neither were you."

"Is that why we're meeting?" asked Sarapen. "So you can warn me off starting trouble for the clan?"

Dominil looked at his face. His experiences in the elementals' dimension hadn't changed his appearance, apart from the scarring round his jaw, which was more prominent than she remembered, as if the heat had darkened the scars.

"No. I didn't ask you here on clan business. It's a personal matter. If you're not planning on starting a new feud right away, I have a suggestion. You could help me to stop taking laudanum."

Dominil was slightly gratified by the way Sarapen's mouth opened in surprise. It wasn't easy to shock the great werewolf but she'd succeeded. Sarapen was so startled he was unable to respond.

"Yes, I'm a laudanum addict," continued Dominil. "I have been for a long time. I kept my addiction secret, but now everyone knows. They're going to throw me off the council because I'm a disgrace to the clan."

"You certainly are!" said Sarapen, hotly. "What on earth were you thinking—"

Dominil held up her hand, silencing her companion. "I've already been through the lectures. I assure you they're not helpful. What would be helpful would be your assistance in stopping."

"How could I help?"

Dominil frowned. "I asked Minerva for help but that option's no longer open. I can't go to a clinic. I can't use any of the substitutes humans use to ease withdrawal. So I've just got to stop. It won't be easy." She sighed. "Withdrawing from laudanum is going to involve fever, hallucinations, pain-wracked muscles, vomiting, sweating and who knows what else. For several weeks, possibly. I could do with someone to mop my brow and bring me water. And clean up the vomit."

"It's not sounding like an attractive task," said Sarapen.

"Some reassurance that I'll make it would be helpful too."

"Surely I'm the worst person you could ask? Mopping your brow? Being reassuring? I'd be terrible at that."

Dominil smiled. "Probably. But I'm terrible at that sort of thing too, and yet I managed to help Butix and Delix." She looked into Sarapen's eyes. "I don't know who else to ask."

Sarapen nodded. "I'll do my best," he said. "When are you going to start?"

"Right away, if you have no other plans. I can't stop taking the substance abruptly because that might kill me, but I plan to lessen the dose each day till I stop taking it altogether."

"Will you be better then?"

"No. I'll be ill during the decreasing dosages, and worse afterward, for some time."

They rose from the bench. A few more people had entered the park. They looked with interest at the huge, scowling figure of Sarapen, and the white-haired and beautiful Dominil, as they strode along the path. Dogs cowered in terror and children fell silent.

"I'll drive us to my flat," said Dominil. She trembled a little.

"Are you already feeling it?"

Dominil nodded. She'd taken less laudanum today and she could sense a faint nausea growing in her stomach. Sarapen put his arm round Dominil's shoulders to support her, and they walked together toward her car.

CHAPTER 183

"Vex seems to have made a quick recovery from her boyfriend trauma," said Daniel. "A couple of days and she's back to normal."

"I think she liked having a boyfriend more than she actually liked Pete," said Moonglow.

"You're probably right. Mind you, I still think it was mean of Dominil to just tell her like that. She might have been more tactful."

Kalix, sitting beside them at the table in the living room, smiled. "Dominil isn't very good at being tactful."

Moonglow poured tea into three mugs. "Have you been drawing today?" she asked Kalix.

Kalix was immediately alarmed. "Drawing? Why?"

"You like drawing. You've drawn a lot of good pictures."

"How do you know that? I only showed you one."

"Vex took all the rest from your room," said Daniel.

Kalix went bright red with embarrassment at the thought of anyone looking at her drawings. "I wish she'd stop doing that!"

"Vex doesn't have much idea of privacy," said Moonglow. "It's annoying. But your drawings are really good, I'd no idea you were so talented."

"Thanks," mumbled Kalix, still embarrassed.

"I loved your picture of us all sitting on the bed watching TV," said Daniel, sincerely.

They were interrupted by Vex thundering up the stairs.

"Look! Dominil sent me a kilt!" She danced around the living room with excitement. "Isn't it great?"

The dark green kilt was quite small, a children's size. Moonglow and Daniel were impressed with the garment, as was Kalix. "It's the MacRinnalch tartan," she said. "No one outside the clan ever gets that."

"I'm an honorary MacRinnalch!" said Vex. "I'm a werewolf! Owwwooooooooo!"

"Don't do that!" cried Kalix.

"Owwwoooooooo!" yelled Vex. "I'm a Scottish werewolf in a kilt!" She raced upstairs to try on the kilt.

"That was nice of Dominil," said Daniel. "She must have feelings."

"She likes to pay her debts anyway," said Kalix. She frowned. "No one ever sent me a kilt from the castle."

"You wouldn't wear it," said Daniel. "Your legs are too scrawny."

"Hey! My legs are not . . ." Kalix paused. She laughed. "They are quite scrawny. I felt like an idiot modeling these shorts for Thrix."

"You could model more," said Moonglow. "Didn't someone offer you work?"

Kalix shrugged. "I didn't really enjoy it."

"But you could earn money," said Moonglow. "Which would be useful. You know, for your future."

Kalix was immediately suspicious, as she had learned to be whenever Moonglow mentioned her future. "Why?"

"Well," said Moonglow. "It's almost time for you to start college again, and it's your last year, so you should think about what you're going to do after that."

"Do I have to?"

"Moonglow doesn't approve of anyone not having plans for the future," said Daniel.

Kalix felt some twinges of anxiety, and wondered how she'd managed to get trapped so quickly in a conversation she'd rather not have. "I'll probably just wait and see what happens," she mumbled.

"That's never the best plan," said Moonglow. "I think you should go to art school."

"What?"

"Art school," said Moonglow. "You'd enjoy it."

"I think you're getting carried away."

"I'm serious," said Moonglow."

"They'd laugh at me."

"No they wouldn't. They'd look at your drawings and think, *this girl has talent.*"

"I don't know anything about art."

"Well who does?" said Moonglow. "It would still be a good place to go. I mean, what else have you got planned?"

"Wouldn't Kalix need qualifications?" asked Daniel.

"I can hardly even read," said Kalix.

"Your reading's getting much better!" enthused Moonglow. "Another year at remedial college and you'll be right up to standard. And the qualification you'll earn is enough to get you into the foundation course at St. Martin's Academy, or Camberwell School of Art."

"How do you know that?"

"I just happen to have checked."

"Why? Have you been planning my future?"

"Someone has to. You can't spend all your life just being a werewolf with problems. You'd like art school."

"I'm sure I can't draw well enough."

"You're pretty good with these crayons," said Daniel. "Anyway, they do more than that, I think. Don't artists cut up sharks and stuff these days?"

Kalix quite liked that idea. She had a strong prejudice against sharks.

Vex came downstairs very noisily in her new kilt and glacier boots. "What's happening?" she asked.

"Moonglow's planning Kalix's future," Daniel told her. "She thinks she should go to art school."

Vex's eyes bulged. "I want to go to art school!" she screamed, at the top of her voice. "Kalix, we have to go to art school! It's the best idea ever! I'll get more crayons!"

Kalix remained unconvinced. "It costs a lot of money to go to college."

"Aunt Malvie's got lots of money!"

"So has the werewolf clan," Moonglow pointed out. "Your mother would probably pay your fees if you approached her the right way."

Kalix wasn't sure about that. She could imagine widespread mockery at Castle MacRinnalch were it ever learned that she was planning to go to art school.

"You should think about it anyway," said Moonglow, in her most encouraging manner. "You can read some prospectuses. Which I just happen to have picked up for you. Look, here's one for St. Martin's foundation course." She held open a pamphlet showing a picture of three students cutting up sheets of colored paper.

"What are they doing?" asked Kalix.

"I'm not sure. Something artistic, I expect."

"They do look happy," said Daniel.

"I want to cut up paper!" screamed Vex.

"I probably couldn't manage it," said Kalix. "I'll think about it." Kalix took the pamphlets from Moonglow and went upstairs to her room.

"That went better than I expected," said Moonglow.

"I think it's a good idea," said Daniel. "She's got the tortured bit already. Enough depression and anxiety for a room full of artists."

"I'm going to art school!" yelled Vex. "I'm off to ask Aunt Malvie for money." The young Fire Elemental raced out of the room.

"Is Vex a suitable candidate too?" asked Daniel.

"Who knows? But I'm sure they'd let her in. I mean, just look at her."

"True. She's already like a walking art exhibition."

"She might even get good enough grades, with Dominil tutoring her," said Moonglow.

Daniel shuddered. "Poor Vex. Imagine being tutored by Dominil. It's inhuman."

"I asked Dominil if she'd help you too," said Moonglow.

"Very funny," said Daniel. "Wait, you're not serious, are you?"

"She'll really help you with Shakespeare. She's good at Middle English too, and you need a lot of help with that."

Moonglow walked upstairs toward her room.

"I know you're just saying that!" cried Daniel. "Dominil isn't really going to tutor me. Is she? Are you serious?"

Daniel's frantic enquiries were cut short by the sudden appearance of the Fire Queen. She looked at Daniel with raised eyebrows.

"Daniel, could you explain to me why my dreadful niece has just burst into my private chambers screaming about something called 'art school'?"

"It's Moonglow's fault. She suggested that Kalix went to art school and Vex got caught up in the excitement."

Malveria's eyebrows lowered slightly. "Is this art school a proper place of learning?"

"I suppose so. I don't really know much about it. Moonglow has all the information."

"I shall consult with her. My lips are in need of attention in any case."

As Malveria approached the stairs, Daniel had a sudden stroke of inspiration.

"Could you help me?"

Malveria turned. "Help you, Daniel? With what?"

Daniel blushed bright red and immediately regretted his stroke of inspiration. His hair flopped in front of his eyes and he looked down at the carpet. "It's all right, it's nothing."

The Fire Queen advanced. She had always found Daniel's shyness amusing. "Well, young Daniel. What is this?" She scanned his aura. "You want to ask me about Moonglow, yes?"

"No."

"I can see it quite plainly in your aura."

Daniel blushed an even deeper shade of red. "OK, it's about Moonglow. I'm getting nowhere," he said. "Can you help?"

"Clarify 'getting nowhere,'" said the Fire Queen.

Daniel looked hopeless. He raised his hands despairingly. "I'm in love with Moonglow, but I can't make any progress. It's just impossible."

The Fire Queen nodded. "I see. Well, Daniel, this is a difficult enterprise. Your problem—or, I should say, one of your problems—is that you are now very familiar with each other. You have become friends and companions. Transforming from friends into lovers is not so easy. There is no spark, you see. No fire. No thrill of the unknown. To Moonglow, you can never be an exciting new discovery."

Daniel's shoulders slumped. He sat down heavily at the table. "I knew it was hopeless."

"I did not say it was hopeless. I said it was difficult. Too difficult for you to manage, as things stand."

Daniel slumped lower. "How's my aura looking now?" he mumbled.

"Very bad. Another of your problems is giving up too easily. In a way, it is a shame, because Daniel and Moonglow might well be a satisfactory couple. There is something about your auras that does match."

The Fire Queen sat down at the table. She smiled at Daniel. "You have looked after my appalling niece far better than I could have expected. So I am prepared to help you."

Daniel's heart leaped. "Really? How? You'd have to be discreet of course."

Malveria rose to her feet, very grandly. She crossed the small living room, climbed halfway up the stairs, and called out to Moonglow.

"Yes?" said Moonglow, appearing at the top of the stairs.

"Moonglow, please join us. I have some questions regarding Agrivex and her sudden mania for art school, but first I have some words for you and Daniel."

Moonglow came down the stairs, slightly puzzled. "Me and Daniel?"

"Yes. Daniel has been telling me of his hopeless love for you—"

"That's not quite what I—" said Daniel.

"Which he is too young and foolish to do anything about. But Daniel does have many good qualities, Moonglow, which may make up for his deficiencies. If you could overcome them, you may find you make a suitable couple."

Daniel had by now buried his face in his arms on the table. The Fire Queen carried on. "There is a certain meshing in your auras, which does suggest to me you may be compatible. I would suggest you pretend you've just met, and go out on a date, as other young humans do."

The Fire Queen smiled, and looked at Daniel. "Well?" she said.

"That wasn't quite what I had in mind," mumbled Daniel.

"What did you expect? A love spell?"

"Something like that."

The Fire Queen laughed. "A little plain talking was all that was required. Moonglow, you should consider Daniel's request for a date. But before that, could we talk about my niece? Why should I pay money for her to cut up paper and sharks, as she seems so keen to do?"

CHAPTER 184

Two days later the Fire Queen summoned her niece to the throne room.

"Agrivex. I will be absent from the palace for a few days. While I'm gone, you will be in charge. Don't wreck anything and don't spend the palace reserves on ridiculous items."

"Wait a minute!" cried Agrivex. "You can't just say I'm in charge and then leave."

"Why not?"

"I don't want to be in charge!"

"You're perfectly capable. Reasonably capable. Just do your best."

"I can't be in charge of a whole country!"

The Fire Queen studied her niece, carefully examining her aura. She turned to dismiss her attendants. "Agrivex, I know you are not keen to take on responsibility. And I'd rather not burden you with any at the moment. But you must be prepared. I have no other heir at the moment."

"Can't you get one?"

"Not in the space of a few days, notwithstanding the gaggle of aristocrats you've flung at me recently, all of them very unsuitable."

"Maybe you should have tried harder," said Agrivex. "Some sex might make you less grumpy."

"I am rarely grumpy. And my sex life is no concern of yours. I do have a date with a Japanese fashion designer coming up."

"Oh, is he nice?"

"Very nice. I may be in need of a new designer if Thrix does not recover. That is why I must leave the palace. Despite her promises of a new winter wardrobe, Thrix's mind has not healed. She has been too bitter for too long, and has used too much sorcery, sorcery filled with hate and revenge. It has left her drained and unable to function."

"Will she get better?"

"I think so, but it will take some time. I've made her comfortable on the mountain top, and will continue to minster to her. But she won't be designing any clothes for a while. And this is a cruel twist of fate, as I have important fashion engagements coming up, and she absolutely promised me a full wardrobe for next season."

The Fire Queen took a seat, not on her throne, but on a golden ottoman at the side of the room. She motioned for her niece to sit next to her. "I have confidence that you can manage."

"I don't. What if war breaks out?"

"Unlikely. Kabachetka is cowed and we have no other serious enemies. First Minister Xakthan will take care of day-to-day business, and you will probably find that nothing important arises which requires your attention." The Queen rose. "I will be back in a few days. If you wish to pursue this dubious art school adventure, I suggest you study in preparation for your upcoming year at college."

"I would," said Agrivex, "if only I could bring my college books here."

"Fortunately, I have arranged with Merchant MacDoig to do just that," said the Fire Queen. "You will find them all in your room. Farewell, Agrivex."

"Wait a moment, Aunty."

"Yes?"

"About you producing an heir. Do you have to be married first?"

"It would be better. Illegitimate heirs inevitably lead to civil war."

"In that case, why not just marry Xakthan?"

The Fire Queen stared at her niece. "That is the most extraordinary suggestion I've ever heard. Xakthan? My first minister?"

"Why not? If you don't like anyone else well enough, they say you should marry your best friend."

"Who says that?"

"*Elle* magazine. Last month, in their piece about fashionable weddings."

"It seems like a very strange suggestion," said Malveria. "I have nothing in common with Xakthan."

"But you're used to each other. You know each other well enough not to be fighting all the time."

"I don't know about that. Besides, I don't think I'd call Xakthan my best friend."

"He's your best male friend. You've known him since you were a child. You've been on the battlefield together. He's always cropping up in your war stories. Not that your war stories are dull or repetitive in any way."

The Fire Queen shook her head. "I do not count this as one of your best ideas, Agrivex."

Malveria bid her niece farewell, and dematerialized, on her way to Scotland. Behind her, Vex grinned. She didn't think it was such a bad idea. It would certainly never have occurred to her aunt on her own, but now it had been suggested, who knew what might come of it?

I have a real talent for matching people up, thought Vex. It was extra-brilliant of me to demonstrate to my aunt that none of these aristocrats was suitable, and then suggest Xakthan.

The young Fire Elemental was still smiling as she went to sit on the throne, to see what it felt like.

The Fairy Queen of Colburn Woods was irate. She could feel the anger and confusion among the werewolves caused by Teinn's revelations about Markus.

"That dreadful fairy!" raged the Queen. "Does she know the trouble she's caused? The MacGregors are up in arms. So are the MacPhees and the MacAllisters. And this at a time when there are funerals to attend and they should all be together. Now Markus has left the castle. I can sense very bad things in the future because of this. Where is Teinn? Bring her to me."

Teinn was nowhere to be found. She wasn't much troubled by the Queen's wrath, but thought it wise to avoid her for a while.

"I'll go visiting till she calms down. It's a while since I've traveled the country."

Traveling the country would have been a laborious flight for a small fairy, but Teinn had no need to fly all the way. There were certain spots she could reach via the same sort of paths used by the Fire Elementals in their travels. The next day she popped into existence above Sherwood Forest, where she visited her friend Ælfleger, a fairy renowned for her powers of spreading ill health and misfortune. They shared stories of their misdeeds, and laughed together, before Teinn set off again, on her way to visit another friend in Cornwall.

I'll fly over London, she thought. Big cities always inspire me to mischief.

CHAPTER 185

Kalix lay in her favorite clump of bushes in Kennington Park. She stared up at the sky. It was a cloudy night, and there were no stars.

This doesn't feel like I thought it would.

Kalix had expected to die in the attack on the Guild. She hadn't thought much about what might happen if she survived, but she wouldn't have anticipated the feeling of emptiness that now engulfed her.

I thought beating the guild would be a triumph. For the clan anyway.

The MacRinnalch Clan was anything but triumphant. Kalix knew this because her mother had taken the very unusual step of calling her. From the tone of the conversation, Kalix gathered that the werewolves in Scotland were grieving over their losses, rather than celebrating a victory. At least Decembrius was recovering, though Verasa hadn't heard anything more from Thrix. All she knew was that Malveria was looking after her. Dominil too had disappeared. Apparently there was a lot of bad feeling against her.

"That's ridiculous," Kalix had said. "Look at all the hunters we killed. We'd never have managed that without Dominil." Not everyone at the castle saw it that way. Kalix felt annoyed, though not that surprised.

She looked up at the sky. She remembered lying here not long after she'd killed Sarapen. Or thought she'd killed him. Now he was back, she didn't know what would happen. Kalix frowned. She had always hated her brother. She supposed she still did, but she knew the attack wouldn't have succeeded without him. He was so powerful. She wondered if she'd end up fighting him again.

I said I wasn't going to get involved in any violence. That didn't work out very well.

Kalix remembered her plans for self-improvement. *None of them worked. I should have known better.*

The night air was chilly. Kalix shivered, and changed into her werewolf form. *I like this clump of bushes. It's so peaceful.*

Kalix jolted upright as her thoughts were interrupted by a loud crash followed by wailing.

"Help! I'm trapped in the bushes!"

Kalix sighed. "Don't you know I come here for peace and quiet?"

"I like peace and quiet too!" said Vex. "So I've come to join you. But I'm trapped!"

Kalix made her way through the dense undergrowth to help Vex, who had become entangled in thorns.

"Couldn't you start hiding in some place that was easier to get to?" asked Vex, brightly. "I've been ruling the Hiyasta but now I'm back in time for college."

Both of them were due to start their second year in two days' time.

"You were ruling the Hiyasta?"

"It wasn't as bad as I thought it would be. I sat on the throne for three days reading manga and not much happened. Now I'm back. I'm really looking forward to everything! We've got college and then art school."

"Art school? Are you serious?"

"Of course, why not? I've got extra crayons so we can draw everything. And I got some big scissors in case we need to cut things up."

"We might not even pass our exams this year."

"Of course we will. Dominil's going to teach us."

"Dominil's going to teach *you*," said Kalix.

"I've included you as well," said Vex. "I left her a message saying you wanted help."

"Thanks for that."

"It's not so bad. It'll be fun, just you, me and Dominil and a few books."

Kalix thought that sounded anything but fun, but let it pass. Vex made a small spout of flame spurt from her hand. She watched it for a few seconds, then let it vanish. "I never thought I'd be able to do that. Let's go to the café."

"OK."

Kalix changed back to her human shape as they made their way from the bushes into the park.

"The flat was empty when I got back," said Vex. "Is this the big night?"

"Yes."

Vex laughed, and Kalix smiled. They both knew that Daniel and Moonglow had arranged a date, after encouragement from the Fire Queen.

"It was super-brilliant of me to arrange that," said Vex. "I knew I'd get Daniel to ask Aunt Malvie for help if I kept talking to him about dating."

They left the park. It was late evening but the lights were still on in the small café on the corner.

"I love the all-day breakfasts," said Vex. "I'm going to buy two." Vex looked happy. "You'd have to say our self-improvement's been a big success."

"What? I was a complete failure, and you weren't doing any self-improvement anyway."

"Of course I was. And look what I can do now. I can make fire and I can heal people. Well, I'm better with plants really, but it's a start. And you went running and got fit, you managed not to be so bad-tempered with your flatmates all the time, and you won a big fight, and now we're going back to college and then we're going to art school. Even your mother called you and she never does that. How can you say you haven't improved? We should get medals for self-improvement, we're practically world champions."

Kalix laughed. "Well, maybe."

"And I brought you some new Hello Kitty running shoes! I got them specially because you liked the other pair so much."

"Thanks," said Kalix. "I can't wait to see them."

CHAPTER 186

In the middle of the night there was a small flash of yellow light on the roof of Somerset House, above the Courtauld Gallery. Distikka emerged from the shadows, frowning.

I didn't mean to land on the roof. My powers of navigation are far from perfect in this world.

She looked up at the gray sky. There was a light drizzle, which she found annoying, though she'd visited London often enough to know that the rain wouldn't kill her.

Though it does weaken my powers. I doubt I could produce much fire here.

Distikka had fled her own dimension. After initiating a rebellion in the realm of the Fire Queen, and fleeing from a death sentence at the hands of the Empress, it seemed the prudent thing to do. There were other nations in the realms of the elementals, but most of them were allied with at least one of her enemies. Were she to seek asylum, it was quite probable that she would be returned to Malveria or Kabachetka, and promptly executed.

Distikka walked to the edge of the roof and looked down at the great courtyard below. It was deserted. She stepped off the roof, and floated to the ground.

I sill have some power here. Enough to maintain my presence for a while, anyway.

Distikka was thoughtful as she walked toward the courtyard gates. Fleeing to Earth was a no more than a temporary solution. Only the most powerful elementals could spend long periods here. Distikka was strong, but her strength was not at the same level as the Fire Queen or the Empress. Eventually her fire would dwindle, and she would die.

Distikka nimbly vaulted the tall gates, and walked into the dark street outside. Humans survive here, she thought. But I have no wish to become human. They're so weak, and they have such a short lifespan. Anyway, there's no known way of becoming human. Distikka walked down the Strand. *It's unfortunate that I'm an enemy of Thrix MacRinnalch. She might have had some suggestions. I suppose I could ask Merchant MacDoig's advice. They say he's extended his own lifespan.* She would have set off to visit see him right away, but realized, depressingly, that she didn't know how to get there. She knew the address, but couldn't navigate her way through London.

I'll need to wait until morning, and buy a map.

Distikka reached Trafalgar Square. Though it was the middle of the night, there were still people at the bus stops. She sat on a bench, to wait until morning.

My plan should have worked. I lured the MacRinnalchs into a trap. If they escaped, it was down to deficiencies in the werewolf hunters. The Empress should have realized that. Unfortunately, the Empress is a fool. Distikka hoped that Dominil had survived the battle. She thought about Dominil for a while, and then about werewolves in general. They were a strange breed. She'd read a lot about them during her service to the Empress. It struck her that, in comparison with the rest of Earth's population, werewolves were very strong, and very long-lived.

And while there's no known way of becoming human, there is a way of becoming a werewolf. A bite, a blood transferal and a brief ceremony. So it's said, anyway. That's an interesting thought.

Distikka sat on the bench, a small, dark, a fugitive, alone in the world, without any realistic prospects of success, or even survival. Most elementals in her position would have given in to despair, but Distikka was too resilient to despair. She was confident she'd find some means of surviving, and prospering.

Teinn the fairy hopped onto a chair, and looked around the room. Paintings were torn from the walls and there was blood on the floor. The front door was broken, forced open by the police who'd responded to the emergency call following Manny's screams.

They took him away in an ambulance. Teinn laughed. She liked ambulances. Her mischief had been the cause of many an emergency call-out in Scotland.

She sniffed the air. How funny, she thought. That silly Queen of the Fire Elementals has tried to cover it all up.

Teinn laughed again. The Fire Queen's covering spells might have fooled another elemental, or a werewolf, but not her. No one could hide mischief or misdeeds from Teinn. Flying over London, she'd been attracted to the scene, sensing the recent presence of a werewolf and a powerful Fire Elemental. Now she was here, she could picture the events quite clearly.

I wonder why Thrix tried to kill the boy? I should find out more about him.

The fairy hopped onto the windowsill, pleased with her discovery. It held promise for some entertaining mischief in the future. Teinn launched herself into the air, soaring high above London.

How horrible this big city is, she thought. But as she looked down at the vast sprawl of buildings, it did occur to her that there was an almost infinite capacity for mischief here. She had become constrained in the small world of Colburn Woods, and the werewolf estates. Who knew what she might be able to achieve, given such a huge canvas?